Gemini

Introduction

by Judith Wilt

THE ELEGANT WORKING out of designs historical and romantic, political and commercial, psychological and moral, over a multi-volume novel is a Dorothy Dunnett speciality. In her first work in this genre, the six-volume *Lymond Chronicles*, suspense was created and relieved in each volume, and over the whole set of volumes; the final, beautifully inevitable, romantic secret was disclosed on the very last page of the last volume. *The House of Niccolò* does the same.

The reader of *Gemini*, then, may wish to move directly to the narrative for a first experience of that pattern, with a reader's faith in an experienced author's caretaking; the novel itself briefly supplies the information you need to know from past novels, telling its own tale while completing and inaugurating others. What follows, as a sketch of the geopolitical and dramatic terrain unfolding in the volumes which precede *Gemini*, may be useful to read now, or at any point along the narrative, or after reading, as an indication of which stories of interest to this volume may be found most fully elaborated in which previous volume.

VOLUME I: *Niccolò Rising*

'From Venice to Cathay, from Seville to the Gold Coast of Africa, men anchored their ships and opened their ledgers and weighed one thing against another as if nothing would ever change.' The first sentence of the first volume indicates the scope of this series, and the cultural and psychological dynamic of the story and its hero, whose private motto is 'Change, change and adapt'. It is the motto, too, of fifteenth-century Bruges, centre of commerce and conduit of new ideas and technologies between the Islamic East and the Christian West, between the Latin South and the Celtic-Saxon North, haven of political refugees from the English Wars of the Roses, a site of muted conflict between trading giants Venice and Genoa and states in making and on the take all around. Lady Dunnett has set her story in the fifteenth century, between Gutenberg and Columbus, between Donatello and Martin Luther, between the rise of mercantile culture and the fall of chivalry, as the age of receptivity to – addiction to – change called 'the Renaissance' gathers its powers.

Her hero is a deceptively silly-looking, disastrously tactless eighteen-year-old dyeworks artisan named 'Claes', a caterpillar who emerges by the end of the novel as the merchant-mathematician Nicholas vander Poele. Prodigiously gifted at numbers, and the material and social 'engineering' skills that go with them, Nicholas has until now resisted the responsibility of his powers, his identity fractured by the enmity of both his mother's husband's family, the Scottish St Pols, who refuse to own him legitimate, and his maternal family, the Burgundian de Fleurys, who failed his mother and abused him and reduced him to serfdom as a child. He found refuge at age ten with his grandfather's in-laws, especially the Bruges widow Marian de Charetty, whose dyeing and broking business becomes the tool of Nicholas's desperate self-fashioning apart from the malice of his blood relatives.

Soon even public Bruges and the states beyond come to see the engineer within the artisan. The Charetty business expands to include a courier and intelligence service between Italian and Northern states, its bodyguard sharpened into a skilled mercenary force, its pawnbroking consolidated towards banking and commodities trading. And as the chameleon artificer of all this, Nicholas incurs the ambiguous interest of the Bruges patrician Anselm Adorne and the Greco-Florentine prince Nicholai Giorgio de' Acciajuoli, both of whom steer him towards a role in the rivalry between Venice, in whose interest Acciajuoli labours, and Genoa, original home of the Adorne family. This trading rivalry will erupt in different novels around different, always highly symbolic commodities: silk, sugar, glass, gold, and human beings. In this first novel the contested product is alum, the mineral that binds dyes to cloth, blood to the body, conspirators to a conspiracy – in this case, to keep secret the news of a recently found deposit of the mineral in the Papal

States while Venice and her allies monopolise the current supply.

Acciajuoli and Adorne are father-mentor figures Nicholas can respect, resist, or join on roughly equal intellectual terms – whereas the powerful elder males of his real and supposed families, his mother's uncle, Jaak de Fleury, and Simon de St Pol's father, Jordan de Ribérac, steadily rip open wounds first inflicted in childhood. In direct conflict he is emotionally helpless before them. What he possesses superbly, however, are the indirect defences of an 'engineer'. The Charetty business partners and others who hitch their wagons to his star – Astorre the mercenary leader, Julius the notary, Gregorio the lawyer, Tobias Beventini the physician, the Guinea slave Lopez – watch as a complex series of commodity and currency manoeuvres by the apparently innocent Nicholas brings about the financial and political ruin of de Fleury and de Ribérac; and they nearly desert him for the conscienceless avenger he appears to be, especially after de Fleury dies in a fight with, though not directly at the hands of, his great-nephew.

The faith and love of Marian de Charetty make them rethink their view of this complicated personality. Marian, whose son was killed beside Nicholas in the Italian wars, and whose sister married into his family, is moved towards the end of the novel to suggest that Nicholas take her in marriage. It is to be platonic: her way of giving him standing, of displaying her trust in him and his management of the business, and of solacing him in his anguish. Once married, however, she longs despite herself for physical love, and Nicholas, who owes her everything, finds happiness also in making the marriage complete.

That marriage, however, sows the seeds of tragedy. The royally connected Katelina van Borselen, 'characterful', intelligent, and hungry for experiences usually denied a genteel lady, has refused the vicious or vacuous suitors considered eligible, and seeks sexual initiation at the hands of the merry young artisan so popular with the kitchen wenches of Bruges. Against his better judgement, Nicholas is led to comply, for, however brusque her demands, she has just saved his life in one of the several episodes in which his enemies try to destroy him. Two nights of genuine intimacy undermined by mismatched desires and miscommunicated intentions culminate in Katelina's solitary pregnancy. Unaware of this, Nicholas enters his marriage with Marian, and Katelina, alone, fatalistically marries the man in pursuit of her, the handsome, shrewd, and fatally self-centred Simon de St Pol, the man Nicholas claims is his father. Sickened at what she believes is Nicholas's ultimate revenge on his family – to illegitimately father its heir – Katelina becomes Nicholas's most determined enemy.

VOLUME II: *The Spring of the Ram*

Simon de St Pol, the overshadowed son of Jordan de Ribérac, husband
of the bitter Katelina, father of the secretly illegitimate Henry, has
clearly had his spirit poisoned long since by the powerful and malignant
de Ribérac, and is as much pitied as loathed by Nicholas vander Poele,
who sees in Simon something of his own deracinated brilliance. Looking
to find a sphere of activity where Simon and Nicholas can no longer
injure each other, Marian de Charetty, now the wife of Nicholas,
persuades her husband to take up an exciting and dangerous project:
to trade in Trebizond, last outpost of the ancient empire of Byzantium.

It is less than a decade since Sultan Mehmet took Constantinople,
and several forces of Islam – Mehmet's Ottomans, Uzum Hasan's
Turcomans, Kushcadam's Egyptian Mamelukes – ring the Christian
outpost while delegates from the Greek Orthodox East, led by the very
earthy and autocratic Franciscan friar Ludovico de Severi da Bologna,
scour the Latin West for money and troops to mount still another
Crusade. With Medici backing and Church approval, Nicholas sets
out for Trebizond to trade as Florentine consul, bringing his skilled
mercenaries as a show of support from the West – a show that will soon
turn real as the Sultan moves against the city more quickly than anyone
had anticipated.

Nicholas's rival, and in some ways alter ego, is the gifted, charming,
and amoral Pagano Doria, trading for Genoa, gaming with Venice's
Nicholas in a series of brilliant pranks and tricks which include, terribly,
the seduction of the thirteen-year-old Catherine de Charetty, one of
Nicholas's two rebellious step-daughters. Pagano, who is secretly
financed by Nicholas's enemy Simon de St Pol, has invited the adoles-
cent Catherine to challenge her stepfather, and no pleas or arguments
from Nicholas, her mother's officers, or the new figures joining the
company – the priest Godscalc and the engineer John le Grant – can
sway her.

In Trebizond, Nicholas deploys his trading skills while he assesses
Byzantine culture, once spiritually and politically supreme, now calci-
fied in routine, crumbling in self-indulgence. Nicholas must resist the
Emperor David's languidly amorous overtures while he takes the lead
in preparing the city for, and then withstanding, the siege of the Sultan.
The city, however, is betrayed by its Emperor and his scheming Chancellor, and Pagano Doria suffers his own fall, killed by a black page
whom he carelessly loved and then sold to the Sultan. Nicholas has

willed neither fall, yet has set in motion some of the psychopolitical 'engineering' which has triggered these disasters, and he carries, with Father Godscalc's reflective help and the more robust assistance of Tobie and le Grant, part of the moral burden of them.

The burden weighs even during the triumphant trip back to Venice with a rescued if still recalcitrant Catherine and a fortune in silk, gold, alum, and Eastern manuscripts, the 'golden fleece' which this Jason looks to lay at the feet of his beloved wife. A final skirmish with Simon, angry at the failure of his agent Doria, ends the novel abruptly, with news which destroys all the remaining dream of homecoming: Marian de Charetty, travelling through Burgundy in her husband's absence, has died.

VOLUME III: *Race of Scorpions*

Rich and courted, yet emotionally drained and subconsciously enraged, Nicholas seeks a new shape for his life after visiting his wife's grave, establishing his still-resentful step-daughters in business themselves, and allowing his associates to form the Trading Company and Bank of Niccolò in Venice. Determined to avoid the long arm of Venetian policy, attracted to the military life not precisely for its sanction of killing but for the 'sensation of living through danger' it offers, Nicholas returns from Bruges to the war over Naples in which he had, years before, lost Marian's son Felix and contracted a marsh-fever which revisits him in moments of stress. When he is kidnapped in mid-battle, he at first supposes it to be by order of his personal enemies, Simon and Katelina; but in fact it is Venice which wants him and his mercantile and military skills in another theatre of war, Cyprus.

The brilliant and charismatic but erratic James de Lusignan and his Egyptian Mameluke allies have taken two-thirds of the sugar-rich island of Cyprus from his legitimate Lusignan sister, the clever and energetic Carlotta, and her allies, the Christian Knights of St John and the Genoese, who hold the great commercial port of Famagusta. Sensing that, of the two Lusignan 'scorpions', James holds the winning edge, Nicholas agrees to enter his service. He intends to design the game this time, not be its pawn, but he doesn't reckon with the enmity of Katelina, who comes to Rhodes to warn Carlotta against him, or the sudden presence of Simon's Portuguese brother-in-law Tristão Vasquez and Vasquez's naïve sixteen-year-old son Diniz, all three of whom do become pawns.

Nicholas is now the lover of Carlotta's courtesan, the beautiful Primaflora, whose games he also thinks he can control, and he recognises a crisis of countermanipulations brewing between Katelina and Primaflora. Only at the end of the novel, after Katelina's love/hate for Nicholas has been manipulated to bring Tristão to his death and Diniz to captivity under James, after Nicholas and Katelina rediscover intimacy and establish the truth of their relationship, after a brilliant and deadly campaign waged by Nicholas for James has brought him to ultimate tragedy – the siege of Famagusta which he planned and executed has resulted, without his knowledge, in the death of Katelina and the near-death of Diniz, trapped in the starving city – only at the end does Nicholas fully admit even to himself that much of this has been planned or sanctioned by Primaflora, intent on securing her own future.

In the end, too, the determinedly rational Nicholas gives vent to his rage. Punishment for the pain of the complex desires and denials in his private and public history cannot be visited upon the complex and only half-guilty figures of his family or his trading and political rivals and clients. But in this novel, for the first time, he finds a person he can gladly kill, the unspeakably cruel Mameluke Emir Tzani-bey al-Ablak, whom he fatally mutilates in single combat while James, unknown to him, has the Emir's four-hundred-man army massacred in a pre-emptive strike carrying all the glory and damnation of Renaissance kingship.

Like Pagano Doria, like Nicholas himself, Primaflora is a 'modern' type, a talented and alienated 'self-made' person. Unlike the other two, Nicholas has the memory of family in which to ground a wary, half-reluctant, but genuine adult existence in the community. At the same time, however, he avoids close relationships: he has established the Bank of Niccolò as a company, not a family. But, resisting and insisting, the members of the company forge bonds of varying intimacy with Nicholas, especially the priest Godscalc and the physician Tobie, who alone at this point know the secret of Katelina's baby and carry the dying woman's written affirmation of Nicholas's paternity.

Nicholas's only true intimate, however, is a man of a different race entirely, the African who came to Bruges as a slave and was befriended by the servant Claes, who first communicated the secret of the alum deposit, who travelled with him to Trebizond to run the trading household, and to Cyprus to organise and under Nicholas reinvent the sugar industry there. His African name is as yet unknown, his Portuguese name is Lopez, his company name Loppe. Now a major figure in the company, and the family, he listens at the end of the novel as both

Nicholas and his new rival, the broker of the mysterious Vatachino company, look to the Gold Coast of Africa as the next place of questing and testing.

VOLUME IV: *Scales of Gold*

For those who know the truth, the deaths of Katelina, Tristão, and Tzani-bey, the brutal forging of a new monarchy for Cyprus, even Nicholas's alienation from and reconciliation with young Diniz, have stemmed from honourable, even noble motives. But gossip in Europe, fed by de Ribérac and St Pol, puts a more sinister stamp on these events. Under financial attack by the Genoese firm of the Vatachino, the Bank of Niccolò undertakes a commercial expedition to Africa, which young Diniz Vasquez joins partly as an act of faith in Nicholas, while Gelis van Borselen, Katelina's bitter and beautiful sister, joins to prove him the profit-mongering amoralist she believes him to be. They are accompanied by Diniz's mother's companion Bel of Cuthilgurdy, a valiant and razor-tongued Scottish matron who comes to guide the young man and woman and ends up dispensing wisdom and healing to all; by Father Godscalc, who desires to prove his own faith by taking the Cross through East Africa to the fabled Ethiopia of Prester John; and by Lopez, whose designs are the most complex of all. Through Madeira to the Gambia and into the interior they journey, facing and eventually outfacing the competition of the Vatachino and Simon de St Pol.

Like everyone but the Africans, both companies have underestimated even the size, let alone the cultural and religious complexity, of Africa: no travellers in this age can reach Ethiopia from the west, and the profits from the voyages of discovery and commerce recently begun by Prince Henry the Navigator are as yet mainly knowledge, and self-knowledge. There is gold in the Gambia, and there is a trade in black human beings which is, as Lopez is concerned to demonstrate, just beginning to take the shape that will constitute one of the supreme flaws of the civilisation of the West. There is also, up the Joliba flood-plain, the metropolis of Timbuktu, commercial and psychological 'terminus', and Islamic cultural centre, in which Diniz finds his manhood and Lopez regains his original identity as the jurist and scholar Umar; where Gelis consummates with Nicholas the supreme relationship of her life, hardly able as yet to distinguish whether its essence is love or hatred.

On this journey, Godscalc the Christian priest and Umar the Islamic scholar both function as soul friends to Nicholas, prodding him through extremes of activity and meditation that finally draw the sting, as it appears, from the old wounds of family. Certainly there is no doubt of the affection of Diniz for Nicholas, and surely there can be none about the passion of Katelina's sister Gelis, his lover. As the ships of the Bank of Niccolò return to Lisbon, to Venice and Bruges, success in commerce, friendship, and passion mitigates even the novel's first glimpse of Katelina's and Nicholas's four-year-old son Henry, moulded by his putative father, Simon, in his own insecure, narcissistic, and violent image.

On the way to his marriage-bed, the climax and reward of years of struggle, Nicholas is stunned by two blows which will undermine all the spiritual balance he has achieved in his African journey. He learns that Umar – his teacher, his other self – is dead in primitive battle, together with most of the gentle scholars of Timbuktu and their children. And on the heels of that news his bride Gelis, fierce, unreadable, looses the punishment she has prepared for him all these months: she tells him how she has deliberately conceived a child with Nicholas's enemy Simon, to duplicate in reverse – out of what hatred he cannot conceive – the tragedy of Katelina. As the novel closes, we know that he is planning to accept the child as his own, and that he is going to Scotland.

How Nicholas will be affected by the double betrayal – the involuntary death, the act of wilful cruelty – is not yet clear. There is a shield half in place, but Umar, the man of faith who helped him create it, is gone. Nicholas's own spiritual experience, deeply guarded, has had to do with the intersection of mathematics and beauty, with the mind-cleansing horizons of sea and sky and desert, and with the display in friend and foe alike of the compelling qualities of valour and joy and empathy: the spiritual maturity with which he accepts the blows of Fate here may be real, but he has taken his revenge in devious ways before. More mysteriously still, the maturity is accompanied by a curious susceptibility he cannot yet understand, a gift or a disability which teases his mind with unknown events, unvisited places, thoughts that are not his. As much as his markets, his politics, or his half-hidden domestic desires, these thoughts seem to draw him north.

VOLUME V: *The Unicorn Hunt*

Thinner, preoccupied, dressed in a suave and expensive black; pitched between melodrama and satire, between grief and devilry, our protagonist enters his family's homeland bearing his mother's name. Now

Nicholas de Fleury, he comes to Scotland with two projects in hand: to identify the child his pregnant wife says is Simon's and to build in that energetic and unpredictable northern backwater a new edifice of cultural, political, and economic power. Nicholas brings artists and craftsmen to Scotland as well as money and entrepreneurial skill, making himself indispensable to yet another royal James. But are his productions there – the splendid wedding feasts and frolics for James III and Danish Margaret, the escape of the King's sister with the traitor Thomas Boyd, the skilful exploitation of natural resources – the glory they seem? Or are they the hand-set maggot mound, buzzing with destruction, of Gregorio's inexplicable first vision of Nicholas's handsome estate of Beltrees? Is Nicholas the vulnerable and magical beast whose image he wins in knightly combat – or the ruthless hunter of the Unicorn?

The priest Father Godscalc, for one, fears Nicholas's purposes in Scotland. Loving Nicholas and Gelis, knowing the secret of Katelina van Borselen's child, guessing the cruel punishment which her sister has planned for Nicholas, the dying Godscalc brings Nicholas back to Bruges and extracts a promise that he will stay out of Scotland for two years, and so remove himself from the morally perilous proximity of Simon, the father-figure whom he seeks to punish, and Henry, the secret son who hates him more with every effort he makes to help the boy. Nicholas agrees, and turns to other business, mining silver and alum in the Tyrol, settling the eastern arm of his banking business in Alexandria, tracking a large missing shipment of gold from the African adventure from Cairo to Sinai to Cyprus. These enterprises occupy only half his mind, however, for the carefully spent time in Scotland has confirmed what he suspects: that Simon, now infertile, could not in reason be the father of the child whom Gelis has in secret borne and hidden, and who, dead or alive, is the real object of his quest. In a stunning dawn climax on the burning rocks of Mount Sinai, Nicholas and Gelis, equivocal pilgrims, challenge each other with the truth of the birth and of their love and enmity, and the conflict heightens.

The duel between husband and wife finds them evenly matched in business acumen and foresightful intrigue, tragically equal in their capacity to detect the places of the other's deepest hurt and vulnerability. But Nicholas is the more experienced of the two, and wields in addition, or is wielded by, a deep and dangerous power. One part of that power makes him a 'diviner', who vibrates to the presence of water or precious metals under the earth, his body receiving also, by way of personal talismans, the signals through space of a desperately sought living object, his new-born son. The other part of the power whirls him periodically into the currents of time, his mind aflame with the sights and sounds of another life whose focus is in his name, the name he has abandoned – the vander Poele/St Pol surname whose Scottish form, Semple, is startlingly familiar to readers of the *Lymond Chronicles*, Dorothy Dunnett's first historical series.

The professionals Nicholas has assembled around him have always tried to control their leader's mental and psychic powers; now a new group of acute and prescient friends strives to fathom and to guard him, from his enemies and from his own cleverness. Chief among these new friends is the fourteen-year-old niece of Anselm Adorne, the needle-witted and compassionate Katelijne Sersanders, who finds some way to share all his pilgrimages as she pushes adventurously past the barriers of her age and gender. The musician Willie Roger, the metallurgical priest Father Moriz, and the enigmatic physician and mystic Dr Andreas of Vesalia add their fascinated and critical advice as Nicholas pursues his gold and his son through the intricate course, beckoning and thwarting, prepared by Gelis van Borselen. In the end game, as the Venetian Carnival reaches its height, this devoted father, moving the one necessary step ahead of the mother's game, finds, takes, and disappears with the child-pawn whose face, seen at last, is the image of his own.

Yet there is a Lenten edge to this thundering Martedí Grasso success. Why has Nicholas turned his back on the politics of the Crusade in the East to pursue projects in Burgundy and Scotland? Who directs the activities of the Vatachino mercantile company, whose agents have brought Nicholas close to death more than once? Have we still more ambiguous things to learn about the knightly pilgrim and ruthless competitor Anselm Adorne? What secrets, even in her defeat, is the complexly embittered Gelis still withholding? Above all, what atonements can avert the fatalities we see gathering around the fathers and sons, bound in a knot of briars, of the house of St Pol?

VOLUME VI: *To Lie with Lions*

Nicholas de Fleury goes from success to success, expertly operating large structures by the nice application of invisible pressure, as the craftsmen do in the miracle plays in which he has from time to time taken part. Within the theatre of family he has produced the convincing illusion of harmony between himself and Gelis, his estranged wife, for the sake of their beloved, acknowledgeable son Jodi. Within the circus of statecraft, where the lions of Burgundy and France, Venice and

Cyprus, England and Scotland, Islam and Christendom stalk and snarl, the Banco di Niccolò wields a valued whip. Its padrone is a cosmopolitan, virtually stateless man, intellectually drawn to the puzzle of history in the making, but not visibly compelled by the roots of race – although, to be sure, some of his enemies think him motivated mainly by the passion of revenge on his own family.

Free now to enlarge and complete projects in the small, unsteady country of Scotland – which the priest Godscalc, half guessing his intent, had compelled him to abandon for two years – Nicholas carries out two *coups de théâtre* which have consequences and resonances unexpected by their designer. He spends ruinously of his time and the kingdom's money on a nativity play whose single performance, a glory of thought, feeling, and art which makes transcendence of all its illusions and momentarily unites its fractured community, hints at the strength and value of the wounded spirit who has devised it. And he mounts a merchant expedition to the fish-fertile waters of Iceland, whence he lures and bests his old rivals the Adornes and the Vatachino company, as well as a new one, the Danziger pirate Paúel Benecke.

Sharing this adventure are Kathi Sersanders and Robin of Berecrofts, a Scottish youth whose courage, and desire to break free of the bounds of his sturdy mercantile heritage bring him to the magnetic Nicholas as an admiring squire. Together they explore the new world of the North, learn from the hardy generosities of the Icelanders, and, transformed in the end from actors and designers to spectators, experience in awe and humility Nature's own nativity play, the re-creation of a continent in the double explosions of Katla and Hekla, the volcanoes of Iceland.

Nicholas's well-wishers will need this glimpse of his humanity. For in the matters he controls, Nicholas's plans are coming to dark fruition. Gelis has a climactic announcement to make – she has won the war between them because she has secretly been working for years for the Vatachino. But Jordan de St Pol, whose painfully rebuilt career in France Nicholas has undermined once again, brings a devastating illumination: Nicholas knew of Gelis's connection with the Vatachino and skilfully played with it; further, all his projects in Scotland, from the nativity play and the Iceland expedition which brought him a barony, to more secret investments of the Bank's and the country's money in worthless mines, poisoned grains, and debased coinage, were meant in fact to wreck financially the country whose gentry, the St Pol/ Semples, had terrified and rejected Nicholas's mother, and Nicholas himself, thirty years before.

He has carried out this plan because he could: he could not draw back from it because it was his. In this final spectacle, the work of an angry child, of an obsessed artist, even his friends believe they see the death of Nicholas's soul, and desert him. Stunned by his own dire success, Nicholas agrees with them: as the novel ends and the abandoned and pitiless banker allows himself to be carried East by the newly ascendant Emperor of Germany, he seems ready for burial. Or, possibly, resurrection.

VOLUME VII: *Caprice and Rondo*

Nicholas seeks another life in the violent and irresponsible company of his old sea-mate Paúel Benecke, but the quest-shapes of his life are printed too deeply for denial. Already he has set in motion another search for that lost African gold used so cruelly to deceive him in his search for his child. And the worldwide network of correspondence he maintains guarantees that counsellors for the Polish King will come seeking him, that new business projects will tempt him, that the religious and political leaders who have been using him as a bridge between West and East for decades will compel him to responsibility again.

Three times before, Nicholas has been propelled East: to Trebizond, to Cyprus, to Sinai. Now three forces converge to send him East again. Anselm Adorne and Ludovico da Bologna's overt agenda is care of Christian interests in the East, Julius and the clever Countess Anna's spoken mission is to increase their business, but these groups also have covert reasons for drafting Nicholas in to help. And Nicholas's cadets and soulmates from the Icelandic adventure, Kathi Sersanders and Robin of Berecrofts, now married and starting their own family, recognise that he needs a difficult and penitential enterprise to precipitate self-recognition and redemption, and urge him to go.

Meanwhile, those at home who had expelled Nicholas as a congenital 'wrecker' recover their economic and emotional balance, and, impelled to understand him better, turn to trace the mysteries of his birth and early history. The Scottish St Pols who deny his paternity are sequestered in Portugal. Now the maternal de Fleury ancestry comes into focus: the loving and terrified mother Sophie, who bore a dead son and then many months later a live one rejected as a bastard; the uncle Jaak de Fleury, who took the boy into his household at age seven as a menial dependant and subjected him to brutalising contempt; the young 'aunt', Adelina, who came also to the cruel and sensual Jaak in childhood, to be in her turn abused and abandoned. And the grandfather, Thibault de Fleury, long rumored imbecile, whom Gelis and Tobie discover still exercising, despite paralysis and disease, those supreme gifts for mathematics and music, for witty puzzles and detached analysis, which Nicholas has inherited.

Nicholas meets his grandfather spirit to spirit, in an exchange of letter-puzzles, only once before Thibault dies. The dangerous bond between Nicholas and another de Fleury, however, twists slowly and fatally into sight as the long and frustrating journey of Nicholas and Anna into the East and back parallels the increasing illumination of the searching, speculating families at home. The adored wife of Julius, the formidable Countess Anna with the numeracy to run a business and a desire – cold, calculated, yet ultimately intense – to seduce Nicholas, is actually his grandfather's child, his fellow sufferer in the abusive grasp of Jaak de Fleury, Adelina herself.

The obsessed woman plans to unravel not just Nicholas's commercial and political world, but his marriage and the whole structure of his adult life, freezing the two of them in a tableau designed to end in the outlawry of incest before she brings about his death. But Nicholas, master of the interlocking wheels of plot, has in fact recognized the shattered and vengeful Adelina within the stylish Anna, and worked to draw her safely east, away from his imperilled family. Adelina's final attempt to destroy Nicholas becomes the means of reconciling Gelis and Nicholas to full marital partnership, leaving the rash and unrepentant Adelina to die in circumstances left somewhat mysterious.

The caprice and repetition of domestic plot, Adelina's plan to ruin Nicholas as Gelis had also attempted to do, is more than matched by the caprice of princes and the sickening replication of political immaturity which wastes both soldiers and civilians in military adventurism. Nicholas had learned the horrors of war in the sieges of Trebizond and Famagusta. Now, unable to stem the caprices of Charles the Bold, he watches the phantom kingdom of Burgundy disappear from the European stage in the death of its Duke and the wreck of its army in the siege of Nancy. At book's end he is restored to both his private and his business families, and they to him.

But the fading of a potential public life in the East, or in the now leaderless land of his mother, makes him look to the land of the man he believes is his father, and to the questions remaining for him, and Lady Dunnett, to answer in this last volume of the series: as an adult how does one choose a country and foster it, and what is the meaning of 'patriotism' in such a context? If Nicholas is as he now believes the survivor of twin sons born to Sophie de Fleury and Simon de St Pol, what will this mean for the lives of his own so different sons, Henry de St Pol and Jordan de Fleury? And how will the answers to these questions illuminate the meaning of those shafts of insight and foresight hinting at a link between this fifteenth-century story and the sixteenth-century story of Francis Crawford of Lymond?

Judith Wilt
BOSTON, 1999

The House of Niccolò:

Gemini

Dorothy Dunnett

MICHAEL JOSEPH
LONDON

MICHAEL JOSEPH
Published by the Penguin Group
Penguin Books Ltd, 27 Wrights Lane, London w8 5TZ, England
Penguin Putnam Inc., 375 Hudson Street, New York, New York 10014, USA
Penguin Books Australia Ltd, Ringwood, Victoria, Australia
Penguin Books Canada Ltd, 10 Alcorn Avenue, Toronto, Ontario, Canada M4V 3B2
Penguin Books (NZ) Ltd, Private Bag 102902, NSMC, Auckland, New Zealand

Penguin Books Ltd, Registered Offices: Harmondsworth, Middlesex, England

First published 2000
3

Copyright © Dorothy Dunnett, 2000
Introduction copyright © Judith Wilt, 2000

The map on page xxxvi is James Gordon of Rothiemay's Plan of Edinburgh, 1647,
and is reproduced by permission of the Trustees of the National Library of Scotland

Set in 11/12.5pt Monotype Imprint
Typeset by Rowland Phototypesetting Ltd, Bury St Edmunds, Suffolk
Printed in Great Britain by Clays Ltd, St Ives plc

A CIP catalogue record for this book is available from the British Library

ISBN 0-718-14083-4

For Alastair

Sum in-till hunting has thar hale delyte
And uthersum ane nother appetit
That gladlie gois and in-to romanis reidis
Of halynes and of armes the deidis.
Sum lykis wele to heir of menstraly
And sum the talk of honest company,
And uthersum thar langing for to les
Gois to the riall sporting of the ches,
Of the quhilk quha prentis wele in mynd
The circumstance, the figur and the kynd,
And followis it, he sall of werteu be.

AUTHOR'S NOTE

The epigraph, part-head and chapter-head verses in this novel are from *The Buke of the Chess*, a Middle Scots version by a fifteenth-century Edinburgh notary of the *Ludus Scaccorum* of Jacobus de Cessolis. The original work was also the basis for William Caxton's *The Game and Playe of the Chesse*. This text, edited by Catherine van Buuren, is published by The Scottish Text Society, 27 George Square, Edinburgh EH8 9LD.

At the end of this series, I should like to pay tribute once more to the many libraries which have made this work possible, and especially to the librarians of the National Library of Scotland and the London Library. Similarly, of the generous editorial directors who have given me their time and their counsel, I owe special thanks to Robert Gottlieb and Susan Ralston in New York, and Susan Watt and Richenda Todd in London. And lastly, the friendship and support of Anne McDermid and Vivienne Schuster of Curtis Brown have been invaluable in steering this ship into port.

Characters

from February 1477

(Those marked * are recorded in history)

RULERS:
*England: King Edward IV, House of York
*Scotland: King James III, House of Stewart
*France: King Louis XI, House of Valois
*Burgundy, Brabant and Flanders: Duchess Marie
*Pope: Sixtus IV (della Rovere)
*Florence: Lorenzo II de' Medici (Il Magnifico)
*Venice: Doges Andrea Vendramin, Giovanni Mocenigo
*German Emperor and King of the Romans: Frederick III
*Scandinavia: Christian I of Oldenburg; John (Hans)
*Ottoman Empire: Sultan Mehmet II; Bayezid II
*Persia: Uzum Hasan
*Muscovy: Grand Duke Ivan III

HOUSE OF NICCOLÒ:
Present and Former Company Members:
  Nicholas de Fleury of Bruges, merchant-founder of the now devolved
    European Banco di Niccolò
  Egidia (Gelis) van Borselen, his wife
  Jordan (Jodi) de Fleury, his son
  Manoli, Jordan's bodyguard
  Captain Cuthbert, Jordan's master-at-arms
  Lowrie, steward and chamber-servant to Nicholas
  Mailie and Ella, house-servants
  Michael Crackbene, shipmaster
  Ada, his wife
  Tobias Beventini of Grado, physician
  Clémence de Coulanges, his wife
  John le Grant, engineer, gunner, sailing-master

In Germany:
  Julius of Bologna, lawyer and director
  Bonne von Hanseyck, regarded as step-daughter to Julius through his late
    wife, Adelina de Fleury
  Sister Monika, her companion
  Father Moriz of Augsburg, chaplain and metallurgist
  Govaerts of Brussels, manager

In Venice:
  Gregorio of Asti, lawyer and director
  Margot, his wife
  Jaçon, their son

In Low Countries:
  Diniz Vasquez, director, nephew of Simon de St Pol, q.v.
  Mathilde (Tilde) de Charetty, his wife, step-daughter of Nicholas
  Catherine de Charetty, younger sister of Tilde, also step-daughter of Nicholas
  Marian and Lucia, daughters of Diniz and Tilde

DUCHY OF BURGUNDY:
*Dowager Duchess Margaret of York, widow of Duke Charles of Burgundy,
    sister of King Edward IV of England
*Marie, Duchess of Burgundy and Brabant, Countess of Flanders, Holland,
    Zeeland etc., daughter of Duke Charles by a previous wife
*Bastard Anthony of Burgundy, natural brother of Duke Charles
*Philip of Burgundy, his son
*William Hugonet, lord of Saillant, Époisses et Lys, Viscount of Ypres,
    Chancellor of the Duchy, brother of Cardinal Philibert Hugonet in Rome,
    q.v.
*Hugo vander Goes, Ghent artist

Bruges, Ghent and Lille:
*Anselm (Seaulme) Adorne, Baron Cortachy, ducal adviser, magistrate and
    burgomaster of Bruges, Conservator of Scots Privileges. Offspring include:
*Jan Adorne, oldest son, educ. Paris and Pavia; lawyer with Curia; canon of
    St Peter's, Lille
*Antoon, another son, also canon in Lille
*Maarten, in Carthusian monastery of St Kruis
*Margareta, in Carthusian convent of St Andries
*Lewisje, in St Trudo Convent, Steenbrugge
*Pieter, sheriff and doctor in law in Ghent; married, with daughters
*Anselm, unmarried
*Euphemia, unmarried
*Elizabeth and *Marie, married, without sons

*Arnaud, a younger son of Adorne
*Agnes von Nieuenhove, his wife
*Agnes and *Aerendtken, their children
*Katelijne (Kathi) Sersanders, Adorne's niece
*Robin of Berecrofts, of Scottish merchant family, her husband
  Rankin and Margaret, her children by Robin
  Mistress Cristen, her children's nurse
*Anselm (Saunders) Sersanders, her brother, Adorne's nephew
*John Sersanders of Ghent, their kinsman
*Guy de Brimeu, sire de Humbercourt, military leader and adviser to the late
    Duke on finance
*Paul van Overtweldt of Bruges, Deputy to the Estates-General
*Jean de Baenst, seigneur de St George, former Treasurer of Bruges
*Nicholas Barbesaen, former burgomaster and Treasurer of Bruges
*Martin Purves, former Berwick trader in Lille
*Dr Andreas of Vesalia, physician and astrologer
*Andro Wodman, merchant; former Scots Archer in France; successor to
    Adorne as Conservator of Scots Privileges in Bruges
*Louis de Bruges, seigneur de Gruuthuse, Earl of Winchester, Governor of
    Holland
*Marguerite van Borselen, his wife, 'cousin' of Gelis van Borselen; aunt by
    marriage of King James III of Scotland and his brothers and sisters
*Jean de Gruuthuse, Seneschal of Anjou, their son
*Jean Breydel of Bruges, Councillor and Deputy to the Estates-General

Veere and Middleburg:
*Wolfaert van Borselen of Veere, Count of Grandpré, 'cousin' of Gelis van
    Borselen; once married to the late *Princess Mary, aunt of King James III
    of Scotland
*Charlotte de Bourbon, his second wife
*Anna van Borselen, his oldest child by Charlotte, contracted to marry Philip
    of Burgundy, q.v.
*Paul van Borselen, his bastard son

Dijon:
  The Widow of Damparis, niece by marriage to Enguerrand and Yvonnet de
    Damparis, by Dole, friends of the late Marian de Charetty

SCOTLAND:
Royal Household and Officers of State:
*James Stewart (Third of the Name), King of Scotland
*Margaret, daughter of Christian I of Denmark, his Queen
*James Stewart, Duke of Rothesay, their oldest child
*James and *John Stewart, younger sons

*Mary Stewart, King James's elder sister
*James, 1st Lord Hamilton of Cadzow, her second husband
*Robert, Lord Boyd, father of her first husband
*James (Jamie) and *Margaret Boyd, slighted children of her first marriage
*James, Earl of Arran, and *Elizabeth Hamilton, children of her second marriage
*John Hamilton, Lord Hamilton's eldest illegitimate son
*Elizabeth Hamilton, Lord Hamilton's daughter by his first wife, married to
    *David, Earl of Crawford, q.v.
*Alexander Stewart (Sandy), Duke of Albany, Earl of March, lord of Annandale
    and Man, Admiral of Scotland, King James's brother
*Alexander Stewart, Albany's illegitimate son
*Andrew Stewart, one of Albany's two legitimate sons by his first wife, Cath-
    erine Sinclair, q.v.
*John Stewart (Johndie), Earl of Mar, King James's youngest brother
*Margaret Stewart (Meg), King James's younger sister
*James Stewart of Auchterhouse (Hearty James), Earl of Buchan, half-uncle
    of King James; Chamberlain of Scotland
*John Stewart of Balvenie, 1st Earl of Atholl, Blair Castle, half-uncle of King
    James, married to *Eleanora Sinclair, q.v.
*Andrew Stewart, Bishop-elect of Moray, half-uncle of King James
*Joanna Stewart, deaf and dumb aunt of King James, married to Sir James
    Douglas of Dalkeith, Earl of Morton, q.v.
*Annabella Stewart, aunt of King James, married to George, 2nd Earl of
    Huntly, q.v.
*Andrew (Drew) Stewart, 1st Lord Avandale, Chancellor of Scotland; former
    Warden of the Western Marches; life-rent of earldom of Lennox
*Archibald Whitelaw, Archdeacon of Lothian; Royal Secretary; former tutor
    of King James; graduate of Cologne
*Colin Campbell (MacChalein Mor), 2nd Lord Campbell and 1st Earl of
    Argyll; King's Justiciar and Master of the Royal Household
*William (Will) Scheves, Archbishop of St Andrews after Patrick Graham,
    q.v.; former Dean of Dunkeld; medical graduate of Louvain
*Archibald (Archie) Crawford of Haining, Abbot of Holyrood; Treasurer to
    King James
*Alexander (Alex) Inglis, Lord Clerk Register; Edinburgh and Berwick-
    upon-Tweed
*Patrick (Pate) Leitch, former Rector of the University of Paris; canon of
    Glasgow; Clerk Register after Inglis
*John Laing, Bishop of Glasgow; former Treasurer; Secretary to the late
    Queen-Mother Mary of Guelders; Chancellor after Avandale
*David (Davie) Lindsay, 5th Earl of Crawford; Master of the Royal Household
    after Argyll; sheriff of Forfar; son of Margaret Dunbar, cousin of Euphemia
    (Phemie) Dunbar, q.v.
*Elizabeth Hamilton, his wife, q.v.

*Alexander Lindsay, Master of Crawford, his son
*Sir David Guthrie of that Ilk, captain of the Royal Guard; former Clerk of King's Treasury, Lord Clerk Register and Comptroller
*Master Conrad, physician; tenant of Cousland
*Thomas Smyth, royal apothecary

Landowners:
*William Sinclair, 3rd Earl of Orkney and 1st Earl of Caithness, married firstly to *Elizabeth Douglas, Countess of Buchan, and secondly to *Marjorie, daughter of late *Alexander Sutherland of Dunbeath
*Beatrix Sinclair, his sister, married to the late *James, 7th Earl of Douglas
*Another sister, married to the late *George Dunbar, Earl of March
*Euphemia (Phemie) Dunbar, their daughter, Earl William's niece; formerly of Haddington Priory
*Sir David Sinclair of Sumburgh, Shetland, his illegitimate son; Keeper of Dingwall Castle
*Sir Oliver (Nowie) Sinclair of Roslin and Herbertshire, son of Earl William by his second wife; married firstly to *Elizabeth Borthwick, daughter of Lord Borthwick; secondly to *Isabella Livingstone; and thirdly to *Cristina Haldane; cousin of Phemie
*Elizabeth (Betha) Sinclair, Oliver's full sister, widow of *Patrick Dunbar of Blantyre and Cumnock; former supervisor of Mary and Margaret, King James's sisters
*William, 2nd Earl of Caithness, Oliver's full brother; Justiciar, chamberlain and sheriff for Bishops of Caithness
*Eleanora Sinclair, Oliver's full sister, second wife of John, Earl of Atholl, q.v.; cousin of Phemie
*John Sinclair, another of Oliver's full brothers
*Catherine Sinclair, Oliver's half-sister, daughter of Earl William by his first wife; first wife of Alexander, Duke of Albany, q.v.
*William (the Waster) of Cousland, Dysart and Ravenscraig, Oliver's half-brother and eventual 2nd Lord Sinclair of Newburgh, Aberdeenshire; son of Earl William by his first wife
*Henry Sinclair, son of William the Waster; farmer of Sinclair lordships in Orkney
*Cristina Dunbar, Phemie's sister, married to *Alexander Innes, heir to *James Innes of Innes, north-east Scotland
*William, Thane of Cawdor; Constable of Nairn Castle; trading partner of *Hugh Ross, q.v.
*William Cumming of Inverallochy (Marchmont Herald)
*Cristina Preston, his second wife
*Thomas and *Alexander Cumming, Aberdeenshire kinsmen of Marchmont Herald, q.v.; in business with Thomas (Big Tam) Cochrane and Sir John Colquhoun of Luss, q.v.

*Hugh Ross of Kilravock, Nairn; trading partner of Cawdor

*Patrick Hepburn of Dunsyre, 3rd Baron Hailes, Governor of Berwick-upon-Tweed Castle; sheriff of Berwick; grandson of *Alexander, 1st Lord Home

*Alexander Hepburn of Whitsome, sheriff of Edinburgh

*John Murray of Touchadam, by Stirling, temporary royal captain of Dunbar Castle

*James Shaw of Sauchie, Governor of Stirling Castle and of person of Prince James, Duke of Rothesay

*Robert Lauder of the Bass, Keeper of Berwick-upon-Tweed Castle

*Alexander Lauder

*George, 2nd Lord Seton

*Robert, 2nd Lord Lyle

*Andrew, 2nd Lord Grey, supporter of the Earl of Angus, q.v.

*Sir James Liddell of Halkerston, Creich, Dunbar and Edinburgh, steward to Albany

*William, 3rd Lord Crichton, son of *Janet Dunbar; cousin of Phemie

*Marion Livingstone, his wife

*John Ellem of Butterdene, captain of Dunbar Castle for Albany

*John and *Alexander Trotter, supporters of Albany

*William Dickson, bailie of Peebles and *Patrick, *David and *Thomas, supporters of Albany

*John Jardine of Applegarth and Jardinefield, Berwickshire

*Alexander Jardine, his nephew and subsequent heir

*Alexander (Sander) Jardine of Applegarth, his son, supporter of Angus and Albany

*David Purves, supporter of Albany

*James Gifford of Sheriffhall, kinsman of James Douglas, Earl of Morton, q.v.

*Archibald (Bell-the-Cat) Douglas of Tantallon (Red Douglas), 5th Earl of Angus and lord of Abernethy, married to *Elizabeth, daughter of Robert, Lord Boyd, q.v.

*Sir James Douglas, Earl of Morton and lord of Dalkeith, married to Joanna Stewart, q.v.

*John Douglas of Morton, their son

*Joanne, their daughter, married to Thomas, Lord Erskine, q.v.

*Janet, another daughter, married to Patrick Hepburn of Hailes, q.v.

*Margaret Hepburn, daughter of Janet and Patrick, granddaughter of Joanna Stewart, q.v.

*James Douglas, 9th Earl of Douglas (Black Douglas), son of Beatrix Sinclair, q.v. and cousin of Sir Oliver Sinclair, q.v.; pensioner at English Court

*Robert Douglas of Lochleven, son of *Margaret Erskine; Keeper of castle

*Sir John Colquhoun of Luss, shipowner, trader; chamberlain to the King; former royal Comptroller

*Elizabeth Dunbar, Countess of Moray, Lady of Luss, his wife; cousin of Phemie; claimant with James Shaw, q.v., to Sauchie

*Humphrey Colquhoun, their son

*Sir John (Johnny) Stewart, 1st Lord Darnley, grandson of 1st *Lord Aubigny, cousin of *Bernard Stuart of Aubigny; claimant to earldom of Lennox

*Walter Stewart of Morphie, half-brother of Avandale, q.v.

*Sir John Haldane of Gleneagles, claimant to earldom of Lennox through his wife, *Agnes Menteith; kin to Cristina Haldane, wife of Sir Oliver Sinclair, q.v.

*Sir John (Jock) Ross of Hawkhead, sheriff of Linlithgow and Keeper of Blackness Castle; champion jouster and poet

*Egidia (Gelis) Ross, his daughter, married to James, q.v., son of *Sir James Auchinleck

Jordan de St Pol of Kilmirren, formerly vicomte de Ribérac when royal adviser and merchant in France

Simon de St Pol of Kilmirren, his son

Henry de St Pol, son of Simon's late wife Katelina van Borselen, sister of Gelis van Borselen, q.v.

Isobella (Bel) of Cuthilgurdy, one-time neighbour to the St Pols of Kilmirren

*David Simpson (de Salmeton), former Scots Archer in France, former agent of Jordan de St Pol; agent and Procurator for Prosper de Camulio, q.v.

*Dame Elizabeth Stewart, widow of *Sir William Charteris, Perth

*Robert Colville of Hilton, Clackmannan, seneschal of Queen Margaret

*Malcolm McClery, Queen's legal agent; armiger to Earl William Sinclair, q.v., by whom enfeoffed with Garton-Sinclair, Menteith

*Sir Thomas Semple of Elliotstoun, sheriff of Renfrew; son of Sir William Semple

Oliver Semple, kinsman, once factor to Nicholas at Beltrees

*Sir William Wallace of Craigie, Ayrshire

*James Wardlaw of Riccarton and *John, his brother

*Robert, Lord Fleming and *David and *John Fleming, his grandsons and heirs

*George Gordon, 2nd Earl of Huntly, eldest son of *Alexander Seton, lord of Gordon

*Elizabeth Dunbar, q.v., widowed Countess of Moray, niece of George, Earl of March; cousin of Phemie; Huntly's first (divorced) wife

*Annabella Stewart, q.v., Huntly's second (divorced) wife

*Elizabeth Hay, daughter of William, Earl of Erroll, q.v., Huntly's third wife

*Alexander Gordon, Huntly's son, married to *Joanna, daughter of John Stewart, Earl of Atholl, q.v.

*James Ogilvy of Deskford and Findlater

*Sir Robert Arbuthnott of Arbuthnott, married to a daughter of *John Ogilvy of Airlie

*William, Lord Forbes

*William Hay, 3rd Earl of Erroll, Constable of Scotland

*Alexander Home of Home, grandson of 1st Lord Home

*Patrick Home of Fast Castle
*William, 2nd Lord Borthwick
*James Borthwick, his son, captain of Home Castle
*Thomas (Tom) Kilpatrick, laird of Closeburn, captain of Lochmaben Castle
*John, Lord Kennedy, married to *Elizabeth Gordon, former Countess of Erroll
*William, Lord Ruthven, tenant of Cousland
*William, his son
*Alan, 1st Lord Cathcart
*Thomas, Lord Erskine, sheriff of Stirling, married to a daughter of Joanna
    Stewart, q.v.
  Constantine (Conn) Malloch, Borders landowner
  John and Muriella, children of his late wife
  Benedict (Ben) Bailzie, landowner and merchant
*Angus Og MacDonald of Islay, illegitimate son of John, Lord of the Isles,
    and married to a daughter of Colin, Earl of Argyll, q.v.

Religous:
*Patrick Graham, excommunicated Archbishop of St Andrews
*William Scheves, q.v., his successor
*Bishop Thomas Spens, Bishop of Aberdeen, escort of young Albany and
    Scottish Princesses abroad
*Robert Blackadder, next Bishop of Aberdeen
*James Livingstone, Bishop of Dunkeld
*John Hepburn (Herspolz), Bishop of Dunblane
*Robert Colquhoun, Bishop of Argyll; related to Sir John Colquhoun of Luss,
    q.v.
*John Laing, Bishop of Glasgow; later Chancellor, q.v.
*Andrew Painter, Bishop of Orkney
*John Wodman, Prior of May and Postulate Bishop of Ross; brother of Andro
    Wodman, q.v.
*William Elphinstone, Official of Lothian, Archdeacon of Argyll, Bishop-elect
    of Ross
*Andrew Stewart, Bishop-elect of Moray, q.v.
*Archibald Crawford, Abbot of Holyrood, q.v.
*Abbot Henry Arnot of Cambuskenneth, former King's Procurator in Rome
*Abbot James Crichton, Newbattle Abbey
*Abbot John Brown of Melrose
*Abbot George Shaw of Paisley
*Abbot Andrew Cavers of Lindores
*Abbot Henry Crichton of Dunfermline
*Abbot William Bonkle of Arbroath
*Prioress Euphemia Graham, half-sister of the late *Bishop Kennedy,
    St Mary's Cistercian Priory, Eccles, by Coldstream
*Prioress Elizabeth Forman, Cistercian Priory, North Berwick

*Prioress Elizabeth, Cistercian Priory, Haddington
*Alisia Maitland, nun at Haddington Priory
*Prioress, Cistercian Priory, Elcho, Perthshire
*Sir Edward Bonkle, Provost of the Collegiate Church of the Holy Trinity, Edinburgh
*Alexander Bonkle of Bruges and Edinburgh, his brother; merchant
*John (Jannekin) Bonkle, his illegitimate son; once agent, now churchman
*John Bonkle, his nephew; merchant; briefly Treasurer of Edinburgh
*Master of Soutra
*William (Will) Bell, priest, public notary and Rector of Church of Upsettlington
*Brother John Yare, Guardian of the Minorite Friars in Haddington
*Sir William Knollys of Torphichen, Preceptor in Scotland of the Order of Knights Hospitaller of St John of Jerusalem
*John Knollys, his brother; burgess of Aberdeen
*Robert Knollys, Berwickshire, one of his four illegitimate sons
*Prosper Schiaffino de Camulio de' Medici, Collector for the Apostolic Camera in England, Ireland and Scotland

Traders, Burgesses, Craftsmen and Shipmasters:
*William (Old Will) of Berecrofts, merchant
*Archibald the Younger of Berecrofts (Archie), his son
*Robin, son of Archie and husband of Katelijne Sersanders, q.v.
*Thomas (Tom) Yare, merchant, dealer, bailie and chancellor of Berwick-upon-Tweed; burgess and Treasurer of Edinburgh
*Margaret Home, his wife
*Walter (Wattie) Bertram, merchant of Edinburgh and Leith; Provost of Edinburgh; sailed the *Marie* with Henry Cant, q.v., married to *Elizabeth Cant
*George (Dod) Robieson, Customar of Edinburgh
*James (Jamie) Hommyll, King James's servant, envoy, tailor
*Sir Simon Preston of Craigmillar Castle and Lauderdale, merchant
*Margaret Preston, his sister, married to *Andrew Bertram, brother of Walter, q.v.
*Thomas (Leithie) Preston, shipmaster and merchant; with Tam Cochrane and Master Conrad, q.v., tenant of Cousland under the Sinclairs; also in Middle Pitcairn under Lord Ruthven
*Alison Russell, Leithie's wife, formerly married to *Alan Cochrane of Cleghorn and Grugfoot, Tam Cochrane's brother
*Archibald Preston, Leithie's young son
*Thomas Preston, brother of Sir Simon Preston of Craigmillar
*Cristina Preston, second wife of William Cumming, Marchmont Herald, q.v.
*Agnes (Nanse) Preston, nurse to Prince James, Duke of Rothesay; married to burgess *John Turing

*John Preston, burgess of Edinburgh

*Elizabeth Monypenny, his wife, of Franco-Scottish family

*Thomas (Big Tam) Cochrane, mason, dealer, master of defensive building and artillery movement; Constable of Kildrummy Castle

*Robert (Dob) Cochrane, Tam's cousin; Edinburgh burgess

*Edward (Ned) Cochrane, Renfrewshire kinsman serving John, Lord Darnley, q.v.

*James Cochrane, sheriff-depute of Renfrew

*Andrew Lisouris, lay Brother of Cupar, Fife; King's Carpenter

*Walter and *John Merlioun, master masons

*John Bonar, bombadier, Mill of Dron, Fife; member of artillery family

*Alexander (Alec) Brown of Leith, Colstoun, Ratho and Berwick-upon-Tweed, master of the *Marie* and the *James*, trading to England with Thomas Yare, q.v., and others

*Peter Brown of Colstoun, his brother

*Sir Andrew Wood of Largo, Fife; Leith captain and merchant

*Gilbert (Gibbie) Fish, coiner in Berwick-upon-Tweed, goldsmith; burgess of Edinburgh

*William Goldsmith, 'the Halfpenny Man', moneyer, gun-smelter

*William Tor of Tor, hammerman; descendant of Warden of the Royal Mint

*Matthew Auchinleck, goldsmith, Canongate

*Alan Landells, of moneyer family, former occupant of King's secure Blackness house

*Thomas Mulliken, of Florentine mint masters, in Scotland for three generations

*James MacCalzeane, Edinburgh burgess and goldsmith, and burgess brother *John

Alexander (Eck) Scougal, manager of East Lothian stud of Knights of St John

*John of Scougal, East Lothian, cousin of *John Scougal of that Ilk

*Patrick Flockhart, commander of the Archers of the Guard of the French King

*Thomas Swift, merchant, with great mansion in High Street, Edinburgh

*Dean Walter Swift, his brother; Holyrood chaplain; occupant of former Royal Mint

*Robert Grey, butcher, of Canongate and High Street booths

*Isabel (Isa) Williamson, Tolbooth trader; supplier to King James

Lang Bessie, brewster-wife, High Street tavern

*Hector Meldrum, royal macer, of Canongate and High Street booths

*Henry Cant, merchant with booth in Edinburgh; sailed with Walter Bertram, q.v., and kin to his wife

*John Napier of Merchiston, variously merchant, Provost of Edinburgh, Master of the Royal Household; married to *Margaret Preston; claimant to earldom of Lennox through second marriage to *Elizabeth Menteith, elder sister of Agnes, wife of Sir John Haldane, q.v.

*Janet Napier, of the same family, married to *John Wilson, burgess of Edinburgh

*John (Johnnie) Ramsay, heir and probable son of Janet Napier; married to *Isobel Cant

*Sir Gilbert Johnstone of Elphinstone, King's armiger and future Deputy Constable and sheriff of Edinburgh

*Adam, his son, and *Adam, his brother

*James Russell, associate of Johnstone

*John Heriot of Longniddry, another associate

*James Gullane of Newbattle, another associate

Musicians and Poets:
*William Roger (Whistle Willie), English musician long resident at Scottish Court

*Blind Harry, travelling ballad-maker

*John Reid (Stobo), churchman, royal clerk and poet

*Sir Richard Holland, clerk, poet and English pensioner

*Robert Henryson, law graduate and notary; schoolmaster at Dunfermline

*Sir John Ross of Hawkhead, q.v., poet

*James Auchinleck, poet, husband of Sir John's daughter Gelis, q.v.

ENGLAND:
*King Edward IV, House of York

*Cicely Nevill, Duchess of York, his mother

*Margaret, Dowager Duchess of Burgundy, his sister, q.v.

*Elizabeth Woodville, his Queen

*Cecilia, their third daughter, contracted in childhood to son of King James III of Scotland

*George, Duke of Clarence, King Edward's brother

*Richard (Dickon), Duke of Gloucester, sheriff of Cumberland, Warden of the West March, Admiral of England, George's younger brother

*Anne Nevill, Richard's wife

*Dr Alexander Leigh, canon of Windsor, Almoner to King Edward

*Humphrey, Lord Dacre of Gilsland

*Henry (Harry) Percy, 4th Earl of Northumberland, sheriff of Northumberland, Constable of Bamburgh Castle and Warden of East and Middle Marches

*Anthony Woodville, Earl Rivers, brother of Queen Elizabeth

*Sir Edward Woodville, brother of Queen Elizabeth

*Thomas Grey, Earl of Huntingdon, Marquis of Dorset, son of Queen Elizabeth by her first marriage

*Thomas, Lord Stanley, married to a sister of *Richard Nevill, Earl of Warwick

*John (Jack), Lord Howard, King's lieutenant and captain of main fleet against Scotland

*Sir Thomas Fulford, commander of west coast fleet
 Hector, mason

FRANCE AND LORRAINE:
*William Monypenny, Lord of Concressault, a Scot resident in France; envoy
   of French King
 Bernard de Moncourt, seigneur de Chouzy, by Blois
 Claude d'Échaut, his wife
*Dr John Ireland, Scots scholar resident in France; envoy of the French King
*René II, Duke of Lorraine in succession to his grandfather *René I, Duke
   of Anjou, Bar and Lorraine, Count of Provence

GERMANY, HOLY ROMAN EMPIRE, BALTIC STATES AND TYROL:
*Emperor Frederick III of the House of Habsburg
*Archduke Maximilian of Austria, his son
*Sigismond, Duke of Austria and Styria and Count of the Tyrol
*Eleanor Stewart, his wife, aunt to King James III of Scotland
*Paúel Benecke, Danzig privateer

ROME AND ITALIAN STATES:
*Father Ludovico de Severi da Bologna, Patriarch of Antioch, papal and
   Imperial envoy
*Cardinal Philibert Hugonet, brother of Chancellor Hugonet of Burgundy;
   master of Jan Adorne in Rome
*Josaphat Barbaro, merchant; Venetian envoy to Uzum Hasan of Persia
*Caterino Zeno, merchant; also Venetian envoy to Persia
*Violante of Naxos, his wife
 Nerio, her unacknowledged son
*Catherine Corner, her niece, widowed Venetian Queen of Cyprus
*Charla, *Eugene and *John, natural children of the late King James Lusignan
   (Zacco) of Cyprus
*Marietta of Patras (Cropnose), mother of Zacco
*Lorenzo de' Medici of Florence
*Francesco Nori of Florence, former Medici manager in Geneva
*Tommaso Portinari, former Medici manager in Bruges
*Lorenzo di Matteo Strozzi, merchant in Naples

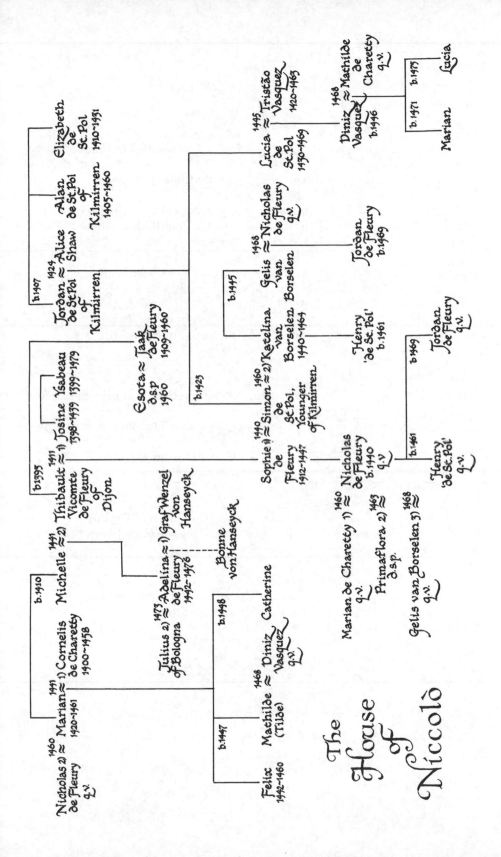

The House of Niccolò

Part I

First rewle thi-self and of thi-self be lord,
Syne rewll thi folk and so it sall accord.

Chapter 1

For euery man desyris naturally
To leir and knaw and heir of novelté

FROM VENICE to Caffa, from Antwerp to the Gold Coast of Africa, merchants anchored their ships and unloaded their cannon and flipped open their ledgers as if in twenty years nothing had changed, and nothing was about to change now. As if old men did not die, or younger ones grow up, eventually. There was no fool in Europe, these days, who treated trade as a joke. All that sort were long sobered, or dead. Or were temporarily unavailable like Nicholas de Fleury, who had removed himself to the kingdom of Scotland, far to the north of the real world of pretty women, and international intrigue, and the benefits of social and financial success.

North of the real world, it was noticed quite soon that Nicholas the Burgundian was back. The first to suffer was the bailie of Berwick, who had a house of three floors and good eyesight, so that he personally observed this big Flemish ship plunging up from the south and bucking round into the mouth of the river. He held his breath until the manoeuvre was finished, for the *Karel of Veere* was the first merchantman to reach Scotland this season, and he had serious need of its news. When the harbour-bell clanged through the gale, Thomas Yare closed his shutters and sent a clerk pelting down to the wharf with an invitation to the *Karel*'s seamaster. Then he had a word with his wife, and strode down through the garden to the red-painted warehouse, where his business room was.

Thomas Yare, an active Scot of burnished acuity, wished to entertain Mick Crackbene of the *Karel* before anyone else. Thomas Yare was bailie and chamberlain of the town of Berwick-upon-Tweed, and the River Tweed was the frontier with England, which meant that one did not bellow sensitive news, even now, in times of miraculous peace. Tom Yare was a native of these parts but, until recently, had earned most of his living in Edinburgh. That was because, until recently, the English owned Berwick. Berwick had switched sides between England and Scotland thirteen times since it was founded. Half its footloose population were spies, and the other half smugglers.

So Yare wanted the big Scandinavian's news for himself. He would get it. They had an understanding. Trade news was worth money. At whatever port they arrived, no matter how high the bribe, Crackbene's men never talked. Unless, of course, first primed by Crackbene. Crackbene or one of the merchants he carried. You never knew who that might be.

There were two with Crackbene today. Pouring ale in his office, Tom Yare heard the footsteps and doubled the number of tankards. When the door thundered back on its hinges and the red-faced master marched in, Yare winced, waved the pitcher in welcome, and then set it down to go forward, hand outstretched. Behind Crackbene was another robust figure of door-cracking capacity: Andro Wodman, the Scots-Flemish consul with his blue jowl and fighting-man's shoulders and twice-broken nose, all of which Yare duly greeted. And behind Wodman approached another of the same breed, heaven help us: so big his furzy brown head and soaked hat barely got past the lintel.

Tom Yare dropped his welcoming hand and also released, very slightly, his business gentleman's smooth-polished jaw as he set eyes on a man he hadn't seen for four years.

Nicholas de Fleury of Bruges. *Ser* Nicholas, do you mind: former banker, former dyemaster, former owner of armies, stepping over nice as a hen and unpeeling a soaked sailing-cloak to stand gazing down (Tom Yare straightened) with that bloody disarming smile and two dimples. They knew one another. The Burgundian had once made the bailie a very fine profit in cod.

The first emotion felt by Tom Yare, and most others, upon meeting Nicol de Fleury, was an urge to be friendly. The next, based on experience, was a heady mixture of horror and glee.

De Fleury said, 'Are you going to be sick?'

Tom Yare, his face warming, recovered. 'Damn you. Why didn't you warn me?'

'I wish I had,' said de Fleury. 'You might have managed something better than ale. *Ale?* Business bad, Tom? Wish you had firm news from somewhere?' It brought back immediately all that fascinated Yare about Nicol de Fleury, and all that he distrusted as well.

'Mick prefers ale,' the Conservator observed, shaking wet from his bonnet. 'Nobody knew you were coming, Nicholas, with your luxurious Persian tastes. How are you, Tom?'

'Dumbfoun'ered,' said Yare with unusual honesty. He opened the door, called an order, and shut it swiftly again. 'Have ye spoken to anyone yet?'

Crackbene's evil smile broadened. The Conservator, Wodman, said, 'What about?'

De Fleury sat down on a coffer, which groaned. 'Can't you guess? He wants to know if the siege of Nancy is over. It is.'

'That's old news,' Wodman said cheerfully. 'He's bound to know that.'

Tom Yare didn't waste time being exasperated. He said, 'There hasn't been a ship from the south since Epiphany. You're the first.'

'It's a good ship, the *Karel*,' said the Scandinavian shipmaster proudly. It was purgatory.

'But you must have had dispatches by road,' Wodman said. 'Wardens' runners. Envoys. Lawyers on business. Wenches with well-informed clients. After all, that's England, over the river.'

'I remember,' said Yare. Men behaved like this, safely landed from sea. Nicol de Fleury behaved like this far too often. Tom Yare was a solid, fit man, but lodged between de Fleury and Crackbene he felt small and thumbed, like a rosary bead. He continued in his soft, deliberate voice, defying the burr in his speech that Margaret always said she found sweet. 'The roads [rhodes] have been closed, and the place is jumping with rumours. Wheat prices are surging already. The word [wuhd] is that there was a disaster at Nancy, and the richest prince in the West is a corpse, with an unmarried lass as his heiress. True [tehoo] or not?'

Someone tapped on the door. Wine came in, and was poured. No one spoke. When the door closed: 'The Duke of Burgundy is officially dead,' de Fleury said, saluting the ceiling and drinking. 'I was there. That isn't a bad little Osey.'

'Tell me,' said Tom Yare. Then he listened to what he was given: the unemotional account of a disaster.

The Grand Prince of the West had been discovered dumped dead in a ditch after a mindless battle with Swiss and Lorrainers. The news had taken a long time to spread. Before de Fleury left Flanders, he had had an audience with the widowed Dowager Duchess, and discussed the future with men of commitment like Gruuthuse, Hugonet and Adorne. For, of course, France would try to reclaim her borders, and the heiress would marry someone who might not suit Flanders at all. So there were implications.

They discussed them. Wodman contributed: he had once been a soldier in France. By the end, Yare had grasped that de Fleury had actually taken part in the fight and been wounded. Most of his companions were dead. Some were captives about to be ransomed, among them two Scots: the gunner John, and that decent young merchant, Robin of Berecrofts, who had also been injured.

Yare said, 'Was Robin hurt bad?' It was the business-man in him that spoke. The noble Anselm Adorne of Bruges bought and sold through his kindred in Scotland, and Robin had wed Adorne's niece. A trading empire was involved.

De Fleury said, 'I don't know. He was shot. It looked serious enough at the time.'

Yare said, 'You'll want to tell his eme and his father in Edinburgh. What else have ye in mind while you're there?'

He was entitled to know. Four years ago, without explanation, the Burgundian had closed all his ventures in Scotland and gone, abandoning the stripling Court which had befriended him. Now he was back, with a trading-ship which belonged to his wife. All the years de Fleury was absent, his wife Gelis had successfully run a good business, as you would expect of a van Borselen of Veere. She had an eight-year-old son by her husband. Tom Yare's own sharp-witted wife admired her acumen, but not what she had heard of her casual marriage. Yare thought de Fleury (in this respect only) a fool. Yare also admired Gelis van Borselen, who was still at home in Bruges and, it seemed, abandoned again. He had met other husbands like this. Men who could sail, but not navigate.

De Fleury hadn't mentioned his wife, except in the context of business. Nor did he now. He said, 'I thought I'd see what was happening. I suppose I'd better report what I've told you. Then I'll probably pick up a cargo and leave.'

Yare said, 'They'll want you to stay.'

'They?' said de Fleury.

'The King. The Council. The merchants. It depends whom you plan to see first.' He let a pause develop unhindered.

De Fleury said, 'Perhaps I should ask your advice about that. As you said, it is sensitive news, and incautious handling could cause damage.'

Yare said, 'What have you heard?'

Wodman glanced at his fellow passenger, but said nothing. De Fleury said, 'Only what reached Bruges before the end of the year. The King's brothers and sisters are young, and occasionally wilful. Sometimes merchants and even envoys find it better to speak first to the older men of the Council, who can then choose the right time to debate the issue with King James or his brothers. But I may have heard wrongly.'

'No,' said Yare. He was aware that he had been spared an explanation he would not have wanted to give. He was bailie of Berwick, but he was also one of the small circle – Scheves, the Prestons, the Sinclairs – who supplied personal service to the royal household; whose ships brought in baby night coats and wine-barrels and salmon, while some of their houses in Edinburgh were grand enough to lodge envoys. He heard a lot of personal gossip and, of course, used it. But he was careful to whom he imparted it.

Now he said, 'What you heard is true. It is a young Court, as you say. The Duke of Burgundy's death raises complex issues which the King's advisers will want to consider.'

'So that perhaps I should see them initially,' de Fleury said. 'But if the King summons me first, there is not much I can do.'

'No,' said Yare. 'Once he knows that you've landed, that is. But you could be sorely held up. It's a bad beat sometimes, north, in this wind.'

'And Mick Crackbene, as we all know, can't set a course. Yes, that's true,' de Fleury said, lifting a brow at his shipmaster.

'If you say so,' the big fair man said blandly. And to Yare: 'I didn't tell you. We've brought your tombstones. Lovely, they are. One for you, one for your lady. Come and see when we get them ashore.'

He promised. As the talk turned to more everyday channels, it occurred to Tom Yare that there was a piece of gossip he should give to Nicol de Fleury. Something heard by Yare's brother the friar, who lived near the Priory that taught the King's youngest sister in Hadding-ton. He would tell de Fleury, in private.

Back on board: 'He didn't notice the chip in the marble,' Nicholas said.

The ship heaved. Wodman said, 'He wasn't really thinking of tomb-stones. He was trying to work out how fast he could get a message to Edinburgh. Whom will he send the news to? The guilds?'

The ship pitched. Nicholas said, 'Christ, Mick: you *have* rigged the sails badly. No. The guilds will come second. First, he'll send to the Lords Three.' They both knew whom he meant. Avandale, Whitelaw and Argyll led the inner council that supported the King. That supported young James and his little wife and the four royal

Gemini

brothers and sisters about whom Tom Yare knew so much that was disquieting.

Mick Crackbene said, 'You mean he'll send to the Council, who will then tell the King that the Duke of Burgundy's dead, and suggest what to do about it? Is that what Yare told you?'

And Nicholas answered, 'As good as. You heard him.' He wished sometimes that Mick were less observant. For many years, the shipmaster had worked, off and on, for Nicholas de Fleury, and sometimes against him, as Wodman had done. But what Yare had said, in that brief aside noticed by Crackbene, had been for no one but Nicholas himself.

Yare had given him news – no, a piece of scandal, which Nicholas was compelled to believe, however unwillingly. He would have to deal with it personally: there was nobody else. But first, he had a weightier errand: to report to the policy-makers of Scotland the facts of the Duke of Burgundy's death. He did not know how long all that would take, or when he could set in train what he had come for, which was not to pick up a cargo. He was not, in fact, perfectly fit; but that would mend. His injuries had been nothing to Robin's.

Landing in Berwick that wild, February day, Nicholas de Fleury had known that he was mad to come back to Scotland, but that it had to be done. And since he had made a computation, as he always did, of all the possible risks, he concluded that the two parties who intended to kill him would not try it at once, but would hope to have some sport with him first.

In which he was wrong.

With the co-operation of the weather, it was not hard to arrive tardily at the harbour for Edinburgh and Nicholas was unsurprised, knowing Tom Yare, to find nobody there but a few unfamiliar harbour- and customs men, who dealt solely with Crackbene, and showed no interest in identifying his patron or passengers. Although it was mid-afternoon, the sky was dim with rain-clouds, and a blustering wind scoured the puddles and seethed over the sandbanks, and collided in spume with the jetties. Officially, they were to stay aboard, with their cargo, until morning. Unofficially, it was conveyed that two persons might land if they wished. Which let Nicholas take Wodman to Edinburgh.

It was only two miles from Leith. Someone hired him a couple of hacks, in a port where once he had had his own stables and lodging. Crackbene's wife stayed in Leith with their children: he didn't know where. Four years ago, he could have named every man in these streets.

Now he and Wodman rode out muffled in scarves, leaving the ship to toss in the gloom of the river-mouth. He had sympathy for the crew, but relied on Crackbene to preserve the fiction that no one had landed. Presumably the harbourmen knew to keep silent. He wondered whether the Council or the Abbot had arranged it, and who would come to escort them to their rendezvous; for obviously someone must come. To arrive unprimed at the portals of Edinburgh would defeat the object of all this performance. Once recognised, he could hardly withhold his news, whatever damage it did.

Out of Leith, the road was a mess. All the land to the north of the river was under the jurisdiction of Archibald Crawford, Abbot of the most important monastery in Edinburgh. The Abbey of Holyroodhouse lay at the foot of the hill on which the King's castle was perched. The town clung to the steep spine between them. He knew every house, every lane in it.

He hadn't been here for four years. He had been growing and changing somewhere else, with different people, speaking a different language. He had never meant to come back, but had done so. Chilled and sore and battered by violent sailing, Nicholas was suddenly positive that he was right to be here; seized by a kind of hope not incompatible with the lunatic joy that he had forced himself to leave. Now he knew what he wanted, and had resolved to bring it about. He meant to succeed.

They had chosen the western, riverside route to the town, because it kept to the Holyrood bailery, and touched the busy hamlet of Bonnington, which led to the Canongate, and was tenanted by yet other Crawfords. Also, being longer, the way was less apt to be plagued, like the Easter Road, with wealthy pack-trains, or ox-wagons stuck in the mud, or by common contingents on foot, rolling their kegs or dragging their sledges of merchandise.

Their chosen path was mostly used by pedestrians, who kept clear of mud-throwing hooves and did not look up as they trudged. To the right was the river, with an occasional mill and its lade, and its service buildings close by, on the rising ground where the thatched cottages huddled. On the left, the ground was rough and uneven, and rose in humps and hillocks towards the high town ahead, with a steep hill between. There were crofts there as well, each with a beaten yard and some hens and a kailpatch among dug-up anonymous workings, or parcels of rough grass and whin and low trees. Nicholas knew what it all was or had been. It had once been his business, and it might be so again, depending on what happened now. He said, 'What d'you think?

I expected someone to collect us by now.' The rain had begun, but the sky was no lighter.

'We're going too fast,' Wodman said. 'We could get to Bonnington and stop at a tavern. You could do with a rest.'

'You stop at a tavern,' said Nicholas. 'If you think you can drink through your scarf. We are meant to be still on board the Christmassy *Karel*, and not spreading good tidings just yet. If you're desperate, I have a flask.'

'I'm desperate,' Wodman said. 'You wouldn't have any food?' In France, he had been a royal Archer, and they were all hearty drinkers and trenchermen. Turned merchant, he made a good, conscientious Conservator, who just happened to know some dangerous people. Nicholas handed over the flask, and dropped his horse's gait to a saunter. The rain rustled down. There was no one on the road at the moment, and nothing to attract anyone either. Between themselves and the river, there were three wattle cabins with smoke drooping down from the heather and childish voices disputing inside. The noise drowned, at first, another sound from behind them, which gradually emerged: he automatically identified it. *Allah-u akbar, la ilaha illa'llah*; the afternoon summons to prayer.

No, of course not: wrong country. Women, singing. Fisherfolk, calling their wares. Sellers, calling buyers to Paradise. *Allah-u akbar*.

Wodman took his mouth from the flask. 'I heard it,' Nicholas said. 'Do you really want food?'

'I don't think so,' said Andro Wodman. The warbling voices were clearer and closer, and there was a rumbling basso beneath. 'Unless they're selling bowls of seethed meat with onions. What are they selling?' They had both turned and stopped to look back. Toiling up the rise was a group of sturdy young people, their faces bright in the rain, hauling sledges behind them. Walled sledges, crowded with hampers.

The wind was from the east. Even without that, you could tell what was in them.

'What about oysters?' Nicholas said. Wodman handed over the flask and jumped down before he did.

There were three sledges, each with two fellows hauling and another couple striding behind. The girls rode with the creels, singing and holding them steady. The men wore skin caps and tunics, with rough over-mantles of felt for the rain. The women were hooded and bundled in hessian and stopped singing as they came up. One of the men delved in a creel and came forward, his hollow hands weighted and dripping.

The oysters in them were the finest Nicholas had ever seen: the sensitive shells, thin as a porcelain rose-leaf, slowly closed as he watched. 'They like to be serenaded,' the man observed. 'If you will sing to them, they would surely re-open, my lord.'

Nicholas laughed a little, for the voice was educated, and the discreet device to attract them was plain. A clerk, a servant of Church or of state, had at last arrived to collect them. The girls, who remained crouched with the creels, were no doubt genuine.

Wodman had realised it also. Dismounting, amused, he was accepting the gift with bravura. Nicholas gathered his reins to do likewise. The same well-spoken man smiled, and stepped round to help him, still speaking. 'But you will need something to open them with.'

The something was naked steel, flashing from under the felt and driving expertly upwards.

It was so fast that only instinct could help. As Nicholas swerved, he shouted to Wodman. They hadn't indulged in an escort, but they weren't crazy enough to have come on this ride unprotected. The swordpoint bit into his cloak and grated across the cuirass underneath, bringing the swordsman close for a moment, his face blank with surprise. Nicholas kicked him under the chin, so that he blundered back and hit someone else while Nicholas dragged out his own sword. The horse wasn't his, but it was a powerful beast and alarmed enough to be ready to rear. Nicholas wrapped the reins round one wrist and hauled, using the bit to drag the horse threshing on to its haunches, and then allowing it to plunge forward kicking again. It couldn't last very long, but at least he didn't fall off, and enjoyed the whistling sound his blade made as he slashed it down on one side, then the other as the oystermen mobbed him. He could hear Wodman making loud breathless noises, but couldn't see him, which meant he hadn't managed to remount. He tried to steer towards him, but it was like jousting in a cone of molasses. Too many men. And he was not at his best.

It was now very noisy, with a lot of shouting and cursing and the flat sound of steel against steel from his blade and Andro's. All their assailants seemed to have weapons. There were three less than there had been: two fell back, bloodied, and someone was screaming continuously. Far from summoning help, the uproar had probably frightened off every traveller for miles. Jolting about in the saddle, fending off the blows to his legs and his horse and the inventive characters who wished to mount up behind him, Nicholas kept track of the sound of Wodman's swordplay, and heard his yell of triumph as someone was spitted. He had never fought beside Wodman before, and was glad to have the benefit of an expert. He wondered if Wodman were wishing he hadn't come.

He fell off, finally, because they stabbed the horse under him and he wasn't expecting it, this being an action profoundly alien to professional robbers. His horse wasn't wearing a cuirass. Nicholas hurled himself off as it staggered, with his sword in one hand and the wine-flask in the other, unstoppered. One man got the force of his shoulder, and two others the remaining wine full in the face while he located where Wodman was and crashed into him, back to back. Wodman said, 'About time.' He was covered with blood, but his sparse teeth gleamed: he was happy. They had been about fifteen to two. Fewer, if you left out the girls, screaming, crouched in the sledges. A lot fewer now, when you reckoned the men on all fours in the road, and even one who looked dead. Say eight to two.

It was worrying, for the fact was that they themselves both ought to be dead. The first man had certainly meant to disable him, but no one had tried to do more – and with those odds, and his shortcomings, it should have been easy. So it wasn't a personal matter. Not handsome David de Salmeton, and his private grudges. Not a minion of the St Pol family, which had thrown de Salmeton out of its business, but shared his hatred of Nicholas de Fleury. Just someone who wanted a ransom, and assumed he was rich, and worth a lot more than a horse. Or perhaps he wasn't the target at all. He said, panting, 'Have you bedded anyone you shouldn't have lately?'

'I was trying to remember,' Wodman said. He was slowing.

If they could get to the cabins . . .

They couldn't hide in the cabins. There were children there.

They were being forced towards the cabins. Their assailants wanted them there. They were going to be killed, but at leisure. Wodman suddenly swore.

'I know,' Nicholas said. 'Any suggestions?' It emerged in gasps, for his strength had suddenly gone, and he had no reserves. His limbs belonged to somebody else, and one eye was shut, he trusted not permanently. With mixed hope and dread, he caught sight of a flash from the cabins: one of the low doors had opened, and men were running out, carrying weapons. Several men. Enough almost to balance the odds. Wodman said, 'Oh deary dear.'

And it was Oh deary dear. The newcomers hurtled straight to the sledgers and joined them. Nicholas was cross enough to try quite hard to kill one or more, but this time he had no real strength, and neither had Wodman. In the end there was too much against them, and it finished quite soon. They were disarmed and flung on the ground, their cuirasses shed, while someone brought rope-lengths to bind them. One or two others embarked on a kicking, which he unwisely resisted. He saw Wodman doing the same. Then the kickers were stopped by a new voice, very gentle, speaking half in English, half in a language Nicholas de Fleury had known all his life.

'*Mais non!*' it said. 'You must not let them die yet. Foolish men! There is no hope of rescue. Who will interfere in a fisher-feud? Everyone knows the mettle of oystermen; how those who own the scalps of Inchkeith will fight the dredgers of Musselburgh. The men who walk this path later will find broken sledges, and blood, and two wayfarers who became sadly embroiled in the dispute. But they will never, of course, find the oystermen.'

The French was irreproachable, with an accent as familiar to him as his own, although it was not Burgundian. The speaker was one of the girls from the sledge, cloaked and hooded in hessian over a fine gown of green. He could not see her face. He could not speak.

Wodman said, 'You didn't even fight, you. You set fifteen on two. If we die, we die with honour at least.' He spoke in English, so that all the others could hear.

Nicholas used English also. Sitting stiff with his bound hands before him, he sustained the gaze of the invisible face with his one unbloodied eye and spoke in a clear, level voice. 'You have planned well, but not well enough. There are men coming to meet us who will not be deterred by a fight, but will feel it their duty to stop it. Also, Andro Wodman is a royal official, Conservator of Scots Privileges in Bruges and the King's familiar squire. The King will not rest until his killer is found.'

'In which case,' said the girl, 'the deed had better be done indoors.'

'But not by you,' Nicholas said. 'You devised this, but others will hang. What will you do when the bailie or the King's men arrive? Are there horses for everyone? Look, your men are worried already.'

It was true. One man had glanced at another. Their momentum was failing. Nicholas addressed the girl evenly. 'There is my sword. Kill me yourself.'

Wodman growled. Even the sodden ground beneath him seemed to stir with unease. The rain stuttered on the uneven group round about them, and on those who had left it, unbidden, to search out the dead and the wounded. The other girls had all gone.

One of the girl's henchmen looked up. A single horseman was racing towards them; not by the road but crosswise, over the hillocks. He was shouting a warning.

Nicholas said, 'The bailie's men are coming. I told you.' The ground was vibrating. It was obvious that he was speaking the truth, even before the outrider arrived.

The girl said, 'Get the horses.' So the mounts had been concealed in advance. As he had said, it had all been well enough planned. If you had resources, you could arrange matters. The men ran; the girl stayed. She had picked up the sword. She had capable hands.

Wodman said, 'Damn you. If she kills you, she's got to kill me as well.'

'But that would be an injustice,' Nicholas said. She had come to stand at his side. The sword, gripped in both hands, reflected into her face, which was swathed to the cheekbones under the hood. All he could see were her eyes, fringed, wide and lovely. All he could hear in his mind was her soft, husky voice. Nicholas said, 'I could have killed you, but I didn't.'

'Because you are a coward,' she said. 'Which I am not.' And slowly raised her arms holding the sword.

Nicholas kept his eyes open, upon her. Kept his single eye open. It seemed fitting that, at this, the ultimate moment of his preposterous life, he should be staring one-eyed at his killer. Like his captain, Astorre, who had died for the Duke. He was probably about to meet Astorre in Hell, and be lectured into eternity about military privies and pasties and women. She might not have time to kill Wodman.

She didn't have time for anything. Her own hired leader, now mounted, had lingered. As she gripped and aligned the sword, the man swore and flung his horse back towards her. She turned, swinging the sword, but he avoided it. Instead, stooping, he grasped her and swept her aside, so that the sword fell and she was pulled away screeching at his flank. He bent and hauled her up into the saddle, and then spurred off, fast, after the others. They took the way towards Edinburgh. The man was not a philanthropist: he simply didn't intend to be named by some frightened employer.

A moment later, the bailie's horsemen breasted the rise and slowed and stared, as well they might, at the trampled mud, the cottages with their imprisoned, screaming inhabitants, and the Conservator of Scots Privileges and Nicol de Fleury trussed and half stripped and blood-stained at their feet.

The bailie said, 'My lords! What has happened? The Abbot expects you!'

Nicholas said thinly, 'A case of mistaken identity. You saved us. A little salve and fresh clothing, and we shall not disappoint the Abbot, I hope.' Every bone ached.

He avoided looking at Wodman. Wodman maintained a welcome silence all the time they were being untied, and Nicholas was blocking auxiliary questions, and inventing explanations as they occurred to him. They were given horses and cloaks and some temporary patching, until the bailie's own household could tend them. The Abbey Farm of Broughton was not very far.

In public, Wodman didn't utter a word. Wodman was forty, and could pass for being exhausted. In private, he waited until they were riding together. Then he said, 'It wasn't a girl.'

'No,' said Nicholas, whose digestive organs were obeying him once again. 'But pretty enough to pass for one. He tried to kill me in Cyprus, and I let him escape. Didn't you recognise him, your old colleague David de Salmeton? You would have, when he flung back his cloak in that hut.'

He didn't have to explain. Wodman knew why Nicholas had come back to Scotland, and had promised to help him. To track down some gold. To end a family feud. To kill a man who meant to kill him. A French-speaking one-time royal Archer called David de Salmeton.

Wodman said, 'You thought he wouldn't attack to begin with. You thought he would play with you first.'

'I was wrong,' Nicholas said.

'But you didn't denounce him to the bailie?'

Nicholas said, 'What, without any proof? Could you swear that was David de Salmeton?'

There was a long pause. 'No,' said Wodman.

'No. And neither could I. But now I am warned. Now I know what precautions to take. And it isn't all loss.'

'No?' said Wodman.

'No. They're bringing the sledges. Are you hungry?' Nicholas said.

He knew, without looking at Wodman, that the words they had just exchanged were like the steps in a dance: a formality. For him, they were bleaker than that. He was watching the sledges jump and slew at the heels of the horses, their creels roused to a silvery rattle, their spillings dancing from timber to timber and sprinkling the unwinding roadway like rose-leaves.

Or like the living creatures they were, male and female at once; lust and tenderness embraced in one heart; each now shut and alone in its shell, because the singing had stopped.

Chapter 2

Get I a gud man as I had in-deid,
Aye of his ded suld I be in dreid.

ARCHIBALD, ABBOT of Holyrood, said, 'You don't look very well,' and handed over some wine. Simply attired, within the privacy of his own chamber, in cap and gown, cross and rosary, he might have passed for an exceptionally well built, brown-haired monk of middle years, until you noticed the provenance of his crucifix, and the coats of arms (gules, a fess ermine), on the ceiling. The side table was covered with grit.

'I don't look well?' Nicholas said, taking the cup, which was solid gold, in the hand that didn't hurt. 'I can't think why. Nancy? The God-awful voyage from Bruges? The little skirmish with fifteen armed robbers? The flaying I've just had from Master Secretary Whitelaw and my lord of Avandale and Colin Campbell of Argyll his own self, at all at all?'

'You don't have the Gaelic? Then learn it, don't treat it lightly,' the Abbot said equably. 'And don't get angry with me. They were only doing their job. They have to be sure, before they decide how to tackle the King. Sure of you, sure of your news, and Wodman's.'

Wodman was in the infirmary, being inspected. There had proved to be a break in his arm as well as his nose. His nose had been broken so often already, it didn't matter. It had been an interesting fight. Wodman had said, once it was over, 'You're not bad,' which was kind of him. As soon as he was repaired, they must make their way back on board ship, as if they had never left it. And tomorrow the King would hear of their presence, and would summon him, to question him about the Duke of Burgundy's death.

The Abbot said, 'Drink up, Nicol. It was never going to be easy, coming back. You made good friends, and left them too suddenly. But I hear you and your wife are reconciled?'

Wodman's rambling tongue, damn him. Nicholas said, 'We were only apart because I was travelling.'

'But you're going to settle together? Here?'

'It depends,' Nicholas said.

'I imagine it does,' the Abbot said. 'You fell out with the St Pols. You know the old man is back at Kilmirren? And he comes here to his town house as well. I'm not having blood and battery break out because you and he are discussing your demerits.'

'He didn't set the robbers on us,' said Nicholas.

'But you know who did? And if you stay here, you'll kill them?'

'No, I won't,' Nicholas said. 'If I stay here, I'll have enough to do managing the King and his family, from all that I hear. Or am I wrong?' He had asked a lot of people about the five royal siblings of Scotland, because he had known them when they were young. Adorne's account had worried him most. Adorne knew a surprising amount, being well briefed by his nephew, Anselm Sersanders, who lived in Scotland and represented Flemish merchants. He was going to have to see Sersanders. And others.

The Abbot said, 'What more do you wish to know? They are not children now. The King is out of his minority, and the Queen is nineteen. Even the lady Margaret is old enough now to be at Court.'

'I heard,' Nicholas said.

'Yes. Then you remember Mary, the King's elder sister, who once stayed with Anselm Adorne. She is little seen, being in the west with her children, and having the advice of her noble husband, mature in years. While he lives, all is well.'

'And the other two?' Nicholas said.

'You heard Master Secretary Whitelaw,' said the Abbot. 'My lord John of Mar, sadly, is no less wild at eighteen than before, and sometimes defeats all we can do. The King's oldest brother is as he was when you befriended him. That is, he is of middling understanding, but can be persuaded to act responsibly on occasion. The King and he do not always agree, but he has the affection of the ladies Mary and Margaret his sisters. He is a man who needs friends.'

He was talking of Alexander, Duke of Albany. Red-haired, impressionable Sandy, now aged twenty-three. Thirteen years younger than Nicholas. And he was repeating what had already been said, obliquely, by the Lords Three in that hair-raising interrogation just now. 'My young lord was once fond of your company, Messire de Fleury. Is it a relationship you aspire to resume?' Well, in fact, yes.

He still hadn't found out what he wanted. Nicholas said, 'I hear the King can be moody.'

The Abbot did not look unduly disturbed. 'He has come into authority. You will notice a difference. And yes, occasionally he will give way to passion. The Archdeacon – you remember Scheves? He also went to Louvain – has some excellent palliatives, should his grace become over-excited.'

Nicholas said, 'All the students got over-excited at Louvain, but I don't recall any palliatives. I suppose we provided our own. Is his grace calm at the moment?'

'Perfectly,' said the Abbot. 'But this is why weighty news requires to be serenely and clearly presented. Tomorrow, you will explain to him with great care all the recent events in Burgundy, and answer his questions immediately.'

'If I can,' Nicholas said. 'So you think I shall be summoned tomorrow?'

'I know you will. But you will do very well. And we shall be there. He is still at the Castle.'

Nicholas knew that. The dust here in Holyroodhouse came from the rebuilding of the royal household's lodgings, which they so often preferred to the windy fort on the ridge-top. Crossing the courtyard to come here, he had had to avert his face, there were so many masons and workmen he knew. Everyone in Scotland seemed to have building-fever. Construction men travelled from palace to palace in jolly companies, like some new, free-drinking monastic order. The Abbot said, 'If you decide to stay, we might find a room here until your family comes. My lord of Albany often uses these lodgings, and even the Queen and her babes.'

And that was too much. Nicholas said something under his breath, which was still all too audible. Then he apologised. His fingers ached, and his guts.

Crawford said, 'At least you excused yourself this time. You are too free with your expletives, my son.'

'I am sorry, Father,' he said.

Father.

The Abbot said, 'No, you are not yourself. You should have gone to the infirmary. I shall send for a potion. Take it once you are safely on board.' And, turning his head: 'Here surely is the Conservator, ready to leave.'

It wasn't Wodman who entered. It was the Abbot's servant, reporting a visitor. And the visitor, it being the God-awful day that it was, proved to be Archibald, Master of Berecrofts. That well-liked merchant, father of Robin, who had found out that Nicholas was here, and could tell him about Robin, and Nancy.

Archie came in very slowly, a neatly made man in his mid-thirties. He and Nicholas had been fellow traders and neighbours through all the nine years during which Nicholas had chosen to inflict himself periodically on Scotland. Nicholas had built his office and home on Berecrofts land in the burgh of the Canongate. When Nicholas left, Berecrofts had bought it back, and taken Sersanders as lodger. Nicholas thought he knew Archie well. He had never seen him so unnaturally pale.

Nicholas rose and spoke without waiting for niceties. 'I have no recent news, Archie, but none, either, that's worse than we know. Robin took a hackbut shot in the battle at Nancy. We were afraid he was dead. Then the message came through that he was safe, but a prisoner. John le Grant, my gunner, is with him. Julius and Tobie have now gone to Lorraine with the ransom. You know them. Julius was my lawyer, and Tobie is one of the best physicians in the world. They will bring him back to Bruges. Kathi is there, with the children. And Adorne. And my own wife, and the whole of the business to call on.'

'I should go to him,' said Robin's father. He sat.

Nicholas dropped to a stool at his knee. 'Take my ship. But you might miss him, if he's already on his way home.' He stopped and said, 'I have letters for you from Kathi. For you and her brother.'

'It would be better for Robin to come,' Archie said. 'To run his business from Scotland. Yare told me the news about Burgundy. I've not to repeat it.'

'That the Duke is dead? It'll be known by tomorrow,' said Nicholas. 'But yes, Flemish trade will take time to settle, especially in Bruges. I'd trust Kathi to decide what is best.' He kept out of his voice everything that he was feeling and thinking. That he would trust Kathi with his life and had trusted her, before and after she had married Robin. That Kathi knew why he was here, and that his enemies were hers and Robin's as well. David de Salmeton had a score to settle against Robin of Berecrofts and his wife Kathi.

Despite that, Kathi might – would – bring Robin home, because it was right that he should be home, in the care of his father and grandfather. So Kathi, like Gelis, was trusting him to clear the way for them all. At which he was not doing particularly well. He said, 'What about the old man, your father?'

Archie looked vaguely up. 'He's frail. He's mostly at Berecrofts these days, or in the west. I've said nothing to Sersanders yet, Kathi's brother. He's here, in the Canongate.'

'You'd better tell him,' Nicholas said. 'I'll come and to see you both anyway.'

Their voices were flat. They were talking for talking's sake. It was still a shock when, without warning, Archie cried out.

'*Where did it hit him?* Could you not have –'

He broke off. Then he said, 'Nicol, I'm sorry.'

The Abbot spoke, his voice kind. 'Nicholas was struck unconscious himself, as I understand it, by the same men who felled Robin. Two of the Duke's sons are prisoners – the Grand Bastard and his half-brother. They'll be well looked after together in Nancy.'

Nicholas pulled himself together, and added all that he could. 'Robin is a fine soldier, Archie. I've never seen a man so in his element. It was sheer bad luck he was hurt. We surprised some mercenaries hunting for booty. I saw him hit in the thigh.' He didn't say any more about it than that, or mention that there had been more than one shot. The boy, Kathi's husband, was twenty.

'Oh, my laddie,' said Archie; and brought up his clenched hand, and wept. When the Abbot signed to him, Nicholas left.

The *Karel of Veere* was where they had left her, but the wind had died down, and the grumbling. Most of her modest complement of mariners were asleep.

Crackbene was gambling against himself in the cabin. 'Christ!' he said, starting up, as Nicholas and Wodman came in.

'You use too many expletives,' said Nicholas. 'The Council didn't like us. They punched us and sent us off home.'

Ignoring that: 'You were set upon?' Crackbene said. 'By the St Pols or de Salmeton? How did they know you were here?'

He hadn't thought of that. Wodman had. He said, breaking a journey-long silence, 'The monks of Newbattle Abbey have gift-land in Leith. Religious men get to hear secrets.'

'But –' said Crackbene.

'But,' said Nicholas, 'David de Salmeton is very religious these days. He's Procurator, isn't he, to the Papal Legate? While pursuing his usual business in Scotland?'

'So it was dear Davie behind it?' said Crackbene. 'By God, I'll give him new battle.'

'I'm sure you will,' Nicholas said. 'And Andro agrees. And now, since we have a big day tomorrow, we'd both like to get to our beds.'

Before he lay down, he tossed off the mixture the Abbot had given him. He felt Wodman's stare on him then, and all the time he was trying to sleep. To hell with Wodman. Expletive.

By first light next morning, as a matter of instinct, everyone in Leith was aware that Nicholas de Fleury had come in with a ship. Whatever they thought of him, no canny Leither would fail to explore this phenomenon. Indeed, the sociability began before dawn, when Crackbene elected to begin unloading the cargo by lantern-light, and the ship shuddered with bumping and shouting.

By the time the sun rose, Nicholas had greeted three merchants, two tavern-owners, a number of fishermen and a man he had last seen in Danzig. He learned from his former landlord that there might be some rooms with a yard, if he wanted them. There was even a warehouse. He was asked what he had been doing, what he was going to do, and how his wife was. He replied with every appearance of truth, and added a crop of very new serial jokes, which he knew would reach Edinburgh before he did, since instant transmission was of the essence with jokes. If they had worked Duke Charles into a motto, the news of his death would have got here like lightning.

On the wharf, they took him aside and asked him if he had been in a fight with the Conservator, and the Conservator, overhearing, joined them and said, No, the only fight had been with that rolling tub of a ship and the poor ale they'd had to put up with. People thrust Hamburg beer upon them. They sent a boy for a loaf and two capons and worked their way back to the ship, ducking and veering as heavy articles thumped to the ground. The jetties were much better kept than when he used to come here. Other things had changed. Once he had disembarked here and the King's brother had been waiting to greet him.

Things hadn't changed. Except that this time Nicholas was on the wharf, and Sandy stood at the top of the gangplank. Alexander, Duke of Albany, Lord High Admiral, Earl of March, lord of Annandale and of Man, looking mean and royal and venomous, with all last summer's freckles yellow as jaundice on his red-head's fair skin, and Crackbene behind him, transmitting an instant non-joke on the lines of *Watch out*.

The King's brother said, 'Am I to be kept waiting all day? I ordered some goods.'

'Pepper, velvet and a pair of Milanese daggers. They will be brought at once, my lord,' Nicholas said. He sounded breathless. 'Your lordship wishes to take them?'

'Of course not. I wish to see if I will accept them,' Albany said. 'Do I know you?' He had dressed rather quickly. The cloak was superb but, between doublet and riding boots, he wore yesterday's silk evening hose.

Nicholas said, 'Nicholas de Fleury, of the former House of Niccolò, my lord.' He paused. 'It is several years since we met.'

'Is it?' said Sandy. 'I am sure merchants come and go. Where are my purchases?' He had flushed. Behind him his factor, Liddell, had come forward, then paused. On the wharf, the crowd about Nicholas had fallen into respectful and attentive silence. Wodman had stood as if frozen, then vanished.

Nicholas said, 'I shall fetch them myself. Perhaps the master might have the honour of seating your lordship in his cabin?'

There was an eddy behind him. A young voice cried, 'The ship stinks! Don't do it, Sandy. They'll give you cheap wine while they're falsifying the scales. Who's this?'

It was John, Earl of Mar, Albany's brother. Standing offensively close, he peered upwards, examining Nicholas. The youth had a short, Flemish nose, a red-bristled jaw and a rash. He said, 'Oh, my mistake, brother. It's the tame ox you used to think charming. Do go. I'll help burn your clothes after.'

He turned, grinning, to Albany, whose hand was clenched on the rail of the gangway. To one side, Wodman had reappeared with a sign. Beside him was the Keeper of the King's own lodgings and arsenal in Leith. Nicholas turned his head back to Albany. 'My lord of Mar is quite right: the ship is not fit. May I bring the goods to the Wark?'

'No. I don't want them,' Albany said. He stepped back, snatching his hand away quickly as his brother unexpectedly sprang up the same gangplank and whirled to bend his bright eyes on all the curious faces below him. The younger man laughed.

'Maybe not,' said John of Mar fondly. He surveyed the crowd. His manner, blithely adjusted, recalled that of a moneychanger about to announce a new rate. He addressed them all, raising his voice. 'But don't you know, men, that this is the first ship out of Bruges since the Duke died? Come and see what it's brought! You can name your own price, or none! No one's going to complain – there's no one to complain to. Come and take what you want!'

The crowd stared. There began an undertow of movement and comment, developing fast into something like a commotion. From its midst, several voices shouted a query. 'For certain sure, the Duke of Burgundy's dead?' Windows opened. On the river, men hopped from boat to rocking boat to land where they could listen.

The youth turned. 'Didn't you know? You'll never get rich if you never take chances. What's that load on the wharf?' He jumped down and, striding across, thrust his sword through a cluster of bales. Several collapsed, spewing white sparkling powder. 'Alum! Who wants some cheap alum?'

'Anyone who wants to be excommunicated,' said Nicholas, using his full speaking voice for the first time. He stepped up beside Albany and turned. 'All those goods belong to the Pope. Look at the seal. Ask the Papal Legate. And the consignment over there belongs to me.'

'This paltry parcel?' said Mar and, jabbing, tossed it in the air. Then he coughed.

He coughed quite a lot, between sneezes, his eyes closing. The circle round him retreated, and someone started to laugh. Mar snatched at his sword, and abandoned it to search with one hand for a house-wall. His head jerked and his upper lip glistened. The contents of the sack, following the wind, pursued and enfolded him, and the ensuing explosions brought to mind a measured attack by good hackbutters. Albany was looking at Nicholas.

Nicholas said, 'I'm sorry. Your pepper.' He was smiling a little. Somewhere, he could hear a distant command, and the sound of trampling feet, coming from the arsenal of the Wark. The crowd, already upwind, began discreetly to melt.

Albany said, 'No. It is for me to apologise. That was supposed to be a secret. The Duke of Burgundy's death.'

Below, solicitous men had surrounded Mar and were guiding him to the Wark. By the time he had recovered, the cargo would be secure. Nicholas said, 'Some fool always upsets the market. It will correct itself. Shall I find the rest of your goods?' He had dropped the extreme formality, but not the courtesy due to a prince.

Albany said, 'You can't be surprised. I meet a thousand people a day.' He was not talking of Mar.

Nicholas said, 'I should have been more surprised had you remembered me. I probably shan't stay very long. You may have heard, I have no banking interests now. I am free to go where I choose.' Albany had walked down to the wharf, and he followed, with the factor, James Liddell. He could hear Crackbene issuing orders and see Wodman, far off, doing the same.

Albany said, 'I expect you know something of what is happening in Burgundy. The King ought to hear, and as soon as possible. My goods can wait.'

'I don't have a horse,' Nicholas said. 'If my lord will allow a moment to –'

'Take John's,' Albany said. 'He owes me for the pepper.' He glanced at Liddell, who quietly moved off to manage matters. Albany paused, eyeing Nicholas, his manner still stiff. 'You are bruised? It was a violent journey?'

'No,' Nicholas said. 'That is, yes. But now it is over.'

Before he left, he told Wodman where and with whom he was going. He had changed his outer dress quickly, and unearthed his unicorn collar. He had nothing to fear this time from thieves. Wodman said, 'Great God, man, I couldn't believe it. It's started already?'

'Why not?' Nicholas said. 'You lay a plan, then you follow it.' Ever since Albany appeared, he had been cheered by Wodman's expression.

'Oh, surely, surely,' said Wodman, wiping the bewilderment from his face. 'Like you laid a plan to get us both half murdered yesterday. They made you sing to the oysters, all right. And what about Mar? *That* wasn't your plan.'

'No. *That* was a stroke of luck,' Nicholas said.

It was reported in Flanders, that February, that the Duke of Burgundy had received a solemn church burial in Nancy, close to the ditch where he fell, the ceremony being attended by his recent opponent, the young Duke of Lorraine, respectfully sporting a waist-length beard of gold thread. In the same month, the King of France's armies occupied Picardy, and began to march into Artois.

There was no word of the prisoners of Nancy, and Robin of Berecrofts had yet to come home to his wife.

Awaiting him, Katelijne Sersanders, aged twenty-three, had moved with her children into the Hôtel Jerusalem, the great mansion of that elegant man, her uncle, Anselm Adorne, whose own surviving sons and daughters were now grown, and elsewhere.

She did not delude herself that he wished his household better run, or to be diverted by the prattle of children. No one could have maintained a great house better than Margriet his wife, who had borne him sixteen infants and, dying, left a régime that ran sweetly still, five years later. Accordingly, lodged out of sight with Mistress Cristen, her nurse, and her family, Kathi devised and maintained a life that was busy, but separate from his. But when France stood to arms, and the fires of dissent and revolt began to flicker through the leaderless Burgundian states, she was glad to be here for her uncle.

Those were the weeks when the little Duchess was held fast in Ghent and, desperate to raise a fresh army, made lavish undertakings to her towns, while swaying in private between the policies of her late father's wife and high officers. One of the latter was Louis de Gruuthuse of Bruges. Another was his trusted Chancellor and hers, William Hugonet. In the initial, cautious approaches to France the little Duchess employed the brains and experience of both, as well those of Wolfaert van Borselen of Veere, who was the brother of Gruuthuse's wife.

These were all friends of Anselm Adorne, and the problems of Bruges were both his and theirs. Shuttling between Bruges and Ghent; returning angered and drained by the narrow-mindedness, the greed, the confusion, Adorne found in Kathi the most patient of listeners, and one who had admired him from childhood for his intelligence, and his looks, and his integrity.

She was glad to be there. And as a further consideration, she was where the first news from Nancy would come.

She was not without support or distraction. The children loved Clémence, who came often, and had been nurse to Jodi de Fleury before marrying Master Tobias, now gone to help ransom back Robin. So, while she spent time with the children, Clémence was ready to talk also of Robin, and Tobie, and Julius, whom Tobie had taken with him. But Julius, of course, had no wife now to worry over him.

Before leaving for Scotland, Nicholas de Fleury had told Robin's wife all he could remember of the shots which had caused Robin to fall. Tobie, also present, had been alarmed by his frankness, Kathi thought. Nevertheless, after a moment, he had quietly taken Nicholas through his account once again and then, after clearing his throat, had explained the kind of damage such wounds might inflict. He was a military doctor, and could quote lucky and unlucky cases.

She had wept in the end, but in a way it was over: she had nothing left to imagine. And it meant something to her that Nicholas had thought her strong enough to bear the whole truth, and that Tobie, who had not been so courageous, yet recognised that Nicholas was right, and had treated her with enlightenment in his turn. And if she knew the nature of the unhappiest outcome, she also knew what to expect of the best. She had a son and a daughter, the elder just two. Robin had wanted a house full of sons.

Kathi had another friend, too, in Gelis van Borselen at the Hof Charetty-Niccolò, home of the Bank and dyeworks which Nicholas de Fleury had formerly owned, and where his wife and son, Jodi, still lived. Kathi went there, on the day she heard that Dijon had fallen to France. Dijon, encompassing Fleury, from which Nicholas took his name, if nothing else. Being in Scotland, he would not even know it had gone.

Gelis, who had been working with ledgers, put the last one away and came to sit down. Viewing herself from the outside, as ever, Kathi was entertained once again by the contrast they made: herself small, brown and sinewy, and indefatigably active, and Gelis fair and supple and shining, and never visibly active at all, while all the time quartering Flanders on behalf of the business. The owner now was Diniz Vasquez, to whom it had fallen three years ago, when Nicholas had divested himself of his holdings. Nicholas had then taken himself to other lands, from which act of understandable but wilful stupidity he had come back, altered, to resume his marriage to Gelis.

To begin his marriage. Even now, weeks after he had left, you could see the incandescence in Gelis: the fires that had been lit in the short time she and Nicholas had had together. They had burned for Nicholas, too; and for that, Kathi was deeply thankful. She did not wish to imagine the force of will it must have taken to sever himself from that haven; to walk away knowing that, once in Scotland, he might not live to return.

And yet – she underrated him, to think of him like that. However fierce his longing for home, he would, characteristically, find some zest in what he was doing, create something worth while, because he could not help it. He was there because he owed Scotland something. Driven by personal hurt to extremes, he had used the most sophisticated of his gifts against a community, simply in order to injure a single family – the St Pols of Kilmirren – which had caused hurt to himself and his mother. Once, when he was a boy, Nicholas had hoped, Kathi knew, to have himself proved a St Pol. Later, it did not matter to him whether he had a claim to legitimacy or not. He had wanted, like a child, to become their friend. And the three generations, Jordan, Simon and Henry, had responded with cruelty, and now threatened his life and his family.

He had gone to Scotland to deal with that, and to make amends for what else he had done. It was something that Gelis understood, as she understood the sacrifice that she was being forced to make also. She must wait, while the way was cleared for her to join him. For he did not only face the St Pols. There was the other enemy, David.

One did not, then, begin to talk to Gelis of Scotland, but of what was happening here. And, listening, Gelis said at the end, 'I'm sorry that Dijon has gone, but I think Nicholas had got quite used to the idea of not being the next vicomte de Fleury. It makes life simpler without titles. Just think, Jordan has lost Ribérac too, so he is merely St Pol, lord of Kilmirren.'

'It still sounds quite grand,' Kathi said. 'Anyway, I shan't let you sniff at the Scottish orders of chivalry. My uncle likes being a Knight of the Unicorn, and I suspect Nicholas doesn't mind all that much. If he thinks about it at all.'

'I don't know what he thinks about,' Gelis said. 'He is so used to being alone.'

Kathi was silent. Until a few months ago, Gelis too had lived behind ramparts. Then the defences had been broached. And now she talked, with moving honesty, of what she cared about. But the reticence Gelis had shown had been different in origin, surely, from the fierce and solitary silence of Nicholas, which could be dissolved sometimes by awe, but not significantly by physical pain or euphoria. Wherever he was, no one would know, would really know what he was thinking, unless he wished them to. Or, rarely, it would happen by chance, as when one accurate note resonates with another. But then there would be no need of words.

They talked. Kathi had chopped up and painted something for Jodi: a miniature tabard to wear in the jousting-field. Nicholas had been amused, in the few days he had been at home, at his son's addiction to military training, and even Gelis tended, laughing, to sigh. But Kathi knew, as Nicholas probably did, that it arose from hero-worship: adoration of his large, fond, magnificent father, who fought against Turks; and love of Robin, the mischievous playmate who invaded his house in the Canongate, and who laughed and fought like a dancer. Jodi had never really taken to Kathi, who had stolen his Robin and married him. When Kathi left gifts for Jodi, they were always in Robin's name.

Gelis put down the tabard and held out a kerchief. 'What brought this on? Don't tell me. I'm avoiding Jodi just now because he reminds me too much of Nicholas. Would you like to talk about weddings? Paul and Catherine have drawn up a contract, but have to wait for a dispensation from Rome. Weeks, in this kind of weather. Children could be born, if Catherine weren't so prudish.'

Kathi laughed, blowing her nose. There was some nominal kinship, for sure. Catherine de Charetty was related by marriage to Nicholas, and Paul was son to Gelis's cousin. Dispensation would come, but Catherine, who once flouted every convention, would behave until then like a nun.

'Poor Paul,' Kathi said. Then she remembered that Paul himself was not exactly legitimate, which might very well tend to make him as cautious as Catherine. She thought it all rather a shame.

She went home soon after that, and saw by the bustle that the baron her uncle was home. She was on her way to her room when he sent for her.

Anselm Adorne sat at his desk, in the finely wainscoted room splashed with colour from the armorial glass in the windows and pinned benignly with unicorn heads. Just before leaving, Nicholas had attended several meetings here with her uncle and the late Duke's advisers, debating how to handle this turbulent interim; how to prevent all that was good in the past from being swept away before the grand marriage came, which would throw what was left of Burgundy into the hands of the Duchess's future husband, whoever he was.

Nicholas had once served the Holy Roman Emperor Frederick, and carried intelligence of many countries, near and remote; at such meetings, he made his own contribution to the state that had reared him. Furthermore, in what time he had left, he had taken Diniz aside and taught him what he needed to know, so that, whatever happened, the business would survive. It should be safe. The new régime would need merchants. And with Catherine's marriage, it would have the support of the van Borselen family of Veere, whom no one offended.

Now Kathi walked in, and sat, and saw the change in her uncle's eyes. She said, 'What has happened?'

And Anselm Adorne rubbed his face and said, 'I'm sorry, child. Someone will tell you, and you had better hear it first from me. It's Ghent. Ghent again. Do you remember in Scotland – you were a little maid only – when the news came of the destruction of Liège, and of how the Gantois submitted in fear to the Duke, and were punished? The people secretly blamed their own leaders, but did nothing about it. Not then. Now they feel they have the power to vent their anger, and have done. All those who held office in 'sixty-eight have lost their lives. My son was not touched, but a man of your family, John Sersanders, was among those who died. No one close. I don't think you ever knew him. But a Sersanders.'

He stopped. Kathi said, 'No. I didn't know him.' Ghent was where she and her brother had been born. It was where all those called Sersanders lived, that radical family into which Anselm Adorne's sister had married. Her own parents were dead, and her brother now living in Scotland. But there was a Sersanders house in Ghent. She had lent it to Nicholas once. Before Nancy. She said, 'But perhaps he was someone you knew? Had you met him?'

'No,' he said. 'He was on the council. Outspoken, of course, like your father, but he didn't deserve that. I mourn him, but I mourn still more what is happening.' He looked up and spoke with a vehemence that came close to savagery. 'I wish you were in Scotland. I wish your husband would come. I have sent again to ask about the delay, but nothing happens.'

'The weather,' Kathi said. 'But look. Those were Ghenters. This sort of madness doesn't happen with Brugeois. You served the Duke, all of you, but you fought for the town and its rights.'

'So did the men who ran Ghent,' her uncle said. 'No. It will settle, so long as nothing hasty is done. There has to be some central control; it is too large to leave solely to the Estates of the regions, when there are all these competing and disparate states. Brabant, Flanders, Hainault, Namur, Holland, Artois, Zeeland – think how different they are. At the very least, the countryside mustn't suffer because of the power of the towns and the guilds. On the other hand, the central authority must work to be accepted; must be seen to be just, and to be able to defend the states from their enemies. It takes time. But we shall manage.'

'I'm sure,' Kathi said. 'Meanwhile, commonsense suggests that you should leave for Scotland, not me. Have you thought of it?'

'No,' said Adorne. 'This is where I am needed. And indeed, I couldn't go if I wished: there are no safe conducts for burgh officials.'

'You are a *prisoner*?' Kathi said.

'Do I look like one?' said Anselm Adorne. 'Or Hugonet, or anyone else? No. Our master has gone; there is a vacuum, or what is perceived as one; and we remain, men of another régime, answerable to an inexperienced girl. We must stay till our place is decided.'

'As it was decided for John Sersanders?' Kathi said. 'If you won't leave, I'm going to call Nicholas back.'

'To take which side?' Adorne said. 'What he is doing just now is creating a refuge fit for his wife, and for you and your family, eventually. Do you want to condemn Robin to what is happening in Ghent, or in Bruges?'

'Ghent or Bruges may not let Robin leave,' Kathi said. 'He is a Sersanders by marriage.'

There was a pause. 'That is true,' Adorne said. 'But they will surely allow him a Scots convalescence? You will sail as soon as he comes. I will hear no refusal: I will put you on board with the children myself. As for me, this is the house and the church I have built. This is the country where my family has lived and been respected for two hundred years. This is where I will die.'

Chapter 3

Suld God haue maid thi cors in quantité
Lyke to thi will and thi desyr to be,
So large of persone suthlie suld thow bene
That all this warld suld nocht thi cors contene.

IN SCOTLAND, it pleased Nicholas de Fleury to make his public entry into the King's town of Edinburgh in a royal cavalcade, passing up the incline of Leith Wynd, and turning his back on the house of Archie of Berecrofts and Anselm Sersanders in order to pass through the portals that led to the High Street. The banner of Scotland flew above him, and at his side rode Alexander of Albany, the King's brother, curtly conversing. Jamie Liddell, politely silent, rode behind him.

As they progressed, Nicholas kept seeing faces he knew. A goldsmith. A shipmaster. A chorister from Trinity College. A man who sold fish-hooks. A man who made traps for devils. As with a person drowning, he appeared to be compulsorily reviewing his past, while all the time attending to Albany's disjointed discourse.

Albany hoped (he said) that de Fleury observed the changes since his last visit – the well-built houses on either side, some of them tiled, and with chimneys. They were better served, too, with royal merchants: Yare and the Prestons and Scheves brought in (he mentioned) all they could want, so that he trusted de Fleury would not rely too much on his favour. They had the dowry arriving, of course, from the young Prince's marriage contract with England, although that would be offset when –

'. . . When?' prompted Nicholas, a little late.

'. . . when Meg's – when the lady Margaret's future is settled. My brother and I are concerned. There are those who wish to see her married in England.'

Albany had spent some enforced time in London as a boy. Some royal prisoners hated it; some looked back on it in a delirium of nostalgia and envy. Nicholas said, 'What does she want?'

'She despises England, as I do,' said Albany. 'I want you to speak to James, and to Mary.'

Christ. A nobleman with two servants glanced up and then stopped, looking surprised. Nicholas couldn't remember who he was. They had come to the open grassland around St Giles, and would soon reach the West Bow, and the domiciles opposite, which had once housed the family St Pol, and sometimes sheltered an elderly lady of whom he was deeply afraid.

Nicholas said, 'My lord, I shall be glad to help, if you think they will listen to me. The King has changed, I am told.'

'You know how to entertain him,' Albany said. 'Talk to him. Put on a play. Bring him a fine hat, or a horse. Then tell him not to trust England.'

He was dreaming. They were riding in public, with their escort about them, and Sandy's fractious voice rising and falling. To be fair, it was not audible to anyone else, except perhaps Sir James Liddell, his henchman. It was the lack of commonsense that made Nicholas nervous. It continued until they had climbed the long slope to the Castle and had been saluted within, to hand over their horses and scale the steep flight of steps that took them close to the crown of the vast, uneven plateau that contained the fortress, and brooded over the loch and the town far below. The King lodged in David's Tower, the new keep that had been building when Nicholas had promoted the crazy ball game on the walls that had nearly killed that courageous young acrobat who, swarming up the tower, had risked his life to protect Nicholas. An acrobat whose career was to finish by twenty.

At the top, the buildings were handsome enough. Painted, gilded, with their coats of arms and decorative windows, they outshone anything in the town below, except the Abbey. Only if you knew Rome or Florence, Bruges or Venice would you praise such things carefully, for there were other men here who had travelled, and who were listening out, seething, for patronage. Someone had been sent ahead, and men had gathered, it seemed, in the audience chamber. A page came to seek Sandy and deliver a message, bowing to Nicholas; and Sandy touched Nicholas on the arm. 'James wants to see you at once. I told you he would.'

Even then, Nicholas thought it was all going to plan, and he was partly right. To reach the chamber they had to climb a steep stair, and then pass through a couple of antechambers. He had not heard, until he saw the Archers lining the walls, that the King had reconstituted the Royal Guard, portentously established some years ago. It had lapsed, partly because of expense and partly because younger sons preferred to join the King's Archers in France, where the wages, the living and the opportunities were all very much plumper. Captains such as Stewart of Aubigny – or Jordan de St Pol – might end up with estates, although they might not always keep them. Others, such as Wodman, or David de Salmeton, now reverted to Simpson, returned with well-filled coffers to sell their training and knowledge in the business world. Behind and below the years of Franco-Scottish pacts and alliances, there had always been a two-way secret underground traffic between the young exiled Archers and the noble families which one day they would rejoin. Well advised of the danger, and the opportunity, Louis of France was lavish with his money and honours. But then he also required the protection of his Guard, which James of Scotland did not.

The faces, then, beneath the matched feathered bonnets, not quite new, and the livery tunics over the handsome half-armour, were of men largely of middle years, and from families all over Scotland: fair Campbells with their close-set blue eyes; handsome Erskines from Stirling. Stewart kinsmen: men from the Lennox, related to Darnley and Avandale and the King. The captain, Guthrie, whom Nicholas remembered as a noble administrator, and far from being a veteran of the field. Little George Bell, once of the King's chamber, whom he also remembered. And one member who was more than handsome: whose beauty of feature would have made him remarkable, even had he not broken the rule and turned his eyes as Nicholas walked up with Albany. Turned, for an instant, his long-lashed, magnificent eyes.

Nicholas slowed, but did not stop. He had thought of nothing else all through the night, but he didn't stop, and his schooled face remained faintly smiling. He could do nothing now. He had the King to handle, in whatever mood he might find him today.

The King, to begin with, was upset. He had planned to go hunting, and instead, the man he generally obeyed had come to invite him to get up because his kinsman Charles, Duke of Burgundy, was dead, and there were urgent matters to discuss. He had actually risen, and got three of his councillors into the room, because he already knew how important it was, from all the rumours he had tried to ignore. Also, Master Whitelaw wore his thoughtful face, which, as a boy, the King had ignored at his peril.

Master Whitelaw, Royal Secretary, had served James's father and, for long years of dire educational hardship, had been tutor to the young James himself. He was the sort of man who often spoke inadvertently in Latin. Colin Campbell, of course, often spoke inadvertently in Gaelic, but the King's sisters thought the Master of his Household exotic, with his wild Highland clansmen and his ice-cold legal mind. The third councillor who entered James's chamber was, of course, his own kinsman Drew Stewart of Avandale, who used the family patois in private, and who had been Chancellor to James's father as well as to himself. Sometimes it seemed to James that he had been conceived in a masculine womb instead of a feminine one, and that he was still in it. Sometimes he rebelled.

Now they were telling him of the various possible consequences of the Duke's death, and how these might affect Scotland's political relations with France, and her trade relations with Flanders, and the management of the present welcome truce with England. He had his own ideas about all of that, and they listened to them, as they always did (as they ought to do), and praised their acuity, and discussed them. The consensus was that before planning further, more exact detail was needed, and that this might be got from a Burgundian who had just arrived back in Scotland. Did his grace recall Nicholas de Fleury?

At first he resented being reminded of Nicol de Fleury, who had behaved like a friend, or rather a discerning subject, and then had disappeared. Indeed, to his recollection, his advice had often been faulty.

Drew said, 'I am afraid that is true, and he knows it. I should take it as a sign of humility that he has returned at all. I gather he does not intend to stay long.'

'I see,' the King had said. 'Then, in that case, we shall see him. Briefly.'

Back in Avandale's office: 'That might have been worse,' Argyll said. 'He had two new hounds to try out. Has de Fleury been sent for? Are we still agreed that we shall use him, whateffer? And that he should not be told what doesn't concern him?'

'I think so,' said Avandale. 'If he moves in too fast, we get rid of him.' There was little more to say. They had made their decision the previous night, after their private interrogation of Nicol de Fleury on the matter of the Duke of Burgundy's death. The precision of the account he had given them had revived memories of what had seemed enlightened about the man in the past: his fertile imagination, his abundant energy, his undoubted intellect, all of which the kingdom could utilise. Also, on the occasion of his four previous periods of residence, he had formed a close but seemly relationship with all the royal siblings, and especially with Albany. Which could be a good thing, or a bad. Yare, in his note, had recommended it, with respect, as an exploitable asset.

The future of Flanders could not have received, in Avandale's view, a more valuable airing than it did in the exchanges that followed. On personal issues, de Fleury had been markedly less forthcoming. His reasons for leaving Scotland were specious; and it was hard to believe that he had relinquished control of his Bank simply in order to travel. He also omitted to mention that, although he passed for Burgundian, he had once tried to claim to be Scottish. It was said on good authority that he had pretended to be the son and heir of Simon de St Pol of Kilmirren, but had dropped the claim for personal reasons. The claim was invalid in any case: it was known from the same source that his Burgundian mother, whose name he now took, had deceived her husband Simon by producing a bastard. It was what they believed in Kilmirren, where the woman's name was anathema.

He had taxed the fellow with the matter last night, since it had seemed coincidental that after de Fleury's last visit, the St Pol family had gone into exile on grounds of fraud and deception. And now, by a similar coincidence, the old man was back, and so was de Fleury. Perhaps that was de Fleury's true interest in coming back?

The Burgundian had sworn, last night, that he had no intention of harming any one of the family. He was here to do business and leave. If he could serve their lordships meantime in any way, he would be happy to do so. They had all listened. Their conclusion last night was summarised by his own answer just now. The man was worth courting a little. And if it didn't work, they would get rid of him, one way or another.

It was what Nicholas, pragmatic as ever, fully expected them to conclude. He was on trial. On trial for all the weeks he might stay, as well as now, before the Secretary, the Chancellor and the Master of the Household, and before James, Third of the Name, who might be moody.

He was certainly haughty when Nicholas was ushered into the room to make the customary reverences, choosing the dangerous Italian style, for the hell of it. He could see Argyll's mouth twitch. His own expression was serious. Knight of the Unicorn or not, a courtier who had left without warning was not going to be embraced by a Stewart. Seated on his chair of state in a velvet side-gown and magnificent chain, below which his riding dress could be glimpsed, the King stared down his long nose. On his right hand sat Sandy his brother, and on his left the three interrogators of last night's privy encounter, gazing at Nicholas as if at a stranger. There was a page at the King's feet, and two of his men at the door.

'So,' said the King. 'I hear you have news to tell us of the circumstances of the noble Duke of Burgundy's death. We are prepared to hear it.'

Nicholas embarked on his narrative, which was clear, and grave, and concealed nothing. The King then enquired whether M. de Fleury believed that the young Duchess, the Duke's bereaved daughter, would marry the young lord, the Emperor's son, to which Nicholas answered, Yes, this was the general view. Asked about Scottish trade, he answered that in his opinion the Staple would desert Bruges for Antwerp or Middleburg. Finally, he reported the wide-held belief that the King of France would now attempt to restore his claims over Burgundy.

The questions were as he expected: obvious, sensible, and deriving mostly from the royal ministers. They were voiced with some resentment. To James, the death of Charles of Burgundy was a severe inconvenience, and reduced his own standing as kinsman. Unlike Sandy, James had not travelled in Flanders or even in England. Princes in conflict praised his offers to mediate, but were not generous with their invitations, unless he promised to come with an army. And his Parliament had always stopped that.

The elder by only two years, the King lacked the haphazard taste for adventure that his brother displayed, but dreamed intense dreams of leading armies, and attracting the envy of chivalrous Europe with his well-placed artillery, and his timely advice, and the great marriages that his children would make. Scotland, at present a place of thatched houses and hens in the street, would become a second Lombardy. Nicholas thought, automatically answering the pre-arranged questions, that James and his brother would probably never understand one another, even though on the surface they seemed so alike. The King was slighter in frame, with a long, reddened nose less attractive than Sandy's, and short, full pink lips. But the auburn hair of the Stewarts was the same, and the curiously innocent appetites. James had tried, once, to seduce Gelis in front of Little Bell.

As if on cue, the King began talking of Gelis. 'And your lady wife. I trust that, if you intend staying, your lady wife will come to ornament our Court? She is here?'

Nicholas took a short, calming breath. The picture in the King's mind was not necessarily an echo of what was in his, but the naïveté of the question was unfortunate: Whitelaw's face, below the grey hair, was pained. Nicholas smiled and spoke mildly. 'No, my lord and great Prince, but I hope to bring her one day. She also feels for your loss, and asked me to add her condolences to mine.'

The King gazed at him as if he had forgotten. Then irritation returned. He said, 'The Duke's death. The lady is kind. I suppose, then, you'll have brought a shipload of expensive black doublets to sell me? Velvet cloaks? Fancy pourpoints? I am sure you think I can afford them.'

Nicholas said, 'Mourning may take many forms, my lord King. The interment is over. All the world knows the grief you carry in your heart. A Mass in the spring would surely suffice, at the time of the usual change in the wardrobe. Your grace's own merchants know what serves best.'

The King looked surprised. On earlier trips, Nicholas de Fleury would have jumped at the chance to press costly goods on them all. Forgetting his stance on economy, the King said, 'Now here is a surprise! The good sire de Fleury cannot aspire these days to a nobleman's cargo, but has fallen on hard times, perhaps? Of what sort is this cargo – some salt and a few sacks of alum, or a few barrels of the cheaper sorts of wine? If that is all, he cannot expect to trade here.'

A man was shouting outside the door, and there came the sound of faint scuffling. The King started, and then said something petulant to his door-keepers, who retreated to the posts they had started to leave. Albany swore. Continuing his undisturbed solo: 'Your grace, I have no expectations,' said Nicholas musically. 'I came to fulfil some orders and, since you were pleased to send for me, to tell you my news. The lady my wife is the trader.'

The door burst open, revealing two men-at-arms and an usher attempting to restrain John of Mar. John of Mar shook them off and, marching forward, slapped Nicholas viciously across the side of his face. Nicholas jerked and recovered, breathing deeply, standing repressively where he had been. His gaze locked with Mar's.

'They could afford pepper,' snapped the King's brother over his shoulder. His entire face was as red as his rash. Where James's hair hung in loose waves, John's was crimped like a thunderstruck wedder. He spat at Nicholas. 'You could afford pepper, couldn't you, you obsequious brute? You weren't smirking and making reverences this morning when you thought you had me alone with your bullies about you. I could have died.' He turned to the chair of state, his voice rising. 'I could have died!'

Someone – Whitelaw – spoke in an undertone, quickly. 'My lord! We can discuss this elsewhere.'

'I am discussing it now,' said the Prince. 'Now the man is here, and can answer for what he has done. Hang him. Hang him, James.'

Albany said, 'Don't be a fool. He's done nothing. James –'

'Wait,' said the King. 'What has de Fleury done? An attack on a prince of the realm constitutes treason.'

The large, grey eyes of the Burgundian glanced at Albany, and then returned to the King. The Burgundian said, 'In the presence of the King and his nobles, my lord, may I confess that what you say is true as the Lord's Prayer? An attack on a prince is a hanging matter. A prince who drives his sword into another man's merchandise and then suffers the consequences must, however, blame only himself. Indeed, he should in law recompense my lord of Albany, whose pepper it was.'

'I told you,' said Albany. John of Mar, with deliberation, set his hands to the thick table below him and heaved, so that it crashed to the ground, sending a candlestick rolling and ringing. Then he turned and raised his arm, fast, once again; this time towards his brother Albany. The Master of the Household, the Highland Earl of Argyll, seized and held it with ease.

The youth struggled. He yelled, 'All right, lick his arse, Sandy. You'll still not get to marry the Duchess. Christ, would you put a brute like de Fleury in front of your own flesh and blood?'

'The law herself so puts him,' said Colin Campbell. 'If you disagree, there is a place to complain, my lord of Mar. But surely it is not here and now, when you are unwell. Let me help you out.'

Others came. Presently the door shut on them all, and the sound of Mar's bawling receded. Nicholas de Fleury rubbed his cheek, which was numb, and collected the silent support of the Council. The King, talking fiercely to Albany, had avoided his eye. The table was righted and Argyll returned, adjusting his robe. He said, 'I am sorry, your grace. Were there other matters your grace wished to open with M. de Fleury?'

It seemed there was nothing, which suited M. de Fleury very well. He had conveyed all he wished to convey. A cynical ear might have noted that there were some details that he did not pass on, such as the precise plans of the leaders of Bruges. He had however reminded the King of their names, causing him to exclaim when he mentioned Adorne. 'My good baron of Cortachy! If they change his office in Bruges, then perhaps he can resume as our Conservator for Scotland? We miss his visits. That is, his nephew and Wodman do well enough, but Adorne was an ornament to our Order.'

It sounded heartfelt. It gave Nicholas reason to remember Mar's antipathy to foreign advisers, who might arrange foreign marriages. The Duke of Albany had aspired to the little Burgundian heiress. No doubt the King had encouraged him, even though he might suspect it was a lost cause. It would suit James to be free of brother Sandy. He probably wished to God he could be free of his second brother as well. A confused King and two rudderless Princes, adrift in a world which they hardly seemed to realise was splitting apart.

He didn't know why he felt quite so dismayed. If everything was all right, he wouldn't be here. He knew why he felt dismayed. It had nothing to do with the Princes.

The interview ended. Nicholas withdrew, after establishing that he hoped to stay for some weeks, and could be reached through the Abbot of Holyrood. He tried to sound grateful for the Abbot's insistent hospitality. Albany left the room with him, which he hadn't expected, but which made the next step easier. Before, he had meant to set out at once on the journey Yare had mentioned in Berwick. It was only an hour after noon. There was time to go and return, and make his call on Adorne's nephew, Kathi's brother Sersanders. Their house was in the burgh of the Canongate, the lower part of the single thronged street that plunged down from the castle to Holyrood. He had passed it, coming from Leith. Dawn and Leith seemed a long time ago.

That had been the plan. Now he had to make one small alteration. Leaving the King's apartments with Albany, Nicholas spoke as they walked. 'Thank you for your support. I found it difficult to know what to do. Does the King fear for his life, that he has a guard now?' They had begun to walk between the armed men, whose captain lifted his sword in salute. His face was unfamiliar. All the faces were unfamiliar. The Guard had changed since he had arrived.

Albany said, 'Against you, or John? Hardly. No. It's only for show during audiences. The men will stand down and eat very soon: they have a place by the wall. Then they'll gamble and drink till the next call.' He smiled at the captain, who returned a grin: they were comfortable with Albany.

Nicholas said, 'It sounds quite enticing.'

The King's brother looked at him. 'Where were you going to eat? We could join them. I don't stand on ceremony.' He paused and said, 'You deserve some ale after that buffet. I'm sorry.'

Nicholas supposed the bruise must be obvious, even among the rest of his contusions. It felt swollen: the face of a thug above the splendour of the unicorn collar. Well, the King hadn't demoted him, yet. He said, 'Rather that than a hanging. Ale sounds good.'

The rough stone lodge for the King's élite Guard was not large, but the rushes were clean, and the big brazier warmed the room where they spent their off-duty hours. Because the windows were small and half shuttered, the light inside came from the blue and red peat-flames and the torches stuck on the wall. A trestle far from the door was littered with pewter and food, and some men were sitting there, eating. One of the Castle dogs rooted for scraps. Four Archers who had finished were using a cleared space for a dice game, while others nursed their ale-cups by the brazier, stripped to their shirts, lolling on benches or stools. The timber roof shot back the talk and the laughter, and the air was thick with masculinity and ale.

Sandy went in, and the seated men got hastily to their feet, and then relapsed slowly when he told them to. You could see they actually thought it an honour. Someone ran out for food, and several got up and started clearing the table while Albany turned to introduce Nicholas.

Nicholas stood in the doorway. Across the room, a slender, an exquisite Archer also stood where he had slowly risen; the candle-flame gilding his hair and the ends of his lashes; his eyes wide and lovely and blue.

'You know each other,' said Albany, looking from one to the other. 'Of course. I'd forgotten. Aren't you even related by marriage? So may I reintroduce to you Henry de St Pol of Kilmirren, our newest member?'

'My dear Uncle,' said Henry. 'You didn't recognise me. You passed me just now without recognising me. Won't you forget your looks, and take out your eyeglass?'

He was sixteen, perhaps. His voice, husky and soft, was full of sweet mischief. Men laughed.

The most patient of men, Nicholas awaited the end of the meal. Seated by Albany, he could do nothing else. Despite Henry's golden attractions, or perhaps because of them, Albany did not offer to the newest and youngest recruit an elevated seat at his board. Henry, court-trained to sense the unspoken, sat and ate in the shadows, submissive and sad, his dulcet voice seldom raised, even when his companions attempted to tease him. Nicholas met the situation by restraining his own performance to match. It was not the moment, in any case, to break into a breathless display of buffoonery, whatever Sandy might have been hoping for. They talked mainly about war. By the end, he knew them all reasonably well, and took his leave of them and of Albany, who was walking back to the tower. Albany directed him to present himself the following day, and Nicholas thanked him. Then he turned to where Henry de St Pol stood awaiting him, derision in the wondrous blue eyes. Henry said, 'After that, how dare I hope to claim your attention, my Uncle?'

'I expect you'll risk it,' Nicholas said. 'Shall we go somewhere and talk? I thought I saw you up there, but couldn't believe it. I admire you. An appointment to this Guard is given only to the best.'

'It must indeed have seemed unbelievable,' Henry said. 'Will you trust yourself, then, to my house? It is just down the hill.'

Nicholas knew where it was. It was where he had first been shown the child Henry by a triumphant Simon de St Pol. Where other things had happened, with other people. He said, beginning to walk, 'Thank you. Your father is still in Madeira?'

'Where your false information sent him? Yes, Uncle. But my grandsire is here.' His voice taunted. 'Do you still want to come?'

It was not what Nicholas had heard; nor, he suspected, the truth. Two days ago, the fat man had been in the west, at Kilmirren, and was most likely still there. Nicholas remarked, 'Should I have a bodyguard? And who else will be there: Mistress Bel?'

'You remember our old friend Mistress Bel,' said the youth, gratified. His hair curled, ducat-gold, from under the tilt of his bonnet, and the guard at the drawbridge saluted him. He said, 'Sadly, no. She stays in Stirling these days, since you threw her out of her house.'

Nicholas had bought her house. He had not thrown her out. He said, 'I can't quite recall doing that. Could it have been David Simpson?' It was what de Salmeton called himself now.

The boy stopped and slapped the side of his own head. 'That was it! After he bought your castle of Beltrees, he took over her land and expelled her. Life in Scotland has become very rough; I wonder you dared to come back. I heard Johndie Mar slapped your jaw. I see he punched your eye also. Did you stand still and let him?'

'I'll blind him next time,' Nicholas said. 'The black eye and the rest came from another fight. As you say, Scotland has become very rough.'

'*Another* fight? When? You only came yesterday.' The boy came to a halt. Two washerwomen and a cowherd stopped at the top of the West Bow, admiring him. A servant of Wodman's, seeing them both, raised his brows and unfurled a hand in some sort of greeting.

'So people started hitting me yesterday,' Nicholas said crisply. 'You might even have been without an uncle if Andro Wodman hadn't ridden out with me. We were waylaid by some rascals. They broke his arm and his nose.'

'I wish I'd been there,' Henry said. 'Your army would have helped: you should have brought them. I remember Captain Astorre: you set me to train under him. How is he? And the gunner, John, wasn't it? He taught me all I know about guns.'

This was true. In return for which, Henry had tried to blow him up, and Nicholas too. As he had tried to kill —

'And Jodi,' Henry said fondly. 'How is your little son Jodi? If you aspire to place him with the Guard, I should be happy to teach him. He is a brave fighter, I'm sure, and could look after himself even in a rough country like Scotland. Ah! Here we are.'

And not before time. A different kind of assault was under way. But he was committed to his own, private injunction: to subdue his personal feelings; to recognise what forced the other to act as he did; to put himself, as ever, in another man's place. And if he could see into the heart of a stranger, he could surely fathom this, the damaged son of Katelina van Borselen.

The servant who opened the door was not one of Bel's. The man stood aside as if he were used to the way Henry brushed past unspeaking, making for the door that led to the parlour. It was a handsome, two-storeyed house with a thatched roof and a curved outside stair. It was built facing the causeway, on the slope of Castle Hill, with behind it a long, shelving garden. At the bottom of that was the Nor' Loch where Gelis might have died, one icy winter, through the self-willed machinations of Simon de St Pol, man of impulse, like Henry. Impulsive as Simon's far cleverer father, fat Jordan, was not.

It was very quiet. The servant, after hurrying, had left him. The door had closed behind Henry. Then it opened and Henry stood there, as he had stood in the guardhouse, straight and fair and defiant. He said, 'My grandfather *is* here. He wishes to see you.'

Nicholas said, 'It's all right.'

'Well, of course it is,' Henry said. He backed, and Nicholas walked past him and into the parlour. Henry shut the door and stood still, his gloved hand on his sword, his chin up, as if on guard for his grandfather.

It was not a large room, and Jordan de St Pol of Kilmirren was the only other soul in it. The stoutness that had come with his wealth had increased over the years since he had lived in France and fought for the King, father of the present King Louis. At seventy he was gross, his bloated chins swathed in the scarves of an old-fashioned hat, his gown falling in opulent folds from massive shoulders, his thick fingers heavily

ringed. Seated in a high-backed deal settle, he seemed to occupy all the
space and all the air, like a portly illumination: a painted initial on
vellum. Our Father. It was no wonder that Simon and Henry were
afraid of him.

His eyes, deep in the glossy cheeks, gazed at Nicholas. 'Are you
disappointed? You hoped to come and quarrel privately with Henry.'

'I can do that any time,' Nicholas said. 'No. He told me you were
here. I am willing to quarrel with both of you, if you insist, but it was
not my intention.'

'A social visit, no more?' the fat man said. 'How inexplicable. Did I
not draw blood, the last time we met, all those years ago? And you
responded by disarranging my livelihood. But as you see, I am back,
and not inconvenienced.'

'That was why I came,' Nicholas said. 'To put it to you that the sheet
is now balanced, and there seems no need for further scoring or friction.
I am willing to let the past rest.' He crossed to a stool opposite the old
man and sat. At the door, Henry cleared his throat. The old man sat
staring at Nicholas. Beneath those cold eyes, he felt his face throb,
quelling the incautious aspirations of his features. It was a handicap,
losing his face, and making do with a collection of bruises, an inflamed
eye and a discoloured cheek, down which ran the thin seam of a scar
that both he and the fat man knew all about.

The fat man laughed, saliva issuing to rest on his lip. He said, 'Does
the trumpet decide to blow truce, or lie like a clod, awaiting the lips of
its master? My dear Nicholas! You have no power to end the *friction*,
except conceivably by cutting your throat. If I ever tire of it, I shall
tell you. Meanwhile, you must manage your life as best you can. Bring
your wife and your child, and let us see who survives. That is what you
want to know, isn't it?'

'Very well,' Nicholas said. 'You relish the feud. Simon doesn't greatly
enjoy it but, being your son, feels committed to waging it. You think
that will not change. But I suggest that my son and your grandson
should be kept out of it.'

'You would send Jodi away?' said the fat man with exaggerated
surprise. 'Force him to live away from the new marriage-bed of his
parents? How surprising, by the way, that crude little reunion was. And
what of poor Henry's new lucrative post? He is to leave it so that you
may feel safe while you deal with – let me see, who are all your other
ill-wishers? John, Earl of Mar, for a certainty. And David Simpson for
another, whom I had to expel from my business, Tell me, are you going
to ask them to be your friends also?'

Henry laughed. He moved from the door and sat down, studying Nicholas as if counting the marks of his failures. He said, 'I want to see you begging for the kiss of reconciliation from Johndie Mar.'

'Did you think I was begging?' Nicholas said.

The fat man turned his eyes.

Henry said, 'I heard you beg us not to hurt that little turd Jodi. You're afraid of my father and grandfather.' There was the curl of a smile at his mouth.

Nicholas said, 'I was also promising not to hurt you.'

'And you think you could!' Henry said. His dense blue eyes shone at his grandfather.

His grandfather sighed, and made a small, cursory sign. Henry, puzzled but willing, jumped up to bring out cups and some wine. He poured, glancing up at the old man, but the old man was examining his rings. When the three cups were full, Nicholas was given one. He said, 'Poison?' It sounded grim, which was the way he was feeling. Grim, and sore.

'I was tempted.' said St Pol of Kilmirren. 'Drink. Look, the child does not understand, even yet.'

Erect and muscular in the embroidered cloth and glittering armour of the Royal Guard, Henry de St Pol stood and gazed at his grandfather. He said, 'I am sorry, my lord? You are not, I assume, speaking of me.' His face was drained.

The fat man glanced up and waved him away. '*Chut!* Don't play-act with me because someone at Court needed money and was willing to sell a man's place to a boy. Do you not understand what this fellow is saying?'

'De Fleury?' said the youth. So far as he knew, clearly, Nicholas hadn't said anything. And, of course, to anyone less sharp-witted than Jordan, he hadn't.

Nicholas said, 'Your grandfather has realised that I know you tried to kill me at Bonnington. From which you will gather that he also must know.'

A tremor ran through the boy. He looked down, and then away, at the window. He drew a long breath to speak.

Nicholas said, 'There is proof. Wodman also knows. No one else.'

The old man still did not speak. Henry stole a glance at him. Henry said, 'He thrashed me in France. He made the van Borselens disown me. He killed my aunt. He had you sent out of France. He made us all go to Madeira. None of you ever did anything.'

'Does it seem so?' said Jordan. 'I am sorry. As I have been trying to indicate, I mean to do my best to make up for it. Or intended to. But do you see what you have done, once again? You have taken an unwise, unauthorised step, without proper advice. It has failed, you have been caught and, as a result, we are all once more in thrall to this man. He denounces you, and you are dead.'

'But he hasn't,' said Henry. He looked at Nicholas.

'And provided you all keep the peace, then I won't. The kiss of reconciliation,' Nicholas said. His unforgiving stare rested on Jordan.

Jordan said, 'You have a strange iron cage of a mind, have you not, which enjoys laying traps? If I knew it, I should probably savour the detail of this one. So you have proof that poor Henry waylaid and tried to kill you. You will publish it unless what?'

'This feud will stop,' Nicholas said. '*Will stop*. No more lives will be lost. And, as from now, Henry will combine his post with another. The shifts are easy; he is allowed to live partially elsewhere. So when he is not on duty, he will live with me. And when he is not serving the King, he will train as my factor.'

'*What!*' said Henry. He had his sword in his hand.

'Put up, you fool!' said his grandfather. And to Nicholas, 'Henry is the heir to Kilmirren. The estate will need him, and that is where his training should be.'

'The estate will have him,' Nicholas said. 'I hardly mean to keep him for ever. As it is I don't suppose he'll average more than a few days in my house every week. But with a training by me, I promise you he will be able to run anything, anywhere, better than he does now.'

'So you are staying?' said St Pol. He suddenly lifted and drank off his wine. Nicholas had not set hand to his.

'For a while,' Nicholas said. 'It depends.' He looked up at Henry, suddenly standing between them.

Henry said, 'So it's settled? Two old women carve out my future. You didn't ask me? Some by-blow wants me as his lackey, and my father's father tosses me over, like a husk to a pig. Well, I won't do it. And when my lord Simon comes home, you'll be sorry.'

Nicholas rose. 'I think,' he said to Jordan de St Pol, 'that I had better leave him to you. I shall send a messenger in a day or two to find out when he can begin. If, that is, my lord of Kilmirren agrees?'

'You haven't drunk your wine,' the fat man said. 'That you drink it is my only condition. I have no other choice, have I, my serpentine Nicholas?'

Nicholas lifted and drained off his wine. It wasn't poison, and he felt better for it. He said, 'No. I trust that you don't.'

Henry trembled. On his way to the door, Nicholas turned. 'You will be asked to do nothing demeaning.'

'Speaking to you is demeaning,' Henry said.

Chapter 4

And for a man, abone all bestis liffand,
Off his barnis has maist the cur on hand
To norys, honour, to cleith and thaim to feid.

WODMAN SAID, 'You're crazy. He'll kill you.'

'No, he won't, you'll stop him,' Nicholas said. 'You did get the proofs?' They were in the guest-house of the Abbey at Holyrood, arranging a bed for his worst enemy barring perhaps three. Wodman said, 'I told you. We tracked down two of the amateur oystermen and reasoned with them until they gave us a notarised statement. You could lock up Henry on the strength of it now. I wish to God you would.'

He had a freshly cut lip. Nicholas quite enjoyed working with Wodman since it had become finally evident that Wodman had no designs on his life. He didn't necessarily trust him over anything else, but he didn't mind dealing with self-contained bastards like Wodman and Crackbene. He sometimes wondered what it would be like if he ever found himself reunited with the people he did trust . . . Kathi, and Robin, and Tobie, and Moriz and John. And Gelis, with whom the war, now ended, had never been real. The problem, latterly, had been that they didn't trust him. And in any case, it was a weakness to surround oneself with a family when busy with difficult tasks. They were a distraction.

He wondered how Wodman managed for women, but knew he would never ask him. He realised why he was thinking the way he was thinking, and shut and locked that door in his mind. Wodman said, 'Are you having second thoughts? Or maybe you want to train someone else? What about John of Mar?'

Nicholas said something offensive. As it happened, the comparison had already occurred to him: the spoiled princeling, the spoiled, wealthy brat. Of the two, you would say that there was more hope for Mar, whose upbringing had been controlled by the wise men who had done the same for his father. But Mar's juvenile rebellions held something within them that should not have been there, whereas Henry, dragged up by Simon, was behaving as any boy would. And behind it all, as any boy would, he wanted the approval of Simon, whom he loved. And nothing must interfere with that.

He gave a snort of laughter, just because it was all so impossible, and, under Wodman's corrosive eye, went off to talk to the masons. He had a journey to make. He hadn't looked forward to making it, but as it was, things probably couldn't get worse.

Nicholas had been to Roslin Castle before, deep in its wooded glen in the loop of a river, ten miles south of Edinburgh. It was an opportunity not given to everybody. He qualified because he had made friends with Betha Sinclair and Phemie her cousin. Both were earls' daughters. Both had helped to bring up the King's sisters. Betha's father owned Roslin.

Nicholas had been introduced to the family at Haddington Priory, not far away, where the female young of the royal house were traditionally brought up from childhood. Once, Kathi, Robin's wife, had been a maid of honour there to the King's little sister. Gelis, his own wife, had briefly attended the elder sister, now married. The Princesses' mother, from Guelders, had been related to the rulers of Burgundy. Indeed, for centuries, the Crown of Scotland had intermarried with Flemish nobility, and Flemish courtiers had settled in Scotland. It was unremarkable that the royal household should embrace Flemish attendants, and that Burgundians should receive Scottish honours.

The Sinclairs accepted Nicholas, however, for quite different reasons. Ruthlessly successful in business themselves, they recognised exceptional ability in others, and had already shared in past years in some of his dealings, such as the rather satisfactory Icelandic coup. In more civilised mode, he knew a lot about manuscripts. Earl William had a fine library, supplemented from many sources, not least through the lords of Anjou. Nicholas de Fleury, ranging the world, had handled volumes in Greek and Latin and Arabic which the Earl intended to own. Lastly, de Fleury's Bank had possessed its own army, implying a military expertise of some relevance to a family with holdings, even yet, in Orkney and the north-east.

Such were the reasons why Nicholas in the past had been allowed to enter the spectacular stronghold of William Sinclair, Earl of Caithness, now presided over by his son. And in his turn, it had suited Nicholas in those years to cultivate this valuable acquaintance, because the Sinclairs were close to the Crown. Indeed, Betha's elder, unfortunate half-sister had been married for nearly three years to the prince Alexander, Duke of Albany. That is, Sandy had two little half-Sinclair sons, as well as a third occasioned by chance.

Nicholas had not mentioned to Wodman where he was going. He felt that it would only have worried him.

On the other hand, after the oysters, he had no intention of travelling alone. It had not been difficult to persuade a work-party to alter its schedule and accompany him to Roslin, even at dusk. Builders were always visiting the unfinished chapel at Roslin, and he knew some of them anyway, from the times when he had been building himself. It made the journey short, because there was plenty to gossip about, and he had had their saddlebags packed with good ale.

By day, the easiest way to the castle was the low one, through the deep gorge and over the bridge by the waterfall that gave Roslin its name. In wintry darkness, a band of lightly inebriated masons chose the high path which skirted the valley and, passing hamlet and chapel, plunged down to the keep from above. The path did not go all the way: just before the castle doors, a chasm had been cut in the rock, offering monitored access by means of a high, vaulted bridge with a fifty-foot drop. There was also a turreted gatehouse with guards in it.

Boisterously delivering their charge to the bridge, his companions were abashed, not to say offended to hear their gentleman Nicholas de Fleury, of lovable conversation and good fame, denied entrance – would ye credit it? – to the bloody castle? Some of them actually crowded into the gatehouse and tried to argue, but they were only chapel bairns, with no influence. At the final rebuff, after consultation, they put up a spokesman to invite Nicholas to pass the night in their cabins. Then, further inebriated by his acceptance, they all set off back up the slope, singing, with a man with a lantern in front.

Nicholas remembered the cabins, put up when the new church of St Matthew was started, and since grown into a small village for the wrights, the masons, the plasterers who were slowly perfecting it, at a speed dictated by the input of interest, money and indeed whimsy by the reigning Sinclairs of Roslin. The nave, not yet started, was meant to be ninety feet long, positing a church as big as St Giles. They had been building for thirty years and had got the choir nearly done, all forty feet of it. As they got to the top of the path he said, 'Lights! Is someone working?' And someone else said, 'It'll be Big Tam and his cutters. Ye mind Tam? He built ye Beltrees?'

He remembered Tam, too. Thomas Cochrane, master mason and architect who, for him, had transformed a crumbling keep into a handsome building, which Nicholas had relinquished, and which had subsequently been bought – deliberately bought – by David Simpson. Since then, it was said, lavish additions had been made, but not by Tam Cochrane. Nicholas wanted to meet Tam Cochrane again, and when he said so, his companions rollicked with him up to the church and deposited him there, with instructions to join them all later. Then they went off downhill, taking his horse. They had all started singing again, but he had stopped. Someone he thought he knew stepped out from the wooden wall that protected the building, and then went back inside without greeting him. When he walked slowly forward, stumbling over the rubble, he found the access door in the wall still ajar. He went in, and stopped in the fretted dark, feeling the building itself staring down at him. Then he moved forward to the deeper dark of the north door, and opened it, and took the single step down into the unfinished church.

He had been here before, too; although not at night. Viewing this, the interior of the chapel at Roslin, he had experienced, and recovered from, amazement and amusement, admiration and exasperation, and finally settled for good-natured acceptance. This ode to the Sinclairs, truncated at either end, aspirationally based on the plan of Solomon's Temple, was not quite of the dimensions to carry the emblems with which it was loaded, coated and smothered, as in a kiosk in Tabriz. Except that here, you would say, the carvers had not been of uniform mind, or indeed of uniform training. The clustered shafts, the carved arcades, the canopied niches, the traceried windows, the figured and foliaceous capitals, the storeyed entablatures celebrated, as was to be expected, the triumphs of every known member of the family St Clair, since it left France to multiply in every promising corner of somebody else's land it could reach, ending up several hundred years ago here.

But among the armorial devices, the country-style Biblical figures – the Dance of Death; the Seven Virtuous Acts – were other strange faces, wild and pagan and snarling, which had more to do with the dark empire of the great Viking Rognvald the Mighty, Jarl of the Orkneys, from whom all Sinclairs claimed descent. Good-natured acceptance was the attitude that Nicholas had chosen in the face of such wanton eccentricity. Acceptance of a benignity that allowed simple craftsmen free rein. A pride, an exuberance that had no fear of excess. The spirit, perhaps, of the Sinclairs.

Now it was dark. It was hard to imagine, indeed, what light had attracted him, for there was almost none now, and no sign of human activity. Seeds in the darkness, working lanterns swayed in the draught from his door, plucking monsters from the gloom. A stone demon sprang into being, and behind it a wild man, with foliage in his teeth. A mask leered. A grinning animal moved. An avenging sword flickered.

Nicholas said, 'My God, you haven't got on very far, have you? Leave you four years, and it's shakier than it was when I saw it last. That pillar's going to fall down.'

The pillar fell down with a smack, rousing all the dust on the floor.

'I told you so,' Nicholas said, scratching his nose and nearly blinding himself because someone, howling, slapped him on the shoulder and two other people jumped out of the dimness and rattled his arm. He grinned, his eyes watering, and shouted back in the increasing noise while, bit by bit, the whole dusty interior came into view as candles were relit and lamps turned up and men gathered round him. There were half a dozen, perhaps: Tam Cochrane's team; and it was Cochrane who had hammered his shoulder, complaining. 'Damn you for a cold-blooded bastard, you're meant to shite yourself then!'

'Then you'll have to use better buckram, won't you? How are you all, Tam?'

'Wait till I tell you. Can ye stay a bit? What're you here for?'

Nicholas explained, and the master listened and snorted. 'More fool you, not to say you were coming. Mind you, Nowie's maybe away. You can try again the morn's morn. And we've got you the now. Ye've time tae come down?'

He had. 'Down' meant down the steps to the sacristy, the drawing-office, the booming underground cavern with the stools and the trestles and the mattresses where the arguing, the gossip, the eating and drinking went on as the work progressed and different experts came to serve their time in the dusty gloom far above. One day it would be the awful, chill heart of the church. Now it was the place for refreshment, creation and recreation: a haven of light and warmth under the ground. Trust masons.

Nicholas lingered as the others began to clatter down the stairs at the side of the Lady Chapel. He had been prepared by Abbot Archie for the changes in Cochrane. He looked as he always had: like a big florid Renfrewshire farmer, keen to drill you into the ground with detail about sheep prices and foot rot and fencing. Thomas Cochrane might have ended like that, for he came from a decent West Scotland family, with several brothers and dozens of cousins of fair education. But then he fell into the company of builders rather than estate managers, and found plenty of places where his knack for numbering made up for his youth. He picked the best masons as masters and travelled wherever they went, beginning with Paisley Abbey and Glasgow Cathedral, and then a lot further afield. His family let him. He worked at St Andrews, at St Salvator's. When a French master mason came over, Cochrane made himself indispensable, and no one saw him for two years after that. Then, when he came back, he was not just building, but designing.

That was when Nicholas last saw him. But an aptitude for organising and detail spills over into other things, if the owner is good enough. Masons need to manage money, and men, and to quantify and import materials. Masons often become perforce their own merchants and dealers and shippers, and the stone and iron and timber, the gunpowder they import for their quarrying are all useful for other things. Good masons make cannon balls and gun-carriages and build and fortify castles. The change in Big Tam Cochrane was not a physical one: it was the overlay of satisfaction and confidence which comes to a man who is extended as he was meant to be extended. And all his enthusiasm, his earnestness, his attention to detail were still there underneath. Nicholas envied him.

It was time he joined the others below. When Cochrane reappeared, Nicholas thought he had come to collect him. Instead, the mason banged noisily past him and shouted into the gloom of the opposite corner. 'Willie! Are ye no done yet, man! Look who's here!'

Nicholas stood where he was. There was a screen at the end of the Lady Chapel. He could hear a mutter from beyond, and then a light appeared: a lamp, borne by a stranger with a willing expression. He was introduced, but did not shake hands. The man's fingers were covered with charcoal. '*Willie!*' bawled Cochrane. His voice, for a big man, was not deep.

'I hear you,' said the man he was calling, and came sulkily out from the same place.

His hair had turned grey: that was the first thing about him. It was no tidier: heaped round his large-boned, lugubrious face with its lips as flexible as two springs. His eyes were angry. In his arms were a rebec, a recorder and a set of bagpipes, and round his shoulder was slung a small drum. There was a glint from something stuck in his shirt cords: a whistle.

Nicholas said, 'I stayed away because I found someone much better than you. Better voice, better pieces, and a damn sight better on the drums, which wouldn't be difficult. Are you playing in churches for halfpennies, now?'

Cochrane said, grinning, 'See our model. We want some angels with instruments up on one of those capitals. About there. He's got a portable organ.'

'Well, that's a relief,' Nicholas said. 'You don't have to go home all the time. Are you sore with me?'

'Yes,' said Willie Roger. He was the King's master musician. He had taught Nicholas all he knew about music and, more than anyone else, was liable to have been hurt when Nicholas left. Roger said, 'How long are you here for?' The instruments winked all about him.

'For quite a long time,' Nicholas said. 'Which is just as well, because you need a porter or you're going to dent all that bloody brass. Give me your organ.'

'You bastard,' said Whistle Willie; and laughed.

Down in the Sacristy, it was about as good as it could be, but necessary to tear himself, hoarse, away from the talk and the laughter to fulfil his obligations to the folk in the cabins. They offered him a bed in the church but, when he explained, they elected to come with him instead, and walk to the village, bearing lanterns, with Willie playing his pipes in the lead (*Cibalala du riaus du riaus/Cibalala durie!*). All the builders turned out at the noise, and were both flattered and flustered to find the master mason and his team among their guests for the evening. Then they found they had brought their own food and drink and a choir and a consort, and settled down in the dormitory for the best evening yet.

There wasn't much privacy. Alone with Cochrane for a moment, Nicholas said, 'I hear Davie Simpson is at Newbattle. David de Salmeton.'

'Aye. He is. He doesna like you verra much,' Cochrane said. 'Nor me. I wouldna play up to his fancy notions. Plenty of money, though.'

'That's surprising,' Nicholas said. He waited, then said, 'But he didn't buy the rest for a barony?'

'The land wasna for sale,' Cochrane said. 'My lord Semple got some, and the King has the rest. There's no title or barony now.' He paused and said, 'It was a pity you went.'

'I needed to go,' Nicholas said. 'And I needed to come back. Tom Yare told me something.'

'Oh?' said Cochrane. It was hard to hear, with the voices and the instruments and the drums. He said, 'Come out a minute.'

Outside, the cold struck at once: there was a moon behind trees, and the grass they stood on was sparkling and slippery. Nicholas said, 'I have told no one. I will tell no one, unless I have permission. That is why I am going to the castle.'

'That is why they didna let you in,' Cochrane said.

'I thought you would know,' Nicholas said. 'Are you working for them a lot?'

'A bit. They're strong on Speyside; you'll know, with the fishing and timber and that. And there's a lot that needs protecting and redding, but young Mar won't listen to sense. And then there's the polite war betwixt Newbattle and the Knights of St John – have you come across that? Oh, that's a beauty,' Cochrane said. 'If you want to get to grips with what's wrong here the now, just ask me some time when you feel you can stand it.'

'I shall,' Nicholas said. Then he said, 'We'd better go in.'

Later, when they were all rather drunk, Willie Roger crossed to drop beside Nicholas. He said, 'You knew I'd be at the church. You sang as you arrived.'

'I thought you might want to escape. I wouldn't have blamed you.' He had sung all night; sung until the hoarseness had vanished like fog and his voice had come into itself. Not for anything complicated or grand: verses that fitted the whistle and tabor, or an impertinent flute.

'I might have done, if you hadn't sung. Has someone been teaching you?'

Nicholas showed the surprise that he felt. 'I haven't been singing. I haven't wanted to sing until now.' He paused and said, 'I am hoping to bring Gelis and Jodi back, when it is safe.'

'It is not very safe at the Castle,' Roger said. 'I play to them, sometimes. Spondaic rhythm in the Hypophrygian mode. Soothing music.'

Pythagoras. 'And you think I should sing to them? Soothing music?' Nicholas said, unwisely captivated by remembered delight.

'It doesn't matter. I'm glad you're back. Be careful,' Will Roger said.

Next morning, presenting himself with a sore head at the castle bridge, Nicholas de Fleury was admitted, and escorted over the courtyard, and up to the apartments of Sir Oliver Sinclair, whom Thomas Cochrane (who had left early that morning) called Nowie.

Former Vikings, former Normans, the Sinclairs all ran to fairness and bulk, and Nowie was a large man like his elderly father, who had resigned Roslin and much else to this, his third son. Sir Oliver exclaimed, his gentle face marred with anxiety, 'Your face! What has happened? Is this my fault as well?'

'Hardly, my lord,' Nicholas said. 'An attack on the highway to Edinburgh, already forgotten.' It was true. He kept forgetting how he must look. Reminded, he discovered that his face ached as well as his head.

Oliver Sinclair said, 'Then I am doubly sorry. Please sit, Nicol. I may still call you Nicol? Can you forgive me? When I gave orders not to be disturbed, I had no idea you were coming. Did you have an abominable night?'

'Noisy. I've had worse,' said Nicholas, sitting. He could smell the aroma of the wine that was being handed him: it was of the same quality as the Turkey wall-hangings and the tiles under his feet. He seemed to recall assisting the Sinclairs quite a bit in their extravagances of four years ago: books and salt-pans and similar knick-knacks. They could afford them rather better than his other victims.

Sir Oliver said, 'I am sorry, all the same, to have so squandered your valuable time. To have first-hand news of Burgundy must make you the most sought-after merchant in Scotland. I hardly dare keep you to put my own questions.'

Payment in advance. Fair enough. Nicholas settled down.

The short exposition he produced was that which, with appropriate variants, he had already delivered to the Abbot, the Lords Three, the King, the Royal Guard and Big Tam Cochrane, even, with music. It had provided a valuable study in reactions. Oliver Sinclair did not react: he asked one or two charming questions to indicate that he was still willing to listen, and at the end fell into a long silence, which Nicholas didn't bother to break. Nicholas had mentioned Adorne, and the trust placed in him by the little Duchess of Burgundy. The Sinclairs dealt with Adorne's nephew, Sersanders. Nicholas remembered that he still had to visit Sersanders, and wished, with sudden violence, that he were somewhere else. He drank off his wine.

'Yes. I see,' said Oliver Sinclair, as if he had spoken. He stirred and, leaning over, refilled Nicholas's cup. 'So you yourself have come back without plans. But you might one day wish to set up a trading house? With Sersanders and the Conservator, perhaps? Or with me?' All his teeth, although uneven, were intact, even back to the molars. They said there wasn't a girl in Orkney his father hadn't bedded, and he was the same.

Nicholas said, 'That is not why I am here. I am troubled by what I hear, and what I see in the King's apartments. I wished to ask my lord's advice about his grace the Duke of Albany.'

'Do you think this is a subject for you?' Sinclair said. The courtesy was unimpaired.

Nicholas said, 'If I may risk my lord's displeasure. The death of Burgundy threatens all existing alliances. Your peace with England has brought many benefits. His grace the King and his advisers wish to maintain it. The ladies his sisters and the Princes his brothers may not agree, but only Alexander of Albany is of an age or of a . . .'

'Maturity?' Sinclair suggested. His expression had not changed.

'. . . of a maturity to act on his feelings. May I speak of his marriage?'

'You appear to be speaking without restriction,' Sinclair said.

Nicholas began to experience faint feelings of gratitude. He said, 'The King's marriage deprived your father of the earldom of Orkney, but brought him compensations, including Albany's marriage to your lady half-sister. Had the Queen proved to be childless, Albany's sons might hope to inherit the throne. But she has not, and so the Duke has become restless. Either he seeks power at home, or through some great foreign marriage.' He paused.

'So?' said Oliver Sinclair. He signed to his attendant, who left the room. His manner changed to one more precise. 'So perhaps you should know that his sons my nephews were never eligible to inherit the throne. And that the divorce which, no doubt imminently, will separate the Duke of Albany from Catherine will, by its nature, bastardise the same boys and the child she is carrying now. I have to say,' added the lord of Roslin, tenting his fingers, 'that I cannot greatly blame Sandy. Like her brother, the woman is addled.'

'I had heard,' Nicholas said.

'And you are suggesting what?' Sinclair said. The door opened 'Ah,' said Oliver Sinclair. 'Come in. Master Nicol, let me reintroduce you to one of the several of my sisters who is not addled. Betha?'

Betha. There, as Nicholas sprang up and turned, stood the rotund and positive lady who had been the mainstay of the royal nursery; who had reared the King's sister Margaret at Haddington Priory, when Kathi, Adorne's niece, had attended her. Betha, widowed, stouter, with her three daughters doubtless married, and now brought in to inspect him, or more likely chastise him. She said, 'Who dunted your face?'

'Not I,' said her brother. 'Master Nicol is well able to take care of himself. He is about to tell us why we should allow him to become the mentor and close friend of Sandy Albany. Am I right?' He had poured wine, and now gave it to Betha, who had seated herself at his side. A tribunal of two.

Betha said, 'They are good friends already, from what I hear. Why, Nicol?'

Nicholas said, 'Because he could be a danger, and needn't be.'

'I think I might very well agree with you,' Sinclair said. 'But I wonder why you should care?'

'I want to bring my wife and child here,' Nicholas said. 'And well-run countries can profit from turmoil abroad.'

'And what would you do,' Betha said, 'aside from holding poor Sandy's hand?'

Nicholas set down his cup. 'If you believe that is what I think of him,' he said, 'we might as well stop this conversation now.'

'Forgive Betha. That is her way. But,' said Oliver Sinclair, 'I have to ask myself this. Might you not be tempted, as a friend, to foster my lord of Albany's restlessness, and perhaps even to aid some of his schemes?'

'My lords of the Council do not think so,' Nicholas said.

Silence. The cold blue eyes rested on his. Then: 'I do see,' said Oliver Sinclair, with his widest, most conciliatory smile. 'You might have begun with this news, but I see you felt that you should examine my expectations for yourself. Let me therefore repeat them. By the terms of the renunciation of Orkney, my father agreed that he would henceforth hold no post, nor play any part in the governing of Scotland other than his occasional presence, as an observer, in Parliament. The same applies to myself. I seek no power, and I hold no dynastic ambitions. My half-sister married my lord of Albany because she could hope for no better marriage and because we, familiar to him from childhood, might help to guide him through the years of his growth, as we have tried to do for his sisters. But it has not been easy. And I have to admit, with the lords of the Council, that the time has come where – independent – help may well be hoped for. It seems that you are trusted to do this?'

The voice was amiable. The gaze remained, unblinkingly chilly. As a credo, it could hardly be improved upon, and was mostly true, depending on how you defined the term *dynastic ambitions*. Another of the great Nowie's sisters had married the King's half-uncle Atholl and presented him, to date, with two sons and nine daughters, which was presumably nine daughters more than he wanted, but a tribute to something.

'He'll do it anyway,' Betha said. 'He's just giving you notice.'

Sinclair smiled. 'You have an adherent, my dear Nicol,' he said. 'So why are we wasting time over this? I am to understand that you will be spending time in Albany's company, so long as his fancy permits it, which may not be as long as any of us would desire. And if Andrew Avandale regards you as trustworthy, then so surely should I. And, of course, because Betha says so.'

'And because of the other reason he's here,' Betha said.

Sinclair turned his head. For a long moment, he gazed at his sister, and she sustained the gaze without blinking. He said, 'I think we leave the other reason aside.'

'I don't,' said Betha. 'She's waiting. As for Sandy, why not ask her opinion? She may not know the best or the worst of Nicol here, but she kens more than we do.'

Nicholas rose. He said, 'I will leave if you want me to.'

'Oh Christ, man,' said Betha. 'D'ye think I'd want you to hurt her, or get her to say or do anything but what she wants? She wants to see you.'

Sinclair said, 'It's a pity you told her he was here.' He stood and walked round to Nicholas. 'We are speaking of Phemie, our cousin. You knew her at Haddington, where Tom Yare has a brother. It was Yare who suggested you call?'

'Yes. Then may I see her?' said Nicholas. He looked at Sinclair, but instead was beholding the past: Phemie, and Kathi, and the rest of the brilliant company at the Priory of Haddington. The stalwart Prioress; the gentle nun Alisia Maitland who had helped to control the wild little red-headed princess; the servant Ada feeding her babies, and not yet married to Crackbene. The whole great, unwieldy, teeming Cistercian convent, with its flocks and its herds and its orchards; its hordes of paying guests and their households; the council meetings for prayer; the visits of the dancing-master, the doctors, the courtiers; Will Roger patiently conducting the singing and playing. Jodi stumbling about, chuckling. Tobie. Gelis. And again, quicksilver masterful Kathi with her fearsome small charge; and Phemie. Phemie Dunbar, daughter of the late Earl of March and cousin of Betha; not yet in full holy orders, and so able to travel, to perfect her gift for music and verses; to discover friendship and laughter. Dear Phemie.

Sinclair said, 'Take him to her.'

The place Betha took him to was warm and bright, a little apartment of several rooms, the first of which had thick paned glass in the windows and a table and prie-dieu, and a leather chair and a stool set before a real fireplace. The fire was laden with peat, the dark sods outlined with vermilion from the cave of heat that shimmered below, and blue flames playing around it. When Betha opened the door the ash blew about, fine as dust from a kiln. Betha said, 'Here he is,' and ushered him in without entering herself. The door shut, and he could not speak for the stone in his throat.

Euphemia Dunbar, daughter of a great family, sat by the window, her embroidery at her side. Instead of the coif she had worn for so long, a white cap covered her hair, and the cold daylight on her pure brow and strong cheekbones and solid nose made her skin seem as pale as the linen. Below, she wore a dull-coloured gown with a fringed shawl set on her shoulders; her hair, not having grown, hardly showed under the cap. The light made it grossly apparent that she was perhaps five months with child.

She said nothing, and he saw that it was because she, also, was unable to speak. Then she mastered it and said, 'Poor Nicholas. Tom Yare should never have told you: this is the last place you must want to be. But thank you for coming.'

She had put his hesitation down to revulsion. He crossed the room at once and, kneeling, took her hand, and then kissed her, his cheek against hers. For a moment she rested against him. Then she set him back and said, 'There's wine over there. We both need it.'

He spoke while he was pouring. 'Tom Yare is a very sensible person, and so is Betha. I wanted to come. Sir Oliver wasn't so sure.' He gave her a cup and sat down, regarding her soberly. 'Are you well? You know that none of us knew about this?'

Phemie said, 'Nicholas. It's all right. I know you aren't here as an agent of Nowie's. And yes, of course I know how well the secret has been kept. I wanted that, as well as the family.'

He drank his wine and listened to what she was saying and how she was saying it. This wasn't someone's frail, frightened daughter surrounded by enemies. This was a cultured, intelligent woman who had had many weeks in which to decide what to do. He said, 'They think they know, of course, the name of the father. But you haven't confirmed it?'

She smiled, her eyes bright. 'Now you have come, perhaps you will shake their convictions. No, I haven't confirmed it. Everyone has been very kind. I lack nothing. But I do need advice.'

Of course she did. It was why he was here. 'If you wish, I shall give it,' he said. 'But you know, surely, what he would want. Would he want you to ask me at all?'

'He would want you to help me,' she said, 'if he knew this had happened. He doesn't know. There is to be a child. I wish to rear it. But I am unmarried; I was in holy orders, if only of the minor kind. I cannot ask him to acknowledge this. I had hoped to keep it quite secret; to go perhaps to my sister's in Moray before it became obvious, but one of the doctors found out. Nowie has been kind: he and Betha brought me here and only a few people know, but already the rumour is growing. I have thought that the best thing might be to have the child fostered, and to return to my family. Scandals come, and are forgotten. I had thought even of saying that I was molested; but it would not ring true. The trouble is –'

'That as everyone knows, you have only ever been fond of one man,' Nicholas said. 'Phemie? Don't you want his son or his daughter? Don't you want to keep it all your life?'

Her eyes were stark, but she didn't give way. She said, 'Of course I do.'

'Then,' said Nicholas, 'don't you think that he would feel the same? Keep the child, that is the first thing. It is yours. And next, let him know.'

'Nicholas?' she said. 'Think. If I tell him, I give him no choice. This is not something he could or would hide. Yet he is a great man. How could I go there, and have him install me in some house, in the same town as his children? How could I force him to consider leaving his home and exiling himself to this place, out of a sense of duty towards me?'

'He is a widower,' Nicholas said. 'There are dispensations; there are procedures which you could follow, I am sure. You could marry.'

'There, you don't know him as I do,' she said. 'It may sound possible, but more likely it would cut one or both of us off from the Church. I don't mind, but for him, that would be terrible.'

'He would have his love for you,' Nicholas said. 'And yours for him.'

There was a space. Then she said, 'Would love not spare him this?'

'Perhaps,' Nicholas said. 'But respect comes into it as well: regard for his beliefs; for his right to decide for himself. I should want that. Everyone would. Phemie . . . give me a letter to send him. Then it is between him and his conscience. But at least he has the dignity of a man, making a choice. He wouldn't want to be spared.'

'No. I see that,' she said. After a while, she continued, 'Whatever I sent – he wouldn't receive it for two weeks . . . a month. And as long for the reply. Longer, if I go north.'

'I shall be here,' Nicholas said. 'Don't go away. Talk to me. I shall come whenever you like. But until you hear what he wishes, no one can be sure of a name.' He smiled. 'You have not spoken one, even yet; and neither have I.'

She released a long sigh, and looked at him in something gallantly close to her usual manner. She said, 'That is certainly true. If I . . . When I . . . Now that I am writing this letter, how will you know where to send it?'

'I shall have to guess,' Nicholas said. 'Or send it in triplicate to three very surprised men. Phemie: he deserves you, and you deserve him.'

Returned to Sir Oliver and his sister, Nicholas was formal and brief. 'I have no more to tell you than your lady cousin has told you herself. There is nothing she wants to add meantime. If and when there is, she will tell you herself. No one could appreciate your present kindness more than she does.'

'But she told you the name of the father,' said Sinclair.

'It was never mentioned,' said Nicholas. 'She has, however, asked me to visit her. Would this be allowed?'

'Allowed?' Sinclair said. 'My dear Nicol, how strange you make us sound. Of course, unless I am away, you will always be welcome. Indeed, there are some matters that you and I might well talk of with profit before you go back. You haven't eaten? Then come along, my dear man, and favour my board.'

Betha was staring at him. He agreed. On the way, she addressed him in an undertone. 'Are ye as wubbit as ye look?'

'Worse,' he said.

'Aye. So you're sending to him, is my guess. And nothing'll happen until he sends back. But meanwhile, you've done that lass a rare service, Nicol de Fleury. I'd kiss ye for it, if ye didna have such a sore face.'

He laughed, but all through the meal he found himself thinking of Phemie Dunbar. He had told her not to go north. So long as she stayed fast in Roslin she was safe. But anyone, seeing her now, could guess that the child was conceived in the latter part of the autumn. And would remember that, during that season, Phemie had not been in Scotland at all, but in Bruges.

Then the meal ended at last, and Nicholas left. He was free to make the next call on his stirring agenda: to visit Adorne's nephew, Sersanders, and tell him how Robin fell. And refrain from telling him anything else.

Oysters, where are you? I want to be kidnapped, tonight.

Chapter 5

Befor the knycht on the left syd suld stand
Ane officer to kepe the tovne, havand
In his richt hand the keyis of the zet . . .
For to this knycht as capitane of the tovne
Thai suld obeye in absens of the crovne.

ARRIVED IN THE dark, as now seemed habitual, at the great
Berecrofts house in the Canongate, Nicholas bestowed suitable drink-silver upon his princely escort from Roslin and
watched them depart. Under the lanterns at pend and at
porch, the engrailed cross of St Clair had made its own emphatic
statement: none of your anonymity here. There were several heads out
of windows already.

As a result, he didn't have to rasp at any doors: one was flung
open at once and Archie's chamberlain came out, followed quickly by
Berecrofts the Younger himself. Nicholas relinquished his horse and
came forward. 'No news. I've just called to see you.'

'Oh,' said Archie, changing colour. Then he swore. 'God's bones,
I'm turning into a woman. Nicol, I'm sorry. Ye look –'

'Wubbit. I feel fine. I've just come from Roslin. I've been talking
business with Nowie.'

'Nowie?' Archie said.

'Well, not yet; but I'm working on it,' said Nicholas. 'Sir Oliver
Sinclair at present. And saw Cochrane and Whistle Willie as well. Now
I remember why I left Scotland. Is Sersanders in?' He was so tired he
felt queasy, but knew from experience that it would pass. There were
two flights of stairs up to the main hall, which was bigger than his had
been. When he had had his bureau in Edinburgh, he had built the
house next door. Just outside the portals to Edinburgh; just up from
Holyroodhouse; just round the corner from the road leading to Leith.

A substantial property, which he had sold, like everything else, and which Archie had bought for Kathi and Robin, his son. And which was now occupied, he supposed, by Anselm Sersanders, Kathi's brother. Or Saunders, as he heard Archie calling him. It was shorter. And two Anselms would be confusing, in trade.

He wondered what name Phemie would give to her child, which none here knew about, and none must suspect, or not yet. Nicholas had Phemie's note to her lover, slipped him before he left Roslin. It would have to travel by ship. He would ride to Leith at first light tomorrow. This was his third day in Edinburgh, and he was sad, and elated, and exhausted. He hadn't realised how easy it had been, surviving in Moscow, or Tabriz, or Thorn. He thought, with despair, that what he actually wanted, imperatively, was a woman. No; specifically, it was Gelis, alone.

Sersanders (Saunders) appeared. He said, 'Nicholas.'

It was not ecstatic. From his point of view, Nicholas had done everything in his power in the past to damage Scots trade, in a successful attempt to harm the St Pol family. Now he was back. The fact that he had been accepted in Bruges; that dowry gold had replenished the Scots treasury; that the St Pols were being slowly re-established had not wholly reassured Kathi's brother. He sat on the edge of a table and said, without shaking hands, 'You've no news of Robin. No. Did you ever find out who made an exercise-bag of your face?'

The answer, if he had been willing to give it, was yes. The minions of Henry de St Pol, who was or was not at this moment in his apartment at Holyrood, awaiting him. Or wrecking it. Or standing behind the door with an axe. Nicholas said, 'I'd forgotten about it. Did you get Kathi's letter?'

Some of the grimness left Saunders's face. He had always had a short temper, perhaps because he was smaller than most men. People underrated Adorne's Scottish agent his nephew, unless they noticed his shoulders and arms, and heard what he could do in a tournament. He was in his early thirties, and ten years older than Kathi. Now he got up and walked to a stool nearer Nicholas, where he sat down. He said, 'I'm sorry. She said you were badly hurt at Nancy yourself. But you seemed to be interested only in trade, and it was my understanding that you had come back to settle accounts with the St Pols and de Salmeton. Until you do, it seems everyone is in danger.'

Adorne must have written before Christmas. It was natural. Nicholas said, 'I need a reason to stay, and some pieces to play with. It's a little early to expect anything else, but I haven't forgotten. In fact, I've made a reasonable start. I've muzzled Kilmirren himself, and taken his grandson into my household.'

'What!' said Archie. He sat down. 'He'll kill you.'

'That's what Wodman said. He'll watch out. I wondered if Saunders would also like to give me a hand.'

'With Henry de St Pol!' said Kathi's brother.

'He's going to despise common management and deal-making, but he reveres the chivalric arts. If I set up a few exercises, would you give him some show-fights?' said Nicholas. 'Or am I asking something too dangerous?'

'Against that little braggart?' said Saunders. 'Dangerous for him, I can tell you. I couldn't hold back if he provoked me.'

'But you could teach him?' Nicholas said. 'The Guard won't. They're uncomfortable with him: he's too young, and he shows off. He needs someone to practise with who's hard, but fair. Someone he can admire. He'll end up adoring you. And then there's David Simpson.'

'I don't think Simpson will end up adoring anyone,' said Archie of Berecrofts. 'Kathi says he will lay plans to kill you, but not yet. Not, ideally, until your family are here and can witness it.'

'So I have to get rid of him before that,' Nicholas said. 'Will you tell me all you know about what he is doing? He seems very rich.'

'He is, if he has your African gold,' Saunders said. 'Kathi says that you think that he has. But he lives genteelly in Edinburgh, at Blackfriars, most of the time, as agent for the Apostolic Collector, Camulio. You know him?'

'Prosper de Camulio? Yes. He came to Bruges as a Milanese envoy. We did a deal once, in Genoese alum. So they both stay in the guest-rooms at Blackfriars?'

'Camulio does,' Archie said. 'Simpson occasionally lords it at Beltrees. Or he'll spend some nights at Newbattle Abbey. The Abbot likes him. All those Norman families, and David's French Archer connections. I'm told he gives his services free.'

'For what?' Nicholas said, without emphasis. He was thinking.

'Don't the Sinclairs have a lot to do with Newbattle, Nicholas?' Archie said. 'One of the founding families, and next door to Roslin. They still lease bits of land to the chosen ones – the Cochranes, the Prestons, a doctor or two. God, you want to keep in with the Sinclairs and their tribe of physicians, Nicholas lad, if you're going to go on the way that you've started.'

'You've changed my mind. I think I'll stick to trade,' Nicholas said. He went on, in fact, to talk about trade until they had lost their uneasiness. He wanted help, but not until he was ready. Simpson hadn't publicly threatened him, or done anything against him in Scotland as yet: the reverse, in fact. To kill him now would be murder. And that would be unfair.

When he eventually found his way to his chamber in Holyrood, everyone had gone to bed except Andro Wodman, who was visible, fully dressed, throwing illicit dice in a storeroom with a senior carpenter. Nicholas flung his saddlebags down and went to join him.

Round the bandaging, Wodman's face was purple and yellow. Archie had been right. They did need the services of a medical team. Nicholas said, 'I'm sorry. I had to stay last night at Roslin. What's happening?'

'I know. One of Tam Cochrane's cronies came back.'

The carpenter, by which term was understood a highly trained, blue-blooded expert called Lisouris, said, 'And you're going into business with Nowie?'

'Sir Oliver Sinclair to you,' said Nicholas sourly, in the knowledge that Lisouris certainly did call Nowie Nowie.

'And still got your arms and your legs? Watch it,' said Lisouris, who looked like a dancing-master.

'So what about Henry?' said Nicholas. If he sat down, he wouldn't want to get up. He recalled, with amazement, believing at some point that he wanted a woman.

'He's asleep. In the next room to yours. Sweetly sorrowful because, having invited him, you weren't there.'

'So what did he do?'

'Went to Mass, made sexual advances to one of the monks, and was dragged in front of the Abbot. He's leaving tomorrow.'

'Oh,' said Nicholas. He sat down.

'Well, it's what I expected him to do,' Wodman said. 'He didn't. It makes you feel anxious, doesn't it? Whatever he's planning, it'll be a lot worse than that.'

'You bastard,' said Nicholas, and got up. It was as difficult as he had expected. Bed, when he got there, was blissful. He was almost asleep when he remembered his saddlebags, and a passing impression, as he emptied them, that something was missing. He lay for a moment, swore, sat up, and then stood. By the dying light of the brazier, he could see something that he hadn't noticed before, pinned on the wall. A square of paper.

A letter.

No, a drawing. A careful drawing, beautifully done in two colours, of a fox and a hare and two dogs.

'I thought,' said Henry's voice from the door, 'that you liked to look at it, maybe, at bedtime. You sleep better, don't you, with a little something from home? I have an old bit of blanket, myself. Good night, Uncle. Sweet dreams.'

The door shut. Nicholas crossed over and looked at the drawing, then took it down. Apart from the pin-holes, it was perfectly smooth and intact. For a moment, he had an impulse to crush it; then sensibly didn't.

He had been going – he was still going – to Leith, to send it tomorrow, along with the other letter, which was next to his skin and had never left there. The letter, in Phemie's level writing, to Anselm Adorne.

To Gelis van Borselen, looking back to the halcyon years, Bruges had seemed a fine place to rear a child, with its ranks of handsome brown and red houses, ribboned with silvery water and knotted with bridges and wreathed about with its churches, its abbeys, its gardens. Warm and compact and thronged; full of vigour; full of surprises; the richest and most cosmopolitan small business town in the world, Bruges flowered all through the year, but never more so than in September, at the coming of the Venetian galleys, and at Carnival-time, just before Lent. The two marvels of a child's year; of Gelis's year, when she was small. There, up on the Belfry, was the platform from which the speaking-trumpet announced the results of the lottery. There, on the Minnewater, once filled with laughing, tumbling skaters, was where she, a fat child, had first met and been enchanted by Claes the apprentice, soon to be Nicholas.

There, within the walls of the Hôtel Jerusalem, was the lovely church built by the Adornes, where Nicholas, brave and young, had entered into his first marriage, with Marian de Charetty. And there, in the great Palace of Louis de Gruuthuse and his van Borselen wife were the rooms where her own wedding contract to Nicholas had been signed, just a few streets away from where Gelis's sister Katelina had wilfully made him her lover, in the hapless affair that had ended in the birth of a child.

Katelina had died in Cyprus, long before Gelis's own marriage to Nicholas, blighted for eight years, but now mended. Katelina's child had another name, in another country, and believed himself to be another man's son. It was small Jordan, born to Gelis and Nicholas, who should be growing up here as his parents had done, revelling in the whole noisy life of the town: the clack of the looms and the chime of the work-bell; the chanting of children and fullers; the barking of dogs and the cry of the moneychanger wheeling his cart. The rattle of horses bearing officials and merchants about their business. The thunder of wagons and carriages crossing the drawbridges and entering the various portals. The creak and splash of the mills on the water; the rickety chorus of the mills on the walls. The market smells of fish and fruit and butcher-meat. The odour of paint from the book-stalls and the workshops and Colard Mansion's window, and of ink where the printing-presses had been set up. A town of merchants and artisans. A town where children lived with their parents. A family town.

It should have been like that, but the Duke's death had brought Lent in Epiphany. Mourning did not enter into it: every municipality, every province with whom the late Duke had been at odds instantly saw a chance for advancement, and seized it. In Bruges, there was a disturbance almost at once, only reduced when the little Duchess, advised by Louis de Gruuthuse, assured them that their traditional privileges were secure. To keep Bruges calm and safe, she appointed four captains, one of whom was Anselm Adorne, lord of Cortachy.

It had worked, for a bit. Even when the Estates of Holland, swept by local fervour, proposed to end the tenure of Gruuthuse (not a Hollander) as their Governor, Gruuthuse merely acceded, and the office was passed, without fuss, to his brother-in-law. Wolfaert van Borselen was cousin to Gelis, and so was Gruuthuse's own wife. She still felt safe.

Then had come the ill-advised attempt to cajole or buy off the King of France, or at least win time to rebuild the Burgundian armies. King Louis, that masterly tactician, had received the pitiful letters of the little Duchess and the Duke's widow the Dowager; had listened to the Burgundian envoys – Gruuthuse, the Chancellor Hugonet, Wolfaert van Borselen – and had finally lent ear to the worried envoys from Flanders, who were not in immediate danger from the advancing French armies, and who were thriftily unwilling, as always, to pay for yet another Burgundian war.

The King of France had responded very simply by demonstrating, with sorrow, that the little Duchess had no intention, whatever happened, of consulting the Estates-General of the Low Countries about her wars, her future marriages or her alliances, but was obediently following the advice of her (English) stepmother and her late war-crazed father's advisers. The storm over that blew up in Ghent, where the little Duchess was being politely immured by a number of strong-minded officials. But already Gruuthuse had been forced to leave Ghent to help

Anselm Adorne deal with the situation in Bruges, where the clacking of looms was giving way to the sound of arguing voices, and merchants gathered, low-voiced, in private rooms over taverns, and fewer men than usual ran out of their houses when the work-bell clanged, and sometimes those who did were visibly being pushed by their wives. Adorne took the leaders into the Hôtel Jerusalem and talked to them, and they were given a proper hearing in the Hôtel de Ville in the Burg, where Gruuthuse and the Provost of St Donatien listened to them, and made certain adjustments and certain promises, and in the end it died down. But for a while the communal cavalry and the companies of archers and crossbowmen had been waiting uneasily on call: uneasily because most of them, too, were merchants, and those who were not were now supposedly employed by a girl who didn't know what she was doing.

About this time also, the Dowager had been compelled to move out of Ghent, which left the little Duchess alone there. What was not yet commonly known was that the same little Duchess, entertaining her suitors, had (on Gruuthuse's advice) remained loyal to her late father's scheme to marry her to the Archduke Maximilian of Austria, son of the Emperor Frederick. And that the Emperor had not only reaffirmed the contract, but was sending an Imperial embassy to clinch it.

France wouldn't like it.

It was a simple choice between two husbands: between encroaching France and paternalistic Germany, you might say. Personal proclivities didn't come into it. Maximilian was two years younger than she was, and inexperienced at that. The Dauphin was not quite seven, and a hunchback. It was what God liked that mattered.

By then, it had become advisable to keep children off the streets of Bruges, and Gelis did not allow Jodi out, even well guarded, any more than Tilde risked her two little daughters beyond the yards and gardens of the Hof Charetty-Niccolò. Living with Diniz and his family in the great house that had once belonged to Nicholas, Gelis employed her time, profitably, in the company's business, and took what precautions seemed sensible. At least no one now had to be concerned about Tilde's sister Catherine who, miraculously certificated and married at last, had left for Veere, her new home in Zeeland. For Gelis herself, it was also an option, in the last resort, to go to her kinsmen at Veere, but the last resort had not yet occurred. And no one had yet heard from Nicholas.

This was natural. It was not so long since he had sailed. And now, although it was March and the gales had abated, a wintry cold had returned which, she knew, slowed down cargo handling and the transit of goods. She suffered the unending questions of Jodi, who was not interested in frozen rigging, but who knew that ships could sink, and that the Narrow Sea was full of French and English and Polish and Portuguese pirates. She told him of his father's friend Paúel Benecke, who was a professional freebooter and would never harm papa.

She did not tell him that the ship from Scotland, when it came, would not bring his father, but only news of what he was doing. His father had gone to Scotland for his sake and for hers, to deal with the men who had become the stuff of Jodi's nightmares: the fat man of his own name, who had once had him captured at knife-point; the handsome man known as David, who had caused the death of Raffo, Jodi's friend.

Nicholas could not be expected to deal with it quickly; until it was safe, she and Jodi had to stay. She had promised. Had she been alone, she would have broken the promise.

As it was, during the day, Jodi experienced no nightmares, being busy with his books or his riding lessons or his exercises with his small bow. Jodi worked hardest of all when papa was away, so that papa would not be disappointed when they were together again. Gelis was not envious of the bond between Nicholas and his son, but anxious at times, feeling Jodi too young to bear the passion of love that he felt.

Kathi, observing it, had reassured her. 'At the moment, it's all trained on Nicholas, and fortunately Nicholas is a good teacher as well as a parent. He will make sure that Jodi learns to make his own friends.'

'But if he loses Nicholas first?' Gelis had said.

And Kathi had said, soberly for her, 'He will forget. It might be worse, in effect, if Nicholas were to lose him.'

The thought stayed with Gelis, and frightened her, sometimes.

Then the real trouble started.

It began, one frosty morning, with a change in the quality of noise outside her windows. The Spangnaerts Street house was a big building, office, warehouse, stables and domicile at once, set between the canal at the foot of the street and the merchant club at the top, which in its turn was a dog-leg away from the slope of the great market, the Grand' Place of Bruges. Because the canals conducted speech, upraised voices were audible in several different directions, and very clearly from below her own windows, where groups of men were hurrying uphill. From the Grand' Place itself, a breathy sound spoke of a sizeable and increasing crowd.

Diniz came in. 'Trouble. I'm sorry. I've called everyone in and barred the doors, and sent a runner to warn the dyeyard. Kathi and the children are safe at the big house, and Adorne spent the night down the road and is up at the Poorterslogie, trying to knock sense into the eminent brethren of the White Bear.'

His olive skin had darkened to red. Ever since Africa, Gelis had owned to an aunt-like tolerance for Diniz, who was half a St Pol, and who loathed the corpulent Jordan, his grandfather. He was a year younger than she was. She said, 'What are they agitating about this time?'

Diniz said, 'Oh, the usual. Past ducal injustices? Specifically, the good people of Bruges would like the Franc's special privileges stopped, because they're competing too closely with us. If the Duchess does rescind them, of course, the Franchosts will be out there complaining instead.'

The Franc, the Liberty of Bruges, was a collection of neighbouring parishes with inappropriate feudal affiliations and a controversial free-dom from tolls. Ostend and Sluys were among them. The Franc was under the direct control, not of Bruges, but of a lieutenant answering to the late Duke. Gelis said, 'You'll be all right. Rich merchants won't break down your doors.'

'No, but their employees might,' Diniz said. 'And the said rich merchants won't stop them. Tommaso Portinari is in there, complaining with the best. The Duke died owing the Medici Bank six thousand groats.'

'Stupid Tommaso,' Gelis said. 'But it must have been good while it lasted. If Tommaso breaks your windows, I'll send someone to spit on all the oils of himself that he commissioned.'

'You couldn't even count them, never mind spit on them,' said Diniz. 'Damn!'

She also had heard it. Breaking glass. Painted glass, expensive as painted gold. 'It wasn't Tommaso,' said Diniz, beginning to move, 'but I'd better find out.'

Gelis went to the counting-house, then to the kitchens, then went to Tilde's rooms and found Clémence and Jodi with Diniz's wife. Gelis said, as she'd said to everyone else, 'It isn't personal, Tilde. We represent a rich business that won't be worried by competition with the Franc, and they resent it: it's as simple as that.'

'I'd feel safer with something more logical,' Tilde said. 'Some day they won't let Anselm Adorne calm them down. They'll get their pikes out and start wrecking in earnest.'

There was another crash. Jodi looked from one face to the other. He said, 'Papa will save us.'

Clémence said, 'I'm sure he would, if we needed saving. But that's just window-glass breaking, not us. And the door is barred. No one can get in.'

It was true. It would also be true of Kathi, behind the high walls of the Hôtel Jerusalem, well away from the centre of town. But other houses were less well protected.

Diniz came in. 'Good news. Adorne sent to Gruuthuse last night, and he's bringing an armed troop from Ghent.'

Tilde said, 'Won't that make it worse? If they feel they're being rounded up before being given a hearing?'

'He knows the dangers,' Diniz said. 'Adorne does understand his people, and they respect him. All it needs is some face-saving. An excuse to stop the violence and talk.'

When he left the room, Gelis went with him. It would be dark by late afternoon. If the unrest lasted longer, they would keep all the staff overnight. There was food, and bedding of sorts. She wished that Andreas was with them, a wise man as well as a doctor, but he was somewhere in battle-torn France, called to the side of some friend in distress. Dr Tobie, Clémence's husband, was in Nancy. It didn't matter. They were hardly going to need doctors.

She listened. Now the noise from the south was coming in waves, suggesting single voices followed by massed shouting. Diniz said, 'Adorne's troops and Breydel are at the Grand' Place, protecting the way into the Burg. Look, I'll have to go and help. Don't tell Tilde.'

The Burg was the Duke's territory. A fortified square, washed on two sides by the river, it held the prison known as the Steen. Also the Hôtel de Ville, the Duke's collegiate church of St Donatien, and the elaborate, defenceless town hall of the Franc.

The prison held prisoners, ripe for releasing by compliant jailers. The Hôtel de Ville held the burgomasters and magistrates of Bruges, including those appointed by the late Duke. The church of St Donatien, although bearing the ducal arms on its doors, had yet objected so strongly to paying the last lot of ducal war taxes that half its canons had ended up in the Steen. And, finally, the Palais du Franc was a sitting target to everyone.

Gelis said, 'Diniz, one man won't do much for those odds.' Clémence had quietly joined them.

'If they break through, no one can stop them,' Diniz said. 'Or not until Gruuthuse comes. But if they can't break through, they'll try something else. The arsenals. The Belfry – it's got the town seals. The houses of men from the Franc. I can take some men and reinforce the worst places, or get people out.'

'They don't know Gruuthuse is coming?' Gelis said. 'It might even stop them. Or – Who holds the keys to the gates? Adorne and the other captains, I suppose.' There were five miles of ramparts and nine gates into Bruges, each with its drawbridge and portcullis, and some with a depot of arms. The Ghent Gate, by which Gruuthuse would come, was approached by a bridge and consisted of a collection of massive drum towers, battlements, platforms and spires, with a gold weathercock trembling on top: come quickly, Louis de Gruuthuse; the wind has changed.

She said, 'The Carpenters' Guild looks after the Ghent Gate, doesn't it?' There were fifty-two trade-guilds in Bruges. She knew the Dean of the Carpenters.

Diniz said baldly, 'No.' Then remembering whose wife she was, he said, 'If one man couldn't help in the Burg, then one woman couldn't help in a hand-to-hand fight at the Gate. And not even you could change the Dean's mind in front of his own guild.'

'I could watch,' she said. 'And report, if you'll tell me where. A servant's cap, and a cloak and an apron, and I can go where you can't. If it gets difficult, I have places to go – the van Borselen house in Silver Straete, and Gruuthuse's own place, and the Hospital of St John – Adorne's son might even be there. Arnaud.'

'He will be. It's one of the chief arsenals,' Diniz said. 'I can't let you. Think of Nicholas.'

'Do you imagine he is thinking of me?' Gelis said. 'He is doing what he has to do. And I am doing the same.'

Clémence said, 'That is true. Before he went, Nicholas took care for Bruges. It is not to say that, then and now, he does not think of you, as you think of him while you breathe.' She smiled, and Gelis, remembering Tobie, looked at her with softened eyes, and smiled in return.

To Diniz, she said. 'Thank you. But whatever you say, I am going. Nicholas would understand.'

It was worse, outside, than she had expected, partly because of the gloom. It was hardly midday, but windows glowed orange behind her, and at the top of Spangnaerts Street, every floor of the White Bear was lit, casting flickering light on the congealing mud on the streets. The streets before and behind her were empty, but massed roars ahead, by their compact nature, made her think that the crowd was still in one pack, and had not yet broken through to the Burg. Adorne of Cortachy and Jan Breydel and their firm, loyal crossbowmen must be holding it. The third officer, Gruuthuse's own son, might also be there. Holding on;

trying to make themselves heard; offering to talk over their grievances; restraining their impulse to respond when the first missiles started to come. Gelis sent them a silent message of goodwill.

Her hope was that the Ghent Gate was open, and that the porters would be keeping slack watch. They would stop any horseman from leaving, but a woman on foot might slip out. And a woman with money could pick up a horse of sorts, once outside, and ride to meet her good cousin Louis with an exact report of the situation in Bruges. And then might return, in equal secrecy, with Louis's orders.

But first, what was the situation in Bruges? She knew where the arsenals were. Walking swiftly and quietly, head down, she turned up towards the Grand' Place but did not enter it, sliding westwards instead through the deserted egg-market and taking the street that ran past the Princenhof. The great gates were closed, behind which she had feasted with Nicholas on the Duke's wedding day, and her own. She could see guards, and there were some silent groups in the street, looking up, but no threat of assault, or not yet. She slowed, crossing the street and turning at last to the south, into Silver Straete.

Here was the house rented once and now owned by her family. By her cousins: she had no family now, since her parents and sister were dead. Correction. She had a family she did not deserve, better by far. And as Clémence saw, she was attempting to do what Nicholas would have done, and what Jodi, one day, would hear she had done.

She did not stop there, other than to register that the doors and the shutters were closed. Men who turned against authority might turn against the van Borselens, too. But of necessity, surely, she could shelter there. She walked on.

Ahead lay the Palace of Louis de Gruuthuse, with the church of Nôtre Dame beside it. Within, a bridge of convenience ran from the house to the church, and underground, there were two other, more secret connections. No one, even a king, would be trapped in this place. Again she saw barred doors and a guard, but not a large one. Louis de Gruuthuse and his wife were not there, and his household militia were at the Burg, supporting Adorne.

Now she was almost ready to strike fully south for the Ghent Gate. She lingered, listening. This was an area where the streets were deserted of folk, and the winter dirt on the paving was crisp and whitening under her feet, with few lights about within the rows of huddled, dark houses. The sky, which had seemed full of snow, lay on the roof-tops like lead on a casket, and the occasional voice, from a window or yard, piped like the cry of a bird. Behind her, too, the shouting had dulled to the sound of a rookery, broken by small stabs of sound: someone was issuing orders through the Belfry's official speaking-trumpet. She had sallied forth like a ship giving battle, and there was nothing for her to do. The mob was being contained. When her cousin came, with his orderly troop, the people would quieten, and tomorrow would send their elect to the bargaining table.

She hesitated, but being set on her course, decided to finish it. Louis should be told what was happening, and the Gate, now, should be easy to pass. On her way, she could still check on the two arsenals, the first at the Hospital of St John, where Dr Andreas once used to serve. The other was farther on, at the Abbey of Eckhout, better known for the great processions of May, when the White Bear jousters marched from the Abbey. Adorne had won the Horn from the Duchess one year, and Breydel the Spear. She hardly needed to visit either place, except that they lay on her road to the Gate. If there had been any trouble, she would be able to hear it from here.

She had almost come to the Hospital when she realised that there was a change in the air, but that it came from behind, not ahead. The faint sound of the rookery had altered. Straining to listen, it seemed to her that it had become uneven, and louder, as if it had found some sort of focus; had become an expression even of panic as well as rage. She turned, her heart beating, facing the quiet streets, her back to the vast hooded doorway of the Hospital complex. Then she gasped, for someone laid hands on her shoulders. Whirling, she saw that the door behind now stood partly open, and that Arnaud, one of the younger sons of Anselm Adorne, had her in his grasp, and was trying to hustle her towards it. He spoke breathlessly. 'I saw you from above. Come quickly. In here. Someone has warned the crowd that Gruuthuse is coming. They'll man the gates, look for arms. Will you *come*?'

The noise had swelled. Gelis ran, and the great doors of the Hospital slammed shut behind them.

Nearly four hundred years old, this was a hospital for the poor sick of both sexes, accommodated in clean, spartan halls tended by nuns of the Augustinian Order and brethren of the Knights Hospitaller of St John. It accommodated, from time to time, wounded soldiers. And because it was thick-walled and ancient, it had become, like all sacred buildings, a safe place to store arms. It was, after all, in the Order's tradition to defend the Christian right. And Anselm Adorne had close connections with this particular place: thirty years ago, the Hospital's guardian had been his father Pieter Adorne, Receiver-General of Flanders and Artois.

Arnaud had a young wife and a daughter born only last year. Phemie Dunbar had come from Scotland to care for them. Gelis said, 'You shouldn't be here,' and he smiled and said, 'Do you think I would have brought you in, if there had been an alternative? There isn't time to go anywhere else. Listen.'

And now the roaring was loud.

She said, 'Will you let them have what they want? There are sick people to think of.'

She had always thought of Adorne's family as curiously ineffectual: from the eldest, a church lawyer in Rome, to the adolescents who had made their way, one by one, to this convent or that monastery. Two sons and two daughters had married, but were either childless or had only daughters. Margriet Adorne had died from trying to give him a last fertile, vigorous son who would bring him the grandsons who would continue his line. It seemed that all the spirituality of the Adornes had become invested in their descendants, and none of the other attributes: the courage, the wit, the authority of Anselm Adorne. Which existed, too, in Adorne's young niece, Kathi Sersanders.

Arnaud said, 'It seemed possible that this might happen. Father helped us move all the arms yesterday. We are to pretend we don't understand, and hold the doors as long as we can. Father says that it will buy time until someone can rescue us.'

The Adorne courage was not, then, truly lacking. Gelis said, 'How can I help?'

Soon enough, she had to maintain her own courage, when the torches were massed outside the door, and stones were cracking against the speckled brick and the elderly, exquisite carvings and the canopies of the small, adhesive shrines. That was when they were still parleying, and someone of sensibility had shouted crossly for the stone-throwers to cease. Then Arnaud, from his upper window, had reiterated his plea, on behalf of the sick, to be left in quietness, and had conveyed, for the second or third time, his incomprehension over what he was hearing. An arsenal? But that was long ago. Handguns and crossbows and culverin? Surely not.

'Then let us in. Let us see for ourselves, and we'll go!'

Then the Almoner took his place at the window, and a physician, and the crowd were told sternly to disperse. They didn't, of course. They sent men round the back, who got in over the walls and ran between the ranges of buildings and smashed in the big door at the back, and came racing through all the dormitories, opening doors and flinging back the lids of the chests.

There were not so many patients to suffer the noise: Adorne had evacuated all but the dying, and those lay at the end of one hall, where one or two monks held them close, and a priest, on his knees, intoned softly. Gelis remained with the weeping maids in the kitchen, listening as the place was ransacked; hearing the shout of triumph as the underground storehouse was found; the roar as it proved to be empty. She wondered what rescue Arnaud expected. Any men his father could spare would certainly have been sent to the Gate, and to protect the arsenals that had not been evacuated.

This store was empty. Having been made free of the place, the attackers were not likely, surely, to endanger their souls by harming holy men and innocent people. They could only vent their disappointment on wood and stone and glass.

So she thought until, the noise receding, she was tempted to leave the kitchens and go seeking Arnaud. She found him on the floor of the dispensary with a doctor bending over him. The floor was spattered with blood and strewn with shards of smashed jars. She exclaimed.

The doctor said, 'They wanted to know where the arms were. Then some horsemen came up the road, and they left him and ran. He's taken a beating. He'll be all right.'

Arnaud looked up and grimaced. He had lost a tooth, and everything about him looked painful and battered. Gelis said, 'If you knew, you should have told them. By the time they find it, Louis will surely be here. Do you know how near he is?'

The physician looked round. 'At least two hours away, these men were saying. They have better spies than you'd think. And whether they trace Master Arnaud's arsenal or not, the mob have found some artillery somewhere, they say, and are going to use it at the Ghent Gate. I'm afraid your cousin is going to have a fine welcome.'

Gelis got up. Arnaud rose on one elbow. His mouth was bleeding. 'Gelis, you can't do anything.' It emerged as a lisp.

She said, 'I can try. That's what I was going to do. Get out through the Gate somehow and go to meet Louis. Mobs are often divided. Not all of them may want violence. The Gate may be open.'

Someone said, 'The spokesmen may want to be civilised, but the rest don't. The portcullis is down, its cable cut. You won't be able to get out that way, Gelis.'

It was Diniz Vasquez. He brushed past her and knelt. 'Arnaud?'

'It's nothing,' said Adorne's son. He sat up, the doctor supporting his back. Then he said, '*Kathi!*'

Gelis turned. It was Kathi, Arnaud's cousin. Kathi, her eyes large and darker than hazel in a colourless face, within a long hooded cloak that shrouded her small frame like a quilt. Kathi, who had been safely locked with her children in the Hôtel Jerusalem, on the farther side of the town.

Diniz said, 'I had to bring her. We've had some news as well. From the other direction, from Damme. They knew Gruuthuse had set off from Ghent. They also knew of someone else on the road: another party well on its way, and likely to get here before them. Gruuthuse's is a troop of armed cavalry. The other is an ordinary convoy of wagons for Bruges, with a small escort, but no arms to speak of. They set off before Gruuthuse. They don't know anything's wrong.'

'If it's dark, the Gate will mistake them and fire,' Gelis said. 'Or they'll be caught in the crossfire against Louis. Can anyone warn them?'

Then she saw the look on his face, and on Kathi's.

'I hope so,' said Diniz. 'The carts are from Nancy. Robin is with them.'

Chapter 6

Come of hir husband that was went fra hame
A fals tythand: hir husband suld be deid,
Scho wepit so and swownit in that steid
As sho ourcome and went furth at the zet,
All sudanly hir husband that scho met.

ONCE, A BOY of eighteen, Diniz Vasquez had travelled and argued and fought with Gelis and Nicholas and a woman called Bel on a journey to win gold in Africa, and there had discovered a hard-won maturity. Before that had come the long apprenticeship on the island of Cyprus, when Diniz had lost his father and watched Gelis's own sister die, and had formed the undying bond of love and respect that he felt for Nicholas. It was Diniz who had saved Nicholas at the battle of Nancy.

Now, standing in the ravaged Hospital of St John, he said, 'That is why I am here. Lord Cortachy sent me. To make sure you were safe. And to get outside the town somehow with a warning. It must be done. And you will both wait here for me.'

Then Gelis said, 'I will come with you.' And when Kathi said 'No!' she rounded on her with roughness. 'There must be two: one to go for horses and the other to keep to the road. And it must seem innocent, as it might with a woman and a man. And you are not to go because if you and Robin both die, then what of your children?'

The large eyes were chilled. Kathi said, 'And I know the other reason. You think it is cold enough for the Minnewater to be bearing again.'

It was what she had thought. She had not said so. It was how Diniz had lost his mother, long ago: drowned in the broken floes of a little river by Berecrofts. It was how Gelis, too, had nearly died, below the ice of the Nor' Loch of Edinburgh.

It did not matter to her. It did not matter, either, to Diniz. He looked at her, struck. 'Of course. You know the Minnewater, all the canals from your childhood. You will know where it freezes up first.' And, of course, she did.

They went quickly, then. Kathi came to the postern and caught Gelis and kissed her, just before she stepped through. 'That is for you,' Kathi said. 'And for Robin, if you see him.'

It was different, now, from the dark empty roads outside Spangnaerts Street. As the day grew towards dusk and the cold hardened, the chilled crowds had left the stinking, unprofitable barrier of the Burg for the warmer business of smashing into the places where pikes and hatchets were stored, and helping to drag the small culverin that someone had found, and cheering on a barrow loaded with gunpowder bales and some hackbuts. The roads to each of the southernmost gates were filled with determined people, and the way to the Ghent Gate was packed.

Gelis was dressed as she had been, and Diniz had cast off his half-armour and helm and wore a servant's gear from the Hospital: a cap with flaps and a rough felted cloth over a worn leather tunic, hose and boots. Soldiers alone or in small groups could do nothing in this sort of crowd. Adorne must have had to regroup: leaving part of his force by the Grand' Place and sending the rest to protect what they could; avoiding fire; avoiding bloodshed; spinning out time until Gruuthuse should come; hoping that darkness and cold would take the heart out of the rising. Battling through the crowds, anonymous in the flickering gloom, Gelis glimpsed now and then the flash of plate steel in the distance, where men were travelling swiftly to one danger point or another, to mass with their weapons. Some carried trumpets, and she saw saddle-drums: ready to rally, and parley. But the mob voice might prevail before then.

Diniz, his arm in hers, was half running now. They had faced death together before, but with Nicholas sharing it with them, and sharing the sense of exhilaration, of comedy, of high adventure which he brought to everything he did. She thought of a dangerous, exuberant piece of play-acting on an enemy ship in an African anchorage, and the sheepish joy in the eyes of Diniz and Nicholas, lurching on board from a night at Tendeba. Diniz said, 'I wish Nicholas could be here,' which made her look at him, beginning to smile. Then, ashamed, she saw that her mind had been seduced into a dream, while he was facing reality. They had to cross out of the town. They had to get horses. They had to waylay and stop everyone on the road, beginning with the slow convoy from Nancy, so near home at the end of its journey. And at best, in the darkness and cold, to turn it aside to find shelter while the battle between the town and the Duke's former men played itself out. She did not speak, and neither did Diniz, for soon they were leaving the crowds and turning into the dark, by the water.

There were few people there, and those who laboured past, going home, were the elderly or the disenchanted or the cautious, who preferred not to see a protest escalate into a killing. She and Diniz were not the first, obviously, to try to cross the waterway since the gates had been blocked: the frosty grass on both banks was well trampled, and the canal lumpy with re-congealed blocks and a frozen litter of planks and random possessions. In war, the town employed men whose sole duty was to break up the ice to preserve the town from invasion. This drop in temperature had come too quickly for that, and in any case the ice was still soft. You could see black water swirl in the centre It was seven feet deep.

Diniz said, 'Where?' and Gelis said, 'Follow me.'

You learned, as a child, which bits froze first; where the eddies were. The nearest place, the shallow pool that lay still, was not here, but far down the bank, where there were no people or lights. She had brought, tied in her apron, two pairs of footed leggings in wool from the sickroom, to drag over their footwear and offer some purchase. If there was enough ice, they would help. Diniz took her wrist as they stepped from the bank, and held it as they edged forwards.

One step; two.

At the first sign of a crack, they could help one another. Lucia, his fair, silly mother, had been riding, unaware that there was ice under the snow. When it gave way, the weight of the horse took her straight down, and the cold of the water had ended it. At first, they had thought Nicholas had driven her on to the river, thinking her to be Simon, her yellow-haired brother, but it was not so.

Two steps; three. How close was the convoy with Robin? It might arrive when they were still in mid-river. But no. In this flat country they would see it. They would hear, far away, the shouts from the watchers on the gatehouse battlements, who would certainly see it. She realised that John, the other prisoner, would be with Robin, and Dr Tobie, Clémence's husband.

Three steps; four. Five steps; six. She slipped, and Diniz's hand tightened and held her, and she steadied. She had been thinking of Jodi. If she died, he had Nicholas. If Nicholas died . . .

She slowed. If she and Nicholas died, and Tobie didn't survive, there was something else; someone other than Jodi whom she had forgotten about. She said, feeling foolish and frightened and cold, standing in the middle of the ice, 'Listen. When my sister died, you were with her. You know that Nicholas has another son? An unacknowledged son by Katelina?'

She heard him draw breath. It was a difficult place. Then he said, 'I guessed. No, I knew. But I haven't told anyone.' He paused, and the ice rocked. He said, 'Don't worry. You're doing better than I am.' He had begun again to draw her across.

She followed, still talking in gasps. 'Tobie knows. There is a paper, lodged with Tobie's notary.' Step, slide and step.

'I see,' Diniz said. 'But you speak as if Nicholas is going to die, too. I'm sure he isn't. Gelis, can you jump?'

They were in the middle, and there the ice was soft, with water spilling and lapping about it. For five feet, or six, perhaps. Beyond that, it looked firm. There was no guarantee. Diniz said, 'I'll go first, and catch you. If I don't manage, don't try to help me. Go back.'

'All right,' she said. It saved time. She wouldn't leave him.

He withdrew his hand, and settled his feet, and balanced, and jumped. She saw him land on all fours, and slip sideways, and then thrust himself over and over, rolling away from the glistening gruel. She could hear him breathing harshly when he got up. He held his hands out, and she jumped as well, into his arms.

He hugged her and said, 'On a tightrope next, with a hoop,' and seized her hand and began leaping, this time, towards the far shore. And arrived there.

There was a little cover: some frozen bushes, the shanks of a sparse piece of woodland. They had already made their plans: he to race off to the nearest farmhouse; she to keep close to the road and make her way, fast, in the direction of the oncoming travellers, where he hoped to join her with horses. It was almost fully dark now, and the road glimmered hoar and white as its surroundings, defined only by the uneven cleared ground at its edge. The cloud had lifted, and there were stars in the sky, except over the town at her back, where the smoke haze had turned red from the massed torches.

Diniz said, 'About what we spoke of. I shall remember. But Henry isn't alone, you know. He does have the St Pols.'

So he did know. He kissed her briefly and went; she set to walking. When she felt safe even from the eyes on the battlements, she picked up her skirts and ran.

Her attackers crept up so quietly that she heard nothing until one sprang before her and the other seized her arms from behind. They were armed, with metal under their cloaks. One of them said, 'And who are you spying for, jonkvrauwe? Or is it really jonkheer?' His hands delved; she kicked him; he gasped, swore and hit her. She bit her tongue: through watering eyes, she glared at him, and then addressed him in vicious, clear French. 'Listen to me, son of a pig. I have escaped from the town. I have urgent news for Monseigneur Louis de Gruuthuse. I am Egidia van Borselen, his wife's cousin. Take me to him, and you may not be hanged. Indeed, you might be rewarded, if I ask it.' Then she said it again, this time in Flemish. Far in the distance, she heard hooves. Diniz, with one horse from the sound of it, and about to rush up and be killed. And further off, surely, the rumble of a great number of riders. And wheels.

It was either Louis, or the convoy. The men holding her were either scouts from one of these, or two of the disaffected from Bruges, and whichever they were, they were very likely to dispose of her now. It was a gamble, but she had nothing much to lose. She drew a breath and screamed, 'Diniz! Go and get Louis to help!' and received another blow as Diniz came hurtling into view, saddleless on a horse like a carpet. He had his sword drawn. The two men released her and drew theirs. She kicked one, and achieved a lock on the other, her knife at his neck. She said, 'Move, and I'll kill. This is Diniz Vasquez. Friend of mine. Friend of Monseigneur's. All you have to do is come with us to Monseigneur.'

'I know you,' said one of the men, staring at Diniz. 'He's who she says he is. So why are you here then?'

'To tell my cousin that the portcullis is down and there are cannon at the Ghent Gate. They're expecting him.'

'Bloody hell,' said the man. 'Why didn't you say so?'

'I did,' Gelis said, lowering her knife and awarding him a single, smart blow on the ear. 'You weren't listening.' Then the rumble of hooves became thunder, and a mass of horsemen filled the Ghent road ahead. The banners were the ones she had hoped for, and the blazon was plain now in the torchlight on the sleeves of the two scouts as well. The blazing twin cannons and the motto, *Plus est en vous*, of Gruuthuse.

It had been a long ride; he must have been tired; but he was an exceptional man, Louis de Bruges, seigneur de Gruuthuse, Earl of Winchester, Prince of Steenhuse, first chamberlain and chevalier d'honneur of the Duchess Marie, Countess of Flanders; and the splendour of his plumed helm, his silver cuirass, his velvet housings and jewelled harness was only the outer manifestation of his quality. The conference was swiftly held there, on the spot, that was to determine what was to come, and all the rest – the surprise, the censure, the commiseration – was relegated until later. With his lieutenants about him, he gave his orders, and only finally turned to his cousin. 'Go behind to the wagons and wait. I am sorry the night is so cold, but it should resolve itself soon, and then you can come in and be comfortable.'

The wagons. It was not just Gruuthuse's troop they had met, it was both the parties expected that night. Gruuthuse had overtaken the convoy from Nancy.

She did not know that she was weeping, mounted on the shaggy horse behind Diniz as it plodded slowly down from the head of the troop, past the massed ranks of armed men. She did not think of what she had just heard, or consider, just yet, the fate of the town at her back, and all those within it: Adorne and his men; her own son and Tilde's daughters at the Hof Charetty-Niccolò; Kathi's children in the Hôtel Jerusalem, separated from the mother who waited with her cousin in the Hospital of St John, among the blood and the shattered glass. And then, yes, Gelis stopped weeping, for this was what Kathi was waiting for.

There were four carts, and perhaps eight men on horseback, dismounted at present, with the reins in their hands, talking in low voices by the roadside. Six were escorts, and two were better dressed: former prisoners well enough to ride. There were two other horses, loosely tied to one of the wagons. The wagons themselves were well made, and quilts and straw and pillows could be seen in the darkness under the hoods, and the muted glow of travelling braziers. Everything possible had been done to make the journey bearable, but of course nothing could help the vibration of the unyielding wheels on the frozen ruts of the road, or prevent the cold air from whining through crannies. There was almost no sound from inside the wagons. Later, Gelis realised that Tobie had been sleeping, exhausted, with his patients slumbering about him. At the time, she saw only John le Grant, grimly awake, silently busying himself in the ultimate wagon, cleaning and setting out handguns. There were only four, and some crossbows. The freed prisoners of Nancy had not expected a fight.

At the sound of the hooves, the engineer set down his rag and looked up, clearly anticipating one of the escort. Then he stayed very quiet, looking at Diniz, and at Gelis seated behind, her hand on his shoulder. Finally he said, 'Is Kathi with you?' and lifted his head a little when Gelis shook hers.

It was Diniz who saw what to do: dismounting with Gelis and extending his hand until John took it, stepping heavily down to the

road and moving across to the side, where they all three stood, apart
from the others. He did not look dirty, or wounded, or starved; simply
very much older, with the vigour gone from his hair, and lines bitten
into his skin. He said, 'I'm sorry. They say we can't get into Bruges
because of some rising. Ghent is the same. The Duke seems to be doing
as much damage dead as he did when he was living, the bastard.'

Gelis said, 'It shouldn't be long.' She added, 'Kathi is waiting with
Arnaud quite close, in the Hospital of St John. We'd only just heard
you were all coming. Then we were afraid you might be involved with
the fighting. But Louis will do something, I know.'

John said, 'I thought you would be in Scotland.' It seemed to be
beyond him to say what had to be said.

Then she saw what he was in fact saying. She said, 'Nicholas is in
Scotland, intent on behaving like the Mastiff of Brittany, as usual. I
shall take Jodi there later. Kathi might join us one day, with her children.
The Berecrofts family would want her.'

She saw that somehow, at last, she had helped him. John said, 'He
is still alive. He's in there,' and nodded towards a dark wagon. 'Tobie
is with him.'

She climbed in gently, Diniz behind her. A brazier glimmered,
softening the cold. Far at the back, the shape under the quilt on the
makeshift mattress of straw was still and silent, and the face of the man
lying there was invisible. Nearer at hand, the doctor lay on his back in
deep slumber, his hat askew on his pale, balding head; his creased cloak
and rucked doublet and jacket far from the standards expected by
Clémence. Diniz said, 'He's all right as well. They've only got to get
through these gates . . . They can't stay here all night.' His face was
wet.

Tobie opened his eyes.

Kestrel's eyes, pale round the dot of the pupil. *There is a problem. I
am assessing it.* He looked exhausted. Gelis said, 'We're outside Bruges,
waiting to clear the Gate and get in. Diniz and I came out to see you.'

Tobie sat up. 'You've seen John, then.' They were speaking in
whispers.

Diniz said, 'He told us Robin was here. That is all.'

'That's all right then,' Tobie said. 'He's sleeping. What's happening?'

Diniz looked at him and at Gelis. 'I'll find out,' he said, and took
the horse and rode off. The cohort ahead hadn't either moved or
dismounted. Sitting in the wagon by Tobie, Gelis watched Diniz ride
its full length and vanish. Tobie didn't speak and, being at a loss what
to do, she was silent. Then suddenly there was movement ahead, but

not what she expected: one of Louis's captains, with Diniz, riding quickly towards them. They stopped at each of the wagons, ending with hers. Diniz looked different. He said, 'It's over.'

It was over because Louis de Gruuthuse, out of hearing and sight of his troops, had ridden alone to the Ghent Gate of Bruges, a torch in his hand, so that they might see without doubt who and what he was. And there, when the shouting had died, he had told them that they could have what they wanted, and that, if they came to the Hôtel de Ville in a day, they would hear read out the Duchess's promise that the rights of the Franc of Bruges, as the Fourth Member for Flanders, would be suppressed.

He was surprised (he said) that they had put Lord Cortachy and the good Master Breydel and his son to such trouble, for between friends, it was only necessary to talk. And, especially, he had hoped to find a welcome this day, when he had come expressly from Ghent to escort men who deserved better from Bruges than to be held up in the cold and the dark while some petty matter of money was settled.

He asked the burghers of Bruges to open wide (he said) the gates of their town to the heroes of the town. The wagons, toilsomely come the long journey from Nancy, which contained the men who had fought for the Duke, and had suffered for it. Those who had given not merely money but their liberty and their health that the states of Burgundy should remain proud and free. 'Will you welcome them?' said Louis de Gruuthuse. 'Will you open your gates, and let them see that they have not fought in vain?'

Ahead of Gelis, the wagons were already lurching into motion. The horsemen remounted, John and Tobie in silence among them. Those who could, sat up in their carts, their cloaks wrapped about them, and peered out as they rocked past the troops and made for the stretch of white road that led to the bridge and the great Gate of Ghent. Gelis and Diniz, separately horsed, rode behind. As they approached, it could be seen that, with effort, the carpenters had raised and secured the portcullis with chains. The mob, weapons forgotten, took their torches and lined all the way, bridge and drawbridge and archway into the town, shouting and singing. And the carts, rumbling, passed over between them and entered the avenue that led to their homes. The people followed. Only then did the troops of Louis de Gruuthuse stir, and without drum or trumpet silently enter the town and disperse as commanded. And Louis himself, after commending all his stalwart captains and the troops of the Burg, took Anselm Adorne and set him in the great chamber of his own Palace, his best wine at his side.

'Seaulme, what would I do without you?' he said. 'And we've brought your Robin home.'

Inside the town, nothing of all this was known in advance. Within the Hospital of St John, time stretched out, and Katelijne Sersanders occupied herself with dogged persistence: rallying the frightened women; setting the carpenters to work; making up the beds that might be needed, should the inevitable happen. She had sent Arnaud home to his wife and, after demurring, he had gone. She did not see how, after all this, it could end in anything other than gunpowder and bloodshed and misery far into the future for Bruges. And in the midst of it were the prisoners, freed at last to face such a homecoming. She did not allow herself even to conjecture that Robin, alive and well, would still be among them.

When the cheering began, she unbarred the door herself, shaking, to permit one of the servants to slip out. When they let him in again, he was too excited to speak. Then he told them that the fighting had stopped. The lord had come alone, and stood at the Gate, and promised Bruges all that it wanted. And the prisoners had arrived and were entering first. The lord had read out all their names, and the husband of the lady Katelijne was among them.

Then the cart had turned in under the archway, with Diniz and Gelis and John le Grant, mounted, beside it, and Tobie was already beside her, talking in a kind, chattering voice about Robin. A long, tiring journey. A bed. A quiet room here, in the Hospital for a day or two, before going to the Hôtel Jerusalem. If she liked, he would have Robin installed, while she took and saw to this list he had written. It itemised drugs that were needed; certain ointments from the Dispensary. If she waited there, he would come to her directly.

Silently, she took the paper and went.

The Dispensary had been cleaned out and swept. She found most of the things on the list, but they did not reveal a great deal by their properties. Tobie would know as much. Tobias Beventini of Grado, friend and physician to armies, had dealt, through the years, with many hundreds of widows and wives; and knew that he had conveyed enough for the moment. She was to see Robin in bed; not before. The others, they told her, had gone. Clémence, too, would be waiting. She thought how tired Tobie had looked, and was stricken.

When he came, she had found some wine for them both, and made him sit.

He smiled a little. 'I am being cosseted.'

'It is about time,' she said. She looked down, and then straight at him. 'The wounds are as Nicholas said? Or did he not tell it all?'

'He didn't know it all,' Tobie said. He waited, and then spoke with simplicity. 'Nicholas thought he saw Robin die. He is experienced and, ordinarily, he would have been right. The shots should have killed. But Robin is young, and he is here for you, alive. He is here, and he is going to survive. Do you understand that?'

'Yes,' she said. 'And whatever you are going to tell me, it doesn't matter.'

His face altered a little. 'I know that, my dear. Here it is. There were several shots. The first was as bad as we feared, and has lost him one leg. The others hit higher. They could have killed, but they didn't. He has his sight, and his speech, and his hearing. They didn't alter his intellect by a shred. But they have deprived him of movement, from shoulder to foot, on one side.'

'On which side?' she said.

'On the left. The side of the leg he still has.'

'Is he in pain?' Kathi said. 'No, how silly. Of course.'

'It is getting less. It will go.'

She said, 'Does he wish that he'd died?' and was surprised when he laid his hand on hers.

Then he removed it and said, 'Yes, at first. Then he remembered you, and the children, and us. I think he is grateful, now, that he didn't. But he needs time.'

And us. She thought how wise Tobie was, in some things. Dear as she was to Robin, and he was to her, they shared their trust and their friendship with others. She said, 'Is he ready to see me?'

'For a little,' Tobie said. 'Then he must sleep.'

He took her to Robin's door, but she went in alone.

He lay on a low pallet bed, looking up. Tousled brown hair; deep eyes; wrist and finger bones frail on the coverlet; and the young, young face full of calm.

'Kathi,' said Robin of Berecrofts. 'I'm so sorry. I can't walk.'

'I know,' she said, and sat carefully down, and slipped her hand into his, which tightened a little. The other was under the cover. She said, 'If you can't suffer it, then you needn't. But we all hope that you'll try. Will you try?'

'It's why I came back,' he said.

Then she laid her cheek on his, and stayed there, her hands curled at his neck, her weight where nothing could harm him. When she kissed him, he closed his eyes, and did not open them again for a long time.

On Friday, the seventh day of March, 1477, an orderly crowd, ranged below the balcony of the sugar-spun Hôtel de Ville of Bruges, heard read out in French and Flemish a solemn undertaking, on behalf of the Duchess Marie, Countess of Flanders, to return to the town all its communal liberties, its commercial monopolies, and its lordship over Sluys and the other towns of the Franc, including superiority over the commune, now the new town of Middleburg. This was followed by a joint announcement by the Deans of the trades, to the effect that their members, having laid down their arms in their guild-houses, were now free to disband. The bells rang, the crowd dispersed, and those who had lost money by neglecting their work over the past few days returned to their workshops and tables, while preserving their privilege to meet, as had become the custom, to further develop their opinions over an ale-pot in their parlours and taverns.

Anselm Adorne ceased for a while to frequent the Poorterslogie at the top of Spangnaerts Street, but took the chance, over several days, to visit his son Maarten's Carthusian convent, to call upon his daughters similarly immured in Sint-Andries and Steenbrugge; to visit his youngest son Antoon, who was training for the priesthood, and to confirm that his married son Pieter in Ghent was still safe. He knew that his eldest son Jan, in Rome with Cardinal Hugonet, was frustrated as ever, but secure. Elizabeth and Marie had good husbands who would protect them. And of course, first of all, on the very night of the rising, he had gone to comfort Arnaud, of whom he was proud. Arnaud's wife was of the good blood of the Nieuenhoves, but frail after the birth of her daughter. It did not look as if she was preparing for another infant just yet.

The rest of his time, Adorne of Cortachy spent in conference with Louis de Gruuthuse and the other officers of the Duchess and of the town. When he could not avoid it, he went home.

In the recesses of her mind, his niece Kathi registered his absence, and understood it, and was grateful for the prayers that she knew had begun, and would continue, wherever her uncle had friends. For the rest, the King of France and his armies might be ruling Bruges from inside the White Bear, for all she knew or cared.

At first, Robin remained at the Hospital and, hour by hour, Tobie taught her how to care for him. While Tobie slept, John le Grant took his place at her side. It was as if he could not keep away; as if, weary as he was, his only relief lay in maintaining the same dogged routine that had kept Robin alive through the long weeks of their joint captivity. It was Tobie who persuaded him that Robin belonged to his wife, and that John should seek proper rest and recuperation in the Hof Charetty-Niccolò. Then, also at Tobie's suggestion, Kathi brought her invalid back to the Hôtel Jerusalem. There, better than her own house, she could keep the children's household apart, and the nuns who looked after her uncle were at hand. So, too, was Mistress Cristen, the children's own nurse, and Clémence came often, in between the visits of Tobie. At first, indeed, Tobie had continued to stay all day, every day, until she took him aside and asked what he thought she was doing wrong. John le Grant and Gelis, who never came without sanction, were the only other persons she admitted. This was not a matter for communal management. This was between Robin and herself.

She knew, because she understood him so well, that now was not the time to be bracing and jocular. It was not the time, either, to be tender and warmly compassionate. They were two people with a difficult problem, in a situation which involved, or could involve pain and resentment and anger, or at the very least an unending affliction of petty embarrassments; leading to lessening confidence, a growing sense of inadequacy.

They held no soul-searching talks; they did not need to. They took the situation and worked at it together. Then, at the end, they would admit the public. In those days, it was their friends who wept, not Kathi or Robin.

The day after he came home from Nancy, Tobie wrote a letter, with Kathi's consent, to Robin's father in Scotland, and another to Nicholas. He hoped Nicholas was alive to receive it, since no one had heard from him since he left. But then, it was still barely March.

It was still early March, and the repercussions of the Duke's death had not stopped. Going about her business, with the silent company, on occasion, of John, Gelis brought back fragments of information to add to that already reaching the counting-house. It was, as ever, from Ghent, where the departure of the Dowager Duchess had been followed by an upsurge of French-fostered suspicion. Who were these men, asked the Gantois, who were making pacts in the name of the state, but without its sanction? Causing towns to surrender to France, arranging unsuitable bridegrooms for the Duchess, betraying their office? Once more, executions began: of minor malfaisants, or former unreliable officials who had abused the town's trust. Gruuthuse rode between the two towns, and Adorne, it was known, was deeply anxious once more about his son.

'They won't do more,' Gelis said. 'Easter is coming.'

Easter was coming, and the Governor of Bruges sent to Middleburg to import cannon and gunpowder. Easter came, and the people of Ghent, invoking the law, arrested not an elderly alderman, but the great and learned ducal Chancellor William Hugonet, lord of Saillant, Époisses and Lys, Viscount of Ypres, close confidant of the little Duchess and her father; staunch adviser at Trèves; saviour of the Duke's reputation in crisis after crisis. And with him, they had arraigned another of the Duchess's suspect inner circle, the Knight of the Golden Fleece Guy de Brimeu, sire de Humbercourt, who led the élite squadron of ordnance at Neuss and who, with Hugonet, had taken part in the negotiations with France, and so could be blamed, however groundlessly, for the consequences.

Arrested them, questioned them for six days on the rack, found them guilty, and, on the third day of April, hanged them on the public scaffold in Ghent, which also saw the slaughter of the papal protonotary, the ducal Treasurer for Ghent, and sixteen other servants of the late Duke.

The news came to Bruges, accompanied by a summons to action. Now is the time to clear your town of the miserable agents of ducal corruption! You too have been exploited! You too have been asked to shed your blood for your country while those noblemen laugh in their palaces, who took your money, took your young men to die for the whim of the Duke! Act as Ghent does! Refuse to fight until your town has been cleansed! The burgomasters of those years, the Treasurers: all, all must pay!

This time, hearing the roar of the crowd, Gelis van Borselen did not go seeking help, because no help could reach Bruges in time. On the other hand, the waterways were now clear, and the Hof Charetty-Niccolò had a boat that could be carried down to the canal and launched, with herself and John le Grant and eight armed men to propel it. She had left Jodi behind, in a house that was full of men, and well protected, and in no danger of serious attack. Diniz had never held civic office. In the Hof Charetty-Niccolò he was safe, and so was she, wherever she was. She was a van Borselen.

The walls of the Hôtel Jerusalem were manned, but she was recognised and allowed into the grounds. In the house, they were met immediately by Kathi. She said, 'Go back. The town guard is coming, and we are not to defend ourselves, or resist. Our men are there only in case others try to burst in.' She was without colour, her eyes enormous as they had been in the Hospital.

Le Grant said, 'Where is your uncle?'

'Here,' said Kathi. 'They are coming to arrest him. They have found some authority; he says it is necessary to let the law take its course. He is here to surrender, so that there will be no reason to harm the rest of us.'

'You have a boat,' Gelis said quickly. 'We have ours. We could take you all and escape.'

A little of the starkness left Kathi's face. She said, 'Thank you, but no. We should be caught, and it would only cause bloodshed. And there are the children, and Robin.' She paused and said, 'You are such good friends, to have come. I'm sorry to seem ungrateful. I thought Uncle should escape too, but he won't. He says he will stand by his record. After all he has done for Bruges, they will surely be ashamed, and release him.'

John le Grant said, 'I don't understand how they can make a case of any kind. Is he the only one?'

'No. He isn't the only one,' Kathi said. 'They're rounding up the magistrates, the burgomaster who worked with him – Paul van Overtweldt, Jean de Baenst, Barbesaen . . . everyone in office when the Duke was raising money for his wars. My uncle gave money himself – do you think they have forgotten the forced levies? Two hundred, two hundred and fifty pounds he paid for the Duke's wars out of his own pocket. Even Dr Andreas had to pay.' She broke off. 'They're not all mad. He has only to stand up in court, and it will all be judged in his favour. But it would be best not to be here when they come. Please go, John. You saved Robin for me. I can't let you do more. He'd blame me if you did.'

John le Grant was red-headed, and Scots. He said, 'I'll go if Adorne tells me to go.'

'You know he will,' Kathi said. 'Not to resist is our best protection. And as someone who fought at Nancy, you can speak for him better outside prison than in it. Do you want me to wake him, do you want me to disturb Robin so that they may both tell you that?'

'No,' said John. 'If you're sure.' Since he came back, he had changed.

Gelis said, 'John has to go. But, Kathi, would anyone object if I stayed? An innocuous female? Would you mind?'

'No,' Kathi said. 'Please stay.'

John le Grant went, silently, taking Diniz's men. Gelis waited to make sure that he did. Then she turned back into the house, where Kathi waited. She said to Kathi, 'Does Robin know what is happening?'

Kathi said, 'It would be rather hard for him not to know.' It sounded like a rebuke, and she caught herself suddenly. 'I mean it's best, if you think of it, to tell him everything. He isn't fond of being protected.'

Of course he wouldn't be. Gelis thought suddenly of how he must feel, a man helpless in the presence of another man's crisis and even, by his impairment, preventing the other from flight.

But no. Adorne had stayed not because of Robin, but because he was a magistrate, and had spent his life upholding the law. He must trust the law to uphold him now.

They stayed in the public rooms, she and Kathi, from which the road could be watched. They talked, in a desultory way. Occasionally Kathi would leave, to reassure the rest of the household, to visit the children and presumably Robin. Gelis thought that Adorne was in his own room, and was startled when, drifting over the courtyard alone, she opened the door of the church and, walking into the quietness, found him there.

He had been kneeling at the altar, alone. He raised his head with composure and turned. Then he said, 'Ah Gelis, my dear,' and rose to his feet.

He did not look very different. The fine bones of the face were perhaps starker than usual, and the amusement gone from his mouth and his eyes. But the well-cut doublet in rich, sober cloth, the velvet cap on the crisp silver-fair hair were the choice of a well-born man of authority, not a self-seeking petty official. He wore none of the emblems of the King of Scotland or the Doges of Genoa, but only a crucifix. And he knelt in the church whose foundation stone he had laid as a child, before the bone-white sculpture of the Passion; beside the rectangles on the floor where his wife's sarcophagus and his own would eventually lie, if mob rule did not first destroy both his home and his church.

Gelis said, 'I didn't mean to disturb you. Forgive me.'

'No. Stay,' he said. 'You have come to be with Kathi? I am glad. But it is dangerous outside. You might have been better in Scotland after all. Although I still think that Nicholas took the right decision. He must deal with those who have threatened you, or who would use you and your son as a weapon. And here, anyone from Veere will be safe. Have you heard from Nicholas?'

There was a cross-stool by the wall which he held for her, before taking another himself. He was not booted, like a man about to ride far: his calf and thigh, extended in the fine hose, were shapely. She wondered how often Kathi was brought up now by something as trivial. Robin, loose-limbed and agile, would never wear fine hose again. She said, 'Nicholas? No. But they will tell me if a ship comes with a letter.'

'It might come into Veere,' Adorne said. 'Send to Wolfaert. He will make sure the message comes quickly, no matter what's happening. You wouldn't go to Nicholas then?'

'No,' Gelis said. 'It would only make it less easy for him. And I want to be here.'

'I'm glad you are,' he said again. He had been listening. 'But now –'

Behind her, the door had opened again, to the sound of booted feet. It must have been what he was waiting for when she came. A man started to speak. Adorne rose. He said, 'I know why you are here. I am coming. Only let me take leave of my niece. The lady with me is leaving.'

She stood beside Kathi and watched as he left. She said, 'He will be back. They will let him go. Nicholas will come and plough Flanders with salt if they don't.'

'I know what you mean,' Kathi said. 'It is what I was thinking as well. I suppose it is a tribute to something. Simple, childlike, hot-headed justice, which everyone expected of Claes. But he does things rather differently now. And in any case, he's in Scotland, doing them to David de Salmeton and others, I hope.'

The letter from Nicholas did come to Veere, and was sent by her cousin Wolfaert to Gelis by courier. By the time she received it, Anselm Adorne had been in prison for some time, and facing, with his fellow accused, a process of questioning which did not rule out the possibility of torture. The date for a tribunal had not been fixed. To all the protests and demands of the ducal officers, the magistrates simply replied that there was a case to answer at law, and that the law would decide.

Well, they would see about that. Wolfaert van Borselen would see about that. Sitting in her room in the Hof Charetty-Niccolò, breathing shakily, with the packet in her hands, Gelis thought of all the times that Claes, the happy-go-lucky apprentice, had been beaten and thrust into the Steen by edict of Anselm Adorne. They had been on opposite sides, Nicholas and Adorne, many times, but Nicholas had never borne grudges for punishment he knew he deserved. In those days, he tolerated even undeserved punishment with good humour. But not now.

At first she gripped the packet without tearing it open, deferring the moment, savouring the fact that he had written, and so must be safe. Then she cut the strings and unfolded the outer paper to find, surprised, that inside there was less than she thought: a small note of one page for herself, and a larger one folded in half, and covered with a very fine drawing of a fox and a hare and two dogs, signed by T. Cochrane, and obviously destined for Jodi. Well, thank you, Tam Cochrane. Without you, he would have sent a much smaller package. She unsealed the note to herself.

It was in code. Busy Nicholas. Market secrets already?

She was good at codes, and hardly had to look up anything. It was one particular to themselves, so that she translated the last few lines first, which proved to be the only personal ones in the note, but which could hardly have been more specifically personal. She flushed, and choked to herself as she read them, because he would know very well the disturbance he was causing. She hoped he felt as frustrated himself when he wrote it. Then she deciphered the rest of the letter and sat, deep in troubled thought, for a long time. Finally she turned back, with rather more care, to Master Tam Cochrane's generous drawing.

It consisted of more than one folded sheet. Sealed between them, and freed only by a very sharp knife, was another note, addressed, in handwriting she did not recognise, to Anselm Adorne, Baron Cortachy.

Gelis rose and went to find Tobie's wife Clémence, whose wisdom she respected, and who could keep a secret, as he could, to the grave. Clémence went out. Later that day, it became known that Lord Cortachy seemed unwell, and Dr Tobias had undertaken to visit him. His visit was short. Leaving, he made his way, as might be expected, to the Hôtel Jerusalem, to reassure the sick man's niece, Katelijne.

To Kathi he said immediately, 'He isn't ill. It was a ruse, to let me hand him a letter from someone. This letter. Your uncle wants you to see it.'

He watched her read it: young Kathi, whom he knew so well, and who had shouldered the burdens of others all her short life. And then Robin. And now, this.

He had found before that men of a certain class, of a certain birth, were careless in the matter of bastards, as servants were not. Or were hungry for heirs, even base-born ones. Or sometimes a girl would fib about taking precautions, in the hope of a child. Or yet again, sometimes love, or lust was so intense that the experience was supreme; the consequence nothing.

Whatever the cause, the consequence now was painful to contemplate. Phemie Dunbar of Haddington Priory was with child by Adorne, and would give birth in July to a bastard child whom everyone would know to be his. Dispensation could not be summoned in time, even if it were deemed proper to give it. And support from Adorne there would be none, for he was here, and on trial for his life.

Kathi said, 'Where was he when he read it?' She hadn't looked up.

'Alone,' said Tobie. 'I paid for a room.' He had been inescapably there as Adorne read the letter. The doctor had stared hard through the bars of the window until he heard Adorne force his breathing under control. Then Tobie had turned and said, 'What do you want done?'

'Or undone?' Adorne had said. His lashes were wet, but his face was as disciplined as his voice. And had added, 'I would have nothing undone. I would have made her my wife. I will do it still.'

And Tobie had said, 'Then will you give me a letter for her? And do you want Kathi told? No one else knows, but Gelis and Clémence.'

'They should all know,' Adorne had said.

After that, he had written a letter, a short one, with the writing materials that Tobie had brought. Tobie had been shown it. A formal acknowledgement of the child, and of responsibility for its upbringing. A promise to marry. And words of love, no less believable for being restrained. When he had finished, Tobie had said, 'I have some bad news. Barbesaen has confessed on the rack, and has been condemned. He is to hang.'

'And so may I?' Adorne said. 'You are asking who will look after the child?'

'No. I shall, or I shall find someone. Leave it to me.'

The man had been whiter than white, but still intent on mustering his thoughts. 'At least, not Kathi. She has enough. She ought to go away as it is. I have told her already. If they turn on me, they may turn on her next. And Robin should be with his family. If he can travel?'

'He could sail,' Tobie said. 'But they wouldn't go.'

'They will, if I make them,' said Adorne.

Now, telling Kathi, Tobie awaited her answer. He could see her weighing it up. She knew Adorne, and his pride. She knew when to override it. She also knew Robin. She had children, in a town full of danger. And there was something else which Adorne had not asked of her. There was Phemie and her child about to be born. Adorne's child, Kathi's cousin.

After what seemed like a long time, she said, 'I think we should leave, if he really wants it. Does he?'

'Yes, Kathi, he does. He has a hard way before him, and it will be easier if he treads it alone.' He thought, saying the words, that it was what Nicholas in Scotland had also chosen. Then he said, 'Gelis will be here, with all the van Borselen power to help him. Gruuthuse will move heaven and earth. Andreas will be back, as a friend and a doctor. And he has his family.' He ceased speaking. Adorne's family. His older family. But not, of course, his eldest son Jan, who was employed in

Rome by the brother of that Chancellor Hugonet who was now dead, executed in Ghent. Who remained obdurately at Rome.

Human nature, that was all. One had to understand it, and tolerate it, and try to forgive it. Tobie said, 'It may be a son. He deserves one.'

Chapter 7

And quhen this lord and his folk was on sleipe,
The oistis man that suld the stabillis kepe
Staw in quhar at this lordis horsis stud
And put his hand to tak awaye thar fud.

THE YEAR ADVANCED. Clement weather, dutifully visiting Scotland, winced from the spectacle of Nicholas de Fleury, exporter, who no longer envied Tam Cochrane, being fully extended unsupervised in a theatre of his own choice, with a cast of thousands and an unimaginable profusion of Secrets. Those who believed they knew him were filled with foreboding. The few who did know him (including two women) carried in silence an anxiety bordering on pain, since it was they who had released upon Scotland this masterless man; they who were trusting him, in order to prove that he now had a master – himself.

To an unbiased observer, there was no evidence as yet, either way. In fact, below the surface of his intense and soul-satisfying preoccupation, Nicholas was quite aware that monsters lurked. That in Bruges, Anselm Adorne would have received Phemie's letter, and must be preparing an answer. That Gelis and Jodi were there and not here, where he wanted them; and that the parting might be a long one. He was conscious of the absence of news from and about Robin in Nancy. In Scotland, he knew, because he visited Roslin, how Phemie was faring. He also knew, because he suffered him daily, how Henry was nursing the venom that one day would erupt, and would force Fat Father Jordan into action. He knew, although he had not yet met him, that David Simpson had opened his campaign, because of the presents.

These had begun to descend on him in March, just after he had leased a house in the Lawnmarket of Edinburgh, and another in Leith, with a warehouse for his gathering cargo. Henry had been sardonically happy to be free of the monastery, although Wodman had objected, especially when introduced to the spacious, timber house near the head of the Bow, with its service buildings and stable behind, in the terraced ground that plunged down to the Cowgate. It was on the opposite side of the road from Kilmirren House, Henry's home, and a shade further away from the Castle.

The altercation between Wodman and Nicholas delighted Henry, coming upon it as he dutifully entered the house, fresh from guard duty one day, and negligently unstrapped his armour, his eyes dancing, his golden hair lit by the sun.

'Dear Uncle. Poor Andro. He's afraid he can't protect you, but really, you ought to be safe. One steward, one manservant, two grooms, three people to wash and clean and cook for you – does your wife pay for them all? You must be a true Flemish stallion, Uncle Claes, between the sheets. But can you keep it up? And if you can't, what will you use for money? Mind you' – changing mode, since Wodman had left and Nicholas was paying no attention – 'you could always sell the silver. David Simpson's sent you another piece. What arc you doing for *him*, Uncle, between the sheets?'

And sure enough, on a table, was an opened parcel, with silver gleaming inside it, and a note.

'Damned if I can remember,' Nicholas had said. 'What does the note say?'

'For your eyes only,' was the dulcet reply. Henry's insults, in the early days, had a schoolboyish quality that reminded Nicholas sometimes of his own boyhood, to his annoyance. In Henry's case, it was misleading. Behind the crudity was a dogged bulwark of incohesive and violent emotion, liable to break out in any form, against anyone, but mostly against this man to whom he owed all his present humiliation. He watched Nicholas lift the card from the parcel.

It was unsigned, like the rest. Henry, by implication, should not have known who had sent them, but claimed to have glimpsed Simpson's man at the door. For Nicholas, the contents of the cards were enough. This, like the previous two, contained only a few words in Spanish, which Henry might translate, but fortunately couldn't interpret.

Henry said, duly translating, '*A thousand kisses from Ochoa*, again. Ochoa, your Persian wife, I think you explained. And the second time, your African mistress in Cairo. So this time?'

The article was heavy: a silver-gilt pitcher worth a great deal of money. Having registered as much, Nicholas heaved it over to Henry, who let it fall, as he had the two previous gifts, although this time with a fraction less confidence. 'God knows. I called all my ladies Ochoa,' Nicholas said. 'Well, pick it up and put it with the rest. I give them all to you. You'll get a better price if you beat out the dents.'

There was hardly a pause: the boy was quick. 'I don't want them!' said Henry with surprise. His expression changed to remorse. 'Uncle! You were training me to catch, and I didn't try hard enough!'

'That's all right,' Nicholas said. 'I'm thinking of asking Davie Simpson to call, and you can try catching them when he throws. Meanwhile, we are going to Haddington, you and I. Half a turn of the hour-glass, in front of the house, with the horses.'

'I don't think so,' said Henry.

'Look across the road,' Nicholas said; and waited until Henry went out, his mouth shut. Obliquely over the road was the house of Jordan de St Pol, to whom Henry had already appealed during the first days of his servitude. He had been sent straight back to Nicholas.

When in his right mind, Henry was afraid of his grandfather. Nicholas, despite his mild threat, knew that (unwisely) Henry felt no particular awe for the Archer he had known as David de Salmeton, who had joined his grandfather's business, and left it abruptly after a misguided display of ambition. Anyone disliked by the lord of Kilmirren could be sure of Henry's securest contempt. Kilmirren's firm, called the Vatachino, had been allowed to disperse, but then so had its rival the Banco di Niccolò. Now, as everyone knew, Jordan's income came from his estates and from distant Madeira; Simpson's from his service to the Papal Legate Camulio, and that of Nicholas from desultory trading on behalf of his wife. The last, at least, being all too true. For the moment.

Preparing to leave, Nicholas gave some thought, briefly, to the problem of the silver. Henry did know that Simpson was hostile to Nicholas, as well as to Jordan, and that the so-called gifts were therefore some sort of challenge. To Henry, anything that promised trouble for Nicholas was spellbinding. To Nicholas, the messages were awesome in their effrontery, for Ochoa was not the name of a woman. It was the name of the Spanish sea captain associated with Nicholas's African gold. The gold captured by the Knights of St John; deftly buried in Cyprus, and, rumour said, secretly removed, unknown to the Knights, by Davie Simpson. And these gifts and these messages were a brazen admission of the kind that only Simpson would make. *I have your gold. Try and prove it. Try and find it. You can see how rich it has made me – I can afford to toss scraps to beggars.*

And much more than that: *Shall we not have sport on your way to the block?*

Wodman, experienced man that he was, had been surprised by the ambush at Bonnington, thinking it uncharacteristic of Simpson. Nicholas had affected to disagree but, of course, Wodman was right. David Simpson would try to protract the game – extend the separation from Gelis, for example, until his new-found marriage weakened and broke, or he was forced to bring her to Scotland. And if Nicholas left for Bruges, of course Simpson would follow.

He had already decided what to do. Dismissing the matter, he collected some papers, spoke to his manservant, who was also his clerk, and checked that Henry was already outside, receiving the saddled horses from the groom, who came from a farm at Lochwinnoch. The groom was speaking, and Henry, fondling his beautiful roan, was smiling at him. The hour-glass emptied. Nicholas turned from the window and swept down.

Before bringing Henry, Nicholas had several times recently visited the Cistercian Priory at Haddington; partly on business, for he wished to speak to Lisouris the carpenter and Conrad the physician, both of whom were often found here, and partly to make sure of the Prioress's silence. But no convent accustomed to training embryo princesses was likely to depart from discretion by discussing young women recently returned to their families. Phemie was spoken of vaguely but fondly by the kind nun of the Maitland family who had once helped teach the King's little sister, and the various donations by other members of the family Dunbar were referred to with gratitude. Anything more personal was unthinkable.

The visit with Henry, when it took place, was of the kind Henry appreciated least: when, grimly carrying tablets, he followed his base-born uncle from field to workshop to desk, making notes of fells and fleeces and hides, honey and cloth in the piece. Paperwork bored him, and so did stock-rearing and inducing plants to grow in the ground. The pace at which artisans were trained to work also annoyed him: Henry had never known anyone who expected to cover so much in any one day – in any one ludicrously long day – as Claes the Bastard. Artisans also, it appeared, could operate on a meagre ration of sleep and no sex: after a furious row, in which the Bastard had entered Henry's cubicle and flung out the girl who was (temporarily) resisting him, Henry had tried very hard – had paid several unsavoury girls to lie in wait for his uncle, without success. The Bastard was probably impotent. The only thing Henry had enjoyed so far in his whole time as a student of management had been a bad-tempered afternoon in the field with Anselm Adorne's nephew Saunders, who had run a battering course with him to test out a shield. In a place like Haddington, Henry couldn't even enjoy being admired, when the only women were servants and nuns. It didn't seem to stop dear Uncle Nicholas, who got smiles and even hugs everywhere he happened to go. It was obscene.

All the same, the young cadet of St Pol was the opposite of pleased to discover, halfway through the afternoon, that while he had been left counting stinking hides with the factor, Uncle Nicholas had temporarily vanished. Then Henry found out where he was, and all his growing suspicions were confirmed.

The stud of the Knights of St John lay not far from Haddington, in rich well-watered meadows where mares could graze, and the choice stallions brought over from Flanders could maintain the line of stout, biddable horses bred to serve a militant Order. In truth, they were more in demand by the great lords and the royal household of Scotland, not to mention the better-off burghers, and selling them kept the Lord Precentor free of debt, if he had ever been close to it. Once, Nicholas had encouraged Anselm Adorne to breed horses, but that shrewd man had blandly abstained. He had been right: it would have lost him money. But not in Scotland, and not now. There was a lot of profit in horses, if you knew what you were doing.

Alexander (Eck) Scougal did. By-blow of an East Lothian family, he was built like a Tartar, squat and thick in the leg, with powerful shoulders and a stallion's mane of black and white hair over a jutting nose that no Tartar would own. In the old days, Nicholas had bought nowhere else. Now, he had been through all the fields, looking at foals, and was sitting chewing a blade, watching Eck, on foot, put a whole-coloured two-year-old through its paces. It had pricked ears and a lofty trot of the kind that screamed breeding.

'That would do you,' Eck said, running easily after the horse to the left, whip in right hand, reins in the other. 'It depends how long you're going to be here.' He receded. 'Wa-a-alk on.'

'I don't know. What about the others?' Nicholas called. 'Would you sell off some mares?'

'They'd cost ye,' cried Eck. At the end of the field (Ha-a-alt) he changed hands, tried some commands, and came back at a different gait, cracking his whip to keep the pace even. He approached.

'Then I'd need time,' Nicholas called. 'Unless you'd take something other than money?' His voice, like the horse, lost momentum. He turned.

'Knollys likes money,' Eck remarked, turning too. He brought the horse to a halt, and stood looking.

'Well, Uncle,' said Henry. 'And I thought you had no interest in horses?' He had entered the gate and was leaning against it, with the ineffable grace – the blue, languorous gaze; the long limbs – that made the rest of mankind look like bison. He had left his jacket behind, and the spring sunshine lit his lawn shirt and unbuttoned pourpoint and the svelte line of thigh, knee and calf, where hose met the close-fitting edge of fine leather.

Nicholas allowed himself a long, baffled sigh. He said, 'Horses? No. A waste of money. I told you.'

'Really?' said Henry. 'Well, if you say so, of course. Then why are you here?'

Scougal opened his mouth, but Nicholas answered before him. 'To get a horse for myself, as it happens.'

'Like that one?' Henry said with compassion. 'Uncle, you'd fall off.'

'Probably. Not like that one,' Nicholas said. 'Eck is training that one for himself. You should get him to show you some time what he does with it. Did you finish the hides?'

'Yes. So where is your horse, Uncle?' said Henry.

'I didn't see one that I liked. So we can go.'

'Can't I see the horses, Uncle?' said Henry.

'Why? You don't know anything about breeding horses,' said Nicholas. 'Eck, I'm sorry I've wasted your time. We'll see ourselves out.'

There were two more calls; one of them to the coal mines at Tranent, which provided fuel for the salt-pans on the coast, and for the Castle. On the seventeen miles back to Edinburgh and their final engagement, Henry tried to exclude from his awareness the voice of de Fleury, taking each of the day's meetings in turn and summarising its course, his conclusions, and the action it ought to engender. Occasionally, the voice suspended itself, and Henry became aware that he was expected to comment, or answer. He amused himself at first with effusive apology, and then increasingly moved on to the facetious. Finally he drew up his horse saying, 'Do you mind, Uncle? My head bursts with over-excitement. I really think I ought to make my way back alone and lie down.'

'I do agree,' Nicholas said. 'Indeed, why not lie down here?'

There followed a few crowded moments, at the end of which Henry's horse had galloped riderless into the distance, the Bastard had ridden on, and Henry himself was lying dazed in the road, with labourers pensively gathering to view him.

Since no horses came by, he walked back.

Nicholas called, as appointed, at the great double Berecrofts house in the Canongate of Edinburgh with, instead of the liveried escort of Sinclair, Henry's captured horse at his girth. He handed both mounts to the groom, and ran up the foresteps with his mind on something other than a business meeting with Sersanders and Archie. It had already occurred to him that, without Henry, he was free to discuss rather more than he would have risked otherwise. But that didn't excuse what had happened. He couldn't believe that he had lost his temper with Henry: something so predictable; so easy to avoid. But now that he had, it was for him to turn it to some sort of advantage. He cleared his mind, walking with Archie's chamberlain to the bureau, talking about the Easter processions. They were almost there when a man came running to stop them. Master Archibald was in his private chamber with Master Saunders, and begged Ser Nicholas to come there on his own.

He *was* on his own. 'What has happened?' Nicholas said. The staff didn't know. But he knew, as soon as he entered the room and saw the letter between Archie's hands. 'Robin?' he said; and sat down, as young Sersanders brought it to him to read.

He absorbed the contents in seconds, but did not at once speak. It was all very comprehensive, in Tobie's crabbed doctor's handwriting. He was used to Tobie in connection with other people's written effusions: the list of accessible girlfriends in Milan; a recipe for camel-cough, or for a vile death on St Hilarion, or Famagusta. A document about the birth of a child. Henry, and Robin.

Archie said, 'It's all right. Read it again. Robin isn't dead,' and Nicholas looked up, disquieted to find that he had somehow attracted Archie's compassion. Archie said, 'I know you two are close. I've been thinking. There's a house over the way. They could have that. We'd widen the doors for lifting him out. And the same over here. Once up the steps, he could lie in Saunders's office; run the core of the business; keep it all going. It's not his head that's astray. Ye don't need your feet for a business.' He paused. 'And doctors don't know it all. If the power comes back, he's got ae leg. Like yon peg-leg Florentine. He could walk.'

He had assumed Robin was coming home, with Kathi and the children. The letter said nothing of that, or what was happening in Bruges.

Sersanders said, 'It came from Leith. The ship's clerk had a few to deliver. Were you going back to the High Street?'

Coded message, which Archie, thank God, didn't pick up. Nicholas said, 'Eventually. I don't suppose we need go on with this meeting just now. What do you say?'

'I don't know,' said Archie of Berecrofts. 'I don't know. There's more than ever to discuss, don't you think? Now we can expand even more. Make a good life for these two little childer.' His voice broke on the word.

Nicholas said, 'Yes, of course. Let's begin planning.'

It was dark when he left to walk up to his house in the High Street. Sersanders walked with him, for reasons other than courtesy. As Nicholas had divined, there was another letter from Tobie: it would be awaiting him there. And this one might have truths that Robin's father had better not know.

He had expected to find Wodman at home, and was not sorry to learn that he was out. He remembered Henry only when he ushered Sersanders into his parlour and found the boy half lying there, disposed over a settle, freshly changed into velvet; the pure, pale skin showing its one violet bruise. The letter from Tobie lay open and thumbed on the table.

Henry said, 'Uncle! Saunders, what can I say? To find the living dead in your own family! To see your pretty sister bound to a mindless half-man for life, performing for him every service but one, I should suppose. What have the Adornes, the Sersanders tribe done to deserve this?'

Sersanders took one stride before Nicholas stopped him, his voice harsh. 'It is my fault. I acted childishly, and Henry is returning the compliment. Come to another room.' He picked up the letter. It was much longer than Archie's, and not in code. Nicholas said to Henry, 'Have you shown this to others?'

'To everyone I could think of. Did you think you could keep it secret?' Henry said. 'If little Mistress Kathi has another child now, they will know whom to blame, won't they? Or what about your own wife, and Cousin Diniz! What a close-knit family we all are, to be sure!' And he laughed.

Nicholas did not then know what he meant, but Tobie's letter explained it. Studied in Nicholas's own room, and shared with Sersanders, it contained the medical details that the writer had spared Robin's father. It also contained an account, for Gelis's husband, of the true circumstances of Robin's arrival in Bruges, and all that Gelis had done, helped by Diniz, to warn her cousin, and the convoy from Nancy. Reading it, Sersanders had exclaimed, and then had the sense to go on talking until Nicholas recovered his sense of proportion. It was ridiculous that, for a moment, he had lost it. Gelis and he had lived apart for months, for years. Gelis had experienced far greater dangers than this. But now they had what they had, and he could not bear the idea of losing it.

After that, he and Sersanders reread the rest of the letter, and discussed it painfully but thoroughly, as it deserved. It was perhaps the most adult conversation Nicholas had ever had with Kathi's brother. Presently, Sersanders left. Tobie had not referred to Adorne, save to say that Kathi's uncle was determined to do everything possible for Robin.

Phemie's letter, of course, had barely left Scotland when Tobie's two missives were written. If it were otherwise, and Tobie had mentioned it here, Henry would now know the truth about Phemie. The thought turned Nicholas cold.

As it was, Henry's words were a cruel distortion of what Tobie had said. Robin could not walk, that was true. But he had the use of part of his body, and was not mindless: his intellect was unimpaired. Tobie had said he had made himself Robin's personal physician, and would remain so. He had said that Robin would need lifelong attention, and Kathi's presence was paramount. He had added that naturally all Robin's friends would have some part to play, but that he did not think Robin could survive the next months without Nicholas.

Sersanders had looked at Nicholas then, frowning a little. 'Of course, you did so much together. But now? Won't he be jealous of us all?'

'I don't know what Tobie means,' Nicholas said. 'But of course I shall do all I can. Do you think he'll come home?' Tobie had said that he should.

'It will break his father's heart if he doesn't,' Sersanders had said.

After he left, Nicholas waited, thinking, for a space. Then he went and tapped on Henry's door.

'Yes?' said Henry's voice. 'If it's you, Uncle, I'm sleeping.'

Nicholas opened the door and closed it quietly. He said, 'I've come to apologise. It was not your fault that you found business tedious. I should have let you ride off.'

'Uncle!' said Henry. The candlelight rested on the smooth, fair planes of his face and made his deepened eyes bright. 'Is this remorse? Or fear of retribution to come? There but for the grace of God go I, a one-legged cripple unable to fuck?'

'It doesn't happen very often,' Nicholas said. 'Men usually die from wounds as bad as that, partly because they want to. Robin wanted to live.'

'You sleep with his wife,' Henry said. His lips sneered, contradicting his eyes.

Nicholas said, 'No, I don't. But you might think I would say that anyway. You have to judge for yourself.'

There was a pause. Henry lifted himself angrily in the pillows, his tangled hair shadowing his cheek. He said, 'I want to know why I am here. You haven't real proof that I attacked you. You couldn't really harm me, although Grandfather thinks that you could. I'm really here as a hostage, amn't I? You think if I'm here, you can force my grandfather to do what you want?'

There was an easy answer. *Your grandfather, Henry, is one of the cleverest devils I know. If he thought as you do, you would not be here now.*

Nicholas said, 'It's not very difficult. I *can* prove you attacked me. So your grandfather is right: whether you are physically with me or not, I can still dictate to him. To begin with, I thought I'd deprive him of your company. I'm willing to send you back, if you suggest something else he'd hate more. You tell me. Money? Kilmirren?'

Henry laughed with something suddenly close to real pleasure. 'You think he'd give you *Kilmirren*!'

'To save your life?' Nicholas said. 'As soon as I denounce you, you will be condemned. Wodman is a royal officer. I'm a Knight of the Unicorn, come to that. You don't try to kill unicorns every day.' He paused. 'I don't think you're doing too badly. What are you grumbling about? I promise I'll hit you only every third week.'

'I'll knock you off your horse next time,' Henry said sharply.

'All right. Wager you one of the bloody bashed jugs you don't. Are you on duty tomorrow?'

'No. Yes,' said Henry. He looked slightly dazed, as he had on the road.

'Oh. Well, don't get too drunk on that,' Nicholas said, producing and dumping a flask by the bed. 'Salve for the wounds. Good night.'

Henry said nothing, only stared as he left. But he didn't fling the wine after him.

Nicholas returned to his room and, ignoring the bed, walked to where the other flasks were, and pulled down the first, by his chair. Then he set it aside with one clumsy hand, as the first wave of reaction overwhelmed him.

He was too far from childhood, at thirty-six, to expect comfort. Eventually, he resorted, instead, to the wine-flask.

Like father, like son.

Prosper Schiaffino de Camulio de' Medici of Genoa, once Milanese diplomat, now a nuncio of the Pope and the Apostolic See, and Collector for the Apostolic Camera in the realms of England, Scotland and Ireland, had first bustled into the orbit of Nicholas some seventeen years previously, and had subsequently entertained him in Milan, and in Bruges. Their common interest had been an illicit one, in the chemical alum. You would suppose that, now in holy orders, Camulio would have abjured every form of chicanery but you would, of course, have been wrong. Debts and misguided patriotism, between them, would always talk louder than God.

At just over fifty, he had begun to weather, in the way that run-about envoys usually did, whether representing a Duke or a Pope. Nevertheless, his black eyes beamed upon Nicholas, entering his comfortable guest-room in the monastery of the Dominicans, Edinburgh. Nicholas, who had never minded Prosper de Camulio, beamed back. He said, 'I like the robes.'

Camulio plucked at them. He said, 'It is a living,' and laughed, and waved Nicholas to a seat. A serving Brother, in humble black and white, poured some very good Chios wine. 'I thought it appropriate,' the Nuncio said. 'I hear you have just returned from the lands of my forefathers. I wish to hear about Caffa, and the Adornes. And, of course, about your own circumstances, these disturbed times. Ah! Perhaps you even miss the days when you were a simple apprentice called Claes!'

'I am constantly being reminded of them, at least,' Nicholas said; but he smiled. They had a lot in common. And it passed the time until he could ask about the Nuncio's splendid new procurator.

'David? But you are his close friend, of course. How sad he will be to have missed you. No doubt you were dazzled, as was I, by the gifts he was anxious to send you. What great service did you perform for him in Cyprus?' Camulio asked.

'Not the one you're thinking of,' Nicholas said, and waited while the Nuncio cackled. It was easy to confirm, talking further, that Camulio knew something of Simpson's past history, but nothing of his long campaign against Nicholas. There was no reason, indeed, why he should. Simpson, as a Scot working abroad, had the sort of disconnected career that was hard, even for the Curia, to examine completely. And he had no public blemish on his character. David Simpson had left the Scottish

Archers in France at the same time as Wodman, and had followed him into the service of Jordan de St Pol. Even his dismissal from the Vatachino company had not been publicised; Wodman professed not to know why. Nicholas thought it was obvious. The traitorous Simpson would be tolerated by Henry's grandfather in Scotland, just so long as Simpson aimed to kill Nicholas. When Nicholas died, no doubt Simpson would be seen off immediately. It made his own threat against Henry fairly useless.

David Simpson, it transpired, was at Newbattle. From politeness, Nicholas protracted the interview, eliciting, from habit rather than anything else, all the Roman gossip that might be relevant, and a diatribe about Germany: Prosper had once been attached to the Emperor Frederick as agent and councillor and had loathed every coarse, ill-fed moment. If the Emperor's son married Burgundy, Camulio's prospects would shrink. And, of course, there was nothing but rebellion and political turmoil in his adored native Genoa, since the assassination of the last Duke of Milan. You did not have to speak to Camulio for long to know what he thought of Milanese rule in Genoa.

Nicholas listened from politeness; from expediency; and because Prosper de Camulio, long ago, had been considerate in his dealings with Marian de Charetty, and forbearing with Felix her young son, now dead.

Before he left, he arranged to entertain the Nuncio in his own house, in advance of the Nuncio's forthcoming brief vacation from Scotland. Nicholas extended the invitation, at second hand, to his good friend David Simpson. He didn't mention throwing big jugs at Henry.

While he was feeling responsive, Nicholas undertook, that same day, the short journey to Newbattle Abbey, and found that, sadly, the good Master David had left for Beltrees. He had feared (said the sub-prior) that he might miss his dear friend Ser Nicholas, and wished him to know that Ser Nicholas would always be welcome at Beltrees, where he would notice many necessary and delicious improvements.

Since he was there, Nicholas asked to be received by the Abbot and his steward, and opened a number of business matters which met with an instant and enthusiastic response, leading to a number of gratifying proposals which he took away, promising early decisions. The Abbot escorted him to the doorway, still talking. Outside, everything was covered with building dust. The epidemic was growing. The Abbot viewed the wreckage and said, 'Ah! I had almost forgotten. You know the wretched pirate Paúel Benecke? Master David wished me to tell you that, most happily, he has now departed this earth. Knowing his bestiality, the Procurator asked his French friends in particular to look out for him. The ship he was captaining was seized, and the man himself killed in the struggle. Master David said you would be pleased.'

Nicholas gazed at him. Then he said, 'I am glad to know. Thank you for telling me. I shall find a way to thank Master David when I see him.'

Paúel, too. But then, the Tough Seabird had been disappointed in his hopes for the future. Drunk and defiant and reckless, he would have made a fine target.

The day went on. It was no longer young, but on the other hand it was still free of Henry, whether Henry was on duty or not. It seemed to Nicholas a good time to embark on one of his regular calls on Mistress Phemie. These days, he had no trouble entering Roslin Castle. It was having nothing to report from Adorne that was the difficult part.

Phemie was alone, so that he was able to talk right away. 'No word yet. But for what it's worth, I have a letter from Dr Tobie. He's back in Bruges, and gives all the news, but not yours. If Anselm had your letter, I think Tobie would know, and would tell me.'

'So it is still too soon for an answer, that's all,' Phemie said. She was right. It was only a month since she'd written, and she was too sensible to expect the impossible. Indeed, since his visits these last weeks, her cheeks had begun to carry more colour; her manner had regained some of its natural edge. Now she said, 'But Nicholas, how are you? You begin at once on my affairs, and never mention your own. Or –' She broke off. 'Tobie is back from Nancy? Nicholas? Is it bad news?'

'Not for Kathi,' Nicholas said. 'Robin is alive, but can't walk. He can think, and hear, and speak, and see. Apart from that, he has the use of one side, and he may be able to sit. He'll be like that for life.' He didn't go on.

'But Kathi will manage,' she said, after a bit. Phemie Dunbar had lived with the King's sister and Kathi in Haddington. She had stayed with Kathi's uncle in Bruges. She knew Kathi, almost in the way that Nicholas did. She added, 'And so will Robin. Or he would not have come back.'

'That's what I thought,' Nicholas said. 'Now we have to build a business here for him.'

'We?' she said. In her face was the distress they all felt.

'Robin's father. Kathi's brother. And me.'

'And Nowie,' she said. 'I hope you had thought of asking him.'

'Should I?' Nicholas said. It was best to be frank.

He had taken her thoughts, for the moment, from Robin. Phemie said, 'What has happened to me was at my desire. Even if he knew, Nowie would never deny help to someone I loved, or to his family. As it is, he knows what Betha and I both think of Kathi. He will help. I shall come with you just now and make sure of it.' She lifted herself from her chair and stood, examining him. 'And don't look so doubtful. He knows what I think of you, too.'

Nicholas altered his expression, which concealed apprehension rather than doubt. It might be weeks before Phemie heard from Adorne. If Adorne didn't support her, this whole scheme would blow up in his face, and in Robin's. But if it worked, it would achieve a number of small, desirable miracles.

This time, the session with Sir Oliver Sinclair of Roslin was not one of assessment; it was exhilaratingly dangerous. Very soon, Phemie dropped out of the exchanges, but not because she did not understand, Nicholas thought, what the issues were. She had brains; she had helped run a large and complex Priory. And she was a teacher, with all that implied. Adorne would have chosen no one less.

As for the discussion, it had the quality of those he had already had recently; with Adorne and Hugonet and Gruuthuse, with Abbot Archie at Holyrood, and supremely with the Lords Three. Argyll's sibilant shrewdness; Whitelaw's precisely filed portfolio of finnicky experience; Avandale's masterly overview from the summit. He had spoken to a lot of rich, clever men since he came back, but more than most he enjoyed talking to Nowie.

Now, hearing of Robin, Sinclair listened in silence. Then he said, 'I am extremely sorry to hear this. I imagine you are quite right: his will to live will depend on the challenge of work. I wish to know first, do you have the permission of Berecrofts and Anselm Sersanders to reveal the state of their business? For unless I know this, clearly I cannot advise on its future.'

Nicholas had their agreement, and figures would follow. He didn't have, at this stage, very much more. He didn't know whether Kathi and Robin would come home, or what they would plan to invest if they did. He was simply exploring the field, so that if they returned, there might be something of value in prospect.

'I am flattered,' said Oliver Sinclair, 'to be entrusted with such a sensitive charge. And what investment are you making, Nicol?' The large, fair face bent kindly eyes upon him. Phemie sat still.

'My ships,' Nicholas said. 'Or rather, my wife's. We have never been part of the Berecrofts-Sersanders business. That would remain a family company, for which we should act as agents and carriers, if wanted.'

'If wanted!' said Nowie. 'But of course they will want you. Of course you must benefit from any expansion, since you are taking such trouble for Robin.'

He turned his head, because Phemie had stirred. She said, 'Nicholas hesitated to come to you, in case it seemed that he was exploiting Robin's misfortune.'

'And that is why you are here: I see, Phemie, my dear. But Nicol could hardly avoid doing so, could he, even with the purest of intentions? A merchant must collect information, and what will benefit Berecrofts will advantage him. You have been to Newbattle, I hear?' He had turned back, politely, to Nicholas. 'Did they make you any noteworthy propositions, might I ask?'

Nicholas said, 'Yes, Sir Oliver. But we need not pursue this. I know you are closely connected with the Abbey.'

The pale eyes considered him. 'We helped to found it,' said Sinclair. 'But their decisions these days are their own, as of course they should be. I should be interested to know, none the less, what they said.'

Nicholas told him.

'And you propose to accept?' Sinclair asked.

'No,' said Nicholas.

There was a long silence. Phemie glanced at her cousin, and smiled. He returned the smile with an absent-minded one of his own, and reverted to Nicholas. 'You are exceedingly wise. Yet this was presented as a serious offer?'

'Or as a form of subtle discouragement. They have been warned, perhaps, against trading with me. In which case of course I should not do so. Directly.'

'I see,' said Oliver Sinclair. 'I wonder if I have this correctly. You are asking me to conduct business for you under my name.'

'Not for me. For Berecrofts,' Nicholas said.

'And if I were to agree, you might even tell me who has warned Newbattle against you? Or is that a secret?' asked Oliver.

'Not a very great one,' said Nicholas. 'But it is best that – officially at least – you don't know.'

'Hm. Well, then. What were the arrangements that you hoped for from Newbattle, had things turned out differently?' Sinclair said.

He had won. He had expected to. He spoke, making sure that the commercial case that he made would serve the Sinclair family at least as well as the Berecrofts. At the end, the lord of Roslin ceased making notes and sat back. 'So. And what does Phemie think of all that?'

Her cheeks were pink. Meshed into his neat, professional project had been opportunities for Phemie's own extended family: the husband of Cristina her sister; the two Tom Prestons, and Marchmont Herald, who had married one of their sisters. Also Tam Cochrane, who was becoming an ally.

Phemie said, 'I think, Nowie, that you should accept his suggestions. I also think that you should tell the Lords Three to compel this man to settle in Scotland. Chain him, if need be.'

'My dear, your eloquence gladdens the heart. Indeed, you might almost persuade me. Nicol, I think she has almost persuaded me to help you. What do you think?'

Nicholas said, 'I think we should both thank her, Sir Oliver.'

'What a nice speech. Doesn't he have a nice turn of speech?' the other man said. 'So I think that, yes, I might do as you ask. And by the way, my name is Nowie, dear Nicol. (A glass of something?) If we are to work together, of course you must call me Nowie.'

Crossing the bridge, rather drunk, Nicholas was stopped, not very surprisingly, by Tam Cochrane, who wanted a word in the sacristy. At the end of it: 'Mares,' said Cochrane, who by this time was drunker than Nicholas was.

'What about them?' said Nicholas, who was playing with a plumb line. He dropped it.

'The clack was ye were buying stud stock frae Eck Scougal. Now he says they're all going to some client in Renfrewshire. So would you like me to get you some others?' Cochrane knew about horses.

'Never mind. I've changed my mind. I'd better go,' Nicholas said.

He supposed that, back in Edinburgh, his groom would have departed already. Up and down, up and down like the pendulum.

'It's a shame about the young laddie. It's a shame about Robin,' said Cochrane.

Chapter 8

'Quhy has the se thé thus misluffit maid?'

 PRING CAME, to mend the brutal geometry of space. A ship arrived in Sluys bearing a poem, of which Gelis van Borselen took sasine:

> *Suspendit gaudium*
> *Pravo consilio*
> *Sed desiderium*
> *Auget dilatio.*
> *Tali remedio*
> *De spinis hostium*
>
> *Uvas vindemio.*
>
> (Delay . . .
> A perverse tutor
> Suspends joy
> But redoubles longing.
>
> So we
> From evil thorns
> Shall harvest grapes.)

Below this artful translation, her husband had written: *Be patient. I am not.*

*

It was the first communication from Nicholas since the coded note about Phemie. With the poem came several pages of news, characteristically scurrilous: about people she knew; about where he was staying. She gathered that he had been accepted at Court and elsewhere without too much trouble; that Davie Simpson had failed to surface; and that he had had a non-lethal meeting with Jordan de St Pol which boded reasonably well. There was an idiotic story about one of the King's brothers and pepper. The letter was dated mid-March, and when it was written, it was clear, he had received none of the letters she had been trying to send him since February. His ended with a careful reminder that, despite all this good news, she was not to come back as yet. No grapes. Also in the packet was a budget for Jodi of everything he was accustomed to receiving from his roving father: letters, verses and drawings, puzzles and questions.

She assumed she was being told perhaps an eighth, perhaps even a quarter of the truth. Kathi, consulted, agreed, but added that Nicholas would be much comforted by the belief that he was sparing her, and Gelis must simply suffer in a good cause. It did not occur to Gelis, then, that Kathi might know more than she did.

By the end of April, there were two further letters from Nicholas, written later in March, and after he had received some of her own. It appeared that Tobie had told him something of her share in the Ghent Gate arrival, and Nicholas was frightened enough to be angry, which touched and pleased her: tit for tat. She read, with awe, his plans for Robin's business, and learned that he had met Prosper de Camulio, but not Simpson, so far. He mentioned Adorne, and asked Gelis whether she had received a letter in code. He did not know, of course, that Adorne was in prison, or how delayed Phemie's letter had been. He must be waiting, with more and more disquiet, for Adorne's reply.

He would have it soon. By mid-April, when that cautiously worded enquiry reached Gelis, Kathi had left, braving the seas to take Robin and her children to Scotland, and Tobie and Clémence with them. And taking, too, the precious document, newly written by Anselm Adorne, which accepted with joy Phemie's child, and which asked her to marry him. It brought to Gelis's mind that other, older affirmation whose existence she had confided to Diniz. Then, there had been no question of marriage, for the child's mother, her sister, was dying. This was different. Now she must pray that Adorne, the father, would survive.

Now, with Kathi gone, Gelis was alone with her anxieties in Bruges. But no. Of course she wasn't alone. She had Jodi. Diniz was here, and his family. John had travelled to Sluys, as she had, to see Robin and the others depart; but, returning, had withdrawn into silence, sitting in corners with clerks, engaged in the final, dreary paperwork to do with the ending at Nancy of the mercenary company of which he had been master gunner. Outside, she had acquaintances: Bruges was full of people who had known Nicholas from boyhood. Letters came from the managers who had been friends – Gregorio in Venice, Father Moriz and Govaerts in Cologne, where they had been joined by Julius, direct from his successful visit with Tobie to Nancy. And with them (and long might she stay there) was Julius's step-daughter Bonne.

Gelis had no right to repine, and indeed little time, for she was occupied with the closing of Robin's affairs as well as the normal business of the Hof Charetty-Niccolò. And above all else, she set to work for the survival of Adorne of Cortachy, who was still under duress, untried, despite all that she and Wolfaert and Gruuthuse had so far been able to do. The little Duchess, temporarily freed for her inauguration, was applied to, but Gelis herself – tellingly escorted by John – had seen her only briefly, and left with no promises and a feeling of helplessness on both sides. Their protests had, however, borne some kind of fruit: the execution of Adorne's condemned companion had been delayed, and so had the trial of the others, as well as his own. But that was also to keep matters quiet during the visit of the Imperial embassy, come to Bruges to arrange for the Duchess's wedding. And then there had followed the actual contract of marriage, which required the Duke of Bavaria, representing the groom, to lie down with the Duchess in bed, both being fully dressed, with a naked sword lying between them. Thus, to keep the land safe from King Louis, was contracted that union which would yield Burgundy, bit by bit, back to France, and would ensure that for three hundred years the Low Countries would belong to the Habsburgs.

That day, it was not wise to walk about Bruges, where drinking was fierce and tempers ran hot and high. When the caller arrived at the Hof Charetty-Niccolò, he had passed through the streets with some difficulty, and before that, through France itself with even more trouble, so that his return had taken many weeks. The bright-eyed, middle-aged figure whom Diniz introduced to the parlour where Gelis and his family were gathered was the astrologer Andreas of Vesalia, physician, guild-brother and friend to Anselm Adorne, and – in his time – Court physician in Scotland.

His first words were, 'I have been to the Hôtel Jerusalem! What has happened?' And at the end, 'It has begun then. I was afraid.'

Diniz, a sceptic, was silent. But Gelis knew from Nicholas, who had the power to divine minerals, the narrow boundary that lay between the occult and the rational, and was prepared at least to listen to astrologers; especially those of the worldly sort with a much-cherished mistress in Blois.

On the other hand, listening to astrologers was not always productive. Dr Andreas had been touched by no premonitions, it transpired, about Anselm Adorne. Speaking of him, he expressed the same angry anxiety that they all felt. This trial was iniquitous. Its effects would be felt by the unborn as well as the living.

Gelis, distrusting the phrase, changed the subject. Tilde returned to it. What did he mean, It had begun? Pressed, Dr Andreas made a non-specific reference to Scotland.

'So what about Scotland?' said Diniz sharply. 'Is there something we should know? Or Nicholas ought to be told?'

'He will find out before we could tell him,' the astrologer said. 'He has experience of the King and his kindred. So has Dr Tobias.'

Gelis stared at him. The King and his kindred? But before she could speak, the door opened on John le Grant, and the chance was lost in an exchange of fresh greetings.

When she questioned him later, Dr Andreas was willing but not much more informative. He had formed an attachment for the ruling circles in Scotland, and had sensed a certain increasing tension in recent years. So far as he knew, M. de Fleury was not endangered. He did not know why he had connected the ills of Scotland with Lord Cortachy's present predicament.

He said nothing of Phemie. He probably knew nothing of Phemie, but his sixth sense had told him that something was wrong. She did not blame Dr Andreas. She knew, through Nicholas, how perverse that gift was.

That perverse gift. That perverse tutor, Delay. That dire master, redoubled longing.

She wished she were where Kathi was, sailing to Scotland.

Be patient. I am not.

I cannot wait much longer, Nicholas.

Unfortunate the doctor who, sick at heart, is also sick at sea. For nearly three months by this date, Tobias Beventini had been physician and shepherd to others, protecting Robin of Berecrofts and John while Julius argued for their release; caring for them when Julius had gone. Now Tobie was moving away from home, away from Bruges, away from the Italian states where he had grown up and trained, and towards Scotland, and Nicholas. And Robin was still in his care.

Fortunate the doctor who, sick at sea, has a highly trained, much younger wife as formidable as Clémence, and a dear young former patient such as Kathi, to tend the sick man, and the sick doctor, and the sick children.

They put in often to shore, and allotted themselves time to recover between the ceaseless storms and the buffeting. Only a journey by land would have been worse. England was at peace with both Scotland and Burgundy, and they had safe conducts from the little Duchess herself. But always Robin, appealing in whispers, was anxious to hurry and Tobie, deeply disturbed, had to weigh the effect of a refusal against the damage already inflicted by an elderly, badly packed vessel in tumultuous seas.

Which was when Nicholas sent the *Karel* to collect them.

Already anchored and waiting at Berwick, Crackbene had scattered drink-silver and threats through the fishing fleet and set off at the first word from the south. At Newcastle he found the slime-heavy vessel and boarded it with distaste, discovering Tobie emerging from his shoddy cabin. Tobie said, '*Mick!*'

'Not much of a seaman, are you?' said Crackbene. 'Well, Mistress Sersanders? And these'll be the young sprouts? How's your husband?' And presently, sitting by Clémence at the crippled man's side: 'How did we know? We guessed you'd have enough sense to come, and not enough to choose the right ship. I'm to take you to Berwick and wait there for your father and Nicol to join us. It'll give you a good rest, and some nourishing food. I've got some on board, too. I'll wager Master Tobie's missed his fried minnows and seethed mutton gobbets. And I've got a nice bit of pork belly in lard.'

'That wasn't fair,' said Robin, in his light, gasping voice. He was smiling. Tobie would have been pleased, had he still been present to see it.

'Oh well,' said Crackbene. 'You're one up on him: you're not seasick.'

Cushioned and comforted, they were in Berwick in days, and passed from the *Karel* to Tom Yare's big house at The Ness, to wait and to recuperate. Tom and his wife made them readily welcome, although Tobie perceived on their faces, in private, the expressions Robin would learn to confront for the rest of his life. And he did not tell Robin, as they rested, what he had learned about Nicholas on the voyage.

Had Nicol not thought to tell them? Crackbene had asked. Well, they had better know now. Remember that little rat Henry? Well, Henry was not only in Scotland, but now living with Nicol after trying to kill him and Wodman. Remember old Jordan, the grandfather? Well, where was he but in Edinburgh, planted over the road, breathing murder. Remember the King's brother, Mar? Well, Nicol had riled him again, and there he was, wanting his blood.

It had come out, and, to Tobie's displeasure, it had also come out that Kathi knew this already. Wodman had sent an account of it all to her uncle. But her uncle being in prison, she had opened and read it.

And then, of course, Crackbene had exclaimed, 'Prison!' and listened in turn, deeply startled, to the news from their side.

Watching then, Tobie deduced that Crackbene knew nothing of Phemie's involvement. He continued to watch. In Berwick, later, Yare happened to mention her name, but only to say that Mistress Kathi's friend had left Haddington, and was now biding with her cousin at Roslin.

So the pregnancy was not public knowledge.

No doubt Kathi had made the same deduction. She never spoke of it. In public, she led Tom Yare rather to talk of what was happening in Scotland, and Yare, responding, conveyed caustic details, in his soft Berwick burr, of the great tournament that was to end the royal English Almoner's current visit to Scotland. He'd heard her brother was involved with the jousting, and Nicol of course – anything for a ploy – and Big Tam *and* Dob Cochrane and that wee hoor St Pol. Even Davie Simpson had been recruited, they said, to give them the benefit of his grand Archer's training.

'So when is all this?' Kathi had enquired brightly.

But Yare didn't know. The Almoner wasn't staying in Yare's house, thank God, and it was up to the Governor to see to him on his way south. Anyway, even if Nicol or Archie were delayed, Master Robin was comfortable here. They were free to wait here as long as they liked.

Kathi thanked him, with warmth, and so did Tobie. Inside, he felt seasick again. Nicholas. Simpson. *That wee hoor, St Pol.*

Tobie didn't like Henry either. Only the wrong people liked Henry. For Henry's own sake, the boy should have been settled, for life, in Madeira. As it was, he was being used as a pawn. Tobie could imagine Simpson at the King's ear: 'Why not let the boy home? What would look better in this élite corps than a golden beauty like Henry?' The voice of malice which, by chance, had achieved more than the speaker could guess.

And so Nicholas had taken Henry into his house. And now he, Tobie, was bringing him Robin.

*

Granted this romantic view of himself, Nicholas would have reminded Tobie of Tobie's age (forty-seven), and observed that he himself was as yet perfectly capable of dealing on or off the tournament field with sixteen-year-olds, twenty-year-olds, and even Davie Simpson, who was a year older than he was.

He was probably right. He was never to find out, as the trial took place during the rehearsal for the passage of arms, and not the tournament itself, which he never saw.

He had not been greatly surprised, on the eve of the event, to find Davie Simpson sitting in one of the half-erected rough stands, smiling in his direction. Well, at last. Nicholas smiled back, wading and leaping over the exercise ground. The fifteenth horseload of mixed sand, earth and straw plodded in and disgorged itself at his feet, plus some inadvertent manure: he skidded round it. Orchardfield lay in the lee of the royal Castle: the smell rose to its windows, winking in the mild midday sun. Practice performances were supposed to take place at Vespers, but Will Roger had squashed that, having the music and the procession to rehearse, while the carpenters had to be reminded that the fence posts were still piled in the huts.

He had tried to get Nicholas to take part in the singing, the fighting, or even just to dress as the Shepherdess, but Nicholas had refused, while being foolishly pleased to be asked. He shouldn't have been here now at all, except that he knew Henry was coming; and the two Cochrane cousins had urged him to watch. They were defending the Shepherdess. It was only part of the programme, none of which would be carried out properly until tomorrow: traditionally, the Vespers rehearsal was for young tyros and townspeople, cheered on by their parents and friends. He sat down beside Simpson, nodding to the others also taking their places, and turned his full attention to the only enemy he possessed who was not a St Pol. It struck him as embarrassing that, having caused havoc over three continents, he should end with a small, winsome Scot as one of his ultimate adversaries. It was true that most of the others were dead. It was also true that David Simpson was a highly skilled soldier and dealer, who had threatened Gelis, and who had already, in the past, tried to dispose of Nicholas and wrest away Jodi.

Simpson was dressed in clerical black and, below the shallow black hat, it could be seen that the black waves that once brushed his neck had been finely shorn by a craftsman. Below the brim, the lazy, brilliant eyes smiled. Nicholas said, 'Davie! Do you have a tonsure as well?'

He didn't raise his hand very fast, but in any case, Simpson's iron fingers took his before they reached the edge of his hat. Simpson said,

'My dear, don't give me away. Prosper would hear, wherever he is, and be devastated. How are you?

'Enjoying your hollow-ware,' Nicholas said. 'Has Camulio gone? Laden with profits from investing with Newbattle?'

'Of course,' Simpson said. 'Your loss was his gain. I do understand your timidity: your wife will demand an explanation, I know. And what will she say about the loss of your brood mares to young Henry de St Pol! His account to the Guard, so I hear, was quite convulsing. Persuading Eck Scougal to sell him all the beasts you had chosen, and lifting your own groom as well!'

Nicholas knew the account had been convulsing. Henry had given it, under his nose, one day at the Castle, when surrounded by some of his rather young, drunken friends. Taken to task later on, he had been impudently unrepentant. 'You always said I should interest myself in new projects for Kilmirren. The Abbot of Melrose wants horses. So does Knollys. I thought of looking into shipping arrangements at Leith. You wouldn't mind that? You haven't bought Leith, Uncle?'

To David, now, Nicholas merely said, 'It's all right. I've taken out shares in a peat-face.' Henry had walked on to the field, with a group of the same younger friends, and one or two older members of the Guard. No one of great importance was here: he was free for once of Sandy Albany and Liddell, now almost coaxed back to the trust he had enjoyed before leaving. He saw Sersanders, one of the organisers, talking to Roger.

He noticed, with mixed feelings, that Henry's horse was not the usual kind, bred to stand the shock of the joust, but was the one that Eck had trained for Nicholas himself, and kept after he'd gone. He wondered whether, in such a short time, Henry could have mastered its management, and concluded, again with mixed feelings, that he probably had. He had seen how Henry could ride: straight-backed and austere as a knight, or low in the seat like a Tartar, horse and rider a single, flexible unit, moving as one. Even for someone riding from birth, he was good.

Simpson said, 'Take your eyes off him, my dear, or people will wonder why you have invited him into your house. Indeed, I wonder myself.'

Wodman had spurred on to the field. Nicholas said, 'Well, it was either Henry or you. I'd rather know where to find my assassin. Although I can't understand your timidity at all. I shivered last year when Gelis reported your threat; and now I find you are leaving the job to a boy.'

'I am leaving the *attempts* to the boy,' Simpson said. His vivid, dark features glowed, and he drew his open hand in the air to explain himself.

'You don't really think, Nicol, that I expected him to succeed? No. These are the Vespers. The genuine event will occur when your wife and son join you. I pin my hopes, my dear Nicol, on your marriage. She will come, sooner or later, if only to see what you are doing.'

'I expect she will,' Nicholas said. On the field, they were lining up for a mêlée. 'But will you be there?'

'I plan to be,' Simpson said. 'And if by any chance I am not, you would not survive to profit from it. I have my protectors. I should add also, perhaps, that I do not keep objects of great worth at Beltrees . . . Shall we watch?'

Once, when Henry was seven, Nicholas had watched him take part in a children's mêlée, which had ended in a near-fatal quarrel. John of Mar had been involved. Old Berecrofts had been sitting beside Nicholas then, gazing with pride upon Robin, his graceful young grandson.

This contest was nothing like so elaborate: just a field full of young horsemen banging at each other with clubs. A flourish of trumpets began it, and another, crossly repeated, signalled that the happy contestants were now supposed to disengage. It was patent that Henry had learned to manage his horse, which had been trained for Persian riding and responded to aides of great subtlety. The effect was spectacular, although the horse, used to ball games, was nervous. Nicholas could see Wodman speaking to Henry as they all trotted off.

Simpson said suddenly, 'Why . . . Good day, my lord. We are honoured.'

He was looking past Nicholas, towards someone whose settling weight made the bench shake.

'Such, I fear, was not my intention,' said Jordan de St Pol's indolent voice. 'But in the open air, I can bear company I should perhaps find intolerable under a roof. I came to speak to Claes here.'

Nicholas turned, not very fast. Where two spectators had been, the fat man now sat at his elbow, engulfed in a voluminous gown, his wide hat shading his eyes. The lower face, seen more clearly in sunlight, was firm and clear as an apple: without blemish and almost without wrinkles. Seventy years had marked a line between his thick brows and one on either side of his mouth, that was all. Fat had smoothed out the rest. Fat, or the freedom from care that went with freedom from conscience. They had not met since they had reached their adjustment over Henry.

Nicholas said, 'And then you are going to take part in the jousting?'

'No more than you are, my cautious Claes,' Kilmirren said. 'Or our mutual friend here, Love's Lover. Have you seen his bodyguards? There, and there. And, of course, Claes, you have your own: stout

Sersanders over there, who would come running at once, but might not be in time. Indeed, if David and I did not dislike each other so much, we could sheath our knives in you at once, David on that side, and I on this. What do you think?'

The question was addressed, past Nicholas, to David Simpson. And Simpson, his voice sweet, said immediately, 'Of course. And as the senior, my lord, please take the first stroke.'

It was like listening to Henry. Nicholas, seated foursquare in the middle, recognised, as Simpson did not, all the cold amusement behind the flat tones of St Pol's ironic suggestion. And in Simpson, more than twice Henry's age, the same faint thread of uncertainty, as he contributed to what he thought was the dialogue.

The dialogue which – *I came to speak to Claes* – was in fact conveying something, with supreme effrontery, at this moment. Which was saying, unless Nicholas was mistaken, 'My dear Claes! Much as we hate one another, Simpson and I, we have cause to detest you far more. So we have joined forces against you. Afterwards, of course (admire the bodyguards!) poor David will have to watch out.'

Was it possible? Or was he manufacturing fantasies?

Jordan de St Pol smiled into his eyes. He said, 'Forgive me, dear boy. I did not mean to spoil your enjoyment. Let us watch the field.'

He had been right.

The field contests continued, and Nicholas remained where he was, tranquilly flanked by the fat man and Simpson. Willie Roger brought on a choir, which fell below his requirements. There was some shooting, then a foot contest with blunt swords, then a short interlude with musicians, while the barrier was put up. That was followed by some jousts proper, with lances fitted with coronals. Sersanders took part with Henry, who was repeating his success on the same Persian-trained horse. Groomed by Adorne, Sersanders was a fine jouster, and out of courtesy spared Henry a little, to Henry's displeasure. After a jarring encounter their contest was stopped, and another couple rode up.

Throughout, Henry's grandfather said nothing but watched, his eyes narrowed. He, too, had once been a champion jouster, and had commanded the King's Archers in France. He kept his lips shut, but his stare, following Henry, was that of a pawnbroker assessing a bankrupt. Nicholas turned his back on him, but made no effort to leave.

The riders wore padded linen, without blazons. It would be more formal tomorrow, but not much. When denying his services to Willie Roger, Nicholas had pointed out amiably that it wasn't as if Willie had to provide for a Royal Grand Entry. It was only the English dowry money arriving again: third instalment, two thousand crowns, delivered this year by the Canon of Windsor. The dowry belonged to the Princess Cecilia of England, aged eight, who was to marry James, Prince of Scotland, aged four, but not yet. No one brought a sword, naked or other; just money. And since the envoy came every year, a romp at Orchardfield and a banquet or two were good enough. Although, as it happened, Nicholas had helped Willie with something for the finale.

A small number of trim, confused sheep had arrived on the field: it was nearly time for the Pastoral Passage. The Shepherdess was a part often played by a man, and normally, Nicholas would have agreed to dress up. He had done it before, because he liked clowning. When he did it now, it tended to be for a reason, and because it let him create something distinctive. But not today.

Today, in place of his chosen candidate, Willie had simply installed the largest of the town's brewster-ladies, and appointed Tam Cochrane and Robert his cousin to defend her. They were two hefty, country-built men, but Lang Bessie, six feet tall and pure brawn, was their equal: when they stood holding hands for the fanfare, they could have passed for a hanging arcade. Being an Edinburgh man and an unmarried burgess, Robert (Dob) Cochrane knew Lang Bessie even better than Tam. He slapped her buttocks and got on his horse, and the sheep ran about, bleating, and getting sand on their newly washed fleeces. The spectators settled down in expectancy.

There was supposed to be a series of duels, in which each of the Cochranes fought his way (for the Shepherdess) down a short queue of ravening seducers. One of those waiting was Henry, on his favoured agile, small horse, now lathered with sweat. Wodman was another, along with Leithie Preston, whose wife had once been married to Tam Cochrane's brother. There were one or two friendly masons, clearly designing a happy bash at their fellows. There were some hammermen, including Will Tor of Tor, whose forebear had been a Royal Mint warden. Coiners had been popular contestants in tourneys for as far back as the time of King's father. It seemed appropriate now, on an occasion to celebrate money. And, lastly, there was the odd bailie from the Knights of St John, who had a lot of property to defend, and liked to keep their reflexes supple. The Lord Precentor's bastard was one of them. That is, one of the Lord Precentor's bastards was one of them.

The trumpets blew, the Cochranes pranced forward, blunted swords in the air, and the contest began.

By this time, a lot of drink had gone round, and the spectators were boisterous. Beside Nicholas, the old man held aloof but Simpson engaged with his neighbours in a stream of light witticisms, invariably critical. His remoter neighbours responded, but Nicholas failed to contribute, although he appreciated the old man's occasional grunt of explosive disgust. Under other circumstances, he might even have goaded St Pol into making some comment, but the standard of fighting was not high enough to interest an expert: the disgust, he well knew, was against Simpson. He wondered how good the old man had really been. Simon, his son, had once been a professional jouster. None of them fell off their horses.

The Cochranes, used to rough sport, were doing remarkably well. Tam had seen off two bailies, and Dob got rid of a liner and accidentally cut the face of a very small flesher on a big horse that got excited at the blood on the sand and lashed out at a sheep. The sheep lay on its back, complaining, until the Shepherdess strode forward and, lifting it in both muscular arms, handed it to a young page, who dropped it. Meanwhile Dob had felled the flesher who lay winded while his horse galloped away and the next contestant moved up.

Willie Roger, arriving like a spent bolt behind Nicholas, said, 'They're drunk.'

'I don't think so,' said Nicholas. Beside him, Simpson turned round. The old man grunted. Nicholas added, 'I liked the last piece. They were all in tune, nearly.'

'Not the singers,' Roger said. His hat had come off and his grey hair lay about his long face like frayed rope.

Nicholas stared at the field. There was a roar. Leithie Preston had just felled Dob Cochrane. The big burgess lay on the ground, with his man running up, and an apothecary. Everybody else looked sober, including the three contestants still left in the queue. The youth in the middle was Henry. Nicholas said, 'They don't look drunk to me. Maybe dead.' Cochrane stirred and was dragged off. Not dead, but out of the contest. Leithie stood aside, grinning, and Willie Tor moved up to fight the remaining Defender, eyeing the Shepherdess. The Tors had their domain close to Tayside, and the laird of Tor had never had the pleasure of Lang Bessie's acquaintance. He waited, sword in hand, as Tam Cochrane rode forward, and Jordan de St Pol unexpectedly spoke. 'There is someone who can fight.'

This was true. At the side of the field, Leithie Preston's joy had clearly moderated as he took thought. If Tam Cochrane was bested, Leithie would have to fight Tor for the Shepherdess.

Willie Roger said, repetitively, 'The riders aren't drunk. It's the pigs.'

Nicholas, his mouth a little open, was watching the contest. He said, 'You're making it up. It's an old story. I've heard it. I don't want to hear it twice. *Christ!*' Beside him, Jordan grunted again. For the second time, Cochrane had been hit by a powerful blow to the chest. For the second time, he rocked in the saddle. Roger looked across, irritably. He said, 'Tam isn't going to last very long. And then, I'm telling you –'

He was stopped by a roar louder than all the rest. Nicholas jumped to his feet, as did everyone else but the heavy man at his side, who sank back defeated behind a phalanx of backs. Nicholas yelled at him, over his shoulder. 'Tor is out. He was coming for Tam fair and square when his horse pecked. Tam's lance spun him out of the saddle, and the poor devil's flat out on the ground.'

'He fell over a sheep?' St Pol said. His voice, for once, held ordinary amusement.

Nicholas thumped down and grinned. 'No. But you'd wonder if all they say about Preston witchcraft is true. Mags Preston, remember? She never had to settle her debts because no one could take her to court while she was under process and sentence of cursing. Leithie's almost as bad.' He was being frivolous. But there was no doubt that the accident gave Leithie a chance at the prize. Tor was out, and Henry, spurring forward, was not a very likely conqueror. Which would leave Preston just the exhausted Cochrane to fight.

Then he remembered there was one more contestant, and got up to look.

Jordan de St Pol's long-sighted eyes had identified him already. He said, 'What a surprise. You have royalty, Roger, at your display. My lord John, Earl of Mar, has favoured us by entering the contest.'

'Mary, Mother of God,' said Will Roger piously, and, vaulting over the bench, kicked Nicholas until he made room for him.

Simpson removed himself slightly, but smiled. He shifted the smile to the fat man; his voice was consoling. 'I am sure, my lord, that you need not be anxious. Although Cochrane is tired, he will perform very stoutly: it will be simple for Henry to lose. Certainly, I should not like to be the man, or the boy, who stood between Johndie Mar and the lady. I believe he has been commanding her in vain for some time.'

Roger swore. 'I didn't know that.'

'You didn't know that Mar was coming,' Nicholas reminded him. 'Anyway, even if Henry wins against Cochrane, he'll lose against Leithie. And Leithie is a cool little bugger, who'll make up his own mind whether to give in to Johndie or not.'

The fat man on his other side stirred. 'What prompts you to think that Henry will lose against Cochrane?'

Nicholas swung round. Until you looked at it closely, the smooth, contemptuous face with its chins seemed unchanged. Their gaze met. 'Look at his horse,' Nicholas said. Then returning to Roger: 'So. Drunk?'

Fright and anger left the musician's face. He leaned towards Nicholas. Placing a thumb in each dimple, Willie Roger carefully kissed the other man on his pursed mouth. 'Very drunk,' said Will Roger fervently.

Henry de St Pol won his fight against Cochrane, simply because he was determined not to lose. He did not need to be told of the consequences. He would have to fight Tom (Leithie) Preston next. And if he won that (and Leithie would make sure that he did), he would have to fight the King's crazy young brother for Lang Bessie, whom Johndie Mar wanted and Henry didn't.

The alternative was to give up. And Henry de St Pol would never do that. Not with his fat Chamberpot grandfather sitting there gloating. The shock of seeing the old man, and de Fleury, and Davie Simpson all sitting together had scared Henry silly. Johndie Mar was nothing after that.

Which of course, was not so. John Stewart, Earl of Mar, was a fair, well-grown youth of eighteen, nearly three years older than Henry, wearing no armour at all, and riding a fresh, sturdy horse bred for tournaments. In place of a helm, he wore a felt cap with the royal badge pinned to its side. You couldn't touch him without killing him. You couldn't kill him, because he was the King's brother. The crowd, which had cheered Henry's two brave successes with increasing warmth, now observed a cool silence. The trumpeter swung his instrument to his lips. Henry looked across at his grandfather. De Fleury had gone. But Jordan de St Pol was still there; and as Henry looked, his grandfather gave him a nod.

Henry flushed. When the signal rang out and he set his neat little horse to its duty, his blue eyes were bright as the sky.

The Earl of Mar knew who Henry was. Since Johndie was ten, sycophantic courtiers had pointed out the wretched child who had attacked him on this spot. Where he could, Mar made Henry's life inconvenient, and had opposed his selection for the Guard. He had not thought it worth doing more, until now. Mar wanted Lang Bessie.

Wearing no armour, he assumed all would be well: an initial leisurely course during which the brat dared not hurt him and Mar would deliver one nicely judged blow, to send him toppling to the ground. And then look out Lang Bessie if she tried to escape him again. It amazed Johndie Mar, therefore, to spur his horse down the lists and see, on the other side of the bar, the opposite lance driving nearer and nearer, and not clearly intending to deflect its first blow at all.

A prince could not dodge. Mar waited until the last excruciating moment and then swung his lance sideways, battering the other weapon off course and allowing both combatants to reach the opposite ends of the lists with no damage. Mar turned his heaving horse and bestowed a menacing smile on the Shepherdess. The Shepherdess, surprisingly, smiled back, thus disguising the fact that a small sheep had escaped from her fold.

This time, the two riders had almost met, each lance aimed for the jugular, when the sheep ran bleating under their feet, pursued by three dogs. Mar's horse stumbled and fell. So did Henry's. Both the riders got up. Johndie Mar drew out his blade, which was sharp.

'Your grace!' Will Roger called. Sprinting on to the field, he carried two whalebone swords. Henry took one and Mar, slowly replacing his steel blade, took the other. They squared up to fight.

Now it was Henry who had the advantage. Whalebone wouldn't kill, but it hurt. Fitter than Johndie, in fine practice from Sersanders's grudging training, Henry advanced on Johndie Mar and began to rain blows on his body. And Mar responded by dropping the whalebone and drawing his own magnificent sword.

A gasp travelled round the spectators. In the stand Simpson smiled, and the fat man sat still, his face stolid. At the end of the list, there was a rumbling sound. Mar turned round. Willie Roger, excusing himself, stepped forward and whipped the sword from the Prince's fingers, handing it to a page and offering the whalebone instead. Mar punched it away: 'What d'you think you are doing?' At the end of the lists a line of carts had appeared.

'If my lord would finish the fight?' Roger said. 'It's the pigs. They can't wait much longer, and I'm afraid the pig-wives have got at the drink.'

'What?' said Mar; just as Henry's whalebone sword knocked him down. He tried to get up, and found three dogs endeavouring to herd him. He got his sword and knelt, hitting at Henry, but Henry, politely not hitting back, kept gazing anxiously at the end of the list and Mar realised that, unless he got up and ran, a line of pig-asses, bells jangling, was about to run him over. He got up and jumped, and the pig-asses swept erratically by, their carts thunderous with fountaining pig-shards and their drivers' whips cracking. The drivers, in short skirts and striped headgear, were all female, and tipsy.

They raced to the end of the lists, and someone was awarded the prize, to much cheering. In mid-field, Mar faced Henry. 'Now,' said Mar.

'I'm sorry, my lord,' said Will Roger, appearing before them. 'It's over.'

'What gave you that idea?' said Johndie Mar.

Nicholas appeared. Nicholas de Fleury, the Burgundian. The Burgundian said, 'I am sorry, my lord. But three courses were run. One inconclusive, one where both contestants fell, and the last exchange on foot, won by St Pol here.'

St Pol glared at the Burgundian. Roger looked meek. Mar threw away his practice sword for the second time, and looked for his own.

It had gone, and the page with it. The sheep had gone. The dogs had gone. At the end of the field, the painted platform was empty. Lang Bessie had gone as well.

'Where is she?' said Mar.

'Why, my lord?' Nicholas said. 'The lady is the prize of St Pol.'

'Damn St Pol,' said Johndie Mar sweetly, and drew his knife, and lunged at him.

Henry skipped aside. Everyone skipped aside, for the pig-asses were thundering back on a victory circuit. And by the time they had reached the end of the field, Henry had gone, the swords had gone, and even Nicholas de Fleury was absent.

'Pigs!' said Davie Simpson admiringly, as the spectators rose, stretched and prepared to go home. 'Pottery pigs. Pig-asses to carry the shards. Pig-wives to drive them.'

'Drunk pig-wives,' Nicholas said. 'They'll never remember who put them up to it. Is my lord going home? Henry is waiting.'

'So I see. And Mar?' Jordan de St Pol enquired. He rose to his full height and gazed at Nicholas. Simpson, smiling, had gone.

'He knew one of the pig-wives,' said Nicholas. 'One who is less particular than Lang Bessie.'

'So I suppose I should ask, where is Bessie?' The pursed eyes never left Nicholas's face.

'I think,' Nicholas said, 'you would have to ask Willie Roger. Or even Dob Cochrane, if he's well enough. I'm sure Dob Cochrane could tell you.'

'Thank you. I am sufficiently answered,' Kilmirren said. He paused. 'I am sorry about the horse. It was misused. The boy should be thrashed.'

Nicholas, too, had seen the pretty, Persian-trained horse, lying where it had dropped, and where it would never display its young rider's beauty again. He said, 'You have to break eggs to cook them.' He saw a flash of contempt, and the other man went.

He had expected, then, to run down and join the exuberant, arguing crowd round Whistle Willie. Instead someone was coming quickly towards him. Sersanders, followed by Archie of Berecrofts. Sersanders cried, 'Nicol! Archie's just heard. He's come! Robin's come! He's at Berwick!'

Behind him, Archie's healthy, good-natured face was a mixture of crimson and white. He said, 'So I'm away. Are ye coming?'

Nicholas grasped his shoulder and shook it, relief and pleasure tingling through his own blood. He said, 'Of course I am. Try and stop me.'

A little later, when they were shouldering their way through the Horse Market, Nicholas asked a question of the Master of Berecrofts. 'The message . . . did it say who else Robin had with him?'

Archie stopped. 'Man . . . I'm sorry. I should've told ye at once. Your lady's not there. She stayed in Bruges as you told her. But Kathi and the children are with him. And Dr Tobie and Clémence.'

'Then he's being well looked after,' Nicholas said. He gave a large smile, and began moving again. 'And it's all that we hoped for. He's home.'

Chapter 9

Thar was a Roman takin in the weir,
And fred agane.

WAITING IN BERWICK, Robin was frightened.

Kathi guessed, and perhaps Dr Tobie suspected, but no one could have known for sure. The pride that kept the sick boy alive saw to that. And there was nothing that even Kathi could do to alleviate it. Robin was afraid to meet his father, for his father's sake. He was afraid to meet Nicholas for his own.

Kathi also felt pain. In the five days of their stay so far, she tried not to project upon this abused and struggling harbour, the wide, shoaling river, the green hills, the foreboding that came whenever, as now, she had time to think. She, more than perhaps his other friends, had been responsible for releasing Nicholas into this arena. Three months had passed since then. On what happened now depended not just Robin's future, but the future for all of them.

After they all first arrived, they saw little of Crackbene or Yare. Tobie had stayed, and taken time to persuade her to leave Robin sometimes and walk out with Clémence and small Margaret and occasionally that active lady, Tom Yare's wife, to see the trading-vessels unload at the wharf, and the sea-fishing boats coming in, noisy with gulls, to meet the flashing knives of the gutters. Then they would stroll by the swift stream that turned the town's mills, and through the portals in the massive walls to the fields beyond, with early flowers in the new grass, and patches of arable heaped with dank, salty seaweed. Past the walls and the great ditch were those other walls, which encircled the castle where the Almoner Leigh would stay after the final great tournament.

Once, she and Clémence, carrying Margaret, walked along the river-side and watched the small wooden cobles laying the sweep of net that would bring in the salmon. *Contra Nando Incrementum* – against the stream we multiply – was a local fishing-town motto. Very soon after that, they turned back, for she never wanted to leave Robin long, or the baby.

The baby was now a year old. Robin had wanted sons, and she had given him only this one. She had braced herself one day, and asked Dr Tobie a straightforward question, to which he had replied in the same way. It was not impossible. But it could only be done if – as Tobie had said, with the delicacy doctors kept primed for these times – Robin surrendered his sovereignty.

She understood. She also understood that, whether he was physically ready or not, she must wait until his pride would allow it.

Towards the end of the period, she was too uneasy to stay away, and remained in the large, comfortable house, talking to Robin or reading to him. Outside, the yard was busy with horses most days: every time she heard a fresh clatter of hooves, she felt Robin grow still, and made desultory conversation until the riders' voices told that they were strangers. Until the fifth day, about an hour before noon, when Kathi strayed to the window and was looking down as four horses came in: two travellers with two grooms. The grooms were nothing special. The men – she knew, without even seeing their faces – were Robin's father and Nicholas de Fleury. Archie dismounted heavily and looked up. Nicholas said something, and Archie looked back at him, as if caught by surprise. Then he moved forward alone. Nicholas also glanced up at the windows, but it was no more than a flicker, after which he turned back with the grooms to the stables. They were all talking. It struck her to wonder if Crackbene was there, out of sight somewhere.

Robin spoke her name from the bed.

She turned and said, 'Do you have second sight? It was your father.'

He couldn't even be propped up: not yet. He could only turn his head and look anguished. 'But Nicholas,' he said. 'I heard Nicholas.'

She crossed and knelt, smiling. 'You heard Nicholas being tactful,' she said. 'He has retired, to leave the field clear for the family. May I stay?'

She had hesitated even to ask. He saw it and, as ever, understood the reason, and gave her one of his sudden smiles. He said, 'I think you'd better, don't you?'

And then his father was standing in the doorway, his hands loose, his eyes on his son's face, saying, 'Oh, my laddie! Thank God, thank

God, ye've come back to us!' And somehow he was on the floor by the
bed, Robin in his embrace, and they were both weeping.

Which was the best way of all.

Kathi stayed, her eyes wet, through the first of it: when Archie,
recovering, took a stool, and Robin asked questions, and his father
began to explain, in a torrent of eagerness, all that he had prepared for
his homecoming. Only, after a while, Kathi saw Robin's eyes flicker
towards her and away. Smiling, she backed to the window and sat there,
without looking round. A few moments later, there came the rattle of
purposeful footsteps and a bang on the door, which opened on Nicholas.

Robin's eyes left Archie and his pale face coloured deeply. Archie,
looking round, got up from the stool and gestured, offering it. Settling
into his face was the first distillation of the last fifteen minutes: an
expression of pride and relief and, above all, joy. It did not go unnoticed,
Kathi thought; nor did her own presence. But the odd, intent look on
Nicholas's face was only for Robin. Nicholas said, 'I'm so bloody sorry.
And so bloody glad.' He sat down.

Robin's lips trembled. He said, 'That about sums it up for me, too.'

Nicholas studied him. 'So what happened? I saw you shot. How did
you get there? And what happened next?'

While Robin was speaking, Archie quietly made for the door. Kathi
made to rise too, but a glance from Robin asked her to stay. The door
closed, and she came and sat down on the other side of the bed, so that
she could listen to all Robin was saying. She hadn't heard it before. No
one else had dared ask him. At one point, speaking of the battle, his
colour high, his eyes bright, Robin suddenly burst into tears and lay
gasping, before lifting the hand that could move and wiping the wetness
away. When he removed the hand, he was smiling. 'I'm sorry,' he said.
'I'm so happy.'

'We'll soon alter that,' Nicholas observed with casual fondness.
Ceaselessly, from the first moment, he had dispensed boundless,
ineffable comfort. Only Kathi had seen, at Robin's cry, that Nicholas's
hand had clamped shut like an animal.

The same tightrope that she walked, hour by hour. Is this right? Is
it wrong? Have I destroyed him?

After a while, she went and got her hostess, and wine came, and the
others – Tobie, Crackbene, Archie again, and Tom Yare himself. She
stayed until the noise was at its height, and only lingered on her way
out when she heard Robin ask about the tournament. The answer, in
Nicholas's inspired re-enactment, wrung comedy out of elements she
could only imagine with horror: the presence of both Simpson and

Jordan de St Pol, of the boy Henry and John of Mar. It rose to a climax.

'*Pigs!*' This time Archie was weeping with laughter.

'Oh, we've got pig-wives in Berwick,' said Tom Yare. 'And muggers. They bring round the mugs frae the piggeries. Terrible rough types they are. Jump on ye for your purse.'

'They've got them in Bonnington, too,' Nicholas said. 'Andro and I nearly lost more than our purses. But our muggers were oyster-muggers, it turned out. Mongers. Mussel-men with a nasal impediment. Which reminds me. Did you know that oysters like to be sung to? Repeatedly?'

'The more you eat? Responsorial chants?' Robin said, wheezing.

'With hockets,' said Nicholas. 'And they appreciate double-sexed love songs. Come on, Tom. *Ah! I die; ah! I die; ah! I die* . . . I'll sing it. You follow me.'

'You're drunk,' said Tom Yare cheerfully.

'I am only drunk to my oysters,' observed Nicholas superbly, against Tobie's wail of resistance. 'Sing. This is your scalp-mail. Until you've paid it, no beds.'

She left, shutting the door on the laughter, and had a small weep herself, in seclusion, because she too was relieved, and proud, and full of joy.

He came to speak to her late in the evening, when the house was quiet and the men were dispersed, thinking of bed. They were to sail in the morning.

She had said good night to Robin, and to Tobie who shared his room in this house: they had found a bed for Archie nearby. Crackbene was on shipboard already. Here, Kathi slept with Tobie's wife Clémence, but she had gone first to the children's room and found Nicholas already there, his doublet over one shoulder, gazing down at her children. Cristen, her nurse, stood smiling beside him. He looked up.

Boundless, ineffable comfort, dispensed hour after hour, with intervals for fast-talking planning and others for vulgar hilarity. Until now, there had been no sign of effort. He smiled and said in a low voice, 'I hadn't seen them since January. One a Berecrofts, one an Adorne. That seems fair.'

The children slept, plump and healthy and beautiful. 'They are too young to understand about Robin. It's a blessing,' she said. 'Clémence is not using her room, if you wanted to talk.'

The nurse smiled at Nicholas as they left. Another of the friends he made so easily, when he wanted to. It was not the case with his own servants, with whom his relationships were even, but distant. But then, moving about, he had been surrounded these last years by strangers. And loneliness was another name for self-sufficiency.

Walking from one chamber to the other, she wondered what he needed to say, and what she dared say. He had spoken to Clémence, and would have all the news about Gelis and Jodi. For the rest, Tobie and Crackbene between them had told him everything else: about Bruges; about Robin; about her uncle. She knew as much from Tobie, who had drawn her aside and said, 'In case you find yourself in private with Nicholas . . . I've given him your uncle's letter for Phemie. He was very thankful to have it, but extremely concerned for Adorne. I told him all you and Gelis had done.'

'Gelis more than any of us,' Kathi had said. 'I'm glad you told him.'

Now it was almost the first thing he spoke of when they entered the small, empty room. Even before he found a seat for her, he drew her round and said, facing her, 'You are tired. I shan't keep you. I just wanted to ask if there was anything more I could do or say now that would help.'

'About Robin? You saw him come alive today,' Kathi said. 'That's enough for the moment.'

He still stood. 'And about your uncle. I'm so sorry. I would have stayed in Bruges if I'd known.'

'I know. But you were here, for Phemie.'

'She did need someone,' he said. 'Most of all, she wanted to hear from your uncle. But now? Do I tell her he's in prison? I think I have to. She would hear.'

'Do you want me to see her and judge?' Kathi said. 'You don't need to be careful. I do have room for someone other than Robin, and she was a very good friend.'

Nicholas said, 'I didn't want to ask, but it would mean a lot. You might want to see her alone. You might want to take her the letter. Or your brother, once you have told him.'

'Saunders?' she said. 'I think Saunders might need some time. This is not the way he wants to think of his uncle. But I can deal with all that, I think.'

'Can you? Or shall I?'

'Goodness, no. This will be an Adorne affair in his eyes. I could always manage Saunders. Well, nearly always. So,' said Kathi with finality, 'I think you and I should see Phemie together. Then she can be sure, if anything happens, that at least she has one Adorne to rely on, as well as you.' She paused: 'Are you standing because you've ridden too far, or because you want to get away fast?'

Then he pulled a face, and seated her on the only chair while he found a cushioned coffer for himself. There he rested back on the tapestried wall, as he had when he was a prisoner in her uncle's house, and she had visited him. She said, 'We are all tired,' and he answered, 'I know. But meeting you is like being rewound.'

They had known each other ever since she was fourteen. Their minds had always been close. She felt an ache because it was so much simpler to talk to someone whose eyes – over-large and sleepless and direct – were on the same level as her own, and whose whole, co-ordinated body was an extra instrument of subtle communication. His physical presence was one of the instantly memorable things about Nicholas. In another man of his background, the unusual height, the powerful shoulders and limbs might have seemed uncouth or unwieldy, but through his adventurous life, he had been moulded to grace by many hands. Against that, the broad-blocked face, with its large eyes and repertoire of expressions, had nothing classical about it, or even remarkable, unless it were the two deep dimples, absent now, and the scar given him as a boy by Jordan de St Pol.

You would say, at first glance, a comely man; then an ugly one. Then you might change your mind yet again. The ambiguity was what had first attracted the attention of David Simpson, and no doubt Gelis van Borselen, who had also known him as a child. Gelis had passed through a fire of her own making in order to earn the right to live at his side. Now she would face anything for him. Yet, in all that, there was no rivalry between Gelis and herself. She, Kathi, had Robin. What bound Kathi to Nicholas was quite a different bond. And, today, perhaps also a lifeline.

Nicholas said, as if he had followed her thinking: 'I've spoken to Tobie about Robin. He requires permanent care. But he will have to learn to think for himself.'

'I know,' she said. 'We smother him. But he will need us less, soon.' She hesitated, and then said what she wanted to say. 'I have told Robin that he is free, if he finds it too much. Tobie says you can't tell yet whether he'll manage, because he's so young. He has to find a method of living, but at the moment he's tired, and his wounds are not fully healed. It will all take a while.' She stopped again. 'He has asked me if I think you will stay in Scotland.'

He said, 'Who asked? Robin or Tobie?'

She smiled. 'Both. I said I couldn't say. I gather they didn't ask you.'

'Everyone else does,' he said. 'The answer is, I don't know. I can't be sure I can keep out of trouble. I need time, like Robin, to be sure I can manage myself. If this attempt is successful then yes, I should want to stay; but the decision must come from all of you, not from me. From my victims.' His face, an untrustworthy witness, was rueful.

'Would you let me tell him that?' Kathi said. 'Would you let me say that you have allotted yourself a certain length of time within which you mean to teach yourself . . . to . . .'

He made to stand up, and then didn't. His face, a trustworthy witness, showed shock. 'No, Kathi, no! It isn't a parallel. Christ, he's a boy fighting back from disaster, none of it his fault. What is wrong with me is my own fault entirely. If I fail –'

'Yes?' said Kathi.

He clearly hadn't thought of it before. He said, 'If I fail, I can simply go back to the dyevats, where I can't damage anybody. He doesn't have an alternative.'

'So, knowing that, you will feel bound to help him through his trial,' Kathi said. 'And if you talk to him as you have talked to me, he may well think he can help you. At least, knowing Robin, he will try. And isn't that what we want, to engage him with something? Business by itself won't be enough.'

There was another blank silence. Then Nicholas said, 'But if I failed, I should bring him down with me. He would lose his guide-rope as well.'

'I'm glad you see that,' said Kathi. 'For if you stray, a lot of people are going to be hurt badly again. Robin won't be alone.'

His face had stilled. He said, 'I see.' He didn't inflect it. If he had, she thought she would have heard despair. He said, 'I think you must be the hardest person I know.'

She said, 'That's what Robin says, too. Anyway, you were hard enough on the multi-talented Master Yare. Tormenting him with the Latin version. Making him sing the song with the Rs.'

She could see him manacle his thoughts in order to follow her lead. His face slowly became untrustworthy again. 'Dame Music and her less well-endowed scholars. Tom didn't mind. He has such a wonderful burh. *A! mohrioh; A! mohrioh; A! mohrioh* . . . Robin enjoyed it, at least. And about oysters.'

For a moment, she had forgotten the connection between singing and oysters. Then she said warily, 'What?'

'Just this,' Nicholas said. There was a little suede bag in his hand, which he brought across and, kneeling, emptied into her palm. 'The fair stone Margarita which dwells there. For Margaret. The Icelanders reduced it to Groa, but I think Margaret of Berecrofts sounds better. I don't know what to get Rankin. I'll think.'

The pearl lay in her palm, lustrous and creamy on its fine chain. After a while, she looked up.

'I sang for it,' Nicholas said. 'Perhaps one day Margaret will sing for it, too. I must go, or Clémence will chastise me.'

She followed him to the door, and he touched her fingers, and left.

She sang the pearl a short, suitable song, and went to bed. And, surprisingly, slept.

In Edinburgh, the English envoy departed, with many fine gifts, on the heels of his moderately successful farewell tournament, and David's Tower shook with dissension. Messengers seeking Nicol de Fleury waylaid him outside his house and took him up to the Castle where he was pitchforked, with no visible pleasure, into the private lodging of Sandy Albany. Standing inside the door, Nicholas said, 'My lord. Forgive my dishevelment. I have just ridden from Leith, and have not so much as entered my house.'

'I know. What were you doing in Berwick? I wanted you here.'

'I am here now,' Nicholas said. Liddell was also in the chamber: steward turned watchdog who had not been so credulous as Sandy, renewing this relationship, but who was, Nicholas thought, at ease with him now. And then he saw there was someone else – a young woman. A short, rounded girl of sixteen or so whose hair rippled red on her shoulders, and whose fierce young voice he had first heard on the sands of Leith, when she was eight. Margaret, Sandy's young sister, once the illustrious charge of Kathi Sersanders.

She stood, feet astride, glaring at him. Her slippers were scuffed under her gown. She said, 'Sandy said you had good ideas. Then when we needed you, you had gone. I don't want to be married.'

'Highness,' Nicholas acknowledged. 'The English envoy brought an offer?' He emerged from his second reverence. From where he stood by the window, Liddell cast him a glance, almost of sympathy. Albany, sprawled in a chair, scowled at his sister.

Albany said, 'If we find the situation intolerable, we shall deal with it in our own time. We are not short of ideas. We merely wished to test public opinion. The offers, such as they are, come from our side. His grace my brother has proposed that the lady Margaret and I marry the English King's brother and sister. That is, that I should be contracted to Margaret, the widowed Duchess of Burgundy; and that the lady Margaret should console the Duke of Clarence, who lost his wife in December.'

Nicholas said, 'I am not sure, my lord, that I follow. This is surely a gesture, no more. Neither marriage, however splendid, would suit English policy.'

'Of course you are right, but James doesn't think so,' Albany said. 'He is determined to abase himself before England. If this doesn't succeed, he'll marry Meg to some high-born English bab in the cradle, and she will be tied to London for life. Why were you in Berwick?'

'Because Berwick is full of spies,' Nicholas said. 'And I had an excuse. I went to meet Katelijne of Sersanders and her husband on their way home from Bruges.'

'Kathi!' said Margaret. She stopped tramping about and looked pleased. 'Did her husband die? Perhaps she would return to our service.'

'She has two children. No. Her husband was badly wounded at Nancy, but hopes to continue in business. They are in the Canongate, opposite the old Berecrofts building.'

'I shall send for her,' Margaret said. 'She will want another interest if he is sickly, or dying. And she also has good ideas. You helped my other sister with her marriage. Sandy is sure you can help us.'

But Sandy's mind was on affairs other than marriage. Sandy was Warden of the East Marches and Earl of March, which meant he possessed control of the south-east of Scotland, down to the walls of the fortress of Berwick-upon-Tweed. The fortress and the town were the King's. The King's money paid for their fortification and repair, and the King recouped from the customs paid by foreign merchants. The King's wine and the King's luxuries were conveyed by his merchants from the quayside at Berwick. Just recently, since the treaties with England, the King had made gifts of land within Berwick for his own state officials who now merited a presence there. The Lord Clerk Register and the customs controllers had joined William Scheves, and Wattie Bertram, that eminent citizen of Edinburgh, and those others who were already there: the Keeper of the Castle, the bailie and chamberlain, the representatives of the monasteries of Melrose and Newbattle, and Sir William Knollys of the Order of St John. Everyone upon whom the King's favour shone obtained a place of honour in Berwick. To visit Berwick was to proclaim yourself a King's man.

Albany said, 'Spies? The biggest spy in Berwick is Tom Yare. I see his riders coming in through the ports and down to the Cowgate to have a quiet word with my lord of Avandale, or up the High Street to Argyll's tavern, or disappearing through the pend to catch Master Secretary Whitelaw.'

'It depends how you look at it,' Nicholas said. 'At least they're spying for Scotland. It's the English sympathisers I should be interested in myself. But it disturbs you, my visit to Berwick. And Sir James can probably tell you more than I can.'

The easy flush came to Albany's skin. He said, 'I am not disturbed. I expected you to be here, and you were not. That is all.'

'I shall try not to disappoint you again,' Nicholas said. He was tired of standing, and perhaps they noticed it, for he was given a seat and some refreshment while the lady Margaret set herself to discover, to her own satisfaction, all the pertinent details of Messire Nicholas's disconnected married life and present amatory liaisons, if any. It came to her, with delight, that naturally, Messire Nicholas had rushed to Berwick to enter the embrace of the demoiselle Kathi, to console her for the crippled, the dying, the incapable husband. Was this not the truth?

Neither Albany nor Liddell was interested enough to rescue him, so he had to devise his own means of countering it all. It reminded him of the old days at Haddington, and Kathi, aged fourteen, driven to wild exasperation by this same shallow, wilful inquisitiveness. And yet there was no malice in it. Bleezie Meg, the small royal hoyden, was as natural now as she had been then, and was not deserving of harshness, so he showed her none. It dragged on for a long while, and by the time it finished, he was too late to call and see how Robin had settled, so he walked down, in the lamp-studded redolent darkness, past the descent to the Horse Market and on to his own house in the High Street.

Lowrie, the latest in the long line of chamber-servants, had already unpacked the saddlebags brought from the ship, and the wall-sconces were trimmed, and some dishes set out under cloths. Nothing in parlour or bedroom appeared to be smashed, torn or burned, although Master Henry, said Lowrie, had spent that day in the house, and was in his chamber at present. Nicholas, not entirely depressed by the news, did not at the time observe the man's slight hesitation when dismissed. He was disposed, deep in thought, on the window-seat, the candles dimmed, the elements of his small feast strewn about him, when the door opened silently and Henry came in.

From the window, his head lodged in a resigned way against the wainscoting, Nicholas could not read his expression. As Henry said nothing, he spoke. 'I'm sorry I had to go without warning. It was to bring Berecrofts back. There is some pasty left, if you want it.'

'Not particularly,' Henry said. His voice sounded blurred, as if he were drunk. He added, in the same blurred voice, 'But you should be pleased. Are you pleased, Uncle? Your friends did this to me, once.' But before he had halfway finished speaking, Nicholas had crossed the room and was confronting him with a muttered word that would have earned him short shrift from the Abbot of Holyrood. Then he turned the boy to the light.

The bones of the face were intact. The skin clung to them in glazed and discoloured pillows; the eyes were slits; the lips bloated and shapeless. And the bruising ran down below the throat of his shirt and was part of the reason, no doubt, why he held his shoulders so stiffly. When he moved, he moved with a limp. Of all his beauty, only the golden waves of his hair were untouched.

'Who?' said Nicholas.

'You don't need to know,' Henry said. 'I am going to kill him tomorrow. I only wanted you to note the provocation.'

'I am noting it,' Nicholas said. 'Strip. I want to see the rest of it.'

'It has been seen,' Henry said. He detached himself, concentrating a little, and let himself into a seat. 'There is nothing broken.'

'How many?' Nicholas said.

'Oh, thank you,' said Henry. 'So you don't imagine I just got the worst of it against a very big man?'

'Not unless you've wasted every penny spent on your training,' Nicholas said. 'So when, where and how many? And, of course, why?'

'I upset people,' Henry said. 'There were six of them. Paid bullies, of course. In the dark, on my way home. Someone came by and interrupted them.'

The words emerged from the fluffed lips with all the old insolence. Looking down, scanning all he could see, Nicholas recognised, as he always had, the kind of courage that was greater than other people's, because it was not instinctive. He said, 'I'm going to try and give you some wine. Does your grandfather know?'

'No,' Henry said. 'That is why I am telling you.'

Of course. His grandfather would try to stop him – would stop him. Nicholas, the enemy, wouldn't.

He could drink, after a fashion. It turned out that he was hungry, and Nicholas sent him back to his room and found bread and milk and some honey, which he melded and brought him. He had not offered to undress him, and the boy had done so himself. He sat up in bed, commenting, 'You make a good servant, Uncle. Might we make a permanent arrangement? All my meals, when I want them? A ready hand to empty my privy?'

'A ready hand to find an unbruised place and bruise it,' said Nicholas equably. It was not how he felt. He had just realised who had ordered this punishment, and whom Henry was proposing to challenge tomorrow.

While the boy ate, Nicholas left the room. When he came back to collect the empty bowl, he leaned over the bed, to Henry's amusement. Then the amusement turned to rage, for there was cord slipped and knotted across Henry's bruised chest and round his wrists and the bedposts, and while he was straining painfully against that, Nicholas took his hammer and nails to the shutters and lifted the key of the door.

Henry said, 'What do you think you are doing? You can't keep me for ever. You can't keep me for a day – I'm due on duty tomorrow.' There was puzzlement mixed with the rage. 'What's it got to do with you?'

And then enlightenment. 'You're going to bring him. You know who he is. You're going to bring him and let him do what he likes.'

'I know it's John of Mar,' Nicholas said. 'And that it's because of what happened at the Vespers. I'm not going to bring him. I'm going to tell his brothers to deal with him.'

'The King? Of course, he'd listen to you!' Henry said.

'Or Sandy Albany, for preference. If they control Mar, I'd have to undertake that you wouldn't revive the quarrel by challenging him.'

'You expect me to accept this without challenging him?' Henry said.

'It's a rule,' Nicholas said. 'Everyone is excused from challenging princes. He is brought to order by his family, and honour is satisfied. And if you refuse, I'll tell your grandfather all about it tonight.'

He cut the cords, neatly, as he was leaving, and got the door shut and locked before Henry could blunder towards it. Henry shouted in a painful, muffled way for a while, and then stopped. Nicholas lay in bed listening. He had meant what he said. He had to go to see Avandale in the morning, and Avandale would do what was required. Nicholas hoped not to have to tell Jordan de St Pol before then; afterwards, it shouldn't be necessary. It would be known soon enough that Mar had initiated a cowardly attack, and had been reprimanded by his royal brother. A challenge would be forbidden. Of course, it wouldn't end there. Mar would try again. But Henry wouldn't be here.

Towards dawn, Nicholas fell asleep at last, but not for too long. Today was his meeting with Avandale. Today he had to take Adorne's letter, and Kathi, to Roslin.

Today was another day without Gelis, and Jodi, who did not have golden hair and blue eyes, but who had learned how to show love, and receive it.

And still it was not safe. It was not safe for them to come.

Chapter 10

Thir iudges suld richt veill attend
Fra pryvate luif and faynd thame to defend.
Sentence of luif evermoir bein blind,
As in a proper actioun ay ve find.
Erar a man to de thairin forquhy,
His is proper luif him blindis suddanlye.

ALL THE WAY to Roslin with Kathi, Nicholas did what he never did, and presented her with a detailed report on all his activities.

This marked a nerve-racking departure. It also represented the aftermath of a short, stormy scene with her brother who, after a night spent largely pacing the floor, was still in no mood to condone the wiles of some sluttish nun who had trapped his ageing uncle into a lucrative marriage. When Nicholas appeared, he received the full blame. If Nicholas bloody knew, why hadn't he told Sersanders? If Nicholas bloody knew, why hadn't he stopped it?

It was vain, at this point, to reiterate that the lady was an earl's daughter and richer than their uncle Anselm. Kathi had shut him up finally by recalling that if their uncle were to be executed, there would be no problem at all. Then she had ridden off, grimly. Catching up with her, Nicholas had called across, 'I shouldn't worry. He's going to be so busy soon that he'll want to recruit the child as extra staff when it comes.' And, dropping his voice, had proceeded, as they rode, to invite her into the innermost sanctum of his planning.

It sounded smooth, but it went across the grain of all his old habits, and must have been difficult. As her own perceptions cleared, Kathi also discerned that something had happened that he wasn't telling her: when she asked about Henry he brushed the subject aside. In every other way, however, she revelled in sharing his mind.

All of the background she knew: she had been on first-name terms with the royal kindred since her earliest visit to Scotland. But now she listened hungrily to all Nicholas had to say about recent developments: about the loyalties and lucrative projects of Sir Oliver Sinclair (*Nowie?*) of Roslin; and about Sandy Albany, who was divorcing Sir Oliver's sister, and whose dislike of the English peace was shared by his royal sister Margaret. From time to time she interrupted the fast, close-packed report with questions which he answered at the same even-voiced speed. She had forgotten, attuned to the sickroom, what speaking to Nicholas was like when he and she were alone.

'How will it help, if Sandy thinks you're spying for him in Berwick? If I go back to Meg, won't it increase the rift with the King over the English peace?' Then she said, 'Ah, I see. You need to know what Sandy is plotting. And you also need to know what the King thinks. If I'm at Court, I can tell you.'

'You might also tell me what David Simpson is doing,' Nicholas said. 'He has worked very hard to recommend himself to the King, but has been a little hampered so far by his papal connection with Camulio. Now that Camulio's gone, he will want to strengthen his grip.'

'*Now?* Not *while?*'

'An informed guess. And I'm not throwing Robin and you to the wolves. You'll be safer from Simpson the closer you are to the Court. Whitelaw and Avandale and Argyll will look out for you. There are some others as well: officials, advisers, doctors. I'll tell you who they are.'

'You've discussed all this with them?' It was like the Play. It was like unwrapping the canvas, and opening a coffer of dazzling secrets.

'About Simpson and Albany, yes. I saw some of them this morning. It's important, of course, that none of the royal brothers and sisters know that their councillors discuss them with foreigners. These are the men who have kept the kingdom steady for twenty years; they mustn't lose the King's trust.'

'And Tom Yare is in touch with them?' Kathi said. 'So why do they need you in Berwick as well?'

'They don't,' Nicholas said. 'But Albany thinks he does. And Liddell and Purves and one or two others. I had to choose whether to associate with the King or with Albany, and I had some influence with Sandy to build on. The pity is that there is no one except Davie Simpson attached to the King and, indeed, the Queen.'

'But James has his personal merchants, and he trusts Avandale and the rest, surely?'

'He needs someone closer than that. The . . . the boon companion,' Nicholas said.

She waited. When he didn't go on, she said, 'A dangerous role. Do boon companions ever die in their beds?'

'Do they want to?' he said. And because he had followed her thought, 'Whatever kills me, it is unlikely to be Albany's excess of affection.'

'Where have you lived?' Kathi said. 'Excess of affection always kills.'

Then they were at Roslin. For an hour, for the first hour since January, she had thought of something other than Robin.

Nicholas, sending ahead, had arranged that they should see Phemie first, before anyone. Phemie herself accordingly had some small warning, and received them, labouring up from her chair in the sunny room, her eyes moving from Kathi to Nicholas, but resting on Nicholas. The cordial, wimpled colleague of the Priory had gone, but the same positive mind read his smile. Few men could radiate happiness as Nicholas could. Phemie opened her arms and he moved forward and caught her and hugged her. Then he set her apart and looked down. 'Phemie? He is so delighted. He loves you. He has written to you.'

Later, when she had read the letter, they talked about Seaulme Adorne, and about the rising in Bruges. Listening to what she was told, Phemie was disturbed, but not unduly apprehensive. Men like her uncle, Kathi said, might be subjected to a token imprisonment but, by now, it might well be all over. Of course, Phemie could not travel at present, but had begun to speak of joining Anselm after the birth. It was only two months away. He might even travel to fetch her. Then she asked about Robin.

There, Kathi held back nothing, but balanced the bad news with the good. He could never walk, but could be strapped in a chair. One side would always be dead, but the other was not, and the living intelligence that made him was unimpaired. Kathi was in Scotland to stay, but her life henceforth would depend on Robin's determination to rediscover his place in the world. Phemie, she thought, understood.

Then it was time to open the door, and announce Phemie's news to the world. For whereas yesterday she was an earl's daughter, illicitly pregnant, today she was the promised wife of Anselm Adorne, Baron Cortachy, and could now quietly reshape her life.

Nicholas stayed for a while, as did Kathi. It was partly because Phemie wished it, and partly to savour the moment when Nowie was told. Consummate performer that he was, Sir Oliver moved from relief to chaste satisfaction, expressing delight at his dear cousin's choice, mixed with the faintest censure for the gentleman's hastiness. He gave her his blessing. It was even possible, since he had certainly guessed it all beforehand, that the satisfaction was genuine. Reminded of recent events, Kathi murmured to Nicholas at her side, 'You made her very happy just now.'

'I wanted to,' Nicholas said. 'I knew how she felt.'

'How?'

'When I first heard I had a son.'

He spoke very softly. It was so unlike him that she thought at first she had misheard. She said, on a light breath, 'Where were you?'

'In a convent. I left. I was thinking about him when they attacked me, or I should have escaped. Abrupt awakening.' He gave a laugh, still very soft.

'Who attacked you?'

'Men of Jordan's. Jordan de St Pol. It doesn't matter. But I know how she feels.'

He said nothing more. Kathi thought crossly, No one knows. No one knows what has happened to him. He hardly knows himself. Only this moment of happiness suddenly came back to him now, because of Phemie.

Then she had to step forward, for Betha rushed in, followed by young Will Crichton's mother, another cousin. And that was only the beginning. As word spread, the castle would fill up with relatives. No one, dear God, could say the Dunbars were not well connected. Among her second cousins, Phemie counted some of the King's staunchest friends in the north-east. The earldom of Moray was once a Dunbar's; a Dunbar was Keeper of Darnaway Castle. Phemie's sister Cristina had married into a family that held the rents of all the royal fishing on Speyside, for which at Lammas each year they had to present to the King three and one half lasts of salmon, *full, round and sweet.*

So Nicholas had told her. The same rights, of course, obtained in salmon rivers elsewhere. Tom Yare held tack of the River Tweed fishings for life. The Knights of St John held salmon rights in Peterculter, Aberdeenshire. Monasteries, great and small, all had their privileges: the extraction of salmon, which then required to be salted, barrelled, and conveyed to their markets. Andrew Lisouris, that peripatetic carpenter of noble birth, shipped down the King's salmon with timber from Darnaway forest for barrels, for building. Timber often accompanied salmon, and coal, to fire up the salt-pans.

The keys to the future of Scotland, Nicholas called them: what would weld guild-brethren together, what would fill the royal Treasury; what would draw the eyes of the siblings from England; what should occupy, above all else, the attention of Archie of Berecrofts and Robin. And now Phemie and Adorne would be at the heart of it. And their child.

Before they left, she overheard a single exchange between Sinclair and Nicholas which was not about salmon, or timber.

'Adorne is in prison?'

'He was, in April. Gruuthuse and the little Duchess were determined to have him released.'

'I am told,' Sinclair said, 'that the Duchess ran crying into the square when they executed Hugonet. It did not stop them . . . You know that Albany has begun a consanguinity divorce against my half-sister? Ostensibly so that he may marry the Dowager Duchess?'

'But your reading is different?' Nicholas had said.

'I may be wrong,' said Nowie Sinclair. 'I am sure that if a miracle happened, Sandy would bed the Dowager with equal delight. But if she declines, he is then free in the marketplace.'

'But not as the heir to the Scottish throne,' Nicholas said. 'King James has two sons.'

'Both called James. How fragile is life. How unpredictable is life,' Sinclair had said.

Returning to Edinburgh with Nicholas, Kathi allowed the conversation to find its own level, and soon it dwindled to nothing. Ahead lay the long, rolling range of the Pentlands; beyond the plains to the right lay the sea. From time to time she glanced at Nicholas, who was riding at a hard, steady pace, his face absent. They passed Newbattle, and rode down and up from Dalkeith. She kept what she wanted to say until they were close to the green crag beside Holyrood, and the Castle shone, small and clear on its rock.

'Nicholas? Why did Jordan allow Henry to join you?'

Then, he glanced across. 'I told you. I threatened him.'

'And he agreed meekly. I know. So Henry is spying for Jordan?'

'And I am feeding him false information. Yes, all of that.'

She hesitated. 'I thought he tried once to claim you molested him.'

'In Bruges, when he was young. It didn't stick. He'd look a fool trying it now: an armed Royal Guardsman unable to escape the advances of a man twice his age?' His voice lightened a little. 'In fact, it's the other way round. He was kind enough to mention that his wittier friends had accused him of falling in love with me. I won't tell you what answer he gave them.'

'It seems to me,' Kathi said, 'that you won't tell me anything. I *am* able to direct my weakened mind to subjects other than Robin: I've proved it. Now I want to know what is wrong about Henry.'

'John of Mar tried to kill him,' Nicholas said. 'Avandale and Sandy have gone to see Mar, and I have locked Henry up, until he agrees not to challenge him.'

It had been the only way to get an answer. With Nicholas, you didn't do that very often, and it hurt. 'I am suitably abashed,' Kathi said. 'That, then, was what you were doing this morning. Was Henry injured?'

'A painful mauling, but it could have been worse. Next time it will be.'

'So Jordan will want him back in his house?'

'When I left, Jordan didn't know,' Nicholas said. 'And I promised not to tell him.'

'Because Henry is planning to do something nasty to Mar, and you don't mind if he does?'

'Because I know that a secret like that can't be kept. I'll wager anything you like that Jordan de St Pol of Kilmirren is enthroned in my house at this moment, brooding until I come back.'

There was a silence. '*Anything* I like?' Kathi said. 'May I come and see if he's there?'

'No,' said Nicholas. 'Go home to Saunders. By the way.'

'Yes?' She knew the tone, and was thankful.

'Ask Saunders why he used to go to Berwick so often.'

'*Berwick?*'

He didn't answer. His gaze dwelled on her, restored, and she felt the responsive colour tingeing her nose, not her cheeks. 'All right. Berwick,' she said.

Lowrie said, 'I'm sorry, my lord. They brought a hatchet. I had to unlock the door.'

'So Master Henry has gone, and my lord of Kilmirren is still here?' Nicholas said.

'Merely to make Master Henry's excuses,' remarked Jordan de St Pol from the parlour doorway. 'You expected it.'

He filled the doorway. It became light when he retreated and sat down. Nicholas followed him in and took the same place on the window-seat he had occupied only last night. Someone had cleared out the food. Nicholas said, 'Since I lost my leverage, yes.'

The fat man was smiling, today. 'Quite. The law will be happy not to pursue a case against Henry, provided Henry drops his complaint against Mar. The men who attacked you at Bonnington will, alas, remain for ever unpunished.'

'Mar will try again,' Nicholas said.

'Of course,' said St Pol. 'What can one do, except hope my poor Henry survives it? You can't imagine I care?'

'Then why take him back?' Nicholas said.

'What shall I say?' said Jordan de St Pol. 'He reported a few of your minor business dealings but, really, not enough to be worth it. You learned even less, I am sure, and indeed suffered some loss. You have no idea what plans Henry now has for his horses. In fact . . . I have a theory. I think you were trying to suborn Henry from his grandfather's bosom. Should I be right?'

This time, the smile of the fat man was lavish; the eyes bright, the lips a voluptuous rose. He waited. It was so quiet that Nicholas could hear the beat of his own heart.

'No one could do that,' Nicholas said.

The snowfield stilled; the hissing springs drained; far off under the glacier, Hekla breathed.

'I should have killed you,' said Jordan de St Pol; and rose; and walked out.

Nicholas remained on the window-seat. Presently, since there was a great deal to do, he swung his feet down and went to his desk.

Primed by the padrone himself, Kathi Sersanders was able, more than most, to appreciate what was happening during the following weeks.

Over the road, Robin's father, in his level way, had resumed business; and the grandfather had retired, at last, to the family estate at Templehall. Saunders, under the impact of the murmured word *Berwick*, had ceased to be ashamed of his uncle, although he hadn't brought himself to meet Phemie yet. Nor had he said what had happened at Berwick, save to mutter that it was years ago and irrelevant.

In their own house, the children had settled with Cristen, and Dr Tobie and Clémence had made a home of their building in the same yard. Robin was mobile now, wheeled from one room to another, and often over the road to Saunders's office. It had once belonged to Nicholas, and had its own door. The counting-house, which was not so easy to reach, was upstairs. If Crackbene was about, he sometimes carried him.

Once installed, Robin would sit listening with frightening intensity to what was being said, and would take a determined part in all the discussions. To begin with, Archie steered these into areas with which Robin was conversant, but Robin soon noticed, and recognised when his ignorance was being treated with tolerance. Very soon, with ferocious dedication, he had set aside pain to master all they could tell him. And when Nicholas visited, which he did within their old house, Robin would test himself further, disputing over the developing business, which had once taken second place in his heart to the active world he had lost.

As he had been to Kathi, so now Nicholas was candid to Robin. Again, for the first time, he laid before the boy in the chair all his thoughts and his plans, and listened to Robin's views. With Nicholas, Robin dropped the curt, probing manner he used with his peers, and relaxed into the low-key, speculative style that Nicholas encouraged. Only, as had happened with Kathi, Nicholas did not talk to him of Henry, or of anything personal. In some respects, no one could blame him. But he should, she believed, share some of his apprehensions with Robin – over the St Pols, for example, and Simpson. Robin wanted to help.

For the moment, though, he was fighting his way along the path they had designed for him, and it seemed to be succeeding, even if Dr Tobie sometimes left Robin's bed, frowning, after one of the excursions over the road. You would say that Robin was learning to become used to his disabilities, except for those times when, talking business, someone would lift and flourish a paper, or cross the room to a map, and Robin would instinctively make a half-movement. Then he would drop back and lie, his lips tight, his eyes full of cold rage.

As much as she could, Kathi shared in it, and absorbed the news that came from abroad, much of it from men who still worked in the disjointed establishments of the former Banco di Niccolò. Julius, the handsome lawyer, wrote from Germany and so did his partner Father Moriz and Govaerts their deputy. According to Julius, all business was suffering in the interregnum between the old Duke and the little Duchess's new husband. According to Moriz, Julius had become the most popular widower in Cologne, to the amazement of his step-daughter Bonne who, of course, was still mourning her mother. They both expressed anxiety about Adorne, and about Robin.

News came from England: the King's brother Clarence was under a shadow, and both royal marriage proposals were politely turned down. Meg was free. Kathi, who had made a first, cautious response to the cordial invitations from Court, found that Meg still possessed the attributes of eight, and assumed that Kathi was permanently fourteen. It was quite pleasant, in a confused way. The older sister, Mary, was absent, but Meg presented her to the Queen. It was less pleasant to be called *Katelijne Sersanders of Bruges: the crippled Berecrofts boy's dame, you remember?* The Queen, however, had retrieved her good-sister's gaffe with some skill, and when addressed in her own language, had expressed pleasure, but not the painful relief of her first years. She had been twelve years old when she came from Denmark to Scotland.

Will Roger dropped in. Once he brought a large hearty choir, and made it sing under Robin's window. The children cried. Brought indoors, choir dismissed, he performed on the whistle and drank, and exchanged stories with Nicholas, so that Robin's head switched from the one to the other. Robin said, 'I'm supposed to have *soothing* music.'

'Well, if you're out of your head, I'll give you it,' said Whistle Willie, his grey hair on end. 'But if you're not, please excuse me. I get enough of that in the Castle. That young Johndie Mar is a devil.'

'With drink?' Nicholas said.

Kathi got up from her stool. 'Do you remember Hugo the painter in Bruges? Hugo vander Goes? Dr Andreas said he's having to go into a monastery. He drinks, and thinks he can't paint, and they play soothing music to help him. He's doing Canon Bonkle's altar-piece.'

'It doesn't sound as if he's doing it,' Robin said. 'So why is Willie playing up at the Castle? Are they all moody?'

There was a little silence. Kathi glanced at Nicholas and said, watching him, 'Dr Andreas said something in Bruges. Something he suspected, or divined about their health. He didn't say what it was.'

'So come on,' Robin said. 'You're the diviner. What's wrong, Nicol?' He had taken, recently, to this style of addressing Nicholas, and no one had commented, least of all the man he used to call 'sir'.

Nicholas said, 'Short tempers, poor concentration, varying amounts of intellectual capacity. They're very like one another. Ask Tom Yare's friend Scheves. And a streak of lunacy, if you want to throw in John of Mar.'

'And the recently excommunicated Archbishop Patrick Graham, whom your kind offices elevated,' said Willie Roger. 'He went clean crazy, and thought he was the Pontiff. And he was a second cousin, wasn't he, of the King's?'

'Is,' Nicholas said. 'Sad things are happening to him even as we speak. So who's mad in your family?'

'Me,' said Willie Roger. 'When I don't get what I want. And what I want is *that*, sung immediately.'

That was a piece of hideously difficult music, scribbled on ecclesiastical vellum. The composer, said Willie, was one of the Arnots. Nicholas sang, and Robin became very silent, so that they went back to chaffing again.

Nicholas, too, spent this time observing and learning. Henry de

St Pol, returned to the home of his grandfather, did not go out until his face healed. After that, he divided his time between his guard duty, his new stud, and Leith, where he had begun to take a keen interest in coastal shipping. Having lived in and about Portugal, he was not unused to vessels, and a few of the skippers took him out now and then to practise his skills. At sea, he was not a bad companion (so said Crackbene's spies), and the lads let him take part in the May King of the Sea contests, one of which he nearly won. Between that and looking out for Johndie Mar, he had no time, it seemed, to create pitfalls for Nicholas; and the deep hostility of his grandfather, which seemed immutable, now manifested itself only in contemptuous silence. Nicholas had not ended the feud with the St Pols, but he had its measure, at least.

David Simpson, passing one day, called on Robin, but was regretfully turned away, on medical grounds, by Mistress Clémence. He did not trouble to return and Nicholas, informed, recognised it for the cynical nudge that it was. Comfortably surrounded by bodyguards, David was waiting. David had relied on the St Pols to make life insupportable for his victim but, failing that, might condescend to provoke Nicholas into action himself. As Nicholas, of course, was presently proposing to do for friend David. But not until Robin's future was as secure as might be.

In all of it, he had the support of Tobie and Clémence. The medical care that had brought Robin alive from Nancy was still there, bolstered now and then by unobtrusive help from the Castle, from the circle of physicians who still, no matter what their ostensible offices, watched over the medical needs of the Crown. Soon, as Robin grew self-sufficient, Tobie would profit from a wider circle of interests, rediscovering the clients and friends of his previous stay. Now he was beginning to emerge from the nausea and weariness of the journey, and to rediscover the satisfactions of disagreeing, often, with Nicholas. He found the battles stimulating, and Nicholas quite often lost. Only occasionally would Tobie revert to the wretchedness that lay behind him, some of it evidenced in his concern for the other prisoner, John le Grant. Unhurt in a camp full of injured, alive in a field full of dead, John had at first retreated, as Tobie had, into the single-minded campaign to save Robin. That done, he had withdrawn into himself. Tobie had advised Gelis what to do, before he left.

'What?' had said Nicholas.

'Nothing,' said Tobie.

Nicholas himself, unmolested, began to move out of Edinburgh, to Stirling, to Dundee, to St Johnstoun of Perth. He, too, was interested in shipping. He was interested in currency. He talked to goldsmiths, and carried his findings not only to the Master of Berecrofts and Robin, but to the Councillors of the King. He began to know Argyll well, and understand some of his tongue and appreciate his subtlety. He held Avandale in the kind of respect that he had given, as a boy, to Adorne. But Avandale was royal, and you didn't forget it, any more than you forgot the Orkney antecedents of Oliver Sinclair. Royal, but without the royal flaws, as Bishop Kennedy had been.

So there was a lull. It wouldn't be permanent, but it let him establish the groundwork of what he wanted to do. With the lengthening peace, the country had a chance to start building. In England, in France, in Burgundy, the effects of the Duke of Burgundy's death, of the Duchess's union, were surely being assimilated by now.

Even when the news came, in June, that Prosper de Camulio, the Papal Collector, had been arrested by the Milanese as a traitor and was not therefore returning to Scotland, it seemed to Nicholas that Simpson, with his own position to consolidate, would not change his tactics towards his victims just yet. Robin was slowly responding, Phemie was flourishing, Nicholas himself was doing what he had set himself to do. He beguiled himself with the idea that if Phemie's child were born in July, he might even sail with her in August to Bruges, and spend time there with Gelis and Jodi. But that would excise two full months from his programme, and lengthen this interminable separation in the end. Also, David might follow him. It was Gelis for whom David was waiting.

All the time, Nicholas thought about Gelis; for these days, every sense was her messenger.

Chapter 11

As cald with heit and richt so heit with cald,
Ioye with sorrow richt so the contrar wald.

IN BRUGES, the cells in the Steen, even the better rooms, were
rank, now, with over-use. As the arguments and counter-
arguments pounded on, the law hung suspended, and Anselm
Adorne and his fellow magistrates lived from day to day in the
prison, passing the time in the quiet pursuits of reading and card-playing
and talking, the more timid taking their example from the courage of
the rest.

Locked away from the fluctuating temper of the mob, they were
treated with pointed aloofness by the gaoler, the bailiff, the turnkeys
who supervised the cleaning of their privies and fetched the rough food
that was all their staple. The provisions they relied on were those
brought from outside: money gave them access to that, as well as to
rooms on the upper storey, and bedding, and freedom from manacles.
It did not buy exemption from torture. Not all had suffered; Adorne
so far had been spared, together with two of his own closer friends:
Paul van Overtweldt, who had been his First Burgomaster two years
before, and the magistrate Jean de Baenst, who was related to Margriet,
his late wife. Others, less lucky, had come back silent and limping
and scarred from their questioning. Out of sixteen burgomasters and
treasurers to be accused, the sole condemned man, Barbesaen, was
guarded elsewhere.

As well as provender, they were permitted visitors, who brought
them clothes, and news, and received instructions for the family or the
business left masterless outside. In the case of Adorne of Cortachy, the

routines established by his niece continued uninterrupted after her departure, and the household of the Hôtel Jerusalem, under his chamberlain, did their utmost to ease his imprisonment. His groom or his bodyservant passed to and fro with satchels and baskets containing ink and paper and letters, books and linen, and his chaplain from the Jerusalemkerk paid anxious visits, as did the religious of the churches in the other places – Ronsele, Viven and Hertsberge – where he had inherited seigneurial rights. He had been a liberal patron, and they were rightly anxious. His family visited, assiduously, and the nuns his daughters all wept.

Gelis, making her own regular calls to the Steen, avoided them if she could. Most often she was accompanied by Dr Andreas, who had moved into the Hôtel Jerusalem, the better to campaign for its master. Andreas of Vesalia bore a name that carried some weight: his father had been town doctor of Brussels and Rector of the University of Louvain; his late half-brother Everard had been doctor to the little Duchess herself. But more important even than that, he was a respected member and doctor to the leather guilds, bound by their trade both to Genoa and the Adornes. All his life, Adorne had been generous to the guilds, and a popular member of the merchants' club, the White Bear Society. Diniz spent all the time he could spare at the White Bear, pursuing support for his uncle. Andreas did the same with the skinners and glovemakers. And Gelis used her influence with her van Borselen relatives: on Wolfaert, the Governor at Veere; on Gruuthuse here, on whom the Duchess depended.

On advice, she did not try to speak directly to the Duchess again, and John le Grant, who had once accompanied her, did not offer to do so now. Since Robin and Tobie had gone, the engineer had lost what little interest he had had in the winding up of the mercenary company, and had begun to exchange his desk for the quayside at Sluys, or even the wharves as far off as Antwerp, where there were always men whom he knew, and taverns to meet them in. He had his share of the company money, and was free to live as he chose: Tilde kept his room and Diniz accepted his wandering without comment. It was understandable that, now, he did not want to exchange one responsibility for another.

Within the prison whose outer walls he had protected such a short time ago, Adorne received his friends and their reports with unfailing courtesy, and a wry sense of humour. Since his wife died, he had made a fresh will, to replace the one prepared years ago, before his trip to the Holy Land. He would not, now, be leaving his best sapphire to the

Bishop of St Andrews, because Bishop Kennedy was dead, and his nephew Archbishop Graham had been arraigned before the law, as he himself was. And it was unlikely, now, that twenty-four porters of the weigh-houses would wear new robes and carry new torches to his lying-in-state, amid hangings of black and white and grey linen, or that the bells of his three churches would be permitted to ring, to remind Bruges that he had died. Waiting now, a little more spare, a little more pallid than he had been, Adorne passed his time well enough with his fellow magistrates, but was glad, as they were, of any diversion. Reports on the altering political climate were important to him, for they affected his chances of life. But dispatches from Scotland were what he was waiting for.

Gelis couldn't tell, yet, whether he had broken the news about Phemie to his existing family. Since he could not marry as yet, perhaps he would wait. He wanted to know, always, what news she had of Nicholas, and she told him whatever she heard. Then, in the middle of May, there came word of Robin's safe home-coming in a letter from Kathi and with it, at last, a joyous response to his letter from Phemie herself. That afternoon, Gelis returned to the Steen with something from his own house: the lute upon which he had so often made music with the Scottish friend of his heart. He took it from her and then, leaning forward, kissed her cheek. 'Nicholas is fortunate,' said Anselm Adorne. 'And I am fortunate, to have known you both.'

He was a brave man with few delusions, who knew that, hard as they might work, his life hung on a thread.

Early that month, the Estates-General had accepted the Imperial marriage as valid, and were even now waiting for the Archduke Maximilian to set out from Vienna. The signs were that the country was becoming reconciled to 'the rude German' against whom King Louis had warned. If so, they would wish to put their house in order before he arrived. They would wish no sign of dissension in Bruges.

The little Duchess made sure there would be none. A letter of remission was posted in June, absolving the Brugeois from *alle mesdaden, offensien, mesgripen ende abusen*, which satisfactorily excused the summary execution of the sentence on former burgomaster Barbesaen, at last.

Adorne's family rushed to the Steen. Dr Andreas presented himself at the Hof Charetty-Niccolò. 'They are to hold a final Tribunal. I have done all I can. So have you. Now all we can do is pray.'

It was Gelis who stood before him and spoke. 'We don't need to pray. You can tell the future. You know what is going to happen.' None of the others said anything. John le Grant for once was in the room, as well as Diniz and his family.

Dr Andreas shook his head, with its bright eyes and its fresh, big-featured face which seemed compatible with human appetites rather than spiritual ones. 'I draw up birth charts. Sometimes they hint at what is to come. But not everyone wants to know his own fate. My lord of Cortachy asked me to refrain from compiling his horoscope. So did your husband.'

'Nicholas? But he can tell the future,' said Gelis.

'Can he?' said the doctor. 'It would surprise me. He can divine, as many people can, what is lost, or under the earth. He may be able to communicate, in a simple way, with those to whom he is close. But if he has some window into the future, I should like to know of it.' He paused. 'I have reassured you. It is not certain, then, what he sees? Or he sees unwanted splinters, of no meaning?'

'That,' said Gelis. 'It disturbed him. So did the pendulum. But perhaps both have stopped.'

'One may stop using a pendulum,' Andreas said. 'He has probably made that decision: you are right. But the other is not within his control. He is only the recipient.'

She stared at him. 'Of what? Someone else has chosen him? Someone else with a pendulum is deliberately –' She broke off. 'This is nonsense.'

John le Grant spoke. 'Of course it's nonsense. A pendulum never saved anyone, or visions or prayers that I know of. If anyone was sending messages to Nicol, they didn't do him much good. Or Robin. Or Astorre.'

'I agree,' said Andreas. 'But do we blame the unseen for what happened? No one is consciously trying to reach Nicholas from beyond the barrier of life. If such intangible transmissions exist, they are involuntary, and harmless. Should we not be thinking of Lord Cortachy, rather than this?'

'I was. I am,' Gelis said.

'Then pray,' said Dr Andreas. 'John does not agree, but for the rest of us, there is comfort in prayer.'

The word came later, from the courtroom over which Anselm Adorne had himself presided so often, before judges who once were his equals or underlings, and now were not.

The prisoners Anselm Adorne, Jean de Baenst and Paul van Overtweldt had all been tried, and found guilty. The last two were stripped of all they possessed, and immured in a monastic community, to be separated from their families until death. Anselm Adorne was disgraced. His punishment was to walk in solemn parade, dressed in mourning before all those he had deceived; and to be excluded for ever from all the public activities of the city of Bruges.

'But his life!' Gelis said. 'He has his life?'

'They all have their lives. Through the intervention of the Zwaer Deken, the Council of Grand Deans of the Guilds.'

'And Phemie can come here then? They can be married!'

It was Diniz who said, 'Gelis, he is disgraced. Don't you understand? After two hundred years of his family's service to Flanders, he has to walk like a beggar before his own people, apologising for something he didn't do. He can never hold public office. He can belong to no clubs, no societies, and soon will lose all common ground with his friends, and become an embarrassment. They might as well have killed him.'

'That is going too far,' said Andreas. 'Time may bring a change. He is not incarcerated. He is not in a convent. He must face something, for sure, that I would wish on no man; but his reserves are profound. With a new young family to accompany him, he can go on to make a new life.'

'Here?' said Gelis.

'It would take time. But yes, why not here? Or with the van Borselen at Zeeland, or with his son Jan in Rome or in Naples? Only Genoa, for an Adorno, would be unwise. He could survive anywhere else, and return when he pleases.'

She looked at him dry-eyed. 'I am afraid to go and see him,' she said. 'I think he will think as Diniz does. Two hundred years in Flanders. That great house, freely lent to the state whenever the state wished to borrow it. That magnificent church, draining his personal pocket, built on Flemish soil as a replica of the Holy Sepulchre, to the glory of God and this town. All his illustrious forebears; all he has brilliantly achieved to make them proud of him; all to end in this. He will think, too, that they might as well have killed him.'

'No,' said Andreas. 'He is stronger than you know. You have travelled with him in times of adversity. During these last weeks he has accepted you as a friend. But you have not stood in opposition to him, for example, as your husband has. Your husband knows the measure of Anselm Adorne.'

Euphemia Adorne was born into the world in the last days of June, and was carried to the private oratory within the Castle of Roslin, where she was baptised. As the child of an unmarried mother, she was privileged to be received into the Church by the compassionate hands of the churchman-physician who was to be Archbishop of St Andrews, and she was held at the font by her first cousins, Anselm and Katelijne Sersanders.

From there, she was returned to her cradle, while those who had attended her walked over the bridge and climbed, in silence, the winding, tree-shaded path to the unfinished church of the Sinclairs, where the northern door was hung with black and white and grey linen. And inside they knelt, still in silence, before the casket that stood at the altar, and looked upon the calm, closed face of the child's mother, Euphemia Dunbar, lady of March, lying in death.

So they were found by Anselm Adorne of Cortachy, come from prison to Roslin to claim a bride, and a child.

By then the music had started: grave, spare statements in harmony of the kind that only Will Roger could induce from a choir, and then only when sung from the heart. Of all those surrounding the catafalque, it was Katelijne Sersanders who first detected the faint patter of hooves approaching outside and who, with a premonition of doom, rose to her feet even before the sound ceased and two men came to stand on the step which led down from the sunlit archway of the north door.

Her brother jumped up. Around them, Oliver Sinclair also rose, followed by Phemie's cousins and sister and all those others who had come to welcome the child, and to mourn.

Willie Roger, after one glance, slowly swept up one arm, and smoothed the music down into his fist. Silence fell.

Anselm Adorne walked into the aisle, Dr Andreas behind him. With a glimmer of silks, the Archdeacon moved slowly forward and stopped.

Adorne said, 'They gave me some news at the castle. Is it true?'

Will Scheves was a humane man, and a skilful one. He said, in his quiet, ordinary voice, 'It is true that you have a daughter. It is true that the mother who gave her day is now at peace with her God.'

'May I see her?' said Adorne. 'May I see my wife?'

She was not his wife. The affirmation, before all the company, was a challenge. In the gentle beams from the high southern windows, Adorne's face was grey; and he faltered, once, as he walked forward. With a light hand, Dr Andreas guided him to the coffin, from which everyone else had drawn back.

Oliver Sinclair said, 'Let us leave him with his family,' and led the others away, so that only the priest and Katelijne and Sersanders were left with Adorne in the circle of candlelight. Behind them, in the dimness, the singing had begun again, tender and close-knit and low.

Dr Andreas came out, and joined Oliver Sinclair where he stood, massive and frowning, in the helpless consternation that gripped them all. In the quietness of the green empty meadowland, with the abandoned masons' marks under the grass, there existed small disparate sounds: birdsong; the hiss of the waterfall deep in its gorge; the cry of a lamb; the rustle, now and then, of the hanging linen in the warm air. Andreas looked worn.

Sinclair spoke to him quietly. 'I am sorry. It happened yesterday. One would have wished very much to spare my lord of Cortachy this distress. He came, of course, expecting to see her? The Tribunal has freed him?'

Andreas stirred. He said, 'He expected to make her his wife. He is free, so far as it goes. He is debarred from office in Bruges. The Duchess has made him her personal envoy, so that he could come for his marriage and stay until he had decided where his future would lie. How did it happen?' His questing gaze had found the other professional, Dr Tobias.

Tobie said, 'A premature birth, and a rupture. Everything possible was done for her.'

'I am sure it was,' said Andreas. He looked back at Sinclair. 'I hope you know that my lord of Cortachy was unaware of all this until recently, and has been mortally anxious to make amends.'

'We are not about to be harsh,' said Oliver Sinclair. 'There is a burial to arrange, and the infant's future to think of. If he wishes to stay here, then he may.'

'There is also my house,' said Archie of Berecrofts. 'Or Kathi and Robin's. Dr Andreas would be welcome as well.'

'Or either could come to me,' said Nicholas de Fleury. He had remained in the background, as he had ever since he arrived at the castle. He was not related to Phemie. His gaze, all the time he spoke, was on the doorway into the church, as his thoughts were on Adorne. He added, 'He will take this very badly.'

'It is the final blow,' Andreas said. 'You must speak to him. But not at your house. The others will all be there by now. John le Grant was taking them there, straight from Leith. They will know nothing of this.'

Nicholas, beginning to speak, was overridden by Tobie.

'*John?*' said Dr Tobias. 'John has come to Scotland?'

'He decided, eventually,' Andreas said. He was already moving towards Nicholas, who was standing quite still.

Nicholas said, 'What others?'

'Your wife and son,' said Dr Andreas. 'Forgive me. Of course, you couldn't know; I had forgotten. Adorne and I left the ship to come here. Your wife and son have gone with le Grant and their servants straight to Edinburgh. They will be there when you reach it.'

The doctor had taken his arm, as if something in his face gave cause for alarm, or as if he, Nicholas, were Adorne. At the door of the chapel, the hangings parted as a small person quickly emerged and looked about. Kathi, hunting him. She darted over. 'Nicholas! Gelis and Jodi were on the same ship.'

'I've just heard,' he said. 'Why?' His voice cracked.

'It doesn't matter why,' Kathi said. 'You can protect them. They're here. *They're here.*' She looked round. 'Tobie?'

'I'll go with him,' said Tobie. 'Sir Oliver, you don't mind if some of us leave? M. de Fleury's wife is in Edinburgh.'

He didn't say, as he might have done, *And so is David de Salmeton, who has been waiting for this. And the brat St Pol, who has already once tried to get rid of Jodi. And Robin, who is not ready, yet, to share his protectors.*

Kathi, with the aid of a groom, was dragging over Adorne's horse, and Andreas's own. 'Take these. They can come back with yours.'

Her voice was not cracked; it was fierce. Nicholas drew breath, and walked across, and curled his hand over hers as it lay on the reins. He said, 'I've just realised what you said. Gelis and Jodi are in Edinburgh.'

Oliver Sinclair studied de Fleury. He had a remarkable facility, the Burgundian, for switching expressions. The light in his face was reflected, Sinclair observed, in the young woman's; the light, still mixed with the pain.

The young woman, Adorne's niece, said, 'You should listen.'

For Gelis, disembarking and travelling to Edinburgh, this was not a first marriage she had come to consummate, nor even a second: she and Nicholas had already marked with a few days of desperate happiness the end of their war of eight years. Since then, five months had gone by, and she could bear it no longer. Adorne's departure had presented an opportunity. Against orders, blindly rebellious, she had come. *So we, from evil thorns, shall harvest grapes.*

The day seemed as radiant as her mood. Seagulls gleamed; the sea whispered over the bar; banners rustled in the warm breeze. John, subtly provoked by his old mistress the ocean, had arranged the disembarking with abrasive efficiency and a touch of reluctance that gladdened Gelis's heart. Then they set off, John and herself with their servants on horseback, and Jodi riding beside her, sharing a saddle with Manoli, his friend and his bodyguard, whose presence, with John, was meant to reassure Nicholas. *Look, we are safe. Between you all, how could we possibly come to any harm?*

A boy of eight remembers a place where he once lived with his father and mother and Mistress Clémence who used to be his nurse, and kept a parrot, and played in gardens, and slid on ice, and got sweetmeats for being ill, and marchpane from his wee Aunty Bel, and sat on the knee of a man called Whistle Willie in the Queen's room up at the Castle. Jodi said, 'Will we see Whistle Willie?'

'Yes,' said Gelis.

'Will we see Aunty Bel?'

'Yes. I hope so.'

'Will we see Robin? Will he be better?'

'He'll want to see you. He is better, but he has to lie in his bed.'

Silence. 'So who else will I see?'

They had been over all this a dozen times. She had told him, on Nicholas's advice, that his silly cousin Henry was up at the Castle, so that Jodi would never even see him. She had told him that they would visit Dr Tobie and Mistress Clémence very soon. She had told him that Henry's fat grandfather sometimes came to Edinburgh, but that he was too old to harm anyone now, and Jodi had to be sorry for him. She had explained that Robin's father now owned both the big Canongate houses, and that the other house had been sold. Jodi was going to meet papa in a splendid new house in the High Street.

It was possible, of course, that Nicholas would not be there, since he had no idea that they would be coming. That is, a message they had sent from the harbour would hardly arrive much before they did. Gelis had, nevertheless, no qualms about the capacity of a de Fleury household to receive all of them without warning, if necessary. The world was strewn with Nicholas's efficient former establishments and well-trained ex-servants. There would be no fuss.

They passed the Holy Trinity Church, and turned up Leith Wynd into the Canongate.

Now Jodi, warned against emitting loud personal comments in crowded streets, had settled for watching the houses, bright-eyed, and the children and the chickens and the stalls and wheelbarrows and dogs. It was steep, unlike Bruges. It had no flat canals, as Bruges had. If you twisted sideways in the saddle you could see that the lanes on the right plunged down and down to a hollow, and then up a low ridge, and beyond that, you could see the sea. You had to go three miles before you could see the sea outside Bruges. He had been promised a boat.

Gelis watched the road without seeing it. After the wedding it had been she who had waited for Nicholas, and Nicholas who had come to her through the streets, walking with his friends, a little drunk. She wondered if he were at his desk now, very sober; or interviewing someone on business; or perhaps entertaining a friend. He had many friends, men and women. She didn't fear them. She knew what she was to Nicholas, and he to her.

He might, then, have been entertaining a friend when the message came from the harbour. At first, he might not believe it, but only at first. He knew, as she did, how terrible the separation had become. He would understand that she had reached a conclusion: that nothing mattered but that they should be together. Then he would make some excuse to dismiss whoever was with him and, throwing orders at Lowrie his steward, would come, on foot, striding down the High Street to meet her.

Or no. That was not how he would want their first meeting. He would wait. But not as once she had made him wait.

He had described the house: she could see it. It was timber and tall, and stood near the Bow, past where the High Street merged into the Lawnmarket. Because of its site, it had been expensive, and he had taken care to explain why it was necessary. The money that had leased it was hers, as were all the funds that had financed his journey. In fact they were his: they represented the wealth he had bestowed on her at their marriage, which she had since used to restore the fortunes of the Bank he had left. Now that was done, and the investment returned to her with interest. She was rich, but he had his fortune to make all over again. There was irony in it as well. He had had no desire for wealth or position, but had acquired them as a prize, to lay at Marian de Charetty's feet. And now he would not rest, Gelis knew, until he had earned and repaid every groat that she had given him. Her heart wept for the pride she felt for him.

Now they were near. The windows were sun-struck and blind. She saw two or three men in newish dress hastening out from the courtyard, looking towards her, preparing to lead in their horses. John, riding quickly, bent and called to them. She heard his voice and theirs. She heard what he turned and called to her.

'Nicholas is not at home.'

It was just as well. Her riding gown was filthy with dust. The roar of the packed streets was deafening. The sun, beating down, released the stench of the town, which she had forgotten during fresh weeks at sea. When she dismounted, the ground swayed, reminding her that she had had a long, tiring journey. It was a relief, in the end, not to have to manufacture some sort of greeting. Jodi was silently crying. John put his arm round him. A brawny middle-aged woman emerged and ushered them into the house, explaining something in a broad accent. She wore a white cap and apron, and a heavy gown of the same stuff as the livery doublets.

John, who came from Aberdeen, said, 'Apparently Nicholas left home early this morning, for how long no one knows. Our message came later, and rooms are being prepared. Lowrie, the steward, had to go out, but they say he'll be back, and ask us if we would like a refreshment in the parlour. One of the girls is coming to look after Jodi.'

They were inside the house, and the woman had turned and was encouraging Gelis to follow. 'Just a step this way, my lady. You've had a wearisome journey, but you're home now. And I ken who'll be richt glad tae see ye.'

The man behind bringing their baggage muttered something, and the woman turned on him, hands on hips. 'And why for should I not say what I think?' And to Gelis, 'Am I being familiar, my lady?'

The noise had receded, the air had become cool; the smells inside the house were of seasoned timber, and scented wax lights, and something fragrant, cooking. Gelis said, 'You are being welcoming, and Master John and Jodi and I are most grateful. What is your name?'

It was Mailie. The girl who came next was called Ella, and was introduced to both Jodi and his bodyguard. A few questions more, and the first steps had been taken towards integrating with her new household. She kept it friendly and brief, and at the end was left in the parlour, with John and Jodi, and some dishes of pastry and marchpane, and some wine.

John said, 'Well done. Well done, Jodi, as well. By the time papa comes, you'll be as much at home here as he was. He'll be astonished.'

No one knew where my lord was. Mailie said that this was unusual: that everyone knew, as a rule, what his movements were. She would take a wager that Master Lowrie, when he came back, could say.

After a while, Jodi fell asleep in his corner, and Gelis felt her own eyes beginning to close. She sat up. The engineer was standing at the window. Gelis said, 'Do you want to wait for him?'

John le Grant turned. 'I'd like to go and see Robin. Would you mind?'

She didn't mind. In anyone other than John, it would have been tact. Before he went, he carried Jodi up to his new bed, accompanied by Ella. Jodi hardly woke. Below, Gelis walked round the room, touching cushions, lifting books. She had glimpsed Nicholas's office with the desk in it, efficiently marshalled. It was much as she had imagined, except that he was not there. She had seen, too, the chamber with its wide, canopied bed which she saw he had made half his own. She had had her coffers put there, but hadn't opened them. She would have to ask Mailie to find her a servant. Or the absent Lowrie.

She was tired, but she would not lie there, to be found. This time, he must take her.

Soon after that, the absent Lowrie arrived. She heard voices outside; then the steward tapped on the door and came in.

He was hard to assess: a neat man with a collected manner. Only when he began to speak could you guess that he was a clerk, as well as a man who managed the house and its master. She realised he was saying that he had brought someone to see her.

She had no wish to receive anyone. She said, 'I should like to hear first, please, about my husband.'

'That is why I brought this lady,' said the man Lowrie. 'She will tell you.'

Someone stood in the doorway: someone short and plump and not very young whom Gelis, rising, recognised as if four years were nothing. Bel of Cuthilgurdy, sharp-tongued neighbour of Jordan de St Pol, and once friend of Jordan's dead daughter Lucia. Bel, who could live in Kilmirren House, and yet prove a staunch friend of Nicholas, and herself, and young Jodi. Bel of Cuthilgurdy here – why?

The round shapeless face gave nothing away. Bel said, 'I mauna stay. I'll not spoil your homecoming. I'm fair pleased to see you, but ye've come on a bleak day, my hinny. I've something to tell you.'

Lowrie slipped from the room. Gelis, rising to rush forward, stopped. *Nicholas.* No, of course not. Not in these words. Then she said, hesitantly, 'Robin?'

'No.' The small woman came forward, and kissed her, and pulled her down beside her on a settle. She said, 'Anselm Adorne went to Roslin. I ken why. So do you. He went to see Phemie Dunbar. He'll see the bairn: it's born; he has a wee daughter. But Phemie died yesterday.'

The silence stretched on. Anger was the first overwhelming emotion. But for the ingrates of Bruges, Adorne would have been with her; would have shared her joy at the coming child; would have made her his wife. Even if death had come in the end, they would have had that. Now he would arrive and find he had lost her by a day.

Then she realised why she was being told. 'Nicholas is there?'

'The babe was baptised this morning, in private. They were all there:

the Dunbars and the Sinclairs and Phemie's good friends from the Priory. Jamie Liddell, for Albany. Not Robin, but Kathi and Saunders, of course. Adorne would find them, at least, when he arrived. And Dr Andreas would be with him.'

'And Nicholas? You know what he –'

'I ken what he did for Phemie Dunbar. Love and pity have aye been the key to the puzzle of Nicol de Fleury,' said Bel. 'And yes, he'd be stricken, but he'd be among friends, as Adorne would. I'd trust one of them to bring him back to you, for he'll know by now that you're here: Adorne or Andreas will have told him.'

Bel stopped. 'That's all. I'm going. If you can stand that old besom Kilmirren, that's where I'm staying. I know that ye canna fathom how I can thole him, but I've kent Jordan de St Pol for a long time, and I'm used to him. Will ye be all right, now?'

'No,' said Gelis. 'But I know what I owe you. Nicholas too. He wrote that you hadn't come to see him, or sent.'

'No. I had my reasons,' said Bel. 'But now I'm just over the road, if you want me.'

In the event, it was Tobie's stalwart wife Clémence who rode with Nicholas to his new house in the High Street, and saw, as he did, that there were extra horses in the stable, and a familiar saddle set to one side. 'So she's safely here,' Clémence said. 'Now there's Lowrie, who can tell me where Master John and Jodi might be. You go to the parlour.'

He disliked being organised. He was trying, very hard, to keep his breathing even, and the turmoil within him under control. Gelis had come. Whatever it meant in terms of extra anxiety – and it would increase his burdens tenfold – was outweighed, as she had realised too, by the necessity that they should be together. Now he had let go; now he had given into her charge all the part of him that found expression in physical love, he could not manage without her. With her, he could do anything.

So he must leave her in no doubt that he wanted her. The desolation he felt must be set aside, even though it ensured that, for all time, he could never explain what the death of Phemie had truly meant. But one did not repeat one's mistakes. This time, Gelis came first.

She was in the parlour, and alone. Her face was paler than it had been in winter, and her eyes marked a little with strain and want of sleep. She looked as if she had waited there a long time. She rose, and stood still, and said, 'Nicholas. I have come at a bad time. I am so sorry.'

Of its own accord, his throat jammed, leaving an ache like a sprain. 'You know?'

'About Phemie, yes. Bel told me. But Adorne, arriving like that . . . What happened?'

'*Bel!*' He was still bewildered. He said, trying to recover, 'Adorne came, with Andreas, and found her in the chapel. Scheves was kind. Kathi and Saunders were there. He'll stay at Roslin until the burial. No one knows what will happen after that.'

'He meant to stay in Scotland for a while,' Gelis said. 'Until the baby could travel. What have they called her?'

'Euphemia,' he said. 'She'll have a plethora of nurses. Cristen. Clémence. Ada. Nanse Preston, even.' He broke off.

'What?' said Gelis. She walked forward and drew him down to the settle, as Bel had done with herself.

He said, 'I wonder what Robin will make of it? Another rival. He needs so much . . .'

'And now Jodi and I are competing as well for your care. Nicholas, you can't be everyone's crutch. You don't need to be. I'm here as well. So is Kathi, and Tobie and Clémence. You walked into all this alone, and you've managed for five months. But now we are all with you.'

He said, 'But I was meant to –'

'You were meant to prove that you could hold to a straight line on your own. You have sustained it so far. I'm prepared to trust you the rest of the way. So are the others. Nicholas, Nicholas, don't.'

This was how, stemming his grief, she had held Jodi all through his childhood, wishing that he were Nicholas. Now it was Nicholas.

Presently, when the positions had courteously got themselves reversed, he said, his voice still disconnected, 'I meant this to be different. I haven't even told you yet what I feel about seeing you.'

'Perhaps later,' Gelis said. 'You did say that Clémence was with you? She must be running out of small talk by now. Unless she's found Jodi?'

She had found Jodi. Exploring, Jodi's father and mother discovered the two of them, deep in a game. Then Jodi looked up and saw Nicholas, and the game flew to the floor.

Much later, Clémence asked, with some briskness, if anyone would mind if she removed Jordan to her own house for the night, as there was something Dr Tobie was waiting to show him. Jodi said No, and then Yes. Gelis kissed Clémence, even before she kissed Jodi goodbye.

Mailie came to say that my lady must be tired, and she had made up the bed.

Nicholas discovered that he also was tired. He said, 'I have an idea. I go to bed first, and you follow.'

'It doesn't sound very seductive,' Gelis said.

'They do it in harems,' Nicholas said helpfully. 'Anyway, you followed me here.'

She said, 'What made you think I was coming to you?' They were upstairs by now. He noticed that Gelis's coffers had been unpacked, and some of his own belongings moved to the room next to the marital bedchamber. Clémence had been busy.

He said, 'Well, for one thing, no one has claimed you. Which is just as well, because now you can't go.'

'I can't?' she said. He was thankful to see that she was shaking as well. He shut the door of the bedchamber.

'No. It's a convention. It's like not leaving before the end of a dinner, unless you can plead you've a nose bleed.' He was suddenly shattered. 'Of course . . .'

'No. I don't have a nose bleed,' she said. 'You've gone white.'

'That's because –' He broke off. 'Do you suppose we could just get there together?'

'Where?'

'On the bed. Anywhere. Oh God,' said Nicholas, 'there isn't time to undress.'

She was laughing, and so was he; and then there was no room even for laughter, because they were as one at last: joined in lust but also in love; knit together in love, but also in constancy.

Part II

And be thow nocht, as nocht sone sall thow be;
Forget thi-self and in ensample se
The lyoun, king of bestis, as thou sayis
Sum tyme is fude to megis and to fleis.

Chapter 12

Welcum he was, and thar he baid all nicht

h APPINESS, THAT MOST childish of states, is infectious. Furthermore, in its innocence, it will not be hidden, even when tempered with sorrow.

In the weeks that followed, none of his friends required to be told what had happened to Nicholas. Most, like Kathi, were thankful. Others took longer to welcome it.

A growing son, available once more to his father, expects his father's attention. Nicholas, rather desperately, did what he could, but it was Mistress Clémence who swept Jodi off and embroiled him and his minders in the raucous young community of the Canongate, from whose expeditions of fishing or fowling he returned ragged, filthy and triumphant. Occasionally, he would be sent to exhibit some bedraggled capture to Robin, but never stayed long. Robin, like Jodi's father, was a deity whose services tended, as now, to be moderated or withdrawn without warning. Usually, someone else was to blame.

At eight, Jodi himself was too young to detect the same reaction in Robin. As he welcomed Jodi, so the bedridden young man greeted Gelis when, friendly and practical, she came to call as she had done in Bruges. She went alone, and so did Nicholas, and neither appeared before him with Jodi. The tact this time, it seemed, was too obvious: Robin showed his annoyance by driving himself and everyone else into a morass of business minutiae, displaying a lightly cutting insistence both in the counting-house and in private with Nicholas.

It was Andro Wodman, the veteran Archer, who diagnosed the root of the trouble and, one day in the Berecrofts house, put it to Nicholas, who had called. While Adorne remained with Andreas in Roslin, the double house in the Canongate had become home to several new people: the home and offices occupied by Sersanders now housed John le Grant as well as the Conservator, and opened its doors to the frequent visits of the sailing-master Crackbene, and Dr Tobie. At present, the inhabitants were merely a coterie. They were also, you might say, a company in embryo, awaiting instructions from two very different men.

Both of these, for personal reasons, were at present preoccupied; and the Conservator, like Kathi, was not censorious. Nevertheless, when Nicholas, crossing the road, raised the problem of Robin, Wodman gave his opinion. 'Of course he's moody. That's because you and Tobie are wrong. Robin doesn't want to talk about business at all. He wants to talk about war. So does John. They just don't realise it.'

John wasn't there. John, since his return, had resorted to the same pugnacious isolation he had adopted, according to Gelis, in Bruges. Nicholas stared at Wodman, whose damaged nose, since the oysters, lent a hooting quality to his lightest remark. 'You think so?'

'I've seen it before. You're the one they're afraid of. You'll have to take the lead.'

By now, Nicholas knew that there were men who were afraid of him, because he intended them to be. Applied to John or Robin, it was mad.

Except that, God knew, fear took different forms, and arose for different reasons. Pride, for instance. He said, 'Then I suppose I'd better go and talk war to them.'

'That's right,' Wodman said. He had looked grim. 'Hold an inquest.'

He hadn't said any more, and presently Nicholas left. Thinking it through, he realised how right Wodman was. He *had* led Robin through such an interrogation at Berwick, but that was not enough. Men subjected to horrors require to talk about horrors, but also to try to find in them some meaning. Men whose imagination, fired by chivalry, still idealised war didn't want to be offered some well-meaning substitute: *now this is all you can manage; forget all your dreams.*

That was Robin's private misery. John's must be different. John's wars had been like his own, the happy exercise of a gift for ingenuity, with no particular bias, reprehensibly, towards either side. Until – a little older, a little less footloose – John had found and respected Astorre's company, and had also discovered a reason to think about causes.

Unlike Robin, John had other passions. He could take to the sea, or make a name with his devices. But he also needed first to digest what had happened at Nancy; to pass this immovable block through his spiritual gut and get rid of it.

Kathi, when Nicholas took the idea to her, was unimpressed by the metaphor, but examined the theory in silence. In the end she said only, 'I wonder. If you want to do it, they're in there together just now, Robin and John, talking about the price of slab iron. It wouldn't be hard to go in and alter the subject. It might help them. It might put them through hell on the way. It might do that anyway, and not help them.'

'I know,' he said. 'That's why I asked you. I may have been doing the wrong thing all this time.'

She shook her head. 'You couldn't know. None of us could. What Robin needed at first is not necessarily what he needs or wants now. If we have fenced him in, you can show him that there is a gate in the fence.'

'I'll go to them,' Nicholas said, and got up. 'There are a lot of possibilities, you know. All we have to do is to find out what he wants. Then, I promise you, I'll see that he gets it.' He paused, and winced.

'I know,' Kathi said. 'Apart from a body replacement. Nicholas, be careful. Of him, but also yourself. You are not Robin. Don't try to be.'

'I know,' he said, in echo, and stood, looking down. In a year or two, Jodi would be taller than Kathi was at twenty-three. She looked spent, as she had done in Berwick; her face full of slight, sharpened bones and the ends of her mouth curled in irony rather than mischief. Always, Katelijne Sersanders had treated her strength as a boundless commodity; a wind-blown orchard, spinning winter and summer with blossom, in which the fruit never took time to set. In that, he and she were alike.

But now he had Gelis, who had an ability – noticed before, when they had worked side by side – to render the impossible possible, and to divert him from his enthusiasms, before they exploded from white heat to ashes. Only now her devices were different.

Kathi was smiling. She said, 'At least, if John and Robin collapse, you will remain firm as a chimney. Nicholas, you look as if you could walk on water.'

'That,' he said, 'is an illusion.'

He had Gelis, but Kathi had nothing. That is, she had a doctor, she had Tobie. And she had Robin. She would have Robin, for he was going there now, to sit with Robin and John, and force them – and himself – to talk about Burgundy. And then about the late Duke. And then about how he had died. And that would be the beginning.

It was a beginning. It was about war; and about leadership; and about responsibility. It was about how peoples were ruled, and might live together. It was not, this time, about the sights and sounds of the battlefield, although that was its provenance. It disposed, for all time, of the unalloyed enjoyment of war for its own sake, although it couldn't banish completely their instinctive love of a fight. They were men.

Afterwards, he did not seek Kathi out: he had no wish to share this experience. He went home. Later, his balance sensationally restored by quite a different experience, he was able to turn his mind to other things, such as the news that Jordan de St Pol had gone back to Kilmirren, leaving the old lady, Bel, in his house. It was Clémence who told him, recalling the old fondness between Mistress Bel and young Jodi. Nicholas owed a great deal to Bel of Cuthilgurdy. Her opinion of him, he knew, was not so high. Nevertheless, he would take Jodi to see her. It was safe: even Henry was not there, but lodged with a comrade. He would go, when he had time.

He did not immediately have time. It was remarkable, during this period, how little time Nicholas had, and how unpunctual he had become. He also fell asleep, now and then, at his desk. He had a suspicion that Gelis spent part of the day, every day, recovering her sleep. In fact he knew that she did, for once or twice he had returned to the house of an afternoon and found her fast asleep in her chamber. Which had made him late for something again. He was gripped by carnal delight to a degree of shocking intensity – an immersion in glorious lechery which still retained, at its heart, all the uncomplicated joys of his boyhood, kept for the only woman who matched him exactly in this. For this was her music, this ferocious deployment of instruments; each development unexpected; each thoughtful progression reaching for a different climax.

He gave himself to it, for it would never happen again, or not to this degree. And when it reduced itself, as it must, to the safer levels of marital happiness, he would be enabled, charged with this power, to master anything.

Then Adorne came back from Roslin, and Davie Simpson from the north, where he had been engaged in Cistercian business. He was made welcome, as ever, by the Abbot of Newbattle.

There were two things to be done before the matter of Scotland re-opened, with all its new players. Nicholas descended one of the paths to the Cowgate, and fulfilled a serious appointment with Avandale. Then he set off to return to his house, to fulfil his intention of taking his wife and his son to see Bel.

He hadn't reached home when he was stopped by someone from his own household. 'Ser Nicol. I was to ask gin ye'd come. Young Maister Henry's arrived at the house, and won't budge till he's seen you.'

The man's voice was low. Nicholas turned him, smiling; and resumed the steep climb in his company. 'Did my lady send you?'

'Oh no. It was Master Lowrie was worried, my lord. Mistress Gelis is fine. She could heckle on Satan himself and never mind it, begging your pardon.'

'I know what you mean,' Nicholas said, with genuine amusement. Then he sent the man off, for they were approaching his house, and he could hear, muffled, the voice of Henry de St Pol raised in contention inside.

The confrontation with Satan, aged sixteen, in the full panoply of an Archer of the King's Guard, had begun a short time before, when Kilmirren's grandson had arrived on the doorstep and the demands had begun. Even when Gelis had him admitted and he saw for himself that she was alone, Henry had refused to leave. She had time to be thankful that she *was* alone: that Nicholas for once was spared this; that Jodi was elsewhere, doggedly perfecting his martial arts, and would not be required to face the cousin who had once tried to kill him, a baby of three. She knew why that had happened. She supposed that Nicholas knew as well.

Meantime, Nicholas was away, and here was . . . Here was his other son, about whom Diniz knew, and Dr Tobie, and Father Moriz, and Nicholas and herself. But no one else.

His beauty was breathtaking. Enhanced by young manhood, the fine skin, the brilliant eyes, the gilded hair were carried now by an athlete, slender and straight-backed and graceful. She did not know, she would never know why her sister Katelina, wilfully importuning the servant she took him to be, had contrived to bear this glorious infant to Nicholas but had not allowed him to claim it. Instead, she had found a surrogate father, and married him, and passed the coming child off as his. Simon de St Pol believed that Henry was his only son and true heir. Henry would fight to the death anyone who implied otherwise, and despised Nicholas as a bastard. She, Gelis, had come close to spoiling Nicholas's life and her own over her jealousy. She had forgiven Nicholas, who was the victim of his own generous nature (*so happy, so often*). It had taken her longer to forgive her dead sister.

Now the boy, white with hatred, confronted her, cuirass glinting under his tunic, powerful sword sheathed at his side. He had flung his plate gloves aside, scoring the wood of a table. 'Well?' he said.

She sat in a chair with a back and arms: always an advantage. She tented her fingers. 'Henry, you heard me the first time. I don't know where your uncle is. I don't know when he'll return. You don't want to come back another day?'

'No.'

'You wouldn't like him to come and see you?'

'No.'

'You don't want to tell me what it's about?'

He stared at her. 'It amuses you? It won't if I send the Guard to roust through every tavern and house till they find him.'

Gelis said, 'The Guard? Henry, I'm sorry. If it's as serious as that, then let me go myself to Sir David. I'll get my cloak. You should have said. In fact, I think your uncle is with the King at this moment. I was told not to say so, but if Nicholas is to be arrested, then it must be made public.' She had left her chair and was already crossing the room. She stopped beside him. 'What has he done, Henry? He's killed somebody? Will it harm you, because you're related?'

'I'm not related!' he said.

She frowned. 'But you always call him Uncle,' she said. 'He told me. I know he likes it. And I'm your aunt and he is my husband.'

Henry smiled. He backed to the door and stood against it. 'You are clever,' he said. 'I grant you that. No, you're not going out. Neither am I. Suppose we both sit over there, and you tell me about all these delightful family ties. You are his wife, but you slept with my father. Of course, everyone did. So whose son is Jordan? Do you know?'

'He happens to be mine,' Nicholas said from the door. 'So who is your mother? Do you know?'

Gelis drew in her breath. Nicholas, in the grip of real anger, for a second had a look of his son. She said sharply, 'Stop it, both of you. Henry, he didn't mean that; he was only protecting me. Sit down, let me send for some wine, and let us deal with this properly. And for Christ's sake take off those swords. You're not going to use them, and you look just as close to real men without them.' She marched off to give orders, but stayed within earshot.

Behind her, Nicholas gave a half-laugh, and her heart eased. He said, 'That's marriage for you. I'm sorry. Begin again. What was the matter?'

'Tell her to go,' Henry said.

'She's bringing the wine,' Nicholas said. 'And I'll only have to repeat it all anyway. Is it Mar?' Gelis reappeared.

'*Mar!*' said Henry. 'Why should I come to some failed out-of-work mercenary for advice about Johndie Mar? No. I want back the horses you stole from me. With three more, to compensate for my trouble. And if you don't tell me where they are now, I'll get that woman under me the way that my father did.' He had his sword in his hand. Nicholas started slowly to move, and then stopped.

'Well, about time,' Gelis said. Lowrie, entering with a tray, laid it down, caught Nicholas's eye and left. She said, 'Sit down, both of you. You can't drink, Henry, with a sword in your hand. Why on earth should your uncle steal horses? Nicholas, if you don't sit, I shall take Henry at his word and carry him off to the bedroom. And *that* will frighten him silly.'

Nicholas started to laugh, and did sit. Henry reddened. Gelis walked across with a cup and stood before him. His jaw was set, and his lashes were as long as a woman's. She said, 'I heard how you bought Nicholas's horses. It was a trick, but it was legitimate. If they're stolen, I suppose you might at once think of him. But why should he do it? If he didn't complain then, and he didn't, why should he invite trouble now? You were bound to want redress. The theft was bound to come to light.' She paused. 'You have his groom, haven't you? What does he say?'

'He's off sick,' said Henry. 'But I'm told that if I make you come with me to Eck Scougal, I'll find the horses all right.' He looked down at his wine, and suddenly drank some.

'Deliberately placed there?' Nicholas said, half to himself and half to Gelis. 'No. Eck would never allow it. In any case, the horses don't matter: someone will have locked them up somewhere and we may or may not find them again. It was all just to get you to call on me, and hope that youth would prevail over a failed out-of-work mercenary.'

'You were meant to fight one another?' Gelis said. It was hard work.

'I suppose so. Henry, who told you I'd taken the horses?'

The boy set down the cup. 'No one. I still think that you did.'

'All right,' Nicholas said. 'Then you make a proper complaint, and the Lords in Council will conduct the enquiry. We'll go now.'

'I'm afraid,' Gelis said, 'that something else is going to happen.' Her voice trembled. 'Henry, did you say something about a squad of armed men?' She could see them through the panes of the window. Lowrie was outside, expostulating once more. She looked at Nicholas, who had very seriously poured himself a second cup of the extremely strong wine. She knew how he felt.

Henry said, 'I didn't tell anyone to come.' He stood up.

The door crashed back on its hinges. A man, rather more heavily armed than Henry and considerably older, stood on the threshold. 'Ser Nicholas de Fleury of Bruges? I have an order from the Reverend Abbot of Blackfriars to take and place you in detention forthwith.'

'Why?' said Nicholas, rising.

'It isn't horses?' said Gelis. 'I can see horses outside.'

'Is it horses?' said Nicholas. Henry's head turned from one to the other.

The armed man said, 'These are horses, yes. They brought us. We are to escort you to Blackfriars.'

'But the horses came from Kilmirren,' Gelis said.

The man was becoming impatient. 'They are from the stables at Blackfriars. I do not know where they belong.'

'Henry?' Nicholas said. 'Could the Abbot have stolen your horses?'

There was a moment's pause. Then Henry said, 'By mistake, of course. But it's always possible. Could I see them?'

'Could he see them?' said Nicholas. His face was alight. Henry's blue eyes had started to sparkle.

The captain said, 'Why? I am not here about horses. I have orders to –'

'But you have come at the right time. We are investigating the theft of some horses. A little wine?' Gelis said. She held the cup under his nose, whose ripeness she had already registered.

'Well . . .' said the captain, sitting down. 'Mind you, I can't help you about horses.'

From the door, Gelis gave certain orders and returned. There was a glint of a tray, seen among the squad outside the window. Gelis said, 'There's been a theft of horses from Master Henry's home at Kilmirren. As a member of the King's Guard, he would naturally feel beholden to helpers. Perhaps you could pass round the word, if he describes them?'

Henry described the horses. Nicholas and the captain both drank. Gelis kept her eyes demurely on her lap. After a while, Nicholas said, 'By the way, I'm sorry, you came to tell me something?'

The captain, with some trouble, adjusted his expression but did not rise, as his fourth cup was still full. He said, 'As to that, I'm sorry, m'lord. But the arkshekels went mishing, they say, just after your loship called on the Pipple-Pebble Collector. And I have sworn statements that all of them have been seen in this housh.'

'What kind of articles?' Nicholas said.

The inventory meant nothing to Gelis, seeming to consist of various flagons, flasks and pots, chiefly of silver.

Henry suddenly said, 'Could I see the list?' The captain handed it over. Nicholas's eyes wandered over the room, without meeting hers. The boy said, 'But these weren't stolen. They arrived in this house as gifts.'

'How d'you know?' said the captain. He said it in a mannerly way. This St Pol might be no more than a lad, but he wore the royal cipher.

Henry said, 'I was living here when they arrived. I saw them all.'

'A gift, who from?' said the captain.

Nicholas brought his eyes down, and Henry met them. Henry said, 'No one knew. They came directed to Ser Nicol, along with small unsigned notes.'

'Oh? 'Sha pity no one kept 'em, then,' said the man.

His expression odd, Nicholas was gazing at Henry. He said, removing his eyes, 'As a matter of fact I did keep them. I have all the notes. I hoped, of course, to thank the sender, but never found out who he was. So I passed the silver to the Abbot of Holyrood.'

'Eh, what?' said the man.

'To the Abbot of Holyrood. They were really too expensive to keep, and I could think of no one better. Good Lord,' Nicholas said with surprise. 'If I'd chosen Blackfriars instead, then all this nuisance could have been avoided.'

The man left, his cup empty, and the soldiers outside helped him into the saddle and left. Nicholas had not been arrested. A visit would be paid to the Abbot of Holyrood, and the two monasteries would reach an accommodation in private. The captain was heard to remark, with queasy laughter, that knowing those two wily bashtards, he wouldn' guarantee it wouldn' all end in blushet-blushid n' murder.

Coming back from the door, Gelis said, 'I think you were both a disgrace. The Church will never recover. Henry, seriously, what do you want done about the horses? It wasn't Nicholas, but then you'd expect us to say that in any case.'

'I was mistaken,' Henry said. 'That is, the person who told me was mistaken. I'll look for them myself.'

'I'll help you,' Nicholas said. 'So will that poor man-at-arms you beguiled. And Eck has brood mares coming from Flanders. If you send to one of the Browns, they'll keep back some for you at Berwick. Have you been down to Berwick yet?'

'I thought of going,' said Henry.

'Well, the *Karel*'s busy,' said Nicholas. 'But you'd get a ride on the *Marie* or the *James*, if you keep out of the way of John le Grant.'

It was risky. Henry's eyes narrowed. 'I'm not afraid of John le Grant.'

'No. But he's bloody afraid of you,' Nicholas said. 'In fact, he's forgotten what happened. You're in Scotland, your own country now. You can't put a foot wrong. You can't put a foot right, either, after all the drink that you've had. Neither can I. Gelis, we need to be helped.'

'Whenever didn't you?' Gelis said.

In bed, holding him in her arms, she said, 'Davie Simpson?'

'Yes,' he said. It was warm, and the bedding was all over the floor. 'At least, he sent the silver, although I can't prove it. I suspect he stole the horses and set Henry on me as well.'

'Henry spoke up for you,' Gelis said. She turned her head. 'The first time. The very first time.'

Against her skin, his face became still. His eyes were open. Then they flickered and he said, 'Don't count on it too much. It comes and goes. He didn't report that the silver was Simpson's, although he knew it.'

'He doesn't want his grandfather to know,' Gelis said. 'One hint of that unholy alliance, and Jordan de St Pol would kill Henry, or Simpson, or both.'

'Perhaps we should tell Grandfather,' Nicholas said. There was a strand of bitterness in it.

She said nothing. His rough hair, damp from exertion, lay under her chin, and below that she could see the sturdy curve of his cheekbone, and the scatter of lashes, so unlike the thick, silky sweep of his son's; and the severe nose with its curling, fastidious nostril which was yet another part of his chaotic heritage.

After a long while, he said, 'Of course not,' and after another short space: 'I couldn't do this without you.'

She said, 'You can. You have done.'

'But not by way of laughter,' he said. 'He let himself enjoy that. He can't be my son, but perhaps he could be . . .'

'What?' She was very gentle.

'It doesn't matter. A friend. Gelis? I love you in so many ways.'

'I know. Lie quiet,' she said.

He took his other son, without Gelis, to see his wee Aunty Bel.

Now Jodi did not have to be lifted to rap on the front door, and he took off his cap without being prompted as he entered the parlour of the St Pol house over the road.

His wee Aunty Bel looked much the same: short and plump inside a lot of wide cloth, with her face like a loaf set to rise, and her hair all bundled into white napkins. She held out her hand, and kissed his cheek when he came over, and then sat with her arm still about him, looking up at his father. She smelled tasty, like fruit cooked in sugar. He turned his head to sniff her neck better. His father came to her other side, and when she lifted her face, bent quickly and kissed it, almost as he kissed Jodi's mother. Aunty Bel said, 'Well, well. So ye've got yourself sorted out at long last. Go and sit there, and here's a stool for your big son.'

'Captain Cuthbert has a hackbut,' said Jodi, taking his seat.

'You remember the hackbut!' said his aunty. 'And what else does Captain Cuthbert have? Have you tried the crossbow yet, now?'

He had. They had an interesting discussion about weapons, and hunting, and dogs. The question of dinner came up. Aunty Bel thought, for some reason, that his father must be hungry these days, and she was proposing a little something to eat. 'So, Jodi –'

Jodi said, 'When I'm at home, I usually eat with everyone else.' He looked at his father.

His aunt said, 'Well, of course you do. But since it's so clement, I thought we might have our wee bite in the garden, and Isa's bad with her legs, and could do with a hand with the dishes. Can ye set up a table?'

Jodi jumped up. He remembered Isa, and something to do with marchpane, but the desire for information came first. 'How is she bad with her legs?'

'You ask her. We'll be there in a minute. I only want to ask your da here about poor Sir Anselm. Ye ken he's got a wee baby?'

'It's a girl,' Jodi said.

'Do ye like lassies?' said Aunty Bel. 'Well, there's a surprise. Tell Isa I sent you.'

When the door closed, she turned to his father. 'A manful wee laddie. Well-grown, well-mannered and happy by nature, I'd say. He's a credit to both of ye, Nicholas.' Her smile grew. 'Ye ken Henry's taken a keek at him on the quiet? Came back fair cackling because wee cousin Jodi had grown up the image of his common big father de Fleury.'

'I expect he said Claes,' Nicholas said. 'And Jordan has gone home? Why?'

Bel looked surprised. 'I thought it was something you said. If you dinna ken, I'm not competent tae inform ye. He came back right red-wad after seeing you.'

'And Simon?'

'Is still in Madeira, and we all have to hope that he'll stay there. The house is empty, Nicholas. You can say what you want to say, and so can I.'

He rose then, and walked forward, and took his place quietly at her feet, on the stool Jodi had used. She was in her late fifties; old enough to be his mother. Younger than his real mother would have been. He said, 'What happened at Roslin. I was able to share it with Gelis, instead of having to choose. How did you know?'

She said, 'I loved Umar, as you did, and this was no different. You think a man, or a woman, dies only once? They die afresh every time a friend hears of it, and be they ten years in the tomb, that is the day that the new-bereaved friend gets to mourn them. You gave Umar his due: the shame was that you knew he was dead, and Gelis didn't. I made sure it wouldn't happen again.'

He said, 'You knew Phemie.'

'I didna know she was childering. You were the one she trusted with that. But I was here at the sickbed when Adorne's wife lost her wee bairn, and so was Phemie. I was there in Bruges with Phemie and Margriet when the Princess had her first son under his roof. I spent time with them all many times over, and I would have been glad to see Anselm Adorne share his life with that lady.'

'Have you told him so?' Nicholas said.

'You think I should have been at the kirk,' Bel of Cuthilgurdy said. 'And so maybe did he. But I've seen him, and Archie. I've seen Robin, too.'

Nicholas said, 'The last time we met –' and broke off.

Bel stared at him, her fists on her two knees, her mouth set like a saw. 'Christ fend us, Nicol de Fleury, is this all that ye can make of it? Four years ago, Robin thought ye were God. I charged you to use your influence right, and you did. Get that straight in your mind. I've no time for the self-centred man: him that's aye off in a corner, squeezing the plukes on his conscience. What you've done wrong is done: God'll judge you. It's what you do now that everything hangs on.'

'Including me,' Nicholas said. He started to laugh. 'I've just escaped a charge of ecclesiastical theft. Davie Simpson.'

'Do you tell me?' said his hostess. She released her fingertips and scuffed absently at some dog hairs, which fell from her chest to her lap. 'And that's a hanging matter, you say? I'd say more like being tied to a board at a horse's tail. So Davie Simpson played a prank on you, the wee naughty man. Ye ken he pitched me out of my house?'

'I heard. He'll pay for it,' Nicholas said.

'That's why I mentioned it. How?'

'Andro Wodman will tell you,' said Nicholas. He made it sound like a kindly reminder. 'At least, I assume he will. You sent him to Flanders, didn't you, to watch David last year? May I ask you something?'

'Air's cheap,' she said.

'Yes. Andro and Simpson were in the same company of Royal Archers in France. Wodman killed a man, and he and Davie both left and joined St Pol, who had once been an Archer and was now settled and wealthy in France. I've asked Wodman, and now I'm asking you. Did anything happen that would give Simpson a hold over the old man?'

'What did Andro tell you?' she said. It was a waste of time. He could tell.

'That he killed the man, Cressant, in a hand-to-hand fight over a personal matter and that St Pol offered him a lucrative job that tempted Davie also to leave. He had to pretend to have leprosy.'

'Aye. That's about it,' Bel said. 'And you're not thinking straight, Nicol. If Jordan de St Pol had anything to fear from Davie Simpson, he wadna have dismissed him. He wouldna even have employed him before that. He would have killed him.'

'But there's more,' Nicholas said. 'There must be more. Why do you always . . .'

'Keep my own counsel? I'm entitled. But I wouldna hold back what would harm you. This is the truth. St Pol will do just what he wants to do. Davie Simpson has no way of controlling him.'

'But you arranged for him to go to the Tyrol,' Nicholas said. He felt like saying it. 'How did Simpson get on with the Duchess?'

It sounded innocent, but it signalled his discontent. Eleanor, Duchess of the Tyrol, was an elderly Scottish princess who knew Bel, Nicholas believed, far far better than she knew Nicholas himself, even though he had worked for her over a season. He waited to hear what Bel would say.

She said, 'Have you ever been chamois-hunting?'

'Once,' Nicholas said. The hurt faded. Oh Bel, Bel.

'Well, ye ken what it's like. It's not the chamois, it's the corruption and riotous merriment afterwards. Cartloads of lassies, they say.'

'Do they?' said Nicholas.

'Aye. And they had a gentleman's bonspiel, big fires and bare scuddies, and Davie wasna that smart at the sooping. And the Duchess took him hunting a lot.'

'Oh my God,' Nicholas said.

'As you say. Also, there's a strong drink she serves . . .' She gazed at him. Her eyes were small, round, and the colour of gravel.

'All right. I had it. I know what happens,' Nicholas said.

'Well, I hope she didna make you do what she did with Davie Simpson,' the dame of Cuthilgurdy observed. 'She's a strong-minded body, the Duchess, and unchancy to cross. I canna think why she took against him, but she did. Of course, he and Buchan her brother were there to offer peace on Duke Charles's behalf: a civil gesture belike; except that no one had told them the Duke had been at peace in superior company these several weeks past, which made them look a wee bit provincial. Well, are ye stuck there, my Ignaures, or d'you want something to eat?'

She had sent David to the Tyrol, and he had learned nothing. Just as Nicholas had learned nothing now. But now, he didn't resent it.

By then, the table was set up in the shade in the garden, and a cloth on it with dishes and flagons, and Jodi had found all the dogs and a few other things besides, including a sturdy bow just his size, with its case and its arrows.

'It was your cousin Henry's,' Bel said, stringing and stretching it with one short, formidable arm before handing it over. 'Mind you, he was a strong loon at eight, and no shame if that's a wee bit beyond you, but . . . Well, fancy that!'

Jodi had shot, and the arrow had flown straight to the wooden target that Isa had put for him.

'It's all right,' said Jodi, in a casual treble. 'A bit on the small side, perhaps.'

'But it'll do?' said his Aunty Bel hopefully.

He put his arms round her neck. 'It's really just right,' he said.

Afterwards, he carried it away in his arms, while his father lingered a moment. He said, 'You see two blithe men.'

'Aweel. I like the gender,' said Mistress Bel. 'Come and see me in Stirling. Bring Gelis and Jodi.'

Nicholas said, 'When Jodi was young, I planned to confide him to you, if I lost Gelis.'

She stood very still, there on the threshold, with her hands like two balls of yarn clasped before her. 'I would have reared him,' she said. 'I would take him now, but he needs a man's house.'

'Your son is lucky,' Nicholas said.

'My son is dead,' Bel of Cuthilgurdy answered. 'That was what kept me away.'

The life of the street swirled behind him. He believed her. He even understood, he thought, the terrible impulse that had forced her to blurt it out now. He signed to Jodi and slowly came back, stepping up to the dim hall beside her, where he took her by the hand, drawing her away from the light. 'How, Bel?'

'A fever. It was quick. I dinna want to say more.'

He tightened his grip. 'You have grandchildren,' he said.

'Oh, yes. But I have a wee place for Jodi as well, if he ever wants it. And for Gelis and you. And that's enough on the subject. Looking backwards makes for poor steering.' She took out her hand, looking away.

'Bel,' he said again. He thought of Umar, and Phemie, and what she had said, and drew breath. She turned back to him, smiling.

'No,' she said. 'I was talking blethers. You canna mourn a lad you don't know. Come again. Send Jodi. Tell me when he wants to go coursing. Those moulting bitches need exercise.'

She had collected her courage again, and he would not disturb it. He kissed her dry cheek, and left.

Chapter 13

That to his knychtis neuer mor he said:
'Go furth or go,' bot: 'Knychtis, fallow me!',
So that mor plesand suld thar laubour be.

LATER THE SAME day, Colin Campbell, Earl of Argyll, left his lodging over the tavern he owned in the High Street and took the same path Nicholas had earlier taken, down the steep incline to the grand house of his colleague Andrew Avandale in the Wellgate, that they now called the Cowgate. He took two torchbearers with him, to protect his dignity and light his way back, for although the sun blessed the land through the long redolent evenings of summer, Archie Whitelaw and Will Scheves were joining them, and the meeting was not likely to be short. On the other hand, Drew Avandale kept a good table and a range of reliable clarets, imported regularly direct from Bordeaux. It was a thing you could do, when you came from the Lennox and had shipping friends on the Clyde at Dumbarton. Argyll had one or two such arrangements himself.

In the event, there was a cushion of veal, and a piquant stew done as he liked it, together with such dainties as hot pears and wafers; and an hour and more had gone by before the four of them settled down in Avandale's own private chamber, with the rest of the claret and some platters to keep starvation at bay: nuts and apple-oranges from Spain; cherries and lumps of coloured glazed fruit of the kind Archie Whitelaw could never resist. Will Scheves was a good raconteur and Argyll himself was a better: it was with a showman's reluctance that, as the laughter died down, he acknowledged Avandale's glance and, sighing, reverted to the voice of MacChalein Mor, King's Justiciar and Master of the Royal Household. He was the youngest man there, but not the least powerful.

'Yes, we forget, so hospitable is our host. I apologise. There is business to do. So you saw de Fleury, Andro. And Will has spoken with Adorne briefly at Roslin, and has had a session with our good Dr Andreas. So now we are here to decide what to do about our Burgundian friends. Will?'

Will Scheves said, 'The poor man was in no state to question at Roslin. But it's my understanding that he's here for temporary sanctuary. I see no political purpose in this sad affair with Euphemia. The child has been placed in a convent, and both the Dunbars and the Sinclairs seem to have agreed to forget what has happened. I would guess that with nothing to keep him, Lord Cortachy will return to Bruges as soon as he thinks the new rule will accept him.'

'But meanwhile he is here, and perhaps for some length of time. In what capacity, we must ask? As an asset, or as a liability?' said Whitelaw. He had a grating voice: in a Gaelic-speaker's opinion, all German-trained orators enunciated like corncrakes. There was a drip on his gown. Nevertheless, behind the chopped pied hair and the croak existed several decades of experience, which no one, under that abrasive black gaze, could ignore. Whitelaw continued.

'Financial standing. Ser Anselm Adorne has presumably brought no bullion with him. Nevertheless, he was once much esteemed by the King and the Princess Mary his sister. If Adorne retains their favour, he may expect a modest continuing income from his life-rent from Cortachy and his other lands. He might supplement this by joining his nephew, and sharing in Andro Wodman's consular work. He is likely, therefore, to be self-supporting and no more a charge on the kingdom than he has ever been.'

'So long as the King continues to allow him the barony,' Argyll said.

'That is so. Secondly. Is he potentially useful? So long as he has the regard of the Duchess, he forms a diplomatic link between Scotland and Burgundy. He is an experienced administrator and judge, and adept in both financial and military matters. He has a son in the Curia, and another who is a Knight Hospitaller of Rhodes. He himself is well thought of by many rulers abroad, including His Papal Beatitude. He has traded in England, and his late daughter served the English King's mother. The answer therefore is Yes, the potential is there. But, we must ask, is the implicit risk worth it? In short, he is either a paragon on limited leave, whom we may wish to tempt to remain; or a paragon with personal ambitions to fulfil, and a young and impressionable monarchy through which to fulfil them. In which case we devise a reason for him to depart.'

In short. Argyll began peeling an orange.

'These indeed are the issues,' Avandale said. 'So what of his character, Will? He performed his office of Conservator, as I recall, with integrity, and without ruffling too many merchants – apart, that is, from those who thought him too close to the King.'

Will Scheves set down his cup and rubbed his classical nose: a comely-faced, round-shouldered medical man whose even humour and quick wits and energy had brought him within sight of the Metropolitan's chair. Colin Campbell enjoyed an intellectual skirmish with Will Scheves. Master Whitelaw had less use for frivolity, but set aside time, now and then, for a long, civilised conversation with the Archdeacon on some abstruse subject. Fortunately Will, although privately pretending to wilt, could give Whitelaw good measure. And, because of his student friendship with Andreas, Will Scheves could draw on an insider's view of Adorne.

'Dr Andreas is of his household, and loyal, but is not alone in his good opinion of the gentleman. In Bruges, Lord Cortachy has always been severe but respected. The town may have discarded him for the service he gave to the Duke, but no one has ever proved him dishonest. If he settles here, he will serve this country as well. On the other hand . . .'

'He loves his peers?' Avandale said. Though born illegitimate, Drew Avandale was of royal Stewart blood, and had suffered his share of sycophancy. And all of them knew, Will Scheves most of all, how readily this King responded to a personable man with a confident manner.

'We all do,' the Archdeacon said. 'But there's a little more to it than that. This is a nobleman: his kinsmen are Genoese dukes. He is drawn to remind them, perhaps, that he walks in the same eminent circles. But the book he presented to the King was by Jan, his son, and I think that patronage for his son was what he chiefly hoped for. I'm not sure what my lord of Cortachy now expects of the King, but I can promise you that it will take very little to revive the King's liking for him. And after that, you will not be able to reject him.'

Argyll said, 'That was what I was thinking. It was what we feared with de Fleury.'

'Our decision, as I understand it, was to encourage my lord of Albany's friendship with de Fleury,' said Whitelaw. He had taught the King in his day, but not Albany: Argyll sometimes wondered, with amusement, how he'd got out of it.

Avandale said, 'That, I think, is where my reasoning is tending. If we trust these two men, then there is something to be said for placing them in opposite camps. One will balance the other.'

'And do we trust them?' asked Colin Campbell. 'What did our agile young Burgundian say, in this latest friendly encounter? I trust it was friendly?' His hands were sticky. Scheves stretched out an arm and proffered a bowl and a napkin from the side table. The water was scented. Avandale's house always had everything.

Avandale said, 'Encounters with de Fleury could be said to be wearing but friendly: I am sometimes made to feel, Colin, that I am conversing with you and Archie at once. I am sure he will address me in Gaelic one day. Meantime, he reports regularly, which was the condition of our arrangement. On the business side, he has put in place a skilful structure, supported by Nowie, which co-ordinates the landing and marketing of salmon along the length of the east coast of Scotland, from the Moray Firth down to Berwick-upon-Tweed. It will be run by Adorne's nephew, in partnership with the Berecrofts family and with Wodman's blessing. He will contribute ships, managed from his own second tenement in Leith, and then from overseas if he goes back. He talks of links with Dumbarton, through Colquhoun. He is also looking into Darnaway timber.'

'A word of warning,' said Whitelaw. 'As I have frequently mentioned. De Fleury has displayed these qualities before. His performance before was inconsistent. You say he has changed. But the greater his success, the more our native merchants will lose by it.'

'Unless they join him,' Argyll said. 'I hear that Berecrofts will consider anyone who wishes to make the minimum investment. Tom Yare will tell you. Several of the shipowners have enlisted, and some well-known names from St Johnstoun of Perth and Dundee. Others think it too risky.'

'And Adorne will join this?' said Whitelaw.

'That is something no one knows,' Will Scheves said. 'Or not yet. It would fit. Adorne and his nephew were burgesses of St Johnstoun of Perth at one time. His family church has Charterhouse connections. I imagine de Fleury is waiting to see what Adorne himself wants. And what we want, of course.' He paused. 'I should say that de Fleury has asked me, quite recently, about the health of his lordship of Mar.'

He caught the eye of Argyll, who treated him to a sardonic smile. Argyll had said all along that there was no point in counting on secrecy. A man had only to look at the number of royal physicians to know that something was wrong. And grotesque things were happening. Instead of an unpleasant feud between de Fleury and the St Pols, the old man had left town, de Fleury had reached some sort of truce with young St Pol, and Johndie Mar was the fool who was attacking them both. Argyll said, 'As I have frequently mentioned —'

Scheves grinned. Whitelaw looked up and grunted. Avandale said, 'I still propose to say nothing yet. They may guess: they don't know. I want them deeply committed, Adorne and de Fleury, before I will present them with secrets of state. Now. We have gone over the ground. What is your advice? Does Adorne stay, and if so, on what terms? Do we continue to accommodate Nicholas de Fleury, with the provisos laid down? He has brought his wife and son now.'

'A beautiful woman. Why not send de Fleury away, and keep the family?' Argyll said.

Whitelaw plunged his hand into his finger-bowl and then used the napkin, muttering, to mop up his lap.

Lord Avandale said, 'There is something to be said on both sides. But my inclination is to propose that we continue to review de Fleury's position each month, and that we invite Adorne to join us at Court and in council, with appropriate emoluments. It will please the Duchess, and enhance his standing if and when he does return home.'

'Also, he will renew his acquaintance with both their graces. And if a difficult decision has to be taken,' said the Earl of Argyll, 'here are two clever Burgundians who may help us to take it.'

'End of synopsis,' Nicholas said. 'That's what Avandale said. That's what he'll discuss with the others tonight. And that's what I think they'll decide.'

'You've been casting runes,' John le Grant said. 'Along with Andreas and Scheves, and every second gargoyle from Nowie's chapel at Roslin. And you're wrong. They won't let us stay. They'll send us home.'

Nicholas wished he were drunk. *They'll send us home.* As he'd outlined it, there was no question of anyone being expelled from Scotland except himself and Adorne. In the eyes of the Lords, John was an asset and Robin was nothing.

Robin lay, his eyes open on John. They were alone, the three of them, in a room in Tobie's house. Nicholas had come to have this settled once and for all and he was going to do it. He said, 'Do you want to go home?'

It was blunt. Robin flushed, but John answered. 'You want to stay, Nicholas, for your own reasons. Everyone understands. But we're not needed here. I'm glad to have come and met old friends. Robin is grateful to have seen his father and grandfather. But there is work for us back in our own country.'

'This is your own country,' Nicholas said.

John said, 'It used to be. But I've made my career, as you have, elsewhere.'

'Doing what? I thought you'd given up war.'

This time, John's freckled skin reddened. He said, 'I thought I had. But there are mercenary companies. Or gun-casting. Or sailing.'

'Robin can't sail,' Nicholas said. He didn't look at the paralysed boy.

'What do you know of it?' the engineer said. 'You would have him lying here in the dust, counting barrels and pennies in ledgers. That's no life.'

'He didn't say so in Iceland,' Nicholas said. 'I assumed he wouldn't say so in Scotland. Especially when I tell him what is happening. He and his father are going to hold in their hands the greatest salmon monopoly ever known. The stakes are so high that ordinary merchants can never compete. But we can. And from salmon, the contracts spread to salt and to coal and to timber. Have you never wanted to be rich, really rich? We can buy land. We can buy up businesses. We can build ships and arm them, for offence or defence, like Benecke did. And then, when we want, we can leave.'

'Is this true?' John le Grant said.

Robin was staring at Nicholas. He said, 'We've drawn up a plan. There has been a plan to acquire fishing rights and . . .' His voice died. His nostrils were wet, and there wasn't a handkerchief he could reach. He said, in a clear voice, 'But not to drive out everyone else.'

'But surely that was understood?' Nicholas said, with smiling patience. He took out his handkerchief. 'There is no point in taking over half an industry if you can have it all. And then it could be run perfectly well from Bergen or Veere.'

He laid the handkerchief within easy reach. Robin ignored it. He said, 'We didn't give sanction for that.'

'You've forgotten,' Nicholas said. 'Or you didn't happen to get to the meetings. If you aren't interested, then you ought to go home. Your father will send you your profits.' He could see the boy straining to move and, of course, failing.

John le Grant said, 'You're doing it again, aren't you? Damn you, Nicholas, you're making a midden of Scotland again. Then to hell with it. I'm going. So's Robin. If he can't sail, I'll find him something to do.'

'No!' said Robin.

'What, no?' said le Grant. 'You hate it here. You've told me. There are grand things still to do in a war. Your bairns will grow up in their mother's land, and you'll be out among men, as ye should be.'

'And what will be happening here?' Robin said.

'I think,' Nicholas said, 'that I can probably manage without you. Although I don't quite see what Robin is going to do among men on the battlefield. Are they supposed to run about carrying him? Or do they put some stones in his hand, and let him throw them till captured? Or might he even have to lie in the dust, counting barrels and fodder in ledgers?'

'You cruel bastard,' said le Grant. 'Stop your mouth.'

'Why?' said Nicholas. 'You've talked about war. You've wept upon one another's bosoms. You're cured of your anguish. That's good. But Robin isn't cured, is he? All you've done is arrange to make a freak of him. He can't move. There's no point in taking him anywhere.'

Even then, Robin didn't cry out. But John's temper had long ago snapped. Nicholas saw the fist coming, and made a half-hearted gesture. He didn't realise quite how much he had miscalculated until the blow landed, and the next one, and several more. He was lanced by excruciating pain, which doubled and redoubled until he stopped thudding about, and lay supine. Robin was screaming, and John was gasping something over and over. Nicholas heard the sound of the door being wrenched open, and Tobie's voice, at its angriest, saying '*What?*'

What, indeed. Thankfully, Nicholas experienced the departure, one by one, of his senses. The last thing he heard was Robin's voice crying, 'It was my fault, all my fault, all my fault.'

Someone was saying, 'It was my fault. It was all my fault. I'm sorry.'

John.

Nicholas opened his eyes. He said, 'I should bloody well think it was.' He was in John's bed, and John was kneeling beside him, pounding the bed with a freckled fist, which he then pressed and squeezed over his face. Behind him stood two of Nicholas's grandmothers. Tobie, naturally. Kathi, even more naturally.

Kathi said, 'Well, it was your fault in a way, but Nicholas didn't give you a chance. At least, he gave you too much of a chance. But he didn't explain.'

'Explain what?' said Tobie.

'Well, that Nicholas would have dropped just as fast if he'd breathed on him.'

'Why?' said Tobie. You could tell that Tobie's mind, to that point, had been on other things. Rigid with bandaging, Nicholas felt like Tam Cochrane's collapsed buckram pillar. Lying flat in the dust. Reading ledgers. To hell, to hell with it all.

'Why did Nicholas want you to hit him? To make Robin feel sorry for him,' Kathi answered herself. 'He's gone grey again.' She spoke calmly. Her eyes had darkened.

John said, 'Nicholas?' and Nicholas opened his eyes with reluctance. He was trying to breathe very shallowly. He even thought of dumb language, translated by Tobie, but his hands were trussed up. He said in a secretive voice, 'It's all right. I meant you to do it. Look, of course it's all right if you want to go home. But Robin has a Sersanders wife; it would be dangerous. And if Kathi went, Adorne would have to follow them both.'

John was still masking his face with one hand. He wiped his lips with the back of the other. Nicholas said, 'You saw what I didn't see. He doesn't want to be a merchant; he wants the excitement of war. You gave him back his dream, for a bit, and he came close to trying for it. If he decides against it, then it's his own decision, not yours or mine.'

'Based on a piece of play-acting,' Tobie said. He sneezed furiously.

Kathi said, 'But we are all acting, Robin included. We're pretending to attitudes that haven't yet come about, to bridge the gap until they do come about. Do you think Robin doesn't know the trials, the humiliation that his dream would really entail? Now he has an excuse to stay. Now Nicholas must make sure that he creates a life for him that makes it worth while. War has a lot of different faces. Chivalry is one of them. Teaching is another.'

'I could help,' John le Grant said. He wiped his eyes on his sleeve. 'Nicol, the hurt that ye cause.'

'It was probably the only way,' Kathi said. 'But though we'll all help, it's Nicholas who will have to take the responsibility for Robin. And for himself. I gather you are grinding the faces of the poor once again?'

'It was havers,' said John. 'I knew it was. I just thought he was making it up to punish Robin. And, by God, it did.'

Nicholas was looking at Kathi. She said, 'Robin was badly upset. But mainly because he was the cause of your quarrel. You can put that right.' She paused. 'Why don't we bring him in here? Tobie can take John away for something strong in a flask. And I might even go with them.'

This time it was Tobie who was trying to send worried signals. Nicholas heaved a sigh and achieved a small nod. Running an overdue personal check, he registered a splinted left arm, two bandaged hands, a pad at the side of his head and something truly terrible when he breathed, which was presumably another lot of cracked ribs. There was also a motley assortment of throbs and pangs from bruised flesh and strained muscles. The idiot had kicked him.

Of course he had. Nicholas had asked for it. The whole thing had got out of hand, that was all. John said, 'I've made you the same as him.'

Nicholas said, 'We all got into his hell for a short time. My fault, if you want to award points. Now we're all going to get out. Including Robin.'

Robin said, 'You don't mind my lying here?'

The others had gone, and Nicholas had wakened to find himself still in John's bed, propped with pillows, and Robin of Berecrofts equally propped at his side, gazing at him with his earnest, schoolboy face and fall of fine hair and pellucid eyes. He wore shirt and hose, whereas Nicholas wore hose and bandages. There was a foot of space between them. The bed was a Genoese four-poster, its carvings running to cherubs. The hangings were silk, and all round the tester pranced dimpled infants with wreaths and pert fundaments. Robin said, 'You look terrible.'

There was something in his voice. Nicholas looked at him. Robin added, 'I hope John apologised.' The candlelight flared, and his eyes glinted.

Nicholas said, 'So did you. You took it bloody seriously at the time.'

'Then I hadn't had a chance to think,' Robin said. 'Of course, it wasn't true, about the business deals. You wanted to stop me from leaving, and you were right. I didn't think what it would mean to Kathi and her uncle. Even to John. He was only going to go back for my sake. Now he'll stay.'

It hadn't worked. Robin was too clever, or too clear-sighted, or both. Nicholas said, 'We could play it all over again, with a different ending. I pulverise John, and you rush back to Flanders, revolted. John follows, Tobie follows, Adorne follows, and you all join Gregorio in Venice and become wealthy.'

'No,' said Robin. He was smiling a little.

Nicholas shifted, then stopped. 'You all join Julius in Cologne?'

'No.'

'Simon de St Pol, harvesting grapes in Madeira? Now there,' said Nicholas, 'is a future for anyone who likes to lie in the sun being hated. Don't smile. I render jokes from an abyss of guilt. Whatever you decide, I shall feel responsible and you will resent it.'

'I have resented kindness,' said Robin. 'And love. I might do it again. But not now. Not when you're here with your arm smashed because of some daft –' He broke off, but recovered at once. 'So what do you suggest? I am going to stay. It makes you feel guilty. What are you going to do about that?'

'Enable you to do whatever you really want to do,' Nicholas said. 'Gambling? Drinking? Women? There is a whole world of activity that is not yet beyond you, so far as I know. And if you're interested in war, so is the King. Adorne may be invited on to the Council. You will hear a lot discussed in your father's house that has nothing to do with trade.' He shifted again. It didn't help.

'I shall present you,' said Robin, 'with an agenda. Meanwhile, if you would stop talking, we could make a start with the ale. The tankards are on your side and the bottles on mine, but we each have one good arm, and should manage.'

At first, they crossed swaddled limbs with some caution; the drinking was not without mishap, but contained moments of ritual elegance: the sacred ibis in slow dance with its partner. By the time the second bottle was empty, they had become more ambitious. Nicholas's two feet brought a fiddle back to the mattress. With Nicholas wielding the bow, and Robin pressing the strings, they got some tavern choruses out of it, sung by Robin to spare Nicholas's violated rib-cage. Then Nicholas returned from John's travelling chest with his praying forearms full of glittering prizes: a whistle, two bits of plate-armour for cymbals, a tambour effected from a chamberpot and some lead hackbut pillocks. He stuck John's helmet back to front on Robin's head, with the green feathers tickling his nose, and put on the earrings John always carried in case he met somebody. He banged on things and Robin carolled. They had both forgotten how late it was, and didn't hear Tobie at first when he opened the door, rather red in the face, and shouted at them.

Robin, always courteous, expressed his apologies and allowed himself to be conveyed, still talking, back to his room, where he advised Nicholas to go home, since Gelis would worry.

'We sent to tell her,' said Kathi. 'Tobie will give him a bed for the night. Are those John's things? His whistle?'

'Christ. They once were,' said John, who had also appeared. His face was still worn, but had recovered, oddly, some of its usual character. 'I don't want the whistle.'

'You do,' said Kathi, slapping it into his hands. 'And your leg-armour. And your . . . How many bottles of that ale have you drunk?'

'None,' said John, aggrieved. 'And it was mine.'

'I wasn't talking to you,' Kathi said. 'Nicholas, say good night to Robin.'

'Good night to Robin,' said Nicholas. He was standing, by now, his wrapped paws in the air. He said, 'I could shake feet.'

'Show me,' said Robin. 'You couldn't even stand on one leg. Take your cracked ribs and go.'

He looked up and Nicholas looked down, both of them flushed; and for a moment, their eyes met and held. Then Nicholas went; and Tobie with him; and John. Kathi retired to her room, while one of Robin's two capable servants prepared him for the night and then left. Then she came back to see how he was. The sight of him, pink and happy and bright-eyed, made her smile. He said, 'Come to bed.'

When his wound was still raw, they had not shared the same bed. Later, he sometimes lay in her arms through his nightmares, but his greatest need often was privacy. Since he was wounded, he had never spoken like that.

Kathi said, 'I was hoping you'd ask. After all that finger-work, do you think you could help pull this off?'

It was only a taffeta night-robe, its embroidered edges held by a clasp, soon undone. If she knelt by the bed, one gentle hand could (and did) smooth the light stuff from her shoulders, and the same throbbing touch could (and did) draw it down and down, when she stood.

It dropped. The mellow light of the candles curtseyed once, and then played, bright as the flute, on the slight, bare body of Kathi Sersanders, cream and brown, with the silvery marks from two births on her skin. Only two.

Robin had begun to breathe quickly. The smile had gone from his eyes.

Kathi said, 'I know what you know. I know what I want. May I take it?'

He spoke her name.

When she touched the sheet at his throat, he caught her wrist, then slowly released it. She drew the white linen down, ushering the travelling light over his smooth, moulded skin. Her own body shared in its radiance.

When he pulled her close with his arm, the kiss that followed was the kiss of their marriage night. And with all the tenderness of their marriage night, she cared for her husband; and he for her.

Chapter 14

His richt hand furth to welcum and to call,
And in his left hand breid and wyne withall.

FOR A SHORT while, with the greatest reluctance, Nicholas de Fleury arrived punctually at all his appointments.

Anselm Adorne, Baron Cortachy, was welcomed at Court and confirmed in his current possessions. He was given additionally, by the Queen, a small, profitable concession connected with her Palace at Linlithgow, and received permission to build a modest mill at the east end of that town, to the profit of himself and the convenience of the tenants of the King's farms. He was invited by the King to appear as a guest judge at the November sitting of the Lords of Council in Civil Causes. Departing from Roslin, Lord Cortachy adopted rooms in his nephew's large house in the Canongate, accompanied by his nephew's associate Andro Wodman, the official Scots Conservator, with whom Adorne would now work in tandem. His daughter, Efemie, was placed in the care of a nun and a wet-nurse at Haddington, on the earnest instructions of the Queen, and Crackbene's wife, Ada.

Mistress Bel of Cuthilgurdy left Edinburgh, and rode west to see Jordan de St Pol at his castle of Kilmirren, Renfrewshire.

She was not well received. The porter, whom she did not know, at first returned to say, a little perfunctorily, that his lordship was away.

'Oh, indeed?' said Bel, who might be wee, fat and grey, but who had a tail of four armed men at her back, and a tongue like a graver. 'And who's that, pray, who was keeking out of yon top window a minute ago, like the wae combless capon he is?'

'The demoiselle is mistaken,' said the man. 'I am sorry. It is always best to send word in advance.'

'Aye. If I'd sent word in advance, he wouldna be here. Aweel. Do we fire off our hackbuts, or just take you in with us with a knife at your neck?'

'Bel?' Across the courtyard, the monumental person of the lord of Kilmirren himself had arrived in the doorway.

The porter turned. 'My lord! I am dealing with this!'

The fat man descended the steps. 'If you go on, I am afraid she will kill you.' He walked over. 'Let me give you some instructions for the future. If Mistress Bel of Cuthilgurdy appears on the road without warning again, you are to ring the alarm, send a courier to the sheriff of Renfrew, and call out the local militia. Is that clear?'

'Yes, my lord,' said the porter, who was a highly trained soldier and did not enjoy being dragged into a family joke.

'Good. Come in, Bel. How kind of you to call. May I persuade you to honour us with a stay?'

Bel of Cuthilgurdy turned her back on him and spoke to the porter. 'Ye did quite right. He was anxious not to see me. But he's right as well; if ye'd tried to stop me, I'd have got them to fire. What's your name?'

This time, she had his full attention. He said, 'Oswald, my lady.'

'Well, Oswald,' she said. 'If he turns ye off, you come to me.'

Indoors: 'You came to purloin my staff. You see how my caution was justified,' said the fat man. They were in the chamber she knew so well from the old days, when she had come across from her house to sit here with Jordan of St Pol and Lucia his daughter. And before that.

Bel said, 'What did he say? What did Nicholas say that so angered you?'

The fat man sighed. Today, instead of his gown and swathed hat, he wore a cap over the long tangle of once-flaxen hair, and a linen shirt under his house-robe. He said, 'I knew that was why you were here. When shall I ever persuade you that I cannot be angered by Claes? He may irritate me for the moment. He may inconvenience me, so that I take some pleasure in reprimanding him, in whatever degree the injury warrants. It is not impossible that I shall kill him one day, although I am increasingly moved to leave that task to the delectable David . . .'

'Davie Simpson tried to kill me, the last time we met.'

'But Wodman prevented him. Or the child's bodyguard, as I remember. It won't happen again.'

'Won't it? Can you tell me to my face that you haven't made a pact with Davie Simpson to harm Nicholas?'

He gazed at her, mildly surprised. 'Did de Fleury say that?'

'No, he didn't. I guessed, for I know you. It's true?'

The surprise changed to a display of mild pleasure. 'Simpson thinks that it's true. Otherwise we might have seen some rather crude, precipitate action. Now the circumstances are right, and I am quite content to leave the perpetration to David, God's Darling.'

'But will he let you do nothing?' said Bel. 'He helped lift the charges that let you come back to Scotland. He proved you didn't stash away French money, someone else did.'

'I wonder who?' said St Pol.

'It's all past. But I know you. You've come back, and there's nothing to do, and you're restless. And Davie won't leave you alone. Whatever he's planning for Nicol, he'll implicate you. You expelled him, remember.'

'So what is he planning?' said the fat man.

Bel looked at him. 'Ye ken what he's doing. What Nicol did, for other reasons. The Court loves him. The King spends evenings with him at the lute or the dice; Mar goes whoring and hunting; the Princesses listen to French tales of illicit lovers, and let him translate Latin books he smuggles in for them. I'm told his delivery's a treat. And away from Court, he's using Newbattle to build himself a trading empire, so that he can invest the profits in land.'

'It sounds familiar,' St Pol said. 'The Daffychino, would you say? He always thought he should be the head of my recent company. Fortunately, he hasn't the brains.'

'Sometimes,' said Bel, 'ye can do mair harm without brains than with them. If he brings you down, he brings Henry too. If he brings Nicholas down, he brings Jordan.'

'Who, I am now told, resembles Nicholas more than he ever did. Henry is greatly relieved,' St Pol said. 'He always feared that Jordan was born of his father and Gelis. You were saying that Simpson is cultivating John of Mar?'

'I was. And Mar – are ye surprised? – is pursuing a feud against Henry. If ye do nothing,' said Bel, 'ye'll fall to Davie Simpson's hand, one way or another, so soon as he's got rid of Nicholas. And then he'll step in, and add Kilmirren to Beltrees.'

'Bel,' said Jordan de St Pol. 'As you know, I am a great admirer of your acumen. If possible, it improves with the years. I think your reading of the situation is flawless. I only wish to say that, if you have thought of it, then Claes certainly has. And that all you describe will only happen if Claes himself succumbs to David Simpson, which seems unlikely to me.'

'Under normal circumstances, yes,' Bel agreed. 'But just at the moment, he's as sharp as the Holy Dead. What with one thing and another.'

'Of course. The cripple, and the all-too-vigorous helpmeet. Between the spearpoint and the sword-edge indeed. Are they subject to breeding impulses, do you think?' asked the fat man. He had finished the mutchkin he had been drinking when she arrived. She had refused refreshment. 'Is it merely a transient pairing, or are they proposing to multiply?'

'I have no idea,' said Mistress Bel shortly. 'So what will you do?'

'I thought I had told you,' he said. 'I wish my importunate Claes to be chastised. I am delegating the task to David Simpson. If it is beyond Simpson, he will die. If it is not beyond him, he will still die, for I shall kill him myself . . . What was it you said of me always? That I wasn't worth the baptism water? And what are you worth, Mistress Bel? Standing on a revolving lectern, complaining? Have you told Claes anything?'

'No,' she said. Then she added, 'I have told him my son's dead.'

His face changed. He said, 'I should have begun – I failed to speak of it because of other things. Forgive me. I was very sorry.' He paused and said, 'Where will you live?'

'At Stirling,' she said. 'And in Edinburgh at your house, if I may.'

'Or here,' he said. 'Simpson will not sell back your own, but there are – what shall I call them? – the family rooms here.'

'You may need them,' she said, 'if Simon comes back.'

'He won't,' he said. 'I have forbidden him.'

She said, 'Then why don't you go back to Madeira yourself? You need a business to run.'

'I also like watching puppets,' he said. 'Tell that to your friend Claes, when you see him.'

'And what else?' said Bel. 'You never said what you'd do if Davie died, and Nicholas didn't.'

'God at his eye-window knows,' said Kilmirren. 'I haven't decided. I like to surprise myself.'

'I think,' said Gelis, 'you should do something about Davie Simpson. Are you as uncomfortable as you look?'

'Wait,' said Nicholas. 'No, that's worse. I *am* doing something about Davie Simpson.'

'What?'

'What he's doing to me. Upsetting his schemes where I can.'

'It doesn't seem to be very effective,' Gelis said.

'It isn't. That's the whole idea. Then he launches a really big scheme to display his infinite superiority.'

'Like Fat Father Jordan. He created the Vatachino expecting to crush you before he got rid of you.'

'That's right. He doesn't have many original ideas, David. It's no good.'

'I know it's no good. It's too soon to try. But at least, whatever you did, it's made Robin happy. Tobie says he's transformed.'

'Well, I bloody wish I hadn't done it,' Nicholas said.

Towards the end of that year, free at last from restraint, Nicholas recognised this period of incoherence for what it was: a bridge that led from the catastrophe of the Duke's death to a new and as yet dimly realised future. He had come to Scotland with clear objectives but had not yet attained them, partly because he had been side-tracked by circumstances. And now he seemed committed to something much more challenging and protracted, with responsibility not only to his own family, but to the men who had left Bruges to join him. He was not short of plans. He faced the future in a state not far short of euphoria. But, imperatively, he must talk to Adorne.

Gelis would have had him do this at once, but instead, Nicholas had waited. He had made his reconnaissance. Adorne must do the same. Only then could there be any profit in talking.

In the end, it was Adorne himself who approached him, by means of a gift – a high-tempered, light-footed horse of the kind Nicholas had watched die in the lists at the Vespers rehearsal. It was brought, with an invitation, by a groom in Cortachy livery whom Nicholas sent back, rewarded, with an answer. Presently, he made his way down the High Street to the substantial house to which Adorne had now moved, together with Dr Andreas and Andro Wodman. There was enough space, in its several storeys, to house a young child and its nurse, as well as public rooms and offices and service quarters. It seemed to Nicholas, met and escorted upstairs by a chamberlain, that Adorne was preparing for a stay of some time, at least. It was what he expected.

Adorne received him alone before the fireplace in the most private reception room in the house, his own bedchamber. In all the years Nicholas had known him, he had changed very little. The wry, fine-boned face was perhaps leaner, the hair curling between his feathered cap and strong neck was paler than flax. But his shoulders had not lost their set of authority; his doublet, of pleated black cloth, was fresh and well-ordered; and his rings and shoulder-chain showed that he had just come from Court. Only his voice had altered, as he came forward, hand outstretched. 'Nicholas.'

'Sir.' Nicholas inclined his head and took the hand, which closed on his and then held it.

Adorne said, 'I hope this means that you accept what I sent you. You will have been told what your wife did for Robin, and what she and the van Borselen family did for me. I probably owe her my life.'

'She was glad to do it,' Nicholas said.

His hand was freed. 'And I know now what you did for Mistress . . . for Phemie.' He cleared his throat.

Nicholas said, 'It was its own reward. But since the gift marks what it does, I am glad, sir, to accept it. And I hear the small demoiselle flourishes.'

'Some good has come of it,' said Adorne. 'Perhaps there are other things to be redeemed. Come, if you will.' There were two fine chairs by the fire, and wine, which he handed himself, while he regained his composure. It shocked Nicholas that he had lost it. Then they were both seated and he felt himself under that level, magisterial scrutiny, so often experienced.

Adorne said, 'I have watched you grow, with such pleasure. I have enjoyed crossing swords with you, as you mastered and entered my particular empire. I did not always appreciate it when you bettered me.' He paused to smile.

'Or when I stupidly injured you,' Nicholas said. 'Or when I made a fool of myself in this country.'

'Shall I tell you my mistakes?' Adorne said. His eyes were clear and fine drawn, set between heavy lids in his narrow face. He said, 'You have been here for most of a year, for half of it without supervision. You had no need to return. You did not do so to exploit the country, or you would have had to do so at once, before you could be detected and stopped. I am satisfied that you wished to make amends for what you had done. So far, you have devoted your skills to founding a future for Kathi's husband, and having care for my lady. I merely wish to say that whatever else you wish to do, you can depend on my help.'

Nicholas lifted his eyes. 'I am grateful. My understanding also has been limited.'

The clear gaze still rested on him. 'But now we are two men,' Adorne said. 'And you are a person who has experienced what is good and what is bad in many parts of the world. I am going to describe to you what I make, this time, of this country of Scotland, and its future. And if you will trust me with it, I should like you to do the same for me, as if it were an assessment of the court of Uzum Hasan, or of the Doge of Venice, or of Louis of France. Then, if you are willing, we might share our conclusions.'

Nicholas looked at him. Adorne said, 'But, of course, you may have decided to make your future in one of these countries. Flanders is my home. I will repay Scotland's hospitality to the last drop of my blood, but when the doors are open for me again, be it within one year or two, I shall go back.'

Nicholas said, 'My plans are less clear. But it seems likely that I shall be here at least as long as yourself. And yes. I should like above anything to compare notes.'

Then they talked until it was dark.

Adorne had the advantage, which Nicholas lacked, of years of dispatches from Sersanders and Wodman, and of the kind of overview of mercantile business that his former Conservatorship conferred. Also, he was a nobleman. It made a difference, at Court and in council, and in the great homes of those families from France and from Flanders who had poured into England four hundred years ago, and then, a hundred years later or less, had followed King David north. Some had dwindled, or produced only daughters. But the rest of that rich, virile stock was still in Scotland, often at war with itself, but still with a sense, running below, of the bond of blood they all shared. Adorne, son of Genoa, was of the same kind.

Nicholas was not. Nicholas was endowed with the intense experiences of his previous visits; a practical acquaintance with individuals of every station; and an intuitive understanding of the young, including the young of the Castle. By now, also, he had matched himself against many men, and knew the extent of his ability. This was, however, the first time he had used it in partnership with someone of similar intellect, instead of in opposition. It was like getting drunk, to hear Adorne's exposition, so like his own, and to then add his own, and realise that Adorne had been silenced.

Then Adorne said, 'I have, of course, been fatally stupid. Why didn't I ask you to come and work with me for the Duke?'

'Because, quite rightly, you didn't trust me,' Nicholas said. 'Anyway, as it happens, I did work for the Duke. I was fighting for him when he died.'

'You despised him?' Adorne's enquiry was soft and a little blurred.

He had discarded his chain and doublet and was resting, as Nicholas was, in shirt and hose. His hair was damp.

Nicholas pulled a face. 'There's little point in despising what you can't alter. You try to cushion the consequences, that's all.'

Adorne said, 'And here?'

Nicholas said, 'Here there is everything to fight for. You've just said it all. Thorough, hard-working people. Growing trade. Growing towns. A structure of law and of education and of government ready to build on. And a decent team of veteran councillors to keep the throne steady.' He made a deliberate space. 'The single threat is the one thing no one mentions.'

When Adorne spoke, his voice sounded flat. 'You have heard the rumours.'

'I have used my eyes,' Nicholas said. 'But no one will trust me yet with the truth. You have been to the Castle. You have had a chance to compare what you found when you last came, and now. There has been a change in the King and his family. I think Mar is sick. I think the others share in the affliction, and that it is not a disease, but something hereditary. Their father stabbed a nobleman to death in a quarrel – a king, a man at other times perfectly sane. Your friend and their relative the Archbishop Patrick is said to be mad. All of them are volatile beyond reason. If we are to make any design for the future, I need to know what is wrong. Do you, sir?'

Adorne rose and walked to the window. The panes were dark but outside, Nicholas knew, the stair-lanterns would be glimmering now on either side of the causeway that led up to the Castle, and there would be men and women passing up and down and pausing to chat and call to one another, while children who should be in bed were leaping the common gutter and playing hopping games on the flags. Adorne turned. 'They haven't trusted me either, but Saunders has seen what you have, and I was concerned enough to ask Dr Andreas.'

'And?' Nicholas said.

Adorne came back and sat down. 'There is a certain hereditary ailment. The symptoms – a red flush, some unexplained pains, other signs – could be those of this condition, which affects the mind and the temper. It is sometimes mild, and sometimes intermittent. Sometimes it simply becomes worse. And it cannot be cured.'

'There are five of them,' Nicholas said. He could hear the horror in his own voice. 'Two sisters, three brothers. And if these were debarred from the throne, the children might also be unfit to follow?'

Adorne said, 'Nicholas. There is a fractiousness in the Stewart family, but it is not certain that this is the cause. It is feared, certainly, which is why it is not spoken about. But even if John of Mar is afflicted, your Sandy may be luckier. And if the lady Margaret is wild, her sister Mary is not.'

'And the King?' Nicholas said.

'He is wilful,' Adorne said. 'But, I think, manageable. Perhaps too manageable. I don't care for David Simpson's prominence at Court. Nor, I suppose, do you. I plan to counter it. I think, between us, we may even ease the Councillors' burden with these young people, as you are already doing with Albany. But it must be done carefully. And we should plan it together. Such activities are easily confused with high treason.'

He was smiling a little. Nicholas said, 'Surely not. But leave David Simpson to me.'

Adorne had ceased to smile. 'I am sorry. This is dangerous for you, as well as for Kathi and Robin. What has happened so far? The St Pols at least are not troubling you?'

'Neither is Simpson,' Nicholas said. 'Or only in minor ways. I thought I might attract a stray arrow at first, but that would have brought in the law before he had disposed of the rest of us. And now we have met, and he is enjoying life at Court, and seems in no hurry to plan a grand quietus. It may not happen. Discontent sometimes fades.'

'Discontent!' Adorne repeated.

'Why, what else would you call it?' said Nicholas. 'It is not rooted in conviction, like hatred.'

'But you have experienced hatred,' Adorne said.

'Very seldom,' said Nicholas. 'It's usually discontent. I don't work on a grand scale.'

'I think you underrate yourself,' said Anselm Adorne.

They talked for an hour more, then Nicholas left, walking carefully. He felt apprehension. He also felt very happy. As much as anything, it pleased him that, within minor as well as major ways, Adorne had placed their new and different relationship on a basis which would take them unembarrassed into the future. His name, to Anselm Adorne, had undergone no spurious change, and remained formally Nicholas. Equally, it had been established that Anselm Adorne was to be addressed, as he always had been, as 'sir'.

The requirement was the reverse of what it seemed, and was taken by Nicholas as a compliment. It affirmed that the world was a place of order, which he found reassuring.

The whole encounter did more.

It confirmed to Nicholas de Fleury that he had arrived where, and when, he was needed. It indicated that he had been given something to do for which he was qualified; for which indeed he had been prepared, by all that had happened to him so far.

Chapter 15

No man of craft suld haue inwy at vther,
Bot luf his fallow as he war his brother.

TIME PASSED; and the Master Melter, you would say, had
stooped to the furnace, and cast all the world into gold. Or
so it seemed to the temporary exiles in Scotland, to whom
life became fair.

It was a measure, very likely, of past wretchedness that, despite the
frustrations and dangers, despite the threat from one vain, silly man,
the crowded vennels of Edinburgh became the proving-ground of a
new group of companions very close to that once created, out of adventure, out of love, out of pride, in the name of Marian de Charetty in
Bruges.

Witnessing concordance arriving at last, Tobias Beventini found
himself thinking of the missing members of the Banco di Niccolò –
Julius and Father Moriz in Germany; Gregorio in Venice; Diniz in
Bruges. But in their place were Robin and Kathi and Dr Andreas,
Robin's father and Wodman, Kathi's brother and her uncle Adorne.
Except that, in the delicate strategy Nicholas had settled upon with
Adorne, the bond between all of them was not obvious. Adorne and
his family continued to trade as they had done in the past, and to make
themselves welcome at Court. Nicholas, with John as his sailing-master
and gunner, and partnered by Gelis, spent as much time at Leith as in
Edinburgh, and more time than he probably wished riding the Marches
or hunting with Sandy Albany. Yet even that was less than true. Nicholas
was as ungrudging with Sandy as he was with Kathi's children, or Jodi,
or Robin. His business was managing people.

He came to see Robin often; but was as likely to meet him at the Castle, where the Master of Artillery found it congenial to spend an evening with John and Nicholas and anyone else who liked war, drinking ale and discussing stratagems and scratching out scale drawings and maps. Sometimes the gathering was down by the Tron, and you would find a hard-drinking bunch of masons and hammermen, a Merlioun and a Lisouris and a Bonar perhaps in their midst, bursting with talk about pattrens and deal boards and cornishes, but equally ready to listen. The chair they'd made for Robin had wheels on it, and his own man pushed him about wherever he wanted, often with Margaret or Rankin riding with him, or running screeching with joy at his side. They saw nothing out of the way in it all: they didn't remember him walking. When he had mastered that, he had bigger wheels made, so that it could bounce really fast down the High Street, and John fashioned another identical chair, so that they could have races.

By then, Robin had recovered his interest in business, and spent some time across the road, if not quite as much as before, and without the same over-intensity. Adorne had given some money towards equipping a set of butts and a practice-ground at Greenside, beyond the hill on the way down to Leith, and a small club had formed, which called itself the Society of the Unicorn. Youngsters went there – Jodi and Jamie Boyd often among them – and the masters-at-arms gave their time. It was encouraged. These were the leaders of the future. Even the Royal Guard sent someone down now and then to instruct and encourage. Henry de St Pol went once or twice. But by then he had already come face to face with his cousin Jodi.

It happened at Leith, on a day full of wind-gusts and rain, when Gelis was enjoying herself supervising goods lumbering in and out of the warehouse: a task at which, like Marian de Charetty, she was rather good. Nicholas and Jodi had temporarily boarded the *Marie*, which had come in with Tom Yare and a cargo, and was about to leave, loaded, for Berwick. Hindering Gelis were a number of friends, such as Leithie Preston and Tam Cochrane and Alec Brown and Mick Crackbene's jolly wife Ada, in whom the constant attentions of Mick and the birth of eight children, five of them Mick's, had engendered a voluptuous increase in bulk, all of it bountifully inviting. Gazing, periodically, at Mick Crackbene and his springing step and solid, satisfied vigour, Gelis was gratified to be reminded, quite often, of Nicholas.

The dulcet voice of Henry de St Pol, insinuating itself through the hubbub, was therefore something of a shock. Gelis abandoned the sledge she was supervising, broke off a raging argument with Tam and Leithie and swung round to locate the speaker, who stood in the doorway. As ever, a small silence fell, in tribute to Henry's hair, his eyes, his smile and his stance of heart-breaking, insolent grace. 'Lang Bessie?' he said. 'My darling aunt, did I hear you speak in defence of Lang Bessie?'

'You did,' said Gelis, recovering. 'Someone put out the fire under her malt, and she's raised all her prices.'

'For beer?' Henry said. He was looking about.

'Well, that too,' Gelis said. 'Did you want Nicholas?' It was called taking the bull by the horns. Nicholas had always convinced himself that since Henry, as a boy, had been murderously jealous of Jodi, his two sons were better apart. Cornered, he had agreed that, since they were both in one town, Jodi should at least be prepared for an encounter. Further cornered, he had agreed to speak to him, and had done so. After all, the boys were supposed to be cousins. They *were* cousins, born to Gelis and her sister. They didn't know that Henry's father was not Simon but Nicholas.

Henry said, 'I've just put some fells on the *James*. I wondered what you were loading for Berecrofts. Won't Bruges refuse to take goods from Adorne? I thought he was nearly hanged for misappropriating ducal funds.'

Big Tam Cochrane had finished Gelis's job on the sledge and was now planted, hands on hips, gazing at Henry. 'Weel, man, ye maun tell the Duchess of Burgundy. She's made Lord Cortachy her personal envoy. But then, no one's free of mistakes. I heard you were thrown out of Veere, but I dare say you're still hoping to trade there.'

Henry reddened. Gelis said, 'If you want to see what we've got, Nicholas is on the *Marie* just now, and could show you. Master Brown here will take you. He's sailing it.' She ignored Alec Brown's stare. The Browns were related to the Berecrofts clan, and protective.

Henry said, 'I dare say I can find it myself. Don't trouble.' He walked out.

After a moment, Brown said, 'I'd better go,' and followed him. Gelis gazed after them both. If Henry knew Nicholas was here, he would know that Jodi was with him.

Leithie Preston said, 'They should have drowned that one at birth.'

It was a common view. On the other hand, all the Prestons talked like that. They were a strong-minded family. Gelis said, 'I don't know. I expect they said that of all of us at that age. I think we should find him a girlfriend.'

'Lang Bessie,' said Cochrane. 'If he can afford her. What are you grinning at?'

'Man,' said Leithie Preston, 'if ye could hear the note in your voice. Mope away. Yon same wee rutting bantling's hardly been out of Lang Bessie's skirts since that time with Johndie Mar and the pig-asses. And according to rumour, it's *her* that pays *him*.'

The loading finished. Tam and Leithie left. Gelis went to the office and became lost in the paperwork. No one came. The guard who always protected her eventually tapped on the door and brought in one of Tom Yare's men, with a bit of paper and a message. The message, from Yare, was to say that the *Marie* had sailed, taking Ser Nicholas and the two young men with it. The note, from Nicholas, said, *Gelis, I'm sorry. Only to Berwick, and I'll bring him back safe.*

He had reassured her about Jodi. Perhaps he didn't realise how disturbed she felt about Henry as well. It seemed puerile, after all that, to experience a sudden, deep pang at her next thought, which was that she was bereft of her lover, for the first time since she had found him again.

The thought had occurred to Nicholas also, inducing a surge of involuntary protest that perhaps even exceeded her own. But it was too good a chance to forgo. He knew it as soon as he saw Henry approaching, his fair face upraised, and Alec pointing to where Yare stood at the top of the companionway, with Jodi beside him. They were in the outermost part of the harbour, and would cast off when Brown was aboard, and Nicholas and Jodi had left. The gangplank shifted up and down as the ship swayed. The *Marie* was big as Leith ships went: a hundred tons, requiring sixteen mariners to handle the sails and the oars and the freight. There was a pilot boat waiting to ease her out of the shallows.

Henry was on board. He spoke to Yare, and then glanced at Jodi, throwing him a word as he passed. Jodi said something, looking after him. Then Yare had taken Henry by the shoulder and was directing his gaze to the top of the mast, where Nicholas rocked. Nicholas waved, without moving, and Yare shouted up. It was something about tides, but it didn't matter. Ten minutes wouldn't hurt. He had climbed to the basket, as he often did, to give himself a last view of the ship, and the wharves, and the port. Of these, as he sometimes recognised, it was the ship that meant most to him. These last weeks he had been surprised – and shamed by the surprise – to find that it was the same with Jodi. With both of the boys, he was beginning to think.

He leaned out, signalling, and when Yare sent up a man, dispatched him back with an invitation. Would Henry like to join him aloft? There was room. There was room for more than Henry.

Now there were two faces peering up. Then came Jodi's young voice, and a movement. Jodi had repeated the invitation to Henry, and Henry had suggested, languidly, that if Jodi's father wanted company, Jodi should ascend. Which, as it happened, was no trouble to a boy whose father had a ship and a house and a warehouse in Leith. Jodi laid hands on the ropes and swarmed up.

He didn't look down, but Nicholas, handing him up the last foot, saw Henry's expression. He saw it alter. And, as, breathless and proud, Jodi settled beside him, Nicholas saw Henry begin the long climb.

He had done it before. Living on the western island of Madeira, he must have spent half his leisure on the ships of what had once been the cane-sugar company of Vasquez and St Pol, and which Simon de St Pol still ran in the Portuguese island. Henry would have climbed rigging, but of a different kind of ship, and in calm, blue waters. And not perhaps for a year. It was a gamble. But against that was the co-ordinated, beautiful body, and the will-power, and the pride.

Henry de St Pol was pale when he arrived, but he arrived. And Nicholas, pulling him in as if his own breathing had not stopped, began talking at once of the rigging, the cargo, the sailing qualities, punctuated after a moment by breathless comments from Henry, and Jodi's eager voice. Then Yare shouted again, from below, and Nicholas said, 'Mind you, it's even better out at sea, but perhaps not with this wind.'

'I've been out in worse,' Henry said.

'I suppose we all have,' Nicholas said. 'But if we sail, we couldn't get off until Berwick. The King would dismiss you.'

'I have three days free,' Henry said. 'More, if I wanted. I could send a message.' His knuckles were white, his eyes dark.

Nicholas said, 'Wait a moment. No clothes! And Jodi and I were going home.'

'I like Berwick,' said Jodi. 'Master Yare or Master Brown would have clothes.'

Nicholas looked at them, frowning. 'Dammit,' he said. 'Shall we sail?'

The ship leaned over and back. 'I don't mind,' Henry said.

Nicholas didn't keep them long on the top: only for so long as it took for the *Marie* to edge out of the Water of Leith and head south. Then he took them below and remarked that he was hungry. So were they. Jodi said, 'I'll tell Master Yare,' and went off.

Nicholas, peeling off his boat-cloak beside Henry, said, 'Thank God he's reasonably good at this stuff. You don't mind keeping an eye on him? You must have done a lot of small-boat sailing as well. What's the water like round Funchal?'

Then food came, and ale which Henry rather indulged in, so that when Nicholas, his meal over, left to make a quick round of the ship, he returned to find the representative of the King's Guard fast asleep on a bench, with someone's old cloak wrapped about him. Tom Yare had carried off Jodi.

Tom Yare said, 'No, I don't mind, and neither does Alec. But I thought the St Pols were after your hide? You might woo the boy, if you're lucky, but what if something goes wrong? Accidents happen. If Henry is buried at sea, his grandfather will have you buried on land.'

'You sound as if you can't sail this ship,' Nicholas said. 'Nothing will happen. Neither are we going to fall in love and marry each other in three days. Henry may not commit actual murder, but he'll still offend the crew, and madden Alec and you, and snap at me or Jodi whenever he's worried. On the other hand –'

'I know. You can't help admiring him. There were sixteen men down here watching the style of him as he worked up those ropes, however nervous he was. A comely man draws the eye, and makes men lenient.'

'All right,' Nicholas said. 'So long as no one gets too excited. His grandfather will bury me also if he finds I've diverted his line by implanting a new taste for sailors.'

All his predictions were correct. He kept Jodi beside him, so that the boy had some protection when Henry lost his nerve or his temper. But Henry let fly with his tongue, not his sword or his fists, and never at any time was Veere mentioned, or anything that had happened between Henry and Nicholas in the past. And Jodi had been well primed. When an argument arose, he just opened his grey eyes on Henry and said, 'I don't agree,' and walked out. And when Henry said, 'Oh yes! Run to your father!' Jodi just said, 'Well, you're older than me.' And quite often that silenced him.

The best times were the times of danger when, triumphant after some crisis, Henry would joke with the crew, as he heard his captain joke with the Guard after a contest, and join Tom or Alec or Nicholas over a tankard in the cabin and talk it all over. Once Nicholas said, 'Does everyone call you Henry? No short name?'

'There aren't any,' the youth said. 'Or just Harry, which is all right if you're blind. It's a van Borselen name.' He stared Nicholas in the eye.

'Well, I think I prefer it to Wolfaert,' said Nicholas mildly. 'I suppose you're right. All the good Henry names are Italian. But remember the problem, when you come to baptise your first son.' He added, with vague hopefulness, 'There was some talk of trailing a bladder, and shooting at it, for money?'

'You think you can beat me?' said Henry.

'Jodi can beat you,' said Nicholas scornfully. Henry was beginning to recognise jokes.

In fact, Jodi was remarkably good: so much so that Henry remarked tolerantly, 'You've been practising.'

'No. It's your bow,' Jodi said. 'I brought it with me. That's what I'm shooting with.' He paused. 'You don't want it back? Aunty Bel said you didn't.'

'Aunty Bel?' Henry repeated. It was sharp.

'Mistress Bel. Not his real aunt,' Nicholas said. 'Bel of Cuthilgurdy.'

'I don't imagine she's anybody's real aunt,' Henry said. 'And if she was ever a Cuthilgurdy, it was forty years ago, my grandfather says. The land's long since gone to somebody else. So how do you know her? Because she used to hang about my father's sister?'

'She went to Timbuktu with us. You were too young, perhaps, to remember. You would have enjoyed it.'

'I've been to Africa,' Henry said.

'Jodi hasn't. Where?' Nicholas asked.

Later, they fished.

Later, Henry settled down to dice with the crew, and lost badly, and accused them of cheating. Later, he either ignored Jodi or sneered at him. Then the wind rose to gale force, and they lost a spar and had to cut a sail free and Alec broke open a keg of strong ale and they were all uproarious again.

Up and down; up and down. No, they were not going to fall in love and marry between Leith and Berwick; but at least they arrived in Berwick, all of them, rather soiled, rather damp, but undamaged in flesh and in spirit. Yare sent Jodi up to his house, from which he and his father would ride home with a good guard next morning. Nicholas stood with his other son on the riverside quay, watching the partial unloading begin. He said, 'You don't fancy sailing on to Middleburg? It would let you mend fences with Veere. Wolfaert can be an ass, but he's quite a powerful man in these parts. Or you could sell your fells directly to Antwerp.'

'You want to know what the competition is?' Henry said. He turned from the river, his blue eyes held wide, as if by some new resolution.

He said, 'I heard you tried to drown my father's sister at Berecrofts. I heard you thought it was my father, and held her under the water.'

'I was there when she drowned,' Nicholas said. 'She tried to cross a frozen river in snow. Why do you think I would kill her, or your father?'

Henry said, 'Because you wanted to be one of us.'

Nicholas said, 'I wouldn't have minded being one of you, although not for the inheritance. I had enough money. But in fact, I couldn't be a St Pol without harming my own family, and I wouldn't do that. If I *were* one of you, my marriage would be void, because my wife and your mother were sisters.'

'So that wasn't why you wanted to kill my father,' said Henry. 'It was because he knew what a slut your mother was. He was a boy when he was made to marry her, and she cheated. Everyone knew.'

Men shouted; horns blew; winches creaked. If you listened, you could hear the surf far away on the sandbanks. Nicholas said, 'Everyone believed it, certainly. Your father and grandfather made sure of that. I think they had their reasons.'

'I'm sure they had,' Henry said. He laughed.

Nicholas said, 'I meant that your father was fifteen when he married, and my mother was nearly twice as old, with a child on the way. He probably felt trapped and resentful. Does it matter? I have my own wife and son. I have no designs on your family. I was hoping that you would talk about it, like this, so that I could tell you so.'

Up, and down. Henry said, 'You think I want to hear your pathetic excuses? Pardon me. You've dragged me on this squalid trip, and that's enough. You won't, I hope, expect me to come back in your company.'

'No. Do you want me to lend you some money?' Nicholas said. 'I did better than you did out of the cockroach championship.'

Henry's blue eyes gleamed. Then he said, 'Go to hell,' and walked off.

Up, and down. But his welcome back home, after the busy, talkative journey with Jodi, was worth it all. Ah, his welcome.

His feast day came and went, signalling that he was about to become a year older. On the Eve of St Nicholas, there was a Mass at the Abbey Church of Holyrood, and Sandy Albany gave a feast for him in the royal apartments. Ten days later, on the day he stubbornly maintained as the anniversary of his birth, Kathi provided a repast, pleasantly set out for him and for Gelis in the big upper room of her Canongate house, and shared with an amazing number of the persons whom he knew and liked best, including those who set to noisy music, on demand, the scurrilous words written by Robin on the underside of their platters. And among the adults were the children whose lives were now also part of his own: Margaret of Berecrofts, a rosy, formidable character of nearly three, in the patient charge of her adored Jodi, with Rankin pattering behind. And in an upstairs room, brought for the occasion, a wicker cradle containing within its muslin freshness a sleeping infant called Efemie Adorne, with her father's hand pensively guiding its sway.

Leaving the room, Nicholas had found Kathi just outside, waiting to take him downstairs. He said, 'He is glad to have her. I was afraid he would resent it.'

'No,' she said. 'Mind you, it's some time since any uncle of mine had a close acquaintance with babies. If she wakes, he will rush out and be replaced by three nurses. Have you heard about Honoria?'

'It's going to be something crude,' he said hopefully. 'One of the dirtier bits from Davie Simpson's selections from Ovid?'

'You *are* having a good birthday,' Kathi said. She negotiated the stair and halted on a small landing, whose window gave a view of Tobie's house and a courtyard. 'Don't you remember Loathsome Ben Bailzie, the assiduous suitor?'

'No. I knew it was going to be a dirty story,' said Nicholas. 'Look. I can see Tobie crossing the courtyard. He's carrying a duck.'

'He's carrying a goose. It's your present. You must remember Ben Bailzie. He was on my marriage list. He was practically in my marriage-bed. You used to encourage him.'

'Oh, him!' Nicholas said. It was a goose. He said, 'And there's Clémence. She's got a goose too.'

'Well, remember,' said Kathi with irritation. 'The Bailzies all want to be rich, and no one ever wants to marry them, so they have a family policy of foisting parenthood on very young virgins of both sexes and then offering nobly to marry them.'

'It's a nice thought,' said Nicholas. 'But *two* geese? Anyway, if Ben Bailzie is the fellow I'm thinking of, I'd be amazed if he could seduce a virgin of one sex, never mind two. You aren't thinking of oysters? They'd go well before geese, if there's time to cook them before he arrives. Or maybe he's come?'

'No,' said Kathi carefully. She put her hands on the window-sill and sat on it. '*Honoria* has come. Ben Bailzie's daughter. He got a rich young virgin in the family way and then was reluctantly compelled to marry her. Result, Honoria.'

'And I encouraged him?' Nicholas said, dragging his eyes from the geese. 'You mean, if I'd succeeded, you might be Mistress Katelijne, spouse of Bailzie and precipitate mother of Honoria? Margaret and Rankin wouldn't like it at all.'

There was a silence, during which Katelijne Sersanders coloured from her brow to her throat, and Nicholas took a breath and then let it out slowly, for he had made the connection; had belatedly realised why she was talking this nonsense. And he was not in a good timber house in the Canongate of Edinburgh at all. He was standing in flickering darkness by the bank of a river, while behind him flames rose from the place of a would-be seduction, attempted by a fierce, lonely man recently dead. Pursued by the same lurid light, Robin, lissom, mobile, an anguished young husband, was seeking help. And before Nicholas, lying where she had been carried, was Robin's wife, Kathi, looking up at Nicholas with the same look in her eyes: the look that even her husband had not yet read.

It was not dark but light, and a matter for joy.

Nicholas said softly, 'My dear?'

And she said, 'Yes. You are the second to know. And I want to tell Tobie.'

Then he gave her his hands, and brought her to stand, small and still slight, against him, within his embrace. 'He must be so proud of you. You must be so happy.' And when she made a choked sound, he added, practically, 'And if it is a girl, you must call it Honoria.'

Then she snorted, and wiped her eyes, and stretched up to receive his salute, to be swept aside by the small, solid person of Margaret, dragging Jodi to see her second cousin Euphemia. Nicholas held Kathi steady, while gazing with her at the retreating children. He said, 'There goes a very happy big-sister-to-be. I like your progeny, Kathi.'

'So do I. Isn't it lucky?' she said.

Down below, rejoining the riotous crowd of their friends, the first thing Nicholas noticed was Robin's gaze, bright and defiant and proud, fixed on him from afar. He must, then, have sent Kathi to break their news to him quietly, tonight. The best gift, the greatest pledge of friendship he could have devised.

A better time to acknowledge it would be found. But now Nicholas went across swiftly, and knelt, and, unobserved in the uproar, said to Robin what could not wait to be said, so that Robin flushed, and lay back, and laughed with brilliant eyes. Then Nicholas rose, and set out to make his birthday one that everyone there would remember, including himself.

*

Dr Tobias Beventini, who now knew and approved of the reason, watched him do it. The guard-geese, which had been bought with considerable trouble, furnished the central motif of the celebration, if not of the table; and Tobie, given over to contentment, enjoyed creating ever more extravagant explanations of their duties and skills. Eventually, watching the birthday guests depart amid a bobbing crowd of servants and torchbearers, with the geese screeching and hissing amongst them, Tobie linked arms with his wife and turned back to where Robin was lying, half-asleep, with Kathi moving softly about him.

The children had gone, with their nurses. Clémence, once Jodi's nurse, was now Tobie's.

Clémence and he had no children. They did not discuss it. It was something much desired by them both, but if it did not happen, then Tobie's life, for him, was still complete; and he thought it the same for Clémence. He wondered sometimes whether Nicholas would now extend the family begun abruptly so long ago, but began to think, as the months passed, that either deliberately or by chance, that door had been closed. He thought he understood. There was the threat posed by Simpson, of course. There was also the age of the children now living. Jodi would soon be nine years old. Henry was already grown, and on his way as a man. And in Germany there was someone else: a young maiden called Bonne, who was supposed to be the step-daughter of Julius, and who was being reared, by her own choice, in a convent. She might never emerge. Tobie hoped that she wouldn't. He hoped that Nicholas might be allowed, now, to proceed with his life without Bonne, without Julius, without Simon de St Pol. Without more children, if that was what he wanted. Nicholas was his own gift to the world. He needed no replication, as Robin did. Or, as someone had said, the family he had was sufficient.

The day, with all that it signified, came to a close. The day closed; the year turned; and the geese screamed, but no one heeded them, yet.

Chapter 16

First of the chekker sall be mencioun made,
And syne efter of the proper moving
Of euery man in ordour to his king.

IN THRALL TO their purpose – that the kingdom of Scotland should be made and kindly wrought, as it were a pair of gloves – the statesmen took note, or failed to take note of the news that now came, filtered by distance, from the outside world.

First of the great rulers to leave, that tall old man Uzum Hasan, Prince of Diarbekr, Lord of High Mesopotamia, chief of the White Sheep Tribe of the Turcomans, took to his bed and died on the Eve of Epiphany, upon which three of his sons immediately strangled their Christian-born half-brother. His motherless sisters escaped. Josaphat Barbaro, the dead ruler's companion, fled in disguise and began to make his way home to Venice. Sultan Mehmet of Turkey gave praise.

Kathi said, 'You went there. At least you went there, Nicholas. It prolonged his life and saved others, that promise of help from the West.'

'Ludovico da Bologna went there,' Nicholas said. 'According to rumour, he was asked to go back by the Pope after Russia. If he did, he'll be dead.'

'So what will happen?'

'Ask your uncle,' Nicholas said. 'Venice will make peace, tellement quellement, with Turkey. It will mean competition for Genoa. Gelis?'

'But opportunities for alum,' Gelis said.

The Bank of the Medici was the next of the great institutions to stagger. On Easter Day, in the Cathedral of Florence, the twenty-nine-year-old head of the Bank and his brother were attacked at Mass by assassins with some help from within, the pre-arranged signal being the elevation of the Host. Lorenzo de' Medici escaped, but his brother died, as did Francesco Nori, who once represented the Bank in Geneva and Lyons. The killers were from the rival banking firm of the Pazzi, encouraged, it was said, by Pope Sixtus, who meant to confiscate the Medici wealth in the Papal States, and end their alum monopoly. Later, under pressure from France, the Medici decided to close their debt-burdened office in Bruges, which Tommaso Portinari had already abandoned in order to live in Milan. Offered the Bruges business on affordable terms, Tommaso declined. About the same time, by chance, another of the long-ago band of young foreign exiles in Bruges was doomed. Lorenzo Strozzi, smitten by a lingering illness, was destined to die in Naples, leaving two little sons by Tommaso's wife's sister, and an older, richer, successful brother in Florence with an illustrious future.

Anselm Sersanders said, 'It always seems better than it was. I know: I remember Felix as well, and all the stupid things you and Julius and everyone did, with the Duke's bath and the ostrich and all those lecherous girls. But everyone has to grow up. Tommaso always did overspend, and what about Nori? You haven't met him since Geneva, and I thought you . . .'

'You thought I disliked everything about Geneva. You should get the whole story, next time,' said Nicholas.

Then he said, 'I'm sorry. Nostalgie de bain. I should probably regard it with horror if someone actually re-created the past. But at least none of us had any money in the Medici. I wonder how Davie Simpson got on?'

'He took out his deposit and lent it to the Abbot of Newbattle,' said Sersanders. 'Who, of course, is one of our rivals in trade. Neat.'

'Oh, I don't know,' said Nicholas.

In Bruges, the young Duchess of Burgundy bore a son to her still younger husband Maximilian, Archduke of Austria. The Habsburg succession was secure.

In Venice, the Doge Vendramin went to his account, and the Turks efficiently captured Lemnos and Croia in Albania, while Scutari starved. The Signoria, which still ruled in Cyprus, felt itself increasingly threatened by the presence of the noseless mother of the late monarch Zacco, and of Charla, Eugene and John, the King's much-loved natural children and only remaining descendants. Of these, it was said, young Eugene (Tzenios to his father) was adored not only by men, but by the very stones of the island. By decree of the Council of Ten, they were all uprooted from Cyprus, and taken to Venice, where they died.

John le Grant said, 'That's why Simpson told you. To make you react.'

'*I didn't,*' Nicholas said.

'*So why smash things now?*'

'*Because I can't find my toy sword,*' said Nicholas. '*It's all right. I've stopped. Would you like to go away and be adult with somebody else? I'm sure you'll find someone.*'

At home in Scotland, meanwhile, there was no respite for busy men. Alexander, Duke of Albany, received notice that his marriage to Nowie Sinclair's half-sister was annulled on the grounds of consanguinity, freeing Sandy for anything, and bastardising those of his sons who were not bastards already.

Within the same bracket of celebration arrived the news that the King of England's brother had been arraigned for treason, poison, sorcery and generally antisocial behaviour, and had been discovered drowned in his bath. Or (according to the current cheap plebeian joke) boiled in a butt of good malmsey, instead of the ale-vat or kettle of your ordinary villain. Whatever, the Duke of Clarence regretted, for sure, that he could no longer observe his obligation to marry the young lady Margaret of Scotland.

The ecstatic young lady Margaret, with her brother Sandy, their friends, and the inventive help of Davie Simpson, Procurator for the Papal Collector, set off to terrorise Castle Hill, the Lawnmarket, the High Street, and Leith Wynd on horseback, blowing horns and preceded by a full pack of hounds which chewed up everything in sight, barely stopping at children. They were halted at the foot of the Wynd by twenty armed men and Bishop Spens, who was building a chapel there, and was also, as yet unreported, arranging with the other responsible lords to contract the ripening Meg, fast, to Earl Rivers, the English King's brother-in-law.

With the Bishop was Nicholas de Fleury, who happened to be passing, and Will Roger the musician, who had just come from a rehearsal at Trinity College, preceded by the College's aforesaid tithe-collecting armed team. The hounds, misled by some ill-judged commands from the Procurator, were inclined at first to be rough, but then the fleshers' porters arrived, with a dripping sack paid for by Nicholas, and the dogs barely moved after that, even when clubbed. When Nicholas peaceably suggested they should all go on to Greenside for some sport, Meg and Sandy acceded at once, although the Procurator found himself left behind, detained by some demand of the Bishop's. By the time he got to Greenside, the others had gone back to the Castle, and he couldn't get at them.

Nicholas himself stayed at the Castle for a bit, until things had quietened, and ended up, as he often did, in Will Roger's quarters. He picked up a guitar. Roger said, 'I suppose that might have been worse. I never thought I'd say this, but I wish Camulio would come back.'

'What's he doing?' Nicholas said, sucking his hand. The string had snapped. He wished he led the kind of gentleman's life that would allow him ten reposeful perfect nails that didn't get scuffed and split and broken on sword-handles and rigging and lathes. He cancelled the thought as pathetic.

Roger said, 'Camulio? According to Bonkle, he's being sent from one court to another; the statutory Genoese, inviting the Emperor and the Tyrol and Naples to fight for the Pope against the Regent of Milan. Before that, he was in prison for months, accused of stirring up Genoese exiles. For all I know, Davie Simpson helped put him there. In the end, the Holy Father hauled Camulio out, Fisher's Ring round the gills, and promptly retained him to work for the See. Clipped and ringed Camulio; free Davie.'

Nicholas fixed the string and sat back. Adorne, kinsman of the Adorno, had never tried to conceal or to justify Genoa's fight to shake off Milan. After a half-baked revolt, which had caused the then Governor to lock himself into the Castelletto, Milan had got Prosper Adorno out of prison, unringed, and sent him to Genoa as the new Vicar. Prosper, delighted, had promptly begun plotting with Naples. He had offered amnesty to all recent miscreants, raised six thousand ducats by common endeavour, and paid the army that brought him to leave. Now he was waiting for money and galleys from Naples. Shocked Milan; free, queasy Genoa.

Will Roger said, 'Shall I tell you what else Bonkle said?'

Edward Bonkle was Provost of Trinity College, and owed his career to Thomas Spens. Edward Bonkle had just come back from Flanders, where he had commissioned an altar-piece featuring the King, the Queen, a token prince and himself, done from life. While there, he stayed with his brothers (or his nephew, or all the other Bonkles with houses in Zeeland and Bruges) and assiduously gleaned all the gossip. Nicholas and Lorenzo and Sersanders and Julius and Tommaso used to go about Bruges with Jannekin, the Provost's illegitimate son, now prudently a son of the Church. Remembering made Nicholas think again of his nails. He said, tearing a noise out of the guitar, 'Yes, tell me.' Then he looked up, changed expression, and resettling the instrument, made it trip a small, flouncing tune in the silence. 'If you please?'

Will Roger said, '*That* is a musical instrument. You are not. Don't confuse the two.'

Nicholas laid it down. 'I'm sorry. What did Bonkle say?'

Roger didn't always relent. This time he did. He said, 'About the Pope. Sixtus wants help. If you have a shopping list, this is the time to present it.'

Henry Arnot, Scottish Procurator and fiery small Abbot of Cambuskenneth at Stirling, had come back from Rome with the same message. It was one of the reasons why the necessary deposition of the Archbishop had been completed so smoothly. Archbishop Patrick Graham, that poor, silly man, now in the care of Wodman's brother. Mad Patrick Graham, whose job Bishop Spens should have been given.

Nicholas knew who else had a shopping list. He said, 'It may be necessary, for Adorne. Would Bonkle find that objectionable?'

'Within reason, no,' Roger said. 'There were other hints in the air. How much would you pay to have Camulio back?'

'Sitting in Blackfriars?' Nicholas said. 'Telling David Simpson what to do? Name your price.'

Afterwards, Gelis thought, in an exasperated way, that Whistle Willie must have got them both drunk, the way Nicholas burst into the house crying, 'Listen to *this*!' Then he saw her face and said, 'What is it?' in a way that left no doubt as to his sobriety.

'It's all right,' she said. 'No one is hurt. But someone has gone to the stables and killed all the dogs, including Jodi's. He wants you.'

He didn't smash anything this time. He just went to Jodi, and caressed him until the sobbing became less, and then chatted. But at the back of his mind, he knew what he wanted to do to David Simpson.

David Simpson himself did not observe that he had made a mistake until the Duke of Albany rode into Newbattle, snarled at the sub-prior and confronted Abbot James himself in his inner sanctum, to which David was summoned. David, his fine eyes wounded, his cultured voice humble, expressed horror that villains should so have attacked the de Fleury household, and even greater dismay that my lord of Albany should connect him to such barbarism as the wanton killing of hounds.

There was no proof: he had been careful. Still, it was unpleasant. The fool Sandy didn't believe him. The Abbot did: the Collector's Procurator was proving a godsend to the Abbot's glorious plans for the monastery, and must not be distracted by baseless accusations. James Crichton was not a shallow or an ambitious man: he was one of the best professors the University of Glasgow possessed. Nevertheless, his mind on loftier things, he was apt to address his peers, without thinking, as students. He could not understand how anyone could be so stupid as to doubt David Simpson. He said so. Albany whirled out of his presence, pale with rage and uttering improbable threats. It was disappointing.

It was disappointing because David had hoped to lure the young ass from de Fleury, to compensate for his own lack of success with St Pol. At one time David's secret admirer, the boy Henry had actually been alienated by the trick with the silver; and the horse dispute had fallen mysteriously flat. The youth was fickle. Sometimes he seemed to want nothing more than to injure de Fleury. Sometimes he seemed not to care.

It appeared to David Simpson that the time was coming when he should concentrate instead on allies he knew would not fail him. He departed to spend a self-indulgent few days at Beltrees, his sumptuous castle so convenient for the Friars' Moor of Newbattle with its precious lead mines and its lavish grazing, so close to the Kilmirren of Jordan de St Pol, with its erratically improved stock and its struggling stud farm. Then he returned, groomed and fragrant and wittily conversant with all the most intimate details of all the cruellest scandals, to devote himself to the serious cultivation of John, Earl of Mar.

After the first, involuntary separation because of the *Marie*, it became more normal for Gelis to work apart from Nicholas from time to time, as well as closely with him. She found she needed both. It still left her breathless, the speed and precision with which Nicholas acted, the volume of energy which compressed itself into each hour. She took his place sometimes, at meetings in the High Street, in the Canongate, in Leith, and was fully accepted, as she had been in Bruges: many women – Cants and Yares, Prestons and Williamsons – helped to run family businesses in every degree, from manufacturing the goods down to shipping them. She made herself get on well with them all; then suddenly found that she liked them.

She worked with Nicholas, twice, on small dramatic productions which echoed the great one that he and Roger had once created for the King. These were also for the Court, with the difference that the Court was to perform them.

It was part of the design, in which they all played a part, to influence the King and his brothers and sisters in small ways which were not open to their official counsellors. The King, for example, was prone to bursts of activity between periods of relative quiescence. Whereas his counterparts on the continent moved their courts to remote regions

daily, hunted, interviewed envoys, held council meetings, dictated letters by the score to their local commanders, James would possibly rally
his forces and leave Edinburgh if some trouble broke out in the north
or north-west, but was as likely to leave Colin Argyll to deal with it.
Most of the time, he went nowhere if he could help it, except to hunt,
and filled the evenings with indoor social pursuits in which gambling
and drinking played a fair part. At the same time, he had shown in the
past a vivid interest in pushing elaborate claims to lands in France and
in Guelders, much as his father did when even younger; and was the
first to offer to mediate in any high-level dispute overseas. The only
time he displayed an interest in building and furnishing was when
foreign envoys were due, and, to that end, he had become deeply anxious
to make money. Some of the ways in which he did it were questionable.

Will Roger said, 'He's timid. All his bishops, his merchants, his
foreign-trained statesmen bring him back tales of the glories of
fifteenth-century civilisation, and the fearful blots like poor, boorish
Vienna. His grandfather married his daughters all over Europe. The
Kings of Scotland have always been courted by everybody because they
can make trouble with England. Now he's at peace with England, and
he wants to make his mark, but won't take advice. Play-acting, he
needs.'

'I thought you said kings shouldn't do it,' Nicholas had said. They
had come together, as usual, in a room off Trinity College Church, and
Bishop Spens had come across from his new hospice, with smears on
his robes.

'I said the confident ones shouldn't,' said Whistle Willie. 'It gives
away how well trained they are. They've got to be. It's like being a
bishop. They're on show all the time. They've got to be trained how
to speak and to dress and to walk, but it's got to seem natural. Yes,
Bishop?'

'Well, everyone has to act in this life: it's good manners,' said Thomas
Spens. A clever, incisive man, he would never tread boards himself:
age had given him a stoop like the crook of his crosier. 'But part of
James's trouble is envy of Sandy. You'll have to write a play with no
parts for young brothers. How is Sandy, Nicholas?'

'Restless,' Nicholas said. In front of Gelis, he didn't always go into
detail about how he was handling Albany. It was another form of good
manners. She knew, however, that he listened to Spens, who had spent
a year as an English captive with the ten-year-old Albany, and who
knew the court at Bruges that Sandy had loved. Spens was deeply
familiar with Bruges, as Bishop Kennedy had been. Gelis remembered

him there, at the Hôtel Jerusalem. It was why he had given up his Linlithgow sinecure to Adorne.

Spens said, 'I repeat, cultivate Liddell. He is mindlessly loyal, but in other ways a sensible man. I hear there is a proposal to make a grand tour of the Marches. I hope you will go with them.'

She hadn't known that. Nicholas said, 'Not before the play. The play with parts for one man and twenty-five women.'

The play was written, and performed, and Nicholas was harried by Will into using his voice, which as usual reduced Gelis to silence and Kathi, who was unwontedly vulnerable, to tears. The King and his courtiers, flattered, agreed to take part, and some of the children who had played seven years before. Young Malloch's voice had now broken, but his place was filled by his sister Muriella, a vision at twelve, commanding the willing attention of all the male adolescents in sight. The performance took place, and was received with ecstasy. Then, before anyone could tell whether the King had emerged from the experience talking like Socrates, Kathi went into labour and produced a son.

Gelis went with Nicholas to visit, and found Kathi up, and Robin asleep, with the infant also asleep on his chest.

'It all got too much for them,' explained Kathi, who appeared to be lit from within like a lantern. 'Guess what he's called.'

'Well, not another Aerendtken,' Nicholas said. Departing from custom, the right to name Robin's first child had been lovingly ceded to Kathi.

'I don't know,' she said now. 'It was quite hard to decide. But in the long run, we felt we might as well give him the same name as Robin. That is, Robert of Berecrofts. Little name, Hob.'

'He looks like a Hob,' Nicholas said, gazing down. 'You could boil a pot on him, really. A small one. What did Robin say? When he could say anything?'

'That now Rankin would have someone to fight with,' said Kathi. 'It wasn't quite what I had in mind, these last weeks.'

'No,' said Nicholas. 'He meant that now *Margaret* will have someone to fight with. Would you like a lot of very fine claret? We've brought some. And also some extremely good news. Do you remember Prosper de Camulio?'

'The alumnus of Genoa? Davie Simpson's absent employer? He's been sent back to prison?'

'No! No!' Nicholas said. 'The Pope likes him! The Pope also likes Scotland, and Scotland has done some rather kind things for the Pope, so that it has been laterally agreed that Scotland should help the Pope reward Prosper de Camulio. He's been made Bishop of Caithness.'

'*What?*' said Kathi. Robin woke up.

'Caithness in Scotland. Bishop. He's busy touring abroad. But once he comes back, Davie will be hard put to it to do as he likes any more. Isn't it wonderful?'

'What?' said Robin. The baby woke up.

Nicholas said, 'I was just saying, isn't Dame Nature wonderful. It's got Kathi's nose and your chin, and can sleep anywhere, like Old Will.'

The baby opened an arched, gummy mouth and pantingly started to snarl.

'He,' said Robin, 'objects to being called it. But you wouldn't know, you're too old to remember. Was there some talk of wine?'

'I brought it for Hob,' Nicholas said. 'But if you insist, you can have some.'

Throughout, Gelis sat, sharing their happiness, but saying little. Sometimes, Kathi, Robin and Nicholas formed, unintentionally, a small unit upon which others did not intrude. She imagined it had been like that, at other times in his life, with other friends: men and women who felt they knew Nicholas, and indeed did, in some special way. She was never jealous; not now.

Fairly soon after that, she began to handle business, as Nicholas did, out of Edinburgh, and with a powerful escort. For her first expedition to the west she had even better protection, for she travelled with that eminent Stewart, Andrew, Lord Avandale, the King's kinsman and Chancellor.

She knew him, of course, from her previous visits, as she was herself known to most of the higher officials. She had served in the royal household; her cousin Wolfaert van Borselen had been married to the King's royal aunt; she was the wife of the Flemish prodigy Nicholas. Once, she had been too close to Simon de St Pol, and had attracted the interest of the King. It had ended in shame and embarrassment for Simon and for James, rather than for her, and the King had since accorded her guarded respect. Latterly, she had been accepted in more general terms, in her own right, since she knew how to conduct herself, and had an excellent grasp of the inner niceties of business. That is, she always knew who was preying on whom, and was an intelligent listener.

She knew by heart, as Nicholas did, the inner structure of the Court. You had to recognise everyone in power. Titles were not a safe guide.

The Master Cook was not a man in an apron. He was the administrator who ensured, if the King wished to travel with five hundred members of his household to greet an incoming embassy, that there would be fleshers and fishmongers, cattle and poultry, cooks and cooking utensils and ovens to provide all they needed for as long as they needed it. He accompanied the monarch to war, and if the King elected to honour a subject with a visit, the Master Cook would present himself and his staff to the host three days in advance, and would be responsible at the end for distributing drink-silver to all the hosts' servants. Master Cooks were honoured with lands and privileges and frequently moved to other eminent posts. Ushers of the King's Chamber Door were equally versatile. They could be Keepers of Royal Castles and pay the King's debts, collect his dues and arrange for his personal luxuries, imported in the Usher's own ships, or those of the King. Master tailors handled everything to do with woven cloth, from outfitting the entire court at Yule, to constructing tents for the King and his army. The new Archbishop of St Andrews dosed the King and imported his books and his medicines. Thomas Cochrane, master mason, built castles for comfort and war, and designed and assembled what was needed to furnish them, both for comfort and war. There was no clear demarcation. They acted, and were rewarded, according to their various abilities, and the order of these was very high.

Of the Lords Three, Gelis had found some affinity with Mr Secretary Whitelaw, who knew Cologne as she did, and possessed a practical knowledge of law which she seldom tired of dissecting. Colin Campbell she usually left to Nicholas, who could match him in malicious urbanity. But Avandale, riding beside her just now, equated more closely to the courtly lords of Brabant and Burgundy, Zeeland and Flanders whom she knew, as deft in the field as when negotiating a marriage in some foreign throne room. A handsome man for his years, Andrew Avandale spoke with disarming enthusiasm of his preferences in music and poetry, and entertained her with faintly scandalous stories of prominent figures they both knew, and brilliantly scandalous stories of courts overseas. About the monarchy, he had no tales to tell. He had been an astute Warden of the West Marches in his time, and guardian of at least two of the great castles of the kingdom. He told her an anecdote, not to be repeated, about the present Bishop of Argyll (a Colquhoun), which made her laugh aloud.

They were riding towards the country of Lennox from which his rents came – the disputed rents from the earldom of Lennox which were his for life, but which might also be claimed by Stewart of Darnley, or even by Haldanes and Napiers. It was a measure of Avandale's character and standing, and also that of Lord Darnley, that the situation, however irregular, had been accepted on all sides, if without particular pleasure. Stewart country such as the Lennox was historically loyal to the throne, and, in this instance, encompassed the salmon fisheries of Loch Lomond as well as the great castle of Dumbarton, built where the river Clyde opened out to the estuary.

Gelis was going to Dunglass, the stronghold of the barony of Colquhoun, two miles short of Dumbarton, in order to talk about cargoes. The Chancellor was to stay overnight also. She had promised Nicholas not to leave the right bank; not to go near either Simpson or St Pol, even if she came across a heap of dead horses. It was hardly her fault therefore that, when she arrived obediently with the Chancellor on the rocky mount of Dunglass, the first face she perceived was that of Henry's fat grandfather Jordan, standing beside Sir John Colquhoun.

'Ah! My dear Gelis. Formidable as ever,' he said. And, turning to his host: 'My son's sister by marriage. We last met in Trèves, when the Duke was alive. How strange to think that all that then seemed so hopeless has now come to pass! The Duke's daughter wed to the son of the Holy Roman Emperor, and with a son of her own. Your own marriage to your Flemish swain refreshed and renewed. Your son Jordan and my grandson his cousin merry shipmates, so they say. Only Julius, your lawyer, has suffered a sad loss, I heard. His lovely wife took her life in a fit?'

'She is buried in Ghent. We are indebted to my lord of Gruuthuse for his care for her,' Gelis said. 'And you, my lord? What good fortune have you had since you came home?'

'Why, none,' he said, 'that compares with the joy of this present encounter. But you, perhaps, are less happy, demoiselle. You hoped for a private talk with Sir John? Perhaps I should offer to leave? Although I have been most hospitably invited to supper.'

Colquhoun said, 'I am sure we all hope you will stay. Our business will not take long, and my lady will be happy to entertain you until we are free. If you do not mind?' He was a capable gentleman, Sir John Colquhoun of Luss, as well as being a man with a trading ship, and a house in Berwick-upon-Tweed, and all the connections you would expect of a former sheriff of Dumbarton who had once held the post of Household Controller and was still a trusted officer of the King's. Whose wife was Elizabeth Dunbar, widow of the forfeited Archibald Douglas, Earl of Moray, and first cousin of Adorne's adored Phemie. And whose niece by marriage was the wife of Oliver Sinclair.

Gelis had come to talk to him, and to his lordship of Darnley, principally on the subject of salmon, and fully expected the Chancellor to be present. Darnley and Avandale had worked together to prop up the throne since the King's father was a young man, and all three had interests on the western seas: imports of the best wine (such as that directed to Hob of Berecrofts) came through Kirkcudbright or Irvine or Dumbarton. But the east coast led straight to the big buyers, and it was equally natural, given the Dunbar and Moray and Sinclair connections, that Colquhoun of Luss should have joined his kinsmen and friends in northern ventures in salmon and barley and timber. The Cochranes, canvassed, had put forward Tam, inconsequentially amassing wages in Nairn, to support at least one promising venture, and others had joined, like Ross of Kilravock and the Cumming brothers, who were intermarried with one of Leithie's innumerable Prestons. Finally, of course, they all needed agents, and shipping-space, and Gelis had those. Although, of course, Colquhoun and Darnley were no strangers to French ships and shipmasters, and knew several who owed them a favour. On the quiet, Gelis had a word about that.

It ended. Men rose, and the chat became general. Bringing her wine, Colquhoun asked if she would object if his wife joined them, with Jordan de St Pol. Avandale intervened.

'Johnny, the family is not well regarded. I gather the gentleman invited himself. Your lady has shown him great kindness, but I think the demoiselle here might be excused.'

'Why,' said Gelis, 'I am pleased to have had this meeting in private, but there is no reason now to keep us apart. The two families are not close, but they are not enemies.'

'Really?' said Avandale. 'I know your husband hoped to achieve as much, but I heard he had failed. Some business of valuable stud horses stolen, and hounds wantonly slaughtered?'

'I am afraid,' Gelis said, 'both were acts of a mischief-maker known to us all. No. If you wish my lord to join us, I have no objection.'

Colquhoun touched her and left. Avandale said, 'Who was the mischief-maker? The gentleman we discussed?'

'Yes,' said Gelis.

'I see.' The short, elegant Chancellor watched the door. 'He is a formidable figure, Jordan de St Pol. I have seen men cringe before him.'

'Not everyone,' Gelis said. 'Even women have been known to hold their own, sometimes.'

'Yourself, naturally. And, of course, the indomitable Erskine. I was sorry to hear of the loss of her son. But Cuthilgurdy had already been granted elsewhere.'

The words were perfectly casual. It wasn't a test. He wasn't even looking at her as he spoke. Gelis made a great effort and kept her voice casual, too. 'Bel? We were grieved as well. I never knew which branch of the Erskines she belonged to.'

'I can't remember. Not, obviously, the main line. Her people all died out years ago, and her husband hardly survived the birth of their son. It seems hard that his name now dies, too.'

'Yes,' said Gelis. Then the door opened and the Lady of Luss made an entrance, with Jordan de St Pol.

The supper that followed was profuse, as befitted a household entertaining the Chancellor. With an equal degree of stately aplomb, Jordan de St Pol ignored the place he had been given and seated himself beside Gelis. 'So,' he explained, 'that we may treat one another with our usual courtesy. *She who loves peril, into peril shall she fall.* Regard the noble Andrew, scion of kings. He attempts the duck: it is a shade too sweet. The plovers? Insufficiently sauced. I had the pleasure, once, of being entertained at one of his banquets and found it hard to know what tribute to bring.'

'Your presence, I am sure, was sufficient reward,' Gelis said. The duck *was* too sweet.

'It was hard, certainly, to excel. But I went to the limits of refinement. I brought him a gift of the first migrating lark,' St Pol said. His chins shone.

'Was it a success?'

'I suppose so. He ate it. I always wondered,' said the fat man, 'what you found interesting in the young Claes. Your beauty, of course, should receive its due tribute, as should his manlier qualities; but what else?'

Pears in crust had arrived, with roast veal. 'What a question!' said Gelis. 'His restraint, perhaps? Although provoked, he does not always retaliate. And whatever appetites he may have, he lacks the vice of real greed. Given your lark, he would not have eaten it.'

'Why, no. He would have tried to make it into a friend. This perpetual desire to be loved. You are wrong. He is greedy, and that is the form of his greed. *The soul is a widow who has lost her husband*, they say. He yearns for heaven on earth.'

'Then he is not alone,' Gelis said. 'Tell me something. Why did David Simpson come to see you?'

'You feel I have attacked you?' he said. 'I hoped, I suppose, that you would be stirred to joust on your husband's behalf, but I see that you wish to disengage. Very well. Master Simpson wished to make mischief, through me. I have been forced to point out, for the last time, that my plans are not his, that he has no means to persuade me to make them so, and that if he attempts to associate with me again, I shall be forced to have him removed.'

'Thank you,' she said. Beside her, Lord Avandale continued politely to present her with his back.

'My dear girl,' said Fat Father Jordan. 'My dear girl, you mistake me. If I remove him, it is only because he is obstructing my view. Why look! Pigs' teats in milk. May I offer you one?'

She set off next morning, and was back in her house in two days.

All was well. Jodi was safe, and Kathi and Robin and their family. Only Nicholas was absent, having departed on a tour of the Borders with a large group of armed men, led by Albany.

Chapter 17

To be a lord but maner or but micht
It is a scorne to euery mannis sicht.

WARDEN'S EXCURSIONS with Sandy Albany had much in
common with the peregrinations of the Court of Savoy.
Setting out with a hundred armed men, accompanied by
minstrels, secretary, chaplain, chamberlain and quarter-
master, Nicholas felt as if he should be attired in boiled leather and
adorned with ribbon knots in the Hungarian style. They had with them
twelve barrels of wine, two baskets of cheeses and a small herd of sheep,
to provide gifts for their hosts and alms for the poor, the religious and
(according to Sandy) prostitutes in distress. *Viva Savoia.* By comparison, the departure of the Lord High Chancellor with Gelis had possessed
the prosaic air of a rather rich sheriff on circuit. The sheriff's food,
Nicholas suspected, would be better than Sandy's.

He missed Gelis, and then didn't, because there was so much to do.

He didn't mind the management of the young. It would take a long
time to accustom red-haired Meg, Albany's sister, to the idea of another
English royal marriage, but, given a chance, he thought he could do it.
He had also begun to re-open, with care, that tenuous relationship with
Mary, the elder Princess, begun during her first marriage and exile to
Bruges. His part in all that had not harmed her, and had even benefited
the kingdom. Despite the lapse of years, and her second marriage, she
still appeared to regard Nicholas as a mentor in whom she could confide.
She now had two sets of children: the son and daughter born in Bruges
to Thomas Boyd, and another daughter and son born to James, Lord
Hamilton, more than twice her age, and now frail.

She did not dislike her second husband, although she was younger than some of his children. Boyd had been the love of her life: she did not seek to replace him, and was content that she had been allowed to remarry a Scotsman; she had not been contracted abroad. Hamilton was courtly and competent and one or two of his bastards were merry company. Her situation only disturbed her, now and then, when she wondered how she was to provide, once a widow, for the dispossessed children of her first family, whose father's land had been forfeited to the King. Anselm Adorne had been allotted a part of it, after he had housed and sustained her in Bruges. When James went to his reward, she was going to require some of it back. Sandy said it was hers. He said that Adorne had certainly made himself useful, but always when he had something to gain.

'Don't we all,' Nicholas had said. 'But the Unicorn Society was a good idea. Jodi enjoys it.' He had seen Jamie Boyd there as well. He was eight, a year younger than Jodi was now. The Hamilton son was only three, a little older than Kathi's Rankin. Both the lady Mary's sons were called James. The lady Mary said, 'I've been thinking. Sandy agrees. Why don't you give me your Jodi to train? He can bring his own man, and he and Jamie can both learn under Jamie's instructors.' She had paused, and then said, 'My brother Mar does not visit Cadzow or Draffane. He and my lord disagree. But Jodi would be welcome.'

Some such offer had always been likely. He had discussed it with Gelis some time ago. 'Sandy will try to persuade both his sisters away from the King and Adorne. This is one way I can counter it. But only if you think it would be good for Jodi. He will be in a royal household, as a page.'

And Gelis had said, 'Thank you for asking me. But you wouldn't even have suggested it if you hadn't been sure. If it's good for Jodi, then yes.'

And now he was trotting beside Sandy – beside Alexander Stewart, Duke of Albany, Earl of March, lord of Annandale, lord of Man, Lord High Admiral of Scotland and Warden of the Scottish March – with all these cheeses and wine barrels bouncing behind, and a hundred men-at-arms, happy to be away from the wife, and ready for anything.

The plan was quite simple: to begin at Dunbar, the chief stronghold of the earldom of March (Sandy's pride), and proceed south by the coast, calling on the controversial Homes at Fast Castle and the other obdurate Homes of Coldingham Priory, and spending some days with the criminally adept population of Berwick-upon-Tweed. Then, following the course of the Tweed and the Border to the east, a ten-mile sweep would be made via a number of good fishing pools to the church and lands of Upsettlington at the Carham ford, the place between the East and Middle Marches where Border disputes were usually settled. Then they would turn for the north, and return to Edinburgh, calling on the Abbot of Melrose (to whom Alec Brown was related), and by the village of Lauder to the hospice of Soutra, which had a good vegetable garden and a sound set of latrines, and a house beside Bonkle's in the Cowgate of Edinburgh.

When Border truces failed and war broke out between England and Scotland, the area about Lauder was a popular mustering-place: it was where, four years ago, an excited Albany, aged twenty, had gathered an army to repulse a threatened English attack led by the possibly superior, possibly cynical, possibly simply ambitious Richard, Duke of Gloucester, not yet twenty-two. The attack didn't come.

There was a theory (held by Bishop Spens and Gelis, for example) that Sandy Albany, one of five royal siblings, sometimes modelled himself on Richard, one of seven. They had first met at Greenwich Palace, the home of Richard's mother in England, when Richard was twelve, and Sandy was ten and a captive. Then Sandy and Bishop Spens had been allowed to come home, and Richard had been sent to the Earl of Warwick's. Richard had gone to Bruges as Sandy had, but not from choice; he had been exiled when he was eighteen with his brother the King. They had stayed in the house of Louis de Gruuthuse, whose wife was a van Borselen. Then they had come triumphantly home, in a ship of the Admiral Henry van Borselen, Sandy's great-uncle by marriage. The Lancastrian King was defeated, and Richard acquired honours and a great household and was appointed Admiral and, two years ago, became the right high and mighty Prince Richard, Duke of Gloucester, Warden of the West Marches for the defence of Cumbria, based in Carlisle. But of course he didn't need to stay at Carlisle, having Lord Dacre to deputise for him; and the Middle and East Marches were looked after by Harry Percy, Earl of Northumberland, with whom Sandy was supposed to discuss all the tiresome frontier matters of purloined horses and cattle, and infringed fishing-rights and wanton injury and destruction, and failure to pay damages or return hostages.

It was stuff for lawyers, and half the time Sandy sent a deputy. He was here just now out of pique, because Percy had called a meeting and then cancelled it, just when Sandy had proposed to attend it. So Sandy decided to go on tour anyway, and visit those sheriffs and baronial officials who dispensed local justice in peace-time, and were supposed to supply him with troops in time of war. And check, as he should, that the decrees of the last March truce meeting had all been obeyed. And observe (his private intention) just how much illegal activity was taking place on both sides of the Border where English and Scots, comfortably distant from central authority and mostly related by blood, were pursuing their own sports and their own interests with blithe disregard of anyone's rules.

Nicholas let it all happen. Once on the road, you couldn't argue with Sandy. But his friend and steward, at least, saw the dangers. It was Jamie Liddell who warned Nicholas that the excursion was mooted, and who kept to himself, in due course, the fact that Nicholas had dispatched a discreet warning to everyone on their route. Sandy could be tactless, especially in the company of Homes.

It seemed at first to promise well. At Fast Castle, no one killed anyone else, although words were exchanged. At Coldingham, Nicholas diverted questions about the future of the monastery, which the King wanted to change, in order to finance his royal chapel music. After the arguments died, Nicholas tracked down those monks who were genuinely interested in music and obtained their approval for one or two new choral pieces, which happened to be signed by Whistle Willie. In between, he visited the scriptorium and had a long talk with the monk in charge of the archives. Sandy came out with a whole skin, and Nicholas came out looking thoughtful.

In Berwick-upon-Tweed, having called on Lauder of Bass at the castle, they repaired to the Browns' roomy mansion in St Margaret's, and got Sandy's bard to perform while they ate. It had surprised Nicholas, in the past, to find that Henry de St Pol had ever heard of a blind poet called Harry, since that particular bard was unwelcome at Court. It had not surprised him, subsequently, to discover that the minstrel, an acerbic veteran best met in the open air, had been adopted by Sandy for parading in taverns and among certain types of patriotic society. He had even, in Nicholas's presence, got the old man to recite the bloodier bits of *The Wallace* for Meg, his unmarried sister, who had burst into tears. Nicholas had felt like bursting into tears himself, but for different reasons. He had no objection to the fifteen contradictory versions of the life of Sir William Wallace, great Scottish hero and martyr, whose left arm had ended up nailed to a gateway in Berwick, any more than he objected to the fifteen lives of Alexander the Great or Robin Hood or King Arthur. He did, however, become disenchanted with Jamie Liddell's deep compulsion to verify facts, which doubled the length of the sessions.

'Where did you hear that? I've never heard that.'

And the old man would bridle. Encased in lid-leather, his eyes looked like pigs' knuckles. 'What would you know? That was a Latin book, that was from.'

'Then the Latin book was by some idiot romancer who didn't know his Ayr from his Alva. Shall I tell you what really happened?'

'Don't,' Nicholas would beg. 'Just don't.'

But he always did.

That night, it was the Lord Clerk Register, Alex Inglis, who entered the room just as Harry was vicariously slaying an Englishman:

> *Wallace tharwith has tane him on the croune,*
> *Throuch bukler, hand, and the harnpan also,*
> *To the schulderis, the scharp suerd gert he go.*
> *Lychtly raturnd till his awne men agayne.*
> *The women cryede; 'Our bukler player is slaine.'*
> *The man was dede; quhat nedis wordis mair?*

The bard broke off. Alex Inglis remarked, 'Good evening, my lord. I see we are preparing to contribute to the peace in our usual fashion.'

Sandy looked furious. It was customary for a representative of central government to accompany the Warden on his visits, which was partly why so many had lodgings in Berwick: the Clerk Register lived in Hidehill in style, as befitted a man who expected a bishopric. The said Clerk Register, at the moment, was suppressing much the same annoyance as Sandy, since he was supposed to be working in Edinburgh, and indeed had been, before Nicholas rousted him out and advised him to speed down to Berwick.

Nicholas caught Liddell's eye, and they began hastily to mend the situation, with partial success. When they all left for Upsettlington and Melrose, Alex Inglis was still with them; but so was Blind Harry.

Back in Edinburgh, Nicholas called first on Anselm Adorne, even before he went home to Gelis. It was safe: Sandy had gone to the Castle and Liddell and Inglis to the Cowgate; Nicholas slipped into Adorne's house in the dark. Adorne was the friend of the King and the Queen and the Knights of St John. Nicholas was a fellow Burgundian, but not a recognised courtier. He was Sandy's friend.

Adorne was there, springing up from a card game with Andro Wodman, who rose also to greet him with what might even have been satisfaction on his broken-nosed face. Nicholas himself didn't want to eat or drink: he didn't even want to be given a chair, but sat on the step of a prie-dieu in his rubbed boots and travel-stained doublet, listening as Adorne told him that Gelis was back, and the gist of her news and his own.

Since the storms of the previous year, news from Flanders had not been cut off, and Adorne was the recipient, as was Nicholas, of many quiet dispatches from unusual sources. They knew that the Medici outpost in Bruges had now closed, and that London was closing. Tommaso Portinari was still in Milan, from which city Adorne had been surprised to receive a small bale of Genoese alum bearing Tommaso's seal and a Biblical text, which those who knew him found faintly alarming.

The van Borselens wrote. Some news percolated from Jan Adorne in Rome, but not overmuch. The many adult young of the family Adorne had had little to say since the arrival of their father's small daughter. Even the cherished Arnaud had merely sent a stiff note to announce the birth of his first son Aerendtken. Nicholas, in his new understanding of Anselm Adorne, judged what it had cost him to confess such a thing to his children, and thought them ungenerous.

He himself had found it sufficiently oppressive to send the same news to his former manager Gregorio who, although now happily married with his own son, had once had a fondness for Phemie. He had had to use less discrimination writing to Diniz in Bruges and Moriz in Germany, neither of whom would be over-surprised. Julius, of course, would not only be unsurprised, but avid for details. Nicholas trusted Moriz to keep Julius fully occupied in Cologne, and not where he could rampage about, upsetting the delicate balance in Scotland.

Relating now the essence of the journey with Albany, Nicholas had cause to remember just how fragile it was. He was not interrupted by either listener until he mentioned Melrose, upon which Adorne caught him up suddenly. 'Davie Simpson had been there?'

'Supposedly on Newbattle business. Of course, it's the daughter-house. I couldn't find out why. Alec Brown's kinsman the Abbot was away, and Alec and both his brothers have this love-hate relationship with Newbattle over the salt-pans and Bathgate. There was also some talk of John of Scougal, the laird, and a law suit.'

'That wouldn't be surprising,' said Adorne. 'They're a litigious family. And friendly with your Alec Brown among others.' Adorne was also friendly with Browns. He had lodged one of them in Bruges, when James had wanted him taught to master the lute. The tasks of a Conservator were multifarious.

'Fertile ground for our Davie,' said Nicholas. 'Andro, both the Browns and the Scougals have sent sons to be Archers in France. Do they know anything about Simpson that we don't? Do you know anything that we don't?'

There was the usual silence. Adorne said, 'Nicholas. For the hundredth time. Simpson did nothing in France that could give us any hold over him. He contrived to leave the Archers when Andro did, in order to share a lucrative post with St Pol. Now that St Pol has turned against him, don't you think he would have exposed any misdemeanours by now? I sympathise. We know that Simpson is planning something. We shall find out what it is. And meanwhile, there is the *Star*. It should be here by Christmas, Gelis says. It is at least appropriate.'

'And Camulio comes when?'

'The word is,' Adorne said, 'that the Reverend Father in God, the new Bishop of Caithness, will return to Scotland in the spring. So Simpson will act between now and then.'

'Or, most likely, between Twelfth Night and then. Good,' said Nicholas. 'I think it is time we finally parted company with Davie Simpson. A public parting. The kind of parting that even the Princesses and Albany will have no qualms about. And then we can begin to bring them all into the fold.'

'You have Albany now,' Wodman said. 'Or most of him.'

'No one has most of him,' Nicholas said. 'Not even Sandy. But losing Simpson will be a beginning.'

Quick as they were, it was late by the time Nicholas left, and reached his own home. Gelis forgave him.

After she had forgiven him, she stroked him for a long time, causing him to sink into a beneficent calm. He thought, through the haze, that if he could stand it, he might even leave home more often. Then he laughed, and pulled on his shirt, and found them both something to drink, and asked about Avandale and Colquhoun. Then he told her what he had told Adorne. They had somehow settled back into bed, sitting folded together.

'It was difficult. Inglis was a great help; Alec less so. Alec doesn't care what happens, so long as he can trade. And I couldn't act the schoolmaster to Sandy, or I'd lose him. I had to let him disappear, twice. That was when he met Archie Douglas. Angus, Earl of.'

'You had him followed? Did Liddell help?'

'Liddell disappeared when Sandy did. I don't know if he likes Angus very much, but that same Archie Douglas is Liddell's landlord in Forfar. Angus rents out a lot of property there, next to Cortachy. And Angus's wife is a Boyd, Tom Boyd's sister. Adorne got some of their land.'

Gelis stopped drinking. Her shoulders against him were moist. A drop of wine from the base of the cup made a glittering bead on the curve of one breast, and began slowly to find its way down. When he stemmed it with two broad, coddling fingertips, she trapped them against her. 'No. Listen. Wasn't the first Tom Preston killed at Forfar? At the sheriff court during a quarrel?'

'Ask Leithie, Thomas the Second. Yes. Thomas One died five years ago. That was when Adorne had gone back to Bruges, and was about to be sent on Burgundian business to Poland.'

'So the quarrel was over his land?'

'I couldn't find out. Someone in Edinburgh knew there was going to be trouble at Forfar and tried to cancel the meeting, but the message didn't get through. Again, justice courts are notorious for dangerous squabbles, and Preston might have been killed by mischance. No one else died. Like everyone else, Preston had been raising money for trade by handing over recoverable assets to people he could trust to return them eventually. People like his own Craigmillar family, and James Shaw, with bits of the old Colquhoun lands of Sauchie. When Preston died, they got to keep them, of course.'

There was a pause. Gelis said, 'Jordan de St Pol's wife was called Shaw.'

'So are a lot of people. She was dead long before Preston was killed. I don't think it's relevant,' Nicholas said.

'But you don't know for sure. Did you know that Bel's last name is Erskine?' She had not lifted her eyes to observe him. Her head pillowed against him, she was watching the pulse in his throat. The two joys of living with Gelis: the challenges and the love.

Nicholas said, 'Yes, I knew.' He stirred his fingers within hers, so that this time she looked up. He said, 'Gelis. I know what we agreed. The only safety for you, for me, for Adorne, for all of us is to be open with one another. To lodge a record, in triplicate, of everything that we do. You know all that matters about me, except for one or two secrets that aren't mine; and nothing about them will ever worry you.'

She held his gaze for a long time, and then smiled. 'No other children with dimples?'

With Gelis, there were no barriers now when he was conveying a truth. Shaking his head, he let his smiling eyes answer. Then he returned freely to nonsense.

'How did you guess? Five in the Curia alone, all upstanding young priests.'

It sounded flippant. No one else could know that something caught in his throat as he spoke. Something very small and remote, like a secret.

It was strange, then, that she lay still at his heart, and didn't smile, or retort, or embark, as only she could, on another complex, ardent, sensual triumph. It was strange and mortally comforting that, instead, she said only, 'I'm here.'

Despite knowing what everyone else knew, Tobie also was happy.

His charges were well. The birth of Hob had transformed Hob's young father. What had been done grimly before was now done with exuberance, including a robust way with his wheelchair which had added astonishing power to the muscles on his active side. With an attendant, he roved Leith and Edinburgh and even, with a contrivance of John's, got himself on a horse. The attendant was as irresponsible as he was, and not much older; they got into scrapes from which Kathi would herd them both home, trying to sound stern while dissolving in thankfulness.

Clémence assisted, while comfortably dividing her time amongst the infants Hob and Efemie, and the older children. She also regularly helped the Princess Mary, which meant that she could be continually astonished by the progress Jodi was making, while checking his lapses in manners. It made Jodi feel safe, if the casual visits of his father had not already done so. Tam Cochrane also dropped by, and bullied him.

Now that he was less needed at home, Tobie had begun to establish a practice. Some physicians, outwith a great household, operated from their homes. Most followed the custom of Bruges and rented rooms in a tavern, which were also used by other professionals, such as scribes or lawyers or notaries. Himself, he liked the Argyll inn, because he admired the great Campbell who owned it. He claimed to be astonished at Clémence when she suggested that the chief attraction might lie with the hostess. But truly, you would search St Johnstoun of Perth and Stirling and Edinburgh before you found a brewster-wifie as good as Lang Bessie.

It was an innocent dream, for a once-randy doctor. As a medical man, Tobie admired the splendours of Bessie, but that was all, for he was also part of a team. Argyll's tavern made just the kind of meeting-place Nicholas wanted, when he needed John or Andro or Tobie to tell him what was happening, or to meet Colin Campbell himself, or Scheves or Whitelaw or Avandale outside their houses. Women couldn't so easily come there, or Robin, but other places were found. It was like it used to be: a team of experts in Bruges. It was better than it used to be: for Nicholas was at the centre, well-liked and well supported; with even Anselm Adorne content to be his partner. Burgundy had been too big; so had France. Tobie himself had once chosen Urbino. Scotland was like Urbino: it was the right size for them all. They could help, here.

He even got to appreciate Conrad, the formidable doctor who had once looked after Jodi. He respected Scheves, not because he was now an Archbishop, but because of the medicine he had studied at Louvain. As for Andreas, the other Louvain graduate, Tobie had long since identified a common streak of levity which had banished all their old rivalry, although he shied from the other man's charts and would not let him talk of astrology. Nicholas plumbing the earth had been bad enough. Tobie was thankful, he mentioned to Clémence, that the lad's divining had stopped.

Tobie didn't realise how much Clémence worried, on his behalf, in case anything happened to Nicholas. Or that in Iceland, long ago, Kathi too had been struck by the place Nicholas held in their lives, and had been afraid for them all, and still was. Kathi, active and chattering, often helped Tobie with his visits. Margaret also wanted to come, but was to wait until she was four. Margaret didn't like being without Jodi.

Yule came, and they all received presents.

The King gave his physicians thick scarlet gowns, and caps with lappets.

The Queen got a new hat from five murders, the King having discovered that he could raise money by pardoning crimes. He had begun (he jested) to pursue some slight misdemeanours for small clothes.

Tam Cochrane received a gold chain. So did Adorne. Nicholas got a fancy engraved ring from Sandy, and another, elegant in its restraint, from Adorne. He felt embarrassed by Sandy's and touched by Adorne's. He wore neither.

Gelis gave him a drawing, once torn and now lovingly pieced together. It was of himself, young and laughing and nude, and it was signed by Donatello, who had added a certain word under his name. Nicholas showed it to John, who went away and didn't come back for a while.

When he did, it was simply to say, 'It's all right. I'm not going back. Or not yet.'

The lure, the enchantment of the world they had left. The enchantment of beauty: of glorious buildings and exquisite gardens, of fabric and carvings; of music and poetry and paintings. The sublime significance of the sea, and the snows, and the deserts.

Nicholas said, 'I know. I know. Some day perhaps. But not yet.'

Sod beauty. The messy significance of sorting out people.

*

The sire de Fleury and his friends were invited to join the Court, which had settled at Craigmillar Castle for the festive weeks following Epiphany.

It had been an open winter. Ships sailed into Leith with tall stories. Lowrie brought a messenger to speak to Nicholas. He had ridden straight from the port, and was frightened and breathless.

'*The Star of Bethlehem!*'

Sir John Colquhoun's ships dealt in French wine and salt, and usually returned to the west coast, not Leith. But, of course, any news from the Narrow Sea would speed, skiff by caravel by barge, to these parts. 'What?' said Nicholas.

It was all that he hoped. The news would have reached Simpson by now. Nicholas sent word to all who should know, and presently set off, in grand cavalcade, for royal revelry at Craigmillar Castle. With him went Gelis and Tobie, John le Grant and Andro Wodman, robed and gloved and jewelled as the festival required, but avoiding Venetian extravagance. Arms were not carried. Anselm Adorne was among the many already in residence at the castle, as was his niece Katelijne, lady of Berecrofts. They had already met the Procurator of the Bishop-elect of Caithness, David Simpson.

Crowning its own hill to the south-east of Edinburgh, Craigmillar had been built by the Prestons of Gorton, who had come from Roslin more than a century since, and who guarded their doors with the Roslin device of a bridge over rock. Craigmillar was halfway between Roslin and Leith: from Craigmillar, as from Roslin, you could see the Pentland hills and the sea. From Craigmillar, you could also see the crag of Arthur's Seat and the David's Tower of Edinburgh Castle, upon which Craigmillar was modelled. The Sinclairs and the Prestons were kinsmen, and had been King's men since before the first King James and his Sinclair guardian were imprisoned in England together. The Prestons' heraldic device, repeated all over the castle, was *argent three unicorn heads erased sable*: hail James Stewart and Anselm Adorne and the late Duchess Eleanor. And, of course, Nicholas de Fleury.

Both Prestons and Sinclairs had houses in Edinburgh. The defensible keeps were outside, on their baronial land, useful for war and for feasts and as a bolt-hole from the pest. Craigmillar, being healthy and convenient for Edinburgh, was frequently commandeered by the Court, which used its secure rooms for its treasure, and caused to be erected massed ancillary buildings for its household. In return, the Prestons enjoyed well-deserved favours, most of them to do with profit margins on luxury goods, but encompassing such imponderables as forgiveness for outspoken females. They shared the same type of posts as the Sinclairs: Nanse Preston now nursed the Queen's children. As a family – a prolific family, fruitful in Thomases and Simons and Wills – they were also rich. A generation ago, a Sir William Preston of Craigmillar had brought back the armbone of St Giles for St Giles. Bruges already had an armbone of St Giles in its St Giles. Edinburgh was almost upsides with Bruges. One of these days, Edinburgh would be the equal of Bruges. Only Gibbie Fish, who fashioned the reliquary case, could have told them that both were left arms.

Tobias Beventini climbed up to the drawbridge and stepped over with the kind of emotion he imagined Nicholas and Willie must have felt long ago, when the curtains swirled back to introduce their famous play. The time had come, and was prepared for. It was a relief and a terror at once. It was a guess, but an informed one, that Simpson would be impelled, at last, to strike against Nicholas. It had been their concern to forestall him.

There were two public apartments in use, of which the upper was that presided over by the King, with his host and his house-guests and family. Below was the temporary hall filled by local guests like themselves. It was one of the advantages of Craigmillar that none but the favoured required beds.

Adorne, it transpired, was upstairs with the King and the Queen, and with the King's brothers and sisters. Bursts of music suggested that Willie Roger was somewhere there also. Periodically, a gentleman of the chamber would appear and invite a group from the lower precincts to ascend to the hall which, although charming, was not very large. Awaiting translation, Tobie mingled with bevies of Prestons, Leithie and Thomas Three among them; and with Sir John Colquhoun and his wife, and Sir Oliver Sinclair and his, and Cristina Dunbar and her husband. He was slapped on the back by Tam Cochrane. It struck Tobie, not for the first time, how many persons of rank were related to Adorne's much-missed lady Euphemia. Adorne, he had reason to think, had hardly noticed this. Nicholas had, for it happened to matter.

You noticed, now, when Nicholas was present in a room. Or you did if he wanted you to. Disapproving, Tobie knew how it was done: how Nicholas could alter his walk so that the weight of his open robe took the eye, offering glimpses of velvet and embroidered lawn and hose-silk; of all the sheaved muscle from the round of his thighs to his ankles. He knew how the candelabra were engaged to illumine the broad, dimpled cheek and muscular neck, and the intimate, smiling grey gaze. And how, when Nicholas moved, the unforced, flexible voice would carry with ease, as over the chatter of rattle-mice. When thus, he drew life to wherever he was, eliciting animation and laughter. It might have been disquieting unless you knew, as Tobie did, how different it could be. 'Stone on one side,' Mistress Bel had once said of Nicholas, 'and skitter-raw on the other, like a badly baked cake.'

Tobie had seen Gelis, conducting a meeting, employ something like the same arts. But now, pale and golden and shimmering, moving smiling among all her friends, she spoke quietly, her back to the room, a foil for her husband.

David Simpson said, 'How we all love him. Zacco's darling, do you remember? If Nicholas came to my bed, I dare say I would take him tomorrow, lout though he is. It is a dangerous magic. It is a magic? No one could pretend he is handsome.'

Davie Simpson was handsome. He stood before Tobie now: a short man with a large-eyed, beautiful face, and loosely waving black hair below the velvet brim of his hat. With swordsman's shoulders beneath the pleated silk doublet, showing the Holland shirt sewn with white silk at the throat, and archer's strong fingers playing with the intricate buttons which were jewels.

Tobie said, 'I like your dress. Not short of gold, then?'

'Not while I have naïve friends,' Simpson said. 'Oh, look! The Princess Mary has sent down her page to summon us all to the Presence. Do you recognise him? The doting small Jordan de Fleury, come to collect his own parents.'

It *was* Jodi, in miniature yellow taffeta and kersey hose, gazing up with glowing grey eyes at his smiling father. Tobie felt cold. Yet they had foreseen this. Simpson would be here: that they knew. So would Jodi. So were Nicholas and Gelis and himself, John and Kathi and Wodman. All of them abhorred by Simpson.

Simpson had been reading his thoughts. He said, with exaggerated relish, 'You are quite right. I have decided that life is too short for tolerance. If something irks me, I remove it.' He looked amused.

Jodi was leading the way to the stairs, which were of the steeply spiral variety that led Gelis to fear for the seams of her skirts. She clutched them, twisting, and climbed. John and Wodman were ready to follow. Nicholas did not at once move. It seemed to Tobie that the other man had been touched by his fancy, and had seen the curtain float back, and had even glimpsed what stood behind.

Then Nicholas saw Simpson, and smiled.

Chapter 18

*And confectioun wennomous it suld nocht
To sempill folk be nother sauld nor bocht.*

UPSTAIRS, HEAT AND noise pulsed from beyond the carved screen that guarded the end of the Great Hall of Craigmillar. The hall, being only thirty-five feet in length, became easily crowded, despite its deep window embrasures; and its low painted ceiling repeated all that it heard. Nevertheless, there was a dance in progress, led by the King partnered by Katelijne Sersanders of Berecrofts, who was small enough to make James look gratifyingly tall. He might, clearly, have been taller, had he not been taught to ride at too early an age. Kathi, chattering to the King, cast an anxious thought in the direction of Rankin's legs, which had not yet embraced a horse, being as yet almost as wide as they were short. Behind her, the Queen pattered along, talking Danish-Scots to Hearty James, the King's uncle. The players, led by Whistle Willie, blew and plucked and banged as stylishly as if the whole room were silently listening, which was only politic. Contradicting this was Whistle Willie's face, which was wearing a hat and a scowl, both unfortunate. The screen door opened, a staff thudded, and Jodi walked in, followed by Nicholas and Gelis.

The sight of Nicholas and Gelis, these days, tended to make most people smile: something they themselves had not as yet noticed. Kathi beamed, and found her greeting being returned by Tobie, which delighted her further. She wished Robin were here. He attended most events, but not those involving dancing, for which he preferred to leave his wife free. Anyway, Willie always came round a day later and played all the music, while Kathi relayed all the gossip, so that he wasn't really deprived. The rest of the time, he was in the counting-house, blithely contradicting his father or Saunders, or chivvying youngsters at Greenside, or showing Rankin how to hold a bow, something at which Margaret was still his superior. He hardly had room for a social life.

Perceiving the newcomers, the King broke off and walked to his chair of state in front of the chimney-piece, causing the dancing to cease, and the music momentarily to straggle, before herding itself gallantly home. His guests presented themselves at the foot of the dais. The King's nod to Nicholas was reserved, and the royal gaze narrowed as, rising, Nicholas was immediately engulfed by a slightly drunk Sandy. Nicholas appeared nothing but pleased: Kathi felt for him. As he greeted Gelis, the King's freckled skin had flushed slightly, as always.

Kathi turned, and found Johndie Mar swaying beside her.

'How's the cripple?' he said. 'Envious of your new son, with the two legs and the busy wee pintle? The very spit of his dad, so I'm told. Do I know his dad, by the way?'

Sandy whirled. Nicholas turned, much more slowly. Kathi held his eyes. Then she said, 'It's all right.'

'No, it's not,' Sandy said, and taking his brother viciously by the arm, propelled him staggering out of the room. Liddell joined him. The door slammed. Talk died, and then surged, somewhat aimlessly.

Jodi's voice, rather shrill, made a comment. 'Hob isn't like Robin at all. Neither is Rankin.' He was looking at Nicholas. Kathi swallowed.

Nicholas said, 'Come on, you're not supposed to be listening to men's jokes about pintles. What are they teaching you in this household?'

The grey eyes slowly relaxed, and the mouth. 'Mine's bigger than Jamie Boyd's,' said the boy. Colquhoun's wife, moving up with Cristina Preston, heard him and laughed. Gelis, out of earshot, nevertheless turned, glanced at them all, and came steadily over. Before she arrived, the way opened for the King's sister Mary who, touching her page on the cheek, laid a kindly arm round Kathi's shoulders. She began to talk, and so did the others. Kathi turned her gaze calmly from Nicholas, who drifted away, taking his son. Unaccountably, the musicians had begun playing again. Nicholas joined Tobie.

Tobie said, '*Christ*, what a court.' He was as red as his gown. He was staring at Mary's sister, the red-headed Meg, who was being entertained in a corner by a deferential man with elegant shoulders. Once, Kathi had been maid of honour and good friend to Margaret, before Margaret's betrothal to the late Duke of Clarence. The possessor of the shoulders, Tobie suddenly realised, was Davie Simpson, Procurator to the Apostolic Collector. He drew a harsh breath.

'I blame the doctors,' said Nicholas. 'And if you make a scene now, I shall *personally* cut your throat. Come and talk to Whistle Willie. Jodi, I'm sorry: Manoli is glaring at you. Should you be somewhere else?'

Jodi reluctantly left. Tobie said, 'What are you thinking of? Jodi shouldn't be here.'

'Maybe not. But I'd rather have him under my eye. There are four people doing nothing but watch him. Who is still to come?'

'That was sickening,' Tobie said. 'What Mar said to Kathi. Sickening. Sickening.'

'I said, Forget it. Who else is to come? Henry?'

'He's on duty till later. The Scougals are downstairs, talking horses with Knollys. So is Abbot Archie. And Abbot Henry. Remember Henry Arnot in Rome? He's back in Cambuskenneth for a bit. But none of the Lords Three; they've scattered to do their duty at home. Some of these will go home as well. This room will only hold about fifty in comfort, and the wine's going round. They expect the Queen to retire.'

Nicholas had not been near the Queen since his entrance. She was Adorne's perquisite, as the young were supposed be the targets of Nicholas. With the exception of Johndie of Mar. He said, 'And Adorne?'

'He's lodging here. You know how well he gets on with them all. He'll come later. Andreas is also here somewhere, and Conrad, and Scheves.' He was making a point. The timber guest accommodation outside must be full. All the Court physicians and apothecaries were in attendance, as ever. And Tobie himself.

'Good. Now talk to Willie,' Nicholas said. 'I know he's blowing his trumpet, but that never stopped him from speaking: I've heard him perform on a pair of brass urinals and order a marrow tart with the same breath. Agreed, Willie?'

Whistle Willie gave a virtuoso bray and laid down his instrument. The other players caught his glare and continued. A dance was beginning. Nicholas said, 'I sent you some verse.'

'I don't need your putrid verses,' said Willie. His chin was wet and the brim of his beaver, descending over his brow, was resting on the ferocious grey ridge of his brows. He added, 'I've got my own writer now. John of Stobo. Doesn't make blots.'

John of Stobo was a royal clerk. Tobie had once heard one of his poems. Moral tales aimed at the King were generally devoured for their gossipy sub-text. This one hadn't mentioned Phemie in the same breath as seduction, but had slipped her sister's husband's name into the story. Tobie said, 'Stobo? Willie, it's tumpety-tump. *This officer but dout is*

*callit Deid; Is nane his power agane may repleid; Is nane sa wicht, na
wyse, na of sic wit –* '

'*Agane his summond suithly that may sit.* Tobie, stop talking,' Nicholas
said.

'Why?' said Tobie robustly, and then stopped and said it again.
'Why?'

'I don't know,' said Nicholas. 'But just stop.'

The argument broke out fairly soon after that, when more fiercely
spiced wine had been brought, and the reek in the hall – sweat and
ginger and cumin, damp fur and pepper and dogs – lay in the mouth
like sour cake, despite all that sweet rushes and kindling could do.
Ill-advisedly, someone had attempted to assuage the consequent
thirst by serving bowls of black, pungent soup which the King drank
earnestly dry, sending Sandy for more. The kitchen was just outside
the screen.

Subject to nasal afflictions himself, Tobie had always suspected some
such explanation for the Stewart disregard of the finer principles of
savour and smell. Unhappily, what the royal kindred did, all must do.
Over the rim of her bowl, the gaze of Katelijne Sersanders, to Tobie's
amusement, appeared perfectly square, while Gelis, occupying a
cushion at a distance, came within a fraction of tipping the contents of
hers into the extremely large fireplace. The Queen by then had gone,
and the King's two sisters with her, Meg with some reluctance. There
was no sign of the Sinclairs. Jodi, returned to the charge of the lady
Mary, bowed to each of his parents, and received a kiss in return, his
eyes rather bright. Halfway to the screen, he broke protocol and ran
back to his father. Head bent, Nicholas received him in a friendly,
murmuring way, his big smoothing hands on either side of the child's
burrowing face until Jodi lifted his head and stepped back, smiling
shakily, and turning, ran to the chamberlain, neatly side-stepping Jamie
Boyd's kick.

The Earl of Mar came in, his eyes lack-lustre, and was contemptuously
filled with soup by his brother Albany, who then let him slip to the
floor with a thump and walked off. The Abbots by then had disappeared,
but Will Scheves, liberated tonight from Metropolitan trappings,
stepped thoughtfully forward and stooped over the youth. Tobie made a
move towards him, and then refrained. Scheves was trained in medicine.
The door opened and Dr Andreas came in, saw Johndie Mar and, after
a moment, appeared to reach the same conclusions as Tobie. He crossed
to Tobie, made to sit down, and then remained standing. 'Soup!'

'It's magnificent,' Tobie said. 'Ask John or Andro. The pot's over there. Is Adorne with you?'

'He thought the King would be going to bed,' Andreas said. 'I was to come and investigate. It looks very black.'

'It tastes quite remarkable,' Tobie said. 'Especially with the spiced wine. Get some and come and sit down.' He watched Andreas go. He found it quite stimulating until the King's voice broke through, a little slurred, a little peremptory. 'Sir doctor! Dr Andreas? We have a command for you, Master David and I. We have a command for all of you.'

Andreas stood where he was; then, bowing, walked to where the King had sunk into a chair not his own and was fanning himself. Nicholas also had risen. David Simpson, at the King's side, smiled and said, 'And you, Nicol. The King wants some magic; and who better to supply it than you, with your divining, and the particular powers of my lord Archbishop and Dr Andreas, disciples of the great astrologer Spierinck? Did he not follow Dr Andreas's father as Rector of the University of Louvain? Were you not there yourself, Nicol, with your young master?'

'You have heard me boast about it,' said Nicholas, a little shame-faced. 'As who would not, when the King's own kinsman the late Bishop Kennedy studied there, and Dr Andreas's father was the Duchess's trusted physician? As for magic' – he flung out an arm – 'none can surpass us. Only bring me a rabbit.'

There was a ripple of companionable laughter, abruptly cut off. The King said, crossly, 'We do not speak of common pursuits, fit for children. We speak of *magic*.'

As he said the word, half the candles went out. The King looked surprised, and then vaguely pleased. Simpson looked merely pleased. The snuffers bowed and retired. Nicholas said, 'My lord King, forgive us. You desire us to leave.'

'We desire you to stay,' said the King. 'And to utilise your pendulum. And tell us when Christ is returning, and when the Pope is expected to die, and how many heron we shall raise in Bathgate bog on the morrow.'

Profound silence fell. Dimly seen, the King smiled. Albany grinned, and everyone present broke into laughter, with the exception of Nicholas, Andreas, Scheves, and some of the Preston family. Nicholas said, 'My lord?'

'Yes?' said the King. 'You mean you wish to be excused? Indeed, we seem to remember that you had little success with your tricks in the past. We expect better things now.' He had shed his furred gown, as most of them had, but although his skin sparkled with sweat, he lay back in the gloom, his lids heavy, his mood one of confused, slightly malicious enquiry. Albany sat at the top of the dais, and Mar sprawled on a step, under the thoughtful gaze of Will Scheves.

Nicholas said, 'I am afraid, sire, that my divining was as poor as you say: I have long given it up. Of course, there was no connection with prophecy, only with underground minerals. Even so, my clerical friends were uneasy and, certainly, the Papal Collector would not approve.'

'That,' said David Simpson quickly, 'is precisely why, with the King's leave, I should like to put it to the test, and on rather more serious matters. Dr Andreas predicted the Duke of Burgundy's death, and it came about. He may have means of telling, even more important to us than the death of the Pope, whether our own lord is in danger. Or can you assure us, Nicol, with your pendulum, that his grace the King will have a long life?'

The candles flickered. Time passed. The King shook his head, as if trying to clear it. He sat up a trifle and frowned, peering at Nicholas. He said, 'We wish you to do this.' John of Mar started to snore and, when touched gently by Scheves, twitched and rolled down a step.

'Then I shall do it,' Nicholas said. He had not given either Scheves or Andreas a chance to speak. 'I shall need a pendulum.'

'Here is a pendulum,' Tobie said. His mouth was dry. He felt as he had at the foot of a mountain in Cyprus, waiting for disaster to strike. What was hoped for was not always what happened. He held out what he had, which was a small silken cord with a crystal, such as he used to test the turn of an eye. Questioned by a practising diviner, a pendulum conveyed yes or no, by its swing. The process took a long time. A voice spoke: Andro Wodman's. 'Nicholas? Here is a bowl.'

The soup bowls had been mainly of pewter, but Wodman's was of bronze. He had rinsed it with wine. Nicholas took it and stopped: the first unpremeditated move that Tobie had seen him make that whole evening. Then he said, 'There are letters on it already.'

'Then you won't have to paint them,' said Wodman. There were letters; Tobie could see them: an alphabet embossed inside the rim. The pendulum, swinging, could spell out its answers.

The fire crackled. The stench hung in the air. Overcome by the heat, some of those further back were comfortably asleep in the dark on their cushions. Two of the musicians were dozing, and Willie Roger kicked them vaguely, his hands slack. Tobie could see Kathi's bright eyes, and the bulk of Tam Cochrane beside her. Gelis had leaned her head on her hand, her eyes closed, and Liddell was blinking. David Simpson said, 'I know it is customary for necromancers to serve up a potion, but you appear to have anticipated us, Nicol. What did you have them put in the wine, or the soup?'

'Wine and soup,' Nicholas said. 'My lord King? Shall I go on?'

'Or doctored wine, as you did once at Linlithgow?' Simpson said. 'Or so I am told.' Albany turned, one hand on the back of the throne. He looked as he usually did, except that he was frowning. Scheves stood up.

The King said, 'Go on!' in a thick, angry voice. Nicholas was looking at Wodman. Then he bent to set the bowl on a stool at the King's feet and, kneeling, looped the silk on one finger.

He had spoken the truth, Tobie knew. Nicholas de Fleury had ceased to divine, not because when he did, nothing happened, but because he didn't know what would happen. He had not chosen the pendulum: for good or ill, the pendulum had chosen him, and had given him its own mindless answers, ever since that day in the Tyrol when, before Moriz and John, the Duchess Eleanor had made him aware of his power. Tobie had seen his hand scored and bleeding where the scything cord and its bland missile had flayed it.

Now the crystal hung, shivering, so that light danced like honey-bees inside the bowl and glimmered in the grey, intent eyes of the diviner, fixed on the King's face. Nicholas had stripped to hose and shirt, like the King, and his throat glittered inside the white, open cambric. He said nothing aloud, but watched the King, and the pendulum. And the pendulum gradually steadied.

Someone groaned. Someone else – Buchan, the King's half-uncle – belched, coughed, and made in a lumbering way to the garde-robe door by the fire. The King said, 'Ask it! Ask it, damn you! When and how will we die?'

It was not a joke any longer. Nicholas lowered his eyes to the pendulum. Gelis, smiling, had fallen asleep on her cushion. As she slipped, Leithie Preston and Cochrane caught her between them, and gave her into the ready arms of Kathi, who settled her with her head on her lap. Tobie saw her glance at Nicholas, but Nicholas had not seen. He was sallow under the sweat, and his mouth was set along its full, curling length, with no puckering dimples. His nostrils looked pinched. There was a small chime, then another; and David Simpson said, 'Ah!' Beneath the theatricality, there was a hint of genuine puzzlement. He had expected nothing to happen, Tobie deduced. There was another small musical sound, and two more: inside the bowl, the suspended crystal was making a peregrination. Then it stopped. Then it vanished, swooped upon and crumpled up hard in Nicholas's hand.

The King said, 'No! It moved! It spelled! Put it down!' His pale eyes were open. He added, 'What did it say?'

Nicholas removed his eyes from Andro Wodman's. His fist was so tight round the weight that his knuckles were white. He said, 'Nothing, sire. I hadn't even asked it a question. It spelled out nonsense, as it does for me now. I can try again.'

'You will,' said the King. 'Here, close to me. And with more light. Sir Simon, we wish fresh candles here, by the stool.'

If his host heard, he didn't answer. It was Big Tam who came forward with his powerful hands and thrust fresh wax into the holders, while Leithie and the Third Thomas brought more. Surrounded by shadows, the King's chair stood alone, pooled with light, and canopied by flickering gleams on the rafters. Tobie wondered if the Prestons had all done this before. Rumour said that they had. But not with a rod or a pendulum, and with women taking part. They were a hearty, rumbustious family, the Prestons, with powerful friends.

There were no women here now, except the sleeping Gelis and Kathi. Nicholas looked round, and Kathi touched Gelis's flushed cheek with her fingers and smiled. Behind the smile was something else. Tobie felt it as well, looking at Nicholas's face. Nicholas said, 'My lord. It is late. If I have any power, it is gone. Might I try for you tomorrow?'

The King said, 'I require it now. I wish to know my fate. Do it.'

Now John had moved and settled by Wodman and Tobie. Whatever was wrong, Nicholas had no means of letting them know. The pendulum should give him no trouble: a small exertion of pressure would produce any message he wanted. In this room, they were safe. All those out of the room were protected. They had gone over these plans again and again. Nicholas had been putting off time, as David was. And now he wanted to leave.

Wodman said, 'Perhaps the reading was wrong. Let me hold one of the candles myself.'

Nicholas returned his finger over the bowl, and let the weight down, steadying it with his other hand. It was no sooner free than it began swaying. Andro bent, his blue jowl and misshapen nose and dripping black hair stark in the light. Within the bowl, they all heard the first of the chimes. The King said, 'I cannot see. Sit back, you.'

Nicholas said, 'It is just the same. The same bowl. It's an echo.' He was looking at Andro, his face haunted.

Wodman said, 'I'm going. Stay. Tobie, stay with him.' He scrambled up, leaving the light where it was.

David Simpson said sharply, 'Stop him!'

John le Grant said, 'It's all right. He felt sick. I'll hold the light for you.'

'You don't need to,' said David Simpson. 'I know what it says. It says that the King is meant to die now, at the hands of his kindred.' He had moved forward and now knelt, swiftly, at the King's feet. 'My lord, protect me. You have been given poison to drink. You and your friends and your brother of Mar. But for me, you would be dead.'

'*Poison!*' exclaimed James. He swallowed. 'By whom?'

Simpson looked round, gilded with light. 'By the Burgundian Nicholas de Fleury, the man who holds that unholy wand, and who dare not let you see the true, the evil thing that it tells. By his fellow wizards, Andreas and the Italian Tobias and even this counterfeit man of the Church, who still brings you your drugs. And by the man who has befriended them all, and instructed the poisoner to kill you; the man whose name I dare not speak. Look about you, my lord. Those who are sick are your friends. The rest wish you dead.'

The King said, 'Who is their master, and the poisoner? My kinsmen, you said?'

David Simpson rose, his face full of pain. 'The poisoner is Anselm Adorne, the other Burgundian. His niece sits there, sharing his triumph. The man who paid them is your brother Albany. I am sorry, my lord.'

The screen door had opened. The men who filed in from the turnpike were armed, and healthy, and wore the Preston of Craigmillar livery. Nicholas rose. The bowl fell with a clang. Simpson said, 'I asked our host, Sir Simon, to help me. The poison was deadly. It came to Lord Cortachy in a bale, supposedly from the Medici, but in fact chopped and dried by his family in Genoa. It is a mushroom used by so-called religious. It mortifies the body and brings the illusion of ecstasy. If you doubt me, look at your brother. I found a way to dilute the poison, but John had already taken too much.'

The King stood. He staggered once, and then mastered his balance, a young, long-nosed, auburn-haired man of medium height, gazing across at the only brother that mattered: the wayward, sulky, athletic brother who possessed the freedom a king did not have, and used it in ways a king often envied. The King said, '*Sandy?*'

Albany had fended himself off the high chair. 'You don't *believe* it?' he said. 'My God, I never thought you'd believe it.' He looked amazed.

On the steps, Scheves hadn't moved. Near the bottom, Johndie Mar suddenly shouted. Tobie looked at Scheves, and away.

The King stood, breathing fast. Then he swept his arm round. 'Don't I have to believe it? Look! Who else could have done this? They said you would poison me. They said you would poison me, Sandy.'

'Who?' said Albany. The amazement was giving way to slow rage. He said, 'You fool, you've been duped. This man Simpson has duped you. But for Nicol, I would never have known. We let him carry out his plan, just to show you what he could do.' He laid his fists on the chair back and shot his face forward between them. 'He hasn't succeeded in poisoning you, has he? By God, if I wanted to kill you, James, I'd have done it.'

'Seize him!' said the King. He was white. Preston's men looked at one another. The King raised his voice. 'Send for my Guard. Bind the Duke, and de Fleury, and throw them both into prison. And the rest. Anyone who hasn't taken the draught. Cochrane is awake. Thomas Preston. The lady, Cortachy's niece. Who else?'

Davie Simpson looked dazed and happy at once. He looked about, his fine skin bright, his lashes dark on his cheek. 'Dr Beventini?' he suggested. 'I cannot guide your grace in the matter of the Archbishop. But Master Roger did not partake.'

'I did,' said Will Roger. 'I've just been sick. Look.'

'I'd rather not,' Kathi said. Gelis opened her eyes.

The King returned curtly to Simpson. 'Where is Cortachy?'

'Here, my lord,' said Anselm Adorne from the door. Moved by the wicked precision of timing, Tobie quelled an unnatural impulse to laugh. Alone of them all, the Baron Cortachy was coolly and properly dressed, his hair brushed under his cap, his fine-boned features serene. There was a page behind him, carrying something. At a sign, he placed it at the feet of the King. Adorne said, 'The bale from Milan. It came unsolicited, with a false seal and note from Messer Portinari. Its opening was witnessed, and the contents certified to be alum, and not agaric. The drug was not imported by me, but by someone else. It is unusual, and can no doubt be traced. Some of it has certainly been cooked and served in some form tonight, although the ill-effects that you see are largely due to the measures taken to counteract it. I am sorry that my lord of Mar has been unfortunate.'

The Papal Collector's handsome agent turned to the King. Then he knelt. 'Kill me,' said David Simpson. 'Burgundy has always been powerful here. You cannot risk offending her. You will believe these two foreigners and their friends, but you will not believe me, who wished to protect you.'

He looked up, his magnificent eyes full of anguish. 'Can you think I would harm you, my lord? Can you believe a tale such as this? That your own brother truly means you no harm, but would allow the whole Court to be poisoned, simply to entrap one supposed murderer?'

'But we weren't poisoned,' said Will Roger's reasonable voice. 'At least, I didn't get any mushrooms. There's my kerchief. You can look.'

'Willie,' said Nicholas. 'Put it into the fire.'

'It's evidence!'

Albany said, 'We have plenty of evidence in the kitchen. The doctored soup was identified, and other means found to produce an effect of discomfort. Master Simpson thought his plan had worked, and implicated himself, as we hoped. Only some of the soup got to Johndie, although he got rid of most of it.'

'You gave it him?' the King said. A great flush had spread over his face.

'Master Simpson gave it to him,' said Adorne. He looked at the kneeling man, who slowly rose. 'He hoped to remove both my lord's brothers and their friends, as well as myself, the King's servant. There would remain David Simpson, spokesman for a Bishop, and the King's sole close adviser.'

There was a silence. John of Mar had stepped to the floor and rolled over. He then attempted to walk. Adorne continued in the same civilised voice. 'His sight is blurred and his senses distorted: he does not know what is real. It is dangerous. He should be watched until he recovers.'

The King said, 'This drug is known in your family?' His voice was strained.

'It is found in convents, your grace. A member of my Genoese kindred so used it, when she resorted to perpetual fasts and became a religious visionary, in response to her husband's philandering. It has no bearing on this, except that it suggested a drug and a trick that would implicate me. I must say again: my lord of Albany is quite innocent of plotting against you, and so are de Fleury and myself. The plot is Simpson's alone.'

'So you say,' said the King. 'We find it difficult to imagine why. And what of the pendulum? What was this fateful message that the pendulum was supposed to deliver? What of that?'

Nicholas answered. 'It was meaningless, sire. The so-called magic was just Simpson's device to fill time until the drug took effect. Then he could denounce his personal enemies as poisoners. My lord of

Cortachy and his family. Others who had offended him in Egypt. My wife and myself.' His attention, Tobie saw, was half on the door. Someone had gone to call up the Guard.

'He accused my brother,' said the King. He searched behind him, and finding his gown, dragged it on over his shirt. Then he strode to the steps and set foot on them. Albany moved away from the throne. James said, 'Was this what you wanted? Perhaps Simpson wanted his enemies dead, but perhaps you did as well? With your King gone, you would never need to wait for orders from me. Then you could challenge your counterpart Gloucester as much as you like, and waste the country's strength in picking fights with those allies you don't agree with.' He was shaking.

'No,' said Albany. 'Yes, I enjoy fighting and you don't. Yes, I want to fight. No, I didn't plan to kill you. Can't you understand? Can't you understand what we're telling you?'

Nicholas suddenly moved. Tobie saw that the royal Archers had come and were thrusting through the door, no doubt expecting some band of assassins. He discerned, among the silvery helms, the determined fair face of Henry. Then he saw Andro Wodman attempting to enter and being stopped. The Conservator made a single, violent sign towards Nicholas, who started towards him and found his arms pinned at his back.

The King said, 'Not yet, sir. No one leaves yet.' Henry, sword in hand, had noticed Nicholas, and Gelis behind him. His face changed. His captain, looking about, also came to a halt.

William Scheves said, 'We are glad you have come. No one is armed, apart from Sir Simon Preston's own men. A circumstance has arisen which needs resolving, and until that is done, his grace would prefer that no one leaves the castle. By your leave, my lord?'

It was bold, for Scheves himself was still under suspicion. He stood, as he had throughout, on the ascent to the dais, although he had descended two steps so that the King, sitting abruptly, was still his superior. Without his ceremonial robes, Will Scheves of the pleasant long face and round shoulders had reverted to a different, well-practised authority: that of the efficient physician-dispenser, the well-read natural statesman who had long served the King. The King looked at him for a space, and then nodded.

Nicholas bit his lip. David Simpson, by the King's vacated chair, bent and straightened, causing a threatening rustle which seemed to amuse him. He held the fallen bronze bowl, cradling it in his manicured fingers. 'Alms, Nicholas?'

His voice was bantering. The beseeching figure of a moment ago had quite gone. The King had not responded and David Simpson had understood, Tobie supposed, that he was not going to succeed. However angry and uncertain James might be at this moment, there were witnesses, there was evidence, and very soon it would be plain what Simpson had done, and he would face the penalty, which was death. The final reward for a petty, miserable life.

And yet his voice was teasing, amused; and Nicholas was looking at no one else. As if they were alone in the room, Simpson said, 'You must forgive me. I had no idea you could truly divine. What a convenience!'

'I am glad you think so.' The King was looking elsewhere. Nicholas added, 'And with accuracy, as a rule.'

'Without any doubt. You saw Andro. I left a message. They will wait for me till sunrise tomorrow.'

'Where?' Nicholas said. Mar was shouting again, and men were trying to restrain him. The drowsiness was leaving the room: as the King's voice rose, issuing orders, the stools and cushions were kicked aside, and the innocent afflicted were encouraged to stand to one side, preparatory to leaving. Among them was Gelis who, to Tobie's eye, had drunk nothing at all and had simply been overcome by sleep. Then she was masked by the trailing shambles of Willie Roger and his musicians, one of whom brushed against Nicholas, who took the chance, presently, to rearrange his shirt-sleeve. Within it, if the doctor were not mistaken, was a small sharp instrument normally used for the trimming of strings.

Then Tobie and Nicholas himself were lashed by the wrist and herded with the other suspects to the opposite side. Simpson, his hands tied, walked beside them, together with Anselm Adorne, as yet unbound. Katelijne and John le Grant followed. Coming close to Simpson, Nicholas spoke, as if continuing a conversation, which indeed he was.

'Where?' he said; and the Procurator, smiling, answered, 'Your castle, where else? How proud he will be, to die there, at sunrise, for you.' Then he was pushed aside.

Tobie murmured, 'What?' But it was Henry de St Pol who usurped what he had been going to say, nodding to the guard who held Nicholas by the free arm before thoughtfully dismissing him and, twisting the arm, taking his place. Nicholas swore.

Henry said, 'Yes, what? What have you done this time, dearest Uncle?'

'Nothing,' said Nicholas. 'It's the Blackfriars silver all over again. Do you know what I want?'

'To escape?' said Henry, and laughed.

'No. To have David Simpson escape. His men have taken a hostage. If Davie doesn't join them by sunrise tomorrow, the prisoner will die.'

'Who?' said Tobie; but he knew. He had heard the five letters that made up the man's name. He was still trying to digest that catastrophe when John of Mar burst through the door to the turnpike. There, instead of descending, he set off, screaming and lurching, to scale the spiral steps to the roof. The flat, stone-flagged roof from which you could see the sea, and Edinburgh Castle.

The King shouted. Men raced to follow. Nicholas swore. Tobie, coming to life, said, 'Mar didn't help you. You can't help him.' Something ripped down his sleeve and parted the rope that bound him to Nicholas. He saw, to his utter astonishment, that David Simpson was one of those who had leaped for the door. Simpson was free. Simpson had been freed by Henry, who had now vanished. A hand, belonging to Nicholas, gripped Tobie hard and propelled him likewise to the door. As men bounded up the stairs, he and Nicholas bounded down. At the foot they saw no sign of David, but Henry de St Pol sprinting up with three horses. Behind him were two riders already mounted: Andro Wodman, looking displeased, and Gelis.

Nicholas stared at her. He said, 'Why not? So where are the Chapel Royal Singers?'

Henry grinned. Gelis said, 'I'm coming. And you'll also need Henry and Tobie. Get up.'

Henry said, 'You could send the doctor away.'

But Nicholas said, 'No, we can't.'

He didn't explain. To Tobie, he didn't have to explain.

Five letters. Robin.

Chapter 19

Sen thow has maid this cruell instrument,
Go preif it first, for this is myne entent.

THE WINTER SUN rises late in the north, and does not care whether it looks upon the new-born, or the expiring, or the prisoner whose execution it has brought. A party of five active people had set out to find a young man by sunrise, but to do this, they had to cross sixty miles of moorland, ravines and hills in the dark, following indistinct muddy tracks and stopping only to change their tired horses where they could, and to snatch some food and drink to keep them in the saddle. There was no time to rest.

Gelis, dame de Fleury, had ridden far and fast on business before, and had helped to manage a tough band of mercenaries before the battle that destroyed her husband's company, as it had half destroyed Robin of Berecrofts, in whose cause she was making this journey. She had ridden far and fast, but rarely in darkness, like this, in a group of which Nicholas became immediately the leader, even though Wodman, his elder, was there.

Wodman and Tobie, she supposed, were in their forties. Henry must be barely eighteen. She was not sure why Henry had chosen to come. He had long since become disenchanted with Simpson, and had displayed a ghoulish delight in the scenes at Craigmillar. Yet he had freed Simpson immediately when Nicholas asked him. It might, of course, have been for the sake of the hostage. Perhaps. More likely, Henry had elected to reverse last year's episode of the oyster-sellers for his own entertainment. Nicholas had told her enough about that to explain Andro's thrice-broken nose, and the present scowl over and under it.

As yet, Henry didn't know who the hostage might be, except that he was clearly important and rich. Nicholas claimed not to know either. In fact, they all did. That was why Tobie was here. Tobie was not going to see squandered the long struggle to bring Robin safely back home and to give him a life of his own. He fulminated, and Gelis sympathised, for she could not understand, even yet, how this had happened. There existed iron-clad rules for protection, especially on occasions like this, when Nicholas and Simpson might be together. Ever since the Milanese bale, they had been on guard against poison. Yet Robin, in the care of his father, of Sersanders, of Clémence, had been captured – the least likely victim, you would think: helpless, difficult to transport, of little importance to anyone.

So your normal bold plotter might think. But Davie Simpson knew Nicholas, and knew Kathi. Davie Simpson had been in no doubt what threat would bring Nicholas most quickly, apart from one to his family.

And now what? But she did not have to think of that, for Nicholas himself talked it over as they rode.

He took Henry beside him, since Henry was a member of the Royal Guard, and would make the arrest when they found Simpson. He also consulted Henry and Wodman at the various places he halted: at Malcolmston, to borrow cloaks and spare hacks from the Browns; at Bathgate for torches and food. There were blankets strapped to the saddles that Wodman had brought; Gelis had made no change to her wide-skirted gown, and observed the wreck of its nap without regret. She listened to Nicholas, talking.

'Andro found out the hostage was going to Beltrees, and sent two men on ahead. The hostage will be there by now, but Simpson won't. He has to get there by daybreak, he claims, or the hostage will be killed. It may be true. It may be that he has told his men to wait a while longer. But if the morning wears on and he doesn't arrive, his men are going to think he has been captured or killed, and flee themselves, after killing their prisoner.'

'How many men does he have?' That was Wodman.

'Oh, I don't think you need worry.' That was Henry. 'Half a dozen servants, who'll run, and not more than twelve bowmen and grooms he brings in when he's in residence.' Alone of them all, Henry wore a plumed helmet, cuirass and greaves, and carried a sword. He added, 'If your men are so far ahead, why didn't you tell them to catch Simpson and bring him back to us?'

Nicholas answered before Wodman could, in a thoughtful way. 'It's possible, but, as I said, time is the problem. Simpson will have to stop now and then, if only to try and pick up fresh horses. It's my guess that he'll follow the Newbattle route. The monks travel this way all the time, and are well thought of in the cots where they stay. The same places will welcome Davie, and perhaps hinder us, if he's told them some story. I think we'd be better avoiding them meantime. I'd like to know when he's close to the tower, and then take him before he gets in. After that, it's his life in exchange for the hostage's.'

Henry said, 'He wouldn't agree. If he did, you'd just besiege him and kill him.'

Gelis said, 'Or what about swearing an oath? If he has the hostage brought out, you will let Simpson and his men escape to wherever they want. They could ride to Dumbarton and take ship.'

'Dumbarton wouldn't do,' said Nicholas. 'In fact, none of it will do, because he wouldn't trust us.'

'So?' said Tobie. She had thought he had gone to sleep in the saddle.

'So,' said Wodman, 'it's not worth talking about, because he's got a head start, and the chances are that he'll get into Beltrees long before dawn, while my men are still trying to track him. In fact, he may not be going to Beltrees at all. His prisoner may be somewhere quite different, and we are not going to get there by daybreak.'

'So we go home,' Henry said. The sneer was familiar.

'We could,' Nicholas said. 'Or we could think it through a bit further. Beltrees is where Simpson has protection, on a route that he knows well at night, and far enough away to dodge large-scale pursuit. He's likely to go there. And he's likely to have told us where to go, because above all else he wanted me to follow. Now he's got Andro and Gelis and Tobie as well, he's going to be ecstatic.'

'Why?' said Gelis. The streaming torchlight showed Wodman looking surprised. Men.

'I suppose because he wants them all dead,' Henry said. 'I rather think I come into that category too. So we may have to storm the tower? We could do with more men.'

'I thought of sending to Semple,' said Nicholas. 'He's the sheriff of Renfrewshire. We'll get there before he does, but it might help.'

Wodman said, 'I told you. I sent to Semple while I was waiting for you. Then I wondered if I'd done right.'

'I'm sorry. It must have been the soup,' Nicholas said. 'No. I'm sure it was right. We'll get there first to negotiate. Then the heavy troops can come up.'

Very soon after that, Wodman's first henchman appeared out of the darkness to tell them that Simpson had been seen. He was still riding west, and on a route that would take him to Renfrewshire.

The messenger was reeling with tiredness. Wodman kept him for a bit, then sent him off to beg an hour on the hay in some farm. Henry helped him find one.

While he was away, Gelis moved beside Nicholas. He said, 'Are you tired?' There was no weariness in his own face. He looked calm, and steady, and competent. He was concerned for her. He did not show what he might be feeling for Robin.

Gelis said, 'Yes, of course, but not beyond reason. Nicholas? This is all because Davie wants you to face him. Wants you more than his own life, perhaps.'

'It's the one problem,' he said. 'What will Henry do when he discovers, too late, that the prisoner isn't a prince with a marriageable daughter?'

'Blame you,' she said. 'Then act like any careless superior, throwing a crumb to some once-favoured cripple.' She paused. 'Not as good for his character as you'd like.'

'You can't have everything,' Nicholas said. Behind, a faint drumming told that Henry was now catching up. Gelis prepared to drop back. Nicholas said, 'No. Stay. To hell with Henry and his character. It's one of the privileges of being married, to ride with one's wife. Especially when being shown so much leg. I like that one.'

'I've got another just like it,' said Gelis.

He smiled: the great, glorious smile she remembered from Bruges, and suddenly she was fresh, and supple, and tireless once more.

'Remind me, some time,' he said.

She loved him. She loved him also for what he had said without words. *You are my beloved wife. You are one of this group, upon which a man's life depends.*

Fatigue, however well managed, cannot be held off for ever. Towards the end of that night, the cold deepened, and the mud stiffened, so that the worn horses stumbled and slid, and riders, half asleep, were jerked awake. Nicholas increased the number of halts, and then didn't. Simpson was racing somewhere ahead, and ahead of him rode the soldiers carrying Robin, chilled and jolting and helpless. If Robin had survived the long night at all.

Travelling west, Gelis noticed, Nicholas avoided not only the route of the Newbattle monks but also the castles which might have been expected to succour them. Templehall, the ancient home of Old Will of Berecrofts, was thirty miles to the south-east of Beltrees, and too far away for a messenger. Nearer but also ignored were Hamilton's Draffane, and Avandale's place by Strathaven. It was partly, she supposed, for Robin's sake, for Simpson's capture would matter more to these men than his prisoner. It might even have been for the opposite reason: that the position of Simpson, of Albany, of Nicholas himself was not yet legally clear, and the King's men should not be asked to commit themselves.

As their destination drew nearer and the hour became later, however, Nicholas did call on some friends. The Cochranes, where they crossed the Black Cart, provided their last change of horses, and a Johnstone brought out wine and would have given them arms, if Nicholas had allowed him. Their previous stop had been a short one at Paisley, where Gelis had been brought indoors by nuns, but had refused to stay. When Nicholas left, he had a sheathed sword at his saddle-bow, and had given another to Tobie. Gelis didn't ask any questions. Nicholas had once presented a window, she recalled, to the Abbot. In honour, she further recalled, of the now disgraced Archbishop replaced by Will Scheves. On the other hand, Paisley traditionally cared for the sons of the monarch, and those who befriended them.

It was there that they heard of a horse litter, travelling fast, which had called at another hospice that night. It had been making west also, but very much earlier. Poor soul, a sick man having to journey that way, in the dark. God be good to him.

Gelis heard Nicholas's voice as he thanked them, and saw Tobie's face. She felt like that, too. They were following Robin, and he was alive.

The sky was lightening.

Nicholas said, 'It's all right. We shall be in time.' He must know, as she did, that the Cochranes would now rouse their neighbours and that, inescapably, armed men would join them sooner or later. All Nicholas was really concerned about was reaching Simpson before them.

She had realised, long since, what the bargain was going to be. So had Tobie and, she thought, Wodman, although his manner throughout had been one of reserve: a powerful, silent lieutenant. Henry, the youngest, the least tired, had made his opinion known several times. 'I've told you! Simpson has twelve men, twenty at most! All these families will turn out and help us take them!'

'So you stay and bring them,' Nicholas had said, the last time. 'I want to get Robin out first.'

'*Robin!* Robin who?' Henry had said. Tobie and Wodman had exchanged looks. It was the first time the name had been mentioned.

In the ensuing silence, Henry's face had grown scarlet. He had said, 'Berecrofts! The living corpse who thinks he helps with the training at Greenside? I'm here – You got me to release Simpson because of one cripple who happens to be married to Anselm Adorne's niece?' Then he said, 'And you knew it?'

'I knew it,' said Wodman. 'I didn't tell you. I didn't think that it mattered. I want Davie Simpson brought to justice. So does everyone else. Getting Robin out is Nicol's affair.'

'Why? Because he cuckolded him?' Henry said.

'Of course. That's why I don't want him killed,' Nicholas had said. 'So you stay behind and come with the local reserves. It isn't your fight.'

'Yes it is, since you made me free Simpson,' Henry said. 'He might escape you. I'll see that he's taken.'

'That's what I thought,' Nicholas said. She could make out his eyes as he said it. And the deepened lines by his mouth, and the deliberate set of his shoulders, moving only to the gait of his horse. She could make out woodlands from moor, and then sky from a line of low hills in the distance. In a long black hollow, water glinted. By the time they reached it and turned their horses up the slope from its banks, points of light could be seen, and the shapeless smoke of newly stirred fires, grey in the darkness.

She knew where she was, for she had taken this way to Beltrees with Bel. The path they were climbing led to the ridge above Simpson's castle, which had once belonged to Nicholas. And the dark blur they had passed at the loch-end was Elliotstoun Castle, the home of the Semples.

It was empty. They knew as much from Wodman's second scout, who had discovered it lightless and unresponsive when sent ahead to find out what he could. The same man, casting about, had found a herdsman to tell him that a party of horse had arrived some hours since, and made its way up the same ridge they were climbing, followed after some time by a single rider.

It could be anyone. They had to believe that it was the detachment carrying Robin, followed by Simpson himself. In which case, Simpson's plan had succeeded. He was locked in his tower, waiting to bargain with Nicholas.

Nicholas said, 'I think we dismount. Henry, you glitter. Stay here with the horses and Andro's man. Gelis –'

'I'm coming,' she said. They spoke in murmurs. The harness chinked, and was still as the tired horses drooped. Their footsteps sank into grass. It was so quiet that a raucous pulsing of gulls' cries was shocking. A blackbird uttered a query, and was answered, and far below, on the water, a line of duck rose with a paddling splash. Tobie trudged up the slope with her, and they lay down beside Andro and Nicholas at the edge of the ridge. Below, she recalled, was a gentle hollow, sunlit by day, but a pool of darkness by night. Beyond was the sky, free of cloud to the south and east. The stillness before dawn in the country; the hour that refreshes the soul.

Of course, they were expected. Approaching, they had put out their torches, but the sound of their horses would carry. Simpson's scouts would have seen them, and reported back to the fortress. We can negotiate. There is only a handful of men, and a woman. Gelis closed her eyes, and opened them, and looked down not into darkness, but into the searing bright bower of elfland, standing open, and vile, to receive her.

She choked. Then Nicholas's hand closed over hers, and she looked again, with her mind.

The tower of Beltrees lay like a courtesan in its gardens below her, coruscating with light; garlanded with lanterns; set with lamps and torchières and candelabra which sparkled and flickered and danced in the clear, icy air. A whimsy; a seemingly innocent gesture; a welcome from a dangerous man who wished to indicate that he, and he alone, was master here. She understood. Her heart slowing, she set it aside, and studied the buildings.

She had last seen this place as Tam Cochrane had designed it for Nicholas: the old keep restored and embellished; and the guest-houses, chapel and hall added in harmony with it, spare of ornament and simple in line, round three sides of a square. All the extravagance had been reserved for within.

Now she saw what David Simpson had done, through the architect he had employed in place of Tam. Cochrane's refusal no longer surprised her. In remaking Beltrees, Davie Simpson had debauched his own tastes to achieve a work of outrageous vulgarity. Now the walls, patterned, coloured and gilded, had grown upper storeys with lavish dormers encrusted with foliage and offensive grotesques. False chimneys, gnarled with sculpture, rose into the sky. The stables looked like a brothel, and the old keep itself had lost its discreet ornaments and its dignity in a welter of painted accretions.

At this moment, it mattered to none of them. What mattered now was what the brilliant light was meant to expose: that every door of every building stood open, and every shutter as well. That there were no horses left in the stables or dogs in the kennels or birds in the mews. That there were no men to be seen, for the place was deserted.

The light from the great double doors spilled down the steps, augmented by the bright lantern above them. The yard before them showed the trampling of many boots, and the stable-yard was deep in freshly churned mud. The exodus had just taken place.

Wodman said, 'You thought he would wait for you.'

'Maybe he has.' It was Henry, arrived glittering where there was no point in concealment. 'Maybe it's an invitation. So what do you think, *Uncle?*'

Nicholas didn't answer. Tobie said, 'I don't think I can get up. I certainly don't think I can get on that horse and follow them. Do you think they know that?'

'I don't know. Stay here. I'll go down.' Nicholas had got to his feet and stretched a hand for the reins. Henry kept them.

Henry said, 'I rather think that may be what he's hoping for. Why don't I go first and see? Since I do have some protection?'

There was a pause. 'All right,' Nicholas said. 'You go first, and I'll walk behind you. The others can wait. If they have artillery, you might as well all go away.'

'They don't,' Henry said. He should know. Kilmirren was not far away.

Wodman said, 'Don't be a fool. We'll all come.'

Again, Nicholas didn't argue. She supposed that, like them all, he was thinking of what he might be going to find. If the nature of the challenge had altered, David would no longer need Robin.

They mounted, and achieved the ridge and rode down to the trampled forecourt, and across to the steps, where there were tethering-rings. Wodman's man took the horses. Nicholas said, 'Let's not walk through the front door to begin with. Let's start somewhere else.'

'You've done this before,' Andro said.

It was Andro he kept at his side during that swift and vigilant tour, with Henry strolling behind in supercilious mode, and Tobie and Gelis to the rear. Beginning with the outlying quarters, Nicholas walked through each room, finding no one, and leaving the keep to the last. Then he entered that, from the cellars, and began to make his way up. The rest followed.

They had seen nothing: no vibrating crossbows, no threatening weights. No douches, no iron birds shrilling, no traps that opened, where mattresses should have been laid. This time, Gelis was forbidden to lead, and Tobie held her arm as they walked. There had been kegs in the cellar, labelled and sealed and laid beside other crates, all clearly merchandise. Some of them contained artillery powder, but there was no actual artillery, only a store for hand-weapons, which was empty.

Nothing else had been removed. Inside, the castle was as Davie Simpson had furnished it, which was as a palace owned by a prince. Nicholas, squandering money, had packed this building with expensive objects, now gone, and Bel had done the same, in her dogged efforts to drain his resources. The furnishings purchased by this owner – the sumptuous inlaid patterned beds, the Flemish paintings, the Italian sculptures, the painted coffers, the Turkey rugs and the knotted pile carpets from Naples, the arras, the Florentine glazed terracotta, the velvet pillows and the tooled leather cushions, the tall, carved chairs and the plaster-work, the painted glass, the carved, gilded cupboards, the walnut firescreens and the embroidered Venetian hangings were the *chefs-d'oeuvres* of craftsmen from all over the world, commissioned, chosen, assembled by a master, in deliberate contrast to the carcass that housed it. It appeared priceless. Gelis could guess what it cost. She knew where the gold came from.

Of course, Nicholas also would know. He showed no awareness of it. Only, as the ascent led towards the more private chambers of the keep, he became more withdrawn. When he reached the door to the small hall, he stopped dead.

Wodman looked at him. Beside Gelis, Tobie also had come to a halt, his gaze sharp. She couldn't see what was wrong. The cressets guttered. The stairway above was now dark. Below, dim in the powdery air, there swam the rose-coloured ghost of some window.

The reason why they had stopped she now saw. Unlike all the rest, the door they were facing was shut. Wodman started to move, but Nicholas was quicker. Before he had taken a step, Nicholas had closed his hand on the knob and pressed the heavy door open. When it was wide enough to admit him, and no wider, he entered.

A voice said, 'This is a knife, my lord. Come in, alone.'

A soldier's voice: unknown; peremptory. Nicholas halted. Wodman put his hand on his sword.

A second voice spoke. 'I am afraid you are too late, Nicholas. Dawn has come.'

The dulcet voice of the owner of Beltrees, David Simpson.

Henry, also, had silently drawn his sword.

Then the third voice made itself heard. A voice of authority, faintly amused, faintly languid, wholly contemptuous. 'It has been a night of disappointments, has it not? My good Claes, come in and give up your sword, unless you want to be killed. I shall also accept my grandson and Andro, disarmed. Your lady and the doctor must wait. My men will show them where.'

The silence of the castle was broken. Running down the stairs from above there came men in light armour, with a familiar crest on their sleeves. The crest of the speaker, Jordan de St Pol, lord of Kilmirren.

There were too many to fight. Driven back to the stairs, Gelis eventually did what she was told. So did Tobie. Then the door closed on Nicholas, and Andro, and Henry.

Chapter 20

Oftsys in perrell and oftsys ar thai tynt,
Slauchter is wrocht and landis braid ar brynt.

SIXTY MILES THROUGH the night without sleep is no particular feat for a fit man, such as Nicholas de Fleury, who has been careful to eat and drink little, and who has prepared himself for most things, even this. This had always been possible.

The door closed, and he stood still, assimilating the room. It was not full of soldiers. There was no one before him but Simpson, standing alone in the centre, and Kilmirren himself, ensconced against the far wall in a chair by a brazier, sipping wine. Even the man who had disarmed them had gone. Nicholas remained, with Wodman and Henry behind him, and wondered, mildly, what the odds really were.

The hall before him was familiar enough, but not its contents, which glittered under the sconces. There were so many lights that the growing pallor outside hardly showed; and the exquisite David stood illuminated like a small, revered object, of the kind generally attached to a basin of flowers. That he was also a murderous swordsman must not be forgotten. Unlike Nicholas, he had had time to change from travel-stained court dress, and wore a quilted tunic and shirt which did not quite hide his muscles. His hair was uncovered, and his lips curled above the dark, dimpled chin. He said, 'You did want Berecrofts dead? I was counting on it.'

Nicholas said, 'Naturally. I counted on your counting on it.' He could tell where Henry was from his grandfather's eyes. Wodman also stood without sound, but close enough to a table for his reflection to shimmer across it.

Nicholas couldn't decide whether the helpfulness was deliberate or not. He had mostly considered it genuine, the enmity between Andro and David: the ugly black man and the beauty, both of whom had once fought side by side in the King of France's Royal Guard; both of whom had once worked for the fat man now watching and sipping, watching and sipping over there.

Jordan de St Pol had expelled David, who had exceeded his orders and entertained hopes of usurping his business. David had briefly recruited Gelis to the same company, and no doubt once hoped to share in her wealth. David had not enjoyed her rejection, or her cleverness, or the fact that Wodman had kept St Pol's trust when he hadn't. David could not comprehend or forgive the success, financial or sexual, of anyone who did not look like David. Wodman didn't look like David. Neither did he.

And Wodman? Wodman had given personal service to the old man, and to the French King, and now was independent of both, with a high position owed to Adorne. Andro Wodman had fought beside Nicholas. He had saved Jodi's life. He had protected Bel. He had also collaborated with Nicholas in protecting Henry. He could not possibly know whose son Henry was. Without Wodman, they wouldn't be here.

Henry didn't know whose son he was either, and never would. You didn't have to consider whom Henry would choose, because it was a foregone conclusion.

So you weighed up the chances, and played accordingly. You tried to forget Robin, for what was done was done. Afterwards, if you lived, you could afford to be human. Meanwhile –

Nicholas said, 'If we are talking, do you mind if we sit by the brazier? There are some terrible draughts in this room. I always used to keep a screen there. So now tell me . . .' He walked across and sat down by Kilmirren. The other two hesitated, and then did the same. Nicholas repeated, 'So now tell me. What did you think when you heard of the *Star*?'

He was concentrating, with a pleased air, on Simpson. 'I do hope you heard of the *Star*? *Star of Bethlehem*? Taken by pirates in the Narrow Sea? Colquhoun hopes to get the ship back, but I fear for the cargo. I heard it represented all your reinvested Florentine savings.'

'There are laws,' Simpson said. He let the three of them pass and sit down, and then walked to a settle and leaned on it. Drawing him, Donatello would have fainted.

Nicholas managed, without difficulty, to forget Donatello. He said, in the same friendly way, 'Not in wartime. France is blockading Flanders.

Remember the problems with Benecke's mixed English cargo? Poor Henne's altar-piece is in Danzig yet. I shouldn't be surprised if this consignment hasn't gone the same way. Paúel's widow and daughter will be rich.'

'I'm happy for them,' Simpson said. 'Is this a way of expressing superiority? If so, I am tempted to mention a matter of gold.'

He sounded, as Nicholas had, perfectly calm. Henry blinked.

'My gold?' Nicholas said. 'I don't see it here. Have you buried it?'

'In a way,' Simpson said. 'It has been converted. It has rebuilt and furnished this house. You are sitting on it. You are standing on it. It has clothed the walls and painted the rafters above you. In your hands, it would have been dross.'

'I sometimes suspect Ochoa had the same theory,' Nicholas said. 'So when you die, where does it go?'

'To me,' said Jordan de St Pol lavishly, from over the brazier. 'As you have guessed.'

It was the first time he had spoken since the beginning. His morning beard, a silvery nap, coated the unconfined rolls of his chins. His eyes above it were fixed on Nicholas.

'I hesitated to broach the matter,' Nicholas said. It emerged sounding bemused. He removed his own gaze, a shade late. He felt giddy, actually giddy, with relief. *The bastard. The bloody-minded old bastard.* The fat man's eyes did not change.

Henry said, 'What do you mean, Beltrees will be ours?' It was rare, these days, for his voice to split.

The old man said nothing, nor did Simpson. Wodman was still looking down. Nicholas explained, like a good marionette. He said, 'As a reward for capturing Master Simpson, and stopping him from blowing everyone up. The King will confiscate Beltrees, and Sir Thomas Semple will request that it be passed to the neighbouring owner, your grand-father.'

Henry said, 'I sent a man to my grandfather, while we were all riding to Beltrees. I told him where to find Berecrofts and Simpson. That was me.'

Nicholas said, 'Well, it was risky, but it worked.' He hoped Wodman wouldn't speak.

Wodman said, 'Good God, I warned Monseigneur well before that. It let him join up with Semple and come and clear this place out. Am I right?'

'Yes, you are right,' said the fat man. 'Sir Thomas surrounded this tower with his men and mine. All the Beltrees men surrendered, and

are now locked in Kilmirren. Their captive was found, and used to
entrap David, in turn, when he arrived. David, of course, is my prisoner,
thanks to Andro.' He turned his indolent eyes on his grandson. 'That
was him.'

The bastard, indeed. There was nothing to be done.

'And Berecrofts?' Nicholas said. It was not yet time to be human,
but he could legitimately ask, and sustain the answer, and get Tobie to
help him, very soon.

'Ah, Berecrofts,' Kilmirren said. 'Our crippled friend Robin of Berecrofts deceived us all. A condition of helplessness is, of course, disarming, but sometimes deceptive. The young man tricked his family
and actually ensured that he would be taken to Beltrees. He left a
message for Andro.'

'Why?' Henry said.

'He felt Master David here threatened his family. I am not sure I
agree. I have always believed a sustained plan to be beyond our dear
David. However. He guessed that David dreamed of confronting de
Fleury, and was willing to assume the position of hostage.'

Wodman said, 'It was quite a sacrifice.' He was looking at Jordan de
St Pol.

'Oh, his chances were better than you might suppose,' the fat man
said. 'Which reminds me. This interview, so far as it has gone, represents
one generous undertaking I have given: that David could remain, as he
has done, to confront de Fleury in person, and even to fight him, without
hindrance, if that was his choice.'

'I don't remember agreeing,' said Wodman. 'Or Nicholas.'

'How strange,' said the fat man. 'Perhaps this was because your
agreement was not deemed to be necessary. David? I offer you justification, or single combat with this – what shall I call him?'

'Knight?' said Wodman.

'Of course. Of the Unicorn. A curious order of horse. David? What
do you choose?'

'To fight,' David said. Justification meant execution under the law.
His delicate features were set.

'With what weapon, if any?'

'With one dagger each. There is a pair over there.'

There was a slender box on the same table that Wodman had stood
behind. If Nicholas and Simpson were going to fight, the centre of the
room would have to be cleared. Nicholas slowly rose. He had not yet
agreed; but as the old man had pointed out, agreement was not necessary,
any more than victory was sure to be recognised. Outside the door were

Kilmirren men, and inside were St Pol and his grandson. This was a duel which neither antagonist might win.

Simpson was smiling at Nicholas. He said, 'Supposedly so brilliant, my dear; yet you could not foresee this? Shall we choose our weapons together?' He had kicked off his soft boots and risen, collected and lithe in the long hose and white shirt and russet tunic. His feathered brows above his dark eyes were raised in amusement, but there was no colour in his fine skin.

Nicholas said, 'If you had taken ship, you would be free.' The windows, now, were as bright as the candles. Wodman, with a glance at the old man, had begun to lift away stools and coffers. After a moment, Henry helped him. Henry, too, was keeping an uneasy eye on his grandfather.

David Simpson said, 'Free for what?' He paused and added, 'I became very tired with some of the things that you did, you and your friends. You should have listened to me. I could have told you something worth hearing.'

'Surely not,' Nicholas said. It was unwise, he knew. The more he heard, the less likely he was to survive. Suddenly, he realised that this was why David was talking.

David said, 'What would you like me to tell you? About your birth? You are a bastard. About this embittered old patriarch who set us all to spy on his family? St Pol will kill you if I don't. But before he does, ask him about his dead wife and the old woman, Bel. Or ask Andro Wodman what it is he isn't telling you.'

They had arrived at the table. Jordan de St Pol stood behind it, with his ringed hands on the box. Nicholas recognised one of the rings. He bore the mark of it on one cheek.

Nicholas turned to David Simpson. He said, 'If you know me, you know that none of these things matter.' He was not really addressing David Simpson. He was speaking to Henry.

Simpson said, 'You mean you don't care if Monseigneur kills you, if I don't?' He stopped and said, 'No. Of course you care. But other things seem more important. We are very alike, you and I.'

No one laughed. No one spoke. Nicholas said, 'You mean if things had gone otherwise, we should have been soul-friends?'

The fine eyes studied his, gravely. The Archer said, 'But isn't this true of most antagonists? We dislike our own flaws in others. We resent those whose admiration we want. Only sometimes, if we are blessed, we may reverse the process.'

He stopped.

'I am sorry,' Nicholas said.

The box was open, and the two daggers lay there, side by side. David Simpson said, 'I was sent to Cyprus, and told to beat you in business, and make sure you went home. But for this old man, we should have been friends.' And lifting one of the knives, he drove it into the breast of St Pol.

It grated on steel. The fat man fell back, staggering. Henry screamed. Simpson dragged back the dagger and lifted his fist to slash it across St Pol's bloated neck. Nicholas snatched the second blade up. It cracked against the first, diverting it from its path, and, when Simpson turned, Nicholas used it again, plunging it into the other man's arm. Blood sprayed, and Simpson gasped. It was not a duel. It was a face-to-face struggle, with the edge of a table before them, and Wodman and Henry running up from behind. The fat man straightened and said, 'I'm all right. Go on.'

Henry and Wodman stopped running. Nicholas stepped back. Blood pumped from Simpson's arm, crimsoning the shirt and falling on to the floor. He made no effort to stem it, or to transfer his dagger, which hung from his fingers. His lashes flickered.

Nicholas said, 'Do you concede the fight?' His voice was hard.

Jordan de St Pol spoke, his voice quite as harsh. 'He concedes. His other arm is useless. He was stabbed by your helpless cripple as he bent over his bed. An unreliable soldier, David de Salmeton. Flockhart always said so, in France. They were glad to get rid of him.'

'To hell with you,' said David Simpson in a clear voice. 'With all of you.' Nicholas saw a flash, and a thick spray of glistening blood hit the table and floor, followed without grace by the other man's body. The wonderful eyes, when Nicholas stooped, were still open, but the life within them had gone. The knife was still sunk in his heart, where he had managed to push it himself.

Lifting him, Nicholas saw now the bandages under his shirt from the earlier hurt. David Simpson could not have fought with a sword, and had only one hand for a dagger. He had not wanted, perhaps, to fight at all. He had meant to kill the old man, and himself. And the old man, perhaps, had even guessed it.

St Pol had found a seat, and Henry, sent for wine, was bringing it slowly, his eyes on the bloodsoaked burden being laid down by Wodman and Nicholas. It was not a charlatan's body. Nicholas thought it a pity that Simpson had had to hear those last goading words of the old man. From what Wodman had said, they were not true. For one thing, St Pol would never have employed an incompetent.

Then he remembered what Simpson had done, and had tried to do, and was not sorry. Perhaps old age would have been unkindest of all.

St Pol was watching him over his glass. There was no change in his face, although the blow to the chest had been considerable, and a mail-shirt was no protection against pain. Nicholas said, 'You could have kept him under arrest at Kilmirren. Why risk this? For the amusement of seeing us fight?'

'Dear me,' said St Pol. 'If so, I should have been disappointed, should I not?' He emptied his glass and held it out. 'No. I had in mind a small test. I thought your evaluation of Simpson was faulty, and his of you quite mistaken. I was right.'

'You were?' Nicholas said. Wodman, refilling the glass, was quite silent.

The fat man said, 'Of course. He persistently attracted your attention. He wanted you for a friend. It was time you showed him that remarkable core made of metal. You and I are very alike in that respect, my dear Nicholas. Only, of course, in that respect.'

The man lay dead, by his own hand, in the same room. Nicholas said, 'So you hardly needed the armour. You almost make me have second thoughts.'

'No,' said the fat man. 'You may think so, but no. You would do the same thing again. And if he had not killed himself, you would have killed him, even had he had both his hands; even though he was the better swordsman. For you should know that you are that kind of man.'

Nicholas drew a short breath. 'No,' said the other man. 'It is enough. Finish what you have to do. I am tired of you.'

Nevertheless, he had called him Nicholas just now, as he had once done in his own house in Edinburgh. *My dear Nicholas*. Why?

For Henry's sake, naturally, both times. They had both been performing for Henry.

Later, Nicholas walked through the door and up to where Gelis and Tobie were waiting. They were not alone. Laid within the silks of a four-poster bed, Robin of Berecrofts was talking eagerly.

There were circles under his eyes, but otherwise you would hardly guess how far or how roughly he had travelled. Or what else he had done. When Nicholas came in, they all stopped speaking.

He was no longer covered in blood, and someone had found him a shirt and an extraordinary garment lined with wolfskin, which were all that came near to his size. He didn't know therefore why silence fell, unless it was something in his own face. It was hardly reverence for

Simpson, whose end they already knew. Nicholas looked down at Robin and said, 'Your father and Saunders are going to flay you, and you deserve it. You know you saved St Pol's life and mine? If Simpson had had the use of two hands, he could have killed both of us. How the hell did you stab him?'

He had, it seemed, carried an armoury inside his bandaging. No one ever remembered he had one arm that worked. It had given him some satisfaction, when the bugger had started to taunt him. He wished he had managed to kill him himself.

'Well, he did the job for you,' Nicholas said. 'For all of us. Now all we have to do is get home. That is, I'm proposing to have a day's sleep followed by a night's sleep followed by a leisurely journey from one side of the country to the other, accompanied by a wagon full of provisions, and another full of girls.' He smiled at Robin. 'We've sent a very fast, fresh groom to Kathi, and another to Scheves. All is well.'

He actually thought that was true. He fell into bed in a room which had once been his own, but now looked and smelled different, and was not disappointed or surprised to find that Gelis was sleeping elsewhere. It was not just that they all needed rest. It was to do with the building, and what was in it, and what had taken place there. It was not a place for that kind of joy.

He might have stayed the threatened whole day and night, or he might have decided to leave, if nothing had happened. Jordan de St Pol had returned with his men to Kilmirren, and Henry and Wodman had gone with them. Semple had come, and asked questions, and removed Simpson's body. No one talked very much, now it was over. They were all too tired.

In fact, he woke later that day, and decided to rise. He was dressing when he thought he heard horsemen outside, and voices calling. When he opened his door, it was to find Avandale's man come to find him, and Drew Stewart himself down below, having ridden post-haste from Strathaven.

Drew had heard about Simpson. This was other business.

By then, Tobie and Gelis had joined them. 'What?'

But Nicholas had guessed. First, the immediate news from Craig-millar: Adorne had been released, vindicated, with all the rest; Simpson's guilt had been proved. All the victims were well, although John of Mar was still under treatment.

Then Avandale's courteous voice had made pause, impelling Nicholas to ask, 'And the Duke of Albany?'

For, of course, it was all about Sandy. Hurt, dismayed and upset by all that had occurred at Craigmillar, Albany had found Nicholas gone, and had promptly set off himself in the opposite direction. With all the men of his lordship, he had ridden off to the Borders, with the stated intention of showing those bastards the English who was master.

'And the Earl of Angus?' Nicholas asked.

'Probably. Archibald. Purves. Jardine of Applegarth. There are a number of good friends whom he'll call upon,' Avandale said. 'Your David Simpson left him with a few unwelcome ideas. It is really rather unfortunate.' He looked puzzled.

Sometimes the Chancellor was explicit. Sometimes it was all done with silence, and charm. Nicholas said, 'Do you want me to follow him?'

And Avandale assumed a conjectural look, as if assessing a new kind of taste, and said, 'We leave you to do anything, my dear Nicol, that you think to be wise. But we should rather like you to come back to Edinburgh.'

We. Argyll had been out of town, as Drew had. It was serious enough, then, to have brought them all back.

But of course it was.

Avandale left almost at once. Nicholas gathered his party and vacated Beltrees that same day. They would rest at Paisley that night, and next morning he would race on alone, leaving Gelis and Tobie to follow with Robin.

There was no one in Beltrees when they departed. Semple had taken the guards, and there were no servants left to tend the glorious chambers with all their exquisite treasures which their owner could no longer enjoy. The doors were locked, the shutters closed, the gates barred, and the churned mud of its mishandling left around it. Arriving, Gelis had looked down upon a glittering travesty. Departing, in the low afternoon light, she was thankful to leave it behind in the darkening hollow, this detritus of gold leaf and obscene gargoyle, with the old, seemly tower standing raffish and shamed in its midst.

They were a mile away when the thunderclap came, which set the horses kicking and stamping and caused Tobie to look back and swallow.

Thunder had not caused the black smoke that blotted out the red sun at their rear. Nor was it the lurid glare of the sun that mounted the sky, broadening and brightening, and then blasting again into fury.

Where, in this douce countryside, was there a place of terror like that; a mine powerful enough to erupt in that fashion, or to burn with such fury?

There was one place.

Gelis spoke in a whisper. 'The kegs in the vaults? Why was the gunpowder there?'

Tobie looked at her. She said, 'And slow-matches. I saw slow-matches, cold.'

'Simpson meant to set them,' Nicholas said. 'Once we had arrived and his own men had gone.'

He had dismounted to soothe Robin's horses, and answered without looking up, his arms on the back of one shivering bay. 'Semple thought he probably intended to stay and die with us. You, and Robin, and Tobie, and Wodman and me. And Henry, of course, as it turned out. Next to St Pol, he would have been pleased to take Henry with him.'

The smoke rose. Another explosion reverberated through the air, and another. Those would be the stores. Then, as the heat took hold, there would be the other objects that would turn white, and melt, and explode. The painted glass and the majolica tableware and the tiles. The tapestries would singe and then burn; the silks flare. The carved chairs and coffers would burst into crackling flame, and the plaster ceilings blacken and fall, as the rafters caught fire, and the precious things from one room crashed down to the inferno below.

There was no human life there; there were no animals. Only a fortune in gold, converted to inflammable artefacts.

Someone spoke, very low.

> '*I take my refuge in the Lord of the dawn*
> *from the evil in what He created,*
> *and from the evil of the dusk when it envelops,*
> *and from the evil of witches who blow on knots,*
> *and from the evil of the envier when he envies.*'

Robin said softly, 'Nicholas?' And Gelis, dismounting, went to her husband, who stood smoothing the warm hide of the horse, over and over.

She said, 'Come here.' And when he turned, folded him into her arms.

He spoke presently, his lips in her hair. 'It was built for all the wrong reasons. I should have destroyed it the first time. But instead, someone else came, and made it worse. I couldn't leave it at that.'

She released him. 'No, you couldn't,' she said. 'And here are three people that agree with you. Nicholas?'

Tobie had come gasping beside her, and she could see Robin, his fist flung up like a wrestler in victory; caught, as she was, between weeping and laughter.

She said, 'Nicholas . . . Jordan de St Pol will be so very annoyed.'

He didn't ride after Sandy. It was too late, for one thing. The repercussions of all Sandy was doing were already reverberating through Edinburgh when he got there. He did visit a few men who owed him a favour, and a number of them rode off south – willing, amused or cross according to temperament – to visit, placate, explain, and gather what information they could. Tom Yare had already raced back to Berwick in a shower of Browns, with instructions to get hold of Jamie Liddell, no matter what. Alec Brown was at sea with John le Grant. The Prestons and Sinclairs stayed out of it. Colin Campbell came back from Clackmannan, not having, thank God, lost himself in the wilds of Lochfyneside, and called a council of war in his tavern. Lang Bessie presided. When Argyll hosted a meeting, all he ever served was drink and rough fare. At Avandale's house, there would be nothing short of a banquet. It amused Nicholas and, he deduced, Colin Campbell of Argyll. Some of us are more royal than others.

There had been some contact already between them: a brief encounter between Nicholas and Whitelaw to establish what was known, and what still had to be done. Nevertheless, the Duke of Albany was not the first thing that they spoke of when they met in the high back room of the handsome timber-built tavern, with its stone gable and smoking peat fire.

Through the low door was the bedchamber that Argyll occupied, for convenience, when he wanted to remain in the High Street. The reason was usually a business one, although he had no objection to the company of women. Nicholas had met the pleasant Highland heiress his wife, who came to Court for the regular festivals, as did some of his nine children, from their various households. They all spoke Gaelic, and enjoyed trying to teach him. He could see Colin watching him, sometimes, trying to calculate how much he knew.

Colin. Drew. Master Archie. Now their footing was changing, it was even more necessary to remember, in public, the formalities which the Lords Three forsook sometimes in private. And even in private, Nicholas took no liberties, especially now, after Craigmillar. Exposing David Simpson had become a political necessity: his influence was becoming too strong. Sandy had been delighted to be part of the plot. It had gone astray for other reasons: that a trace of the poison, by some means, had reached the company; that the King, misunderstanding, had been moved to accuse Sandy in public. That he, Nicholas, had been forced to divine.

Colin . . . The Master of the Household was curious about that little episode, and held up the meeting to enquire. 'Tell me now. Is it a true gift that's in it? Or does it perform as it pleases? Or as you please, perhaps? What did the pendulum really say?'

He could have lied. He didn't. He said, 'It spelled the first name of Simpson's hostage, Robin of Berecrofts. It was how the Conservator was able to trace him so quickly. And yes, it is usually correct, but it can be misleading. I prefer not to use it.'

'I think you are very wise,' Avandale said. 'These things may confuse. You showed the King all its drawbacks quite plainly.'

'He has an astrologer,' Nicholas said. 'As far as the Court is concerned, I cannot divine. And the truth is that I won't. I can't tell you what is going to happen.'

'Or, I imagine, you would have thought twice before blowing up Beltrees,' said the Chancellor, erupting in silvery laughter. 'What do you think, Archie? What will the law say to that?'

The Secretary took off his spectacles and held them out to Nicholas who, in a recently established routine, pulled out a clean kerchief and worked on them while the owner rattled through his opinion, mostly in Latin. Plain words appeared from time to time: the Council, the Sheriff Court and the Justiciary. Diets for proof of destruction and spuilzie. Multiplepoinding.

'I beg your pardon?' Nicholas said. If they were enjoying it, he didn't mind. He handed the spectacles back, splashes removed.

'It's irrelevant,' said Colin Campbell. 'Truly. But go on, Archie. What else?'

Crown gift of tack, heirship moveables. Conjunct infeftment and bairns' rights –

'But David Simpson had no relatives, did he?' Avandale asked. 'In which case the *ultimus haeres* is the King, who is therefore, at law, the injured party. Is that correct, Colin?'

'*Concessum*,' said Colin, who was not only a lawyer, but Lord Justiciar South of the Forth. 'But Archie, the lucky one, remembers much more of it all than I do.'

Master Whitelaw, serenely continuing, mentioned restitution, reversion, and remission for arson in exchange for security. He added something about Wrongous and Maisterful Action by Strangers.

Nicholas stopped listening. When it ended, he just said, 'So what is the penalty?'

Argyll looked pained. Avandale said jovially, 'Whatever the King and his counsellors wish to make it, not excluding death. If, that is, you blew up the building, and a witness felt compelled to confirm it. Otherwise, it must be regarded as natural combustion.'

Everyone looked solemn, including Nicholas. Whitelaw said, 'In which case, we might return to the business in hand.'

In the next hour, there was very little frivolity, as they discussed the effects of Albany's raids over the Border. Accounts were still coming in, but everything pointed to the familiar patterns of destruction, and pillage, and burning. The difference was that the perpetrators were the Warden's own force, purporting to execute justice, but acting outside the due March procedures. It had gone too far to stop, and all that was left was to try to contain it.

The English complaints were beginning already. The formal protest would come from the English Warden, backed by the Crown. The question was how best to deal with it. Both countries needed peace. England had been glad to sustain it so far. Negotiations were under way for the marriage of the lady Margaret to Earl Rivers, the English Queen's brother. Dr Leigh would pay his regular visit in March with the annual portion of his Princess's dowry, by which time the Scottish Parliament would have met to compute and agree a similar dowry for Meg. Any local dispute between the two countries must be settled – would be settled, by compensation if need be, before then.

'Which will delight Sandy,' Nicholas said. Three bottles on, they were all on Christian name terms again.

Archie Whitelaw grunted. 'Which will, clearly, return the young man to the state of mind which impelled him on this course of action – anger against the royal policies; misplaced sympathy for his sisters; disgruntlement over his personal standing. It is unfortunate that the earldom of March covers such a large area. Also, youth and vigour and patriotic fervour have their own appeal. I am told he rides attended by the bard Harry. Perhaps he – or someone – will invite Master Holland as well.'

Nicholas said, 'Sandy isn't a Wallace, but he's quite well liked. He's seen as being honest, at least, in his convictions. He is the overlord of many others, as you say, who owe him service, or money. He has less support among those who find him erratic and occasionally violent, and of course among those who can trade and live well without war. His men have followed him this time.'

'Perhaps the falterers could be encouraged,' said Colin Argyll.

'Not by me,' Nicholas said.

Campbell smiled. Drew Avandale said, 'No. Nicholas is right. He must keep Sandy's trust, as we must rely on Adorne and the Queen to moderate the King's language and actions. You have not yet met the Queen? In private session, that is?'

'No. It would be unwise,' Nicholas said.

'It might become advisable,' Avandale said. 'Leave it to me. Meanwhile, it is your influence over Sandy that we require most of all. Find him when he gets back. Re-establish your credentials. And keep him out of trouble, if you can, until spring.' He paused. 'We are perhaps asking too much. But it seems to me, from what I have heard, that your personal difficulties are now over. Simpson is dead, and St Pol and his grandson can hardly pursue their vendetta when you saved the old man, as I hear, from Simpson's knife. Or is there any other way in which we may help you?'

'No. None. I shall do what I can,' Nicholas said. The offer was meaningless. His situation was already summed up in two words. *Natural combustion.*

He decided, when he stopped being annoyed, that he was amused, and even appreciative.

Chapter 21

Tressour to lordis suld thar no thing be
Bot gud maner, honour, and honesté.

BY THAT TIME, Nicholas had also marshalled his personal life.
Ever since the night at Craigmillar, he had been thinking of
Jodi, in royal service far to the west. He was about to take the
decision to go there, when the boy arrived home, on a visit
arranged by the Princess Mary and Gelis. It would only be, Gelis
explained, for a short time, but long enough for Jodi to become discontented, and to notice that his father was never there anyway.

Gelis's return had been another reunion, and Robin had been none
the worse for his journey. Nicholas had gone to see him, and had talked
to Tobie and Clémence and Kathi. The blowing up of Beltrees was
their favourite topic. He was a hero. He saw Robin's father, and Sersanders. No one mentioned David Simpson, or if they did, he discouraged
them. Henry and St Pol were still at Kilmirren, and none of the Semples
came near him.

He went to visit Adorne, who had been told the whole story by
Wodman. He went to see him to discover how he fared, and to discuss
strategy in the light of what was now happening. He also went, warned
by Kathi, for another reason.

This time, Cortachy was not alone, but in his business room, talking
to Wodman and Andreas. The makeshift nursery had gone: since
Euphemia passed her first birthday, she had been returned to the care
of the Haddington nuns, and the presence of other small children,
staggering and crawling together. Adorne visited her very often, with
Kathi or Clémence. But this was not a house for a young child.

Now Adorne rose and embraced him. 'Nicholas! God preserved you.'

'It was my metal core,' Nicholas said. He said it perversely, since he resented both the phrase, and the fact that Wodman had heard it. Then he said, 'I've just come from the Lords Three. Let me tell you what they say, and then I'd appreciate your view from David's Tower.'

The view from the Court, when they came to it, was much as he had gathered elsewhere: the younger Princess rebellious, the King raging against Albany. John of Mar had been under medical care for a few days, but was now better.

'An abbreviated way of saying that we locked him in his room,' Andreas interpolated. 'We don't know whether Simpson gave him any agaric or not, but the effect of whatever he did take was disastrous. He went wild.'

Adorne said, 'If I hadn't been in Scotland, Simpson would never have thought of this drug.'

'He would have found another,' Nicholas said. 'Maybe worse. Or the fit may just have been due to excitement.'

Andreas said, 'We have talked about it, of course. That is possible. It is also possible that what Lord Mar drank exacerbated his illness. Dr Tobie suggested a more regular testing of urine. Sometimes it is normal. Sometimes it assumes a purplish colour, and may be accompanied by the reddened skin and the outbursts of temper. We have found no solution. We cannot treat him with poppy all the time.'

'And, of course,' said Adorne, 'it adds to the tension with his two brothers. I spend an hour with the King, and everything is undone when Mar bursts in with some accusation. It might even be helpful if he spent some time in the north, in his own lands. I could take him. Cochrane is working in the north-east already. Knollys is often there, or his family, on behalf of the Knights. The King is personally known there as well. Argyll will have told you that he went north in the recent campaigns. Colin can often find a way round the King's misgivings, but has no patience with Mar, as you have with Albany. Then when Sandy returns, you can set to work on him.'

'I feel like a tailor,' Nicholas said. 'It sounds a good idea. What inducement can we offer? Viewing his fortified castles? Not, I hope, salmon?' There went through his mind an elaborate consortium deal brokered by Luss and Tam Cochrane, and involving Cawdor, Ross and the Cumming brothers in the Nairn area. But of course Adorne would know all about it. Marchmont Herald, a Cumming, was married to a Craigmillar Preston, who was thereby related to both Leithie and Cochrane. And Cawdor was in the salmon business with Alex Innes, who was married to Phemie's sister. It was amazing what connections Phemie had had.

He had an appealing idea. He said, 'Don't the Bishops of Caithness have salmon rights? Bonar Bridge? That impossibly rich bailery of St Duthac? Where's Camulio?'

Prosper de Camulio, Bishop-elect of Caithness, was moving in a distracted way through Europe, performing unpopular errands for the Pope and King Ferrante of Naples.

Adorne said, 'I believe he is currently moving between Switzerland, the Tyrol and the Emperor, attempting to form a papal alliance against Milan. His plans beyond that are not known. Simpson, you will remember, was encouraged to believe that his employer was returning this spring, but we have no reason to think so. He has been sent a report of Simpson's death.'

He stopped, looking at Nicholas. 'While we are on the subject of Craigmillar and after: no one but Simpson will be held accountable for what happened, unless an exception is made for the destruction of Beltrees. I should like to affirm here and now that I personally will support what you did to the hilt, and will support you at law if it comes to it. Meanwhile, is there need of a lawyer? Should you not send for Julius, for example?'

Adorne could often surprise him. Nicholas said, 'Thank you, sir, but no. Failing the departure of most of the Council, it seems unlikely that anyone will prosecute. Unless, of course, my lord of St Pol has other plans.' He was looking at Wodman.

The Conservator said, 'I left him at Kilmirren, with Henry. I rather think it would be best if you didn't meet again for a very long time. I don't think he will take your throat out immediately, but you know the old man. He keeps his plans to himself.'

As he was keeping Henry beside him. Nicholas could understand that.

Andreas left. Wodman asked about the Colquhoun ship, and the pirated cargo for Benecke's family, and Nicholas told him, without unnecessary details. He had no regrets. If there had been Newbattle goods on the *Star* as well as Simpson's, it was unfortunate, but he was prepared to answer for it. Wodman said, 'I wish I'd thought of it first. But you be careful. I got the impression that Simpson had prepared one or two slow-matches that might be burning away in a corner, all ready to go off one of these days.'

Nicholas thought so as well, and respected the warning. Wodman had said very little about Simpson's death, or about St Pol. It was an avenue that Nicholas, too, was content not to explore. Wodman had always expected Nicholas to kill Simpson for him. Perhaps there was some code of honour that had prevented him from doing it himself. Or perhaps the old man had forbidden it.

There was, however, one thing that Andro Wodman did have to answer for, but not before Adorne. When the Conservator next left the room, Nicholas followed him. He remembered, from the sludge of the past, another meeting in a latrine in Poland, and what had happened immediately afterwards. No, he did not need a lawyer. He leaned against the door and said, when Wodman turned, 'The copper bowl.'

Wodman finished replacing his ties and sat down again where it was most convenient. The misshapen face looked quite undisturbed. He said, 'That's an eerie gift you've got there. Tobie was sure you'd be made to divine. I had the bowl in my luggage. You remember where you saw it last.'

Nicholas knew. Seven years before, at the court of King René in Angers, when he had met a physician called Pierre de Nostradamus at the edge of a chasm full of stinking wild boar. He had been taken from that abyss and introduced to another, where he had been forced to divine, using that bowl. Then, the pendulum had spelled out the same word, *Robin*.

Soon after that, Andro Wodman had come to take him away. He must have acquired the bowl then, or just after. Nicholas said, 'Nostradamus let you have the bowl? Why?'

Wodman said, 'He is an astrologer. Perhaps he knew that it would save Kathi's husband one day.'

'Do you believe that?' Nicholas said. 'Why should he care? He had never seen me before, and would never see me again. And it was of no advantage to the King.'

Wodman said, 'It might have been. Margaret of Anjou is his daughter, and she spent some time in Scotland. But you are probably right. What he saw in his charts may have surprised Nostradamus in some other way. At least he was intrigued enough to follow your movements. And you did meet again, although you may not remember it. When you dwined away by the river at Trèves, it was Nostradamus who tended you.'

Nicholas stared at him. Trèves, and the grand meeting between the Emperor and Burgundy, at which he had been present with Gelis and Jodi. And Anna. And Julius. When he was cornered: when he was compelled to admit, at last, all the devastation he had been planning for Scotland. When there had been a fight, and Jordan de St Pol had run him through.

Someone had carried him to the river. Someone had placed him, later, on the state barge which would take him to Germany.

Nicholas said, 'How do you know?'

And Wodman said, 'Well, how do you think? Or don't you remember even who sent for help, and got you out of the house? I thought she'd tell you. It was Clémence, of course.'

There was no time for more. Wodman left, and Nicholas returned to Adorne, where the private conversation took place that he knew, from Kathi, to be necessary. He left soon after that for his own house and, seeing a lamp in the parlour, entered slowly.

Gelis was alone. She looked up, beginning to smile, and then rose and took his hand, and led him to sit beside her. 'Can you tell me?'

'I am not sure,' he said, 'when I became wholly transparent, but it does save a lot of trouble. I have just been told by Adorne what you probably know already.'

'It wasn't my secret,' she said. 'I hoped he'd tell you. Except that it means they are now sure. Was he very distressed?'

Anselm Adorne had been distressed, but his voice had been steady, and his composure had been unbroken from beginning to end.

'You know my daughter Euphemia is at Haddington now? It seemed better for her to have company. And there is some reason, sadly, for her to have special care. It has taken some months to be sure, but it now seems that her condition is not temporary. Euphemia can hear nothing, not even the loudest of sounds. She is deaf.'

And Nicholas had said, 'I am so sorry. What would Phemie have done?'

'It is what I have asked myself,' Adorne had said. 'Euphemia is whole; she is beautiful; she has no other flaw. I have everything to be thankful for, and I shall not allow this one circumstance to affect me, or affect her more than it must. If she cannot hear, she cannot learn to speak, but there are other ways of communicating. Dr Tobie is advising me. Your own mother's father, he tells me, spoke with his fingers at the last.'

Thibault, vicomte de Fleury, the grandfather whom Nicholas, grown, had never met, lying paralysed in his monastery of retreat outside Venice, and visited by Tobie and Gelis and, before that, by Adorne and his son. And later, they had been told, by Adorne's servant who, you would think, might have observed and reported the finger-talking.

Nicholas had asked, but Adorne had not recalled, he said, sending anyone. Compared with this, it was of no importance, and Nicholas did not refer to it now. He spoke instead of the child, and all the measures the doctors were taking. The royal physicians were accustomed to deafness. Joanna, the third of the King's six aunts, had been sent to find a husband abroad, and had failed because she was deaf and dumb. Married at home, she had raised healthy children who were now themselves of an age to marry.

'I know,' Gelis said. 'Bel of Cuthilgurdy helped the Princess Joanna. Bel is teaching Euphemia now.'

Nicholas was silent.

Gelis said, 'It's common knowledge, Nicholas, that two of the six Scottish Princesses were sent to the French Court over thirty years ago, and stayed there while the French King arranged husbands for them. Bishop Spens, who was an Archdeacon, escorted them. One of the Princesses was Eleanor, who left after three years to marry Sigismond of the Tyrol. The other was Joanna, whom no one wanted because she was deaf. She came back eventually to marry James Douglas of Dalkeith. One of the matrons of honour who served Eleanor and Joanna in their French household was Bel.'

'And that is commonly known?' Nicholas said. He kept her hand, to reassure her, and saw that her colour had risen. She pulled a face, as he might have done.

She said, 'No. But Bel speaks with her fingers, as Tobie does. They have been teaching the nuns. Bel, and Tobie, and Lord Erskine's wife, who is the Princess Joanna's daughter.'

Nicholas smoothed her fingers, watching them. She said, 'I don't mean to pry. Just to tell you what is known, and what others may guess.'

He looked up. 'I know,' he said. 'And as I said before, there is nothing you need be afraid of in all this. There are no dire secrets, just small matters of loyalty and, perhaps, pride. But I'm glad to know, for Bel's sake, what is being said. And doubly glad that the child can be helped. Adorne will be so thankful.'

He broke off. He said, 'We should be so thankful.'

It was true.

The gold had gone. It was better gone. It had caused little but death and mistrust and bitterness, and he could secure for himself all it offered. He had his brain, and his two hands and his health, to provide for the future. He had a strong son – two strong sons – and Gelis. He was free.

Sandy returned, and Nicholas set to work on him. It was like dealing with Jodi. Liddell was easier: Nicholas respected his loyalty, which had to struggle all the time against his better judgement. That said, he could be an idiot like Sandy at times. That was why Sandy liked him.

And it was unfair, too, to describe this operation in terms of the upbringing of Jodi, although there were parallels. Sandy had had nurses from birth, as Jodi had. The caring families, the Sinclairs, the Prestons, gave their nurslings all the continuity that they could not expect from their parents, and the children responded with love. The great René of Anjou had erected a statue to his nurse. The absences of Jodi's mother and father had been no more or less than the separations Sandy had experienced.

But, of course, the time for nurses came to an end. Royal princes lived in separate establishments, both as youngsters and later. Louis of France had no idea what his son looked like, they said, it was so long since he had sent him away. The boy was locked up in Amboise, to prevent his being exploited against his own father, as Louis had been. And many of Sandy's first personal relationships had been shattered by death. His widowed mother had died while he was in Flanders, and the following year, aged only ten, he had lost Charles, his adored older cousin in Veere, and then Bishop Kennedy, his near-uncle. A proud boy, speaking a different tongue, he had found himself a prisoner at the English Court, and thrown into the equivocal companionship of Gloucester. From there, he had come back to Scotland to compete for attention with an older brother who was King, and a younger who rampaged at will. He had been given a Sinclair wife because it was necessary, and had resented it, and had been allowed to annul it in the hope of something better. It was no wonder that he was hard to control, or that his own children, legitimate or otherwise, were not much in his mind. He took more interest in his sister's son, young Jamie Boyd.

And yet he was not out of reach, or uncivilised. Sometimes, Nicholas could bring him round to a new point of view, or induce him to pause a little and think. The rest of the time it was no good, for there were other factors at work. There were bad influences, such as Simpson had been. But mostly the trouble lay with the imbalance in the family itself, and the friction it brought.

Adorne, most often at the Castle, was able sometimes to mediate. The Councillors exerted what pressure they could. Nicholas, after long months of handling, had achieved only some of the acceptance he had hoped for in Sandy: his position was simply that of a person in whom Sandy would often confide, and whose affection he could count on, for most of the time. As Sandy's steward, Liddell had greater authority. But in essence, he and Liddell were to Sandy what Josaphat Barbaro, that wise envoy, had once put into words. They were his boon companions, with whom a prince might relax, after work with his serious councillors, but who were debarred from all matters of state. The trouble with Sandy was that he didn't have, or want, serious councillors.

The winter was hard work. Complaints duly arrived from the English Wardens, and were given soft answers, to Albany's fury. Yule and Uphaly, always useful distractions, spawned that year a series of ferocious entertainments, masterminded by Roger and Nicholas, which dazzled the young and were admired by the more thoughtful of their elders. Those who did not share in the profit were heard to wonder whether the Burgundians were not out to line their pockets again. Roger sent his singers out by the cartload for nothing, and the grumbles died down, except in Newbattle.

The end of the January festivities brought the pest; not the direst variety, but one that encouraged families to move to their country estates, if they had them, while the forests became crowded with hunting-parties. Kathi took her three children and their attendants to stay with their great-grandfather at Templehall, but Robin remained with Sersanders and Archie, while Tobie and Clémence became busy, as did all the physicians. The Court jogged about between Linlithgow and Stirling and Falkland, with Will Roger in attendance, and Adorne, and Nicholas, if Sandy was there. Gelis stayed at the Leith house. The Lords of the Council for Civil Causes held one well-fumigated meeting in the Tolbooth, and dissolved themselves until spring, so that the number of disputes in abeyance began to overflow into several bags. The King subjected himself to a number of meetings with his better-liked councillors, and called a meeting of Parliament for March. In theory, Edinburgh would be healthy by then, or if not, the meeting could be transferred elsewhere. It would not be cancelled, for its chief purpose was to raise money for the lady Margaret's contracted wedding to the Earl Rivers, the King of England's good-brother.

The lady Margaret was not present to comment, having formed the mutinous habit of departing from Court and staying in the homes of her friends' parents, or with Mary her sister. Kathi, descending occasionally upon one or other of the Hamilton castles, took occasion now and then to hold mild discussions with the lady Mary on the advantages of keeping on the good side of England. Like Nicholas, she soon learned her own limitations; and took instead to sitting with the Princess's elderly husband, whom she liked, and whose sickbed was always surrounded by clever sons from his earlier marriage. She saw, with pleasure, how well Jodi de Fleury fitted into that household, and how his confidence had grown. He appeared to be drawing again: one of the Hamiltons always seemed to be teaching him something. Kathi took Margaret with her more than once, to please Jodi, and enjoyed writing long letters to Gelis. She wondered if it was morally wrong to be pleased that David Simpson was dead. They were all free. And Nicholas might be discovering what he wanted, at last.

The pest was over by March, and everyone came home. The Three Estates convened in Edinburgh on a Friday, in solemn procession, in all their great hats and long robes, and crammed into the hall of the Tolbooth to sit before their sovereign and hear who was to pay what towards the Princess Margaret's wedding. The answer, shatteringly, turned out to be more than twice the sum proposed seven years before to send an army to Brittany, the cost to be shared as usual between the burghs, the barons and the clergy, and the first instalment to be paid up by June. It would mean, at the very least, two shillings in the pound of a property tax. To farm out Margaret.

She was present, in velvet and furs, with her long, unbound red hair crowned by a jewelled circlet that cost someone, such as the exchequer, quite a bit. Her attendants and her sister Mary sat beside her.

Johndie Mar, their brother, was seated nearer the throne, and on his cheek was the red mark that spelled trouble. Johndie Mar, everyone knew, didn't want his sister married in England, but that wasn't going to change anything. Violence wasn't the answer. Procrastination, there was a great word, now. And once the marriage took place, there were certain advantages. That girdle cost a pretty penny. And her shoes.

The rest of the decisions were the kind that could be rattled through: to pursue new trading measures with Burgundy; to arrange to keep the peace between the dense crowds of quarrelling families who had abandoned litigation in favour of force. It was just as well. It was just as well to get through it all quickly, after Johndie Mar had had his say.

What had happened was not at first clear to the crowds who waited to see the King emerge from his Parliament ('He's an awful wee man, is he not? And where's Margaret? Where's Bleezie Meg? How d'ye fancy a sonsy big Englishman, hen?'). But as the delegates emerged, and spotted their wives, and began to call out, everyone knew soon enough.

That Johndie Mar. Standing up and shouting that they were selling his sister. And the officers of the house thumping their staffs, and the King going as red as his brother, and Argyll (it was always our Colin) leaping forward to get hold of Johndie and take him away, shrieking still. The Guard helped. (See that bonny yellow-haired lad, I'd buy *him*.)

And then Meg had burst into tears, and been taken out by her sister.

And then Drew Avandale had stood up and made a speech about how the nation had prospered in these years of peace with England, and how important it was to strengthen the links between the two countries, at a time when trade with Burgundy was at its most prosperous, and mischievous intrusion by others should be repelled. Which everyone took to refer to the French, who didn't want England to trade with Burgundy at all, and especially not to feel free to ally with Burgundy to resist the French advance into Flanders. For, of course, there was that. You might feel sorry for wee Meg, but she was performing a patriotic service, going to England, as well as getting her girdles paid for by somebody else. Well, that was what most thought. But here was someone shouting outside the Parliament door, and they had to silence him. Poetry, he was talking. Collecting for Blind Harry, maybe. Here, that was a joke.

The procession afterwards was all the way down to Holyrood, where there was to be a banquet, with guests. The Burgundians were to be there: Adorne of Cortachy, who was a handsome man, the lassies all agreed, with his nephew and niece, and the big fellow, Nicol de Fleury. The one that sang, and put on the plays, and dressed everyone up. He was all right, was Nicol. And a right marrow of Sandy's. Where was Sandy? Where was Nicol, come to that?

Avandale said, 'Speak in a low voice, if you will. You are telling me that it is as we feared? Albany has set out for the Borders?'

Adorne said, 'I am sorry, my lord. With Liddell attending Parliament, nothing so rash was expected But the Duke has collected some men and is riding south, gathering more. He has made no public proclamation of intent, so that there has been no excuse to stop him. Dispositions have been made: there are bands of men at various places who will try to divert him in innocent ways. But we know that he himself has secretly contacted others.'

The Chancellor's square jaw was set. 'We should have arrested him.'

Adorne said, 'With respect, my lord. We did discuss it. An arrest without proper evidence would double his followers, and turn a disagreement over state policy into something much worse. All we could do is allow de Fleury, as he asked, to go with him. Liddell will follow. If they cannot restrain him, de Fleury can send for help when it's clear that the Duke is transgressing.'

'But some damage will have been done. I am not happy. First Mar, and now this. Well, we foresaw it. With your help we have contained it, a little. We can do nothing until we have word. Let us go in to the Abbot. We must not lose our heavenly credit as well.'

Chapter 22

Sa thocht this knycht desyrit to be fre,
His lawté maid him presoner to be,
And for the commoun proffet of the land
He chesit him as presoner to stand.

NICHOLAS DE FLEURY, immured with his charge on the English border at Upsettlington, had by this time no heavenly credit left, unless his state of mind was proof against angels. Riding like a maniac, he had overtaken Sandy at Duns, to be greeted with amusement mixed with triumph. 'We thought we'd see you before long, didn't we, gentlemen? And I expect you've left messages for Jamie as well. So how did the Three Estates fare? Agreed to everything, did they? If England wants Meg, then they get her, and everyone pays through the nose, because it's good for business. That's all it is, isn't it? A pact that's good for business?'

It wasn't Blind Harry sitting in the corner this time, it actually was Dick Holland, long since come down from the north, and an embarrassment to John Colquhoun, who had married into Dick's poems, as it were, at a time when it was not a good idea – *O Dowglass, O Dowglass, Tender and Trewe!* – to praise some kinds of Douglases. Sandy, of course, was not concerned about that. He said, 'All right. Let us have the lecture and get it over with. I'm going raiding into England, no matter what you say.'

'I wasn't going to say anything. Where are you mustering?'

It was Upsettlington, of course. The convenient Border land with its church on the Tweed, just east of Coldstream, and next to the Norham ford. Nicholas said, 'Then can I go with you?'

Sandy could never see anything coming. He agreed, surprised, relieved and touchingly pleased, and told Jamie Liddell at once, as soon as he burst in. Before Jamie had time to react, Nicholas said, 'We'll all go. With this number of men, we can attack ten different places and be back before anyone stops us. What do you want? Cattle? You'd have them taken off you when you get back. Just to make a few townships sit up, before the other Wardens get there? Then let's plan it.'

'I thought you were on their side,' said Sandy.

If you want to convince, keep as close to the truth as you can. 'I am,' Nicholas said. 'But if you want to do this, no one can stop you. I'm just here to help you do it in the way that will cause you least harm.'

'Never mind that,' Sandy said. 'I can look after myself.'

It should have warned him. It didn't. He had to pull Jamie round to his way of thinking and then, encamped at Upsettlington, to go and plant a word in the shrewd ear of Will Bell, the Rector, who had the triple advantage of being a priest, a notary and a friend of the Abbot of Holyrood. After that, Nicholas wandered round, talking to all the hearty Borderers who had ridden in with their men, ready to wipe their English counterparts off the map. They didn't need Blind Harry: they were going to out-Wallace Wallace on an elixir of personal euphoria.

They liked the idea of co-ordinated attacks in different directions. It was agreed that it couldn't be done without central control. It was further agreed that they didn't want the King's men on their tails, once all the local sycophants got wind of what was happening, and that there should be someone in authority to stop them. It was finally accepted, by Sandy, that the central control at Upsettlington should be himself.

It was different, clearly, from his original dream of heading a young army into England, hacking and burning in freedom's great name. On the other hand, if you knew Sandy, you could tell that shreds of normal thinking were already beginning to creep in. If he did that, he risked losing everything, including possibly his life.

Small attacks were less contentious, but also less stirring. He didn't fancy leading a hundred to burn some boats and mills and destroy a few barns. Staying at Upsettlington and outfacing the governesses when they arrived was not unattractive. Provided, of course, that Jamie led the band they had personally brought. And that Nicol, as promised, led another.

It was a Lumsden he rode with: a jolly man he had met before, who didn't frankly care who ruled what as long as he could batter his neighbours when he felt like it. As, of course, they battered him. He could see, and was patient with the high-flown arguments over it all, which Nicholas didn't try to revive. Nicholas merely pointed out, from time to time, that theft was actually better than burning, and they might even get away with it, if they kept off whole herds, but took a horse or two here and there, and some nags that could carry bales of wheat, or malt, or a few kitchen utensils. If the English complained, it was even possible the King would settle up first himself. He had tried to instil the same idea into the other groups, and he thought Liddell saw the point. A lot of dead men, or raped women, or – God forfend – deceased royal or semi-royal noblemen would cause more trouble than even Sandy had wanted. It would be nice if it rained, really hard.

Someone heard, for it rained. It was not the most joyous late winter's day that Nicholas had ever spent but, returning cold and mud-coated and saddle-sore with his bedraggled company, he thought it might have been worse. They were all alive. He carried a few hacks and slashes, as they all did: there had been some fighting, both on horse and off, but nothing too desperate. As soon as they splashed over the ford, Lumsden waved and set off, his men floundering behind with the booty. The banks of the Tweed would be littered for miles. Fortunately, it was not yet in spate. He waited a bit, until his own men returned with the news that Liddell was back, and most of the rest seemed to be over except for the Douglases, who could take care of themselves.

Also, of course, that a troop from Berwick Castle had arrived with instructions to take the ringleaders back under escort. Including Alexander, Duke of Albany, Earl of March, lord of Annandale, lord of Man, with his odd little device of the three booted, spurred feet going nowhere. Albany, Liddell and himself. Except that they were going somewhere, all of them, that was for certain.

It turned out to be Edinburgh Castle. Sandy was locked into his own rooms, tired but happy; Liddell and Nicholas were put in the spare chart-room, which was at the top of David's Tower. Marching up from the gate in the darkness, they had passed Henry, who turned his head, against orders. He looked amazed.

Jamie wanted to talk, and Nicholas let him. After a bit, someone brought in washing-water and strips of fresh cloth for their cuts: Nicholas recognised the servant. Later, Liddell was sent for. After that, it was not too long before the door opened and Colin Campbell came in.

'*Ochone, ochone,*' said Nicholas sourly.

'No. You did very well. Liddell says you don't need a doctor.'

'For my head, perhaps. So what is happening?'

Argyll sat down, a shade less spryly than usual. Nicholas could imagine what it had been like, steering the King and the others. Ordinary fighting was easier. The Controller said, 'The consensus is that England will take the chance to make threats, now they need us much less. James will meet that by disowning all Sandy has done, and announcing that he is now in prison for his failings as Warden. The recriminations will occupy a few weeks if not months, during which time no one would dream of asking the lady Margaret to pass down to England, which removes that immediate bone of contention.'

'We all did you a service,' Nicholas said. 'Yes, yes, I know. I do understand. My lord.'

'Well, who better,' Argyll said. 'You, of course, were never over the Border. The King thinks you rode south to dissuade Sandy; you and Liddell are here to be questioned, after which you will be released. Sandy will stay until we know the damage that's in it, and can see what best to do. Why is he cheerful?'

'Because he's won,' Nicholas said. 'He did what he was forbidden to do, and showed his disagreement with the English peace policy, and quite a lot of March lords agreed to ride with him, at that. I'll give you a list of their names. No surprises. He'll be a lot less cheerful as the weeks go by.'

Argyll said, 'I've asked Bishop Spens to come and talk to him. 'Tis known to me that he's seen as the universal peace-maker, whateffer, but he and Sandy came through that business in England together, and he knows how Sandy thinks. If Sandy would agree to keep quiet, he could disappear into Annandale for a few weeks while this is all sorted out. So long as the English think he's in prison, that's all that matters.'

'But that's all that matters to Sandy as well,' Nicholas said. 'He expects a rap over the knuckles and freedom. If he doesn't get that, he's going to be the noisiest martyr we have all ever known.'

'*Faire, faire!* I wish I didn't believe you were right,' Argyll said.

He left. Liddell came back, followed by a supply of superior plenishments, including writing materials and books. Food arrived, wrapped in cloths, which was rather more satisfying than the Castle's usual provender and came, Nicholas suspected, from the Argyll tavern.

Bishop Spens arrived, wiping his face. 'Man! He's a thrawn devil, young Sandy!'

Liddell got him a seat. 'My lord, it's not from lack of principles, or respect. He's acting as his conscience directs.'

'Aye. I ken,' said Bishop Spens. 'Rogues are easy. Ye can aye sink your teeth in a rogue, but a principled man can be poison. Which reminds me. All yon at Craigmillar is safely over? Cortachy came away without blame, like the rest of ye? That's a good man. I've said before, someone should try to keep him in Scotland. He could earn his keep. He's got my Linlithgow franchise, and welcome. And I've nine and twenty prebendaries floating about in the north that could offer a position for one or two sons, when the time came. Tell him that.'

'I shall,' Nicholas said. 'Although I don't think Lord Cortachy feels he can make plans just yet.' Spens knew that. The previous year, the Duchess of Burgundy had had a son, Philip, delivered with promptitude the summer after her wedding, but her husband had still produced no decisive victory against the French, nor a new form of combined rule for Flanders in Burgundy.

Spens rubbed his big-nosed, high-coloured face. Rising seventy, Bishop of Aberdeen but tied to Edinburgh by his skills as a judge, Thomas Spens was a former protonotary at Rome, a lord of Council, an auditor, a broker of truces and marriages who had, in his time, asked for and received a papal bull which exempted his bishopric alone from the superior rule of St Andrews. He got on well with Will Scheves. He simply liked to go his own way, and had earned the right to do it. Now he said, 'Oh, it'll open out some time, if only we exercise patience. I've every sympathy with Sandy Albany. He's proud of his country, and so am I. How did he take it, the stramash at Craigmillar? The Prestons had a lot to say, I'll be bound.'

Again. Liddell was up, pouring wine. Nicholas said, 'They're a formidable crew.'

'Aye,' Bishop Spens said. 'Yon John, he made a good marriage. Ah! A cup of Bordeaux! Jamie, your very good health, and may this all be settled by Christmas.'

It was March. Liddell laughed, and so did Nicholas, and presently Bishop Spens left, and it was soon time for bed. In the darkness, Nicholas lay thinking. John Preston. Who was his wife? Then he remembered.

Gelis said, 'Nicholas is still at the Castle: they want him to keep Albany happy, and Liddell under his eye. Or that's my guess. Anyway, you're to go up and see him.'

'Why?' said John le Grant. He had always got on well with Gelis van Borselen, ever since she came to the battlefield at Nancy three years ago, and especially since she got himself and Tobie and Robin into Bruges that God-awful night. In fact, his life had turned round since then. He had replaced Astorre and his company with another: with young Kathi and Robin; with Tobie and Clémence; with Adorne and Sersanders and Berecrofts, and best of all with the sea, and all the friends he had made there. He spent most of his time in Leith. He was best pleased, although he would not admit it, when Gelis and Nicholas were at the Leith house, working with him. The news of Sandy's crass raid, and Nicholas's even crasser involvement had roused him to fury: he had fulminated round Robin's chair until even Kathi grew dizzy and told him to stop. And Nicholas wanted to see him.

'Why?'

'He's dying, perhaps? Or he thinks I'm pining, and wants to send me a token of undying love? Or he just wants some fresh shirts. How would I know?' asked Gelis. She sounded as caustic as ever, but looked edgy.

John said, 'It's all right. Give me something of Jodi's. That'll cheer him up.'

At the Castle, Nicholas wasn't locked in, but there was a guard outside the door, half asleep. Inside, Liddell and Nicholas were gambling with the brat, young St Pol. Nicholas said in a welcoming way, 'John. Did you bring any money?'

'Some,' said John cautiously. Liddell, a big, good-looking man, looked worn but reasonably cheerful; Nicholas looked bland. The brat, vivid and bright-eyed, looked triumphant.

'He's winning,' said Nicholas, indicating St Pol with a nod. 'But that won't last long. Go on, then. Sit down. We need a fourth.'

John said, 'Gelis thought you wanted some shirts washed.'

Nicholas looked surprised. He said, 'Well, I could send her some, but they do them very well here. Little thistle stitched in the corner, and a crown on the tail. Is that all the money you have?'

'No. But I need –'

'Put it all out,' said Nicholas. 'I'll write you a note. My God, who would have thought you so mean?'

'He's an Aberdonian,' said Henry de St Pol quickly.

'And you've just lost that round. So go on, what happened?'

The youth had been telling some story. He continued with it, glancing at John every now and then, and eventually forgetting him as the narrative rose in a crescendo and fell apart amid interruptions and arguments. It sounded normal, like anything you would hear round a garrison fire. The game ended and another began. When John left, eventually, it was dark and the youth Henry helped him down to the gateway. No one had mentioned guns.

He found his way to Gelis's house, and she led him in and put him to bed. The next morning, he came down, holding a paper.

Gelis said, 'It's all right. I read it last night. He owes you two pounds, and you have to make some enquiries at Leith, while I find out when and how Sandy could have communicated with the family of Elizabeth Monypenny, wife of John Preston. How secure is that prison?'

'It's not a prison,' John said. 'They've just made Albany stay in his own apartments, and put a guard on the door. That is, if he escapes, in theory the King can tell the English Wardens how annoyed he is, and that he will bring him back as soon as possible.' He paused. 'I'd better get down to Leith.'

'Yes, you had,' Gelis said. 'Where is John of Mar?'

'Don't ask,' said John le Grant. 'Just don't ask.'

Alexander, Duke of Albany, escaped, with the help of his excitable brother, just as soon as it dawned on him that he was not in course of receiving a rap on the knuckles, but was about to be incarcerated for some considerable time. In the guise of a grim, long-nosed woman, he rode out of the Castle with Johndie Mar and down to Leith, where a small boat waited to take him out to a larger.

As he had feared, at the last moment Johndie tried to come with him. Two of Sandy's helpers stood on the shore, holding Johndie's arms, while Sandy's oarsmen pulled off and began to move for mid-river. Sandy was waving a conciliatory goodbye from the stern when a familiar voice spoke at his hip. Nicholas de Fleury, sitting on the thwart just behind him, said, 'I'm sorry, Sandy, but you can't go any further. I have to take you back to the Castle.'

It was so unthinkable that it was funny. Sandy Albany dragged his sword from under his skirts, but it took rather long, and de Fleury was already trying to get hold of him. The rowers, who didn't seem to be in anyone's confidence, had slackened their pace, while the boat jerked under the struggle and continued to wander out to the river-mouth. De Fleury was also wearing a sword, but at least had the sense not to draw it. Against a prince, that was treason. Albany panted, 'Get him off me, will you?' to the oarsmen, and two of them did. Of course they did. They knew they would be rewarded. They jumped on the Burgundian, and dragged him away, and banged his head on the gunwale until he slumped. Then they tied him up, while Albany got out of his cloak and kirtle and hood, and, in no time at all, they were alongside the bigger ship, which was a fishing-boat.

Albany had been going to send de Fleury back in the skiff, and then had a better idea. He had him hauled aboard, after himself, and sent the oarsmen back with a message. 'Tell my lord of Argyll that his plan has failed, and his minion has gone on a journey.'

Hearing that, Nicholas groaned. It was partly sham, for the plan had not, of course, failed. It was partly real, because the oarsmen had over-acted, and his head buzzed. He kept his eyes shut and lay on the bottom-boards, which were fishy. He wondered where they would transfer to a larger vessel. The rolling motion was soothing, and he went to sleep.

He woke off the castle of Dunbar. That was all right. The castle was built over sea-rocks. Bigger ships sometimes changed cargo there.

That was not all right. Another rowing-boat had arrived. Sandy was climbing down into another rowing-boat and he himself, still bound, was being bundled down after and thrown at Sandy's feet. Sandy said, 'So you're awake? Don't you wish you'd minded your own business?'

'Where am I?' Nicholas said.

'Arriving at my castle,' said Sandy. 'Where I propose to wait for the King of France's army to come.'

The oarsmen were grinning, but not because they thought it was a joke. They were proud of the Duke. Nicholas said, 'You might have a long wait.'

Sandy's smile did not change. 'It's spring. I can hold out all summer. Ellem provisioned the castle while everyone was away because of the pest.'

John le Grant had discovered that. Questioned, the masters of barges remembered bringing timber and lead and artillery. Men and food would come later, by sea, by the open back door to Dunbar Castle. The Lords Three knew the castle was fortified. They knew Albany would try to escape. They thought Albany would go straight to France, or if ships failed him, would use Dunbar as a temporary base until shipping arrived. They had all agreed, if this happened, to let him go.

Instead, he had always meant to go to Dunbar. Long ago, he had asked for French help and (of course) had been promised it. Now, he had announced his escape, and invited the French King to send a fleet, bringing an occupying force to Dunbar Castle. And thus supported, of course, Albany and the French would demand an end to this cowardly peace between England and Scotland. It was for Scotland to proclaim her proud sovereignty by declaring war on her neighbour. And if the King still refused, his subjects would know where to turn.

In a rueful kind of *da capo*, the note from Nicholas this time was the same as before: *Gelis, I'm sorry. I'll bring him back safe.* Only it wasn't Jodi who had left home this time, but a prince of the realm. And Nicholas wasn't simply sailing to Berwick: he was a prisoner in a garrison preparing to withstand assault, and bound to go where Sandy went. For whether Sandy wanted it or not, that was why Nicholas was there.

*

It took a fortnight for Sandy's confident message to reach the French Court, and another fortnight for the reply to travel back.

But for Sandy, Nicholas might have had a harder time than he did. Dunbar Castle was packed full of neighbours and henchmen in jubilant mood, at least to begin with. These, the Ellems and the Trotters and the Dicksons and the rest, were apt to remember that Nicholas de Fleury was a Burgundian before they remembered that he had ridden, after all, on Sandy's last raid. And he might not be the King's puppet like Adorne, but he was the one in the boat who had tried to take Sandy back. One of the Lochmaben supporters, Applegarth, made a point of that.

It was Sandy who pointed out that Nicol, alone, could hardly have hoped to get him back to Edinburgh anyway. He might not agree with what they were doing, but all he ever tried to do was talk them out of it. To which he had added that they might not especially want de Fleury, but he made a good hostage.

After that, it was like watching the lettering of a very long invoice, item duly following item, irrevocably, to the final accounting.

The garrison, settling in, began to relieve the tedium with forays into the countryside, lifting fresh provisions, driving off sheep and cattle and adding to the numbers of compliant women. The King's Councillors, having established that Albany was there, and apparently waiting for French help, sent a competent force to camp in the town and fields facing the castle, both to prevent depredations and to dissuade sympathisers from joining the Duke. By the third week, it could be seen from the banners that the companies which made up the force belonged to men of some power and influence in the kingdom, and that they had both handguns and light artillery. A week after that, the rumbling of wheels and the lowing of oxen told that Lisouris or Cochrane or Bonar or maybe all of them had been detailed to fetch the big cannon. Unspoken message to Albany: Even if the French come, what can they do against this?

Nicholas hoped to God that the coastal lookouts had been warned, and Crackbene and John and Alec and Leithie and Gelis's latest admirer the Great Andrew had ships tucked away and ready to intercept other ships, or were telling everybody that they had. There was no possibility, none, that the King of France would send an army to Scotland just now. But Sandy wouldn't believe that. All they could do was persuade him that if an army did come, it would be nullified.

The banner of the commander, flying from a comfortable house in the town, was that of Drew Avandale. It had an avuncular look. Drew

Stewart, in his day, had been King's Guardian to this young King's father. Very soon, if he kept to the plan, he would send his own familiar chamberlain to the causeway gate of the castle, asking Sandy to meet him and talk.

He sent the chamberlain, who was rebuffed but not killed, which was fortunate, as no response had came from France, and the mood within the castle had changed to one of angry anxiety. The failure was no surprise to Avandale, but it had established a channel. He was there, if Sandy wanted him.

Then the reply came from France, brought by sea on an innocent salt-ship. Untied, it kept rolling up. The top said, *Ludovicus, Dei gratia Francorum rex, illustrissimo et praeclarissimo principi Alexander, Albani duci, salutem cum prosperitatis incremento . . . Cher et spécial ami . . .*

The bottom said, Got your message, but No.

Nicholas, trying not to beat someone at chess, looked up and then stood as Sandy erupted into the room. 'Louis won't do it,' Nicholas said, guessing.

'Go on. Say it. You told me so,' said Albany. He was deeply crimson.

Nicholas said, 'Of course he wants to. But he can't. It would be suicide while he's at grips with Burgundy. What else does he say?'

Sandy flung down a paper. 'That the ship which brought the courier will return in a week, and that it is his dearest wish that I should use it to travel to France, where there will be a welcome such as no man ever had, and freedom to live as his guest until the time is ripe for me to bring about that alliance of Scotland and France of which we both dream.'

He stopped. The other chess player, at a look, bowed and got out of the room. Albany said, 'You were right.'

'I don't always like being right,' Nicholas said. 'You will go?'

'If I go,' Sandy said, 'it won't be to stay as his guest. You say he can't spare an army. I say he can spare enough men and enough guns to hold this place for France, until he can send more later. I'll go. And I'll bring them back.' He paused. 'You don't agree. You never agree.'

'I think of alternatives,' Nicholas said. 'If you go, you leave behind all these men who have supported you.'

'They will wait,' Albany said.

'And if you don't come back with your army? Or if they can't hold out until you do? There are some big guns out there,' Nicholas said.

'The trouble with you,' Albany said, 'is that you don't understand the men in this castle. You think that they would prefer to surrender quietly as soon as I've gone, and sell their ultimate freedom for a possible promise of indemnity. They won't. And by God, before I go, I'll make sure that Drew Avandale knows he has a long, weary summer before him, for I have guns, too.'

That day, Nicholas remembered what the doctors had said about this family, for after so long together, it should have been possible to talk Albany away from his plan; even allowing for his frustration, his hurt vanity, his passion of indignation against England. But Albany was now beyond controlling. He ranged the castle, making his dispositions; appointed the captain who would lead the garrison when he had left, and prepared to depart in a blaze of glory.

The enemy must not know he was leaving, or stop him. Therefore they must believe he was still there.

He led a foray out of the castle, noticed by Avandale's scouts, who brought a troop of horse down upon him; but not before he had fallen upon the barns and beasts of a loud-mouthed cousin of Eck's and killed him in the hand-to-hand fighting that resulted. He got back to the castle, but with a toll of wounded that made the raid farcical. Then, his temper further roused, he sent for his gunners and planned to take his revenge for his company's wounds.

By then, Nicholas had forged some sort of relationship with the men of the garrison, and with Ellem of Butterdene the captain, who would carry the burden of all that Sandy did now. They were loyal, but they were not foolish. Butterdene said, 'I know. If we fire, they will fire back. But what else can I do? Refuse him? And there are others who feel as he does. They can't join us now, but one day they will. This stand will further the fight against England.'

Nicholas said, 'They don't want to fire against you. Those guns are there simply to invite his highness to stop. In my view, they would not even prevent him leaving for France. They know that France can do nothing.'

It was reported to Sandy, as he expected, but did no good. The guns began firing one dawn. He heard them from his room. Later, Albany sent for him up on the battlements, where he was made to look across and see what damage had been done. Avandale's banner still flew, but the field of tents on the rising ground opposite showed a haze of smoke in one corner, and scurrying men. It reminded Nicholas of other places, other battles, other sieges that he would rather forget. Of his own tent in flames, because of Henry. He said, 'What did you hit?'

Sandy said, 'We were aiming at the gun-carriage. There.'

'I see the gun-carriage. What did you hit?'

Then it came out. 'They shared a pavilion next to the guns. They knew the risk.'

'They didn't know you were going to start firing for the first time at dawn. Who, Sandy? Who was in the pavilion?'

Wallace of Craigie, the answer was. Ironically, the man who had told Blind Harry all he knew about Albany's great hero, Wallace.

'And?'

'I wouldn't have wanted it,' Sandy said. 'But he had a finger in a good many pies, and those ships of his weren't above a spot of piracy. His wife was a cousin of Cortachy's mistress, wasn't she?'

'*Who?*' said Nicholas repetitively. But he guessed. Sir John Colquhoun of Luss, Gelis's recent host: dead.

He unwisely said what he thought.

Sandy listened. Sandy said, 'You know so much. I'll show you. When I go to France, you go with me.'

'I haven't been invited,' Nicholas said, after a bit. He had served the King of France once, and left him for Burgundy.

'You are not a guest,' Sandy said. 'You are a servant. You are part of my household.'

He tried again. 'I am a Burgundian, Sandy.'

Sandy produced an angry leer. 'I think not,' he said. 'You come from Dijon. And now Dijon is French. I may be a guest of King Louis, but you, Nicholas, are his subject.'

Which was true, as it happened. He said something. The ship was due any day. Without Sandy, they would have the sense, surely, to stop firing. In time, the castle would fall, and all those who defended it would be punished. Without Sandy, one real problem with the management of the realm would be resolved. So long as France was impotent, it was not the worst thing that could happen, to have Sandy resident there. For Sandy would not be content. And France, importuned once too often, might just possibly send him back home. Upon which he might discover that to be Earl of March and lord of Annandale and Admiral of Scotland was not inconsiderable, especially as enthusiasm for his opinions might by then have shrunk.

To begin with, Nicholas thought he was free to choose: whether to go and help guide Sandy in France, and perhaps come back with him; or whether to stay and try and counter the harm he had done. He was free in one sense: he and his family were safe now from predators. He could leave them until autumn, say, if he must. Then he realised that Sandy had meant what he said. Whether he wished it or not, he was probably going to France.

He wrote the note to Gelis, but added a little more than he had done in the Berwick epistle. He left it in his room. He thought of Jodi, and Henry, and wished he could take them both with him. He felt Robin was settled, and Kathi; and that Adorne was prepared now for the decision he would have to make soon: whether to go back to Bruges or elsewhere. The rest of his company needed no nursing: Tobie and Clémence and John. Wodman was self-sufficient. Bel . . . Bel was her own law. And Gelis would understand, for he had talked all this out with her, as he had done with the others. No secrets, now. Or very few, and those he could carry alone. They need never be known.

He had been right. When the ship came, they bound him as he had been bound when he came, and he was forced on board with the borrowed clothes which were all that he had. He would be one of a household of ten. Later, Sandy had him unbound and delivered a series of warnings. Then they sat about talking, and drank a lot, and Sandy said, his face flushed, 'Nicol? I'm glad that you're here.'

Which meant that he had probably done the right thing. Although it seemed mad to have to revisit France as part of his personal programme of atonement for Scotland. He would forget all his Gaelic, for one thing.

Part III

Without kinrik to call a man a king
It is in vayne.

Chapter 23

Thus all thar moving cummis fra the king,
Richt as the rever fro the well can spring.

ITH NICHOLAS GONE, the Flemish colony in Scotland
coalesced, rather as the Bank had once done during his
frequent absences abroad. Yet they were not a single
foreign community, as were the aliens in Bruges. Their
advocate and adviser and judge was Anselm Adorne, now established
as virtual Conservator, with Wodman, a Scotsman, beside him. And
linking him to the merchants were his kinsmen: his nephew Sersanders,
and the Scottish family of Berecrofts, into which his niece had married.
And, of course, the astrologer Andreas, from Vesalia.

Then came de Fleury's own circle: his lady from Zeeland, who
continued his business; and the Scotsman le Grant, who dealt with
guns and shipping; and Tobie the Pavian doctor, whose wife was French,
and as welcome at Court as he was.

And lastly there were the merchants; every man with a house or a
warehouse in more than one of the profitable ports: in Berwick and
Leith, in Stirling and St Johnstoun of Perth and Montrose; in Aberdeen
and far up in Orkney. And did you go abroad, you would find the same
names and the same faces, or ones very like them, attached to well-built
family houses in Veere and Bruges and Antwerp, Lille and Middleburg.
Such men did business with that bonny wife, Gelis, and had no cause
for complaint; no more than had their own wives (more's the pity). It
seemed to them all, just, that without Nicol something was missing, ye
ken? A kind of good humour. He was a great asset, Nicol, once he got
going.

Other resident foreigners were less free with their opinions. There were not so many. The short-term Italian physician; the German gunner. Men like Bishop Hepburn of Dunblane, whose unpronounceable real name was Herspolz. The biggest faction were the French: the skilled artillerymen and scholars and builders who came for some appointment or other, and often stayed; the old families, long settled in Scotland, who still sent their sons, through the generations, to serve the French Kings. The families connected with Newbattle Abbey.

By now, it was fairly clear which individuals sympathised, however discreetly, with France, and which – mainly the traders – had found the peace more to their liking. Both elements, for different reasons, found some satisfaction in Albany's absence; both were puzzled by the actions of Nicol de Fleury. According to some, he was a hostage; according to others, he had been seen raiding with Albany, and far from trying to stop him from leaving the country, had actually plotted to join him. Now he would come back with Albany, leading a French army to take over Scotland.

The Council, echoed in an unconvinced way by the King, let it be known that Nicholas de Fleury had proved a valued mediator between his highness and his royal brother, and was acting even now in the best interests of the realm. Jamie Liddell, now released from the Castle and returned to the stewardship of Sandy's Scottish possessions, said very little. He had long been afraid that de Fleury's allegiance was to the King, and to a continued accommodation with England. But he had been a good friend to Sandy.

On the second day of June, King Louis of France was at Château-Landon, Fontainebleau, from where he ordered the merchants of Compiègne to meet the merchants of Paris on business, and decreed that the merchants of Lyons should convoke with his officials in Lyons in three weeks. He moved to St Cyr, to St Denis, to Vincennes.

On the nineteenth of June, from Coulommiers, the King sent to enquire how fared the leopard that the Duke of Ferrara sent him in April. He summoned Nicholas de Fleury. 'You know about leopards?'

'I have hunted with them, sire.'

'You shall hunt with this one, and give me your opinion.'

On the twenty-fourth of June, from Villenauxe, Nogent-sur-Seine, the King sent a courier to Sigismond, Duke of Austria, to notify him that, with regret, the King was stopping his pension.

'One cannot,' he said to Nicholas de Fleury, 'condone, in a pensioner, the blatant support of one's enemies. The man is a Judas, a *prince aux trente deniers.* On the other hand, one knows how to recompense friends. You fought at Nancy when the Bastard of Burgundy was captured? But now that he has joined us, what does he not have? Castles, towns, seigneuries, a comté. What more could one wish?'

Nicholas agreed, with some warmth. Now was not the moment to mention that the same Bastard Anthony had just married his son to Wolfaert van Borselen's daughter, thus hedging his bets in a subtle van Borselen style that filled Nicholas with yearning.

Louis said, 'And, of course, there is Jean, son of Louis de Gruuthuse, once so admired by this youth Maximilian that he created him knight. But brought in chains as my prisoner, he saw his errors at once, and now is a chamberlain, a knight of the Order, Prince of Struheuze and seigneur of Avelghem, Espierre and Ussé, Seneschal of Anjou, and soon to be the husband of my niece. Do I seem a generous master to you?'

'I am dazzled, sire,' said Nicholas. It was true. If he looked dazed, it was because he was locked in calculation. All that, and the old fox was also paying bags of money annually as bribes to the King of England, for one thing. When Edward sent the Princess Cecilia's dowry to Scotland, it had come warm from the King of France's annual subsidy. Which must annoy the King of France quite a lot.

Put together, his interviews with Louis might appear like a growing romance, but in fact he had been sent for only occasionally since his separation from Sandy in Paris. Welcomed by proxy and handsomely installed with his suite at the Sign of the Cock, rue Saint-Martin, Sandy had immediately collapsed into his bed, and had hardly noticed when the King had sent for the sire de Fleury to ride south to his travelling household. In any case, he had William Monypenny to look after him.

On joining the royal party, Nicholas, a long-time admirer of Louis's acumen, contented himself with playing the simpleton, leaving Louis to guess whether he was Albany's promoter or King James's spy. Louis studied the problem, then, rather than waste time on it, threw open the bidding with a blatancy which was an attraction in itself. Indeed, the chance to observe Louis held, for Nicholas, far more fascination than the prospect of wealth and advancement.

He did not say so, however; and when, the weather increasing in heat, the King remarked on his plans to take his Savoyard niece Louise to Dijon, Nicholas refrained likewise from comment. They moved from Vitry to Méry to Nemours, just south of Fontainebleau. There the King sent for M. de Fleury once more, and honoured him with a discourse on France's great future: the submission of Franche-Comté and Brittany, the conquest of Picardy, the harrying into compliance of the Duke of the Tyrol, assuming that the young Duke of Lorraine would let his troops pass, as he had done for the late, tragic Duke Charles. And, lastly, there was hope of a pact that would usher in peace for a century with England.

After which, wiping his hands (he had been feeding his dogs), the King observed that there was a rumour of plague in Dijon, and he would be grateful if the sire de Fleury would travel ahead and investigate. It was near his grandfather's comté, was it not?

It had been a lesser honour, a vicomté. It no longer existed. He had been given another lure. Another chance. Another option.

He went.

Dijon hadn't changed its name since its conquest, like Arras, but a third of its population had gone. Some of them had been replaced by Louis's nominees, and a number of Burgundian officers had actually stayed to serve under France – they had known Louis, after all, when he was the Dauphin. There had been a popular rising against them, and some had been killed, but the rising had failed. You could see the battering the town had sustained: the capital of all Burgundy was at present too small for its walls, which enclosed great patches of rubble and weeds, rustling with wild and tame animals. It was also very quiet, with an air of artificial orderliness about the areas where town life still carried on. There was no plague.

When he had seen all he wanted to see, Nicholas produced some coins which no one knew that he had, and endeared himself to his escort by procuring for them the unlimited hospitality of a tavern for the night while he went to pay a visit to an old mistress at Damparis. In four days the young equerry, his two soldiers and Nicholas had discovered a great deal in common: the men-at-arms still could not quite understand how his French came to be as normal as their own.

He did not explain that he was not an expatriate Scot, but an expatriate Dijonnais, whose mother had married a Scot, who had disowned her. He had lied about seeing a mistress, but not about going to Damparis, which was thirty miles south of Dijon, and just outside Dole. The manor he meant to visit had belonged to the seigneur of Damparis and his wife, who had nursed his own first wife when she died. Eight years ago, the same couple had been actively kind to the child of his next marriage, but he did not know whether they still lived. Only he had reason to believe that the house was still there, and that someone was living in it. And if there were, he had a question to ask them.

Dole, the capital of Franche-Comté, was in a worse case than Dijon: it had been virtually burned to the ground. He found an inn and methodically bought something to eat, and ate it. Then, rather slowly, he rode the few miles south-west to Damparis.

It was still there: the lodge, the courtyard, and the fine, turreted house in which Marian de Charetty had died so long ago. Marian, the brisk Flemish widow who had taken him into her business as Claes the apprentice, and then had given him the standing he needed by marrying him. She had been alone when she fell ill, travelling south; and had stopped here, at the home of friends of her sister. He had not known. She had sent him to Trebizond, and he had come home triumphant, to lay at her feet all he had earned, in recompense for her trust and her love. And found she had died.

He had set out then, a boy of twenty, to find this place, and speak to the kind people who had cared for her. He had learned enough to be sure that her death had been tragic but natural, and that she was buried in Dijon, beside her sister and his mother, in the crypt that served their linked families. His life had touched those of the owners of Damparis again, when Jodi had stayed in the neighbourhood, and Nicholas had taken him to his grandmother's tomb. Then Enguerrand and Yvonnet de Damparis had opened their house to the child and his nurses, and had made them all welcome. His last enquiries had been made a year later. More recently, Gelis had come, he had been told; but he did not know when.

It did not take long, now, to learn that the two he was seeking were dead. The porter was graphic. The old seigneur and his lady – ah, the amiable couple they were, known and esteemed by all. How it would have broken their hearts to see what had happened to Dole! Their nephew's widow had been hard put to it, as it was, to prevent the whole house from being entered and ransacked, but her workers had helped her, and even these foreign rascals could see that it would serve them better to make friends rather than enemies in Damparis. And yes, the demoiselle was still here, and always glad to see visitors, for the big house was lonely, and she was a lady who enjoyed cheerful company . . .

He had not given his own name, but saw, as soon as he was shown in, that it would have made no difference. This was a talkative woman of sixty, childless, widowed, and largely ignorant of the minor details of the family she had married into. She wanted to hear all about the countries he had visited as a trading friend of the dear Monseigneur Enguerrand, and delivered, in return, a detailed account of all the terrible days of the French attack, and of what had been taken, and what had been burned. Only then did she cast her mind back to happier days, and the generosity of her husband's uncle and aunt. Yes, she remembered the tale of the poor Flemish lady who died. A lady of many friends, to be sure: two of them at least had come to visit her, and express their gratitude for what the sire Enguerrand and the lady Yvonnet had done. The poor lady. The poor child.

'Monsieur?'

Nicholas had looked up. 'I beg your pardon. You mentioned a child?'

'Indeed. A daughter, they said, brought too soon into the world because of her sickness, and soon to leave it as she did. The pity!'

'I am sorry. You are saying that an infant, a daughter was born, but did not survive?'

'So I heard. And the lady herself was dead and buried soon after, with the child in her arms, and something her husband had sent her laid with them both. Is it not touching?' the widow cried.

She could recall nothing more. What she had told him, she had told Adelina – Julius's late, inquisitive wife. Gelis had tested it, since. Even then, he didn't wish to believe it: he had to try and find out for himself. But now, slowly, he was close to accepting that it must be true. Marian had not wanted him to know that he might have had a child, who was dead. She had not wanted him to grieve over her death, in the belief that he had helped cause it. She had sent him away and, pregnant, had set out on that journey so that, if the child failed, he need never know. The letter that, dying, she left him had contained only words of gratitude and of love. And Enguerrand and Yvonnet de Damparis, receiving his visit, had obeyed her last request, and told him nothing at all of the birth. Only this sole successor, their nephew's widow, knew of the rumour; but not of the promise of secrecy.

He said, 'Demoiselle, it is so long ago. Is it certain that the child died? Is there a record of it, or a priest or a physician who might remember what happened?'

But she had shaken her head. 'It is what everyone asks. But I have never heard of any such.'

He stayed as long as was polite, or a little longer, and left. But although he spent the rest of the day enquiring, he could find nothing, any more than he had found in Dijon.

And yet there should have been something, had the child died. Of course, Adelina – Julius's late wife Adelina – had insisted that it had lived. But this lady did not think so. And Adelina had had many reasons for lying. She had been lying. If the child had lived, Marian would have told him.

He rode back to his companions in Dijon, and completed his return to the King in a state of abstraction which, misinterpreted, roused them to jealousy. They found Louis south of Noyers and hunting in Moutiers St Jean: he appeared to intend to move west, and showed no further interest in Dijon. It was some little while before Nicholas realised that he had been sent away because the King was waiting for news of a war. Then word came. Electing to go into battle at last, Maximilian, husband of the little Duchess of Burgundy, had led an army of twenty thousand against the French just north of Arras, and had won some kind of victory. That was, half the French and a third of the Burgundians had died, and the Burgundian army had been forced to retreat because the ground couldn't be held.

Nicholas was allowed to go back to Paris. In his absence, he discovered, the King had sent for his dear cousin Alexander, Duke of Albany, made him officially welcome, and set out the pension he would have, in addition, of course, to a lucrative marriage. Naturally, nothing could be done about Scotland just at the moment, but the time would come very soon.

Listening to Albany's account at the Cock, Nicholas persisted. 'It won't come soon. He's lost half his men. He's got Maximilian against him in person. Sandy, do you want to stay here for the rest of your life? For that's what will happen.' But, of course, it was no good. Sandy had stormed out of Scotland. He wouldn't go back with nothing to show for it. Sandy said, 'You return, if you like it so much.' Nicholas could tell, from the tone, that he knew what inducement Nicholas himself had been offered to stay. It was considerable. It did not include a new wife, but he gathered that Louis was willing to import his old one. After all, Jean de Gruuthuse had a van Borselen mother. To Sandy, his desire to leave must seem indeed like rejection.

Nicholas said, 'Look. I don't need to go back to Scotland at once. There are people I could visit in Bruges. Prosper de Camulio is moving about, and I'm told that the Patriarch of Antioch has just been in Tours. They both serve the Pope. They could both be helpful in ways that France perhaps can't. If the King allows me to go, I could return to you in the autumn, and we could talk again about Scotland.'

The Duke agreed, haughtily. Being Sandy, he was not even as apprehensive as he should be. He could do without Nicol de Fleury. He had arrived in France. He was well fed, well housed, and on affectionate terms with the King. He was still confident. One could only hope, regretfully, that something might occur to alarm him. Nicholas wondered who the prospective wife was. Someone really insignificant, and

Sandy would simply go home. Someone truly grand, and it would be apparent to everyone that Louis was aiming for Scotland and was sure of it, for if he failed, he would have wasted an heiress.

Sandy liked France, for he liked being spoiled. Sandy would never understand the other kinds of fascination it held for the man Nicholas now was, or for the man that Jordan de St Pol, once vicomte de Ribérac, had been. Sandy would never consider that it might be a sacrifice to go, as duty called, to confirm that Diniz was all right in Bruges, and verify that Camulio was remembering his Genoese friends.

Then Nicholas thought of Damparis, and forgot everything else.

Marian de Charetty had died there. Now, beyond doubt, he knew why. A small, proud lady, no longer young, she had intended, he guessed, to bear this baby in private; away from curious eyes. If she lost the child, if she died, he was not to be told what had happened.

He had been very young. They had lived as man and wife for less than a year. It hurt that she had not given him the opportunity to care for her, to prove his maturity. He had felt like that before, long ago, with someone else. Yet to grieve for that reason was selfish. What mattered, what merited anguish, was the sacrifice made for his sake: the silent decision; the ultimate expression of love. She would not have wished the marriage undone. She would not have wanted him present. In a strange way, she herself had died fulfilled. It was he who was left unconsoled, alone on the brink.

It had happened before.

In Scotland, it seemed natural that Nicholas did not at once return. He was softening up Sandy. Once Sandy saw that the King of France could do nothing for him, Nicholas would bring him back.

Now that Sandy was absent, it was less necessary to keep apart from Adorne, and Gelis saw him most days that summer, on matters of trade, or in aiding the Council in their management of the King. She grew to know the administrators well, as Nicholas had done; especially Avandale, her courtly escort to Dunglass, and that active man, John Stewart of Darnley, his kinsman. The siege of Dunbar Castle had dragged on for many weeks after Sandy had left, until, accepting at last that no French army would come to relieve them, the garrison had withdrawn by sea, and the King's troops had entered the castle. In due course, the absent rebels were summoned, but unsurprisingly failed to appear. Then sentence of forfeiture of life, lands and goods was proclaimed against John Ellem of Butterdene, captain of Dunbar, and his twenty companions. It was as Nicholas had predicted. The men who had remained faithful to Albany bore the brunt of the King's wrath.

Sir John Colquhoun's death had shocked every sea-going merchant in Scotland, as well as Avandale himself, who had left the siege for his funeral. The King had also been there, and the men of the west who had been Colquhoun's neighbours, as well as Will Crichton and his Livingstone wife. And Will's relative, Colquhoun's powerful widow, Elizabeth Dunbar, Phemie's cousin (*O Dowglass, O Dowglass, Tender and Trewe!*), glaring at her even more powerful son, the litigious Humphrey. The division of spoils, it was already apparent, was going to keep the law lords busy for a long time, as the business consortia defended their rights. Tam Cochrane, for one, had put a lot of money into these shared timber and salmon ventures. Working up north, he was making more than he was spending.

Tam had managed to persuade young Mar to go with him up to Kildrummy, once he had set the cannon in place for Dunbar. It was a question, as ever, of fortification: to keep the King's castles in order against the sporadic rebellions in the north. Reports that came south indicated that the stay was not likely to be a long one: Johndie had already fallen out with every sheriff, bailie, baron and lord in the neighbourhood, as well as all the local representatives of the Order of St John, and was liable to start a war by himself if not returned soon. While he was away, Gelis tried to make headway with the Princess Mary, whose husband was sinking, and who would soon be her own mistress, which meant open to every influence. It should have been easy, for Gelis had once served the Princess, and Jodi was there. It was so far from easy that Gelis wondered, all over again, what magic Nicholas had performed to persuade this limp little matron to take the right course in the past. She listened to Jodi's joyous boasting about life with the Hamiltons, and soothed his occasional anxieties about his absent father, and rode home, swallowing tears. She ought to be used to being without Nicholas. She was not. It was far, far worse now.

Kathi helped. Now Robin was self-sufficient, and busy, and safe, Kathi seemed to be everywhere at once, darting from her own children to Efemie at Haddington to Nanse Preston and the Queen's children at Stirling; from her brother over the road to her uncle and Wodman in the High Street. She snatched time at Provost Bonkle's hospice with Will Roger, learning new music and listening to sad reports of Hugo's drinking and painting. Occasionally, the absence of Nicholas riled Will. Sometimes she made a mistake, and there would be a crash as Roger flung something. Then he would apologise. 'It isn't that he was a musician. It just came naturally, damn him.' She told Gelis, later.

She also spent time on Margaret, the other Princess, seizing her interest whenever she could. The disaster at Beltrees had put an end, at least, to Simpson's unsettling of Meg. He had set out, perhaps, with a Bailzie-like plan to seduce her, but despite his confidence in his charms he must have realised, sooner or later, that she looked upon him as old. But his admiration, his wooing, the salacious poetry, the French way of kissing and dancing had all reinforced her resistance to the English political marriage that the kingdom required. And visiting Mary, she had her sister's example before her.

Dazzling Margaret with the accomplishments of Lord Rivers was no part of Kathi's intention, but she did mention an Adorne cousin's high opinion of English court life, and the remarkable beds, and how big the dress allowance always was.

What had happened at Beltrees: even now, Gelis could hardly bring herself to remember. She had never before felt truly thankful that someone had gone, and she tried not to think so now, for David Simpson had been a killer most often by default, and not by intention. But his death meant that they were safe. Jordan de St Pol came to Edinburgh now and then: she saw the house was occupied and his personal servants in town. She imagined he was satisfying his curiosity – his endless curiosity – about Nicholas. When it was known that Nicholas had gone, he went back to Kilmirren.

Henry had struck up a sardonic friendship with John le Grant, and in his time off from the Guard could be found at the siege, learning to transfer to artillery what he had already been taught about sailing. She came across him occasionally, upon which Henry would make some acid joke about Nicholas at the French Court in Paris, and she would reply in the same vein. He had quite a nice wit.

Bel stayed in the St Pol house for a while, and then went back to Stirling. During her stay, Gelis never visited her uninvited, but occasionally Bel would cross the road to see her, or call on Tobie and Clémence, or take some sweetmeats for Kathi's children. She never said very much, but was good company, as always. Gelis thought that she, too, had only waited to learn what Nicholas was going to do.

Which was, of course, to go to France, and apparently stay there.

About his lengthening absence, Kathi spoke only once, and then obliquely, for there were some things too painful for words.

'I suppose they will all be in Paris. What a hardship.'

And Gelis had answered, 'I know.'

That was all. What they meant was quite different.

If Nicholas has freedom in Paris, he could contrive a visit outside. And if he reaches Damparis, he will hear confirmed what you and I tried to tell him, and Marian de Charetty hoped he would never find out.

I know. I know. I know.

Even before he obtained the King's sanction, Nicholas had sent to Bruges to tell Diniz he was coming. It was only fair, even if he was quite certain that missives would have raced from Leith to Sluys the moment it was known that he had sailed with Sandy for France. When he arrived, therefore, after some very hard riding, it was to find that the Hof Charetty (newly named but with the same familiar livery) had sent a patient employee to await him at the Ghent Gate, scene of Gelis's magnificent sortie.

It was someone he vaguely knew (Ryke?), which was thoughtful of Diniz and quite surprising, since it was nearly three years since he had left, in no very good state after the battle of Nancy, and he had been in the East for a long time before that. Chatting, as the man walked by his side, Nicholas looked for the changes. The sounds were the same. There were some different buildings, altered in shape or in use, and a lot of strange signs. The town looked a little slip-shod and not quite so prosperous, as happened in time of war: Bruges would be paying for expensive victories like the one Maximilian had just had. But there were no signs of burning or damage. It had not changed hands like Dijon. It had only moved under the authority of the twenty-year-old son of the German Emperor, who had married the Duchess.

He was so intent on his first sight of the house that he almost missed the most welcome piece of news – that Gregorio was here, the good friend who had once been Marian's lawyer and who now owned and managed the former Venetian branch of the Bank. 'Master Gregorio would be so pleased that Monseigneur had managed to come! They were all so pleased!' said Ryke suddenly. He was beaming. It came to Nicholas, with misgiving, that he had attained some sort of legendary status in his own former Bank, despite the fact that all he had done was throw away his money and leave. But he did nothing to destroy the man's image of him, and slipped a coin in his hand as they arrived, and Diniz and Tilde and the girls and then all the staff, it seemed, were hurrying out into the courtyard. And Gregorio.

He looked older, and browner, and thinner, but the narrow face and the bony scoop-nose were the same, and so was the enthusiasm under the velvet hat, which was well made and had no lappets, nor, like the rest of him, anything of the desk-bound lawyer about it at all. Nicholas opened his arms and they hugged, banging each other on the back, while Diniz stood laughing. Then Diniz and Tilde, his wife – Tilde, who was Marian's daughter, though not his. With the years, oddly, she had become paler and less like her mother, although her eyes were still bright and her smile loving. The little daughters, Marian and Lucia, were shy, and he kissed them both lightly and left it at that. Time enough to make them his friends. Time enough if he stayed. Time enough if he came back. And if not, they wouldn't miss him. Then he had to shake hands with everybody else, from cooks up and downwards. He was to visit the dyeyard tomorrow. Old Henninc had gone, but there were plenty of others who wanted to see him. Then later –

He let Diniz talk. Eventually, he would have to explain that he couldn't stay long. Not if he were to go back and get Sandy home before winter.

Indoors, he heard all their news. Gregorio had already decided to visit, after those bastards at the Signoria gave in to the Turk and upset all the merchants. Diniz and he always conferred, even though they ran separate businesses. Then he had got Diniz's message to say Nicholas was coming from Scotland, and here he was, panting. So, what was happening?

He told them, briefly, for the alignment of power between France and Burgundy, England and Scotland affected Bruges. Then he heard their views on Maximilian and the future. Diniz said, 'Do you think Adorne will come back?'

Nicholas said, 'Do you think that he should?'

'It's better,' Diniz said. 'That is, the Archduke is making his own enemies, and the friends of the last administration are less of a target. I wouldn't advise he comes today, but every month makes a difference. If he comes, would you come? Or do you feel you want to do more for Scotland?'

'It would be hard to leave just now,' Nicholas said. 'Ask me again when this little crisis is over, and we're in clear water again. If the next crisis hasn't arrived, that is.'

'You're enjoying it,' Gregorio said. Once, he had worked closely with him in Scotland. He knew Will Roger. He knew what it was like. He added, 'And I hope you got Beltrees back, after Simpson.'

Gregorio had seen it being built. Nicholas said, 'No. The castle burned down, and he didn't have the land, or the barony. The house was rather unpleasant, in any case. I created it for the wrong reasons, and he distorted it further. What?'

'Nothing,' Gregorio said. Then the conversation, as was inevitable, moved on to children.

Gregorio's son Jaçon was aged seven, and flourishing. As might be expected, there had been no other offspring. Gregorio was not far short of fifty and Margot out of her child-bearing years. They had been blessed, to have their one well-made boy.

The same was true, of course, of Jordan de Fleury. He had no siblings. It was not intentional. It was only partly intentional. There was a limit to the number of people Nicholas felt he could protect. Or so he told himself.

Then, of course, there was the subject of Adorne's small daughter by Phemie. 'Does he resent her?' Tilde asked. 'Not just the deafness, but that she took Phemie from him? And, of course, he must have hoped for a son.'

'No. He cares for her tenderly,' Nicholas said. 'I think he feels humble. Last time, you see, he chose to preserve his wife's life and risk the life of the infant, which died. This time, the choice was not his.'

'You sound as if you approve,' Diniz said.

'No. I am explaining how he thinks, not how I think,' Nicholas said.

That night, they all drank together and it was, again, what it had been like when it was all one company. He remembered what made them laugh, and what excited them. It returned him, too, to the bright, merry level, half carefree, half watchful, that had marked all his life here. The torrent of mixed Flemish and French swept away all his Scots. Sometimes they mentioned Gelis. He had expected admiration, but was made silent, for a moment, by their obvious affection for her. When he went to bed, he slept as if felled.

The following day, he called at the palace of Louis de Gruuthuse and his wife, Gelis's cousin, and found there, as he had hoped, the senior van Borselen, Wolfaert of Veere. With them were Wolfaert's bastard son Paul, and his pregnant wife Catherine de Charetty, Tilde's sister.

He had not seen her since he gave permission, in writing, for her marriage. She looked happy and fearful at once, as she should, considering the escapades from which once he had rescued her. Nicholas said, 'I am going to take Paul aside and tell him everything. Paul, she rides like a man, and likes lapdogs.'

'I know. She has three,' Paul said, and kissed his wife, who had gone pale and then pink. He patted her waist. 'And, do you see? A future race of Conservators for Scotland.'

'The merchants of Scotland will love you all,' said Nicholas comfortably, and gathered Catherine and kissed her properly, with all the reassurance that she could want. He thought that Marian would have been proud of her daughters.

Later, there came the serious discussion with Wolfaert and Gruuthuse, where he learned what Diniz was not in a position to tell him, and reported what he wanted these two men to know. At the end, they asked him the same question as Diniz. 'Will you come back?'

He did not immediately answer. Gruuthuse said, 'I am sorry. We did not mean to place you in a difficult position. You have not yet completed your business in France.'

'It is why I hesitated,' Nicholas said. 'But not because of embarrassment. I have been offered a pension, and also my grandfather's vicomté, with the house at Fleury rebuilt, and the estate and title enhanced. I have not yet given my answer.'

'Then we need not discuss it. As you will know, we have each taken precautions, Wolfaert and I. It is done the world over. I should not presume to give you advice, Nicholas,' Gruuthuse said. 'But I should be grateful if you would tell me, when your decision is made.'

'I imagine,' Nicholas said, 'that should I agree, the King will broadcast it before ever I could.'

He had apparently missed Prosper de Camulio, who had touched Bruges for a few days, and gone. Returning to the Hof Charetty, Nicholas found a houseful of guests assembled to meet him, and it was late before he could ask.

Diniz said, 'Prosper? Did you want to meet him, now Simpson is dead? Or – Of course, he's got a bishopric, hasn't he? The Pope wants to reward him for rousing opinion against Milan, and Scotland was pleased to oblige, in return for one or two much-needed favours. Result, Prosper de Camulio de' Medici, Bishop-elect of Caithness. He'll be a credit to you. Robes a little too silky, appendages a little too heavily jewelled, and most beautifully barbered, except for the time they put him in prison. Did Simpson arrange that?'

'I think he helped,' Nicholas said. 'So is he being successful?'

'In persuading rulers to make war on Milan? Well, you know Camulio. Gregorio knows Camulio. You remember him from St Omer.'

'Unfortunately,' Gregorio said sleepily. Nicholas judged that Margot didn't approve of late nights. Then he added, 'No, that isn't really fair. He's a humanist, he's an educated, quick-witted man who is truly passionate about the sovereignty of Genoa, and desperately wants to get rid of Milanese rule. But, of course, he's been employed by Milan in the past, and tried to get work from the Medici, and turned his hand to anything, in bad times, that would make him money. All this recent prosperity has come about because he's a favourite of the Pope's nephew.'

'So people don't trust him, and won't commit themselves to join the Pope and Naples?' Nicholas said.

'It's more,' said Gregorio, concentrating, 'that the Milanese are less disorganised than he is. Cicco Simonetta knows just how to discredit him. Everywhere he goes, the Milanese ambassadors are there before him, calling him names. *Fonticho di puzza* is one of the best of them. He's still esteemed by the Empire and Naples: Frederick appointed him consul to Genoa, and Prosper's son (did you know he had a son?) serves King Ferrante. But France won't listen. And he might be a mixed blessing in Scotland, referred to as *in culo mundi* by Milan.'

'In which case, they should be pleased that Prosper is going there,' said Diniz lazily. 'Did I tell you Julius is joining you soon? Things are dull in Cologne, and they seem far from dull in Scotland, from all you say.'

'No, you didn't tell me,' Nicholas said. 'But I was thinking of seeing him anyway. What is happening tomorrow?'

They told him. It included a feast at the White Bear, and a drinking session with the Crossbowmen. 'And the next day –' Diniz began.

'Diniz, I'm sorry, but I'll have to leave after tomorrow,' said Nicholas. 'If I'm to get to Cologne and then back.'

They were disappointed, and he, too, felt the wrench. His company, his friends were as close to him as ever they had been. It was not there, but outside the Hof Charetty that so much had changed. Without Tommaso, without Lorenzo, without Astorre and Felix and Thomas and Jan . . . without Godscalc . . . without Marian, without Kathi, without Adorne, without Sersanders . . . without Gelis, it wasn't the same. And quite soon, even the Hof Charetty would have gone, for the company was moving to Antwerp. He had advised them to do it, and Diniz, the responsible family man, shrewd and eager and attractive, grown from the distraught boy of Rhodes and Ceuta and Arguim, had set to work to bring it about.

Now Diniz Vasquez was his own man, cut off in every particular from his mother's family; disowning Kilmirren as Kilmirren had disowned him. And yet, earlier that day, he had taken Nicholas aside and asked him to come back. 'You established the office in Antwerp. Yours has been the vision that made the business what it now is. It is yours. I only ask to be your partner.'

Diniz was more than that. He was a St Pol, however he might deny it. He was part of the past: the past that contained Umar and Zacco,

Gelis and Bel, and the deaths of his parents. Nicholas had refused, shaken, as gently as he knew how. It was not a rejection of Diniz, or Marian's daughters: it was the opposite. This was their life. If he came back, he would not interfere with it.

He left a day later, and they talked of him.

Gregorio said, 'I'd forgotten. I'd forgotten what he was like.' He sounded angry, and resentful, and even afraid.

'But he is different,' said Tilde. 'I remember him joking all the time. Now the good humour's still there, but it's more a solid contentment, inside. And he makes time for the laughter, but there are other things that mean as much to him, or more.'

'He is needed. That's the difference,' Diniz said. 'He made a mistake, he went back to make reparation. He found a purpose perhaps.'

'Perhaps,' Gregorio said. 'But he isn't sure yet. And which Nicholas should we hope for? Not Claes: he has gone. But there is a place short of hegemony, surely, for the considerate nature, the gift for happiness which made him such a good friend, such an easy business partner? Or would constraint be a sin, now his arts have developed, so that even rulers begin to depend on him?'

'A life of duty?' said Diniz. 'He obeys his conscience, when brought to it. It is one of the things that I love him for. But a *life* of duty?'

'It depends,' Gregorio said, 'on what you think life is for.'

Chapter 24

Off gret corage he is that has no dreid
And dowtis nocht his fais multitud
Bot starkly fechtis for his querell gud.

JULIUS OF BOLOGNA was in no doubt about what life was for, although others frequently disagreed with him.

At his school for indigenous orphans, it had been for rebellion. In Paris, at the Bologna college of notaries, it had been for drinking and gambling and other forms of light entertainment, which had got him into trouble with his subsequent master, the Cardinal Bessarion. Later, with reasonable qualifications and no money, he had traded briefly on his good looks (briefly, because he was not a particularly sensual man) and obtained this post and that until, one day, he had taken himself in hand, looked at his life, and decided what he was going to do about it.

He had been to Geneva before, during his training, and had been intrigued by Jaak de Fleury's cloth business. They had no vacancies then, and he wasn't yet qualified, but that was where he saw Nicholas for the first time, although they called him Claes, and he was young. Cheeky, and nine years younger than Julius was. By the time Julius came back, aged twenty-four, and became Jaak's poorly paid company lawyer, Nicholas had gone to the Charetty at Bruges, and it hadn't taken Julius long to decide that he wanted to follow him. He had met few people as unpleasant as Jaak, and not many who made him as uncomfortable as did Jaak's wife Esota.

Marian de Charetty, the widowed head of the firm, after some typical female delay, had appointed Julius as notary and also as bear-leader and tutor for Felix her son, who went to the University of Louvain, and was to be killed not long afterwards. Nicholas went to Louvain also, as Felix's servant, which was where he picked up the education he had. Being not only illegitimate but disowned, he would have had little chance otherwise. Then, of course, Nicholas, aged nineteen, had *married* Marian de Charetty, the little whelp, and was on his way to becoming wealthy and powerful.

It was what Julius had always tried to hammer into him, when they were being serious about anything, Julius and Felix and Claes. If Nicholas had discovered ambition, he could thank Julius for it.

And then, after the golden years, Julius had made a disastrous marriage to a woman he thought he knew all about, and found that his money had gone and he hardly knew her at all. Adelina had been related to Nicholas, and when she died, she had been in custody for trying to kill him. It made Julius feel ill even to think of her. He kept remembering that there was a daughter of hers, subsisting at Nicholas's expense in a convent here in Cologne. The girl's name was Bonne, and she was said to be between sixteen and eighteen years old. But then Adelina, who called herself Anna, sometimes said she wasn't her daughter at all.

So now there were no nightly feasts on the lagoon, or music, or dancing, or archery contests with one's clients, and packed baskets of fine wines and dates in comfits and veal-garnished cygnets. There was German food and German beer, and a modest, uninteresting business with Father Moriz and that assiduous man Govaerts, lent by the Charetty to help him run it.

When he heard Nicholas was coming from Scotland, Julius said at once, 'Good. I'm going to join him.'

'Well, it's an idea,' Father Moriz had said. Father Moriz was a short, bow-legged, truculent metallurgy expert who had worked with Nicholas and John in the Tyrol and Scotland. He was German, and didn't mind terrible food. 'It's an idea. Certainly we should discuss it. And consider who would then run the business, and look after the interests of Bonne.'

That was Moriz. No sense of humour, and a fanatic about piddling details. Julius said, 'All right. We can talk about it. But I'm going to ask Diniz to send Nicholas, anyway.'

Picking his way through the streets of Cologne, Nicholas had no trouble in finding Julius's office and warehouse, smaller than the one in which Gelis had stayed in the affluent days, but still close to the river. It felt strange to be here, after Nancy.

Julius and Govaerts were at home, but not Father Moriz. Nicholas had a strong feeling that Julius wasn't going to send out to find Moriz, or at least not immediately. As soon as Govaerts showed him in, grinning, Julius had remarked, 'Ah, Nicholas. Come to visit the poor?'

He was smiling, too; but there was a snap to it that you might have thought unwise, in Julius's position. Whether about to ask a favour or not, what was in Julius's mind at the moment was the fact that Nicholas was enjoying friends, esteem, security and a rejuvenated marriage in Scotland while he was not. Nicholas extended his fingers and fondled one of Julius's buttons. 'You don't seem to be doing so badly.'

'It's old. I haven't had to sell off my clothes, or not yet. Will you have some wine? We can still afford wine,' Julius said. He was recovering.

'Don't listen to him,' Govaerts said. 'The business is doing very nicely, Ser Nicholas. And are you well? It's a pleasure to see you.'

He looked the same. Govaerts had been a good manager in Scotland, and was being a good manager here, which was not so far, after all, from his home in Brussels. Julius looked fit, and his smooth, symmetrical face with its slanting eyes and Roman nose were burned by the sun, as if he had been out of doors a great deal. The last time they had met had been in Ghent, in the violence that attended the unmasking and death of Adelina. Julius must have been glad of a respite after that. But more than two years had elapsed since then, and he was announcing now his intention of returning to Scotland with Nicholas.

'Just when your business is doing so well?' Nicholas said sarcastically. He could tell what Govaerts thought by his face.

So could Julius. Julius said, 'I could sell it. Or Govaerts could run it. Everyone trusts him. He wouldn't mind.'

'And Father Moriz?' Nicholas said. 'He was supposed to be in Cologne to help you. So was Govaerts.'

'Well, they could help each other,' Julius said. 'Or, as I said, I could sell it.'

'Well, why not,' Nicholas said. 'Let's talk about it when Moriz comes in. You couldn't return with me anyway. I'm leaving for Paris, then Scotland, at once.'

For a moment, he thought that Julius was going to claim that he could settle his affairs, do his packing and leave with him too, but even he had to acknowledge it couldn't be done. Which would give Nicholas time to see Moriz. When Adelina died, the rest of the Bank had shored up the Cologne business for Julius. He owed money. He couldn't sell, although he had conveniently forgotten.

Then Julius began to ask about Scotland, and France, and Diniz and Gregorio, and presently fall into recollections of their shared past. There had been good times, there was no doubt about it. In setting out to remind Nicholas, Julius himself gradually warmed to the telling until, before long, the petulance had gone, and they were roaring together as they had always done over some irreverent incident. You couldn't hate Julius. You could never hate Julius for long, he was so innocent. Someone else had said that.

Govaerts went early to bed; Moriz didn't come; and Julius and Claes, the ex-company notary and the former apprentice he sometimes felt he brought up, drank until nearly daylight.

Next morning, Nicholas found Julius already out, fulfilling his business commitments. He would be free and home, Govaerts said, at midday. Father Moriz had been detained overnight, but hearing that Nicholas had come, had sent a note for him early that morning.

'You know what is in it?' Nicholas said.

'The superscription invited me to read it. As you see, Fra Moriz hopes you will join him. You would be back before noon.'

'Then I shall go. But first, perhaps you and I should have a talk also?' Nicholas said; and was glad he had, when he saw the man flush. It had been difficult, here in Cologne. He had not realised how difficult.

Colonia, that great Roman city, was a place for fine churches. Besides its Cathedral, church after church, monastery after monastery had brought its grace here, and had been nurtured by many nations. The Irish monks of Cologne were known the world over.

So were the Franciscans, and especially that severe sect called the Observatines, the particular favourites of Mary of Guelders, who had sailed to Scotland with Louis de Gruuthuse and Henry van Borselen, and married its King, and given birth to five living children, among whom were James, the present King, and the Duke of Albany, his rebellious brother. It was Sandy's royal mother who had brought the Observatine Franciscans from Cologne to Edinburgh, from where they had now spread to Aberdeen, under the devoted sponsorship of Bishop Spens. It was to the house of the Observatines in Cologne that Nicholas walked now, to be admitted and shown to a guest-room in which were two men. One, springing up on his horseman's legs, short and plain as a dwarf, was Father Moriz. The other he had last seen in Moscow.

'Father Ludovico,' he said.

'Deference!' said Ludovico da Bologna, Patriarch of Antioch. 'Is one of us dying? There is nothing wrong with me, so far as I know, but a few bruises and a surfeit of Prosper de Camulio. Did you see him?'

'No. He'd gone before I came,' Nicholas said. He smiled at Father Moriz, who had risen from beside the Patriarch's bed.

'Didn't want to talk about the late David his Procurator. Did he really try to kill the King and his brothers?'

'He was careless with poison,' Nicholas said. 'And deserved all he got. So, how bruised? By the Empress Zoe, when you told her you were leaving Moscow? By the toe of her shoe?' He sat down where Moriz had been.

'He was set upon,' Moriz said. 'Nothing sinister, just ordinary robbers.'

'You don't look rich,' said Nicholas critically. He eyed the Patriarch, who looked as hairy, as unkempt and as poverty-stricken on the pillows as he had ever been from the first time they had met and quarrelled with each other nearly twenty years earlier in Florence.

'They wanted the mule. So you have given up Burgundy in favour of Bordeaux, my fine Nicholas?'

'Well, not at least in favour of Porretta,' Nicholas said. He hadn't meant to talk about Milan. Faced with the most single-minded man he had ever known, he couldn't help it. Uzum Hasan was dead, Cyprus was in Venetian hands, Caffa had been overrun by the Turks and the Tartars, Muscovy remained resolutely Greek in its faith and – the final blow – Venice had made peace with Turkey, thereby wrecking Ludovico da Bologna's life's mission: to remove the Muslim menace from the Latin communities of the East. And what was the Patriarch doing but quartering Europe in the name of a petty feud by the head of the Latin Christian church against Latin Christian Milan. It was to be expected of Camulio. But the Patriarch?

Except, of course, that in the Patriarch's case there would be labyrinthine plotting below the apparent compliance. The Pope would pay for it, and so would the Emperor. Nicholas knew the Patriarch's methods. To fund his objectives, he would make any promise. To command a man whom he wanted, he would employ any lure. None of it was for himself, and he wasted no thought at all upon the men whom he used; an attribute that Nicholas found harshly liberating.

Father Ludovico had been watching him. 'Ah, you are wondering if I have reached the age of confessions, excuses. Am I a Bessarion, about to enfold you to my bosom and whisper advice? No, I am not, although I do not say ignore what he told you. I have little to say to you, except this. If you wish, as I see you do, the mindless life of a comfortable paterfamilias, you could not do better than return to banking in Venice. You will die rich, and you might be of some service to me in the meantime. And your man Julius, so dismissive of Germany, might enjoy living in Scotland in your place.'

Nicholas said, 'Is *that* why Gregorio is in Bruges?'

The heavy face stirred. 'He hasn't mentioned it yet? I thought not. A sink of sentiment. Never rely on a man deeply in thrall to his wife. They exchange genders. Yes, there is an opportunity in Venice. Take it. Or stay in your puddle.'

Nicholas said, 'Let me guess. Josaphat Barbaro is back.'

'You are right.' The Patriarch looked complacent. 'The Venetian envoy to the late Uzum Hasan. Have all the Persian's sons killed each other? I cannot remember. And other friends in Venice, of course. Caterino Zeno and Violante his wife, and her charming footloose son Nerio, whom the charlatan Andreas, I hear, once befriended in Bruges. The new Doge, Mocenigo's brother. And the Cypriots.'

Nicholas said, 'I thought that was a pity. That Zacco's family died.'

The tangled black brows rose. 'Died? You could visit them. They are all living save Charla, the daughter. In the custody of Venice, and never to go back to Cyprus, but alive. Who told you otherwise?'

Moriz's face was curious, waiting. 'It doesn't matter,' Nicholas said.

The Patriarch sighed. 'I see that it does. I see you are another Gregorio, save that I thought your wife was more of a man. You will stay in Scotland. Or you might settle in France. I wish you more luck than I had in March.'

Nicholas said, 'Julius would prefer Venice to Scotland or Germany or France.' The Patriarch knew Julius of old. Indeed, he had known him in his wilder days with Bessarion in Bologna, and had denounced him to the Medici. Nicholas had long since realised that, with the Medici vanished from Constantinople and Bruges and weakened in Florence, the Patriarch was looking for other observers in the East. Once, Nicholas had proposed to set Julius up in Novgorod, as proprietor of the Banco Niccolò-Giulio, but Julius would not go there alone.

He added, 'And speaking of Julius. The death of his wife was perhaps a shock? And of Acciajuoli. Neither survived Moscow by very long.'

'I heard,' said the Patriarch. 'In any case, they both would have ended, in my view, with a stake through the heart, the woman especially. The Florentine had a romantic brand of mysticism which he paraded rather too much, that was all. Have you been divining?'

'No. Yes,' Nicholas said.

'I heard. I thought Father Moriz here weaned you away from it. And did it bring you profit and delight? No. Well, don't blame me for disturbing your illusion of privacy. Others will do more to you, and worse, if you persist. Returning to Julius and Venice. Julius would go anywhere if you made him a prince. He would stay in Germany.'

Moriz said loudly, 'No one has that kind of money.' He had become increasingly restless. The German and the Italian had crossed swords before. It had amused the Duchess in the Tyrol.

Nicholas said, 'And Gregorio is settled in Venice. No, Patriarch. I am useless to you.'

'That's what I thought,' said Father Ludovico with passing discontent. 'That is, you cannot see beyond the mattress, I am told, at the moment. When your caul is removed, you will notice that the King of France is not as well as he might be; and the King of England leads an unhealthy life; and the Duchess Eleanor – yes! I regret to inform you – is in the care of her doctors. Added to which are all the terminating activities of just and unjust Man – the Medici killing in Florence, who would have expected it? The assassination of the last Duke of Milan! The judicial killing – I am told – of the King of England's own brother, following the example of France. The sad royal slaughters in Cyprus and Persia. The decimation of the nobility of the Fleece – there were only five Knights left alive in the stalls, I am told, when the Order held its meeting last year. Sudden death faces us everywhere, and the whole prospect of Europe can change overnight. You know, of course, that Rhodes is about to fall, and the Turk is attacking Belgrade and moving into Otranto in Italy? The King of Naples accuses Venice of making peace with the Sultan merely to punish Venice's Italian enemies.'

'*Rhodes has fallen?*' Nicholas said.

The Patriarch looked at him. 'I thought you would be pleased? It is not quite confirmed. But when last heard of, the Sultan's Pasha had arrived off the island with fifteen thousand men and sixty ships, ten cannon and thirty stone-casting machines, and the Grand Master of the Order of St John was attempting to resist with three thousand five hundred men.'

Nicholas said, 'They attack, or threaten to attack, every spring.'

'But one day – and perhaps this is the time – they will succeed. And without the Knights to harass them, the Turks will go further than the toe of Italy, you may be sure. Then all Christendom will have to start up from its own petty wars and take to arms. Go to Venice,' the Patriarch said. 'Venice needs you. Venice may prove your best hope for the future.'

There was a silence. Nicholas said, 'France will know this?' He saw Moriz shift.

'Ha! Straight to the point. I knew I could rely on you,' the Patriarch said. 'In my view, France has already seen an opportunity in prospect. A distant one, perhaps, but one which will affect all those little countries of which you are growing so fond. I repeat my advice. From a central position of power, you may out-broker the Medici themselves.'

'Perhaps,' Nicholas said. 'But if I did, where would I find you? Can you trust yourself to the Emperor, while your own people in Bologna and Ferrara are supporting Milan?'

'First this deference, and now a touching care for my family! Now I feel old,' said the Patriarch. 'I remember the Emperor's first visit long ago to Bologna, and his childish delight in the spinneries. You dealt in silk. You remember, of course, meeting Queen Carlotta in the days of Sante Bentivoglio, the last ruler of Bologna – the springs of Porretta did him little good, poor fornicating fool: he died three years after. His successor is a much harder man, and a rival to the Marezzi silk merchants, who are always falling out with their German creditors. There is one in the Emperor's prison just now, whom I was supposed to liberate.'

'And have you?'

'I have promises. If they turn out as usual, the man will be released after three years, on payment of four thousand florins of ransom. But the silk merchants will thank me. And the Pope.'

'And then you will go where?'

'Where would you like me to go?' asked Ludovico da Bologna. 'Ah! Do not trouble to answer. The Franciscans here would no doubt say the same. I have an idea or two. But if you were to settle in Venice, you would hear before anyone.'

Nicholas left, with Moriz, soon after that.

On the way back: 'He was already walking with difficulty,' Moriz said. 'I have never known a stronger man, but he is nearly seventy, and has tramped the world for his faith. Like any sane man, I could throttle him, but I revere him as well. That timber merchant's son from Bologna has devoted his life to his faith, travelling further than soldier, or seaman, or merchant, without money or comfort, sustained by his belief in himself, and his Order, and his God. If I were God, I would wipe half the saints off the calendar to make room for that one untidy priest.'

'I, too,' Nicholas said. He was silent. 'You are telling me something. Should I go to Venice?'

'It will not prolong his life,' Moriz said. 'But if you wish to go, go. You have paid your debt in Scotland, from all that I hear.'

It was a short walk, and Julius arrived home soon after. But by then all the necessary news had been exchanged, and Nicholas had listened to what Moriz had to tell him about Bonne.

'You are going to see her? I am glad. I visit her regularly but Julius, as you know, revolted against everything that reminded him of his wife.'

'And she?'

'She is well enough. That is, you pay for her keep, and she is fed and sheltered and trained by the nuns. But she is a young woman now, and is no longer quite so content with captivity. She never speaks of her mother. I think she resents her. This is natural.'

Walking, Nicholas had said, 'In her last moments, Adelina claimed that Bonne was not her daughter.'

'That she was your daughter and Marian's. Yes, I know. She never speaks of that either. If one asks her what she remembers before her mother married the Graf, she says she does not remember. Nor is it possible to tell by her age. She may be sixteen, as her mother once claimed.'

'Or eighteen, as Marian's daughter would have been, had it lived. They say at Damparis that it died,' Nicholas said.

Moriz said, 'Your lady, Gelis, was told so as well.' His voice was gentle, for an opinionative dwarf from Augsburg. He said, 'For what it is worth, I see nothing of you in her. More, I do not think your wife would have borne a live child and failed to tell you. But, of course, she may have been led to believe that it was dying or dead, and it survived.'

'But someone would have told me,' Nicholas said. 'Surely. Surely.'

'I think so,' said Moriz. 'You have chosen the generous part, to take the burden of her upbringing, so that Julius remains only her nominal guardian. He should be grateful. But if he closes the business, a decision must be made about Bonne. I am unlikely to stay here for ever.'

'I know. I shall see her,' Nicholas said. 'But I hope Julius changes his mind. I shall send him all the business I can.'

'It is not business he wants,' Moriz said. 'It is admiration, and courtly society, and money.'

Then they were back, and Julius, arriving, filled the rest of the day with adventures that reminded Nicholas, once again, of the wayward delights that had once made up their lives. Then next morning he left, with Julius's embrace round his shoulders and Julius's words in his ear. 'I miss you, you young lout. Give me a month or two, and I shall surprise you yet.'

As for Bonne, Moriz was right: she did not look like Nicholas. Entering the Abbess's room in her demure robe, hands folded, long brown hair overlaid with white lawn, she could be seen to be tall, but to lack either Marian's bright colour or his own clownish pits. Her eyes were blue,

and her frame was sturdy rather than graceful. She did not look like
Adelina either. She did not look like anyone he knew.

Under the Abbess's eye she answered his questions with a certain
crisp brevity. From the Abbess's expression, Nicholas deduced that
she was deemed to be on the borderline of impertinence. He asked leave
to walk with the girl in the cloisters, and it was granted. He was a
generous patron.

Alone, she allowed the irony in her voice to be heard. 'I am sorry. I
hear you purchase my clothing, but I am not sure for what purpose.
You have bought my wardship and marriage perhaps? For yourself, or
a friend? And if so, might I meet him?'

'You would rather be out in the world, Bonne?' he said.

She said, 'What should I say? I would not have you think me ungrateful. But there is a certain difference in age.'

'Then for a young, well-landed nobleman?' Nicholas asked.

'Perhaps. Or an old one,' she said. He looked for mischief, and found
only continuing irony. He did not know whether to be grateful or not.
It was not Marian's style, or even Adelina's. He remembered Felix
sounding like this, copying the pawnbroker Cornelis his father. Resentment and anger lay underneath.

He said, 'What do you want?'

She stopped. 'Now there,' she said, 'is a question I have never been
asked before.'

'So you have had a long time to think of the answer. What would
you have said to your mother,' Nicholas said, 'had she asked you that,
now?'

'She never asked me that either,' the girl said, and began walking
again. 'I thought you knew her. She was a nobody. A selfish, ambitious
nobody.'

'And who are you, Bonne?' Nicholas asked.

'The Graf's daughter,' she said.

'No,' Nicholas said.

She rounded on him. 'You have proof? Do show me.'

'I am told there is proof,' Nicholas said. 'But perhaps it would be
enough to ask how often the Graf's family come to visit you? Did you
tell them your mother was dead? Did they reply?'

'I think the Abbess will be expecting us,' the girl said. Her voice
shook. 'Is this how you usually court a bride? With aspersions on her
birth?' The cause of the tremble was fury.

'Most husbands will expect either candour or a well-documented lie.
I am sure you are mistress of both, but I am rather short of time.

Discarding myself as an applicant,' Nicholas said, 'do you wish to be married, to be independent, or to continue in the embraces of Christ?'

'I do not wish to be sold off to an unknown,' she said. 'But since you are so short of time, I shall not try to explain why.'

'Perhaps it is just as well,' Nicholas said. 'When you have a clear-cut plan, speak to Moriz. Or one of the nuns would be prepared to advise you, I am sure.'

She glared at him.

He smiled. 'Bonne. Don't be silly. It's not hard to guess how you feel, but you must stop sulking some time, and think of your future. We are only here to help you, and you shall marry, if you wish to marry, only someone who has your approval. I may not come again, but you can reach me through Father Moriz. Does that seem reasonable?'

Her cheeks were scarlet. 'Oh, it seems reasonable,' she said. 'You are paid to broker my marriage, and when I have been sold off, my costs here will cease. You don't really wish to know what I want.'

'Tell me,' he said.

'To be a superior prostitute, like my mother,' she said.

This time, Nicholas stopped. 'No,' he said. 'That is not allowed. One, because it is not true. And two, because she is dead.'

'What difference does that make? She was always dead to me,' Bonne said.

He spoke to the Abbess, and left the convent without talking further to Bonne: child of unknown parentage; alleged daughter of Adelina de Fleury, who was barren, and someone unknown.

He did not believe she was his child and Marian's. Meeting her, he had been conscious of nothing but pity mixed with impatience. He felt responsibility, because Adelina had reared her. He hoped that Julius would recover and take some interest in her future as well. He sensed nothing else: not the tender warmth that had been there from his first moments with Jodi, nor the ache that stayed with him still, through all his agonising dealings with Henry. He would deal with Bonne with his head, not his heart.

Returning to Paris, he paid a call to a monastery just outside Brussels, and another to a religious complex in Lille, by which time his baggage horse was carrying a very large crate. In between, he made his last visit to Bruges.

It was hard, in the end, to tear himself away from the Hof Charetty. It was hardest of all, perhaps, to take leave of Gregorio, who had witnessed Marian's marriage with such cynicism, and had stayed to see her buried with such love. The unskilled swordsman Gregorio, who had once fought Simon for him; whose wife had cared with compassion for Jodi; who – in his precise legal way – had weighed up Nicholas with greater accuracy than anyone else now in Bruges.

Nicholas had said nothing to Gregorio of coming to Venice, and Gregorio himself did not refer to it. Applying Father Ludovico's theory, Nicholas preferred to think that Gregorio would have acted the same way whether he had been happily married or not. Gregorio was older than Diniz. Gregorio, regardless of self, did not approve of the notion of Nicholas settling into the middle ranks of Venetian society and drifting there for the rest of his days. Gregorio had always expected too much.

Sandy was in Paris, but not packing. With him was Hearty James, the King of Scotland's half-uncle, sent to hold diplomatic talks with the King, find out what the hell was happening, and bring Sandy back. He seemed to think it was Nicholas's fault that he hadn't come back long since. James Stewart of Auchterhouse, Earl of Buchan, was called Hearty James because of a certain absence of frivolity in his nature. It is no joke to be only half-royal, with six sisters.

He was feeling in an even less jocular mood now. In the absence of Nicholas, Sandy had finally made up his mind. He was not going home. He objected, as a Scot of royal blood, to the servility which prompted his brother to make an ally of the enemy England. No one pointed out that Sandy's royal Scottish blood was half Flemish, or that his grandmother (and Buchan's mother) were English. It would have made no difference anyway. He was staying in France, all expenses paid, and the King had offered him a wife from a dish full of Bourbons. Wolfaert had picked one. Everybody in France had a Bourbon. They made good middle-range brides, without skimming off the best cream. Hearty James was furious. Wolfaert had once married his sister.

It was not at all clear what, beyond staying in France, Sandy intended to do. The King sent many warm messages to his dear cousin of Scotland, and begged him, once again, to remember how close was the friendship between them, and how France would benefit in her dark hour, were his serene highness to end the English peace and attack the bastards instead. (These were not the terms used.) Were this to happen, it was hinted, a happy reconciliation between the King and his brother could be guaranteed.

The King was also gracious to Nicholas, and hoped to see him return. He knew that he could rely on M. le comte – ah, no, it was still M. de Fleury? – to explain what the Duke of Albany saw so clearly: the hurt to Scotland's pride, her reputation, her glory, perpetrated by this pusillanimous peace.

Sandy said goodbye, in a word, and Nicholas attached himself, and his crate, to the Earl of Buchan's departing retinue. The voyage to Scotland was undertaken in silence: gloomy on Hearty James's part, and contemplative on the part of that European manipulator *Monsieur* de Fleury who, justifying all the Patriarch's strictures, was increasingly thinking of mattresses.

Chapter 25

The tavernar, this man of hostillarye,
Before the alphyne suld he stand, for quhy
In thar placis oftsys discord is sene.
Neir-by the iugis tharfor suld he bene.

T HIS TIME, with a royal prince at his side, there was no hope
that Nicholas could enter Leith unobserved. The King had
sent a cavalcade with his own Guard to fetch them. Henry,
his chin elevated, his gaze straight ahead, was among them.
If you're about to be hanged, I don't know you. They were then delivered,
at a fast trot, to the Castle, Hearty James being accorded royal honours,
and the Burgundian who fled to France with the Duke of Albany being
viewed with suspicion. His crate, being unwieldy, was to follow along
with his baggage.

Rushed to the Presence, he contented himself with endorsing what
he had already persuaded Hearty James was the case. His grace the
Duke of Albany had felt in conscience opposed to his country's policy,
and had hoped to enlist the help of the King of France to persuade his
royal brother to renounce his friendship with England. The King of
France was, of course, sympathetic for many reasons, and proposed to
send an emissary soon to make the same point, and to urge the King
of Scotland to heal the rift with his brother. It was highly unlikely that
the King of France would expect more from this than a polite refusal.
One could see that such exchanges might go on for some time. But the
truth was that the King of France was wholly unable to send more than
an envoy. His war with Maximilian occupied all his forces. Whatever
the Duke of Albany hoped from France, he was unlikely to get more
than a few years' free lodging, during which time the political situation
in western Europe might have radically altered. The Duke was being

offered a bride, and had accepted. He had settled in France and (implied Buchan) might well be left there, to everyone's benefit.

Calm down. It is distressing; he is your brother; but there is nothing to worry about.

Approached with finesse, the King might have accepted it more calmly. As it was, with the impertinence of Dunbar Castle fresh in his mind, James was scathing. Reconciliation, indeed! Was it likely? Of course, Sandy thought that France would send an army to rouse discontented Scots against England. No doubt Sandy thought he would lead it. Once he realised that no army was coming, he would leave France and come back to take his punishment like a man, and settle down.

With variations, this was presumably what the King had been proclaiming ever since the siege of Dunbar. Whitelaw, who was present (his spectacles dim as soiled ice), had no doubt pointed out, with the rest, that any kind of sentence passed *in absentia* would simply drive Albany irrevocably to France. But now, with Albany not only remaining in France but about to be married, the situation might be thought to have changed.

'And M. de Fleury?' the King was saying. 'Why is he here? A Burgundian, a guest in this country, he takes the part of the King's own brother against the King. What did Louis offer *him* to be his man?'

'A pension for life and the comté of Fleury, my lord,' Nicholas said. 'I refused.'

'Because you are to be a double agent,' the King said.

'My lord, the King of France has no need of me in order to obtain information from Scotland. No. I felt, with my lord of Buchan, that time is on Scotland's side. France cannot use force until her own war is finished. Whatever his grace of Albany may say, he will not be required to decide his own future until then. It is why it seemed best to allow him, if he wished, to leave Scotland.'

Nicholas paused. 'I share my lord's deep regret at the loss of life at Dunbar. It was inadvertent, I am sure. My lord Duke's artillery was not accurate to that degree.' Avandale was there as well, but he supplied no support, not even a nod of affirmation. His reasons were different from Henry's. Before the King, they must not seem to be in collusion.

Unexpectedly, the support, such as it was, came from Buchan. 'De Fleury did refuse. It looked genuine. Sandy was furious.' It wasn't graciously put, but it was said, and all the more convincing, perhaps, because it was cursory. Vaguely, Nicholas wondered what the Duchess Eleanor had told Hearty James about him, nearly three years ago. Not vaguely at all, he remembered what the Patriarch had said of the

Duchess's health. He hoped it wasn't true. Both the Tyrol and her own country needed her.

He was dismissed with something like truculence and got out before anyone captured him. Parliament, long since summoned, was due to meet within the next week. Princess Margaret was also due to report for her wedding at Nottingham. What the King should do about Sandy and Margaret would have to be decided immediately. Nicholas had already had a note from Argyll, summoning him to the tavern. When a second messenger came, he tipped him to turn a blind eye and went off to his house.

There was a large crate stuck in the doorway, with Kathi and her brother Sersanders pushing from outside, and his wife Gelis pulling within. Gelis's face was pink with laughter and she exclaimed when she saw him, in an exaggerated mixture of delight and despair. She looked beautiful enough to consume on the spot, and he saw no hope of a mattress for a very long time. He made a suggestion, and very soon the crate had slid indoors, leaving a strong smell of lard on the doorpost and an excited ballet of dogs in the street.

They collapsed into chairs, leaving the box on the floor. Mailie, beaming, came in with a tray. Gelis said, 'Something told me you were back. They haven't put you in prison?'

'It wasn't my fault,' Nicholas said. 'I was led away by bad influences and the glamour of royalty. Is this all we have? I've been eating ship's food for a fortnight.'

'There is more. You could lick the door while you're waiting. So what's happening?' Gelis said. It was fair enough. Sersanders also needed to know, and he would tell Berecrofts and the rest. Nicholas talked as they ate. From Albany and the French, he went on to speak about Bruges, addressing himself to Sersanders and Kathi at the end.

'So you see, it is settling. Diniz suggested that the time is quite near when your uncle might think of going back. But I have one piece of sad news. Arnaud has lost his wife. She didn't recover from the birth of Aerendtken. Friends have taken the little girl and the baby, but he is very distressed. Antoon is helping. He is now a canon of Lille: I called and saw him. And I saw Julius and Moriz in Cologne. Julius would like to come here, but only, I think, because business is slow. With a little help, it should recover.'

Gelis said, 'He might be better out of Cologne. It must remind him of Anna.'

Kathi said, 'What did Moriz think?' He always forgot, when away from her, how slight she was, and how brilliant her eyes. Robin was well, and the children: he had established that right away, as he had been reassured about his superior page Jodi.

He said, 'Moriz has worked hard at the business and is loath to see it abandoned, I think. But it isn't fair, either, to leave him and Govaerts stranded in Germany. Their help was only meant to be temporary. What is happening here?'

He listened to all of them. First the business, then the Court news. Mar was back from the Don and the Spey, fulminating against Tam and all the Cochranes, and everyone's Constables and bailies, including his own. The Queen was pregnant again, and had vacated the marital bed till next summer. 'Ludovico da Bologna was talking about that,' Nicholas said. 'That is, he was discussing the Queen with a clerk in Bologna who wants to write a book about women. Father Ludovico knew her father. He says you and your uncle told him a lot on the journey to Poland. Your uncle thinks the Queen secretly wants to be like the Great Margaret. You know? The one who ruled Scandinavia for ever?'

'It just felt like it, I expect,' Gelis said. 'So you gave Father Ludovico all the gossip? How was he?'

'Hungry,' Nicholas said. 'Rather like me. No. I'd better go. I'm supposed to be reporting to Lang Bessie. Newly home from the sea, I deserve a good welcome somewhere, and she's clean.'

Gelis said, 'That's why you wanted the food? You're going to be drinking with Colin Campbell all evening?'

'That's why,' he said. 'Shall I show you what's in the box?'

'I want to guess,' Kathi said. 'Why don't we all guess? Nearest correct answer gets to run away with the King, maybe? Nicholas, wasn't it risky to go on those raids, and garrison the castle with Sandy, and travel with him to France? You could have found yourself labelled a forfeited traitor.'

'Except that I had told everyone beforehand,' Nicholas said. 'I even made a discreet call at Aubigny, on my way back from Dijon. Everyone but King James knew the plan, and approved it. Once Sandy had made up his mind, he was best out of the kingdom. I could talk to him. There was a chance he might listen.'

'But the King didn't know. You were entirely dependent on the King's trust in his advisers. What if something happened to change that?'

'Then I start on the Queen,' Nicholas said. 'And help her become another Great Margaret.' He was on his knees. 'I need a hammer. And a pair of shears. And something to lever with.'

Ten minutes later, they were all on their knees. 'You win. I couldn't have guessed,' Kathi said, awe in her voice. 'The drinking-man's nose. The eyebrows. The chin. When did he have it done?' And as an afterthought: '*Does* he have wrinkly hands?'

'Hugo always does wrinkly hands. He began it three years ago, before they decanted him over to Soignes. This is just the left outside wing. He's working on the royal portraits now. Does it remind you of a riper Tommaso?' Nicholas said, his head tilted sideways. 'Or is it just the fringe?'

Before them leaned part of the altar-piece for the Trinity Church, painted in a haze of alcohol by Hugo vander Goes in his recuperative retreat at Rosenklooster in the forest of Soignes. Before a dazzling organ (recalling a munificent gift of his own), knelt Edward Bonkle, provost of the Collegiate Church of the Holy Trinity, Edinburgh. The Provost's body was solid. His surplice and amice fell into exquisite lines. His face was, to the life, that of the good-natured father and business-man Canon Bonkle, to whom the King's Flemish mother had entrusted her church. Mary of Guelders had probably known Bonkle merchants in Bruges all her life, as Claes and his friends had known the Canon's bastard son John. One of the Canon's bastard sons, John.

And now this, standing before them: testament to the skills of a magnificent, falling-down-drunk painter, who once raucously vied with them all, turning out coloured escutcheons in the chaotic prelude to the Duke of Burgundy's wedding: *Fourteen puking sols a day for all this!*

Sersanders said, 'Hugo. Oh, Hugo the madman. What can we do for him?'

'I did ask,' Nicholas said. 'He's really best where he is. He has a brother there too. They relax all the rules and let him out, and people visit him – Colard; Maximilian even. But you know Hugo. There's always something. He's not appreciated; he's never going to finish all his commissions; he can't get over Elizabeth. Pass the Rhenish. When it all gets too bad, they play music till his head clears again.'

He stopped. He said, 'He kept talking about the Duke of Burgundy's wedding, and asking who was Duke of Burgundy now.'

'You'd better go to your meeting,' Kathi said. 'We'll take care of it.'

While he had been indoors, the autumn light had begun to fade, and the windows of Lang Bessie's tavern were yellow with lamplight by the time Nicholas ran up the back stairs to Argyll's rooms. With Colin were Mr Secretary Whitelaw in his smeared glasses, and Will Scheves in plain clerkly black instead of the robes of the Primate. Argyll said, 'Nicholas. Sit. Drew is with my lord of Buchan. We wish to hear, obviously, all that you were not able to say at the Castle, as soon as the ale has come. You know Henry de St Pol?'

It was not the non-sequitur it seemed. 'I'm afraid so,' Nicholas said. 'Shall I . . . ?'

'No, no, someone else will bring it,' said Colin Campbell of Argyll. 'In fact, we shall not wait. Tell us your opinion of the Duke of Albany, and what is liable to happen in France.'

He presented his report about Albany. It included a résumé of all he could discover about the size and quality of the French and Burgundian armies at present in the field, their length of service, their armaments, and the finance in prospect for their replacement. Among other things, he had spent a lot of time chatting to bored members of the King's Scottish Archers. And at Aubigny.

To that, as a bonus, he added his opinion of what was liable to happen in countries other than France, and particularly in relation to Rome, Genoa, Rhodes and the aspirations of Turkey. He had verified, before he left France, that the attack on the Knights Hospitaller at Rhodes had reached its height in July and had been resisted. The island was probably safe until the following spring. He did not mention Ludovico da Bologna's determination to seize his attention over that; or the fact that he had not introduced the subject at the Castle, or indeed on the voyage from France. The Earl of Buchan's confessor was William Knollys, Preceptor for Scotland of the Order of the Knights of St John. He did not mention, either, the Genoese Prosper de Camulio, absent Bishop of Caithness. He did not need to.

At the end, no one at first said anything; then Argyll removed his contemplative gaze from Nicholas's face and glanced at Whitelaw. Whitelaw cleared his throat.

'A good submission, sir. We are grateful. We shall assimilate it, and return to you. As to the Duke of Albany: it is evident that King Louis cannot immediately exploit his presence, but will harbour him against the future. You say, and I concur, that King Louis must realise in the interim that the Duke possesses no value as a hostage, and will not be allowed to return merely to foment unrest. The summons for treason must stand.'

'But not a sentence of forfeiture, and certainly not a justification,' the Archbishop said. 'The King would not agree to his death.'

'On some days, he would,' said Colin Argyll. 'But no. I agree. In the light of all Nicholas has told us, we must treat this stage by stage. First,

a continuation of the summons for treason, as you say, which demands
the Duke's presence in Scotland but leaves open the matter of proof
and of punishment. Then a pause, we hope, during which the Duke
comes to realise that he has discarded a princely living in Scotland
for that of a powerless retainer in France. And then, perhaps, the
opportunity for a genuine reconciliation between his grace and the
Duke which embraces the alliance with England. What *is* that noise?'

It came from below, from the galleried front rooms of the tavern. One
of the voices was that of a woman, and one was that of Henry de St Pol.
The third, recognisable to them all, was the voice of John of Mar.

'Excuse me,' Nicholas said.

Fast as he was, Argyll overtook him. 'No. Go back. You are not
supposed to be here.'

It was true. Nicholas stopped. Whitelaw stepped down beside him.
Argyll ran on, and Scheves followed. Of course, they had more power
than he had to halt this. Argyll had men down below.

From the inner stairs, where he stood, Nicholas could witness the
whole scene like a play. So could the customers, two floors below, who
were already beginning to crowd the bottom steps, peering upwards.
The muffled voice of the woman, Lang Bessie, came from one of the
gallery rooms, testily commanding both visitors to go away. The visitors,
John of Mar and Henry de St Pol, were outside her door, glaring at
one another. Mar had a knife in his hand, reversed for hammering. As
Argyll arrived, he turned it blade outwards. Henry's hand went to his
waist.

Colin Campbell of Argyll put a strong, friendly hand on his shoulder.
'*Dhia!* What a commotion! You want a girl, come and I'll find you one.'

'I have one,' said Henry. 'Thank you, my lord.' He was eighteen:
the Prince three years older. His eyes had never left Mar's. His face
was pale.

Mar also spoke. 'Go away.' He was addressing Argyll, and Will
Scheves behind him. In the darkness of the upper stairs, Nicholas and
the Secretary were invisible. Nicholas, finding a pair of spectacles in
his grasp, handed them up, and felt them taken.

Argyll had answered. 'Certainly, my lord prince, if you will come
with me. I have some good wine upstairs. This is too public a place for
these matters.'

Johndie Mar paid no attention. Even in the poor light, you could see
the red flush that coloured the whole of one cheek, and the tension that
tightened his jaw and his neck. A boy came thrusting his way upstairs,
bearing something, a mixture of excitement and fright on his face.

'A second key,' said Johndie Mar. 'Now kindly open this door.'

Behind the boy, three men had appeared. One, at a nod from Argyll, stayed below, barring the stairs to the crowd. The other two slowly mounted the steps. There was no way for Mar to go except upwards. Whitelaw hastily turned and led the way up and into Argyll's office, which was separate from his parlour. Nicholas waited a moment. Below, Argyll had taken the key. He turned it quickly, speaking Lang Bessie's name, and opening the door a short way, pulled the woman out and into the arms of the two henchmen behind him. She looked at Mar as she came, and screamed, for the Prince had steel in each plunging hand, aimed at her face. 'Slut! Any man's filth!'

Argyll was not wearing a sword, but Henry was. The woman escaped, dragged downstairs by Argyll's men. Johndie Mar's dagger hit nothing, but his sword, changing direction, sliced across towards Argyll and St Pol. Henry parried it.

It was, Nicholas was to think later, through no self-effacing wish to protect the Household Controller; the blade was coming towards Henry as well, and Henry was trained to save himself. There was a clash and a blister of sparks in the gloom, and then a mutter, the trample of feet and a flash as Mar changed position and lifted both blades again. The woman had gone. The two servants obeyed a signal to halt. Henry ducked and retreated, sword in both hands, towards what had been Lang Bessie's room, and Mar followed. There was no fear of Henry attacking Mar. There was every likelihood that Mar was about to do his best to kill Henry.

Nicholas suddenly saw that Argyll was going to do nothing. He said, 'My lord?' And when Argyll looked up, threw him down his own sword. Henry saw it.

So did Johndie Mar. He laughed. He said, 'So the Burgundian is your hireling? Whom does he want you to kill, Colin? This pasty-faced heir to Kilmirren, which would suit M. de Fleury? Or me, the King's brother, which would suit every one of you, because I detest England as Sandy and Margaret do?'

'Sire,' said Argyll. Below, men were falling silent.

'Shall I tell you something?' said Mar. 'Shall I tell you why Meg will never marry in England? Why my sister the most serene Princess, lady Margaret, has twice been summoned to her great English wedding, and twice has failed to arrive?'

'My lord,' said the Earl of Argyll, 'are you coming, or do you need assistance with this young man?'

His voice was helpful, not threatening. He had not used the sword

Nicholas had flung him to bring Mar to order. Instead, he was reminding the Prince of his quarrel, to divert him from whatever he had been going to say.

The Earl of Mar said slowly, 'No. I am not coming. Not until I have finished with Master Randy St Pol, and taught him not to take what does not belong to him.' And, turning, he advanced on the youth.

It was a small room, lit by guttering wall-sconces, with one unshuttered range of windows giving on to the street and a low ceiling, unsuited to swordplay. Within it, Henry stood quite still, presenting his sword to his enemy, and to Argyll who stood at the door, with Nicholas now silently by him. Like Mar, St Pol wore only doublet and hose, without other protection, and his bright hair was uncovered. His stance, like Mar's, was that of a highly trained swordsman, but there was a physical balance about him, a grace that Mar lacked. Mar had the advantage of age, and also a knife which Henry did not possess. But looking at the two, it was not impossible that the unthinkable could happen: that the youngest member of the King's Scottish Guard, to save his own life, might be forced to kill the King's brother.

With a flash and a clatter, it began. Engagement; disengagement. A click as sword parried dagger; a slur of shoe upon wood as someone ducked; and a whine as someone swiped and missed. Fast, irregular breathing; an imprecation; Johndie's furious laugh. From outside the windows, the murmur of a gleeful and increasing crowd (It's Johndie, right? And Lang Bessie's bonny wee pet fighting it out); and the same sounds below, rounded by the confines of the tavern. Argyll's men still barred the stairs and the cause of the fight, Lang Bessie, had long ago been spirited away.

Nicholas watched, his face impassive, his hands clenched. By now, he knew Henry's style, having witnessed it in practice at Greenside, and heard Robin's judicial assessments. Since there was nothing he could do, he stood back from the jumping figures and the massive swings of the heavy blades. It was Mar's dagger hand that he followed, and he saw that Henry was watching it too. Then came the moment when Mar feinted and lifted the short blade as well as the long. Henry ducked, missing the sword by a long hissing fraction, and struck at the dagger instead.

It fell. And as it struck the floorboards and hopped, Argyll sprang forward and scooped it up, retreating immediately to the door, where he tossed the little weapon to Nicholas. Mar gave one amazed glance at the Highlander, then he whirled to defend himself against Henry's swung blade. They were even.

They remained even. Circling, swiping, slipping the length of the room, ducking, returning, there was no advantage lost or given for a long time. Young, well exercised, angry, they were more able than most to bear the weight of the great swords, and the jar of repeated impact along their shoulders, their wrists, their backs and their arms. Only Henry, driven by necessity, kept his head, while Mar, as the minutes went by, was seized by mounting waves of fury and resentment and disbelief.

You could see his attention waver. And you could see Henry watch for his opening.

It came. His dark auburn hair wet, the red flag of his inheritance burning over one cheek, John of Mar made a single wide swing that left his heart open, and Henry swept his blade forward.

The killing blow never fell. Nicholas made a single, vigorous gesture and the little knife left his fingers in a whistling arc that ended with a thud in Henry's body, between shoulder and neck. Henry's sword dropped to the floor, and Henry himself went crashing back against the unshuttered windows of the gallery. For a moment he swayed there, his eyes closed. Then his weight tumbled him over the sill and back downwards into the street, where the crowd's chatter rose to a roar. Mar stood, looking surprised. Nicholas swept past him to the window, and looked down.

The storeys were low. Henry had not fallen far, and the packed heads and shoulders had cushioned his landing. Already their battered indignation was giving way to good-natured concern. Nicholas looked down and saw Henry's body tumbled amongst them. As he watched, it began to unfold. Henry's shocked face appeared. His upper doublet was sodden with blood and his face was chalk-white, but he was not dead or dying.

Johndie Mar said, 'What did you do that for? I'll go down and kill him!'

'Do you think so?' said the Earl of Argyll doubtfully. 'That is, there is no doubt, my lord, that you won. He was disarmed. Men will see that he has been adequately punished. Is it worth any more? As I mentioned, my rooms are upstairs, where we can sit comfortably with some very good wine.'

The King's brother stared at him, coughing at intervals. Sweat shone on his face and he stood unevenly, as if in pain, although there was no sign of a wound. For a moment he resisted with petulance; then, driven perhaps by discomfort, he followed Argyll upstairs to his parlour. After a moment, Whitelaw discreetly came down.

By that time, Nicholas was out in the street. Dusk had deepened to darkness: breaking through the flickering circle of torches, Nicholas de Fleury dropped, a shadowy, anonymous figure, at the wounded boy's side. St Pol's eyes were closed, but every time someone touched him, he swore. He had no broken limbs, and you could see that the wound was deep but not threatening. Nicholas rose and stepped back, still unnoticed, as Argyll's men came running out, followed almost at once by an apothecary. Then Henry was expertly lifted and conveyed, not to the tavern, but further uphill, to his grandfather's house. Shortly after, the apothecary emerged, packing his satchel. To enquirers he said, 'Nothing too serious. He was lucky. He is young.' And added, *sotto voce*, to someone he knew, 'Damn the boy. A little more enterprise, and we might have been rid of Johndie for ever.'

Nicholas went home.

It was not, by that time, going to be the second homecoming that Gelis had personally envisaged, but she was far too charitable to object. Even when, stirring at last the following morning, Nicholas greeted her with shame-faced apology, she smiled, coming forward, and, sitting on the edge of the bed, took his hands. 'You asked if I minded if you got very drunk, and I didn't.'

He had told her, in essence, what had happened. Now she said, 'I sent Lowrie to ask how Henry is. The answer seems to be extremely angry, and in some pain, but not in any danger. Bel has been sent for, and word has gone to Kilmirren. The old man may come over, they say.'

'With a knotted whip,' Nicholas said. 'No. At least he will appreciate what would have occurred if Henry had actually killed the King's brother. The joke is that this isn't the first time. I once stopped a quarrel between Henry and Mar, and Henry retaliated. Now he will suppose that I have duly taken my revenge. I don't seem to get very far, do I?'

'You've reassured Mar,' Gelis said. 'And that is surely worth something. As for Henry, you can never hope for too much. You know that. Godscalc would understand it as well.'

'I know. I'm an idiot,' Nicholas said. 'And especially when there are so many other, attractive outlets to hand. One of the few advantages of excess is the *rallentando* it brings to normally urgent affairs. In place of prompt completion, there is an opportunity for leisurely courting, for subtle incitement, for – what?'

She didn't answer. He made a stifled sound. She continued to do what she was doing. He gave an involuntary shout, and then repeated in his ordinary voice, 'What?'

'Nothing. Pick your own pace, *rallentando*,' Gelis said. 'But if you don't mind, I'm making for prompt completion, *sforzando*. I'll tell you what it was like.'

'Like hell you will,' Nicholas said, and crashed her over.

Making love, they always talked nonsense. Afterwards, if they spoke, it was heart to heart, whatever the subject, as if a passkey had been exchanged for a space. At other times, they lay without speaking, enfolded and silent, sharing comfort.

That morning, he was quiet, and she knew he was thinking of Henry. She was dwelling on something else: something that he had told her of his visit to Damparis. He had talked of it quite simply. 'It confirmed what the family told you. Marian had a daughter, who was stillborn or died, and who was buried with her. She did not want me to know.'

'And Adelina's story?' Gelis had said. 'That the child lived, and was really Bonne, whom Adelina passed off as her daughter?'

'There is no evidence,' Nicholas had said. 'I went to see Bonne. She could tell me nothing.'

Then Gelis had said, 'She was younger when I saw her last. But she had no look of you, or of Marian.' She paused and said, 'Did you like her?'

And he had said, 'Liking doesn't come into it. If she is mine, she is for me to look after.' But he had not spoken of friendship, as he had when talking of Henry.

She had said, smoothing his fingers with hers, 'You need to know, and so does she, who she is. There is one step you could take, if you can bear it. The tomb at Fleury. If there is a child in Marian's arms, then Bonne is not yours.'

And he had said, 'I thought of that. I went to Fleury. I went to the crypt.'

He had stopped. Then he had said matter-of-factly, 'I probably couldn't have done it. I didn't have to. The tomb doesn't exist. The church was hit by cannon fire during the fighting, and everything burned to the ground. To below the ground. To ashes.'

His mother. His infant brother. His wife and her sister. And in his wife's clasp, the little gift he had sent her. And, perhaps, their one stillborn child. He would never know.

Except that, as he had said and as she too believed, Marian would have told him. Had she left a living child, she would have bequeathed it to him, with love and with hesitant pride. If she had given a child to the world, she would have made sure that the child would have Nicholas.

He lay still. She had thought he was dwelling on Henry. As it turned out, he was thinking of nothing personal at all. When he suddenly spoke, it was faintly querulous. 'Gelis, do you think Bleezie Meg could be pregnant?'

Her emotions disintegrated; then flew, just as quickly, to their proper places. This was Nicholas, not a child or a lunatic, although he could be both. She composed her face. 'I could try to find out,' she said gravely. But by then, he had reviewed what he had said and started to laugh, in the devastating way that brought her close to tears, she loved him so much.

Chapter 26

Bot so it be throw awentur he wyn.

THE IMMEDIATE CRISIS with Sandy was over; Mar had quietened. In Scotland then, to those negotiating the wolf-ridden currents in the stout barque of communal statecraft, it seemed that the year 1479 was to slide to its end with nothing worse to fear than the threat of an exceptionally cold winter. Parliament met in October, and continued the peremptory summons of Alexander Stewart, Duke of Albany, to answer for the garrisoning of the castle of Dunbar against the King and his other transgressions. They then proceeded to repeat sentences of forfeiture against those others who had collaborated with him. Jamie Liddell was not among them. Nicholas went to see him.

Liddell was bitter. 'How can it be treason? Has he tried to kill the King? Has Sandy tried to kill anyone? Colquhoun's death was an accident, you know that.'

Nicholas said, 'The Duke refused to stand down from Dunbar. He fired on the royal forces. He flouted the King's orders and fought on the Border. You know what else he did. He has to be challenged, or it's an invitation to general anarchy. Whether he will be condemned or not will be a matter for judges. And meanwhile, note, he hasn't forfeited anything.'

'James hates his brothers,' said Liddell.

And Nicholas said, 'No, he doesn't. The King has the family temper, that's all. He can be guided, just like all of them can. Sandy could hold the highest post in the kingdom if he could bring himself to make accommodation with England. For God's sake, we're not taking King Edward as overlord. We're simply observing a useful pact between neighbours. It needn't even stretch to another marriage, if the Princess Margaret objects.'

Liddell said, 'According to Whitelaw, Edward will renege on the dowry for his daughter Cecilia if Margaret's isn't forthcoming.'

'It's possible,' Nicholas said. 'Just as it's possible that the King will spend all the wedding taxes on cannon, or hats, unless someone persuades him otherwise. What about Ellem and the rest who held out in Dunbar? Can they be helped? Will they make representations?'

'Do you care?' Liddell had said.

And Nicholas said, 'Of course I do. Sandy's going to come back. We're all going to have to make things work in the end.'

'We?' said Liddell.

'Well. You,' said Nicholas mildly.

James, Lord Hamilton, died during the first heavy snow, in November, and those who went to his funeral, in the collegiate church he had founded nearly fifty years previously, found themselves briefly immured in that western sheriffdom of Lanarkshire which had been his, and which now fell to his only legitimate son, his child by the Princess Mary.

There were, of course, many adult Hamiltons to receive those who came to do him honour, from his prolific brothers and their wives to his own illegitimate, talented family. Spread among the several Hamilton keeps and towers at Cadzow, Draffen and at the place now called Hamilton in his name were the well-born officers, young and old, who attended the Princess and her husband, among whom was Jodi de Fleury, brilliant of face and eye, moving decorously in his new sable dress to welcome his parents, but waiting only to be swept inside his father's encouraging arm and to burst into speech.

The widowed Princess wept in resentful short bursts, and alternately commandeered Nicholas and shunned him. It was natural. He had engineered one aspect or another of both Mary's marriages. She mostly felt grateful, but she did not want another.

Her Hamilton children were too small to share in the commotion, but James and Margaret Boyd, the son and daughter born to her in Anselm Adorne's house in Bruges, were little younger than Jodi. They knew their stepfather had died, and walked about, eyes lowered, in their black dress, speaking politely when introduced. They came to life a little when Anselm Adorne himself arrived, with his niece Katelijne of Berecrofts, who had once been maid of honour to their lady aunt Margaret. They came fully alive when Jodi's father eventually joined the company. Jodi had never understood who gave Jamie Boyd the right to walk by his father and talk to him. Mistress Clémence, tackled once, explained that it was because M. de Fleury was a friend of the Princess's brother. The Duke of Albany was a hero to Jamie.

Jodi had thereafter followed the doings of the Duke of Albany, which seemed to him more interfering than heroic, and lately had kept his own father overseas for four months. He did not particularly like Jamie's sister, and missed the other Margaret, Margaret of Berecrofts, who was staying with her great-grandfather and little brothers not far away, at Templehall. Margaret was four and three-quarters, but fought like a seven-year-old.

Gelis, aware of the under-currents, was not surprised when Nicholas took them out of their way to stay overnight at Templehall while on their journey to Hamilton, rather than call on the way back. Kathi and her uncle were there. Set in its own wooded park, Will of Berecrofts's ancestral home was a comfortable, extended keep, with its stable and service buildings about it, all deep in sparkling snow. They arrived with daylight in hand, and when they had eaten, and talked to Adorne and the old man, Nicholas swept all the active young of the household out into the white sunlit snow for wild sport. Margaret, with her light curling hair and Berecrofts fleetness, shrieked with joy, returning her uncle Nicol's bombardment, while Rankin, aged three, chopped about in small manic boots, cheeks vermilion, lungs pumping with determined effort.

Indoors, it was Margaret who pushed Nicol to this room and that to examine treasures, the high voice swooping and fluting as she dictated, explained and enquired. Round her plump neck was a chain from which hung a lustrous cream pearl, his gift to her. Before she was taken off to her bath, she had him hear her sing to it. She had a cheerful, sweet voice. Rankin possibly possessed one as well, but it was more often employed as a stockhorn, to advise that he was about to arrive at high speed smack into some part of Uncle Nicol's anatomy: chest or stomach, thighs or legs. Then, clambering, he would wrap his short arms round Nicol's strong neck and announce things.

Gelis, watching, saw Kathi was watching as well, and smiled at her. 'What's the magic?'

Kathi came and sat down. These days, she didn't look worn any more, but content, and busy, and secure. She said, 'It's good for Rankin, rough play. He can't have it with Robin. And how does Nicholas do it? Ask Andreas some time. Intuition. Animal instinct. A sort of physical love, given to everyone, without even having to touch them. A way of conveying physical comfort, and understanding, and fondness, that also puts into their heads, silently, whatever he wants them to do.' She broke off, her head to one side. 'Is that actionable? It probably is. But if you could work out the recipe and bottle it, you could become very rich.'

Her voice had hurried a little. Gelis said, 'It's all right. I thought of it too. Esota.' The woman who had been understanding and friendly – too friendly – to a very young child then called Claes.

Kathi said, 'It wasn't all bad. It was just a pity she didn't find her own Tristan to make love to. Being stuck with King Mark de Fleury would make anyone odd. And speaking of oddities: what do you think the Princess will do now she's widowed? She didn't mind being married to Hamilton, but he was the King's choice, not hers.'

'And now she has a chance to show her independence,' Gelis said. 'Nicholas thinks she'll demand some sort of security for the Boyd children – she'll have to bring them up with the Hamiltons, anyway, without a husband to finance them.'

'That's what my uncle expects,' Kathi said. 'And she'll probably get it: the King doesn't want Mary and Margaret and Mar joining Sandy against him. You asked me about Princess Margaret?'

Rankin had been taken off, objecting, to bed, and Nicholas, mildly dishevelled, was talking to Adorne and Old Will on the other side of the chamber. Gelis said, 'Apparently John of Mar nearly said something, at the time of the fight in the inn. And it does seem suspicious that she keeps missing wedding appointments in England.'

'So everyone thinks,' Kathi said. 'I hoped Dr Andreas would work out a horoscope, but he's been difficult. I have to say that, egged on by the late Master Simpson, she has been experimenting, I think. There would be no shortage of applicants for the post of royal consort and premature father, and no better way of spiting the King for selling her off to Earl Rivers. Opinion thinks that that was the original idea. Opinion further thinks that Meg enjoyed flouting her brother the King; slept with everybody; became rather too fond of one man and now finds herself pregnant by someone she can't actually marry, because he's married already. Abortion (this is guessing) has failed, and she is reduced to hoping that Sandy will ride up in French feathers and rescue her.'

'So, who?' Gelis said.

'I don't know yet,' Kathi said. 'But I can probably tell you the day after tomorrow. Everyone becomes indiscreet at a really good funeral.'

'So!' said Old Will, limping over. 'What are you twa young quines talking about? Courting and babies and weddings, I'll be bound!'

Kathi got up and gave him a kiss. 'You were listening,' she said.

Considering, or even because of the weather, it was an exceptionally good funeral, in that the less flexible landowners and bishops and business-men stayed away, preferring to pay their respects at a requiem Mass in a more accessible setting. For the Crown, Hearty James came with a brother, and Drew Avandale and Colin Campbell were there, with their servants, as well as most of the Hamilton neighbours: Semple and Haldane and Darnley; the Abbot of Paisley and Humphrey Colquhoun and his mother, glaring alternately at each other and everyone else. There were one or two others with houses in Berwick, such as Tom Yare and his fellow Edinburgh burgess, Wattie Bertram. John Doby from the College in Glasgow, which owed its first real building to Hamilton. David, Earl of Crawford, who had married one of Hamilton's two daughters by his first wife. Preceptor Knollys of the Order of St John, which owned land in every baron's domain. And, late and together, Tam Cochrane the (rich) mason, with old Bishop Spens of Aberdeen, his rosy face purple with cold. Knollys immediately crossed and bent solicitously over him.

It reminded Kathi how much she liked funerals, provided the departed was old, and had led a full life, and had not been particularly well liked. Attaching herself, as was only seemly, to the lady Margaret her former royal mistress, she watched with approval as the Baron Cortachy and the sire de Fleury and his lady wife deployed their social skills among the gathering about to issue to Mass. There was no one there with quite the authority of Anselm Adorne: elegant, courteous, moving from group to group with his observant eye and quiet greetings. And few people there who drew the eye as Nicholas did, with his height, the quality of his voice, and the impression of hardly repressed energy that he did not seem to know he possessed. It was instructive, if you knew what he was doing, to see just which people he spoke to, and for how long. And the same was true of Gelis, who chose her own path, and for whom circles opened in welcome. She had won esteem enough for her name and her looks, but nowadays there was more. Men admired her for her ability. They were also right to admire her as a beauty. Physical love had done that.

The music was good, but should have been better: Whistle Willie was stranded up north. It became very hot because of the candles, and then intermittently very cold, as the doors opened to admit some late-comer and an icy draught swept down the nave. Afterwards, break-fast had been arranged in various Hamilton properties, with the sole inn at the Netherton pressed into use for the overflow. With the family, Kathi was returning to Hamilton Keep, closer than Cadzow.

The service ended. The coffin passed, with its procession forming behind. The doors opened on a livid sky and deep, trampled snow. Standing by the doors, just where they had entered, stood the massive cloaked form of Jordan de St Pol of Kilmirren and, beside him, Henry his grandson, disdainful and fair in royal livery.

Kathi said softly, 'Nicholas.'

Beside her, he had already turned back. 'I see them,' he said. 'It's all right. They've missed the Elevation of the Host, and the Pazzis killed the wrong person anyway.'

'But you're terribly, terribly sorry you stabbed Henry,' Kathi said.

'And burned down Beltrees,' remarked Gelis, on his other side, in a murmur.

'What is it?' said Jodi.

All his elders became silent. Then Nicholas said, 'Your cousin Henry and his grandfather are here. Smile, behave nicely, and especially be kind to poor Henry. He has a sore arm.'

It was all the advice that Nicholas gave, Kathi noted, throughout everything that followed. As they left the church, and during the last of the ceremonies, distance separated them from Kilmirren, and the same was true at the keep, where the feast prepared for them was royal, as befitted the King's sister and her late husband. Had the King succumbed to his illness, or been poisoned, had Sandy been judged and justified, Hamilton would very likely have ruled, as regent for James, Fourth of the Name, now aged six.

The little Prince had a good nurse, Nanse Preston, but not a Nicholas, who was at present handling Jodi, nearly eleven, by doing nothing. When the snow had first come to Edinburgh, Nicholas and John le Grant had disappeared down to the workshops at Leith and returned with paint-smeared fingers and discoloured thumbnails, quarrelling noisily and hoarse with shouting and laughter. With them, they dragged four new-made and magnificent sledges, two for adults, one for a child, and one for a wheelchair.

In the event, Robin hadn't come to Hamilton, but three of the sledges were with them, red and blue and gold, and Nicholas had begged Jodi off duty last night to find a clearing and race them by torchlight, himself

and Jodi alone. Kathi and Gelis had watched. Neither spoke. This was
not remotely like the children's sport he had devised for Margaret
and Rankin. It was glorious in its excitement and beauty. It was as it
must have been in Poland. Indoors, later, Kathi had talked of it to
Nicholas.

'That was dangerous.'

'I know,' he had said. 'I'm too old for that sort of thing.' But he had
turned his attention to her.

She said, 'Were you quite sure Jodi could do it? He was very brave.'

'You have to guess,' he said. 'With men, as well. If they're not sure,
you can usually tell.'

'Unless they love you,' she had said. 'Then they will die, rather than
fail.'

His gaze did not change, but she felt rather than saw a reflex movement, slight as that of a sea animal touched. It made her speak quickly.
'No. It may not be so.'

'I don't think so,' he said. His voice was quite clear. 'But I shall
watch for it now. Thank you.'

But now, he had left Jodi alone. And Gelis never interfered, Kathi
knew, with the way Nicholas handled Jodi. She ought not to have
spoken, herself.

During the breakfast, nothing happened. Bishop Spens spoke, and
John, the clever, lame, illegitimate man who was Hamilton's oldest son,
replied in a way that did himself as much honour as it did the long,
controversial career of his father. Among the family, Kathi could not
see that particular Hamilton girl whom, according to fevered report,
Nicholas had once stolen from Simon de St Pol, Henry's father. Nicholas
had devoted a lot of time, in the past, to investigating Simon's discarded
mistresses, but he had had his reasons, as Gelis certainly understood.
Gelis, too, was watching Jordan de St Pol and his grandson, far down
the table. Watching the exquisite golden-haired Henry, wearing the
royal cipher of a King's Archer on his shoulder, and an expression in
his eyes, blue as Simon's, in which amusement barely masked something
darker whenever he looked towards Nicholas.

The meal ended; the Princess and the family withdrew, and the rest
of the company, reseated, waited to be summoned to follow them.
Nicholas rose, and walked down to where Kilmirren sat, chatting amicably to his neighbour. Henry stiffened and said something, and the fat
man broke off and looked round. 'Ah, Nicholas! Come to receive an
old man's thanks for stabbing this moron. Where would he be now, if

you had not? Where would my lord of Mar be! There would be another death for these two sad Princesses to mourn!'

Henry had risen to his feet. 'I am afraid,' he said, 'I feel rather differently.' Below the even tone, you could feel the hatred: for his grandfather; for Nicholas. Around them, seats had emptied.

Nicholas said, 'I expect you do. And Lang Bessie's with Mar now, as well. A heavy price to pay for attacking him, but it might have been worse.'

'It cost rather more than that,' said the old man. His large, firm face with its gleaming chins turned up to Nicholas. 'Quite a large sum of money, in fact. Really, I think I shall have to take steps to have Henry's manhood pledged to something more permanent than brewing-women. Do you have any suggestions?'

He was a devil. His voice carried down the long table where Gelis still sat, and Kathi herself.

Nicholas said, 'I doubt if you need any, unless the entire female population is blind. In my experience, a few years of brewster-wives don't do very much harm, before the nightingale sings. And the Malloch girl is not quite fourteen.'

The fat man looked gratified. 'Indeed! I congratulate you. I hadn't traced the latest conquest myself. Henry, you had better keep to professional engagements for a while. Then we shall consult, you and I.'

'My grandfather indulges in pleasantries,' Henry said. His voice would have iced a volcano. His gaze had left Nicholas. 'But there, surely, is my van Borselen cousin. You remember Jordan, Grandfather Jordan? So tall! Nearly eleven! Just the age, surely, for his first professional engagement? What do you think?'

Jodi de Fleury, in his black Hamilton livery, had just re-entered the room. He paused at the sound of his name, and then glanced at the speaker, and the fat man beside him, and his own father. Then he said, 'Forgive me, sir,' and crossing the room, bent to deliver a message to the guests seated there. Then he returned, and stood before Jordan de St Pol. 'My lord.'

Surprise and pleasure informed Kilmirren's face. 'Eleven! And of such a precocious maturity! Henry is right. The boy should be initiated at once. Why not leave him in Henry's good hands?'

At the end of the table, it was Kathi, not Gelis, who made to rise. Gelis's hand, hard on her arm, prevented her. Jodi, frowning a little, had lifted his eyes to where his father stood, and caught, as Kilmirren did not, the single droop of one eyelid. Jodi's colour returned. Nicholas said, 'Monseigneur! Of course, the offer is generous, but should we discuss it new-come from Mass, with Bishop Spens himself in the room? That is, I am sure Henry would be a considerate partner, but the Church is not sympathetic towards –'

The crash that stopped him came from Kilmirren's great chair, astoundingly knocked aside by his bulk as he surged up and stood, facing Nicholas. The look on his face was such that Gelis's nails dug into Kathi's arm. Henry said, 'Uncle Nicholas is teasing you, Grandfather. That is not what I meant.'

It was the voice they had all heard before: dulcet, contemptuous, but rarely if ever used to his grandfather. Sitting there, struck with revulsion and pity, Kathi was reminded of something she had heard about the old man, long ago, when Tilde de Charetty's first child was lost. Something that she assumed Nicholas knew, but that perhaps he did not. She put her other hand over Gelis's, and held it close.

Jordan de St Pol of Kilmirren stood where he had risen, powerful, composed as if Henry had never spoken. He looked at the youth, whose smile faded, and then back at Nicholas. 'How tedious,' he said. 'Salacious, juvenile banter, in the presence of ladies. A misbegotten apprentice might be forgiven, but I feel less benevolent, Henry, towards yourself. What can we do to remedy this mistake?'

Jodi spoke. 'I have been sent, Monseigneur, to ask you and your party to do the Princess the honour of joining her.' If he had not understood the sense, he had grasped the ominous tone of what was developing. He stood, his back straight, his immense grey eyes meeting Kilmirren's.

The fat man held the child's gaze, reflectively. When he spoke, it was slowly. 'And so, Jordan. Perhaps here is the answer. Many years ago, I am told, my grandson used his seniority to beat you in some ball game. He has been punished for it, but not adequately, or so it would seem. How would you like to be given a better chance now?'

'He is on duty,' Gelis said. 'Today we buried the lord of this house.'

'There speaks a dame of her child. I speak to the young man himself. The snow is deep. We are unlikely to travel today. When you are free of your duties, and when suitable privacy can be obtained, would you not like to engage my grandson in some better-matched bout? And if so, what would it be?'

His eyes held the boy, tight as wire, but Jodi did not attempt to glance to either side. He said, 'Perhaps Monseigneur would choose.' For some things, at least, he now had the language of royalty.

Kilmirren said, 'Or your father? You have been practising at

Greenside, have you not, Jordan? Perhaps you can excel Henry now at the butts, or in the list. What about shooting? Longbow, or crossbow? What does Nicholas say?'

Nicholas said, 'I think my son means that Monseigneur should choose, avoiding those sports which might strain Henry's injury.'

Henry moved. Before he could speak, Kilmirren said, 'Really? I supposed you would have welcomed better odds. There are eight years between them.'

'Then why not a competition in which the chances are even? A sledge race?' said Nicholas.

Gelis's hand slackened and fell from beneath Kathi's. Nicholas did not look at either of them; nor did Jodi.

Gelis said, between her teeth, 'Sometimes I think that if no one else kills him, I shall.'

'I know,' Kathi said. 'Sometimes I feel like that about Robin. It's called a healthy marriage relationship.'

It's called love.

The race was held at dusk, out of sight of the keep, at a place where the heavy oak trees of the Hamilton forest clothed the lower slopes of a long, precipitous hill. A crowd of the younger guests came along with them, some as spectators and some as competitors, hauling any old plank or piece of fencing they could find. Three or four had actual sledges. Since the only matched sledges were brought by St Pol and de Fleury, theirs was the only true race, to be run first.

Henry had assumed that the third matched sledge was for the brat's father, the Bastard. It would hardly be for his fat grandfather Jordan. His fat grandfather, having blamed Henry for what he had started himself, was now back at the house, waiting at ease by the fire, since no one would expect him to climb up a mountain.

But the brat's father, interrogated, had excused himself, surprised, from the race, contenting himself with packing the sledges for weight, which was fair enough. The race didn't depend, then, on strength, so much as on quickness of eye and agility. Beneath the snow there were rocks. And lower down there were trees. Hit at speed, these could kill. And darkness was falling.

Getting ready, his cousin didn't say anything, but he went about things steadily enough, pulling on his red fur hat and thick gloves, and the boots he would steer with. De Fleury talked to him, but showed no special emotion. Perhaps he didn't care if the brat died. Perhaps in private he made out that he cared, and cuddled Jordan when the brat wept, and left him a drink late at night. Then, what else, he would stick a knife in his back. *This* was sticking a knife in his back. In both their backs: Henry's and Jordan's. Henry hated him.

Henry had sledged before, but not very often. It was not an art required of chevaliers of prowess. The sledges, however, were beautiful. He had heard de Fleury say that John le Grant had made them and he believed it: working with John himself, he had seen wood just like this, down at Leith. John wouldn't have known what the sledges were meant for. John could be an overbearing bastard at times, but he was straightforward.

By the time they had finished the long climb to the top of the hill it was quite dark, and all the torches were lit, at the top and the bottom, and fixed lower down to the trees. Some of the trees were thirty feet round, planted like black tabernacles on the ghostly white of the slope. The torch-flames beaded the darkness below, each over its pastille of glistening snow. There was a sharp wind at the crest, which cut through hide and wool and fleece. Henry had been in enough jousts to be brazen about some things. While they were arguing over the sledges he said to the brat, 'I'm going to pee. What about you?' They went off together, but didn't speak again, coming back. Presently, they climbed into the sledges and lay down, while men held them. Then someone said, 'Go!' and the two of them went.

It was too fast for fear. It was so fast that he forgot to steer for the first seconds, and only remembered when he saw the first bump coming up. A little later he realised that the roar of the crowd had receded, and what he was hearing was the wind, and the rumble and hiss of the runners, and a squeak from Jordan as he heeled off something and jerked back immediately. He was a little behind. Then there was a lot of rough territory ahead, and they both had to start to navigate round it.

He lost speed, doing that, and once heeled too abruptly, so that he nearly flipped over, and clods of half-frozen snow slapped his face and his body. His leg muscles were working, and he was panting as if he were running. The brat was still behind, but not by much. He had a crimson hat of dyed coney that reminded Henry of a quintain he had once had, which whirled when you struck it. He had been young at the time, and the master-at-arms had screamed at him when he missed, which was often.

They were on the straight, smoother slope now, and gathering speed. The torches were nearer. To one side, he saw a snatch of smithy-red sparks and heard a crack, as an unseen rock snagged the brat's runner.

For a moment the boy's sledge slewed right and left, then he had it level and running again. The brat would want to win, for his father. The brat's father was waiting below, probably wishing he were at home by the fire with Henry's grandfather. De Fleury had saved the fat old man's life, back at Beltrees. De Fleury and Henry's grandfather were a pair.

The trees came. Not so many, but wickedly spaced, so that you couldn't get a clear run. As he steered, he could hear himself gasping from the vibration. He could see the boy being tossed about, and clinging on. He saw the other sledge tip, as his had done, and right itself, and then tip in the other direction. Trying to right it, the brat had failed to watch, for a moment, what lay further down.

Henry saw the tree, and moved his weight to swerve gracefully round it. Then he saw the red capped head flying past him in a straight line.

He only had to do nothing. He was expected to do nothing. He was tired of doing what he was expected to do. Henry de St Pol changed his weight, and his direction, and brought the sledge round in an arc which sheared the roots of the tree and crashed full tilt into the other hurtling sledge, which fell on its side, throwing its occupant into the snow. The brat yelled '*Zot!*' and vanished into a snowdrift. His sledge slewed and slithered and stopped. Henry stopped his and stepped over into the drift. He found an arm and a collar and hauled. He said, 'Have you never done this before?'

The snow was nearly knee-deep. Climbing out and back to the sledges, they both slipped from time to time on the crust: soon, that kind of spill would crack bones. The brat said, 'You nearly went over too. Do we go on?'

Henry said, 'Well, we'd look a bit silly if we stayed here all night.'

The brat gave a grunt and a passing grin, and knelt back on his sledge. Then he got up. 'I'll push you.'

'Why?' Henry said.

'You saved me,' the brat said.

'More fool me. All right,' Henry said, and lay down, and allowed the brat to push him. After that, it wasn't a bad slide to the bottom, although he never reached such a good speed again. It pleased him to think of the brat behind, scrabbling with his pathetic feet, trying to get the sledge to run off. Serve him right. If he couldn't sledge, he shouldn't have accepted the challenge.

Almost immediately, it seemed, the ground levelled off, there was a blaze of torches ahead, and he could hear some ironic cheering, and even some genuine shouts and applause. He felt stiff, and bruised, and cold, and shaken, and triumphant. That for you, Uncle bloody Nicholas and Fat Grandfather Jordan.

It was cold, too, at the finishing post, despite the people crowded there and the fire someone had started. Indeed, the company and the light were a mixed blessing, as it made the hill itself all the darker, and nothing could be heard through the noise. Standing behind the broad back of Nicholas, with Gelis at his side, Kathi wished she had either owned taller parents, or been born with a step-ladder. They had gathered here early, while the others were still climbing the hill. It would take time, once they reached the top, to get ready. She had no idea how long it would take to come down. It would depend on the manner of coming, she supposed.

It was Nicholas who hushed them all, so that they heard the sound of the horn, far away, signalling that the race had begun. Even then, they all resumed talking almost immediately and he didn't stop them again. Henry was well known, but not wildly popular. Jodi had quite a lot of young friends, but only a few of them were here. The friends of Nicholas and Gelis and Kathi herself were back at the keep, ignorant of what was happening. It was just a typical de Fleury escapade. The excitement was because of the betting.

In fact, the talking began to halt, more or less, when it seemed likely that the two lads had entered the trees. After that, there was a long pause. It seemed to some that there had been a shout, quite far away, but after that, nothing happened. After just so long, Nicholas moved. He had hardly started to run when he stopped. Something glittering appeared in the snow at the foot of the slope and bumped along, while a prone figure knelt stiffly up and began to get out. By then Kathi was in the front of the crowd, and knew who it was before he came forward. It was the blue sledge. It was Henry.

Nicholas passed her, going to greet him. Everyone ran forward, and flung Henry's arm up, and then chaired him. Kathi saw him smile down at Gelis. He looked happier than she had ever seen him: his hat pulled off, his tangled hair tarnished with sweat; his colour flaming; his eyes a deep and brilliant blue. They took him back to the fire and the ale-keg, while half the company stood, waiting for Jodi.

Gelis, who had been talking to Henry, came back and spoke to Kathi and Nicholas. 'The other sledge skidded. He says Jodi wasn't hurt, but might have trouble getting started again.'

'So he just left him there?' Nicholas said. The anger, Kathi knew, was for himself as well as Henry. The next moment, without a word, he had left the island of light and was forcing his way to the trees.

Kathi said, 'I think we should stay. Jodi may not come down the same route. Nicholas will shout if he needs us.' In fact, seeing him go, others were following. Then they all halted, for a second large object had slithered out on the snow and was grating its way to a halt. A battered sledge, with half its rail torn off, and an energetic figure releasing itself into the snow, red cap bobbing.

'I told you,' said Henry. He had come to stand behind, a mug of ale in one fist, his face still brilliant. 'Couldn't drive a sledge if you paid him.' He lifted the hand with his ale, and Jodi saw it and waved back. Gelis had gone to meet her tardy son, in a kind of hurrying stroll with which Kathi had every sympathy. It did seem, however, that no one was injured. The men who had set out floundered back, except Nicholas, who made off in the opposite direction. After a moment, Kathi set her jaw and waded after him, making (as seemed only fair) a great many bouncing, slithering noises, some of them unintentional.

She thought he might elude her, but he didn't seem to have thought of it. She found him sitting hunched in the base of a tree, his arms so tightly furled that it made her want to shiver herself. He said, 'What did you think I'd be doing?'

'Catching your breath,' Kathi said. 'Now come back, Banco. It's too cold.' They were not dressed for extremes as they should have been. Not as they had been in Iceland, where they had expected to die, and Robin had saved them. Robin, young and determined and agile, come at the risk of his life through the cold snow to rescue them, without knowing that one day he would marry her. She shouldn't be thinking of Iceland. Not here, not now.

She knelt to help Nicholas, and he unclasped his arms and drew her close, her cold cloak against the chill of his jacket. He said, 'I know. That was the past. This is the present. It's all right. It's all right.' And he *had* followed her thought; as she remained for a moment, her cheek pressed under his hand, he resurrected something else from that time, and murmured it over and over, as a physician might, or a priest: '*Guds frida veri med ydr . . . guds frida . . . guds frida . . .*' The peace of God be upon you, my dear one.

And something in English from that time, also incomparably soothing. '*All ills shall cease; Baldur shall come.*'

'Poor Baldur. How embarrassed he will be,' remarked Henry de St Pol, looking down on them.

Light-footed and silent, he had given no warning of his arrival. 'So Simpson's stories were true. Dear me, Uncle, are you deaf to God's thunder? No wonder you didn't care what happened to Jordan. The race was just an excuse.' His face, in the glimmering light, was full of contradictory hollows; his eyes dark. Kathi opened her mouth, and then stopped. Gelis was right. This was for Nicholas only.

The arms round her remained. Then Nicholas set her carefully apart, steadying her still with one arm. He had stopped trembling. He said, 'Well, of course. I always make assignations at night, in deep snow, with my wife within call. Is Jodi with you?'

'No. I came to tell you. He collapsed and died after you left,' Henry said. He made no effort to make it sound credible. He added, 'Can I do anything for you? Build you a fire? If not, I think I'll go back.'

'If you know the way, we'll come with you,' Nicholas said.

'If I know my way? Is that going to be your excuse? You lost your way, and the demoiselle came after to find you?'

'Well, no one would believe anything else,' Nicholas said. 'I'm a shy man. We all get caught short sometimes. Then afterwards, I was walking in circles when the demoiselle found me, and we were both very cold. Aren't you cold?'

'Who will believe that?' Henry said.

'Everyone,' Nicholas said. 'You'd be amazed.'

Henry stared at him. Then he turned abruptly and plunged off.

Nicholas prepared to get up. He said, 'Now we'll have to find our own way back.'

Kathi said, 'What will he do?'

'Nothing. Everyone knows he and I have been quarrelling. I joined Mar and Argyll against him; I stabbed him, for God's sake. I deprived his family of Beltrees. I saved his grandfather's life, which to some might seem yet another heartless blow against Henry. Whatever he claims, Henry knows he would be regarded as a young man with a grudge.'

'But he thinks it is true,' Kathi said. He was standing, and had bent to pull her up.

'Yes. Do you mind that?' he said. 'Even shown absolute proof, he wouldn't change, and Robin could be dragged into the argument. As it is, it may do some good.'

A way that puts into their heads, silently, whatever he wants them to do. Kathi said, 'Not to your relations with Henry.'

'No,' he said. 'No.' He was slow in answering. Then he said, 'But it's better this way.'

She said, 'They were waving to one another, Henry and Jodi. That's what you meant?'

'It is better,' he said again, as if convincing himself rather than her. 'Slower, but better.'

Then they went back, to collect Gelis and Jodi and leave. Henry had rejoined his party and could be seen, noisily drunk, celebrating his victory by the fire. He shouted at them as they left, but his words were too slurred to make out. And by the time the company broke up next morning, Henry and his grandfather had both gone.

Chapter 27

Now be the scheris sall ze wnderstand
And be this knyf he beris in his hand.

AFTER HAMILTON, the journey back to Edinburgh was light relief. They travelled in vast, semi-royal convoy, but even so, they stuck in the snow on the way, and had to improvise shelter in and around a small, worried hamlet, initially visible only as three arms of a windmill and eight or nine bleating spirals of smoke rising from mounds in the unbroken snow.

Argyll's men, sent ahead, soon found the unblocked doors in the lee which admitted them, readily enough, to the ripe darkness within; although a few provident scythes could be seen glinting among the folk packed round the fires, and the inside doors to the byres were mostly shut. Once informed of the size and quality of the company, its peaceful intentions, its generosity, and the fact that it carried three cartloads of food, drink, canvas and mattresses, the hamlet dug itself out in a trice, and three of the unmarried girls washed their faces. By nightfall, there was a comfortable camp with braziers, lamps and latrines, and a feast to which the cottagers were invited. Some of the beasts had been invited as well, and turned rosily on the spit, while the chime of coins sang out instead through the thatch-smoke.

It was a sociable affair from the outset. While Nicholas hopped about with Tam Cochrane, hammering stakes, directing the labour force in the setting of planks, lying on top of flapping canvas, with a self-important Jodi streaking about with hammers and hatfuls of nails, Gelis settled herself in one of the cabins with Bishop Spens, and rocked a cradle with one foot while talking across him about teething and then, on the Bishop's initiative, about the effect of the bad weather on planting. When Lord Erskine's wife came and joined them, the talk switched to weaving, and they transferred themselves to the next house, which held a loom with work still in progress. They were still discussing it when they were called out to see their new accommodation. Tramping over a yard with soaked skirts, Bishop Spens addressed Gelis. 'You know a lot about dyes, demoiselle. Ah! The Charetty dyeworks.'

'She knows a lot about a great deal,' said Joanne Douglas. 'We meet at Haddington, to help with Cortachy's little deaf daughter.'

'And does the child progress?' said the Bishop. 'Your royal mother learned quickly. The lady of Cuthilgurdy would make a good teacher, if you have not asked her already.'

Gelis said, 'Of course! You were with them all in Paris, the two Princesses and Bel. Did you stay with them long?'

'Long enough to see them settled,' the Bishop said. 'Not till they were married, of course; that took some time. The lady Eleanor went to the Tyrol. Very young she was. A clever girl, and well read. She missed Bel, I'll be bound. She always supposed Bel would go with her.'

'You know her son died?' Gelis said. She ignored Jodi, who was jumping and calling.

'So sad,' said the Bishop. 'And Cuthilgurdy itself, naturally, is alienated. Andro Charteris has it now. Not that she is without resources. No. Not at all.'

'So her grandchildren are not in need?' Gelis said. Now Nicholas was coming over.

The Bishop said, 'I should suppose not. Do you know, Lady Erskine? No. Forgive me for changing the subject, but is that the Preceptor over there?'

The tall, slightly corpulent form of Sir William Knollys, lord of Torphichen, head of the Knights Hospitaller in Scotland, was indeed, irritatingly, standing motionless in the middle distance.

'He's just come,' Nicholas said. 'He left after we did.' Jodi, drunk with enjoyment, stood just behind him.

In Aberdeen, Bishop Spens did business, like everyone else, with the Knollys family. He had had some relatives in the Order. He had even made the Preceptor his executor. It meant that the Bishop admired Will Knollys's acumen, but not that the two men were friends. The Bishop narrowed his gaze. 'What's he doing?'

'Costing it all,' Nicholas said. 'It seems we are in one of his bailiedoms. The cottagers pay rent to Torphichen. We've just killed his sheep.'

'Dear, dear,' said the Bishop. 'You don't see the Abbot of Newbattle anywhere? No? Just as well. You remember that distressing dispute over whether Lord Hamilton had pillaged their lead mines. I was afraid at one point that they were about to bring it up at the funeral. And then, pursuing the point, to discover some grievance against Knollys. The Abbot would have enjoyed eating the Preceptor's roast mutton. I fear we are not as tolerant, we churchmen, as we should be.'

You could, Gelis supposed, describe a Preceptor of the Knights of St John as a churchman. Vowed to poverty, chastity, and devotion to the sick. One of the parties from Rhodes had been the first to annex Nicholas's gold. Gelis couldn't remember how many extremely active sons Sir William Knollys actually had, or guess what the size of his private empire might be, but was sure Bishop Spens could. Bishop Spens had helped arrange the English wedding, and the English peace that went with it. The Order was managed from London, and Knollys traded with England as Spens did, and the Prestons. Whether they liked one another or not, tolerance was necessary for the good of the Crown, as peace with England was necessary.

Nicholas said, 'They're calling you over to bless them. The King's uncles in the best places, then Argyll, then you, Lady Erskine, with your husband. Lord Argyll's cook will serve, and Tom Yare and Wattie Bertram and I will see to the rest of it.'

'It smells of horse,' Gelis said, inside the tent.

'That's because we're sitting on saddles,' Jodi said. 'If we were fighting, we'd drink out of helmets, and give our swords to the smith while we eat. Tam says he can put up a hut in an hour, and plait a horse shelter as well. They train teams and race. They train teams of gun-wagons too. Tam says it's just as important as training archers, for there's no use having a gun that can't go anywhere.'

'Would you like to build camps?' asked the Bishop.

'I'm not sure,' said Jodi. 'I think houses are better.'

'I'm inclined to think so as well,' said Bishop Spens. 'Tam Cochrane has given me some very good advice in his time. He likes his joke as well. Get your father to take you to Roslin Chapel. You'll see my face there. Next to the gargoyles.'

Then came the meal, at which everyone worked hard to make the thing a success. At the end, someone called, 'Nicol? Well, how about it?'

At most gatherings, Gelis had discovered, sooner or later, silence would fall, and someone would say, 'Nicol! Well, how about it?' Every Court had entertainers. Only Scotland possessed a highly trained adviser and business manager whom they also relied on for excitement. It sprang, she supposed, from his original concoctions of music and drama, and had progressed as his inventiveness became known. He didn't seem to mind. She couldn't remember if Jodi had ever seen his father in action before, and wondered whether or not to be worried. It was the kind of question that Kathi could have answered at once.

The same thought had occurred briefly to Nicholas, in so far as he weighed up most audiences beforehand. Leithie Preston's birthday inside a locked custom shed on the wharf was a different matter from a novelty to divert Alexander Leigh after supper at Avandale's. Colin Campbell was something other again, and he had all these Highlanders.

Colin Campbell had already obtained from Nicholas the return he expected on more serious matters. It had been done, smoothly, at another break in the journey, and away from the Preceptor, and the Bishop, and especially away from the royal half-uncles. When, in a private room, the Earl of Argyll said, 'Well, Nicol?' he was not looking for jokes. He wanted to know whether the English peace might be threatened because the King's sister had become secretly pregnant.

It was too important to conceal, if you knew. Kathi had agreed. Nicholas reported it without stress, as one would any fact affecting the wellbeing of a nation. 'The pregnancy is of about five months' duration. The father is married, young Will Crichton. Grandson of the Chancellor; connected to the Dunbars, and to Luss and to Huntly. His wife is Marion Livingstone, and the child will be born before he could be freed of the marriage on any grounds. For what it's worth, my lord, it doesn't smack of personal ambition. The Princess is by nature indiscreet and defiant. He is young. Both are attractive. Flung together by someone like Simpson, they were very likely to go to extremes, especially if they believed, as two of her brothers did, that the English marriage was wrong and the King was not to be trusted. Although Crichton could hardly have put any reliance on my lord of Mar. Cochrane's tales of what happened up north are quite disturbing.'

'I've heard them,' Argyll had said. 'And what happened in Edinburgh. That's why he isn't here. Andreas volunteered to look after him. Otherwise every envoy from England and beyond will learn about the fallen bride of Earl Rivers from Johndie Mar's frenzied lips.'

'I'm sorry,' said Nicholas.

'So am I. *Is mairg aig am bi iad*,' had said Colin Campbell. 'But that is what we have to work with, and we must do it. When we are back in Edinburgh, we shall confer. And meanwhile, what else?'

He told it, concisely, for what it was worth. Before the snow sealed the highways, there had been some unexplained movements among the friends of Archibald, Earl of Angus, who had been such a good ally to Sandy on the last Border raid.

'He is planning something?' Argyll had said.

'They think so, in Berwick. Perhaps you would care to speak to Bertram and Yare. Yare might also advise about Crichton. They do business together.'

'Tom Yare would do business with Lucifer. So what is de Fleury's advice?'

'Not to worry,' had said Nicholas. 'With snow like this, nothing can happen. Make the most of it.'

And, since he thought that was true, here he was, in a circle of bonfires, dragging a performance out of just about every man, woman and child of those whose shining faces surrounded him; juggling torches while men leaped over hurdles, and others danced to the pipes, and wrestled, and battered each other with poles while balancing on high, twanging ropes tied to roof-poles. Tom Yare sportingly repeated a long piece of verse with a lot of Rs in it, and children chanted and skipped. And finally MacChalein Mor his own self, stripped to the waist, long pale hair whipping, cartwheeled into the centre and danced, with high-flung hands and arched feet, while his men made mouth-music; the sound of it flittering over the snow, light as a wagtail in drink.

When it was over, and the camp was quiet, Jodi drew close to his father. 'Could I do that?'

'What?' said Nicholas cautiously.

'Make dancing-music with my mouth.'

'If you've got enough breath. Two people are better.'

'Could Margaret do it?' Jodi said. 'If you showed her?'

> *Is mairg aig am bi iad*
> *Is mairg aig nach bi iad; co iad?*
>
> *Pity who have them.*
> *Pity who have them not. What are they?*
>
> *Clann.*
>
> *Children.*

Next morning, the messenger burst into the camp, shouting for their lordships of Buchan and Atholl.

Bare in the crackling snow, Colin Campbell got there before they did. '*Be quiet. What?*'

Nicholas, equally unclad, came running.

It was what they had feared. Johndie Mar, knife in hand, running wild.

In Edinburgh, as yet, no one knew. Enclosed in its frozen countryside, the town clung, silently smoking, to its long slope, with the Castle stark and detached on its height, guarding its secrets.

The day before, provoked into a quarrel by some impatient remark of the King's, John of Mar had drawn steel on his brother. Drawn it, distressingly, not as a murderer with a grievance or an assassin for some noble cause, but as a spoiled lad, frustrated, looses a whip at a horse. The blade had pricked the King's skin, that was all, before the Guard had dragged off the Prince and taken his dagger. The King, overcome, had collapsed and lain shivering on his bed ever since, with Conrad at his side. The Earl of Mar had been locked in his room, with Dr Andreas in attendance. Will Scheves, with Master Secretary Whitelaw and the Governor of the Castle, had sworn to silence all those who knew, and had sent to find the King's chief advisers and, of course, his uncles.

Because, perhaps, it was thought unsafe to leave him outside, Nicholas was with that first small party which entered the Castle, and which, as time went on, was augmented by other arrivals as messengers reached those whom the King trusted: his Burgundian councillor, Lord Cortachy; his Chancellor, Avandale; his efficient master of defence, Tam Cochrane. The outlying members of the Archers were called back to duty, among them Henry de St Pol of Kilmirren, whose grandfather also returned, to occupy his Edinburgh house. Gelis van Borselen and her son returned, at a more moderate pace, in the suite of Bishop Spens, talking occasionally of what they had been told, but most often silent, while behind them, marring the snow, lay the churned mud and smoking embers which were all that remained of the hard work and goodwill of the previous night.

While still confined to the Castle, Nicholas went to Dr Andreas's small room, sat down and said, 'Tell me.'

And Andreas, pulling off and flinging aside his red robe, said, 'I can't predict what he'll do. It's what we all feared. It's worse.'

'How is he?' Nicholas said.

'Drugged. Before that, he never stopped shouting and talking. He had pains like an old man in his joints, or his stomach doubled him up. The attacks have always been much the same, but now they're more frequent, and worse. Will and Whitelaw are concerned because the French envoy is almost due. He mustn't learn that the Prince is under duress, or that the King was in danger. At the same time, we can't let the lad loose. You know why. You've found out, I hear, about the Princess Margaret. Mar knows about it as well.'

'It would certainly cheer up the French if Mar told them,' said Nicholas. 'No English marriage for Meg.'

'It wouldn't cheer the English as much,' Andreas said, 'when the French accidentally told them exactly why Margaret can't marry. So Lord Mar has to be kept out of sight, but under medical care, and near enough to be monitored. Blackness is for criminals. Lord Cortachy could keep him at Linlithgow. Or there is Roslin, or Craigmillar. Dundas? Haining? Torphichen?'

'You're not happy,' said Nicholas.

'It is not my unhappiness that matters,' Andreas said. 'As I told you, I don't know what this poor fellow will do. And no one knows whether his siblings are tainted.'

There was a silence. Nicholas said, 'I got to know Sandy quite well. He's not especially bright, and that in itself makes him short-tempered: princes don't like to seem slow. But that said, what he does isn't senseless. Even the killing of Scougal came from a long-standing quarrel, and frustration over everything else. And there are no physical symptoms that I know of, so far.' He waited, then spoke directly again. 'About the King, I don't know, but his physicians must. If you or the others suspect anything, you will have to tell someone. I don't think they hang doctors nowadays.'

'Avandale and the rest know all we can tell them,' Andreas said. 'Scheves has seen similar cases. So has your Dr Tobie. Like Albany, the King can't stand being thwarted, but that's understandable. There are times when he can't keep his hands off women, but then his Queen is in Stirling, preparing to bear him a child, and he is alone. Also, at other times, she isn't generous with her favours. We should be grateful there isn't a stable of mistresses. Lastly, and this is what worries his Councillors, he does retreat from affairs very often to sink into lethargy. He needs to be amused when at leisure. A competitive game, some versifying, some banter does more good than a powder.'

'I thought you looked exhausted,' Nicholas said. 'What can I do?'

'For the King, nothing,' Andreas said. 'You went to France: he's not convinced of your loyalty. But, for the same reason, the time may come when you could help me with Mar. You saved his life in that tavern.'

'If he remembers. He also connects me with Argyll and the rest. But of course, if you want me, I'll come.'

They let him leave the Castle when Adorne had arrived and after they had had a private council of war. Kathi, Adorne said, was safely at home. Riding out between Archers, and under the ice-hung portcullis of the Castle, Nicholas was conscious of nothing so freezing as the stare of his son, his nephew, his enemy Henry.

They moved the King's brother to Linlithgow, and then to Roslin, from which, although closely supervised, he escaped. He was found again, with cries of pleasure, by Nowie, and cajoled into staying at Newbattle, from which he departed again. Since by this time the French envoy was at Blackfriars, the lord of Craigmillar Castle once more admitted John of Mar as his guest, but this time, on orders, locked him into his rooms. For the second time in four weeks, John of Mar fell into a frenzy, and Dr Andreas was called. The family chaplain was already there, to pray for the servant Mar had killed, and comfort the girl he had attempted to force. Dr Andreas sent for his Italian colleague, Tobias Beventini, formerly of the Charetty company, and for Nicholas. They arrived together.

Mar's room was not the cell of a prisoner; it was furnished as for a prince, although the shutters were closed and there was a guard at the locked door. Inside, it smelled like a prison cell, for shock and pain led to incontinence, and Mar's dress and his bedding were soaked. His hands were tied, and he was weeping, his eyes swollen, his red-head's skin blotched. Tobie swore under his breath and went forward, but Andreas spoke quietly. 'He is violent. If you untie him, he will attack you.' And indeed, at the sound of his voice, the sobbing stopped and the bound man turned, painfully and malevolently, glaring at Andreas and then at Tobie. His eyes, reaching Nicholas, remained on him.

Nicholas said, mildly, 'Do we want the doctors?'

Tobie made a cross sound. Mar kept his eyes open. Then he shook his head.

Andreas said, in the same quiet voice, 'You need witnesses.'

'No, I don't,' Nicholas said. 'I need a blanket, and two chairs by the fire and – what? Something to eat? Something to drink?'

'You will send me to sleep,' Mar said. His teeth were chattering.

'Not intentionally,' Nicholas said. 'We'll drink from the same cup, and eat the same food. Tobie will bring it.' He knew, all the time that it was being arranged, that he was being an idiot. He wasn't a doctor, and what Mar needed were doctors. But while doctors were anathema, the patient might talk to a layman. The danger, as Andreas had hinted, was that anything might happen, and there would be no witnesses.

It seemed worth the risk. He went ahead anyway, talking in a rambling way all the time the door opened and shut until at last he and Sandy's brother were alone in the candlelit room with the firelight in their faces, the young man wrapped in his blanket and sharing a bowl of sops in wine, passing back and forth from his freed hands to those of Nicholas.

After a while he said, 'I'm going to be sick,' and was.

Nicholas said mildly, 'Well, that's all right,' and cleaned it up.

After another while, Mar said, 'Will you stop talking?'

'All right,' said Nicholas. 'Imagine I'm God. What do you want from me?'

Later, there was a mild scuffle which Nicholas, being large, resolved without injury. By then, he had started talking again, and once things had quietened, he produced the wine once more, made a little stronger. He could feel Tobie's anxiety shuddering in waves through the door. Andreas, with a different outlook, had probably gone somewhere to sleep.

Eventually, Nicholas went himself to the door and tapped softly until it opened. The guard brought Tobie, who saw the two empty chairs and went straight to the bed, on which Mar's body lay motionless, its eyes shut. He lifted its wrist.

'It looks like sleep,' Nicholas said, 'but I think it's some kind of a faint. He was rambling a lot. The trouble is partly this place. It's linked with what happened before, with poison and violence and murder and all the Prestons' various brushes with the occult, not to mention my divining. The trouble is, where else could he be kept? He does need doctors. But wherever Andreas goes, he attracts attention.'

'There's my place in the Canongate,' Tobie said. 'You bastard. You meant me to say that.'

'You would have said it anyway,' Nicholas said. 'But if you mean it, could we do it now, while he's like this? A horse-litter so far, then a handcart with a few people around it. Cochrane, if you can get him, would disguise it. It'll be dark. Andreas can go to warn Clémence. Then Avandale will have to know, and the King. You'll need protection. Perhaps Preston's men can stay till you get some. And, of course, Robin and Kathi are in the next house. Perhaps Wodman could come down to stay with them.'

'Or Lang Bessie,' said Tobie dryly. 'I have to tell you, I wouldn't mind some bought-in diversion for Johndie, if he's to stay till the French envoy goes. And where after that?'

'I was thinking of the Knights Hospitaller of St John,' Nicholas said. 'But I don't think Johndie's rich enough.'

*

'You're going *where*?' Gelis said. Jodi had gone back to Cadzow, after waiting in vain for his father to dance or walk tightropes.

Later, she said, 'Don't you think Tobie and Clémence will manage without you? They've had a lot of experience. You might have harmed Mar, in Craigmillar, without knowing it.'

He said, 'That's why I stopped. I can soothe him, but I can't keep his attention long enough to do anything with it. It's as if he has his head full of crickets, and he can only capture a thought when they're quiet.'

Gelis said, 'If he were an ordinary person, it wouldn't matter.'

And Nicholas said, 'He struck the King. If he were an ordinary person, he would be dead.'

Because of the weather, the French King's emissary stayed ten more days. Being, like Monypenny, a Scotsman converted to France, he took the chance to see a few kinsmen and fellow graduates, and presented himself, in a well-mannered way, at all the entertainments belatedly devised for him. These were adequate, but less than remarkable, since the excellent de Fleury (at the King's urgent behest) was absent on business, and Will Roger with him.

This at least was true: they were both on a healthy régime in the Canongate, being sustained by Tobie's wife while helping to keep John of Mar out of sight. Occasionally they would cross the yard to spend a short interregnum with Robin, testing one another's wit and eating less healthy food sneaked in by Kathi. These sessions usually ended with music, and when they returned to their duty, Nicholas sometimes found himself continuing to argue across Johndie Mar's bed, on the other side of which Whistle Willie, instead of soothing harp music, would begin to produce angry bits of lined paper, upon which questionable progressions stood in challenge among batteries of even more questionable rests, dug into the page, as if ready to fire.

But that was at the beginning, before Mar fully emerged from his strange, drowsing coma. In fact, music itself was the best antidote; better than the board games, the card games, the dice; the singing and reading which followed. But even music could not succeed when, very soon, their prisoner began to rebel. While the French envoy still remained, Mar demanded to see him and the King. Refused, he smashed and ripped his way through every article in the room. Soon, if left alone for a moment, he would overturn the brazier, or fling the lamps into his pillows, or continuously bang his own head on the door.

Thinking, with Tobie, that confinement itself was the problem,

Nicholas arranged for Wodman and Cochrane to arrive with a guard, and devised secret forays at night: a sail, a ride down to Leith, an evening in Sinclair's big house next to the Cowgate with Betha, his familiar Betha in the room. From everything, with disbelieving anger, Mar tried to escape; and again, a man died at his hand. It was not the fear of confinement, it was the loss of free will that he found intolerable. The doctors conferred. Their next message, of the daily bulletins sent to the Castle, was different in content. The King's brother's health was not improving. They suggested that, despite the hazards, the King should come to see him for himself.

That night, James descended the hill from the Castle to Tobie's house, walking incognito with a handful of men, and avoiding the great sprawl of Blackfriars where the French envoy slept. The King sent no warning ahead. Thrusting aside his brother's guard at Tobie's doorway, he marched into the house, throwing back his icy cowled cloak and demanding Andreas, who was absent in the sickroom with Tobie. Clémence, explaining, guided the King's grace into her parlour and sent for the best glass goblets, and wine. He knew her well enough. She advised the Queen on the care of her children. De Fleury and good Tam Cochrane and the royal chapel musician Will Roger were already there in the parlour, and rose, until signalled to stay. The King, after chatting perfunctorily, grew fretful at the delay, and proposed to make his way to his brother's chamber, if either Andreas or his brother did not come.

De Fleury said, 'Your grace, my lord of Mar would be ashamed to be seen at less than his best. His doctors will prepare him. Perhaps indeed – Ah. Here is Dr Andreas himself.'

Softened a little by wine, the King was not displeased to see Andreas again. The man was worth his keep. Every Court in Europe knew how he had prophesied the Duke of Burgundy's death. He was esteemed by Adorne, whose opinion the King valued. It was a pity that neither medicine nor astrology seemed able to make a proper man out of Johndie. The King greeted the doctor, and listened with patience to some rigmarole about what he might or might not be pleased to say, as if one required to be told how to address one's own brother. Then someone went off to fetch Johndie. His chamber, it seemed, was not deemed fit for the King's grace to visit. The King's grace believed that. Any room of Johndie's looked like a pigsty. Then Johndie limped into the room, with the doctor Tobias behind him. His skin was rough, but his hair was neat under his cap, and he was properly dressed, although he looked narrow inside his doublet. The King said, 'Well, John. Not about to cut our throat this time then, you young ruffian? Have we to immure you for life, or do you expect to get your wits back one of these days? We are beginning to wonder.'

Later, Tobie maintained that it was the second worst greeting he had ever heard to a crazed patient; Andreas quoted three quite as bad. At the time, they all fell silent, simply measuring the space between Mar and the King and preparing to leap if Mar did. Mar said, 'You poisoned me.'

The door was still open. Nicholas closed it. The King said, 'No one poisoned you. You think you are like this because someone poisoned you? You tried to kill me.'

Nicholas said quickly, 'My lord King, these were accidents. The proof is that, God be praised, you are both still living. My lords have great powers. Had either been ill intentioned, the other would be dead.'

The King looked at him. He said, 'That would appear to be so. But had my brother not been put under restraint, who knows what might not have happened?' He turned to Mar. 'Deny it. You plotted with Sandy. You wanted me dead.'

'Doesn't everybody?' said Johndie Mar. He had been given no wine. He took the King's goblet and drained it. 'No wonder Margaret gets out of your bed the first moment she can. I wouldn't want to be tied to a vacant man who has to be supplied like an infant with friends.'

'And what friends do you have?' exclaimed James. 'But raped women and doctors known for dealing with madmen? Why have they let you out? You should be under lock and key, and in chains.'

Those outside could not hear the scuffle. But when the King shouted, his guards broke the door. Inside, they found the King rolling over the floor-tiles unhurt, and my lord of Mar on his face, held down by three pairs of hands, with his smashed goblet strewn on the floor. Now his hat had fallen off, you could see the marks of blows at the roots of his hair, and his wrists were black and blue, as if he had recently struggled against bonds. The King saw his men, and got to his feet. 'Get me out of here. And send a guard down tomorrow. I want my lord of Mar in the Castle, in prison.'

Andreas said, 'But Dr Ireland, my lord King?' Beneath his grasp, and Cochrane's, and the Burgundian's, Mar kicked and swore.

The King paused. 'When Dr Ireland has gone. I hold you responsible for my brother's imprisonment until then. In chains, if necessary. He must not leave this house.'

'I hear you, my lord King,' said Andreas.

'Then lock him up. Now. I will wait until you return.'

There was no alternative. Nicholas made a loose tie round the fallen man's wrists, while Cochrane and Tobie eased him to his feet. He was talking continuously, while his eyes watered and mucus covered his lips. Clémence stood before him with a fine kerchief and tended him, neatly and kindly. Mar and his helpers disappeared, and only the helpers returned.

The King said, 'Enough time has been wasted on this. I am glad you sent for me. It has allowed me to decide what to do. Roger: you will return. Your presence is needed at Court. De Fleury: I believe you were asked to entertain Dr Ireland. You will return with me, and do so. Dr Andreas: likewise, I have more need of your presence than my brother. I want you back at the Castle. Cochrane?'

'I have work to do elsewhere, my lord,' Tam Cochrane said. 'I was leaving tonight. But my lord of Mar needs care, and someone to guard him.'

'I will leave my guard,' said the King. 'And, of course, Dr Tobie, who has generously lent his house so that my brother may be adequately safeguarded.'

Nicholas said, 'My lord, forgive me, but the Earl needs care day and night. It requires several men.'

'That is nonsense,' said the King. 'My prisoners at Blackness and Berwick do not need day-and-night care. They are locked up. They are fed at prescribed intervals. They sleep. I have no more to say. I am leaving. Those I have mentioned will accompany me.' The door opened, and the King led the way out.

The visit was over. The hoped-for remedy, the invocation of childhood, of family, had been a disastrous mistake. Whether James and his brothers were touched by a heritable sickness was not really an issue. The family was already split asunder by shared characteristics of a different kind.

Parting company with Nicholas at the Castle, Dr Andreas was bitter. Nicholas said, 'You did all you could. He thinks a lot of your prophecies. *The lion will be killed by a whelp.*'

'Even that he got wrong,' Andreas said. 'The prophecy didn't mean Mar.'

'How do you know?' Nicholas said. 'I didn't think you still drew up charts. I hope you've done mine.'

'Do you want an answer?' said Andreas. 'I couldn't. I don't know when you were born, or where. I don't even know in which country.'

'Good,' said Nicholas. He believed him.

*

Because his watchers were thus reduced, John of Mar was left for some time on his own, and no one thought to search his inner clothing, where he had pushed a shard of the goblet which he had taken from his brother the King. By the time the door was unlocked, several hours had elapsed since the young man had opened his veins; and his pulse was almost gone. Returned desperately to his side, the doctors fought for many hours to redeem him, but before dawn, he received the last rites from a chaplain from Holyrood, and died without opening his eyes.

The Chancellor was sent for, and arrived, his silver hair ruffled, his cheek creased from sleep. He looked at the body in silence. In death, the angry skin rash had withdrawn, and the long-nosed, bony face with its combed auburn hair held something of unaccustomed nobility in its stillness. He had been a Stewart. Avandale, of the same descent, crossed himself eventually and rose from his knees. 'Poor lad. Poor lad. Whatever he did, it shouldn't have ended like this. And, of course, so far as the world knows, it has not. So, what do we say?'

Nicholas had been there from the beginning, with Andreas. He said, 'There will be talk, especially as the King was recently here. People may put it about that the King has got rid of both his brothers.'

'Albany rebelled and deserted,' Avandale said.

'I know,' Nicholas said. 'But rumours don't flourish on logic. I think my lord of Mar has had a fever and, being brought to his physicians to be bled, has succumbed to a mysterious illness unknown to the finest of doctors. Andreas and Tobie can elaborate. They may even mention the unnatural humours which caused the Prince, against his true inclinations, to attack those he loved.'

'I suppose so,' said Tobie.

'Then it is agreed,' Avandale said. 'And now I must tell the King.' He tilted his head, allowing his thoughtful gaze to dwell on each member of the small group. 'Since we are friends, I ought to say that I often draw comfort from the simplicity of his grace and his brothers. Were they persons of malignancy or cunning, one would serve them with less than a whole heart.'

He was looking at Nicholas. Nicholas said, 'I feel as you do. So does Dr Tobias. Otherwise we should not be here.'

He left Tobie's house in broad daylight, and made several brief calls, before walking uphill to his home. There, he took Gelis aside. 'Something has happened. Come into the office.'

He never had to explain the implications to Gelis. She listened, and spoke at the end. 'I am mortally sorry as well. But it must be contained. When will his death be made known?'

'Avandale has gone to the Castle. Once the King has been told, the Councillors will frame an announcement. Meanwhile I have asked Adorne to come here, and all those who have been caring for Mar, so that they can hear what Avandale proposes to do. Then we have to think of the effect on Mar's siblings. On Mary and Margaret. On Albany, when he hears.' He broke off. 'It is such a tragedy.'

'You were sorry for him,' she said. 'So were we all. But he was ill. He was dangerous. He would have had to be cared for to the end of his life, or face the hangman, as he continued to kill. He may have realised that himself.'

'I don't think he even did that,' Nicholas said. He got up, more deliberately than usual.

Gelis ached for him. Nevertheless, she spoke levelly. 'There is one other thing. You know that St Pol of Kilmirren is in town?'

Nicholas sat down again. 'Yes?'

'I'm sorry. He called this morning to deposit a single piece of wicked news. You remember the Hamilton funeral?'

'Clearly,' Nicholas said.

'In November. Henry left the keep for Kilmirren. There, he wrote and sent off a letter, without telling his grandfather until it had gone. It's on its way to Simon his father, insisting that he come back to Scotland at once.'

There was a silence. Nicholas said, 'Can he? He was exiled.'

'On a medical charge, on the King's orders. Apparently the King later relented, but Simon's father didn't mention it to him. Seemingly, St Pol doesn't want Simon home.'

'Which is why Henry has sent for him. What did St Pol say about that?'

'Just that Henry seemed to believe that Simon was a person before whom brave men shivered in tears.' She heard the chill in her voice as she repeated it. Simon, athletic and fair as Henry was fair, had once been her despised and unknowing tool against Nicholas. But as a fighting man, Simon de St Pol did not deserve his father's contempt. And, of course, he would never have Henry's. Simon's petty beliefs, Simon's vindictiveness would immediately be adopted by Henry. She said again, 'I'm so sorry.'

He said, 'So am I.' He sounded uncharacteristically at a loss. She thought she saw in his face the same look he had worn when coming to tell her of Johndie Mar's death.

She said slowly, 'It's winter. Nothing can happen for a long time. And you don't need to wait for him. You can leave Scotland now with a free conscience. Havens are re-opening elsewhere. Adorne knows it. Even this poor Prince's death has smoothed the way, and so has Albany's absence. The kingdom has had everything you can give it for three years, and they need you less now. It is worth thinking about.'

'And you?' Nicholas said. 'Would you leave?'

'Wherever you go, there I shall be,' Gelis said. 'Although, whatever you suggest, I shall probably complain about it.'

Chapter 28

Leifsum it is this povne him to defend
And no man suld in-to this warld pretend
To lichtly ocht or sic men to dispys,
For oft we reid of pur men in this wys
That wonnyng has the kinrik and the crovne.

THE SUDDEN DEATH of John, Earl of Mar, was announced, but because (as the Abbot of Holyrood said) God in his Ipseity chose to cap the world that winter with ice, it did not immediately cause a furore, even in the country where it happened, although the Princesses Mary and Margaret furiously mourned their young brother, and the King descended into gloom.

The severe weather also cloaked happenings elsewhere. Yule and the following weeks passed in untoward frozen calm, in which families kept to their hearths and saved their energy and their food for the spring and the summer. Only, for good or for ill, Dr Ireland contrived to buffet his way back to France, having warmly recommended to James a reconciliation with his dear brother Albany, and tested the Scottish King's willingness to abandon his friendship with England.

King James, advised by his Councillors, dismissed an accommodation with Albany, and remarked that he could hardly contemplate breaking the peace unless much better provided with gunners and cannon. King Louis failed to take the hint. As a result, Albany remained rent-free all winter in France, and in January married his Bourbon, a lady of quality distantly related, unsurprisingly, to Charlotte, the wife of Wolfaert van Borselen. It was conveyed to the scholarly Dr Ireland that, come the spring, he might be sent back to continue his kind advisory offices in Scotland. Dr Ireland, who admired Louis in much the same way, he suspected, as de Fleury, agreed peacefully.

Unknown to England, Louis of France made secret approaches to Maximilian of Burgundy.

Unknown to France, Edward of England engaged in exploratory talks with the same Duke of Burgundy, largely to elicit whether, if Edward risked his French pension, Maximilian would make good its loss.

England learned, at last, why the Princess Margaret was not coming south to wed the King's brother-in-law. England looked at Scotland's short-tempered King, and at the King's younger brother in France, perfectly in position to spearhead a French war to oust King James and threaten England on two fronts. England laid plans for the first break in the weather.

James of Scotland, unimpeded by his Council, renewed (for the third time) his English safe conduct to take one thousand men through that realm on his way as a pious pilgrim to Amiens. An expensive gold medallion was struck by a rich goldsmith at Berwick and sent to Amiens as a mark of intent. Amiens was well known as the King of France's preferred meeting-place, and the intent, obvious to England, represented a threat which had nothing to do with the shrine of St John.

Spring hovered. On the basis of the last news from Bruges, Anselm Adorne began provisionally to conclude his affairs, which included making secure arrangements for the future of his daughter, who was to remain with the nuns. With his nephew and niece as her guardians, and the goodwill of her aunt on her mother's side, Euphemia would receive the income from Cortachy, and from the several tenements which her father had purchased in Linlithgow, whose Palace was owned by the Queen. There was also the mill he had built, not far from the port of Blackness. It served a prosperous area, and was capable of a good annual return. As for the rest, his own position of service in Linlithgow would devolve on his departure to Sersanders, who would remain as his agent. That is, if the present mood in Bruges remained the same. If, with the past now forgotten, he could take his place once more in the merchant community, if not in civic life.

Nicholas had made no such moves, but because it was bad business practice to say nothing, had let it be known that he would reconsider his future in the spring. No one was particularly pleased, although the councillors and the traders could hardly fault his reasoning on material grounds. He was a talented man, with the right to take his family where wealth and position were offered. He suffered a series of informal suppers with each of the senior judges and councillors, and was taken out and unsuccessfully plied with drink by all the shipmasters and an assortment of the late Phemie's cousins. Adorne had always known the extent of his options but had applied no pressure, although his own strongest wish, it was clear, was to see Nicholas return to his calf country of Bruges.

Kathi took no sides at all, nor did Gelis. The most miserable part of the exercise was introducing the possibility to Robin. Although he could sit, and there had been a faint easement in one stricken shoulder, Robin was now as he always would be, without the use of one side. Frustrated, currently immured by the weather, he had fallen into one of his rare fits of rebellion, when he fought the world as well as his disability. This, one did not treat with sport or diversion, but by becoming an intellectual football. Having floated, at second hand, the subject of his departure, Nicholas waited a day and then hopped and skidded over the packed snow down to the nursery in Kathi's house. There, having swept Hob on to his back, and played a short, violent game with a screaming Margaret and Rankin, Nicholas left the room and presented himself, breathless, at Robin's wheelchair.

'How kind,' said Robin. 'What will they do for proper sport, once you have gone? So have you decided? France, or Venice, or Burgundy? Or even the Duke of Lorraine?' His jaw was knotted through the fine skin.

Nicholas sat down with a bang. He said, 'I'm going to find the man who took your leg off. And then I'm going to ask him to take off the other one. Will you stop this? I may not go away. If I go away, I'll come back. And if I don't, you have a life of your own. We're not bloody married.'

Robin went very white.

Nicholas said, 'You're supposed to think it over, and then give a furious laugh, and then kick me out. That is, you can't kick me out from a wheelchair. So devise your own bloody response.'

'You bastard,' said Robin.

'I know,' Nicholas said. 'But it's a fast way of reminding us both how much we hate one another. I'm going to get beer. Line up your questions.'

Afterwards they argued, but not bitterly, although Robin did a lot of objecting. Towards the end, Nicholas said, 'Anyway, you heard. Simon is coming.'

'And that really frightens you,' Robin said. 'If Henry had known you were leaving, he would never have called Simon back in the first place.'

'Yes, he would,' Nicholas said. 'It's as much about his grandfather, now, as about me. In fact, they can sort it out better without me.' This was true. As he thought Gelis guessed, it was the strongest inducement, among several, for leaving.

'And I thought Julius was coming?' pursued Robin doggedly.

'Then Julius can fight Simon for me. Once Simon's dead, I'll come back.'

'You *are* a clod,' Robin said automatically. He added, 'You know what they feel, Willie Roger and Cochrane and the Leithers? It's like the last time. You turn your back and leave whenever you feel like it.'

Nicholas said, 'Do you think it's like the last time?'

And Robin had the grace to flush, and say, 'No.'

There seemed little reason after that why Nicholas de Fleury should, once home, shut the door of his office and, with solitary application, drink until he could no longer think clearly. The Donatello pinned above him had surely no relevance. He had been just twenty, hardly older than Henry, when it was done. And anyway, John le Grant had already defined the situation with punctilio. 'That was then, when they needed us. Now, they're fine.'

Sod sorting out people. Sod John le Grant.

The snow ceased; the rain stopped; the gales abated and, glittering like a new set of teeth, the landscape was found to have changed.

At that precise moment, spurred by hearty cries of incitement from France, Archibald, fifth Earl of Angus, led an army raised by Albany's friends across the Border deep into England, and for three days set them to burn, kill, pillage and rape, wasting the countryside as far south as Bamburgh.

By the time Edinburgh learned of it, and Angus had been located and brought in for appalled interrogation, the news had reached London. A response was dictated by the King of England himself and sent north, carried by the accustomed if not overjoyed hand of Master Alexander Leigh.

Through many reigns, the measured language of diplomacy had been developed to convey, with the utmost suavity, the outraged demands of the sender. What Master Leigh brought was not a secretary's work. It was an explosion of anger from Edward himself, abjuring diplomacy and even, perhaps, commonsense.

Nicholas carried the news of Edward's demands to Lord Cortachy's house, bursting into the office where Adorne held his weekly meetings with Wodman and Gelis. 'Listen! Listen!' He began to collapse into laughter and then caught himself. 'No. Really. Listen.'

All three looked up from where they sat. Gelis kept her face grave.

Adorne closed his ledger with care, and clasped his hands on the table before him. 'We are listening. King Edward has made his complaint about Angus's raid?'

'You could say that,' Nicholas said. He had come to a halt. By mustering all his considerable height, he had somehow assumed the massive, corpulent form, vast in belly and buttocks, of the once-golden monarch of York. His eyeballs bulged like peeled eggs, and his English accent was conspicuously accurate.

'Edward to James, right high and mighty Prince and dearest brother and cousin, go to hell. *Before* leaving, you will kindly note the following injuries and make reformation. *Item*, despite the great and notable sums of money received for the assured marriage of his son, the King has allowed his neighbour's subjects on the Borders to be invaded, murdered and slain, without cause and against all honour, law of arms and good conscience. This is intolerable. Heads must fly. *Item*, after all our many reminders, James of Scotland wrongfully occupies many of the King's towns and seigneuries, such as Berwick, Coldingham and Roxburgh, having no right nor title to these. We require them to be returned. *Item*, we notice that the King has not done homage unto the King of England, as his ancestors have done in time past. What is he thinking of? *Item*, having received lavish annual payments towards the marriage of his son to the Princess Cecilia, James of Scotland is required to deliver the Prince into the hands of my lord of Northumberland by the last day of May for the accomplishment of the said marriage. (How old is he? Six?) And *final item*, if, my lord, you are so conscienceless as to object to these demands, we – in our noble reluctance to spill Christian blood – will reduce our requirements to two. Send us the Prince. He's Cecilia's. And hand over Berwick-upon-Tweed. It's ours.'

He crashed down. Gelis clapped. Wodman said, 'Christ!' And Adorne, stirring, said, 'Well, at least he moderated towards the end. It's rhetoric, of course, but perfectly understandable, after what Angus did. What will the King reply?'

'They're still discussing it. Chilly disbelief followed by a counter-claim of previous provocation, followed by an offer of compensation, I should think,' Nicholas said. 'There's also an old charge dating from Lisle's death, you remember, and the temporary capture of Henry Northumberland, whose family think Berwick is theirs anyway. And yes, it was chiefly a stroke in response to the King's well-advertised longing to travel to Amiens. *Don't get too friendly with France, or I can make things really awkward*. Bishop Spens agrees, but isn't too happy.'

Gelis said, 'Angus is obeying Albany, then?'

'Angus is probably obeying the dead voice of Davie Simpson,' Nicholas said with sudden annoyance. 'And Albany, of course, is the woolly face on King Louis's left glove. Do we worry? I don't think so.'

'Or not yet,' Adorne said. 'Meantime, I do congratulate you on the performance. Can you do Archie Whitelaw?'

In their state of confidence at the time, it seemed amusing. In no possible way could England execute war on two fronts. The dogs barked; national honour was invoked; threats and promises were scattered abroad; but behind the scenes envoys scuttled about, and nothing of weight had been settled so far. To statesmen, it was less than desirable, but that was all. In any case, Adorne's thinking, these days, was directed more towards Bruges than to Scotland, and Nicholas, too, had begun to feel consciously detached. Among other things, he kept himself well informed about shipping to and from Portugal.

In due course, Alexander Leigh left, with James's reply, and was replaced almost immediately by Dr Ireland, the envoy of the King of France, with renewed messages of love and friendship, although none from Albany, whose sins were still the subject of continuing process under Scottish law. March storms disrupted trade vessels plying in the Mediterranean, and overturned and sank a ship sailing for Scotland with a cannon from the Duke of the Tyrol.

The letter announcing this brought with it news that commanded real sorrow: Eleanor of the Tyrol, sister of the King's father, had died. With the letter came a coffer with a familiar blazon which her sister Joanna, weeping, recognised from the days of her girlhood. The contents, gathered during the Duchess's long, wasting illness, were letters and mementoes for her sisters, her half-brothers, her nieces and nephews. Among the several fine books was one attached to a sealed paper addressed to *Isabelle d'Asquin, dame d'Échaut et Dombereau*: a name no one immediately recognised except Nicholas de Fleury, who kept his grieving to himself, and said nothing.

The news from the Tyrol reached Cologne, mortifying the former Charetty notary Julius, who had planned to visit the Duchess.

'I don't see why,' said his uncompromising German colleague, the dwarf Father Moriz. 'You can't afford to do business with the Duke. The alum deal's finished, and the mining concessions are going to Augsburg. You hardly knew the Duchess. It's nine years since you came with us to Bozen.'

'She was in France as a young woman,' Julius said. 'I told you. She must have known Jordan de St Pol: he was in France too, advising the

King. She could have met Simon. She could even have heard all the rumours about Nicholas's mother. Sophie de Fleury was still alive then, and Nicholas and Adelina lived with her.'

Adelina had been his wife. As a count's widow, under the false name of Anna, she had married Julius, telling no one that she was related to Nicholas, or that she bore a grudge against him. Her life had ended in violence, after she had tried to harm both Nicholas and Gelis. It was so rare for Julius to mention her that Father Moriz immediately felt guilty. Nevertheless, he said, 'You know I don't agree with all this. If Nicholas doesn't want to unearth his mother's secrets, you had better leave them alone. He's given up all claim to be a St Pol. He is reconciled to having been born out of wedlock.'

Julius had been born out of wedlock, and Moriz had helped him get himself legitimised. Nicholas had refused to submit to the process and, shocked, Julius had hit on the typically generous, typically officious idea of marching out to prove him legitimate. Then he proposed to travel to Scotland, and present Nicholas with his findings.

At first, he had expected to go, proof or not, but had been persuaded to put off the journey. The spring campaigns had begun. Depending on how they fell out, Nicholas might very well be back soon among them, his work in Scotland concluded.

Meanwhile, it made Moriz uneasy, all this zeal on Julius's part. To revive Nicholas's claims would also revive the fading St Pol vendetta. There was in addition the question of Henry. Long-standing friend though he was, Julius didn't know the truth about Henry's parentage. If he uncovered it now, he would be incapable, Moriz suspected, of concealing it. And one could only imagine how the St Pols would feel about that. Moriz wished that Julius, with all his charm and good looks, would simply find himself a rich pretty wife and forget about it.

The subject recurred, as fragments of news came from Scotland, supporting the view that the kingdom was settling, and that Nicholas might soon feel his duty there done. Of the King's two recalcitrant brothers, one had departed, and the other, they now heard, was dead. There were indicators, too, of a new confidence. The Princess Margaret's English wedding had not taken place; and King James had refused to send his eldest son south. It meant that Scotland felt able to bargain.

For a while, Moriz felt some relief. If Nicholas came back, even temporarily, he could stop this nonsense of Julius's, and put the business on a permanent footing, which would allow Moriz and Govaerts to leave. Father Moriz did not mind Cologne, but he found it no longer a challenge, and he felt increasingly that some decision should be taken about the future of Julius's problematical step-daughter Bonne.

Shortly after that, alone in the office with Julius, the priest opened and spread out the latest despatch from Sersanders and Berecrofts in Scotland. After the first few lines, he looked across at the other. 'Julius? You mentioned Bishop Spens?'

Julius looked up. 'Yes. I want to speak to him. He took the Duchess Eleanor to France.'

'Then,' said Father Moriz, 'I fear you have lost the chance. He has died, so it seems.'

'Was he ill?' Julius asked. He came over.

'I expect he was. This says he died of a broken heart. He was a great supporter, was he not, of the English peace?'

'He helped bring it about. He was one of those who convinced the King to make a treaty and keep it. Why? What has happened?' He leaned over to read.

'Superficially, a cluster of silly events – Border raids, royal marriage disputes, revived quarrels over sovereignty – which happen to have occurred at the same time as some seriously changing alliances behind the scenes. Result: six years of peace at an end, and Bishop Spens dead.'

'At an end?' Julius repeated.

'Oh, yes,' said Father Moriz. 'King Edward of England, it seems, is now able to review his less convenient alliances. He is to launch a rigorous and cruel war on Scotland, and has set his brother to work as Lieutenant-General of the North. This will change everything.'

'Mary Mother,' said Julius, straightening. 'It certainly will. Nicholas won't stay to fight someone else's war. He's probably sailing already. Adorne, too.'

'Is that what you would do?' Moriz said. He waited.

'You mean he'll stay to make the most of it?' Julius said. 'I see. There is that. They'll certainly need him.'

'That's what I meant,' Moriz said. 'I don't think you need look for him coming now.' He waited again.

Julius might be a lawyer, but he had allowed himself, from boyhood, to be charmed by the lure of adventure. Julius said, 'Well, if Nicholas won't come here, why don't I go and join him? Think of it! We'd all be together again!'

Rising from his prayers that night, Father Moriz hoped that Nicholas would forgive him. Whatever anyone said, Julius would have insisted on leaving. It was May, the start of the campaigning season. There were reputations to be made, and a war with Nicholas in Scotland was going to be a good deal more exciting than a static, difficult business in Cologne. The prospect gave Moriz, too, a pang of uncanonical pleasure, for he felt that, if Julius went, an ordained metallurgist might well offer his services, too. Govaerts could remain in Cologne.

He had not yet decided what to do about Bonne.

Chapter 29

In-till this chekkar is als gret the space
Wnoccupijt as it that thir folk has.
Quhen euery man has place in properté
The kinrik suld our that extendand be.

ATHER MORIZ HAD been right in his prediction. Once, the
gateway from Scotland had promised to open. Now, for Adorne
and for Nicholas, war had closed it. The crazy war that – against
commonsense itself, it would seem – England was now proposing,
and through which James of Scotland must be warily guided.

For the advisers of James, an advantage appeared. War had brought
the King a little closer to Nicholas de Fleury. Previously suspect as
Albany's friend, de Fleury was now credited with having shared in his
attacks upon England. Also (the King was pleased to remember) de
Fleury had taken part in the battle of Nancy, and had fielded his own
troop of mercenaries. Consequently, when confronting his Burgundian
Knights of the Unicorn, James was gratified to learn that both were
remaining. The loyalty, he thought, was to himself; and in a way he
was right. Adorne would not abandon James of Scotland, any more
than he had done Duke Charles. And Nicholas, with much more at
stake, felt compelled to do likewise.

It brought compensations. He and Adorne need no longer work apart,
but could be seen to be partners. With Adorne were Wodman and
Andreas and Sersanders, and Archie of Berecrofts and Robin. They
met, on occasion, in Adorne's house, but more regularly in the prime
Berecrofts home in the Canongate, where Archie's diminished household was small, and there were chambers at need for them all.

The tall building next door, once the Ca' Niccolò, had reverted,
against all probability, to Nicholas, its original owner. The house in

the High Street remained the family home, but the accretions of Gelis's investments and Nicholas's inventiveness had, in three years, profited themselves as well as the kingdom. Nicholas had money now, and some of it redeemed the premises that he had himself built as the Scottish home of his Bank. Nameless ever since, it instantly became known, in the arbitrary Canongate way, as the Floory Land.

Colin Campbell, who did not belong to the Canongate, preferred to refer to it mockingly, as *Tigh a' Nicol*. Since de Fleury's decision to stay, the relationship between himself and the Lords Three had changed in quality, as had that with others. While Scots merchants in England were taking out letters of denization by the score; while agents like Sersanders were being harried by their foreign clients into calling in all Scottish debts, Nicholas de Fleury remained, and consolidated his presence by collecting a company.

The new house was needed, because the men, once of the House of Niccolò, had come back to him. Some were in Scotland already: Crackbene the big Scandinavian shipmaster; Tobias the doctor from Pavia; John le Grant, the Aberdonian gunner and skipper. Where once had stood Marian de Charetty, there was Gelis van Borselen, also from the Low Countries: a business-woman of a different kind, but respected as once the small, gallant Widow had been. And for master, Nicholas the Burgundian, husband of them both.

Then, at the beginning of summer, to these five were added a final two: Father Moriz, to take the place of that other German, his friend, Father Godscalc. And Julius of Bologna, to be what he had been before the wretched days of Adelina: a vain, eager, attractive man of huge and disarming ambition, who had tried in vain to instil the same into Nicholas since he was a boy and had watched, puzzled, as Nicholas seemed to succeed, whether Julius advised him or not.

Seven partners from all over Europe. Reconstituted, the company that had once made its mark in the merchant world – but this time under a man who was not the youth Donatello had drawn, and who was not following the wishes of anyone but himself.

Returning to the country he had left eight years before, Father Moriz concealed his excitement: two weeks on shipboard with Julius could only be endured in a state of deep calm. It seemed sometimes that Julius actually yearned to meet pirates, if not the entire English fleet, hurriedly mobilised to pursue and sink notaries. From Leith roads, with a content heart, Moriz saw again the familiar outline of Edinburgh against the bustling white and blue sky, and welcomed the small, broad-spoken party, equipped with wagons and mounts, which confronted them when they berthed. As he had hoped, news had travelled from Berwick to Nicholas. They were expected. And when they reached the familiar house in the Canongate, Nicholas was there, running down the stairs to greet them both.

He was the same. He was totally different. He was large and easy-moving and well dressed, with direct eyes and a rich, flexible voice and deliberate dimples. There were single lines round his mouth, between his eyes, across his brow that gave pause. There was something else. Nicholas was not now troubling to adapt, where he did not think it necessary. An observer of his fellow men, Father Moriz had always been aware of the changes Nicholas made to conform to his company. He had done so especially with Julius. Now there was no difference in his manner, whether he was speaking to Julius and himself, or to his steward, or to the long-time company colleagues – Tobie the doctor; John le Grant, Moriz's working partner in the Tyrol – whom he had brought to the hall-parlour to meet them. It was as if Nicholas had found his own person, and was not concerned to conceal it. Moriz could feel Julius's guarded surprise.

They were tired. Serious talk was kept for the next day. They ate; they drank; they exchanged news. Later, Robin of Berecrofts came to join them, wheeling himself across the road and up the ramp Nicholas had had made for him. Julius had last seen the boy hideously wounded at Nancy and looked amazed and pleased, which, for once (thought Moriz sourly), was the proper reaction. For a priest, the situation was, sadly, all too familiar. But even while saying all the other, correct things, Father Moriz was moved to think how extraordinarily well this young husband and father had weathered his ordeal. He had the same com-posure as Nicholas.

But of course he had.

Next day, Crackbene landed and came to see them, and they crossed to visit Kathi Sersanders and Jodi's former nurse Clémence, whose astonishing marriage to the doctor was one of Moriz's cherished mem-ories of his time with the company in Bruges. Then Nicholas took them to his own house, where Gelis feasted them, and Anselm Adorne, and his fellow merchant Andro Wodman, and his physician Dr Andreas came later to join them. 'Tomorrow,' said Nicholas, 'will begin the hard labour. This is just to create the impression that we are all easy to work with.'

'He keeps trying,' his wife added tranquilly. 'But we all remember Bruges very clearly. Hell on earth.'

Leaving that night, Moriz lingered a moment with his host. He said,

'I wondered if you were sure of what you were doing. I wonder no longer.'

'Thank you,' Nicholas said, 'but I am glad you came. You think Bonne is in good hands?'

It was Moriz's one nagging concern. He said, 'The convent is impeccable, and Govaerts will supervise all her material needs. It is as much as I myself have been able to do: she does not welcome visits or seem to possess many friends. I don't know what else to advise.'

'Should I bring her here?' Nicholas said. 'Only there is the war.'

'No. No, I think she is safest where she is. Julius prefers not to think of her. Apropos of which . . .' From the street, the others were calling him. He moved to the door.

'Something about Julius?' Nicholas said. For a large man, he trod softly.

'Yes. I ought not to tell you, but I shall. He is hoping, for your benefit, to prove your legitimacy. He thinks that the St Pol family have conspired to deceive you.'

Under the fluttering light of the porch, Nicholas gazed at him. Then he said, 'I'm glad you told me. It hasn't occurred to Julius that this will launch the equivalent of the Peloponnesian War? I will render vengeance to my enemies; I will make my arrows drunk with blood?'

'He wouldn't listen,' said Moriz. 'If you want my advice, keep him busy. And if Simon de St Pol is really coming, keep Julius away at all costs.'

'Thank you, Father,' said Nicholas.

In spite of his worry, Moriz smiled. 'You'll manage,' he said. 'You always do.'

To Simon de St Pol, Master of Kilmirren, one of the most beautiful men of his day, the maritime wars of that summer were of some inconvenience, now he planned to return home to Scotland. He had not, initially, been sure where his future might lie. The whole of Portugal, never mind his island of Madeira, was bristling at the latest English threat to break the Portuguese shipping monopoly off the African coast – a line of trade Simon de St Pol had often thought of resuming, himself, during these last seven indolent, sun-filled years on the family vineyards and sugar estates. Or failing an African venture, there was a man married to the governor of Porto Santo's daughter who wanted to assemble a fleet to sail west to Asia. But the thought of moving only came to him when irritated by some stupidity of the Governor's, or when an affair ended more badly than usual.

To begin with, girls of the better class in Madeira had shunned him altogether, because of the lie that had exiled him: that he carried an infection that made all his partners barren, and had supposedly threatened the marriage of the idiot King. He now carried a copy of a certificate, from the King of Portugal's own doctor, to the effect that his infertility was not due to disease. He objected to the way it was phrased, for he was not infertile. He had sired Henry, for God's sake. And he had certainly got a child on that wretched woman he had had to marry, Sophie de Fleury, although it had been born dead, thank God. All he would concede was that he was not very prolific as a young man, and had had no children at all in more recent years, even by Henry's own mother.

But the certificate, long since transmitted to Scotland, meant that he could expect to return home, when and if he got the chance. And now the chance had come: a letter from Henry which surely indicated that the old man was losing his wits, and that Simon could oust him at last.

He was halfway home before he learned that a state of war existed between England and Scotland, and that a French blockade would stop him from changing ships at Sluys. He landed instead at Dieppe and was forced to wait, with other travellers, until he could find a Scots ship willing to take himself, his luggage and the suite of six men without whom, naturally, he never travelled. Then the master refused to sail by the English west coast because of the fighting round Bristol, and they had to thrash their way up the east coast towards the Water of Forth, with nothing to relieve the tedium but the crass conversation of the other passengers, most of whom soon succumbed to the weather.

For some days, the only exception was the German girl with the nun and the serving-man. The girl was a hooded, silent young thing, but Simon amused himself by gaining the confidence of her chaperone, Sister Monika, which was always the first step. He could feel the wench watching him; and when, in rough weather, she came up alone he was there, ready with some light banter in his disarmingly poor German. It was even better when he discovered that she also spoke very good French. Attracting girls had always been easy, because of his looks. He might be in his mid-fifties, but under the Madeira sun, as he was aware, his gilded hair had become rippled with silver; his slender nose and lean cheeks and noble brow were golden brown, and his eyes were still the same amazing blue.

Even Henry could not compete with his father. The boy, when last seen, had looked like measuring up to his grandfather's height, which some found excessive. Henry's beard, when it became worth shaving, had been brown and not gold, and his single womanish dimple was also, for sure, from his mother's side: Francis van Borselen had been dimpled, they said. Simon de St Pol had no intention, ever, of being outshone by his son, but he was proud of the dynasty he had founded, and meant to arrange for it to continue.

This girl was a German count's daughter, the old nun had said, but had refrained from revealing the family name. It made for interesting speculation, especially as the girl, got alone, proved to have a dry, tough turn of speech which suggested the opposite of the shy little thing he had taken her for. When, at the right moment, he took her hand in both his own, she did not resist, but merely gazed at him with her unremarkable blue eyes, and said, 'I *beg* your pardon?' upon which he unhurriedly freed her, with an appreciative quirk of the lips. It seemed very likely that the girl was a virgin, as his nemesis Sophie had been. He felt the mild twinge of a challenge. It was one of the advantages of his disability that he seldom had to resist a challenge. There were no penalties now.

Then the old biddy came on deck, and that was as far as they got, for they were off the Scottish coast, and every King's ship in the area came out to have a look at them and check that they didn't have an English admiral and a full range of cannon on board. Once into the Water of Forth, they were actually escorted to their destination at Blackness, which was the vessel's home port, and where Simon proposed to disembark for Linlithgow, four miles away, and take horse for Kilmirren. He wanted to find out what was happening. And he wanted, nursing his wrongs, to set out from this place, close to the salt-pans where, eleven years ago, he had so nearly died, and the frozen river where, the same night, his sister Lucia had drowned. Had been deliberately drowned, as he was going to prove, by the brute who also fought and tried to kill him at Carriden: by the apprentice Claes, who called himself Nicholas de Fleury, and whom Simon had come home to deal with, now that his old fat father had failed.

The other passengers disembarked and went off with their carriers. As the port for the Queen's palace and burgh of Linlithgow, Blackness was an anchorage more than a harbour, but was well organised for its size. Dominating the eastern horn of the bay, with its jetties and warehouses, its fisher-cabins and seamen's huts and single rough tavern was the castle, royal fortress and prison, squat on its spit of black basalt rock, running out into the water. Behind the castle, and on the low rise that held the small chapel were bigger houses, neatly thatched and mostly belonging to merchants whose homes were elsewhere. The largest, and the only one with a slate roof, was the King's.

Simon waited on the coarse strand; and so, he noted, did the small German party. He wondered whom they expected. He had sent a note ashore, himself, and was gratified presently to see approaching a small group of horsemen wearing the livery of the Keeper of Blackness and sheriff of Linlithgow, and led by that same man, his old jousting partner, Sir John Ross. A good Renfrewshire man, Jock Ross of Hawkhead, with the kind of clear head, despite his versifying, which might well recall detail, for example, from as long as eleven years before. Anyway, he produced a warm welcome and an offer of horses and dinner at his Linlithgow house, which was what Simon wanted. Indeed, the sheriff went further and, noting the nun and the girl, sent to ask if he could help.

The girl, eyes downcast, approached and answered in French. They wished to travel to Edinburgh, and had sent for a wagon from Linlithgow.

'Today?' Sir John was kind but impatient. 'My dear demoiselle, the sun will set in an hour. You must be content to stay in Linlithgow. Your wagon can take you tomorrow. There are several good inns: never fear, my men will see you safely settled.' He waited, smiling at Simon, as the girl translated for her companion. The nun's voice, croaking fearfully, burst into reply.

'She is not pleased,' Simon murmured. The sea splashed on the pebbles, and kittiwakes wrangled, *kit-kit*, on a rock. A line of distant trees glowed, lime and orange in the sinking sun. From beyond the elevated ground to the south, there swayed a column of smoke.

'Cortachy's mill,' the sheriff said. 'You know Anselm Adorne? It's a sore point with the local landowners, but he's right to destroy it. The first thing any English fleet would do is raid the countryside for food, and that thing was stacked with grain. Quite a gesture: the man only built it the other day.'

'Adorne?' Simon said. 'I thought your Burgundians would be in prison by now. Isn't there a pact between England and Burgundy? I thought Adorne's friend the Dowager Duchess had spent half the year at Greenwich arranging it.'

'Oh, it's open season for pacts,' Ross said. 'And I dare say Adorne, like a few others, had to decide which side he was backing. But he elected to stay, and the King and Queen trust him. He's well established in Linlithgow, and he's taken over Landells's duties in the King's house over there. If the English do sail in, my people won't be sorry to know he's on our side. Like your lad at Kilmirren. He's going the right way to make a name for himself, your Henry, with the troop he's raised, and those horses at stud. I suppose the idea was yours or your father's, but the King is certainly pleased.'

'I'm glad,' said Simon easily. He wondered if Jock, who had put on some weight, hadn't kept a clear head after all. Henry had killed a few mounts in his time, but that was the extent of his interest in horses. The nun had stopped gabbling, and the girl had come forward again. He smiled at her.

She said, 'We accept your advice with gratitude, and regret our ignorance. None of us has been here before.'

'But you have somewhere to stay in Edinburgh?' Jock Ross asked. 'You are not without friends or relatives? Some convent expects you?'

The girl glanced up, and then lowered her eyes meekly once again. 'I am an orphan, sir, whose affairs are in the care of two gentlemen whom war is detaining in Edinburgh. I have come because I feared to be alone. They do not expect me.'

The sheriff frowned, his eyes on the nun. 'Two gentlemen? Where do they stay? What are their names?'

The girl bit her lip. 'There is an address, written here, for the gentleman who is married. But in case of difficulty, Sister Monika has the name of a Priory which will accept us.'

'And the gentleman who is married?' asked Jock. Horses were coming, the sun red on their harness. Simon judged that his mind was turning towards supper.

The girl said, 'It is a French name. The sire de Fleury. Nicholas de Fleury, of Bruges.'

Simon's mouth opened. Sir John Ross, his thoughts called from supper, said, 'Nicol de Fleury? I didn't know that he . . . How did you say you were called, demoiselle?'

She didn't answer at once, but spoke to the nun, who frowned, and then rattled out her reply. Simon stared at the girl without listening: the teenage girl from Germany, who spoke fluent French from an area certainly far south of Paris; who was brown-haired and blue-eyed and impertinent, and who had come *to join two gentlemen who looked after her affairs*. He caught the word Köln. Cologne. That was where the Charetty lawyer's business was. Julius. Julius, who had been married to –

The girl said, 'Sister Monika says I may tell you. My name is Bonne, lady of Hanseyck, and the sire de Fleury is a patron of the convent at Cologne from which Sister Monika and I both come.'

The sheriff continued to frown. Simon presented her, on the contrary, with an expansive, a wonderful smile. 'But what a coincidence! Nicol de Fleury is well known to me! Indeed, I will not hear of your travelling tomorrow to Edinburgh on your own. You must allow me to take you. And then I shall introduce you, if the Sister permits, to my son Henry. He must be just about your age.'

It was the continuous, excruciating shriek of the de Fleury guard-birds, effortlessly piercing the clamour of the High Street, that lifted Jordan de St Pol ponderously from his desk to his window, to witness the mêlée on the lower side of the street before the closed door and empty premises of Nicholas de Fleury. There, the lord of Kilmirren perceived horses, a wagon, and a party of seven men and two women, one of whom was in holy orders. Six of the men wore the livery (a stag and two ratchets) of his own house of St Pol. Stationed before them, in a battering blizzard of feathers, was his only son Simon, stolidly twisting the neck of a goose.

The lord of Kilmirren sighed, and sent for his chamberlain. When, after a short delay, his heir and the two women stood before him, his only expression was one of ineffable patience, and you could not have told – certainly Simon could not have told – whether the girl's identity, cautiously revealed, conveyed anything. In Simon's version, she was simply Bonne von Hanseyck, a German count's daughter, whom he had escorted from Blackness. Simon hoped that was enough. This was Simon's affair, not his father's. He wouldn't have obeyed this ridiculous summons (what was the old fool doing in Edinburgh?) had he not wished to avoid a possible scene. He didn't know how crazy the old man might be. There could have been a standing fight in the street.

It was still impossible to tell, half an hour later, what was going on, if anything, in the old monster's head. The formalities had been normal enough, except for the lack of a welcome. It was four years, for God's sake, since his father had left him in Madeira, and you would think that his reappearance deserved more than a raised eyebrow and a long, insulting scan. In another way, of course, it augured well. As they sipped wine and embarked, without interruption, on a long, tedious recital of the difficulties of their voyage, it began to seem almost likely that the old man had lost his wits, and that Simon and the women could escape very soon. To where, he hadn't yet made up his mind. He had to find out where de Fleury was first.

He hadn't mentioned de Fleury, and trusted, with increasing confidence, that his father had not noticed which house he had been attempting to enter. The fat man was now talking, like some rambling old crone, about babies. The girl was smiling politely. The nun, who couldn't understand English, was just smiling and sipping. Simon waited his chance. It seemed that Anselm Adorne had a bastard daughter. (Who cared? Had the girl ever heard of Adorne?) She smiled. And the King's sister Margaret had had another. By my lord of Crichton, did Simon remember him? Simon, aware this time of surprise, smiled and nodded. And after two Jameses, the Queen had had a third son – not a bastard, of course. Born at Cupar this summer, and this time named John, after the Prince whom the King and de Fleury had supposedly killed. 'Was this,' asked the lord of Kilmirren in the same amiable, discursive manner, 'why the lady von Hanseyck had wished to visit de Fleury? To congratulate him, or give him a commission, perhaps?'

The girl's face became blank. Simon said, at the second attempt, 'I am sorry. This is all new to us.'

'Certainly,' said Fat Father Jordan, 'you are not well informed; or did you not ask Jock Ross the right questions? Mar is dead, as I told you, and there is unrest over it. The Princess's error helped to break the peace pact with England. Adorne's child links him to some of the most powerful families in the kingdom. And, of course, any child Albany has by this French marriage could be more dangerous than all these put together. These are things, my son, I should expect you to know. Or at the very least – descending to your own simple affairs – where else would de Fleury be at this moment, or anyone else of military age, but fighting on the Borders? The large English invasion didn't come – it is promised, they say, for next year – but the Duke of Gloucester's northern army is busy. There have been frontier attacks on both sides. Henry is in the thick of it, on the West March, a trained militiaman, with his troop of fine horse. You can join him in Annan: father and son, defending the Border. After all, that is why you are here, is it not? To fight the English?'

The bastard. The fat, cunning old bastard. Henry had begged Simon to come. Henry had led him to think that the old man was going soft in the head, and was falling under the influence of Claes. Simon had come – of course he had come, to get rid of both the old brute and Claes. And the old man, suspecting it, had been mocking him.

He didn't know what to say. He said, experimentally, 'I heard about Henry. Indeed, I promised to introduce him to the lady Bonne.'

The old man smiled at the girl. 'Henry is a charmer, just like his father. But not, I am afraid, a friend of de Fleury.'

'Neither am I,' said the girl. She caught herself. 'That is, I should not be ungracious. He pays for my keep, since my mother seems to have been related. But I do not know him. We have hardly spoken. He has his own family.'

'Then you must visit them!' said Jordan de St Pol. 'His wife, his son, his household are all in the company house in the Canongate, awaiting the return of their warriors. And, of course, when de Fleury comes back, he will bring his gunner, his doctor, his chaplain, and Julius, your stepfather. I am right? Your mother married Master Julius, de Fleury's friend at Cologne? Or is he not a friend of yours either?'

He and the girl gazed at one another. Her diffidence had disappeared. For a moment, Simon thought that he saw a softening: an inclination perhaps towards tears.

Then she either conquered or thought better of it. Uncloaked, she had a good, compact body, he noticed. More expressive, in a way, than her face. Almost generous, you could imagine. She said, 'My mother died in disgrace. I remind him of her. He avoids me. It is understandable. But I do not think I could ask for shelter in the same house. There is a Cistercian convent. Sister Monika will find it.'

'Well, of course,' said Fat Father Jordan. 'But not today. These things take time to arrange. Meanwhile, I must ask you to accept the hospitality of my poor house. You will be safe, with the Sister. I am an honourable man, as anyone will tell you. And when those gentlemen return who are responsible for you, I shall ask them to call on you here, where you may have support should they seem importunate, and help if they offer you none. Would you give me the happiness of agreeing? If the Sister does not object?'

The bastard. The bastard. The bastard.

They agreed. They rose to be shown to their rooms. The lord of Kilmirren, walking after, plucked a warm little feather from his son's silken crotch.

'So,' he said. 'Has that cooked your goose?'

Chapter 30

The mor that fortoune giffis thé of grace
The war thow art.

RETURNING HOME AT the end of the season, Nicholas brought with him all his men, including Julius, as predicted. He expected to be home for the winter. No one could afford to keep troops in the field for very long, and it made even less sense, if the weather made action impossible. As it was, no integrated northern invasion had happened, but the cross-Border fighting had been serious. He was not sorry it was over, and yet in a terrible way he had enjoyed it. It was the first time, this summer and autumn, that he had ever fought side by side with Adorne, who had ridden south several times with Sersanders and Dr Andreas, and men of less eminence who owed him service. They had made a good team. Adorne was an international jouster, a leader, a man of wide experience whom Nicholas willingly followed; and Adorne in his turn readily gave him his head when some novel idea entered it. Among other things, they created their own style of banter. Tobie noticed it. It occurred to him (but not, he thought, to Nicholas) that none of Adorne's sons ever talked to him in that way. The other who did was, of course, Kathi.

Adorne's was now a voice of authority in the cabinet of men who were handling this war. Rumours had reached them of the scale of the English fleet which Edward was amassing. Scotland was not unprepared. Since Nicholas had returned, funded by Gelis, he had invested all he could in the charter and purchase of ships. These served in peace-time as merchant vessels, sailing from Berwick and Leith and Dundee. They were leased for long-distance fishing. They were there, if the kingdom needed them, for the transport of troops, or for fighting. There were others who were doing the same – the Fife captain cheekily known as the Great Andrew, for one. Discovered by Gelis and Crackbene, he had become a good friend of them all, as had all the skippers of Leith, although some ran closer to the wind than Nicholas thought wise. When you knew both sides in a war, it was tempting to earn money by serving both sides. Master traders such as Alec Brown kept it even, in a rough way, but some day, someone would find out and object. Gelis kept lecturing him.

Now, of course, she wasn't lecturing anybody as, unshaven, unwashed, and straight from the Borders, they all tumbled into the Floory Land, and broke open the kegs, and regaled the counting-house with their tales while the cooks got out all the food they had been saving and started to prepare it. Robin was coming, and Kathi, and Crackbene, and all the company from next door.

The food had had to be saved because the bad weather had caused a poor harvest, and grain was scarce and high-priced. In some places, there had been real suffering, but in its way it had also cut down the killing: without meal, you couldn't provision long campaigns. It was one of the reasons why Adorne had burned his own mill. All its stores had been transported to the far bigger mill at Kirkhill, and the small one at Abercorn had been left meantime. But Adorne's had been next to Blackness: an invitation to under-provisioned English shipping.

Nicholas had asked about Adorne, after disentangling from Gelis and Jodi, and was told that he was next door, and wouldn't mind a quiet word before coming to join them.

He tried to read her face. 'What about?'

There were too many people. She shook her head. 'He'll tell you. Why not take Father Moriz?'

His mind made several connections, all of them unpleasing. 'Oh, Christ,' he said. 'The Peloponnesian War?'

She smiled, but there was ruefulness in it. He could guess why. Simon was here. And, of course, so was Julius.

Next door, Adorne had some very good wine and a lavish hand for those who appreciated it. Father Moriz, still smelling of gunpowder, closed his eyes as he sat back and drank. Nicholas nursed his, and thought as he listened. Not only Simon, there in the High Street, but Bonne. It was his fault. He had left the Abbess with money, in case of an emergency. Bonne had created the emergency. And because Sluys was blocked, she had joined the other travellers waiting for one of the rare ships to Scotland. That Simon had been among them was not an unreasonable coincidence, but it was an unlucky one. He said, 'Just think. Julius will be able to ask them all about my mother, and tell them all about Bonne's. And if they also think that I've appointed Julius to prove me legitimate, they're not going to do nothing.'

'Yes, they are,' Adorne said. 'Julius must be told to drop this campaign. And I have already been to Kilmirren House and talked to St Pol.'

Father Moriz sat up. 'The old one?' Nicholas said.

'Jordan, yes. Speaking, I said, for the Council, he ought to know that his son Simon was here on sufferance, and at the slightest sign of animosity against a man such as yourself, serving the King at a time of great danger, he and his father would both be returned to Madeira. I said nothing of Julius.'

'But you discussed it with the Council,' said Nicholas.

'My lord of St Pol believed so,' said Adorne. He smiled. 'But it is for you now to be persuasive with Julius. What do you suggest, Father?'

The big head had sunk on its chest. 'Deportation,' Moriz said. 'Opiates. Paralysis of the jaw.'

'I thought,' said Adorne, 'remembering Thorn, that my young Kathi, Nicholas, might be as persuasive as anyone? Then, of course, you and Father Moriz must go and see Bonne and settle her future. It may not be easy. She is not a compliant child, it would seem.'

Thorn was in Poland. Nicholas had lost his temper with Julius, and Kathi had, in her impartial way, been a help to them both. 'I shall talk to Bonne,' Nicholas said.

'Yes,' said Adorne. 'I am afraid you will have to travel to do it. It seemed to me unsuitable that the girl, even chaperoned, should remain in a household such as Kilmirren's. You had not yet returned. I therefore took the liberty of asking the Prioress of Haddington to take both ladies temporarily under her care. It is a Cistercian foundation, although not the one which Sister Monika evidently had in mind. It will serve, though, until you have seen the young lady.'

'She is there now?' Nicholas said. He sat and tried to visualise the scene in Kilmirren House: Adorne's bland proposal to remove Bonne; the Prioress arriving with her cohorts. The old man had let the girl go; he couldn't have stopped her. And, of course, Simon had been out, Adorne said.

'You approve?' Adorne said. He was smiling at Moriz.

'More than I can say,' Nicholas said. 'I owe you a great deal, sir.'

'But for Gelis, I might not be here,' Adorne said.

These days, there was a passage between the Berecrofts house and its neighbour. Crossing back to their own side, Moriz stopped just before the connecting door, and drew Nicholas to a halt. 'May I ask you something?'

'From the sound of it, probably not. What?' Nicholas said.

The mountainous face glared up at his. 'You tried to claim legitimacy once, I am told, and then retracted. Now Julius thinks he can try for you again. Do you in fact believe – Do you know that you are Simon de St Pol's son?'

He didn't want to reply. He had said more of his family in the last half-hour than he ever normally did. But this was Father Moriz, who wore the mantle of Godscalc.

Nicholas said, 'Yes. Yes, I believe it. Yes, I am sure it is true, but I don't have proof, and don't want any.'

'Even for the sake of your mother?'

'I have thought of that,' Nicholas said.

'But other things are even more important. I see. But it has occurred to you, while thinking so deeply, that if you are Simon's son, then Bonne may be his granddaughter?'

'She is not mine,' Nicholas said.

'You think not. But are you sufficiently sure to risk a relationship forming between Bonne and Henry?' Moriz asked. 'For Henry, beyond doubt, is your son, and Simon does not know it.'

'There is no risk,' Nicholas said. 'Bonne is penniless, fatherless; her mother impugned. Henry's wife will be a rich, landed heiress, personally handpicked by Simon.'

'Did I mention marriage?' said Moriz.

He opened the door. Since they left, the convivial clamour from the other side had become louder and, it suddenly appeared, less convivial. Wavering above the uproar was a single thickened voice: that of Julius. Shouting it down was another, far more furious, rather less inebriated and also unmistakable, although it had not been heard by anyone there for seven years or more.

'*Simon*,' said Nicholas. He turned. 'Tell Adorne –'

'– not to come,' Moriz finished. He had already spun round.

'And tell Wodman,' Nicholas called after him. It was necessary. This wasn't the lord of St Pol, executing a bold plan of revenge. This was a man in his cups, come to wreak against someone the hatred and fear he could not indulge in at home. This was . . . Simon.

Nicholas walked through the door and slammed it shut with a report that made the walls shudder. The shouting sharpened, diminished and stopped. The voice of Julius was the last to fade, as he belatedly turned. But before that, blue and white and gold, incandescent with anger, Simon de St Pol had dropped his arms and focused his gaze on the door, and then, with increasing satisfaction, on the man standing before it.

Julius hiccoughed.

Katelijne Sersanders said something under her breath, and Tobie closed a hand on her arm. John le Grant sent a swift glance to Crackbene, and Gelis remained where she was, between Robin's chair and the motionless figure of Clémence. Only Jordan de Fleury, aged nearly twelve, quietly set down the mugs he had been filling and, crossing the floor, went to stand by his father. Nicholas smiled at him.

Simon said, 'What a big bang, my poor Claes. Was it to bring your other men running? Well, there is young Jordan, at least, to protect you. You didn't dare come to me.'

'I could come tomorrow,' Nicholas said. 'Or now, when we have eaten. Will you join us?'

It sounded almost normal, even to Kathi. In fact, he was raising a screen; picking words that would guide them all, not just himself, through the dangerous, secret-filled ground.

Simon laughed a little. He was dressed for the field, and still armed. He had probably been called out on duty, as they had. He said, 'Eat with you? Hardly. I want a word with your sad henchman here, and one with you, and then I propose a fair fight between you and me. The King couldn't object, could he, to a fair fight to wipe out an insult? Jordan, did you know that your mother's a whore, and your father fornicates with the cripple's wife?'

Everyone but Nicholas moved. But before the first flash of steel, Jodi had shot from his father's side and flung himself over the room to the speaker. He had snatched a mug as he raced. Now he hurled the contents full over Simon's smiling face.

Simon's arms locked about him, a man's powerful arms, impervious to the struggles and kicks of a boy. Simon licked his lips, in exaggerated appreciation of the ale. Simon said, 'At least Henry would know not to do that. Heigh-ho. So clear the room, please. I want the boy, Claes and Julius to remain. Nobody else.'

Robin said, 'I am not going. He has insulted my wife.'

Gelis drew in her breath. Simon de St Pol said, 'As you please. I'm only one man. I'll kill the boy first, and then as many of you as I can. You decide.'

Robin's eyes turned to Nicholas. The same uncertainty held them all silent. Nicholas answered them all, but looked only at Robin. 'It's best if you go. Robin, no one believes that for a moment. It was one of Simpson's lies. Will you leave your honour in my hands? If you please?'

Tobie stiffened. Kathi said, 'Yes. We go.' Gelis had already begun to move to the door. For a single moment, her gaze had met that of Nicholas, but neither spoke. Robin turned his head aside and Clémence, taking hold of his chair, began to push. Simon spoke, and the door to the next house was locked. The shutters were already closed. Looking back as she left the room, Kathi saw a sudden movement close to the door, as if the boy had tried to grasp Simon's sword. As she watched, Simon struck the lad to the ground and, kneeling, unbuckled his belt and began to shackle him with it. Julius exclaimed, and then subsided at the look Nicholas threw him. When the door closed, and then locked, she was left with a picture of Nicholas and Julius standing together, facing Simon, at whose feet the boy lay. Julius was swaying. Like Nicholas, he carried no arms. They were at Simon's mercy. That is, any axeman could chop down the doors. But before they got very far, Nicholas's son at the very least could be dead.

She wondered if Simon was really prepared to be killed if that happened; or if he thought that none of these men would dare. She knew that if Nicholas had not allowed Jodi to run, Simon de St Pol would be dead, not to mention the inebriated Julius. She wondered by what law of retribution Nicholas was being brought, over and over, to weigh one life, one responsibility against another. She wished she were a man.

Inside the door, Simon de St Pol stood with the boy at his feet, his hair an aureole of gold, and his sword resting point-down next the boy's face, like that of a crusader in effigy. The candles burned, and the thickened air carried the odours of the uneaten food on the trestles, and the ale in the litter of mugs.

Without excitement, Nicholas spoke. 'All right. That's enough.'

'Julius, sit down. St Pol, I am not as unarmed as I appear, and if you touch that boy again, I shall kill you. Now say what you want to say, and let's get it over. Is it about Julius's step-daughter?'

He sounded different. He sounded like Whitelaw, or Avandale, or Nowie Sinclair. Julius blinked. Jodi's eyes became very bright. Simon de St Pol said, 'I think you should speak when you are spoken to. I will ask the questions.'

'Then ask them quickly,' Nicholas said. 'Wodman will have got to your father by now.'

Simon went red. He lifted the sword.

'And if you do anything, you and he will be sent back to Portugal. At the very least,' Nicholas said.

Julius, although bleary, had heard Nicholas mention his step-daughter. He gazed at him. 'Bonne? Do you know about Bonne? He was trying to make out that she's here.'

'It's a long story. She arrived at Kilmirren House while you and I were away. Adorne heard about it, and had her taken to Haddington Priory. I didn't know about any of this until just now. St Pol thinks I did.' He wasn't really speaking to Julius.

'I know you did,' said Simon de St Pol. 'Or why force her away from my house? It wasn't her idea to go. She says you pay for her clothes and her keep. She doesn't know why, but one may speculate. Is she to be your next wife, or your next bedfellow, Nicholas? The Prioress ought to be warned of your character. I could give her a list of your mistresses.'

'I believe you,' Nicholas said. He was becoming tired of it all, or he wouldn't have said it. It referred to a piece of history about which Julius was ignorant. To him, therefore, it was quite amazing that a simple remark should goad Simon into swinging his sword and, abandoning all his point of vantage, launching himself over the room against Nicholas.

Unfortunately for Nicholas, he was exactly as unarmed as he appeared. He escaped the first swipe by vaulting over a trestle and keeping it between himself and the swordsman. He said, 'Julius. Untie Jodi,' and ducked. There was a crash and a splintering of dishes above him. A gelatine slid down his shoulder and he could smell sauce in his hair. Simon tugged his sword free of the wood of the table and was lifting the blade when Nicholas rose, picked up a ham and rammed it on the point of the steel. Then, as Simon lunged, he slid to the end of the table where the pewter cups were, and began to throw them. Simon fended them off with an arm, shook his sword free and advanced.

Further off, there was another crash. Either on his way to or from Jodi, Julius had slipped on the tiles and now lay groaning where he had fallen. The groans sounded more liquid than painful. Simon's sword, glittering, drew Nicholas's attention suddenly back to the matter in hand, and he jumped aside just in time. A chair back exploded in splinters as he wheeled round it and snatched up a stool. Simon's swordpoint drove straight through it, and Nicholas dropped it just in time, backing. The second trestle, which he had feared to find barring his way, turned out instead to be close to one side, with a selection of puddings. He missed with the first one, but the second joined the dried ale on Simon's face and blinded him just long enough for Nicholas to snatch up a tray and another stool and get out of the way as Simon cleared his eyes and thrust forward. He stumbled over a chest.

The chest had not been there before. Nor, Nicholas realised, had the trestle, not quite in that position. A candle-snuffer, travelling rapidly from one end of the room to the other, caught his attention just before he heard Julius's cry and the whistle of air that meant the sword was in action again. It clanged on the edge of the tray, jarring his shoulder, just as an entire stand of candles went out. 'Ha!' said Nicholas, and was answered by the same exclamation, in a much younger voice, from under the table.

He could hear Julius being sick, and Simon gasping and swearing, and a lot of other sounds he didn't immediately pause to identify, being happy enough as it was. He wondered if it was a regression to childhood, or something he had forgotten in Bruges that made everything seem wonderful as soon as it was smashed up or spilt. He was aware of being covered in sauce, and could trace Simon's passage in terms of sweet milk and almond and cinnamon. It was almost the only way he could trace it, as most of the lights had gone out. Then he saw the cauldron of soup.

He couldn't have tilted it quite by himself, but a pair of younger hands helped. The soup fell on Simon, and Simon fell over Julius, and Nicholas took the sword from Simon's hand. There were two muffled rounds of applause from two doors which appeared to have unlocked themselves from the inside.

Nicholas paid no immediate attention, being engaged in a solemn ceremony of self-congratulation with Jodi. Julius, wiping his mouth, clambered to his feet and joined in. Both doors swung fully open and someone carried in lights. Simon, whether conscious or not, had the wisdom to remain where he was, on the floor under the cauldron. Nicholas left him to other people and walked to the nearer door with his tall son who, breathlessly explaining, carried Simon's great sword at his shoulder.

In the doorway loomed a vast and familiar figure. Nicholas and his son stopped. Turned towards Jordan de St Pol of Kilmirren, the two pairs of grey eyes, expectant, self-possessed, were identical.

The fat man said, 'Nicholas. It seems that your son has a native ingenuity that has escaped mine. Whose sword is that?'

The boy swung it down and held out the hilt. 'Will you take care of it, sir? It belongs to M. de St Pol. I think he has a great deal of ingenuity, but today he is not very well.'

Nicholas glanced at the boy, a smile in his eyes. The old man looked first at Nicholas, then at the young face of his generous namesake. St Pol said, 'He has other swords. If he is unwell today, he has no need of this one. You may keep it.'

Nicholas sucked in a short breath. 'My lord. It is too big. And too much.'

'And will cause trouble, you think. You may be right. But after tonight, I feel you are capable of dealing with Simon. The gift marks my dislike of incompetence. It is not, in any sense, Nicholas, the presentation of a family heirloom. As for its size, Jordan will grow into it. Unless he takes too many risks. Or is unwise enough to behave as his father does.'

'My lord my father –' Jodi began, and then stopped; for his father's hand pressed on his shoulder.

'You have performed enough rescues today,' Nicholas said. 'Thank my lord of St Pol, and tell him that you hope to deserve it.' Then he walked past, followed by Jodi, and did not turn back to see in what manner Simon de St Pol was taken away.

In fact, they consumed their deferred meal that night in the fresh rooms of the Berecrofts house next door, regaling Adorne and Sersanders and Andreas with the tale of Jodi's triumphs and Simon's discomfiture all over again. 'He will never forgive it,' said Adorne. 'But his father can control him, I think. If he is wise, he will take him off to Kilmirren. And it is the end, I am sure, of any interest in the girl Bonne.'

Listening, half asleep, Nicholas was inclined to agree. *Is she to be your next wife, or your next bedfellow, Nicholas?* Simon didn't therefore know the tale about Bonne that Julius had been spun by his wife. And after tonight, it was unlikely that Julius and Simon would ever find themselves exchanging confidences about Bonne. Or, indeed, about Simon's marriage.

It had been the first thing Kathi had said to Nicholas tonight, when the fuss had died down and they had a few moments together. 'Now at least Julius can't hope to badger the St Pols for their family secrets. But you know he's still addicted to exhuming your past. I took the chance to point out that you weren't likely to thank him, if it was going to bastardise everyone else.'

'But he wasn't convinced?' Nicholas said. Now it was all over, he had begun to feel very tired.

'He just repeated, with patience, that it could all be taken care of by dispensations. Which is true. But, of course, it takes time.'

She was asking him something. He answered it. 'I don't want to belong to them, Kathi.'

'But you do belong to them,' she said. 'Tonight, you forced yourself to be as much a St Pol as Simon is. You even let him take Jodi hostage. You cleared the room so that bystanders wouldn't be hurt, but also so that bystanders wouldn't hear more than they should. Whether you are their descendant or not, your conscience forces you to behave like one of them. You have all the burdens and none of the privileges.'

'I don't mind,' he said.

'And that is why you are so tired,' she said. 'All that, and Jodi to think of. But, you know, you gave him his chance. He was all he should be, tonight. Go and sit with Gelis, and celebrate together. You deserve it.'

He smiled, and went. She was dear to him, and dearly percipient. His method of dealing with the St Pols was a strain, and sometimes it drained him.

That, and the everlasting pressure of lying.

Chapter 31

Frendschipe for micht is lyk to caf of corne
And bocht to-daye and saulde agane to-morne.

THAT WINTER, the English Parliament empowered its King to raise the massive army and fleet necessary to invade Scotland.

The detail was very soon known. Earl Rivers, once proposed for the Scottish King's sister, was to supply three thousand men, and the Marquis of Dorset six hundred. The Lord Stanley, with a family interest in Man, was to produce three thousand archers from Lancashire. Ten thousand pounds were voted to pay the Duke of Gloucester's troops already in action in the north. There was separate provision for the fleet. This would sail under that excellent state servant and naval commander Lord Howard. The land army would be led by King Edward himself.

In Scotland, the basic counter-measures were already long in place. For Nicholas, one of the headier satisfactions of the past months had lain in the preparation for this war. Plans had always existed, changing week by week and month by month as secret pacts came to light, and balance shifted between England and Burgundy and France; and outside that close triangle of power, among the more distant states whose accommodation and markets they depended on.

Every country had spies. From long experience abroad, Nicholas had a knack for interpretation, for disentangling what was false or misleading. Added to that was his numeracy: the fast, effortless calculations upon which war logistics relied. His team had other skills.

In Burgundy, he had been an outside adviser within a structure

which was already firmly in place, and controlled by a strong-minded
wrong-headed leader whom none could contradict. Scotland was
different. He had been here now for four years, eight times as long as
any previous visit. In pursuit of his own business he had explored every
part of the country, and met all those of importance within it. In these
last months, in common with the macers and heralds, he had quartered
the country, carrying orders, seeking information, holding consul-
tations. He was part of an active, intelligent group surrounding a King
who might be as ambitious as Charles or Louis, but who had none of
the abundant energy, the charm, the innovative imagination that could
have drawn the men of worth to his side, and made every corner of
this small country his own. The well-intentioned lessons in style, in
self-confidence had failed. After decades of quarrelling, the loss of
Albany and of Mar had left the King isolated and astray. His unruly
sister Margaret had deserted him for a lover. His sister Mary, now free
of responsible advisers, had relapsed into emotional planning for the
welfare of her first husband's children, and sent him demands instead
of sisterly compassion. Resentful of guidance, he brooded.

Will Scheves spoke of it to Nicholas. 'Cortachy has been a courtier
and adviser to great lords, and is a delightful companion to men of his
own world. But this young King of ours will not confide in a paragon.
We should have made you the King's man from the beginning, instead
of Albany's.'

These days, he looked oppressed, as did Andreas. Nicholas thought
of the King of France, and his physician-astrologer, whose reputation,
too, depended on the health of his patient. And, of course, his financial
wellbeing. It was said that when Louis fell ill, he paid his doctor ten
thousand crowns monthly to encourage him to prolong his life. Nicholas
said, 'I think worse might have happened if Albany had been left
unsupervised. At least we knew what to expect. And the King has some
friends.'

This was true, for between them they made sure of it. The men of
the chamber were not drinking-companions like Barbaro, or elevated
dwarves, as in France; but they gave the King companionship, and
played cards, and made music with him when he wished it. Had Nicholas
not served Albany, he would have passed his days at the Castle in such
a role. He didn't think that the Archbishop was suggesting that he
should do so now. He didn't possess the King's entire trust, as Adorne
did. If he were to influence the throne, it would have to be done in
some other way.

Himself, he fretted over his distance from Albany. Twice, there had been letters from Sandy in which, either directly or indirectly, Nicholas had been commanded to come back to France. When he had replied with explanations in place of instant obedience, the letters had stopped. Liddell still heard with some regularity: the Duke's estates, after all, were in his hands. Nicholas had appointed Julius to act as a link between Jamie Liddell and himself, so that he might have a sense of Albany's frame of mind, and convey, in turn, what was most useful for Sandy to know. Jamie and Julius had a long acquaintance dating back to Sandy's childhood in Bruges, when the Liddell good looks had impressed the young Charetty girls, as Nicholas remembered. But that was a long time ago. Tilde was married to Diniz, and Catherine was now the mother of Henry van Borselen, a name to conjure with.

Gelis, welcoming news of that birth, had found it hard to equal his flippancy, even though the pang it concealed was his, and not hers. Katelina van Borselen her sister had also named her child Henry – Nicholas's child, whom she had carried to Simon. There was no reason, of course, why there should not be another so called.

He had reassured Gelis, he hoped; she had enough to contend with for his sake. But for him, she would not be here, working day and night in the cause of a country to which she, at least, owed no debt. Jodi would not be here, freed from the royal household since the Princess Mary's bereavement and acting, ferociously, as combined henchman and runner to Robin. It was necessary to remind himself that, for most of the time, they were both exultantly happy. As was he.

In March, the power shifted again, when there came such news from France that all Europe shivered – some with delight, but many with dumb apprehension.

The Great Spider, Louis of France, had been struck down by a fit, and for a space had been mindless and speechless. He had overcome it, they said, but some day he would be seized by another. Louis, who couldn't bear fools, had been touched by a curse that could make a clod of a genius. And the Dauphin his heir was a boy.

From London, King Edward reminded the world that his army intended for Scotland could be quite as easily deployed against France. His sister the Dowager Duchess of Burgundy had not wasted her summer in England.

To Adorne, as to Nicholas, personal considerations faded to nothing during these packed, breathless months. Adorne's family were perplexed. From their various religious retreats, his sons and daughters lamented their father's continuing absence from the house and tomb of his beloved lady their mother. His oldest son Jan, now a canon of

Lille like Antoon, had actually left Rome in the expectation of a welcome at Bruges, and had been mortified to find the family home empty, and his brother Arnaud in Ghent, distracted by grief for his wife, and for his newest loss, the death of the baby Aerendtken.

Adorne wrote to them all, and tried not to take pleasure in his visits to the Priory at Haddington where his little deaf daughter, aged three, was the sunny heart of the nursery.

It was, too, where Nicholas, had met Bonne von Hanseyck during her brief stay the previous autumn.

He had been busy, as they all were without cease, but he made time to call, and indeed had gone first to the noisiest part of the Priory where, as anyone could wincingly hear, Will Roger and his drums were entertaining the same small Efemie who stood, her round cheek buried in the buzzing drumskins, shrieking with delight. Now she could lip-read, Nicholas was teaching her patter-words.

Bonne, when he reached her, had been judicial. 'Poor child. One wonders, though, how the Sisters can concentrate. We shall not be sorry to leave.'

They were going to the smaller Priory at Eccles, which to his mind was rather close to the Borders, but which should be safe enough this side of spring. The placement had been arranged by the Cistercians at Tart, partly because Bonne's late mother had had links with the Priory. As Tobie had so cleverly found out, Sister Ysabeau of Eccles had had a sister married to Thibault de Fleury. Not that Bonne or anyone would learn much about all that now. Sister Ysabeau, now dead, had been too old and deaf in her later years to communicate much about the de Fleury family.

At any rate, the girl Bonne had been determined to make her way to the Priory and remain there, in the belief, as Nicholas understood it, that it would save her from unwanted suitors. He had had no time to thrash it out with her, even though he had not been convinced by the story. He felt, irritably, that it was Julius's place, not his, to explore the problem. After all, Bonne had been part of Julius's household. Anyone other than a self-centred, handsome bastard like Julius would surely know how her mind worked by now. He spent some time with the German nun, and impressed on her that she must call on him, if in difficulty. Then he had left.

That same autumn, Simon de St Pol and his father had moved to Kilmirren, and had stayed in the west ever since. The West March reached down to the Border, close to the Duke of Gloucester's fortress at Carlisle. Gloucester had repaired the walls recently, and even through

winter storms, castles such as Lochmaben and Threave could be subjected to perfunctory raids. It was not long before Simon abandoned
the boredom of Kilmirren to join Henry at Threave, and supervise and
improve the lad's idea of how to manage a troop.

It did not occur to him that Henry would resist this: they faced one
another in surprise and anger and, eventually, an outburst of violence
that left Henry withdrawn and sullen for a week. Then Simon, forgetting, called him out on some expedition involving burning and looting
that proved rather hilarious, with old goats, human and animal, running
about and his father with a whip galloping whooping among them.
They took a lot of booty and got drunk, and when he found his father
in a barn with two girls, he just shrugged and went off and found one
for himself. Henry never had any trouble with girls. He had been
initiated into all that, even before he could do it himself.

And after that, it was much as it had been in Madeira. He had lost
command of the Kilmirren muster, and his father had ridiculed his
venture with horses, but most of the time it was good. Henry made up
a band of local youths and took them on raids of his own.

In Edinburgh that April, Parliament passed the statutes necessary to
put the Scottish nation on a footing of war, to counter the known
resolution of England. The King's castles and Dunbar and Lochmaben
were to be provided with food and artillery, and the same was to be
done in coastal castles of power north of Berwick. Towards victualling
Berwick-upon-Tweed itself, the Three Estates had bound themselves
to raise seven thousand marks in special taxes, one-fifth from the burghs,
two-fifths from the clergy, and two-fifths from owners of land.

Colin Argyll was called to the west, where trouble, not by chance,
had broken out again in the Isles. The King's half-uncle Atholl was to
sail with him. Before he left, Argyll summoned Nicholas. 'I have to go.
Do you want to come with me?'

Nicholas had paused. 'Lord Cortachy –'

'Seaulme can manage without you, unless all your own predictions
are wrong. King Edward is still in the south. So are our envoys, with
the kind of offers which should hold his in talk for quite a while. And
didn't you report that the Cardinal legate is threatening to excommunicate both Edward and James if they commit their resources to anything
other than war against Turkey?'

'So King James has been told,' Nicholas said.

'Therefore he will do nothing rash. Do not feel,' said the Earl, 'that
you are required to come. I have sufficient men for my galleys. Even
Kilmirren the Younger and his son, although I fancy the son will be of

more use at sea than his father. It occurred to me that on such a voyage you could patch up your difference of opinion with that very beautiful youth. He stayed in your house at one time, did he not? And Mar is dead, after all.'

'I am sorry,' Nicholas said. 'There is nothing I should have liked better, but I think I hold with what my lord of Avandale has been saying. We have to prepare for irrational hazards. I want to check the East March without Angus. I am not convinced that the King can restrain his impulses. There is the money. Also, the wind that will be good for you may be less so for us on the east. I may invite you to sail on one of my ships, when you get back.'

The pale eyes had sharpened. 'If it comes to it, you would take part?'

And Nicholas answered, 'I am not declining to come, MacChalein Mor, because I dislike the sea.'

He went to Berwick after that, in one day, calling at each of the east coast strongholds on the way. Julius and John le Grant rode with him, and some of the dozen men-at-arms he now paid. They came from Leith, and were also capable of making themselves useful on shipboard. Crackbene had picked them, with John's approval.

From the beginning, the expedition went well: a good cracking ride down the eastern seaboard through the earldom of March, Albany's country. Nicholas let Julius make all the early running. Because of his friendship with Liddell, Julius was familiar with the landowners round North Berwick, the Bass and Dunbar, and could count on some sort of welcome from the Earl of Angus and his vigilant colony in the rock-fortress of Tantallon.

Angus, perpetrator of the raid which had broken the peace, had fittingly been rewarded with the duties of Warden of the East March of Scotland on the unspoken premise: *you got us into the war, so now fight it.* In fact, being determined to guard his own land, he accepted the post as his due; but remained resentful of intrusive authority, and suspicious of any friend of Adorne's. Julius treated him with easy deference, and gave the impression that he was here to admire, not to examine, the March's defences. These days, Julius was in the most buoyant of moods, all the disgruntlement of Cologne cast aside.

Nicholas let him have his head, and John, too. Archibald Douglas, Earl of Angus, was just over thirty and used to getting his own way. Ill-advisedly, he had married a Boyd, whose father had been adopted in exile by England. The marriage had not helped his career, and had cast temporary doubts on his loyalty. His loyalty to the King was still questionable, but not his friendship with the King's brother and sister, or his readiness to invade English soil, to the point of provoking a war. Which would make him popular with the French King as well.

He had a nephew there at the castle: Jamie Boyd, Princess Mary's young son. Nicholas saw the boy watching him, and sent John over to speak to him. He knew the boy didn't want John, and that common foresight required that he himself should cultivate both the Boyd children. At the moment, he couldn't bring himself to do it. He had meddled enough with that family.

Riding away, he quizzed Julius. 'What do you think? I'd rather see Angus down on the March, but if he's done all he says he has done, then it isn't bad.'

'You heard him,' said Julius. 'There's no movement at the moment in Northumberland. We'll check the rest as we go. But I think it's all right. Liddell says he'll do anything to protect the Douglas estates, and he doesn't want to share them with Boyd or the other Douglas in exile. He'll fight for the King.'

'I suspect he misses Albany,' Nicholas said. The spring air brushed his face; the horses' hooves behind him drummed comfortably. Below him on the left, the sea sparkled, empty but for a small fishing-boat. John had pulled off his steel bonnet and his hair, grey and red, flopped about his raw face. He looked contented as well.

John observed, 'Jamie was saying they heard from his good uncle Sandy only last week. His new wife is pregnant.'

'That's the Bourbons for you,' Nicholas said. He spoke absently. He added, 'Anything else? How is King Louis?'

'Oh, recovering,' Julius broke in. 'Applegarth was telling everybody that. Recovering, but inclined to dwell on his heavenly future, which might be good news for Rhodes.' He looked cheerful. 'Another shift in everyone's policies.'

John grunted. John had been with Nicholas and their army, working for the Knights Hospitaller in Rhodes. He had helped to build the St Nicholas bastion, which last year had accepted a battering of three hundred stone balls from the Turks. It had resisted. It might not hold out this summer. Sultan Mehmet was to lead the assault himself this time. It was why the Pope was importuning everybody to cease wasting their military resources.

The air seemed colder. It came to Nicholas that there was a conversation with John le Grant which he had been postponing, and which he thought John would prefer to take place without Julius. Tonight, after a ride such as this, they would all fall into bed. But tomorrow, perhaps.

Berwick-upon-Tweed had passed through many changes in the four years since Nicholas de Fleury's first arrival in the house of Tom Yare, and that other, miraculous arrival, of Robin.

In his many subsequent visits, Nicholas had noted them all, and had been responsible for some of them. Latterly, it had been men like Bonar and Cochrane and their craftsmen who had been concerned with strengthening the walls of town and of castle, and repairing gates, and fortifying the buildings and mounting the artillery in the castle precincts. Through all this, Nicholas had formed a good working partnership with Rob Lauder of the Bass, the castle's Keeper, and with Patrick Hepburn the sheriff, whose wife, hard of hearing but merry, was another of Princess Joanna's daughters. Aside from these, he got on well enough with the crown representatives, and with the Abbots of the various monastic houses. His other friendships, of the less formal kind, were with the merchants, the skippers, the fishermen of the untidy Tweedside town, with its lumpy waste ground and battered buildings.

Two decades before, a Lancastrian King had handed Berwick to Scotland in return for support against York. And now a Yorkist King wanted it back. It was what Nicholas wished to talk about with John le Grant, who was the only experienced soldier he could trust to help him draw up a profile of what happened when a frontier town was in danger of changing hands. Among other things.

You could see some of the precautionary changes already, walking these hilly streets. The official houses were empty. The Clerk Register, the former Archdeacon had withdrawn their furniture, their arras, their silver, loaded their coffers and paid off their servants, for no ceremonial meetings of the March Wardens would be held this year, or perhaps even next. The hammerers had long gone, as had the coiners with their punches and dies from the castle.

The church possessions in the Ness and elsewhere had also emptied. In the great houses of Melrose, there remained a small group of Cistercians, with their servants, to serve the community while they could. The rest had withdrawn to the mother house, as the monks of Newbattle had retired north.

On the river, the ferries had disappeared, and the King's boats, leaving everyone to splash over by ford. The merchant ships had also departed: most abroad on their trading, but others to ports further north. The merchant-burgesses of Edinburgh and St Johnstoun of

Perth and Dundee – the Colquhouns from Dumbarton, the Prestons, the Bartons, the Sinclairs – had largely returned home as well, emptying their warehouses. The officers and the Keeper of the castle had closed their lodgings in town and retired to the castle. Those who were left were powerful or obstinate enough, like Bertram or Yare, to wait until the last moment, and still be sure of escaping with what they had left.

Others had in mind, perhaps, waiting beyond the last moment. Some were foreigners, although there was nothing here now like the great Cologne and Flemish factories of a century and a half ago, when Berwick was another Alexandria: rich and populous, and earning a quarter of the customs return for the whole of England, it was said. Those who lingered in Berwick now were more likely to be cottars and fishers and herdsmen of no clear nationality who crept back unnoticed after pompous changes of master, and whose skills were in demand. Only a local man knew the whereabouts of the shoals and the fish-pools, or the clay for the pottery, or where the best fowling was. There was always building to be done. Whatever orders were given, those small burghers who had to depart – fleshers and coopers, bakers and brewsters, saddlers and weavers – would first set fire to their houses, and pollute what could be polluted.

Others stayed for reasons they did not disclose. The Browns, for example, still occupied their big house in St Margaret's district, and that night the three travellers drank with them there, although they slept at Tom Yare's. For some shipmen, it was clear, trade never stopped, no matter who was in charge. The great scattered family of Browns had a kinsman in Melrose and nuns at St Bothan, all of them served by the wagons from Berwick, bringing their food and their coal and their salt. The Holland family traded with England, even while Dick composed his verse for the Scottish Court. One of them was an outlaw at the horn.

There were others, as well, who had links with the English, but it was not a subject which came up that evening, or not while Julius was there. Julius, full of wine and bonhomie, had been keen to discuss the potential slump in Tom Yare's own fortunes, but Yare was smart enough to out-manoeuvre Julius on that. Julius had then introduced the name of Anselm Sersanders, and asked if it were true that, twelve years ago, the bright lad had cuckolded Martin Purves the merchant in Berwick, just before he'd gone off to Lille? And was it true that Saunders still blithely called himself Purves's agent?

Yare had looked surprised, John had grunted, and Nicholas had said with interest, 'My God, that must be a first. I never heard of anyone getting Saunders to bed without handing over the equal of a half-share in the Great Customs of Hamburg. Are you sure?'

Which perhaps sowed a doubt.

Later, when Julius had gone off to bed, Yare had gathered John and Nicholas for a round of claret, and had laughed over it, wharring away. 'You lie too well, Nicol. Weren't you in Lille only last summer?'

'I couldn't resist it. She's a pretty little woman as well, with an indulgent husband and an adored little girl of eleven. Stop laughing. And for Christ's sake, don't tell that to Julius. He's already got one daughter too many.'

John stared at him accusingly. 'You're making this up.'

'I'm not. Ask Antoon. You know Adorne's son is being given a prebend in Aberdeen? His canonry at Lille is not apparently proof against political pressure, and with the family wage-earner over here, saving Scotland, it seems only right that Scotland should be helpful. And Lille is a good market for us.'

He hesitated, and then decided to say it. 'Tom, I know Julius was over-curious, but tell me in general. Who stands to lose most if Berwick changes hands?'

'The King,' said Tom Yare. His bright eyes snapped round to Nicholas's, and his burr ripened. 'The King owns the town. We exported [expohted] eighty lasts eleven barrels of salmon the other day. He exchanges some of it for wine: we imported eighteen pipes of yon through England. And the yield from the Berwick fisheries is his. And the land rents. And quite a good bittie more.'

'But he pays for defence,' Nicholas said. John was sitting still.

'In general, yes. The bailie of the earldom of March would see to the castle. Parliament votes extra, as now, in time of war. But the deficiency is made up by the King. It's a fair exorbitant business, maintaining a frontier town.'

'So Berwick isn't and can't be a gold mine, so long as it sits where it does. It's a fortress, and a symbol, like Calais. Therefore James isn't moved entirely by greed when he sets such store by it?'

'No,' said Yare. He got up and refilled their cups, watching what he was doing, and then sat down again. He studied Nicholas. 'No. It's a symbol of his success as a king. It came as a gift, not a conquest, but he's not going to be the man to relinquish it. He was brought to look at it when he was only ten, a wee speug with his big royal retinue. Sandy was haled here as well, when he was just a year or two older. This is your heritage, he was told. This is what your forebears expect you to protect. If England takes Berwick, I, Tom Yare, tine my fees, my perquisites, my position, my easy route to southern markets, but I can retreat and do the same thing in Leith, and I don't have to help pay for lifelong protection. The only traders worse off than me are those who trade chiefly in England, or who'd lose special privileges. The Bishop of Aberdeen gets his fish duty-free. So do the Knights of St John. They trade with England, of course. They send their responsions to Clerkenwell. And their salmon passes through customs for nothing, eight lasts at a time.'

John said suddenly, 'They have important salmon rights in the north. Peterculter, and the rest. Free of customs, as well.'

'Because presumably the money goes to the Grand Master at Rhodes,' Nicholas said. He had been close to having this conversation once with Adorne, but had backed off. He had not been sure how John le Grant felt.

The engineer said, 'All right, you bastard.' Yare looked at him.

Nicholas said, 'You don't need to.'

'Like hell I don't,' said the engineer. He looked at Yare. 'He wants to talk about the Knights of St John, and he knows I'm connected with them. We're Grants from Aberdeenshire, my family. Bailies, a lot of them, for the Knights. One of them was Administrator for all the Order's land-holdings in Scotland – and maybe you can guess how much that is. Twenty-eight properties in these parts alone, Duns and Hutton and Whitsome and Chirnside among them. It was a franchise. The holder managed the property and collected and pocketed all the returns, in exchange for a flat annual payment to Rhodes. It used to be four hundred florins, banked in Paris. I don't know what it is now. You'd need to ask the Preceptor, who has of course taken the vows of poverty, obedience and chastity, but has four big sons to my knowledge, and sits among the barons in Parliament as my lord of St John, and trades in England with his big fancy ships. I suppose Will Knollys is the richest man in Scotland, but the loss of his fine house in Berwick is going to be a dead nuisance to the poor man. I like him. Is that what you wanted to know?'

'Yes,' said Nicholas. 'Why do you like him?'

'For his cheek,' John le Grant said. 'Also because it's a huge job, and he's one of the few men with the brains to do it all. And also because, although you know you can't trust him, he's probably doing the Crown much more good than an honest, stupid man might.'

'Tom?' said Nicholas. Yare, to his amusement, was gazing at John beatifically.

'D'ye know,' said Tom Yare. 'That's exactly what I've always felt, and I've never kent how to express it. Would it be unhealthy to write it all down?'

'Yes,' said Nicholas.

He didn't ask many more questions. He had what he wanted to know: what John and Tom Yare might do, if someone, somewhere, some time ceased to like William Knollys.

He was sleeping, later that night, when Yare flung open the door and shook his shoulder. Tom's face in the darkness was as red as a beacon. His face was as red as the window, which glared with the red of a beacon which, copying its light to another, would leap from crest to crest to crest to the north, waking Scotland.

The beacon that warned, as Tom Yare was trying to tell him, that the whole English fleet was at sea, and was out there, blind eyes in the moonlight, sweeping north to the Forth.

Chapter 32

Thir folk suld be first on the seye, for quhy
Throw waik spreit of thaim that has the cur
Schippis ar tynt, mor than with stormys stur.

OF THE THREE English flotillas in the water that spring, it was
the main fleet of three thousand men under their fifty-year-old
commander John, Lord Howard, which took this, the first
pre-emptive move by King Edward in the war against Scotland. The ships were loaded with bombards and handguns specially
augmented from the artillery caches in Calais, of which Howard had
once been deputy-governor. Lord Howard sailed on the *Mary Howard*,
his flagship; and the fleet included the *Antony*, once owned by the
late Admiral Henry van Borselen of Veere, which ten years before
had brought the King from his exile in Bruges. The Anthony it was
named after, of course, was now a wealthy pensioner of King Louis of
France.

It was, above all, a well-timed expedition. King Edward himself
was demonstrably still in the south. He had given no audience, as
yet, to the Scottish herald and pursuivant sent to patch up the truce
and, in the event, never would. The assumption was that the King
of Scots, while awaiting them, would be inactive. It was correct in
one sense: assured by his scouts of quiet on the Border, the King was
persuaded to call no general muster but to wait on events. Those in
charge of the King's ships (and their own) followed a different set of
propositions.

In Leith, Gelis was roused by the blare of horns and the clatter of
drums just before Crackbene's man banged on her door. Already the
wharves were brilliant with lanterns and as she listened, gripping her

cloak, she could see the bloom in the sky to the south; the pulsing bloom that was code for a sea-attack, to be followed by the canon-bell: one stroke for each ship.

And Nicholas and John were away. Ah well. All the more fun for those who were left.

In Edinburgh, the Castle artillery thundered its warning to assemble, even before the beacon fire took proper hold. There would be detailed news soon. There were more lookout posts on that coast than there were bloody guillemots.

Robin shook Kathi awake. 'Listen! It's started!' In the children's room, Hob started to cry, and Margaret cuddled him.

Father Moriz, dressing hastily, wakened Dr Andreas and Archie of Berecrofts, and vanished across the road to Tobie's house.

In the King's tiled house in Blackness, Anselm Adorne and his nephew were roused by a man from Jock Ross at the castle. While the port came awake, a fresh rider took the news to the Queen's fortified Palace at Linlithgow. Long before, the King's house had been stripped, and its valuables sent to the Palace. There also were stored the costlier contents of the merchants' homes and their warehouses. Now the merchants themselves would take refuge there. The village of Blackness had no walls, and its thatched houses were mostly of timber. Its place of strength, with artillery, was the fortress; and many, like Adorne and his nephew, made their way there. Others – the boatmen, the skippers – were already down at the pier.

The night was cool, with a strong, gusty wind from the west which showed unco-operative signs, towards morning, of fading and backing. This suited, however, the oystermen of Musselburgh who set off to their scalps at first daylight, although only two boats were sufficiently assiduous to linger in the estuary all day.

Nicholas pitched into Leith in the afternoon, just as the first of the enemy fleet rounded the Bass. John and Julius were with him.

'Which?' he said to Gelis. He looked exhausted and drunk, but was probably just exhausted and wild with excitement.

Gelis said, 'If you mean ships, you're too late for them all. No, maybe Leithie would take you. Have they landed anywhere?'

'The English? No. And their army hasn't moved to the Borders, so it isn't a double invasion, it's the other thing, an attack on our alternative harbours. They're signalling that if we don't give them Berwick, they can stop our trade everywhere.'

'Father?' said Jodi.

'I said you'd decide,' Gelis said.

'You want to come? Then come,' Nicholas said. 'But fast. Ask John what to bring. Julius, they'll need you here, at the Wark.'

'That's all right,' Julius said. 'You herd them in, and we'll pick them off. Don't forget the wine-ship.'

'What wine-ship?' said Gelis.

'Never mind,' Nicholas said.

John, Lord Howard, was himself mildly vexed over the wine-ship, which was not his, but which had been bringing eighty butts of sweet malmsey to await King Edward's (postponed) martial arrival at Bamburgh, and had been unable either to get into the Holy Isle, or to turn back to Alnwick or Newcastle. Sailing north, his lordship had considered the vessel, a small merchantman, to be in serious danger of falling into Scottish hands, and had swept it temporarily into his fleet, where it still was. Brown, the skipper, was known to some of his men.

Himself, Lord Howard had eleven sizeable warships. He'd left two more and some small ships in the Narrow Sea, and three under Fulford on patrol in the west, but he'd taken the best, and his best captains for this. His charts to Berwick were good, and for the coast after that he had taken on local men who had traded or fished in the area, and he had the man Brown's advice. The trouble was not so much the damned rocks as the shoals, which shifted from year to year. From tide to tide, heaven help them. When, entering the estuary, he came across this frightened flotilla of oyster boats, he shot a few cross-bolts over their heads until the fishers rowed over, and once they were on board, he distributed them round the squadron as pilots. He distributed the contents of their baskets, as well.

He had been told not to stay long, but to destroy as many ships as he could, obliterate harbour facilities, and put the fear of God into the local exporters. He had seen the balefires; he knew not to expect sitting ducks; if they had any sense (and it turned out that they had), the shaggy brutes would keep what ships they had close to land, and use their fire power to help hold off landings. He continued over the firth and sank one or two fishing-boats whose crews, he suspected, had been too drunk to notice the signals, and then, while the wind stayed where it was, led the way briskly north to the farther shore of the estuary. There, beginning with Crail, he proceeded to nose like a dog along the string of small ports that lined the river, ending with Kinghorn, which would allow him to turn and drift across directly to Leith, if he got the tide right. He wanted everyone to think he was attacking Leith. He knew he hadn't the remotest hope of getting into Leith and staying there, or staying anywhere, without an auxiliary army and long-term provisions. That wasn't the purpose of the exercise.

In fact, it went rather well. Crail produced nothing but sling-shot and shoals, so he veered off; but there was shipping in Pittenweem, and not just fishing-boats. A large, half-unloaded roundship from Danzig floated in the harbour with almost no one on board. Under cover of an exchange of crossbow fire, he got some of his marine soldiers across, threw off the crew, sliced her cables and had her towed out, cutting a swathe through the fishing-boats with a few cannon shot as he left. Of course, a foreign prize would cause endless wrangles between England and the country of origin, which was presumably why the Scots had left the poor ignorant sod in full public glare in Pittenweem. On the other hand, as Howard could have told them, foreign ships would think twice about going to Scotland, unless they had guaranteed safety. As they would have (he could promise them), once Berwick was English again.

Kinghorn was even better, with two ships from Sluys and three quite respectable local boats, all of which he eventually succeeded in taking, losing three or four men and some spars. He was content enough not to land.

By the time all six prizes were crewed and secure, the wine-carrier bobbing among them, the wind was quite strong from the south. He flagged the seven ships which were still at full strength, and led them across the river to Leith, but as he had suspected, the barrage that met him was at least as strong as his own, both from the fortified enclosure they called the King's Wark, and from the ships lined up in the river. He dismasted one of theirs, but took a ball through his own mainsail before he signalled to leave.

The silly louts cheered as he sailed off. He supposed they couldn't see the cluster in mid-water: his remaining ships guarding his prizes. In any case, they expected him to sail home. They must be watching amazed, as instead he turned the opposite way, and led upriver, on the flood, to the port they called Blackness.

'I must say,' Julius said, 'Nicholas is good at reading the English maritime mind. Did he catch Preston's ship? Where is he?'

'At a rough guess, on the other side of the island of May,' Gelis said. She wondered whether to tell him, then did. 'You know Robin's on board?'

'*What?*'

Vintage Julius. He added, 'Isn't that bad luck at sea? Like pigs and whistling?'

She said, 'Leithie seemed to think the sailors could stand it. And it has Tobie's imprimatur.'

'*Tobie* isn't on board?' Julius asked. His voice was annoyed as well as derisive.

'No,' Gelis said. She said, avoiding other disclosures, 'Are you watching the signals? If things go wrong, we are going to be very busy indeed.'

Blackness, of course, was to be Howard's main objective. He agreed with King Edward. It was the port by which arms and fortification material reached Linlithgow, only four miles away. It was an important alternative to Leith harbour, twenty miles to the east. The fortress itself controlled the whole area, including the seaway to the King's other castle at Stirling. Capable of being provisioned by water, it was one of the few strongholds which, like Dunbar, could be taken and held by an enemy garrison, almost without limit of time. And today, forced to spread its men and artillery on both sides of the river, the Scottish command must have judged it necessary to reduce the strength of Blackness.

He surged up, banners flying, on the tide. Around him, in his ship and the others, the landing-boats were prepared and the men waited, armed and eager, to land. From the castle, as they neared, he saw two flags run up. One was the sheriff's, someone told him. The other he had seen before, at the wedding of Duke Charles of Burgundy: that curious chequer, not unlike the flag of the Stewarts, and signifying also the role of the steward, the tax-collector; the man of finance.

Anselm Adorne. Howard experienced surprise. The man, a known supporter of the Knights of St John, had cast his lot, then, with King James. And on the very spot where that great Order had supported Edward of England against the ruffian Wallace, who had occupied their own place at Torphichen. But then, look at Commynes. Loyalty – and he valued it – had to give way sometimes to what was due to one's name.

His ships took up their positions, dropped sails, and anchored. The holding was less good than he had hoped. They were there to present their guns to the fort, and to cover the disembarkation. He prepared to give the order to fire. As if it had been heard by someone else, the face of the fort became covered with smoke. There came a series of thuds, loud enough to make his helm ring. And a series of balls crashed into the rigging and masts of his ships.

His own guns were already replying, their balls chipping the low curtain wall, the thick stone face, the rock of the fortress. The air was dense with smoke, and with shouting, and the noise of the still-falling wreckage. The lowering of the boats had momentarily stopped and he waved it on. No matter what happened, these men would land. And anyway, guns of that size took time to reload.

This was correct. He hadn't expected that Blackness would have not one line of cannon but two, nor that when his men leaped on shore, a crackle of handgun fire would come from the long landward wall. This wasn't a siege. He had no sows or catapults with him. These men couldn't wait to be overrun by troops from Linlithgow. They had to storm the fortress now, and take it, fast.

He withdrew and stood off, one sail in tatters, as his guns prepared to repeat their fire. A vessel behind him had been dismasted: it would have to be trimmed and then taken in tow. At the foot of the castle something was beginning to burn. His land force – good men! – had set fire to the great barge at the pier, and at least one other boat alongside it. The fire rose like a curtain, blowing out in the strong, squally wind which was fighting the pull of the river and threatening to drag them all further from shore.

He gave orders for the sweeps to be redoubled. His men were on land. He trusted them. They were well led, by the man who would captain the garrison once they got in. But they were not going to throw their hearts over the wall under all that gunfire if, looking over their shoulders, they thought they saw their ships lose their hold and disappear.

Jack Howard swore. Then he gave a few succinct orders and a moment later, under cover of gunsmoke, was himself being rowed to the shore.

He had joined the others before he was seen from the castle. He rallied them, and attempted one assault, but didn't waste time on another. There was no chance of a breach on this side, and his heavy fire was hardly denting the sea defences. He set his force to their second objective, and ran with them as they passed from house to house of the village, firing them all. The wind did half their work. Soon there would be nothing, no homes, warehouses, stables, sheds, fencing. Nothing to support or sustain the garrison if and when he got back and laid a proper siege. Then they ran for the boats.

He was lucky not to be killed. Quite a few of them were, even though his ships came in as close for him as they dared. Of course, he wore armour. He even wondered whether, if he knew Adorne's coat of arms, Adorne might know his. The Order, if nothing else, recognised chivalry.

Then they were on board; and raised sail, with a last cannonade, to which the fortress replied. Behind them, the township burned: a beacon that said, not *the English are coming*, but *the English have been*. He had achieved something.

His prizes and the rest of his ships were further off, because of the wind, but he would catch up with them when the tide changed, and meanwhile could see to his repairs. It was not going to be a pleasant flog south – he was going to need sea room and some wearisome tacking, which was always tiresome with an undermanned fleet, never mind one with a cripple in tow. In its way, though, it was quite a triumph – every vessel he had met sunk or burned, save for the six fine ships he had taken. Maybe more, before he got out of these waters. He could hear, when he got close enough, that his men on the waiting vessels were singing. He thought, when they were in order and sailing together again, that he would break out some ale, and they could have a bite of those oysters. He supposed they could let the oystermen go.

He found, as he arrived and boarded the noisiest ship, that the oystermen had gone. He found, crunching on shells, that his crews had already broached the baskets of shellfish. He discovered that, tipped off by the oystermen (was it possible?) the remaining part of his fleet had discovered the nature of their little stray companion's cargo and, being in the way of deserving a celebration, had helped themselves from its hold.

The wine ship, like the oystermen, was with them no longer. Its captain, having made a number of unauthorised concessions, had thought it prudent to retreat out of reach, a decision with which the more sober officers of Howard's fleet had agreed. It had seemed safe enough. They had cleared the firth of every ship within reach. No one could have guessed that some sly enemy vessel, lurking behind the island of May, would actually dart out and race after the wine-ship. When last seen, King Edward's malmsey, of which there remained many butts, was flying north and east before a powerful beam wind and a Scottish pursuer.

'Let it go,' Jack Howard said. 'We can't drag all this lot after, and then beat all the way back, just for that. So. Where is this wine, and where are the oysters?' When it was too late for reprimand, it was best to be hearty.

The wine was superb; but the singing turned sluggish and died, as the oysters had done, from ill-health.

It was a very, very bad voyage south.

Robin, bruised and aching and strapped to a fiendish harness on deck, was speechless with laughter, while Jodi hung over the rail at his side, his dimpled face scarlet with pleasure. The sails creaked, the sea hissed, and far ahead of them in a flurry of spume the English wine-ship was striving, apparently, for Ultima Thule. Nicholas, ending his recital, said, 'I've got some good oysters, *grata ingluvies*, if anyone wants them. No. It was a joke, but they've burned every house in Blackness. And they've captured eight ships, including three good fishing vessels, among the decoys. I saw them take two more as they left.' He was talking to Nowie Sinclair, who was sitting on a hatchcover, looking amazed. Preston was at the helm.

Nowie said, 'I think it's remarkable. I think the whole scheme is quite, quite remarkable. So what about the three foreign ships, you said? They'll blame England, of course, but they'll also put pressure on us, won't they, to cede Berwick and stop the dispute?'

'England thinks they will,' Nicholas said. 'But I know all the skippers. The owners will get the ships back, with compensation, and the cargo is well insured. The good stuff was ashore already anyway.'

'And now, for a bonus, we have the wine-ship,' Nowie said.

Nicholas caught Robin's eye. It had been a surprise, on first coming aboard, to find Nowie on Preston's boat; but of course the Sinclairs were historically the Prestons' superiors, and Sir Oliver probably owned the boat anyway. It was also typical of Nowie's undoubted charm that he had welcomed Robin as soon as he discovered him, and had been equally courteous to Jordan, aged twelve. When, still attired as an oyster fisherman, Nicholas had rejoined them all, it was to find the same mellow atmosphere. At times, Nowie might be a wealthy, spoiled martinet, but you forgave him for his exquisite manners. It amused Nicholas, now he knew him, to recognise the steely deliberation behind every inconsequential question, such as this one.

Nicholas said thoughtfully, 'Yes. The wine-ship. Do you think Leithie Preston could join us?' He turned to the skipper, who was watching him. Preston gave someone the helm.

'You know something about the wine-ship?' said Sir Oliver Sinclair. 'And I see Robin does, too.'

'And me,' said Leithie, arriving. Brisk, acquisitive, humourless like all his Craigmillar kin, he was never deferential, even to overlords. It had never amazed Nicholas that the other Thomas Preston should have been killed in a courtroom quarrel at Forfar. They were all clever seamen. Leithie said, continuing, 'It's an English boat all right, but it's not English-owned. It changed hands the other day, and guess who bought it: that fool Alec Brown. That's him sailing her now, desperate to leave us behind, in case we notice he's carrying wine to the enemy.'

'Is this true?' Nowie said.

'He was brought on board Howard's ship. He didn't recognise me,' Nicholas said. 'We were wondering what best to do.'

There was as much of a silence as there ever can be in the howl and crash of a three-masted sailing ship with a following sea. Robin's smiling eyes were on Jordan, who met them, and slowly ceased looking uneasy.

Nowie said, 'In Berwick, one gathers, this is not unusual. Stupid, however.'

'Very,' said Nicholas. 'Alec has a good memory for troop movements, though. Master Whitelaw calls on him quite often at Ratho.'

'I suppose I could verify that,' said Sir Oliver Sinclair. His fair skin, in the sun, was powdered with freckles, and his frame was as broad as a bullock's. 'At the same time, I fear that his interest is chiefly in profit-making.'

'That is easily verifiable as well,' Nicholas said.

'What, no pressure? How discreet you are being,' said Sinclair. 'I rather like that, my Nicol. I agree, the man is probably doing no harm, although he will hang himself in the end. I do not think he should be allowed necessarily to profit from provisioning the English. Neither do I think he need die, although I do not wish, either, to be associated with his survival. In fact, I think the problem may resolve itself, given time. Are we in any haste to return?'

'No,' said Robin, considering.

'No,' said Nicholas.

'Eh –' said Leithie.

'No,' said his patron, in helpful translation. 'In that case, let us sit back and enjoy a leisurely chase. What have we to eat, besides oysters?'

Far to the north, in the islands of Orkney, the youngest and cleverest Sinclair prince stood on the stone wharf at Stromness and peered out to sea. 'What's that?'

After only a decade of belonging to Scotland, the average Orcadian still spoke largely in Norse. The harbourmaster said, 'It's a prize ship, my lord, in the grip of three Ronaldsay boats. Shall I send out and bring the master ashore?'

'Do that,' said Henry Sinclair. 'And bring him to the house. And if the Bishop asks, he's carrying nothing but ballast.' The Sinclairs might not be Earls of Orkney any more, but they were still powerful land-owners, with favours to hand out, and call in.

It turned out the ship was carrying wine. And what was more, the skipper looked oddly familiar, for a man who claimed to come from

Hull. But the ship was English all right, and so were the seals on the butts. The man was generous, too: he offered to leave all the wine, if he might be allowed to take his ship and sail off to the west. When the young lord pointed out that the wine and the ship were his anyway, the man grew even more agitated. Then someone came in with the news that a second ship was on its way in; a Scots one this time. The messenger added something else in the Master's ear.

'Really?' said Henry Sinclair. 'Then perhaps we should see this gentleman safely bestowed, while we find out what our newest friends want.'

The wine skipper's face, as he was taken out, was sour as bog butter.

For the newcomers, Henry changed into velvet, which was intended to give him a certain ascendancy over the five unkempt persons who were presently brought in to see him. One of them was a boy. One, in a wheeled chair, was a disabled merchant he knew of. One was Nicol de Fleury. One was Leithie Preston. And the leader was his uncle Oliver, last seen in Roslin at his grandfather's funeral, and just before the consequent division of spoils which had proved so very satisfactory.

His uncle Oliver said, 'We were not at all sure that you would be in residence. How very fortunate this all is, and how kind of you to welcome us. Your father, I take it, is not with you?'

Henry's father, an idiot wastrel in youth, had turned out to be a genuine idiot in age. He was now the second Lord Sinclair. His father's sister had married, and been divorced by, the Duke of Albany. Henry said, 'No. Father is in Newburgh, and Uncle David is in Shetland. All I have on the premises at the moment are prisoners. May I offer you a refreshment, or would you care to retire first?'

'Dear Henry,' said his uncle. 'Insalubrious as we are, we should like to sit and talk to you first. We passed a ship at anchor.'

'The English wine-ship,' said the Master helpfully. 'With its master from Hull. Captured by three Ronaldsay boats.'

'Splendid fellows. I know them,' said his uncle, sitting down with a generous measure of wine. 'And fully deserving of the reward they will win. But the ship and its contents, of course, are the King's, and will have to be taken back south. They tell me that three-quarters at least of the wine has survived. The rest was lost to the ships in the Forth, as Nicol here can attest. Indeed, I was sure that I heard that the skipper was killed then as well. The man you have will be a minor seaman, elevated to master? He deserves his freedom, I should have thought.'

'There speaks a humane man,' said Henry. 'But appearances, we all know, can be misleading. A ship, to be three-quarters full, would ride lower.'

Sir Oliver Sinclair rose and stood at the window. 'My boy,' he said. 'I think you are right. If that cargo is two-thirds what it was, it would be nearer the truth.'

'And the mariner?' Henry said. 'Would you care to speak to him, before I turn him free?'

'No, no,' his uncle said. 'Let him take the next ferry south, with anyone else you don't want to feed. Preston here will sail both ships back, won't you, Thomas? Nicol and I have to leave him at Moray. Salmon business – so important, isn't it, and so vulnerable, in the wrong hands. And I want to see Cochrane, if he's there. Am I right, Nicol? The kingdom can do without you for another week? You have performed enough feats of valour for the moment.'

'You flatter me, sir,' the Burgundian said. His face throughout had been gravely attentive. The boy could not quite hide his puzzlement, but had the sense not to speak.

They were to stay two days, to rest the crews and themselves, and pick up fresh linen and such change of dress as they could find. Henry allowed his uncle the run of his wardrobe, for although they were related only by the half blood, they were much of a size. That is, Uncle Oliver, on his mother's side, was descended from King Robert the Bruce (hence the mighty air), and Henry was the son of a man known as William the Waster. But since his grandfather died, and his favouritism with him, it was William of Ravenscraig, the first-born, who was the second Lord Sinclair, and not Oliver Sinclair of Roslin, a son of the second wife. People forgot that.

Henry Sinclair made a point, during those days, of spending time with the Burgundian de Fleury, whom he had met occasionally since he grew up, and remembered from the scandal four years ago over Aunt Betha's cousin and her bastard by Cortachy. At Roslin, de Fleury had always seemed reticent, but in fact he had more of a sense of humour than you would credit him with, and had travelled quite widely. De Fleury knew Caterino Zeno, and his wife, and the gossip about his little bastard daughter, contracted to a rich merchant at Zakynthos. He knew about the Sinclair voyages, and that Henry's namesake had fought for Duke John of Burgundy. De Fleury had been to the tomb of St Catherine in Sinai, and brought back some of the oil. He had been in *Timbuktu*. The stay, which could have been tedious, really passed very quickly, and Henry was quite sorry to wave his uncle goodbye.

On board, Nowie said, 'Thank you. You were very forbearing. He will make a success of the barony, once his father is out of the way. And as the husband of Pat Hepburn's girl Margaret, the Princess's granddaughter, he will consolidate Sinclair possessions, think of it, from Orkney to Berwick. Meanwhile, I think we have preserved Alec? Did anyone see him?'

'I sneaked in,' said Leithie. 'He was right sorry for himself, I can tell you; and sorrier still when I'd done with him. I told him if he didna stop making money out of the English, I'd hang him next time myself.'

'That should keep him quiet for five minutes,' said Nicholas. 'Why are we going to Moray?'

'My dear fellow, I told you,' said Nowie. 'You deserve a rest. And Will Scheves and Drew are cooking up a small scheme which they really can manage best on their own. Or if they can't, you will be there, all fresh and unsullied, to sympathise with the King.'

'Sympathise with him over what?' said Nicholas, jettisoning court manners. The reticence he had once exhibited at Roslin had long since expired.

'Oh, nothing definite,' Nowie said, redoubling the charm. 'A rumour. You wouldn't hear it, in Berwick. The King swore, if Howard attacked, that he'd muster the army and march into England.'

Jordan sat, his eyes huge. Leithie Preston went on with what he was doing, intermittently yelling at his crew.

'But?' said Nicholas, with a certain patience.

'But the Pope has sent to tell both Kings to refrain. And they really don't want to anyway. Drew and the Archbishop have it in hand. Truly, there is nothing to worry about,' Sinclair said. 'Have you ever fished off Darnaway Castle? I assure you, it is an experience fit for angels. The lad would enjoy it as well. And I do think that Tam Cochrane would have information worth hearing. I might even take him with me up north. The good Bishop Prosper has not yet come into his temporalities, and my brother is not only Earl of Caithness, dear Will, but Camulio's Justiciar, chamberlain and sheriff. It is only wise to have a look at Scrabster and Skibo, and have a word with the Constable. Don't you think?' His large, fair brow wrinkled in anxious enquiry.

Nicholas said, 'You think Bishop Camulio will actually come?'

'I don't know,' said Nowie. 'I really don't know. The Pope is grateful. It would have been interesting, wouldn't it, for a while. I don't think he would be spared to us as Bishop of Caithness for long.'

'And afterwards?' Nicholas said.

'Oh, afterwards, I have no shortage of brothers who could provide a successor. What a pity it is,' said Sir Oliver, 'that Phemie's child was a daughter. But no doubt, if she conquers her deafness, we shall find a good husband for her one day.'

Somewhere in the suave voice there was a thread of real discontent. Nicholas looked at him. It had never occurred to him before. Having witnessed the brave desperation of Phemie's pregnancy, it had never entered his mind that the coupling was not, for the Sinclairs, the utter surprise it had seemed.

Sinclair hadn't noticed his silence. Sinclair was remarking, 'In any case, whatever action develops, the north and north-east are bound to play some part. As Bishop Spens and the Knights knew, and your Anselm Adorne assuredly does.'

'Mine?' said Nicholas.

'Ours, if you prefer,' Sinclair said. 'Without you, he would not be here. Without him, I doubt if you would. And we need you both.'

'We?' said Nicholas in the same tone. It was short.

'Oh, yes; I am Scottish,' said Nowie. 'But you are not. You are nothing yet, are you? You *have* been offered some land?'

'Yes,' said Nicholas.

'But you have not accepted it? Why?'

'Because I didn't want it,' said Nicholas.

'You see?' said Sir Oliver fretfully. 'That is what I meant. You will have to make up your mind, my dear Nicol. Adorne will not make it up for you.'

Chapter 33

In gret lawté thir men of craft suld stand
That baith has cur apon the seye and land.

URING THAT TRIP to the north, Jordan de Fleury stepped from childhood and became the son of his father.

It was Gelis, daughter of maritime Veere, who had him taught to swim as a child, but his father and the cool lord of Roslin who took him to fish in the wild spate of the Findhorn and taught him how to use it for sport, following these two mighty men, bare to the sun, plunging through the ravine; swirling in the swift, rock-strewn waters like the lean, agile salmon which a man got to love, and to prefer to the fat lazy fish of the estuaries.

It was his father who allowed him to come to the meetings he had with the Priors, the landowners, the royal servants who leased the fishings, at which they talked not only of salmon, but of general trade and all that might affect it, which seemed to include everything in the world. Beforehand, his father now would outline for him, simply and briefly, what was going to happen, and what he wanted, and what to watch for, and Jordan would sit through the subsequent meeting, giving nothing away, but convulsed with private glee at each point scored and object achieved. He learned to watch people's hands, and their feet, and their eyes. He learned never to despise a man because he wanted something different, and never to underrate him either.

They met Tam Cochrane, after Sir Oliver Sinclair had left them at Speyside, and scrambled all over Auchindoun while he explained its defensive points and its weaknesses; and then rode south to Kildrummy. Master Cochrane was Constable of Kildrummy Castle, which meant that he had to make and keep it defensible. The masons were working there, and the yard was the kind of place Jordan had liked to play in when he was small, with buckets of mortar, and heaps of squared stones and timber, and scaffolding, and barrows, and scratched drawings everywhere. The money for it came from the earldom of Mar, which belonged to the King since the last Earl had died. As a servant in a royal household, Jordan had become quite familiar with earldoms and baronies, and had already attended a baron court, and seen taxes being collected and local men trained to fight, and even to raise their beasts and plant properly. You had to do that, if you had land. Or even if you didn't, his father said, you should know about it.

They climbed over the Buck of the Cabroch while they were travelling, and he was taken into forests, where he saw trees being sawn and made ready for floating. Master Lisouris showed him how to tell good wood from bad, and he helped manage the oxen. Last thing of all, he helped fell a tree. Then he travelled to Aberdeen with his father, and got a place on a boat going to Leith.

His mother was at the Leith house, and came out by skiff to where they were waiting over the bar for the tide. They went back with her. She didn't kiss him or anything, although she held him at arm's length, smiling, and then gave him a quick squeeze on both shoulders. She kissed his father. She said, 'It was a long two-day battle for some people. Even the St Pols got back from Tobermory before you did.'

It was as well she mentioned it, for Jordan had forgotten about the St Pols, and Henry was the first person he saw on the wharf when they came ashore. His father threw him a smile, but Henry turned his back, and his father and mother walked on towards the house. He could hear his father mentioning oysters, and his mother starting to laugh. Jordan smiled. Henry came over.

Henry said, 'He isn't much of a fighter, is he, your father? Ran away from the Forth. Stayed away from the muster. What was he doing? Visiting all his other wives?'

He had been told what was safe and unsafe to mention. Jordan said, 'We were chasing a wine-ship.'

'How exciting,' said Henry. 'Did you catch it?'

'No. But our ship brought it back. My father had business to see to. Anyway, there wasn't any fighting on the Forth,' Jordan said. 'And I thought the army disbanded.'

'It might not have. And someone certainly burned Blackness without you helping to stop it,' Henry said. 'But I suppose you just have to follow your father. You ought to try some real fighting some day.'

'What was it like with the Earl of Argyll and Angus Og?' Jordan asked. He sat on some rope and Henry perched on a bollard and told him. It was quite interesting, and terrifically gruesome: the place where they fought, even, was called Bloody Bay. It was also very serious, unlike John le Grant's tales of Jordan's father fighting the Turks, which were all full of the jokey things that they did, like pretending they were there to cure camels. In the end, the Bloody Bay story ran to a halt, and although Jordan asked some things he wanted to know, and said, quite honestly, that he wished he could do something like that, Henry jumped to his feet and said he really couldn't waste any more time, and just went. He glanced at their house as he passed.

Nicholas saw him, from where he and Gelis stood, half embraced in the depths of the parlour, but didn't say anything. Gelis's eyes were on Jodi, coming slowly along from the wharf. She said, 'What have you done? You have brought back a man.'

'The start of one. It was a longish time for a boy, and he was very good. But now he needs to get back to his friends, and become thoroughly silly and childish. Don't scold him too much,' Nicholas said. His fingers moved to her ear.

As so often before, the mystery of it overwhelmed her. She burst out. 'How do you know what to do? How do you know exactly what to do?' And when he looked down at her, startled, she said, answering herself, 'It is Umar, isn't it? The teacher, the professor, the judge, who passed on all he knew. That, and instinct.'

'He taught you as well,' Nicholas said. 'But you manage reasonably well on instinct alone. Or you used to.'

She felt herself melt as he said it, for she recognised both the mock complaint and the frustration behind it: Jodi was coming; they could not be alone. She also understood, without resentment, that she had reached a small boundary, and had been stopped. There were not many now, and she did not test them for her own sake but for his; reminding him, as best she could, that she was there, if he wanted to cross. If he never did, she still had more than she deserved. She had him safe. He was back, safe, again.

The next attack came in July.

It had always been possible, in spite of the Church's injunction which had persuaded her Scottish son in Christ James to disband his army, and her English son in Christ Edward to cease having to pretend that he meant to come north with any promptitude. Obedience to the Holy Father certainly entered into both decisions, but did not last long on King Edward's side.

Personally, he was not immediately coming north, or releasing an army. Nevertheless, he lent an encouraging ear when Jack Howard, queasily back after his upsetting and unexplained illness, proposed (in a calm, measured way his men found admirable) a return with his fleet, better armed, better provisioned, and with the capability of establishing a base in the Forth which could act as a supply centre for the land invasion, when it came.

The beacons flared, and King James, cheated, betrayed, torn from his assurance of pious security, fell into a rage that even de Fleury could not pacify. The King was left with his priests and a doctor, and his fleet took to the water.

This time, it was a different fleet, with different tactics. 'Your bloody fault, Nicol,' had said John le Grant, when they planned it. 'If you hadn't had your small fishy joke, there would be no need to cater for Howard: there'd be no sense in his coming back. As it is, he'll probably come for revenge.'

'It would be an extravagant form of revenge,' Argyll had said. 'If he comes, it will be because it suits Edward's strategy. A second attack like the last would be worthless. Howard would either come along with a land force, or to prepare for it.' Colin, Earl of Argyll, had come back from the fighting, having quelled the rebellion and arranged to abstract and imprison his own grandson Donald, aged three. One of his daughters was wife to Angus Og, son of the rebel Lord of the Isles.

Much though he esteemed MacChalein Mor, Nicholas understood that it would not matter to Argyll whether his daughter wept for her small son or not: if necessary for the greater good, the boy would spend all his life in captivity, until he was grey. It was not the same as stealing your son from your wife. It was the same, in some ways.

Nicholas had said, 'So this time we confront Howard, if he comes.'

'*Dìreach air a shùil*, just so,' Argyll had said. 'Andrew Wood will draw up the plans. You and Crackbene and the men of Leith will help him. And it is sorry I am, but trade stops from this moment. We accept incoming ships, but none may leave during the season. We may need them all.'

He had been right. Of all the threats they had discussed, Jack Howard's fleet was the one to materialise. They sailed into the Water of Forth, and there found Sir Andrew Wood, with the full Scottish squadron around him.

It was a short fight. The hope of the English, it seemed, had been to establish themselves on Inchkeith, the mid-estuary island which lay between Leith and Kinghorn. Balked of that, they tried nothing further, but turned picturesquely and left, sustaining a brisk rear engagement until well down the coast. After a while, the Scots let them go. No ships had been lost. They had been evenly matched, and Howard's personal animus had not altered the odds. By mid-August, he and his fleet were back in Sandwich.

At the ensuing council in Avandale's house, the Chancellor had an announcement to make. 'Word has just come. The army which threatened Rhodes has withdrawn. The Sultan of Turkey, its leader, has died.'

His voice was grave, rather than triumphant, and it was a moment before anyone spoke. Struck down before fifty, Mehmet the poet, the drinker, the visionary, the amalgam of cruelty and tolerance: the man who, aged twenty-one, had won the legendary Constantinople from Byzantium, and had developed the fleets which had made him the most intimidating magnate of his time.

The driving power behind advancing Islam had gone, leaving a vacuum. Mehmet's eldest son had died before him, strangled on his own father's orders. The other two lived, and would already be vying for power. King Edward of England might well be emboldened to break the peace, and risk papal displeasure. The Turkish war had lost its urgency, for this year at least.

So Edward of England might now feel morally free to attack – but would he do it this year? The verdict, among those debating round Avandale's table that day, was that he would not. Howard's venture had failed. Edward had sent no army to support it, or to reinforce Gloucester, waiting in vain on the Border. There might be – there would be – trouble still on the Marches, where there remained vengeful men with energy to spare while their food and their pay and the good weather lasted. But the main threat from England would come next year. They had time to plan.

The meeting over, Nicholas and Anselm Adorne walked uphill to the High Street; impeded as ever by the onslaught of eager bodies who wished to sell something, or extract news or impart it, or establish a personal forum on a question of public importance. Fresh from the sea, it was a change to be among pigs, and horseflies, and children; and banging from the hammermen's shops, and disputatious clamour from packed, busy markets. Every brosy face on the causeway had a name, or a nickname. However unavoidably courtly their clothes or glittering the chains of their chivalric orders, this was also true of themselves. Everybody called Nicholas Nicol, and quite a few called Adorne Seaulme, an unexpected tribute from the horseless class which he received in good part. Life in Edinburgh was heavily communal, as it was in the Canongate, whose smells and noise were considerably worse. Adorne said, 'Come to my house for a moment.' He meant his own house, in the same street.

Kathi was there. It was an extra pleasure, like the coolness and quiet. Perhaps because he was used to the dyeyards, Nicholas functioned at work without reference to his surroundings: the crowded premises of the two Berecrofts houses shook his concentration no more than did the silence of a Greek cell. When he was not working, it was different.

Kathi looked the same. No, that was not true. Between them, Robin and her children had achieved the impossible: had anchored her to normal living; had absorbed the extremes of energy which had made her life so exhausting, and left her – not calm, she would never be that, but less volatile.

Nicholas himself had once been the same; perhaps still was. Together, they had engendered a form of articulate and genderless lunacy which he did not allow himself to dwell upon now, for it could not have continued, if only because it put her under too much strain. She was still very astute. She was saying, 'How extraordinary, you managed to walk up from the Cowgate without buying anything.'

'I didn't,' said Nicholas, defensively. 'I bought another goose. It's being delivered. Would you like one?'

'I have three,' Kathi said. 'No household containing Hob need ever fear thieves. Come and have some food. Are you wondering why you are here?'

'No,' said Nicholas. 'I am trying to stay happy for as long as possible.'

Adorne said, 'Don't look at me. It's Katelijne's idea.' Already, his face was lighter, as it had looked in the summer evenings this year when, for the first time since Phemie's death, he had begun to entertain like-minded friends, bringing together singers and verse-makers: Jock Ross and his son-in-law, the goldsmith's cousin; the clerk Stobo; the young man from Dunfermline who had studied at Paris with Jan. Even, once, Blind Harry, suddenly welcome at Court and on campaign. With, of course, Willie Roger and his songsters. Sometimes, among the like-minded friends, with the King's approval, were visiting envoys such as Ireland, and Leigh.

Tonight, it was only Kathi, flanked by Nicholas and her uncle, seated before a table of savoury dishes, and attended by polite, silent servants.

The wine-flagon was a fine one, of glass, which Nicholas had last seen at the Hôtel Jerusalem in Bruges. It seemed lucky, when so much else had gone, that it had survived.

The servants performed their last office and left. Kathi said, 'Guess.' There was a trace of mischief in it; yet her face was not perfectly cloudless. And she was here, and not at home.

Nicholas said, 'Julius?'

Her grimace made him want to laugh with relief. He went on, 'Julius and his new zeal to authenticate me as a St Pol? He has been asking questions of Robin?'

Julius had not been with the fleet. Julius, it was plain, had been busy. Kathi said, 'It's my fault. I'm sorry. I didn't think Robin knew anything anybody else didn't know. But he was talking to Julius about France, and he mentioned the time you were attacked and hurt by the Loire, and he visited you.'

'At Chouzy,' Nicholas said. Adorne was courteously listening.

'Robin remembered the name of the family: Bernard de Moncourt of Chouzy, and his wife Claude. He explained to Julius they were relatives of Clémence, and that you had called, since you were passing, because you knew so little about her, and she was so important to Jodi.' She paused. 'Was that awkward? Do you mind Julius knowing?'

'Not at all. I actually went to make enquiries at the convent where Clémence was reared, and arrived at the seigneur's house quite by accident. No, it doesn't matter. I'm sure Clémence wouldn't mind, if she knew. Julius *is* thorough, isn't he?' Nicholas said. 'Who else is suffering?'

'Well,' said Kathi, munching reflectively. 'He went straight to Tobie, of course, but Tobie just repeated what Robin said. Then Julius went and got hold of Oliver Semple. Your old factor? Who's gone back to work for Sir Thomas Semple? He thought he might remember the scandal –' She broke off. 'I'm sorry. This is very difficult.'

'Not at all. It *was* a scandal. Sweet young Scottish lad is tricked into marriage by Burgundian harridan thirteen years older, who gives premature birth to his dead child and, plunging into promiscuity, tries to saddle him with her next. That was what everyone in Scotland was told, and what they believed. I wish he'd leave it alone.'

'He won't. It's what the monks in Paisley were told as well. Julius asked them. They said Simon was notoriously wild, but that the girl he married was shameless. The St Pols said that if she'd tried to come to Scotland, she would have been thrown out.'

Kathi had begun to look rather hot. She said, 'It's no wonder you felt crucified by everyone here, Nicholas, and not just the St Pols. They were told atrocious lies, and they believed them.'

'And Oliver Semple?' Nicholas said. He kept his voice friendly. He didn't know why she was saying all this with Adorne there.

'Bel got to him first: he wouldn't pass on gossip anyway. But, of course, Julius is now hunting for Bel. He knows Bel was in France at the time when you and Adelina were still with your mother, and St Pol was becoming the vicomte de Ribérac. Julius is planning to question the French Archers who have retired back to Scotland. There was an Erskine among them. Even a Lisouris.'

'Kathi, what do you think they could know?' Nicholas said. 'Anyway, to listen to Wodman, they retire with enough claret to preserve them from thinking clearly ever again. As for the two Princesses, Eleanor is dead, and Julius is very welcome to try to talk to Joanna.'

He suddenly realised why Adorne was here. He sent a flicker of apology to Kathi, and spoke to her uncle. 'Julius has bothered you, too? I am sorry.'

Adorne was more tranquil than he was, or Kathi. 'The situation has been created by Julius, not by you. He asked me about Venice, and my visit to Montello, where my brother is buried, and where your maternal grandfather was then being nursed. I saw the vicomte de Fleury at the time, but he could not speak, and I had nothing to add to what Gelis and Tobie learned later. Julius did also ask, however, whether I had sent a servant back to ask further questions, as someone claimed. I had to confirm that I had not. Then he asked me if I had heard any rumours about the old lady called Tasse, the retired servant who died, drowned in a Venice canal while staying with Gregorio.'

He stopped. After a moment he said, 'Nicholas?' Kathi was looking at him as well.

Nicholas said, 'I'm sorry. She was one of the few friends of my stay in Jaak de Fleury's house, and her death was a blow. What rumour did he mean?'

Adorne said, 'Apparently, Gregorio was not satisfied that her death was an accident, and he was right. Investigation showed that she had suffered a blow before falling, and might possibly have been held underwater until she died. But no reason for her killing was found, and no murderer. Julius wondered if the mysterious man at Montello was implicated, and if Tasse had been killed because she could prove that you were Simon's son. In which case, who was the man?'

Nicholas said, 'I don't know, but I don't think it matters. Tasse knew nothing at all of my parents, and if she was attacked, it couldn't have been over that. People get robbed, and then killed. The muddle over Montello was probably just a mistake of the monastery porter's, and Julius is working up fantasies. I think we should all leave him alone. When he finds out it's hopeless, he'll stop. So may I have some pudding and get to be frivolous?'

Adorne said, 'You may not only have pudding, you may drink my health. This is the other reason you are here. Her grace the Queen has just made official my position at Linlithgow. I am to be her servant there, for as long as I wish to stay.'

Kathi was beaming, and Nicholas gazed at them both with unalloyed pleasure. For a long time now, Adorne had been shouldering what were virtually the duties of a Keeper of the Queen's Palace with all that entailed. He had received some sort of payment for that, and for the Conservatorship he still shared with Wodman. But the official emoluments for the maintenance, repair and defence of a royal palace were substantial, involving rents from land and crofts all round Linlithgow, and the returns from the King's coalheugh as well. All that, with his charge at Blackness, made him one of the guardians of that very vulnerable part of the coast.

There were other implications.

Nicholas said, 'I don't know when I've ever heard anything about this royal family that pleased me more. At last, they have done something right. And, of course, I have to ask: does this mean that you are staying in Scotland?'

'It means I can afford to,' said Adorne. 'I can provide for Euphemia. I can, and shall gladly give my services until, God willing, this unnecessary war has come to an end. What happens after that will depend on what happens in Bruges. But yes. For the first time I am truly contemplating spending my life in this country. Does that appal you, after all Katelijne has been saying?'

'If it did, I shouldn't be here,' Nicholas said. 'Your health. Your health, and all it says on that flagon.'

The flagon was Syrian. It said, *Lasting joy, increasing prosperity and fortuitous destiny.*

'I wish him a fortuitous destiny every day,' Kathi said. 'And you know what I'm going to say next.'

'Am I staying. I don't know,' Nicholas said. 'And yes, I've been offered inducements. And yes, you've been talking to Betha Sinclair.'

'No. It is I who have been talking to Gilbert Fish and Landells and Livingstone and MacCalzeane, and Will Goldsmith the Halfpenny Man, and even one of the Mullikens,' said Anselm Adorne. 'Am I not a compendium of information on the bullion trade? You were offered virtually anything you wanted, if you would mount another expedition to Africa and bring back gold. You were offered lands and a barony, if you would stay in Scotland and use your powers for mineral divining. You refused. Why?'

The sweetmeats had been set out by the window. When Nicholas did not immediately answer, Adorne rose abruptly and walked there, turning, glass in hand, to look at the other man. Nicholas took his glass and joined him, more slowly.

Nicholas said, 'I don't want to go to Africa, because I don't want to spend my time that way, and the bullion wouldn't arrive for two years, and the coinage problem is urgent. Parliament won't vote James the money he wants; he's trying to hoard what he has, and raise more by other means, and you and Drew and Colin and Archie have to guide him, as we have to do about war.'

He had used Christian names, forgetting. Adorne said, 'That is what councillors are for.' He sat down, in a collected way, and Kathi came and sat with him.

Nicholas looked down on them both. He said, 'I'm not demeaning the throne. I meant no more than that the King should be advised. There are deposits of silver and lead and perhaps gold about the western moors: we all know that – the Hamiltons and the Crawfords and the monks of Newbattle better than anybody. But it takes time and money and good engineering to raise it, and it may not make all that much difference. I think it's better to sit down with the Treasurer and your mint masters, as you're doing, and plan what kind of coins the country needs to keep trade going, and the Curia happy, and the price of food down. You don't need my sort of gold. If I thought you did, I might divine. If I thought you didn't but felt greedy, I might pretend to divine. I refused because I didn't want to face the decision. If I can't trust my judgement, then I shouldn't stay.'

He had spoken calmly, but Kathi looked troubled. He sat.

Adorne said, 'You mistake me. I am glad beyond measure that you have refused to divine. It is something that came between us in the past. Now, perhaps I trust you more than you trust yourself. I am only concerned that, between us all, we shall drive you away. I know something about defensive war. I know a great deal more about coinage and fund-raising taxes, but success in that – I think you are right – will not depend upon a sudden influx of bullion. It will depend upon the management of a healthy, developing trade that will continue through every political change, clandestinely if necessary. I know manufacturers,

I know shippers, I know dealers, and I know men who are all three. I know of no one who combines them in all their most questionable aspects with the brilliance that you do.' He was smiling.

Kathi wasn't. Kathi said, 'I think you should say to Nicholas what you said to me. That your work needs his, and his yours.'

Adorne said, 'I think he knows that, but I hope he will absolve me from personal pressure. I assume, at least, that you are in Scotland, Nicholas, so long as the war lasts? Are you to be in Edinburgh, or irresponsibly in the thick of the fighting on the Borders? You know, you ought to place that young lady somewhere safe. Eccles is far too near the frontier.'

Nicholas emitted a short, alarmed groan. '*Bonne?* I sent to have her brought north before I sailed. Didn't she come?'

'Not for you,' Adorne said. 'What a shame. I had no trouble taking her from Edinburgh. Would you like me to go down and help?'

'You're not going,' said Kathi positively. 'But someone must. And if she doesn't obey Nicholas, who?'

'She,' said Nicholas, 'will obey Nicholas.' He resumed his ordinary voice. 'I suppose I'd better ride down. And the nun – oh God, the nun.' He brooded, and then brightened suddenly. 'I know. I'll take Julius.'

'Who then can't search for Bel. You *are* obvious, aren't you?' Kathi said.

'It's why he'll never get on. What about some music?' said Adorne. There was a lute to his hand. He drew it over and brushed the strings, lovingly, with his tapering fingers. He began to sing under his breath, and when Nicholas joined him, he smiled, and then again, when Kathi brought in the descant.

It was partly improvised, the best kind of music: concentrated, pure, more demanding than anything the real world had offered that day.

Harmony is a maiden carrying a shield. As soon as she enters the hall, a symphony swells from the shield.

Come. Here is peace. Here is safety. Here are friends.

Part IV

Quhen I was zoung we had a tyrand king.
I askit than that sone he suld be deid
And so he was; a war come in his steid
And als fast than for his deid I besocht.
Syne come the werst that ever mycht be wrocht.

Chapter 34

Richt sad in moving suld thir women be
And of schort space and to no fer cuntré.

NICHOLAS RODE south to Eccles next day.
At first, Julius had refused to concern himself with the
plight of his step-daughter, driving Nicholas to fulminate.
Then came news of fresh fighting on the Border, and Julius,
bribed by the leadership of their small troop of cavalry, agreed to set
off via Eccles, so long as nobody expected him to bring the wench back.
Nicholas could do that, he said, and then return to the sheepfold in
Edinburgh, and keep the King happy. To Julius, sometimes, Nicholas
was still vaguely an apprentice, whose job was to look after children.

Nicholas, who occasionally shared this opinion, took Jordan with
him. At the last moment, he found Willie Roger also applying to come.

He tried to dissuade him. Conducting choirs developed the shoulders,
but the rest of Whistle Willie's appearance – furious eyes, tousled locks
and meagre physique – were more the March hare than the March
harrier.

The insult (sweetly transmitted at once) displeased the musician. 'I
ride more than you do, back and forth to bloody St Andrews. If I can
just bring back some altos, I wouldn't need to ride quite as much.'

'You won't get any altos at Eccles,' said Nicholas. 'If you get three
cracked sopranos, you'll be lucky.' The Prioress, by name Euphemia,
was a half-sister of the late Bishop Kennedy and aged sixty at least.
Ysabeau, the only other nun he had heard of, had died touching eighty.

'Then I'll go to Coldingham,' Roger said.

This was defiant idiocy. The King had enraged the entire wealthy foundation of Coldingham and their patrons the Homes by milking the monastery to fund Willie's Chapel Royal music.

There was no point in going into all that. Nicholas said, 'Well, you're on your own if you do. I'm not going to Eccles by the east coast. And they won't have any altos there anyway: they'll have moved them somewhere safe with their gold cups and their charters.' Crackbene's wife had once worked at Coldingham, in between being a wet-nurse. She was the best contralto Willie had ever had: he used to say her neck resonated down to her navel; a statement with which Crackbene took serious issue, the first time he heard it.

After some persuasion, Willie agreed that Coldingham was too far, but still insisted on coming to Eccles. So be it.

It was a cheerful enough ride: south through Dalkeith and up the steep hill of Soutra, from which all the world could be seen, from the distant smoke of the town to the far hills of Fife, with the flat grey Forth lying between; from the expanse of the wide Eastern Sea to the Bass Rock close to its shore, thumbing its nose at the cone of North Berwick Law. Then they entered the hills. Every track over the Lammermuirs was busy with traffic both ways: troops like their own, going south with their arms and their provisions, and some coming the opposite way, with their service over. There were also elderly people, and younger women with children, of the kind who regularly moved out during raids. Others took shelter in the nearest stone keep of their lord.

Townspeople did much the same. You could defend your town for a while, but it was liable to fall, or be encouraged to surrender. Before that moment came, the provident took to the hills, or got themselves and their goods into the castle. And a long, successful siege of a castle was a different matter.

Genoa was the supreme example of that: the citadel could hold out for weeks, while the town was in quite different hands. Trebizond had done it while Nicholas was there: he had laid the plans that let the Turks overrun the town, while the army stayed safe in the fortress. Edinburgh had employed the strategy over and over, emerging to rebuild its houses once the besieger had gone. And, of course, Berwick-upon-Tweed, like Famagusta, had provided the theatre for most types of assault: the decision by single combat, the pitched battle, the siege, the contingency pact, the dialogue with hostages. It changed with people, and circumstances. It didn't change.

Jodi was looking at him. For a boy, it ought to be a great day: Nicholas emerged from his thoughts and proceeded to make it so. Julius capped all his stories. Willie had unpacked his whistles and drums and was frightening the horses. They rode through the small township of Lauder, or meant to, but were persuaded to stop and eat by some of the farmers he knew, all of them spilling out of the tavern into the yard that sloped down to the merry, chuckling Leader, on its way through its broad vale. Willie took out his whistle and played, sweet as a lark, until he had them singing and clapping at the sheer exuberance of it, and then dancing with each other, lumbering men, while he tripped out a tune, stopping to swill his free ale.

They all knew Willie Roger. Once, before the Chapel Royal filled his life, Willie had been Master of the Hospital of St Leonard, and received his income from the lands of Traquair, both close at hand to the west. Hearty James had Traquair now, but all over Ettrick Forest and Yarrow there lived baritones and basses and even people who were completely tone-deaf who thought they were his family. Their friendship had left Willie himself with a sentimental kind of affection for the neighbourhood, and an expressed desire to return and live there one day, presumably with a full choir and his trumpets, since nothing less was likely to suit a man who earned his income by presenting expensive musical performances in rich urban areas.

Thinking of it, Nicholas jogged along singing with the rest, until told off for taking flamboyant liberties with the beat. Nicholas mimed tragic remorse, and saw Jordan grinning. Recently, Jordan had become a good mimic. Nicholas was quite sorry when the hills gave way to the wide rolling plains of the Merse and, bypassing the castle of Home, they prepared to arrive, spruced up and sober, at the modest Cistercian Priory of Eccles.

Two miles north of the river Tweed, less than six from the Abbey of Kelso and altogether too close to the frontier of England, Eccles protected its nuns with stout walls and anxious local landowners. Two of these came riding out to meet Nicholas. 'My lord? You mean to call on the Prioress?'

Nicholas knew, but did not trust, either of them. He said, 'We come merely to bring away one of her guests, the lady of Hanseyck. Master Julius here is her guardian.' Julius, rather tardily, rode forward.

'The young lady? The young lady Bonne?' said one of the men. 'But she has already left. All those remaining have left, except for the Prioress and her servants. There have been several raids. It was thought best.'

'Where has she gone?' Julius said.

'To a friend of the Prioress. To a neighbouring laird. You know Constantine Malloch?' said the man.

Julius stared. Nicholas said, 'Yes, very well. How very thoughtful of him to offer her shelter. And Sister Monika, I trust?'

Sister Monika, happily, was with the young lady as well. The Malloch property, as my lord of Fleury would know, was not far away. Indeed, one might think it too close to the frontier for the safety of a widower, however hearty, with a son and daughter still at home. In the opinion of some, the young persons should be persuaded to move. At the time, agreeing, thanking and taking his leave, Nicholas did not notice the glow on Jordan's twelve-year-old face.

They called on the Prioress, and confirmed what they had heard. The Prioress had a hooked nose like her late half-brother, which had presumably come straight down via their mother from King Robert the Third. Her manner also was regal. She was dryly courteous to Julius but a little more forthcoming in private with Nicholas. 'You were a friend to poor, silly Phemie Dunbar. The paramour was not an uncaring man: the outcome was a pity, I felt. So, I believe, did Dr Andreas. My brother studied at Louvain with his father. You seemed surprised that I had sent off the Sisters?'

'I thought your cloth would have protected you,' Nicholas said. 'But I can see, if you fear the English so much, that no one can accuse you of collaborating with them.'

The black eyes narrowed, cross as an owl's. The Prioress said, 'Do people say so?'

'Not at all,' Nicholas said. 'That is why I considered your dispatch of the Sisters so wise. I thought perhaps you might have kept the girl, since she is a foreigner.'

'I might. But the lady Bonne is not a nun, and her chastity must be my care. *Is* she the daughter of the Graf Wenzel von Hanseyck?'

'You doubt it?' said Nicholas.

'It is not for me to doubt it,' the Prioress said. 'She may be his daughter, but if so, she has not been reared to her station.'

'Her manners seemed good,' Nicholas said. He was entertained.

'Her manners are *too* good,' said the Prioress. He knew what she meant. He thought, then, that her only interest was Bonne, and that it was going to be all right.

It was later, when Julius came back, that the Prioress asked after Dr Tobias. Such a learned gentleman, from such an eminent Milanese family.

Nicholas welcomed her interest, and began to expatiate on Tobie's wonderful family, whom Tobie happened to loathe. Julius's mind was already otherwise employed. '*Tobie* here? When was this?'

'Well, surely . . .' the Prioress said. 'Six or seven years ago, when he came to talk to poor Sister Ysabeau about the de Fleury family?'

'It doesn't matter, Julius,' Nicholas said. 'She was remotely related to your Adelina, and Tobie had begun to ask questions. I'm sorry. Look, we ought perhaps to go.' Adelina had been Julius's wife, and a subject he did not like to discuss. With any luck, he would leave it.

'She knew about Adelina?' Julius said. 'What else did she know? Did she know about the St Pols?' The old woman was looking at each of them, dwelling a little on Julius. Julius had the kind of classical face that everyone dwelled on. It went with a diploma in obstinacy.

Nicholas said, 'She was deaf. She was a sister of Thibault de Fleury's first wife, and that was all Tobie asked her about. She wouldn't know the St Pols.'

'Well, of course she would,' said the Prioress, surprised. 'If she didn't come across them in recent years, she certainly knew them during her first stay. Elizabeth Semple was a nun here, after serving her noviciate in North Berwick. They used the Scottish form of the name. A French affectation, to change it back to St Pol.'

'Sister Ysabeau stayed here twice?' Nicholas said. It was against his better judgement. He immediately wished that he hadn't.

'As a young woman, and then again to end her days here. She had been fond of Elizabeth. I had no sympathy for the young person myself. She had taken her final vows, unlike poor Phemie, of whom we were speaking, but was of a light disposition: small wonder her brothers came to repudiate her. Her death, to be strict, was not undeserved. And of course, it had, had it not, an unforeseen consequence? Sister Ysabeau made the acquaintance of Elizabeth's brothers, and continued the friendship in France. Hence Elizabeth's nephew Simon came to meet Sophie de Fleury.'

Damn.

The Prioress said, 'But I have been indiscreet. Please forgive me. That marriage, I know, must be most painful for you, Monseigneur de Fleury. It is not as if I could add to what is already public knowledge. Let me merely say that bastardy is no stigma in a noble career such as yours.'

There was a gleam in her eye, recalling suddenly an earlier dialogue. *Mention collaboration, will you? Not to me.*

Julius clearly wished to interrogate further, but Nicholas excused himself. It was obvious, and Julius later confirmed, that there was no more to learn of that marriage. And the rest of it, so deftly touched on, he didn't want to dig up.

She had all the guile, the old bitch, of her forebears. Riding off, Julius was as gloomy as he was. Then they joined Willie Roger and Jordan, and cheered up.

Malloch's estate, as had been reported, was not far away. Nicholas had never been there, but Willie Roger's infallible instinct for stout lungs and cavernous sinuses had led him ten years ago to discover the exceptional voices of Conn and his two motherless children, and recruit them for the religious play he and Nicholas had created in Edinburgh. For a short time, the children and Jordan had all stayed at the Priory at Haddington, but Nicholas had seen John and Muriella only intermittently since, and never at home. Muriella was three or four years older than Jordan, but younger than her brother. The girl might prefer to come north, but the boy was of an age to want to stay with his father and fight.

It was none of his business, or that of Julius. They were here only to remove Bonne and her chaperone to a place of greater safety. Nicholas stood, with Julius, at the gate of the modest keep which bore the same name as its owner, and watched Willie Roger slap the porter on the shoulder and in due course stride forward when Malloch appeared, large and smiling and fair as the Angel of the Annunciation he had played. He showed genuine pleasure at seeing them all, arranged immediately for the comfort of the soldiers, and ushered Willie indoors, with Nicholas, Julius and young Jordan, talking with gusto. The young lady was indeed here, with Sister Monika, and would be charmed to see them, although Muriella would not be so pleased at the prospect of losing her new, kindly friend. The lady Bonne was down by the river, and would be sent for. Meanwhile, would his friends do him the honour of stepping into his hall? 'Muriella! Muriella!'

His daughter came, skipping in her long skirts, pretty as a picture with her fair hair and dark eyes and sparkling tease of a smile as she curtseyed to all the men, with a special glimmer for Willie. When she came to Jordan she smiled and, instead of curtseying, kissed his smooth cheek, which turned scarlet. Then she took his fingers and said, 'You've forgotten, haven't you, that we've met before? I haven't.'

'I haven't, either,' Jordan said. He was still scarlet.

Muriella said, 'Then we shall have to see much more of each other. Are you going to stay overnight?'

'Of course they are,' her father said, before anyone could protest. 'Provided, sweetheart, that you let everyone know to prepare beds for them, and a meal for us all. Off you go. You will see more of Jordan presently.' And she laughed and ran off, while her father shepherded the newcomers into his parlour.

Another guest sat there already and rose slowly, changing colour, as they entered. With a little weariness, Nicholas saw who it was.

'Uncle!' said Henry de St Pol. 'I thought you were defending the Borders from your table in Edinburgh. And *Jordan?*' He ignored Julius and barely glanced at Willie, whom he had met often enough at the Castle.

'They let us out sometimes,' Nicholas said. 'Julius, you haven't met Henry since he went to stay with his grandfather at Kilmirren. I didn't expect to see him here myself.'

'They let me out sometimes, too,' Henry said. 'I act as messenger for the Lord Warden of the West March. When the scouts tell us that Dickon Gloucester is moving, then I help spread the word.' He was recovering.

'Is Gloucester moving?' asked Nicholas. He had heard as much, but he was interested in what Henry believed. The Duke of Gloucester, much admired by his men, was a ferocious leader of skirmishes, but lacked the broader military vision, they said. Certainly he had failed to provide a counter-invasion to balance the attack of his brother's fleet. They were seating themselves. Malloch was speaking to someone outside the door.

'He's moving,' Henry said. 'And Percy of Northumberland. It looks like a gathering at Tweedmouth.'

Tweedmouth was a small English base with a keep and village on the southern bank of the Tweed opposite Berwick. Nicholas wondered whom Henry was quoting so masterfully. John Stewart of Darnley, very likely.

'Just against Berwick?' said Julius. 'Or something bigger?' With all these men-at-arms, he was longing to use them.

'Nothing bigger, not now; but it looks like a gesture at least against Berwick. You've come to fight?' Henry said. 'And Jordan, too?'

'Tell them to let me,' Jordan said. His voice betrayed that he more than half meant it. Nicholas looked at him. Jordan and Henry had talked together at Leith. He wondered what had been said.

Henry said, 'Would it do any good? At your age?' It sounded disparaging, but there was something not unfriendly about it.

'I don't know,' said Jordan, with gloom. He sat down, not far from Henry, and then got up again as the door opened upon the self-possessed figure of Bonne von Hanseyck, followed by Muriella, still smiling.

Muriella crossed to stand between Henry and Jordan and when they sat, sat between them, taking Jordan by the hand. Henry looked at them both. Bonne gave her hand to the three men and sat between Nicholas and Julius, remarking, 'Forgive me for not being present to welcome you. I had no idea you were coming. How gallant!'

'Your stepfather was anxious,' said Nicholas. 'He has some suggestions to make. Then I shall take you north with me tomorrow.'

'It seems a little sudden,' said Bonne, after brief thought. 'In fact, I have been invited to stay for a month, and have accepted. No. I am most grateful, but tomorrow is out of the question.' She looked from one man to the other. 'Unless, of course, you wish to use coercion. I have no rights of my own. I know that.'

If she had shown a trace of passion, Nicholas would have applauded. She merely looked firm. Against her vivid maturity, her strong brows, her self-possession, Jordan seemed like a child. Henry, closer to her own age, was viewing her with stony intolerance. Muriella, who still held Jordan's hand, looked both eager and shocked. Her lips had parted.

'War is sudden,' said Julius. 'Tomorrow.' It could be seen that his nostrils were white.

Bonne said, 'M. de Fleury? I am really not sure which of you has the casting vote.'

'He does,' said Nicholas. 'That is, he will hold the necessary conversations with Master Malloch and Sister Monika, and I shall supply any coercion required to detach you tomorrow. Or my groom will. He is a married man, and will not be at all rough.'

Suddenly, Henry had caught a note in Nicholas's voice, and a light entered his own eye. He said darkly, 'She'll go. She just likes her own way. You should try living in the same house for two days.'

'That,' said Nicholas, 'is ungallant. It is also discourteous to your host. Bonne, I know you appreciate Master Malloch's kindness, and don't wish to disappoint him, but I think you have no alternative. May I take it that you will come?'

'Yes,' said Bonne, frowning a little. 'But to where?'

To where was, at intervals, the question of the evening: through and after the meal, shared by Sister Monika, and in between the pleasant music they made afterwards, with Nicholas and Malloch in harmony, and Muriella's sweet voice entwined with her brother's. John Malloch, entering late, was an elongated, dust-coloured version of the golden child he had once been, serene in manner and grey-blue of eye. Willie sweated and played, Julius looked bored, Bonne and her chaperone embroidered, and Henry sat sulkily watching Muriella. When she asked

Jordan to sing, and then, laughing, began to sing with him, Henry lay back, a little drunk, and kept interrupting. John, smiling, tried to divert his attention, but Henry got up and walked out.

Soon after that, they reached agreement with Bonne over her future. First, a Cistercian convent within reach of Edinburgh, at which Sister Monika might, if she approved, eventually remain. Next, as soon as might be arranged, an appointment in some gentle household, as a preliminary to an arranged marriage. The household and the marriage to be selected, from a short leet, by Bonne.

Nicholas, who had not expected to manage the business in public, was thankful to have it over and to be able to think of something else. He had not actually cursed Julius aloud. None of it, of course, bothered Willie, and Jordan had sat absorbed through it all, when he wasn't being commandeered, in that enchanting lisp, by Muriella. Eventually, she was sent off by her father to do something, and Jordan came back and beat drums for Willie. Nicholas, vaguely uneasy, made an excuse and left the room himself.

He heard Henry's strained, angry voice almost at once; not that it was loud, but because he would know it anywhere. When another young voice replied, he knew he was listening also to Muriella. They were in the room above, leading off the turnpike staircase he was climbing. He stood where he was.

Muriella was angry as well. She was saying, 'You're not my husband! I'll speak to whom I want! He's a polite boy. I hate you!'

'He's a baby! *Jo-dee!*' Henry mewed the name like a kitten. 'He wets the bed. He'll make you his mammy. If you want a baby, I'll give you one. You want a man. You don't want a piddling baby with a goat for a father! Do you know that Nicholas de Fleury isn't de Fleury at all? He's a by-blow. No one knows who his father was. His mother was a tart and his wife is a worse one – did you know that she slept with my father? Do you know that half the cripple Berecrofts's children were sired by Nicholas de Fleury, not Berecrofts? Do you want to play with a boy whose father is dirt?'

Heigh-ho. Those who eavesdrop never hear good of themselves. With some difficulty, Nicholas de Fleury, by-blow, produced and dwelled on this piece of philosophy. The effort almost made him miss a slight noise. He turned, fast, on the step.

Below, his face set and sick, stood his other son Jordan. Nicholas said, softly and sharply, 'Go. Go outside, down to the river. I'll come.' For a moment, he thought the boy would refuse. Then he spun round and went.

Inside the room, Muriella was speaking. '. . . care? Your father's a worse goat than that, everyone knows. Jordan isn't the same as his father. He's not a bastard. He's *kind*. You're not a bastard, but you make fun of me.'

'I don't!'

'You sneer at everybody! You tell fibs! Jordan doesn't wet the bed!'

'How do you know?' Henry's voice hardened. '*Muriella!* How do you know?' Nicholas moved.

The girl's voice said petulantly, 'I just know. I haven't been in his bed.'

'Then he couldn't give you a baby,' Henry said. His voice softened. He said, the cajolery mixed with a kind of off-hand complacency: 'Look. You like to look, don't you? Go on. You like it when we do it?'

A moment passed. The girl said something, obscurely. Her voice was shy.

'And there *you* are, now. And me. Isn't that nice? I'm going to give you a baby,' said Henry, in a soothing voice broken by hurry.

Which was when Nicholas, sick to the heart, encompassed the stairs and, not quite in time, crashed back the door.

They were on the floor, rosily geometrical, and fully and rhythmically conjoined. Henry, blind and deaf, could not at once stop; Nicholas pulled him off and sent him sprawling. 'Dress!' The blue eyes, glaring at him, were like those of a madman, what with near-coition and fury and anguish.

The girl was bare from the waist, her legs thin and white, the place between them apricot-coloured. She was sobbing. She said, trying to bring her skirts lower, 'Don't look!'

'Why? Is there more to see?' Nicholas said. When the boy, part-laced, came at him like a fiend he slapped him hard on the face and then flung him back in a corner. The girl tried to run for the door.

'Later,' said Nicholas, grasping her arm. He pushed her into a chair, and set his back to the door. He said to her, 'Shall I call your father?'

She stared at him, speechless. Henry said, 'Do. We'll deny all you say.' He was still breathing in gasps.

'All right,' Nicholas said. 'We'll call Muriella's father, and if she says this didn't happen, we'll ask a physician to attest her virginity. Yes?'

'No!' said Muriella.

'I don't mind,' Henry said. 'She's been with plenty of others. I've never touched her. I'll tell them.'

She didn't quite understand. 'I haven't!' she said. For a moment, she just sounded indignant.

Henry said, 'You've been with Jordan de Fleury, his son. You told me. He wets the bed.'

She stared at him. Nicholas said, 'You'd swear to it? That she and Jordan are intimate?'

'All the time. Everywhere,' Henry said. In the midst of the horror, Nicholas ached for him. Always, always, no matter whom it hurt, Henry lied to cover his sins. Perhaps it was in his nature, or instilled by the Church. More likely it had its roots in a very old fear: the dread of his grandfather's mockery; and later, of Simon's. Other people solved the problem by admitting to everything.

Nicholas said, 'Then I'm afraid you'd still be proved wrong. Jordan is too young to be anyone's lover just yet. It's just as well, isn't it? You do realise, both of you, that if Muriella became pregnant, you would have to marry? Exactly as your father did, Henry? Unless, of course, you really plan to spend your lives together. But it seems a little early to force Muriella to choose. Especially the kind of coward who will deny everything and put the blame on the girl. Do you want to marry him, Muriella?'

'No! I hate him!' she said.

'It didn't look like it,' said Nicholas dryly. 'Or is it just the attention of the opposite sex that you enjoy? I think it is. I think it is someone's duty to have a serious talk with your father and perhaps your confessor, and suggest they find a husband for you immediately.'

'I wouldn't marry him!' said Muriella.

'Then I shall tell them exactly why it is necessary,' Nicholas said. 'I shall tell them in any case, if Henry comes near you again. Henry, you will leave here tonight. I don't care what excuse you invent. Muriella, you are coming north with Bonne and myself, and you will stay in whatever convent your father may choose. The excuse will be the war, but by the time the war ends, you will be married. Do you hear?'

'Who are you? Who are you to say so?' said Muriella. She was weeping again.

'A goat,' shouted Henry. 'An old rutting bastard who can't bear to see young people getting more than he does.'

'I thought the premise was that I was getting too much,' Nicholas said. 'Never mind. Put me down as someone who happens to know what this kind of thing leads to, and who is going to stop it, whatever you do. And Muriella: you will not meet Henry again. You will not expect to meet Jordan either.'

She was scarlet, her face swollen, her voice choked, but she still managed to speak. 'There isn't any point, is there?' she said. 'If he's just a stupid boy who can't do anything yet.'

By the time Nicholas appeared downstairs, and made small talk, and bought himself time to walk down to the river, the sun had almost gone, and he felt as drained as the landscape in the withdrawing light. The wind had dropped, so that the sound of the water was clear and level and soothing. As he walked down through the grass, a grazing horse lifted its head and watched him, and a rookery at the top of some trees lobbed out some brickbats of sound, and fell silent again. A jaundiced line of swans trundled from one bank to the other, as if pulled on a wire. Jordan was sitting, low on the bank, watching the water. When Nicholas dropped at his side, he didn't speak.

Neither did Nicholas. He hadn't even thought what he was going to say, or not say. He didn't have the gall to compare this exhaustion, this access of mental paralysis with what was Robin's daily portion.

In the end, it was Jordan who spoke. He said, 'It's all right. I know it's not true.' After a moment he turned fully round and repeated it, touching Nicholas's hand where it lay on his updrawn knee. 'Father?'

It was not a form of address Jordan used very much now. Generally he called him nothing at all, unless formal custom required it. To everyone else, his father was Nicol. Jordan said, 'Father, you can't do everything for everyone. It's all right.'

Nicholas looked at him. It came to him that all the time he had been agonising over what Jordan had heard, Jordan himself had been fretting over what he, Nicholas, must be feeling. To Jordan, whether or not Henry had spoken the truth hardly mattered. His father had been vilified, and he wanted to comfort him.

Nicholas took the hand and lay back on the grass, carrying it with him in both of his own. Jordan dropped back beside him. His hair, which was long and brown, lay flattened under his wide, sunburned cheek. His eyes were on Nicholas.

Nicholas said, 'It's all right for me, too. People say foolish things. You don't need to heed them. I was troubled about you and Muriella.'

Jordan's brow wrinkled, in a fine little print under his hair. He said, 'I was silly there. She belongs to Henry, doesn't she? She was just using me to make him feel jealous.'

Nicholas smoothed and bent the flat fingers. He said, 'I think she likes you both, but there was something of that in it, yes. In any case, she's too young to be serious. She'll go off to finish her training, and then her father will choose her a husband. By that time, you should have met twenty more. The world is full of nice girls. That's one of the good things about it.'

'I like Margaret of Berecrofts,' Jordan said.

'I know. So do I,' Nicholas said. 'And remember, I'm a fountain of wisdom on girls. Anything you want to know, or to tell me, just come.'

'You think you know everything?' Jordan said. 'You'll find it's the other way round. One day, you'll just come to me.' He sat up and, retrieving his hand, leaned on it, smiling.

Nicholas said, 'I think I have done, today.'

He was thinking about it when Jordan, bending suddenly, gave him a fierce, intent kiss on the cheek, releasing it slowly. Then he disengaged and jumped up, as if returned to himself, his face full of unexpected, raw happiness. He said. 'Then come on, old man. Race you back to the house.'

They ran like demons. Nicholas won.

Chapter 35

In tyme of weir unto none erdly wicht
Patent suld be thar portis on the nycht.

THE TOWN OF Berwick-upon-Tweed was invested that autumn; its walls battered by guns and its harbour closed to supply ships. The siege lasted two months, and then was called off because of the cost and the weather. The citadel was of course untouched, and the townspeople had mostly remained, knowing that the attack couldn't last long. The besieged had been slightly better fed than the besiegers. There had been two very bad harvests: it made you wonder sometimes what was happening to the weather these days. Julius took part in the skirmishing, and enjoyed himself so much that he stayed till November.

In Edinburgh, the King hanged Alec Brown, outlawed Peter his brother, and offered Leithie Preston a vast sum, which he refused, as a reward for bringing back the wine-ship from Orkney. Nicholas, freed after a murderous journey with two hostile girls and a nun, found Leith in an uproar, and John le Grant in a timber yard, smashing things. He took him back to the Leith house with Gelis. Father Moriz was there, waiting to hear the news about Bonne. Nicholas informed him, in two words. He had already told Gelis all she needed to know.

He listened to what everyone had to tell him, both inside his own house and several others, and including friends who accosted him outside taverns. Then he set off, with John and Moriz and Gelis, back to Edinburgh. Before he went, he had a brief exchange with his own chief skipper, Mick Crackbene. At the end of it, Nicholas had walked away and turned back.

'You said your Ada couldn't read?'

'She can now. I taught her,' Crackbene said.

Gelis had overheard. 'What was all that about?'

'Ask me later,' Nicholas said. He wished he meant it. He wished she didn't know that he didn't mean it. At least she knew – he made sure that she knew – that after Eccles and Malloch, he found it a shattering relief to be back.

In Edinburgh, he saw Robin, left a message for Tobie, and was collected by Adorne for a swift session of the King's inner council, without the knowledge of the King. It was held, for that reason, in the house of the Abbot of Cambuskenneth in Aikman's Close, which led off the High Street just a little downhill from his own house.

They were all there when Nicholas entered with Adorne – eight men of good age, distributed about a low-ceilinged, wainscoted room in their autumn doublets and robes, and guaranteed a fast, incisive meeting with Abbot Henry in the chair, which he was, despite the presence of the highest officers of the kingdom. Years as part of the procuratorial team representing Scotland at Rome, years close to the royal Court at Stirling as Abbot of the wealthy monastery over the river had made Henry Arnot a highly visible statesman, known to churchmen and politicians alike. Small, quick, sharp-featured, round as a pomander, Arnot made chancellors tremble by the speed of his oral delivery, which Colin Argyll once calculated to exceed that of a hodful of hailshot dropped from the spire of Durham Cathedral. In languages other than Latin, it was even quicker. He knew Adorne and his oldest son well. His cousin was married to a Brown of Couston. He commissioned music from Whistle Willie. He was a confidant of the Queen.

M. de Fleury was invited to mention anything relevant to the kingdom's condition, following his findings in the Borders and Leith. He did so.

The company was asked to consider short- and long-term projections and policies for the war with England, taking into account the King's views on Berwick, and the fact, just made public, that Louis of France had suffered a second seizure.

He didn't need to elaborate. Alec Brown had been killed because the King had discovered he was still working for and in England. So were half the other merchants in Berwick. But to the King, Berwick had become a symbol, a token, an obsession.

The English war had declined because of the winter, but also because England was being challenged on too many fronts. Now one threat was receding.

Drew Avandale spoke to Adorne. 'Seaulme. I can see France trying to buy peace with England. Can you see them attempting the same with the Duchess of Burgundy? Would Maximilian agree to a truce?'

'If it were unknown to England,' Adorne said. 'So my correspondents think.'

'So do the traders,' said Nicholas. 'It would free England to invade us next spring. But whatever the King may wish, men are going to hesitate to die over Berwick.'

'What would they die for?' said Henry Arnot.

He was answered by the other Abbot, Archie Crawford. 'Until now, the King, or what the King represents. If that is to continue, the King must hear advice. If that does not continue, in my opinion the country would still unite for one reason only: to drive out an overlord.'

'And will the King hear advice?' said Argyll. 'Or are we here to look for a successor?'

'Hardly, when I am sitting here,' said Drew Avandale. 'Colin, we don't have time to waste. We have a grown king, with young sons to follow him. There may be some who would like to replace him, but if we act as we should, there will never be a faction with popular backing to oust him. We have to find ways to guide him, that is all. Will? Seaulme? Archie?'

It was Adorne who replied; Adorne who, as a charming and experienced foreigner, had been allowed as close to this young King as anyone. Adorne said, 'It is time to ask the Queen.'

'So I happen to think,' Avandale said. 'So, I think, do we all. Abbot Henry? You know her grace better than anyone. Stirling is the home of her children, and where she spends much of her time. She has been trained well; her brother rules Denmark; she is no stranger to statecraft. Would it place too much burden upon her to bring her actively into our plans?'

'She is half there already,' said Henry Arnot. 'She has her own court, her own advisers, her own views. She is loyal to her royal husband, but knows of his difficulties. She would respond. But whoever visits the Queen is bound to lose the King's trust. You must choose carefully.'

There was an hour more. At the end, Avandale and the others went off, and the Abbot, neatly entrapping the Burgundians, invited them to his room for a dish of cheese and imported olives and pasta, which he thought a Genoese might enjoy, while continuing to talk about bullion.

Much of the recent discussion had been about money: tax-raising, coining and, finally, storage. Mints and treasure chests required stout stone houses. In Edinburgh, coins had been pressed in the stone house Adorne had once leased from the Swifts. The tiled house in his care at Blackness had been used as a royal storehouse and mint. The Precentor of the Order of St John hoarded treasure at Torphichen, as his counter-part in England stored the war funds of the English King. The Abbot of Holyrood had confided half the church plate of the monastery to another Swift, chaplain Walter, who had a stone house in Edinburgh. In his reprobate days, Nicholas himself had used part of his premises in the Canongate to mint illicit coins. In places like Berwick and Edinburgh, the merchants' valuables, the coining-irons, the garrison's wages were kept, in time of war, in the castle, not the town. But gold was hidden everywhere; and so were jewels; and expensive garments; and documents worth more than the gold. And faced with an invasion, you had to know where.

Expatiating, the Abbot of Cambuskenneth had noticed his liturgical hour-glass. With an exclamation, he bounded from the table and lit a candle, still declaiming at speed. Nicholas assumed, since it was broad daylight, that this was a prelude to prayer. The Abbot said, 'You had finished? Ah, good. Follow me.' Since Adorne willingly got up and did so, Nicholas left the table as well.

Instead of leading them to the chapel, the Abbot took them down to a cellar. Below that was another. It was full to the echoing roof with large boxes. 'How careless of me. He will be waiting. Now where . . . ?' said the Abbot, to himself.

Adorne, smiling, took the candle from him and touched the flame to others planted about the large, uneven chamber. Nicholas said, 'You've been here before.'

'I haven't had time to tell you,' said Adorne. 'We were only shown it the other day.'

We. A muffled banging echoed from the end of the cavern. Adorne said, 'Abbot?'

'I hear it,' said Henry Arnot. 'Ah. There they are. Good.' He delved into his skirts like Lang Bessie and lifted out a prodigious steel key. It didn't bleat. Holding it, the Abbot trotted past what he had been looking at, which was a stack of brass handguns.

'*What!*' said Nicholas.

'The Queen thought she should have some,' said Henry Arnot over his shoulder. 'Not my field. I needed an expert.' There came the squeal of the key, and the rumble of a door beginning to open, followed by the Abbot's voice showering someone with apologies. The someone came in, punctuating the flow with short, Teutonic reassurances. You could tell who it was, under the dirt, because he strode through the low door without stooping.

'Oh!' said Father Moriz, gazing at Nicholas.

'It's all right; you don't need to worry; he'll take them,' said Abbot Henry. Adorne, damn him, was looking entertained.

'Nicol will?' said Father Moriz. He sounded cautious. Placed in the candlelight, he coughed as the Abbot pattered round him, shaking his tippet and banging off dust.

The Abbot gave him a final blow and stepped back. 'Your M. de Fleury. The Council's secret adviser to the Queen.'

Father Moriz's pleased exclamation coincided with Nicholas's fevered disclaimer. He scowled at Moriz, and at Abbot Henry, and finally at Anselm Adorne. 'When did that happen?' Nicholas said.

'Before you arrived at the meeting. I'm sorry,' Adorne said. 'I know you're tired of handling people. But –'

'No,' said Nicholas.

'You speak her language. She likes you. You would have access to the young Princes –'

'No,' said Nicholas. 'What *am* I, bloody Ada?'

Moriz was examining the guns. Rare in the company of Henry Arnot, there was a short silence.

I want the teachers sprung of your line to help instruct the poor fools sprung of mine. I mean to match you, child for child.

Except that they were not just his children: they were all children.

The Abbot said, 'Well now, Nicol: don't be daft. You'll forgive me if I call you Nicol? They told me in Stirling you'd jib. Your friend said that, if you did, I was to send you to see her and get sorted.'

The little bugger. 'My friend? In Stirling?'

'You've got so many with that kind of relationship? She's been away, not wanting to court lawyer's questions. But if you were to go now, with the guns, you would find her. Bel of Cuthilgurdy. Who in Heaven's name else?'

Who, indeed. She had been hiding from Julius. Moriz, who would realise that as well, had turned and was looking at them both. Nicholas said, speaking slowly because he was thinking so fast, 'Of course, being in Stirling, you would know her.'

Arnot nodded to Moriz. 'Have you seen all you want? Shall we go?' And, picking up the original candle, continued to Nicholas: 'Not as her confessor, more's the pity, but as a real friend to the monastery. Not all mothers feel that way, but she was happy for John. I can't tell you how sad we felt when we lost him.'

Adorne looked puzzled, but Moriz was genuinely astonished. He said, 'Bel of Cuthilgurdy's son was a monk at Cambuskenneth?'

The Abbot said, 'No one mentioned it? Of course, the Charteris family now have the title, but after John's father died, Bel was generous with her gifts to the Abbey. It was kind, for they were young, and not very long married.'

Adorne still conveyed friendly interest. He said, 'I was told she had grandchildren.'

He looked at Nicholas. Nicholas returned a blank face, behind which was sheer mutiny. Moriz said, his grating voice oddly subdued, 'So perhaps she married twice. We should not probe. But, my friend Nicholas, for your own peace of mind, I think you must agree to go to Stirling to see her, at least.'

'And since you are going,' said Abbot Henry, 'you might place us all in your debt by taking a few crates to a warehouse? The goods may be removed from here by night. It is an old smugglers' route. The cellar tunnel leads to the Nor' Loch. We discovered it when we acquired the house for the monastery.'

A smugglers' route, Nicholas would wager, that had seen a few barrels of illicit French wine bundled in by repentant sinners. No wonder there was a gleam in the Abbot's bright eye. And he had induced Nicholas to go to Stirling with the handguns. And see Bel. And, undoubtedly, get involved with the Queen, whether he wished to or not, although that would not, to be accurate, be Arnot's doing. Umar cast a long shadow.

He found he was no longer resentful, but mysteriously lighter of heart. What was being asked of him was difficult. It was bloody unfair to plunge him into yet another quagmire of intrigue when he was barely disentangled from Albany. But it was the kind of adventure, the kind of risks that he loved. And he was good at working with people. And it might make a difference, at that.

It was time to go. Moriz and the Abbot were chattering amicably on their way to the ladder. The light travelled with them. Adorne extinguished the cellar candles and stood, without immediately following. All Nicholas could see was the fairness of his face and his hair and his hands. Then Adorne moved thoughtfully over and surveyed him. 'We place a great burden upon you, Nicholas. It is as well that you have these broad shoulders.' He rapped them lightly, half smiling; then, spreading his fingers, ushered him after the others.

It was when they had all four climbed from the cellars that Nicholas heard someone sneeze, and uttered an unthinking, 'Bless you!'

They all looked at him. The Abbot said, 'Well, thank you, Nicol, but why?'

It seemed that no one else had heard anything. The ghost of Tobie, perhaps. Or of some master smuggler long dead, athletic enough to have swum over the loch. Or nothing at all; in which case he, Nicholas, had left an unused blessing about. From him, blessings wouldn't carry much weight: his forte was giving advice, and you couldn't leave that behind you. And even if you could, there were some people who never took it.

Bel of Cuthilgurdy's town house in Stirling was built of timber, and lay with others at the foot of the castle rock, which was so like that of Edinburgh. It was a district favoured by well-doing burghers: their neatly thatched premises with stables, bakehouse and well-head were set in swept yards and pleasant patches of grazing and orchard and herb-garden. The enclave was central enough, without being subject to the dusty traffic on the ridge leading up to the castle, or deafened by the clamour of the riverside wharves. Dame Bel's house was not held in her name, and Nicholas, having duly delivered his crates, would hardly have found his way there without Adorne's written direction.

Adorne, of course, had seen quite a lot of Bel since she took to visiting his little daughter at Haddington. So had Kathi and Tobie, for the same reason. Even Jordan had called at the Priory once or twice, accompanying Sersanders, or Robin. From wherever he encountered Bel, Jordan always returned with a minding and some new, funny tale of her doings. He no longer called her his aunt, but there was an attachment, clear to see, between the boy and the elderly woman. Only Nicholas, absent in France during Bel's stay in Edinburgh, and carefully absent ever since, had seen less of her than anyone, and had listened without comment to the reports that he heard. It was Julius who wished to excavate the St Pols and their attachments. He preferred to forget.

The servant who opened Bel's door had the speech of a local man rather than one you would associate with the St Pols of Kilmirren, and pointedly left Nicholas standing while he vanished inside with his name. But, almost immediately, the door opened again, and Bel herself stood on the threshold considering him, with her round, pugilistic face puckered about with glistening linen, and her short person as sturdy as when he first met her, companion to Lucia, Simon's sister, in Portugal.

'Aye,' she said. 'Thrawn as ever, I see. Well, ye'd better come in.'

He was never sure what greeting she would allow. Bel resolved it, once in her parlour, by opening her arms. She was the first to break away, gently, and find a seat for him.

'Bloody Henry Arnot,' he said.

'You think so. He's a wise wee soul. It's getting near time to stop all this nonsense. I'm getting too old, and so's Jordan.'

'Which Jordan?' he said.

'The one that didn't have you for a father,' Bel said.

He got his breath back, and said, 'I'm glad I didn't meet *his* father, in that case.'

'Are you? You don't ever apply your brain to the St Pols, do you? If ye think Simon's your father, then Jordan's your grandfather, isn't he?'

'Moriz,' said Nicholas. He had been stupid enough, recently, to put that into words to Father Moriz.

'Aye. He's Clémence's confessor. Remember it. And if Master Julius wanted more evidence, he only has to compare Monseigneur Jordan and yourself, for I never saw two characters more alike.'

'Thank you,' said Nicholas. It was childish to care. It was childish to mind, as he did, whenever Bel talked like this about . . . about Monseigneur Jordan.

'It's no trouble. He gets an idea, and won't leave it. For him, every stitch in the cloth must be perfect. Give him an objective and he won't notice who or what stands in his way till he's finished.'

'I'm like that?' Nicholas said.

'You were. You stayed a feckless apprentice until you were eighteen years old, because you knew that whatever challenge you chose, it would dominate your life, if you let it. Now maybe you've got your demon in hand, and if you have, you have Gelis and old man Jordan to thank for it. They both made you fight; and they both made you grow. Only Gelis did it for you, as well as herself; and Jordan did it for Simon.' She broke off and looked at him quizzically. 'Now you're sorry you came and you want to go home.'

'Not if you're enjoying yourself,' Nicholas said. 'You got a parcel I sent?'

She looked at him with a half-grudging appreciation, in which there was a great deal of fondness. 'I got it. The Duchess Eleanor's book, discreetly rewrapped and redirected, with all the French names covered over, in case. I appreciated the thought but, Nicol, anyone who has the time and the patience and the curiosity can follow my history easily enough. Every Scottish Archer knows that in France, Asquin stands for Erskine, and Échaut for Shaw, and Moncourt for Moncur. And that if my husband was John Dunbarrow of Cuthilgurdy, in France they'd spell it Dombereau. Every Scottish Archer knows; and so do the sisters and cousins of Eleanor of the Tyrol, because she and I went to Paris together when I was a widow, and she was twelve years old.'

'But you didn't go with her to the Tyrol, because you married again,' Nicholas said. 'You had John by your first marriage, and your daughter Claude by your second, in France. John didn't marry, but Claude married a Scot with an estate on the Loire, and gave you your grand-children.'

'Grandchild,' Bel said. 'There is only one left; the one you saw. You didna go to Coulanges that time just to find out about Jodi's nurse Clémence. You wanted to know how she connected with the Moncur family of Chouzy, in the same valley, and how the Moncur family connected with me. You probably found out as well. Clémence is wholly French, and related to another Moncur by a wife's marriage. I knew she'd make a fine job of Jodi, until you and Gelis came to your senses. I didna ken you'd go bursting into Chouzy, or that Robin and Dr Tobie would see you there.'

'You've forgotten. I didn't go of my own volition to Chouzy; I was taken there,' Nicholas said. 'After having my bones smashed by the thugs of your esteemed friend my grandfather. I didn't need to visit your daughter. I'd confirmed it all at La Guiche. I'd even guessed about Andreas's mistress, with the palatial houses in Lyons and Blois. I don't know why everyone fusses about my divining, and no one prevented that pair from breeding. Do you suppose my grandfather was trying to kill me?'

'No,' said Bel. 'If he'd meant you to be dead, you'd be dead. I jalouse he wanted you taught a lesson, or held up, or both, and someone exceeded their orders.'

'And,' Nicholas said, 'does the same apply to Simon and Henry? I have just antagonised them both to the point where one or other will certainly try to commit murder, and Monseigneur will probably let them, perceiving my usefulness finished. I suppose I ought to go back to Flanders.'

He thought she would take him up on that, but she didn't. The battle light left her face, and she exclaimed. 'Ah, no, no, Nicol. Is that what all this is about? Henry? I'm mortally sorry. Simon should never have been sent for.'

'He had to come back some time,' Nicholas said. 'And Henry had to deal with it some time. I just didn't want other issues dragged in to confuse matters. Now, as you say, perhaps it doesn't matter what people know.'

'Because Henry's opinion of you won't alter now?'

Nicholas looked at her. He said, 'Bel: what in God's name do you think Henry's opinion of me matters? Nothing matters to Henry but the approval of Simon's father and Simon. There were other ways he might have earned that, but they're gone. Now, if he can only obtain it by attacking me, then he will. Hence, I do see, an exposé of his family by you, or by me, or by Julius can't make anything worse.'

'It could unite them,' she said. 'It would unite them, of course, for all the worst reasons, but that's maybe better than nothing. Or don't you think so?'

He was silent. 'I don't know,' he said.

'No,' said Bel. 'Even you can't quite think through that one. But loneliness, I have to tell you, is a terrible thing. A man alone will do from a whim what a tribe of villains would rarely do, even for profit. A tribe of adventurers will survive, but very few men can face fear and self-hatred on their own.'

She wasn't talking of Henry; she was talking of the fat, solitary man who was his grandfather. Nicholas said, 'I really don't know, Bel. I want the same thing for them that you do, but I can't do much more. I won't have my family hurt.'

She smiled. She said, 'They won't be. I have seldom seen any family as secure as the one you have made, Nicholas. I have to pray that nothing dissolves it. But if you didn't take risks, the boy wouldn't worship you as he does.'

'So that I am really here to impress Jodi,' Nicholas said. 'That is what you are supposed to be doing: appealing to me to place my dashing services at the small Danish feet of the Queen?'

'No. I knew you would do it,' said Bel. 'You didn't come here for that. You came to find out how I can stomach a man who does what Jordan does, and love you as well.' She stopped, presumably reading his face. She said, 'Did I have to put that into words?'

'It helps,' he said. He cleared his throat. 'I hoped you knew I felt the same. But I couldn't pretend to want to be as close as you are to Simon or his father. Long ago, perhaps; but not now.'

'Then I've not properly explained what I feel for them,' Bel said. 'It's not what you'd call unalloyed love or respect. It's more the same feeling, I jalouse, that you have. You've been harsh with them, as they have with you. In spite of everything, you still feel protective. They're your family. I feel the same, in a different way. I can carry the burden. So can you. Just so's ye ken, as we were saying, that you're not on your own.'

Someone else had said that, when it mattered. The miracle was, he had long since realised, that he had never been alone; even in Poland. You tried to safeguard other people, and, all the time, the lifeline was working both ways.

Chapter 36

A quene suld be richt werraye sapient,
Of gud maner, and chaist of hir entent,
Borne of gud blud, obeyand to the king
And besy in her barnis nurysing.

MARGARET, QUEEN of Scots, received the younger Burgundian in her apartments at Stirling Castle, with the three
men who constituted her private council about her.

She had first met Nicholas de Fleury when she was an
inexperienced little child-bride of twelve, excluded from the family
games of the King and his siblings, and suffering James's untutored
petting through the long evenings when the Court entertained itself,
with the help of amusing, musical friends such as the Burgundian. De
Fleury could speak in the Danish-German of her father and brothers:
she could converse with him. He had been very correct, but also easy
to talk to. Sandy had been smitten.

After that, the Burgundian had come back at intervals, but she herself
had been less at Court; and during the present long stay, she had
followed the policy they had all deemed to be best, and had seen little
of M. de Fleury, except on formal occasions. By this time, as he would
have noticed, she had grown from a pale, sharp-eyed waif to an active
young woman with a mind of her own, and an acquired grasp of
statecraft. It was necessary. The King her father could hardly have
realised how much. It was one of her personal weapons, along with the
stock of jewels and clothes which she obtained through her excellent
revenues, and also from her husband, as she presented him with each
son. To begin with, she had believed that all husbands behaved as hers
did. Then she had discovered what else was different about James, and
his brothers and sisters.

It might have frightened someone without her kind of Scandinavian determination. Only gradually had she come to realise that the truth was also known to the old men who surrounded James, and that they were working, in ways she had not noticed, to make life tolerable for her. Then, as they saw how her nature developed, they helped her choose her own private council, surrounding herself with astute men – Shaw, Colville, McClery – who were agreeable to James, but also attached to her interests.

The King's men had continued to be helpful. It was Dr Andreas who explained to the King how marital duty might damage a pregnancy, and who advised on the required interval of abstinence after every delivery. She was eternally grateful to Dr Andreas, and Dr Tobias, and Master Scheves, who was now an Archbishop. At the same time, too much frustration could send James into one of his painful passions, when he forgot himself. He was always contrite when it was over, and when, as was only right, she had pointed out to him what he had done. Her father – her poor father, who had just died – used to say she was a saint.

She stayed at Stirling most of the time, or Linlithgow. The boys, for their own security, were always in Stirling. All of them had received excellent fostering, and the care of a good married matron in the royal tradition – Mistress Preston, with Betha Sinclair and the wife of Dr Tobias to call upon for advice. As their mother, she herself saw her sons often enough when they were babies, but did not find them interesting, any more than she was personally devoted to important jewels and fine clothes. The production of heirs was one of the requirements of ruling. She took the oldest son in hand when he was five, and she was officially appointed his guardian. Now he was eight, he had his own household and teachers for everything: academic, religious and military. She took care to spend time with him regularly and check on his training.

He had proved brighter than she had feared, and the doctors agreed that the elder Prince, and perhaps even the second (also called James) might have escaped the blight of the Stewarts. The baby, even at eighteen months, gave less promise. The middle child, who was five, had recently been allotted the forfeited earldom of Ross, which effectively denied it to any adult and ambitious baron. Had she been the King, she would have presented the title to their oldest son, but it was not of great moment. That Prince was already Duke of Rothesay and further advantaged, although she said it herself, by his mother's meticulous supervision. If the King did not always see it that way, it could not be helped. Education for kingship could not be left to chance.

Today, but for her mourning, the Queen would have dressed for the Burgundian in the steepled headdress and sumptuous gown which had just been returned from overseas, where her portrait was being painted for the Trinity altar-piece. It annoyed her than the Provost's picture had been completed first. Of course, Bonkle had travelled to sit for the artist, whereas her own likeness and that of the King must depend upon drawings. Because their children were young, and God's will for their family unknown, it had been decided to depict the King's continuing dynasty in the form of a kneeling young man, with what might be termed Stewart attributes. It could represent any child who survived. If all of them died, it could, at a pinch, represent the next incumbent, her good-brother Sandy, who had certainly won through to his prime. If he hadn't, she wouldn't be giving this audience to Nicholas de Fleury.

The Burgundian was really enormously tall, although he knelt at once, and then slid into the seat that was proffered him. His eyes were steady and large, and he had the engaging habit of resting them for longer than most people did on the faces of those with whom he was speaking. She wondered if he did that with the French King, and in the countries of the East where, she had heard, it was a crime to meet the eyes of the lord. He had something Northern about him that was reassuring. She liked his shipmaster, Crackbene, for the same reason. It was good: it made transactions easier; it did not mean that they were your equal.

She said, 'We are obliged to you for coming. You understand that we are about to discuss nothing that is not fully known to our serene lord, the King. We merely spare him the sorrow of referring to his beloved brother, Duke Alexander of Albany, in the context of recent changes in France.'

'I understand, my lady,' said the Burgundian. He used the language of Scotland, as she had done.

She glanced at her hereditary seneschal, who nodded. Sir Robert Colville, from Ayrshire, was a business-man as well as a courtier: all her advisers were. She respected that. Arranging this beforehand, they had agreed that she should do this herself. She said, 'You know the King's brother. You have shown yourself to be his friend and ours. What do you think he will do?'

'Frankly?' he said. He didn't glance at Colville.

She said, 'That is why you are here.'

Then he looked down, as if collecting his thoughts before he addressed her again. Once more, looking up, he ignored Colville. 'He has several choices, your grace. His situation we know. He is in France because he opposed your sovereign lord's friendship with England and tried to break it, even inviting French forces to help him. They did not, but offered him shelter, and a well-born wife, who has now given him a son. My own reading, from my conversations in France, is that this was not something that King Louis especially sought, and that he would have been reasonably pleased had our King sent to invite his brother back, with forgiveness and honour. Failing this, France is sufficiently content to hold the Duke and his family at the moment, as other rulers keep by them the dissident heirs to foreign thrones. There may be no immediate occasion to use them, but they act as a control, and a threat.'

She was not sure what to say. She waited, and let her seneschal intervene.

'And the Duke's view of that?' Colville said. 'Or did he not recognise the true situation?'

The Burgundian looked at him. He said, 'That, as ever, is the difficulty, sir.'

'You talked to him about it?'

'Both then and before, at Dunbar. His hopes were unrealistic. He saw himself as a national leader, breaking the perfidious friendship with England. His Scottish friends encouraged him to think so.'

Colville glanced at the Queen as she moved. She said, 'And now, when the peace with England has been broken with the help of those same friends, what does my lord of Albany think to do? The war he wanted has come, and he is not here. His grace my husband demands that he comes back to answer for what he has done, but does not offer assurances. Should he do so? Forgiven, would the Duke in his zeal come back and lead us to victory?'

The Burgundian said, 'That is the most important question of all. The King would give you one answer, and I would give you another.'

'You are here to give me yours,' she said. She waited.

He said, 'The Duke of Albany is a man who values friendships, and forms attachments. He has before him, as well, the example of the Duke of Gloucester, the English King's brother, and in his mind, his counterpart. My lord of Albany has sent messengers to those he trusts through all the months of his absence. If he thought he had enough friends to win a massive victory against England under his personal banner, and thereafter enchant Parliament into granting him all the land and appointments he would like, he would come back tomorrow.'

Colville said, 'But he has not applied to come. It would appear therefore that he is not sure of his personal following, as his conduct at

Dunbar would suggest. That is, he hesitates to come without a French army. Do we think he may have been promised one?'

The Burgundian said, 'The King your husband has asked France for help against England, and France has not replied. My lord of Albany will have been promised, I am sure, anything that the King of France believes will keep him content until France knows which way to turn. This winter, France will do nothing. Louis is ill. If he dies, there will be a regency, and all his enemies will pounce when the season opens in spring. Then the Duke of Albany might be glad enough to come home, and accept whatever crumbs he may be given. That, I am sure, is what my lord your husband hopes.'

She said, 'But King Louis may recover. What then?'

'Then,' said the Burgundian, 'he may find himself facing a combined assault by the Archduke and England, and will expect Albany to fight for his keep. Or there is the possibility that England and Flanders both falter, and King Louis sees profit in sending an army to Scotland, with Albany as a popular leader, to waste northern England, and drain it of money and men. Again, this is something that I am sure the King our lord would encourage.'

'But you would not?' said the Queen. 'Why?'

'Because if they come,' the Burgundian said, 'the French will expect to occupy fortresses. You would lose Berwick, Lochmaben, Dunbar, as you would otherwise have lost them to the English.'

'The King would not allow it,' she said.

'The King might not have a say,' answered the Burgundian. 'In my opinion, if the French come with the Duke of Albany, they will expect the Duke of Albany to give them all that they wish. And if the King stands in their way, they will expect the Duke of Albany to countenance his removal. Which he will.'

She stared at him. Colville said, suddenly dropping all her stipulated formality, 'You're talking of Sandy.'

And the Burgundian said, with unexpected violence, 'I know I'm talking of Sandy. He acts on impulse. Everything I have been saying may turn out to be rubbish, because he will fall into a temper and do something that makes no sense at all. But I do tell you this. He is fond of his sisters. He is proud of Scotland. He didn't really mean to go to France at all, in his better moments. But he does seriously believe that he is brighter, better, braver than any one of his siblings, and if he is frustrated, he will simply invite all his allies to help him make himself King.'

She said, 'And my lord? And the Princes?'

The Burgundian said, 'My lady . . . At every Court, there are dynastic struggles: the strong prevail over the weak; rivals and siblings are killed. Scotland has had its full share. But this time, as I have said, I think that there is some feeling between the two Princes. His grace of Mar's death was an accident, even though it may not be perceived as such by everyone. I think the King would go to great lengths, when in health, to avoid harming his remaining brother. With Albany, there is a difference. He is ambitious, he is easily swayed, and he does not think clearly. He would depute the King's dethronement to others; he might even stipulate and hope that his brother would abdicate and live on without harm, and would be distressed when others proved less temperate. The outcome is that there is no sacred barrier between the Duke of Albany and his brother. Were France to invade, the King's life could not be assured. His sons, on the other hand, have value as hostages. They might lead secure lives at the French Court.'

She studied him. He was right. It was what the others had said, more obliquely. Colville, choosing the moment, led from that topic to the second they had selected. 'It is, in any case, hypothetical. There will be no army from France. At the same time, we do require to know what is happening there. You say his grace of Albany writes to his friends?'

'This we have also heard,' said the Queen. 'And, of course, to his sister in particular. You were once closely acquainted with the Princess Mary, M. de Fleury, and your wife and son have both served in her household?'

'Sadly, we see less of her now,' the Burgundian said. 'And my son, as you may know, is now back in Edinburgh.'

'An excellent child. Jordan. We remember. You must bring him with you next time: he and the Prince have made sport in the past with the Princess's children. How then would you answer if I suggested that Jordan should return to his post with the lady Mary and report what he hears?'

'I should reply,' said the Burgundian, 'with regret, that my son is too young to spy, and I should not permit it.' His voice was calm. He was used to opening moves. He was not, in fact, taking it seriously.

Colville said, 'In that case, the Queen would be the last person to compel you. We have, indeed, already thought of a substitute. Lord Cortachy's niece served the younger Princess, who often stays with her sister. It will be natural for the demoiselle Katelijne to take an appointment in the Princess's household. While there, she can tell us when the lady Mary hears from her brother.'

The Burgundian said, 'I can see that it would be useful. As a friend of the family, I confess to the same misgivings that I felt over Jordan. It is not a pleasant assignment, and it could be dangerous. Is there no other way?'

'Several,' she said. 'Were you less squeamish, you could renew your own friendship with the Princess, for example.' They were talking of state matters. She had no patience with foibles. She knew, anyway, that Rob Colville would intervene, as he did.

'My lady. Of course, it would be a valuable gesture. But M. de Fleury could not serve both the Princess and your grace, and he has already proved, in this room, how much he can help us. I am sure Mistress Katelijne will come to no harm with the lady Mary. It is a busy household. There are children. Their nurses know one another.'

They certainly did. Every ruler she knew of had to come to terms with that sinister international sisterhood of children's nurses, heaped with honours, pensioned off into comfortable old age to encourage their successors. Nanse Preston, her merchant husband and clever young son drew the revenues from royal land close to Linlithgow which had previously succoured a needy kinsman of Colville's. The nurse's grant was annually renewed by her small charge, as were the words of noble thanks and affection which had been annually placed in his mouth since his infancy. Indeed, James had grown fond of the woman, and would certainly not cancel them now. No one ever offended a nurse in royal circles.

Colville was looking at her. She would, herself, have preferred to make the first interview more explicit, but it had covered the necessary points, and the next should be more instructive. She thought, as she drew the audience to a close, that she would invite the man and his son next time to Doune. He could stay at the castle, and meet the rest of her council. And even entertain her, perhaps, in the evening.

He left very soon, on his way, he told her, to the Priory of Elcho, to visit the orphaned daughter of a kinswoman. She had heard of the girl from Anselm Adorne, who occasionally passed through on his way to Dundee, or even once or twice further north to Cortachy, the Crown lands from which he received his baronial life-rent.

They hardly needed his attention, being looked after for him by proxy. She wondered if this unusual activity signified that Adorne was planning to make his stay permanent. Certainly she hoped his very capable niece would remain, and continue her surveillance of Mary. She had been surprised and pleased by the Burgundian's stated objection to that, considering that there was nothing but friendship, she was assured, between de Fleury and the lady Katelijne Sersanders. They said that de Fleury's wife had his undying devotion, and that other women considered her fortunate. As for herself, it required more than a good presence to impress her these days. It required political acumen. She was glad to see that he possessed it.

Gelis, who had her own opinion of the Queen, was charmed to find it justified in every nuance of the graphic account unleashed upon her by Nicholas, returned in a state of semi-hilarious exasperation from the north. 'First her Danish grace, and then the German Bonne. It was like having dinner with Beowulf and supper with the Elector of Hanover.'

'No sense of humour,' said Gelis. 'They didn't laugh at your jokes.'

'My God,' said Nicholas, sitting down knee-deep in dogs. 'If that were all. No. I agree with the others. If the King doesn't kill her first, that grim determination is going to do more for his future than two dimpled knees and a pretty face. She's got three good men; they're telling her the truth, and carrying her along with their thinking as far as they can. She's rigid; she hasn't got their intellect, but she's bright enough to do what she may have to do.'

'But they think she needs you?' Gelis said. 'Or no. They want her to understand and agree with whatever you may have to do about the King.'

There was a brief silence. '*About* was a nice way of putting it,' Nicholas said. 'Better than *to* or *for*. Anyway, you have the situation in a bombshell. They also want me to help spy on Sandy, and produced several sticks and a carrot. You will be glad to hear that I refused to plant Jordan as a double agent in disguise with the Princess Mary. They're going to use Kathi instead.'

She was very familiar, now, with the many ways in which Nicholas dealt with anxiety. She said now, 'I know. Kathi came, while you were away. We both thought she should do it. It *is* important, and Mary and Sandy are really not very responsible. And anyway, you'll probably learn far more from Julius's remorseless pursuit of Liddell than she will at the Hamiltons'. She did say, if she found anything, that she'd tell you before anyone. So what about the Elector of Hanover?'

Again, it was one of the joys of her life to interpret him correctly, and to receive her thanks, as now, in his face. He said, 'All right. Farewell, Beowulf. Elcho was nothing by comparison. Muriella wasn't there; she had pined, and been sent to stay with friends, with or without a chastity belt. Bonne is putting up with it all, while sardonically unsurprised that we have failed to find her a husband. She will have to come here for Yule.'

'Julius should be back by then,' said Gelis hopefully. 'And John le Grant speaks German.'

'And operates guns. He would need them with Bonne,' Nicholas said. 'I think a little pastoral guidance by Father Moriz is indicated in the near future. And that's all the news.'

'Is it?' she said. She saw by his face that, until this moment, he had genuinely forgotten about Bel. When he bent abruptly to divest himself of the dogs, it was almost as if he was distractedly pressing back other oppressions. She said, 'It's all right. You wanted to put it away. I don't want to disturb it. Just tell me that you found her, and she's well.'

'I'm sorry,' he said. 'Yes, she is well. A little surgical for comfort, but that's my fault, not hers. She's back in Stirling, tired of prevaricating, and quite willing, I think, to tell Julius anything he might want to know.'

'Which would be disastrous?' Gelis said. 'To you? To us? To the world?'

'No. It would just be sad,' Nicholas said. 'Otherwise, it's of no importance whatever. Bel knows of nothing that will show me to be of legitimate birth. No one does.'

'Oh. Good,' said Gelis. She willed him to begin to laugh, and he did. Then she willed him to jump up, and he did that, too.

By the time Julius came back from the Borders, the fighting at Berwick had stopped, and all that was going on was the usual exchange of vicious raiding by the normal denizens of each side of the frontier, which continued into the New Year and increased the hardship already caused by bad harvests. Being Julius, he had a large, fresh fund of personal gossip, but no actual news of what Sandy Albany was up to in France. Nor had anybody else.

To please the King and themselves, Nicholas and Willie Roger filled the weeks before Christmas with the preparation of several small musical plays, aimed chiefly at children, and one large liturgical work by Whistle Willie, with the voices of his friends as his instruments of experiment. As at the time of the great play they once created together, the houses of the various friends and associated members of the projects became littered with paint and paper and illogical artefacts, and untrustworthy artisans such as Big Tam Cochrane and John le Grant and Nicholas himself were to be found in corners with heaps of wire, whistling and cursing.

The differences between now and ten years before were, however, also impressive. Then, they lived in houses that were chiefly offices, and occupied by their lessees or owners for only a few months at a time. They were ornamental and reasonably comfortable: suitable for entertaining and for meetings, and with room for a family. But someone who lived here for five years, and came to spend time in other homes, to frequent centres of learning, and to keep company with men of literary or artistic or musical interests, would gather about himself the products of all these encounters; would have to find room for books, and for pictures and for instruments, and a workshop or office for his own experiments, as well as a table he would not be ashamed to offer his guests. A man who hunted and shot with his friends would have hounds, and horses, and birds. A family man, whether in business or not, would require clerks who paid his debts and collected his income, together with the great circle of his suppliers: the builders, the merchants, the fleshers, the bakers; the water-carriers, the smiths and the lorimers. He would know by name or by sight everyone who lived in his town, and in business, in sport or at his fireside, would rub shoulders daily with most of them.

All the men who had once belonged to the House of Niccolò, including its former owner, now lived in homes which possessed a permanence which the peripatetic life in Flanders had never encouraged. The exception was Anselm Adorne, whose beautiful Hôtel Jerusalem in Bruges had been a testament to generations of culture, and was paralleled by nothing he had attempted in Scotland. Either he did not wish to try; or else his busy life was sufficiently served by his homes in Linlithgow and Edinburgh and Blackness, which were handsome enough, and his use of the Berecrofts house in the Canongate. And certainly, within these parameters, his entertainment was princely; as he himself was entertained, as he always had been, by men of consequence. His daughter, a silent, merry four-year-old, flourished in Haddington.

Nicholas saw his own twelve-year-old daily, but the other son not at all, until the time he took delivery of his new ship at Leith, on a lowering day of wild weather which had frightened off pirates and allowed the *Jordan*, in all its three-masted glory, to plunge round the coast and come to rock in the river.

It was the latest of several ships he now possessed. He had given new names to them all. Ships did not have long lives, and there would never be another *Ciaretti*. Of his acquisitions, one was a converted Hanse fishing vessel, and two were useful Biscay-type trading ships he had picked up at a sale. His flagship, the *Fleury*, was the merchant vessel he had renounced when he gave everything up, and which Gelis had paid to recover. The *Fleury* mattered, because of that. This one mattered, because it bore Jordan's name: the first public manifestation of the young Jordan de Fleury, not the old Jordan de St Pol.

Because of that, it was Jordan his son who was first on board, and Jordan who, once high on the poop, noticed his cousin Henry caught, vexed and impatient, in the press of people on shore. Since Christmas was close, and the Border fighting had slackened, men were coming back to their houses in Edinburgh. Returned to Kilmirren House with his grandfather and Simon, Henry came across now and then to see to his horses. There was a piece of St Pol land near Dunbar which offered good grazing, and removed the stud from the orbit of Simon, who disapproved of the venture. This information (of course) came from Julius via Sir James Liddell of Halkerston in the Mearns, who had a house in Dunbar. It was the only piece of information Liddell seemed to have supplied, in the long evenings Julius spent with him.

The crowd on the wharf were all friends, come to help Nicol celebrate his new vessel. Knowing what was expected, he had opened and stocked up a warehouse with ale, and something to eat with it, and in due course they all packed themselves in, and there were some mock speeches and a lot of coarse jokes. Nicholas, playing his part, assumed that Henry had departed in a cloud of malignancy; until he suddenly saw him outside, looking searchingly up at the ship. At its name. Of course, hell and damnation: at its name.

Nicholas started to leave. As he began to move from person to person, he saw that Gelis had reached the door and was already walking over to talk to her nephew. She spoke, and it looked as if Henry asked her a question. He looked superb, but not dangerous; not with Gelis. They went on talking. Nicholas, half-emerged, hesitated.

Gelis had seen him. She called across. 'You know more about this than I do. I was telling Henry that he should try another sail with you all. But not in this weather.'

'It's a challenge,' Nicholas said. She had spoken, thank God, as if she had never heard of the scene with Muriella. Nicholas, too, adopted a level that Henry would recognise: vaguely impatient but not at all unfriendly. He said, 'Do you want to come on board and look? It's roomier than you'd think.'

'I'm sure,' Henry said. 'No, thank you. I hear you've been to Elcho. The nuns have reformed Muriella then, have they?'

Gelis stayed quiet. Nicholas said, 'It was Bonne I was going to see. After the pike fishing.' He didn't look at Gelis.

Gelis said, 'It isn't fair. He'll believe you.' Magnificent Gelis.

Nicholas said, 'Well, he ought to. It's true.'

'That you went to see Bonne?' Henry said. 'Or didn't you?' He was looking at Gelis, his expression somewhere between pity and contempt.

Nicholas said, 'I didn't really go to see Bonne. Or not especially. I was at the Lake of Menteith for the pike –'

'So you say,' Gelis said.

She staggered slightly as someone bumped into her. Unbelievably, it was Jordan. Incredibly, he was making for Henry, whom he had last met, in brutal circumstances, at Muriella's house. He addressed Henry, regardless. 'I told them you were here. Has he told you about the pike fishing?'

He had caught the word. Jordan was trying to do something, and Nicholas could only hope he knew what. He picked up his cue.

'Nobody believes it,' Nicholas said. He made it sour.

'That's because you explain it inadequately,' Jordan said. Henry's long lashes batted.

Jordan said, 'Let *me* tell him.'

It didn't take long. Nicholas hadn't believed it himself when Rob Colville had first described the whole farce, and then had actually got them to come back to Doune and take part in it. It was a fishing competition for pike. The fishing was done by local geese, with baited lines tied to their legs. Once the goose was dumped in the water, it beat across the loch to the home of its master, hooking its fish as it went. As the goose-owners lived all round the loch, it ensured a good, thorough fishing.

'I don't believe it,' said Henry; but beneath the scathing tone, there lay something more natural.

'We got *soaked*,' Jordan said. 'It's stupid really, for fully grown men.' His two wayward dimples contradicted him.

'It sounds it,' said Henry. 'Did you catch anything?'

'We won!' Jordan said. 'We brought these two geese from home . . .'

'We got another one,' said Nicholas in an apologetic aside. Something told him that Henry had been treated to a graphic account of Simon standing in mid-street wringing the neck of a goose. Henry was biting his lip.

'And they both hooked a fish?' Henry said. He could still manage a drawl.

'They hooked each other,' said Jordan. 'But no one else hooked anything, so we won. They weren't hurt. It's really funny. Of course, it's silly as well. You should come with us next time and see.' He caught Henry's eye.

'You'd have to lend me a goose,' Henry said. His sole dimple appeared, and was banished.

That was all. A crowd suddenly arrived to collect them, and Henry walked off.

At home, Jordan tried to explain to his father. 'I hadn't forgotten, but he doesn't know that I heard him at Malloch. Unhappy people are cruel and tell lies. You never see Henry with friends.'

'He probably kills and eats them,' said Nicholas encouragingly. 'All right. I know what you mean, and it's kind. Keep trying. But don't forget: unhappy people aren't always consistent. Don't get hurt.'

In Kilmirren House, an unwise friend mentioned the occasion to Simon, who later carried the news to his father. 'He's called the ship *Jordan*!'

'There is no law against it, so far as I know,' observed his father. 'But you say Henry was there?'

'Talking to de Fleury and the boy. Someone saw them. He said nothing to me.'

Jordan de St Pol eased his weight in the chair, and the chair emitted a groan. 'I sometimes think,' said the lord of Kilmirren, 'that your technique with that youth could be improved upon. He should be married by now.'

It was an accusation. It was a sign of impatience. It was a sign of contempt.

Chapter 37

Off archerye the rewll allhaile thai beir.
The men with men fechtis apone fute,
And the women with strang bowes thai schut.

I N TIME OF war, every winter is precious. It is the close season; those months when men return home to their families, and celebrate Christmas, even in scarcity, with glad hearts. It is a time for acts of liberality.

Anselm Adorne took his little deaf daughter Euphemia from her convent at Haddington and travelled with her to Stirling to visit the old lady, Bel of Cuthilgurdy, who had made the opposite journey so often to teach, in the way she had learned from the deaf Scottish Princess Joanna. With him he also took Mistress Clémence, the splendid Frenchwoman who had been married to Dr Tobie from his house, and who had nursed Jordan de Fleury from babyhood.

It was an unusual thing for him to do, and Mistress Bel bided her time, entertaining the child and making Lord Cortachy welcome, before Clémence, whom she knew very well, offered to take the child, well wrapped up, to run and slide in the meadows.

The child was very like Phemie, with her direct gaze and abundance of energy; and constant care had given her a confidence denied to most of her kind. A child of many mothers, she was happy with Clémence, as Jordan had been.

'Jordan was lucky,' Lord Cortachy said. 'And now he has his own father and mother, which he appreciates to the full. It was about that, in a way, that I wished to speak.'

'Jordan is very attached to them,' Bel remarked. 'And now, I hear, there is a ship bearing his name. I know who'll mislike that.'

'It is rumoured already,' said Adorne, 'that Simon de St Pol has taken extreme umbrage; especially as Henry his son apparently had said nothing of it. They are at odds with one another, as usual. The youth ought to be married, but every arrangement so far has failed. Not because the maidens don't like him – the opposite! – but their land-owning fathers are shy. Kilmirren thrives in good times, but Simon is not a disciplined man, and the same could be said of the boy. No one offers an heiress to a potentially run-down estate, or to a hapless life in Madeira, at the end of the day.'

'Not while Monseigneur is alive,' Bel observed. 'But I agree. Those bonny blue eyes have been conquering girls since before his voice broke, and his elders have been daft not to curb it. Fortunately, Efemie's too young, and so is Kathi's wee Margaret. Whoever they get for the lad, they'll want her in the marriage-bed quickly.'

'It should be an interesting Yule,' Adorne said. 'Were you thinking of coming to Edinburgh?'

'Not with all that going on,' Bel said caustically. 'After your sixtieth birthday, it pays to be selfish, in my view. And yourself? You're not staying in St Johnstoun of Perth?'

He took a moment before he replied. 'I'm not sure. I'm going to see Master Julius's step-daughter at Elcho. Nicholas wishes to invite her to stay with himself and Gelis for Christmas, but I think he is unwise. Her arrival from Germany caused trouble with the St Pols and with me, as Father Moriz has possibly told you. It might happen again. Julius apparently doesn't want her in the Canongate house. It's a dilemma. Like young Henry, she ought to be married.'

'From all I hear, she's too poor to be considered for Henry,' she said. 'Why does Julius not want her? Because she reminds him of his wife?'

'I think certainly so. And Nicholas, of course, feels responsible because Bonne's mother was a de Fleury.' He paused. He knew, from Kathi, she assumed, what the other possibilities were. He said, 'I don't know if you've met Bonne?'

'No. What did you make of her?' asked Bel.

'We got on very well,' said Adorne, 'so long as she remembered which of us carried the purse. She knows she is intelligent. She will make a good marriage partner for somebody.'

'But not for you,' Bel suggested, her shapeless face innocent.

'Not for me,' he agreed. 'Bel, you know what I am asking. It is for Nicholas. He carries responsibility enough.'

'You are asking me to take Bonne. For how long?'

'Until January,' he said. 'Or earlier, if you are a miracle-worker who can find her a husband. I should like to see Nicholas free of these tangled relationships, and able to get on with his own life.'

'He is free,' she said. 'Julius likes to be inquisitive, but I am not holding Nicholas back. He knows virtually all that I know.'

'As does Mistress Clémence?' he said. 'I suspect you chose her for Jordan. You have never said how you met.'

'No,' she said. 'But you can imagine. She's French, and I was in France with the two Scottish Princesses. I knew she'd be fine for the bairn, but it was the time of the war between Gelis and Nicol, and I didna want to propose her myself.'

It was understandable. Adorne wondered when Nicholas had discovered the complicity, and what he thought of it. He waited, and then said, 'I thought perhaps you knew her because of your grandchildren. You mentioned them once.'

'Did I?' she said. 'Maybe I did. Well, I've only the one grandchild now. And since Henry Arnot kindly let out that my ae son was in cloisters, you have to suppose that I have a married daughter. I have.'

'In France, then,' he said. 'And if Clémence wasn't her nurse, she was connected to your son-in-law's people? The family who couldn't come to her wedding?'

'Ask her,' said Bel.

He studied her. 'But you'd rather I didn't.'

'I suspect Nicol would rather you didn't,' she said. 'But you must please yourself. As for the lass Bonne, I ken nothing about her, but if it will help you and Nicol, I'll take her over the season. Is there anything more I can tell you?'

'You are generous,' he said. 'And in return, I shan't ask the question I'd put to you, if I were Nicholas.'

'And what would that be?' she said. 'Why is an old besom like me so tolerant of a devil like Jordan de St Pol of Kilmirren?'

'Yes,' said Adorne. 'That is it.'

'Aye,' she said. 'There's a half-answer to that, which he knows. There's a whole answer that maybe he guesses. But that's between him and me and St Pol.'

She went to Elcho the following week, accompanied by a doubtful Father Moriz, brought to authenticate her credentials. The Prioress, whose manners were beautiful, charmingly set the small chaplain to entertain Sister Monika in German, while she heaped praise upon Bel for opening her hospitable doors to the poor young orphan, the demoiselle Bonne.

Bonne, brown-haired, stalwart and formidably composed, sat with her hands folded throughout, saying little, but watching the nun and the priest with something close to private amusement. Sister Monika, it had been established, was to stay at the Priory over the festival. Bonne did not look sorry.

The Prioress rose to arrange for refreshments. Left alone with the girl for a moment, Bel said, 'She's a right talker, isn't she? What are the other nuns like?'

The blue eyes turned upon her. 'The same as everywhere,' Bonne said. 'Dull.'

'But safe, I suppose,' Bel remarked. 'I mind being glad of some nuns when I got back from that trip to Africa. What did ye hunt with the Graf? Bear?'

'Sometimes,' Bonne said.

'It's more deer about here, but it's lively, and I ken a man with some falcons. What about shooting?'

'Shooting?' said Bonne. Her voice was mild.

'With a crossbow. At the butts. Have ye not done much of that? And there's snow sports, of course, but that depends on the weather. Moriz!'

'Yes?' said Father Moriz, rising smartly.

'She thinks I'm blethering. Come and tell her Yule in Stirling's not so bad. I had one look at her shoulders, and I knew she was a lass who could kill things.'

Bonne looked for the first time uncertain. The Prioress was re-entering the room. 'Perhaps,' said Father Moriz testily. 'But, my friend, it does not do to scream the fact all round the cloisters. I hope, demoiselle Bonne, that you can put up with this woman. Nations have tried in vain to subdue her, but she still insists on going her own way. You'll have a terrible time.'

Across the room, the Prioress had turned. Sister Monika sat, looking worried. 'Yes, I can see that,' said Bonne. Her face, to a searching eye, had almost cleared. She said, 'You had no need to arrange this. I am grateful.'

'It was Lord Cortachy's notion,' Bel said. 'But don't go and tell the St Pols, or they'll set the pigs on him.'

Settling into her life as a spy, Katelijne Sersanders, lady of Berecrofts, launched into a busy and profitable winter among all her friends, including the ones she was spying on.

Unlike Nicholas, whose qualms she respected, she had no objection to steering her mistress out of trouble. She made no effort to attract the confidences of Jamie Boyd, and was fairly confident that his royal mother would not press secrets upon her lady-in-waiting. Those she proposed to pick up for herself, which shouldn't be difficult. The King's elder sister was older but not much more mature than the girl who had fallen passionately in love with Thomas Boyd, her official husband, and who had allowed Nicholas to orchestrate the escape, the exile, the return which had saved her life, if not her marriage, and brought her back to remarry in Scotland. Mary still thought of Nicholas as her friend, but had been shaken by his desertion of her brother in France. Kathi, who never had problems with interfering in Nicholas's affairs, worked to present the idea that Nicholas, while a firm supporter of Sandy, was deeply concerned to reconcile the absent Albany with the King. This tended to be the view of most of Albany's friends, including James Liddell. The others lumped him with Anselm Adorne as a self-seeking foreigner who had enchanted all the royal sisters and brothers and had probably slain John of Mar. Kathi killed that rumour stone dead wherever she found it.

She still climbed the ridge regularly to her own house, which was officially outside the burgh, but not far from the Hamilton mansion in the Cowgate. She had told Robin what she was doing. As she expected, his first instinct was to forbid her; his second, one of well-concealed bitterness that he could not do this in her place. His third, of course, was to agree. If she hadn't told him, he would always have wondered whether she had been afraid to put him to the test. Robin of Berecrofts was a grown man with a disability, wonderfully managed, and there were few things not within his tolerance now. His friends knew what they were. Paradoxically, that fact in itself was the one that wounded him most.

She liked the Cowgate. It used to be full of rubbish and dung, but as the city spilled outside its walls, tumbling down from the ridge to the long ravine on this, its south side, the richer families and wealthier churchmen began to build on both sides of the stream, and rakers came morning and night to clear the droppings of the town cattle, on their way up the slopes to the Burgh Muir, leaving a clear way for the through-burn that cleansed it. The slopes themselves were being built on as well. Apart from the vast sprawling complex of the Blackfriars, houses were beginning to spring up in the wynd of the Blessed Virgin Mary in the Field, and the ways that led to the south and the west. The Clerk Register's house was on the rising ground at that end of the Cowgate, close to that of James Liddell, where Julius obediently spent so much of his time.

All in all, it was a good place to collect information. You never knew who you would meet, from Nowie Sinclair to the Abbot of Dunkeld, who had the richest single house in the street; or from the Master of Soutra to a Cant or a Bonkle or a Cochrane. Then there were the household attendants like herself, to every degree, from the kitchen-maids to the stewards and chamberlains who managed their masters' affairs, including their personal buying. By now Kathi knew, as they did, the best place to go for a pendant, or a piece of red leather, or a casket, or a new supply of fine shoes. As one familiar with Flanders, she was allowed by the lady Mary to place direct orders abroad. Some-times, the Princess and her sister would prefer to interview the suppliers themselves, and they would be brought to the house – trim, well-doing men and women, not at all shy – to display what they had, and explain it. It was something the King especially enjoyed. His officials might clinch the transaction, but James liked to preside in his closet, animat-edly discussing the merits of this chain or those bolts of rare cloth with one of his familiar suppliers, and perhaps treating the man – or goodwife – to some ale, and a suitable gift when a feast day came round. He enjoyed a bit of genuine argument, but he always drove a hard bargain, of course, in the end.

Today, she was going to the Tolbooth, with a commission which she had been saving for a day when key people, such as Andro Wodman, ought to be there. He had lost his brother John recently; snatched away on the verge of a bishopric, and was only now returning to the consular duties he shared with her uncle. He was also returning to the orbit of Julius's crusade to legitimise Nicholas. As a former Archer and employee of Jordan de St Pol, Andro Wodman must be at the top of Julius's rota by now.

The quickest way to the crown of the ridge was to climb through the burial ground of St Giles, in summer as crowded with notaries and their clients as with graves. In winter, only the custom-built shelters were occupied, but the barking of dogs came from the homes of the Provost and the curate of the church, and the drone of children's voices from the school. She passed Tom Swift's big house, which her uncle had often rented, and which actually stood in the kirkyard, which she had once thought peculiar. Everyone she met greeted her. From the top, you could look down the ridge and see the Firth of Forth, a broad grey band in the distance, with the hills of Fife sprawling beyond. She thought of shellfish and wanted to laugh, with the lightness of heart she always felt when close to Nicholas's house, or indeed when she thought of him, anywhere.

The High Street itself was full of stalls, but she pushed her way past them to the Old Tolbooth, and the expensive booths rented yearly from the burgh Provost, Great Dozen and deacons. Mostly the same traders leased them, but after the Martinmas reshuffle, it always took time to locate everybody. Sometimes they even moved to the town tenement by the kirk style, which had a pair of booths to rent out, and a tavern below. She hoped to find Wodman here.

There were about thirty small chambers, some on the north side of the old public building, and some on the south. Others had been constructed underneath in the vaults, and some were tucked into landings and crammed under the stairs. There were five booths and a desirable cellar fitted into the bellhouse. Sometimes they held back one or two cells for a prison. The privies were old, and luxury goods and documents didn't drown out the smell, so that even in winter, the fleshers' offices were almost welcome. She poked her head in most of the doors, and had a clack with Isa Williamson and Hector Meldrum, a sergeant of the mace who lived in the Canongate and rented the small cellar here, not being able to afford the four pounds Isa paid. Another of the dear booths had gone to Drew Bertram, the younger brother of Wattie, which didn't surprise her, as Wattie was Provost this year. The stairs were crowded, and so were the crames. She had to fight all the way up to the bellhouse loft to see Henry Cant, another of Wattie's fellow merchants and kinsmen (by marriage) who profitably shipped on the *Marie*. She did some business with him, while people came in and out, and pigeons banged on the window, knowing he'd feed them and not knowing he'd cook them as well.

The Cants were like that: prosaic. Originally merchants in Ghent, they finally settled in Flanders and thus become Cants rather than Gaunts. No one knew whether they were originally Scottish or not: like the Bonkles and the rest, they lived and married on both sides of the Narrow Sea. As well as the Bertrams, the Cants were closely connected to the Prestons and the Napiers and the Rhinds. Thinking of Efemie, and the Bonkles and the Knollys family and Lord Avandale; looking at Henry, natural son of Thomas Cant, and young John Ramsay, Janet Napier's slick by-blow, Kathi sought to understand, yet again, why illegitimacy mattered to some people and not to others.

The truth was that if you were lucky, like Julius, and were proclaimed as a bastard from birth, then there was really no problem. The trouble came with people like Nicholas, whose mother had maintained to the death, helplessly, insistently, fruitlessly, that she was innocent. Nicholas did believe in her innocence, as he had believed, against all the odds, the birth-date she had given him. He had been badly hurt by the blackening of her name – and his own – by the St Pols and their fellows. When, for the sake of his family, he had deliberately stopped seeking to vindicate her, it could not have been easy.

To that extent, then, Julius's campaign was justified. But against that, Nicholas had already faced that difficult choice and had made it. And even if he were wrong, it was now very apparent that proof of Sophie's innocence simply did not exist. The whole search was only causing more heartache, in making more and more clear how determined the St Pols had been to shed Simon's wife and her son. A child weaker than Nicholas would never have broken out of his class. And paradoxically, she supposed, it was Julius he had to thank for it.

She hadn't found Wodman or the other person she was hoping to find, although she glimpsed Dr Andreas, official chaplain to the Guild of the Skinners, swirling past in his gown with a wave. Gib Fish wasn't there, although he was on the Council, and neither was Tom Yare, their Treasurer. She had almost given up when she heard Jamie Boyd's voice, speaking to somebody. It came from a booth, one of the wooden pents under the stairs of the bellhouse, next to Hector's cellar door. It had been empty, before. She wouldn't have heard anything now, except that Jamie's high voice hadn't broken yet. He was protesting. 'I wouldn't lose it.'

Someone murmured: a man. The boy said, 'Well, I might forget. Who was it from?'

Murmur, murmur. Even close to the door, she couldn't make out the man's voice. People passed up on the street, their feet squelching, and someone ran up the stairs over her head, dislodging cold puddle water which rapped on her hood. She bent down, as if looking for something.

Jamie said, 'I don't say who it is from. I say that King Edward has sent to France, and offered to fetch my uncle of Albany to England. And promised he would lead –'

Murmur. '– *help* to lead the King's army to Scotland. Is that true?' said the boy. '. . . Well, of course, but she'll ask. You ought to put it in writing. Get my uncle to write. When will I . . .'

'Can I help you, hen?' someone said from the stair. Kathi looked up. Tom Yare's wife, Margaret Home.

Kathi began, 'I was just going to . . .' but it was too late. The door beside her quietly opened, and the man upon whom she had been eavesdropping was standing there, studying her.

She knew him. His name was Rob Grey, and he was a butcher, with a house in the same part of the Canongate as Hector Meldrum and Robin's father and family. He said, 'Mistress Katelijne!' She could see Jamie, standing rigid behind him.

Kathi smiled. 'How are you? I'm sorry to shout in the street, but I'm astray. Margaret was just going to tell me where to find Hector Meldrum, and I think I remember. Down there?'

The man was smiling in return. 'In the cellar. It's a coney-warren, for sure. Is he in? Come back if he isn't, and share our ale. Jamie and I were just preparing a rare surprise for the Princess's Yule table. Are ye suited yourself in that regard?'

'Too well,' she said. 'I've just seen Henry Cant and I'm penniless. But I'll come back for the ale, if Hector's out.'

He wasn't, of course. She had just visited him. She waved goodbye to Margaret and tapped on the cellar door, prancing in when it opened, before the macer could speak. She wished she had taken lessons from the King's Master Spyar, except that the King had dismissed him, along with his personal Guard, when Albany left.

Which would seem to have been a mistake.

Pathetically, it was only after she was safe that she started to shiver. Hector Meldrum actually walked with her down to the Canongate, when she said she had to go there. He left her at her own house, but she crossed instead to the private stairs of what even Hector called the Floory Land. She hoped her uncle was there. At the very least, she wanted to pass on what she knew quickly, to as many reliable people as possible. She was waiting in the parlour for her uncle when Nicholas opened the door and shut it so quietly and fast that it sighed.

He said, 'I saw you from the window. It's all right. Whoever he is, we'll kill him for you.' Then she was in his arms, her teeth chattering, and he went on murmuring absently, holding her fondly and close like a warmly comatose bear with a cub. When Adorne came in, she made no effort to break away, nor did Nicholas; he simply went on talking comfortably over her head. 'Could you possibly pour some of that stuff over there and bring it to her? And maybe keep the others away for a moment?'

Adorne did as he was asked without a word. It was only as Nicholas freed her to take the cup from him that she saw the concern on her uncle's face. Then she said shakily, 'I'm sorry. Listen. Listen. I've just overheard Jamie Boyd being given a message to take to his mother. The English are offering Sandy an army to help invade Scotland. The English. The English. The *English*.'

'What frightened you?' Nicholas said. He was still speaking simply.

'I think they know I heard them,' she said. 'Rob Grey and Jamie, at the booths.'

'But they let you leave,' Nicholas said. He sat her down with her cup and fixed himself beside her, one arm still holding her steady. 'They can't kill us all, and by now they'll guess that we all know. And in any case, you have just acquired an infectious disease, and are not going back to the Princess Mary ever again. Slightly better?'

The cup was empty. It had been spirits, not wine. She said, 'Yes. Drunk, but much better. I'll tell you the rest; then you'd better get the others in. Who is here?'

John and Moriz were there, and someone found Wodman, and brought across Tobie. Then they were all together in the small room and heard her, composed now, repeat her story. Moriz frowned, Andro swore, John banged his fist on his knee and Tobie glared at her. She had slurred a few words.

Nicholas said, 'Well, come on. Assessment?'

Tobie's pale eyes switched to his. He said, 'It can't be true. It's a lie. It must be. Kathi's right in a way. It's a warning to her. They've guessed what she's doing, and this is their way of telling her so. Who would use Jamie Boyd as a courier?'

'Perhaps someone who wanted to be overheard,' Nicholas said. 'But if so, are we supposed to believe what he said?'

Wodman said, 'Not unless we're daft. Sandy's whole quarrel with King James was because James wouldn't make war on England. That's why he's in France, for God's sake. If anyone gives him an army, it's going to be Louis. Who in England would be crazy enough to think Sandy would join an English invasion of Scotland?'

'The King of England, perhaps?' said Adorne. 'He has become very autocratic, we are told, and not entirely reliable. As with ourselves, there is perhaps a limit to what his advisers can do. And he is receiving a pension from France.'

There was a little silence. Father Moriz said, 'Am I interpreting correctly the complacent expression on Nicol's face? His reasoning is the same. Louis is ill; France is beset; she cannot possibly send an army to Scotland, but would welcome anything that would prevent England from sending archers to Brittany or Maximilian. Edward is foolish enough to want to waste his time fighting in Scotland. France, when sending over his pension, lets it be known that he would be very ready, for a consideration, to lend out the Scottish King's brother for any purpose Edward might wish.'

'Such as to overrun Scotland?' said John le Grant. 'Never. That would leave England free to turn her whole attention to France from now on.'

'If she did manage to overrun Scotland,' Adorne said. 'Louis might have a private view about that.'

Kathi felt very happy. She said, 'I think I see. Sandy is restless; the King is unwell and doesn't want to take action, so he hopes to get rid of Sandy and send England off on an abortive invasion to gain time. But he doesn't know – he can't know how much Sandy hates England. As do his sisters. They'd go mad if they thought he'd dream of doing this.'

The large grey eyes of Nicholas were encouraging her. 'But?' he said. 'Louis is not the Universal Spider for nothing. He knows that Sandy loathes England. He and Sandy both know that Sandy won't get back to a rich position in Scotland unless an army puts him there, and Louis will now have told him that it won't be a French army, *mon cher*. So settle down with your Bourbon and baby, or get someone else to make you a king.'

'A *king*!' Tobie said.

'Oh yes. That would be the English inducement,' said Anselm Adorne. 'We know you don't like us, but we are prepared to place you selflessly on the Scots throne, to the joy of your sisters, provided we receive one or two presents.'

'Such as?' Tobie, still belligerent.

'Such as Berwick-upon-Tweed,' said Kathi dreamily. 'Do you know, I thought I was hearing a garbled version of some ludicrous plot. But it could be real.'

'Or it could be a garbled version of some ludicrous plot,' said John le Grant. 'How do we tell?'

'We don't. Rob Grey and his friends will keep us indirectly apprised,' Nicholas said. 'They have nothing to lose: we're at war with England already; we can't forbid them to take Sandy on board. Meanwhile, it drives a wedge between ourselves and France. And if we are foolish enough to tell the King, it will add to the problems of controlling him.'

'Do we tell him?' said Adorne. He was looking at Nicholas. Kathi thought, still caught up in happiness, that in that group of six men, there was no doubt which were the leaders. Leaders, not leader.

Nicholas said, 'That is for his officers, I think. They will have to be told now. No one else, except our own circle. Saunders. Crackbene. Robin. Archie. Andreas.'

'Julius?' Wodman said. 'Liddell must know of the plot. Julius might find it awkward.'

'All the more reason why he must know,' Nicholas said. 'Grey and others will feed us with tales, but we want other sources. At any rate, Kathi can leave the Hamilton household forthwith, and be excused from all further operations. You did prodigiously well. A coup, by God.'

'*De foudre*, by God,' she said, with a certain grimness. 'I wish I could believe you. I was meant to overhear?'

Nicholas said, 'They were probably weaving in and out of booths all the time, trying to find one you'd stop at. Andreas may even have noticed.'

She said, 'Jamie wasn't acting. He hadn't been told it was a ruse.'

'He may know now,' Nicholas said. 'He was born in Bruges, in your uncle's house, don't you remember? He's the godson of the English King's sister. His aunt is married to Archibald Angus. He could be one of Albany's trump cards, if all this is true. At any rate, you are safe. We are not targets, we're tools. Will you miss your august life at the Princess's?'

He sounded mildly cheerful. Her uncle looked satisfied. She realised, woefully, as the fumes of alcohol vanished, that they were reassuring her. For Nicholas, who had given so much of his time to this one, confused man, and to the Boyds, it must have been shocking news, as it must have been for her uncle. She said with sudden resentment, 'Blind Harry. All Sandy's stupid, dangerous raids; his outbursts against *that reiver Edward* and the *Auld Enemy of perfidious England*; the speeches about the dignity and sovereignty of his nation . . . He *shouted* at James for cravenly keeping the peace. He asked people to die for an ideal. They thought he meant it. I thought he meant it.'

Nicholas was quiet. Then he said, 'He did mean it, although it was coloured by other things. This venture too. He may well be telling himself that he will use the English to get what he wants, and then sweep them out of the country with the help of his friends.'

'Having got rid of the King,' said her uncle. 'But, as we said once of the French, an invading army would expect to be given something more than Berwick-upon-Tweed. They would want garrisoned forts from which they could control all the Lowlands. And do enough men admire Albany to rise up and prevent that from happening? He will have been away for three years.'

'I don't know,' Nicholas said. 'I don't think it depends on what the English do with Albany. I think it depends on what we do with the King.'

'These are princes,' her uncle said. You could hear a sharpness.

'These are impaired men who need help,' Nicholas said. 'As are we all. We put them first, because half a million people rely on them.' He and Adorne looked at one another.

Tobie said, 'So what do we do?'

Her uncle stirred. 'Advise the Council,' he said. 'Abide by what it decides. Continue our preparations for war, and pass the winter as best we can, in good heart. We are not dealing with madmen or tyrants, as Nicholas reminds us. We are dealing with limited men who are doing their best.'

Thus the winter was spent. For Kathi, there were no repercussions. The Princess Mary accepted her retiral with grace, and seemed unaware, as did her son, of any untoward reason. Rob Grey continued to wave to her as he passed from his house to the booths, and might have been equally innocent, although she doubted it. Julius, full of glee, had embarked (he said) on a counter-espionage programme which produced not very much, but kept Julius entranced.

Enchantment of a different kind was supplied, over the season, by the Court's personal entertainment industry, headed by the Master of Music and his acolytes. The playlets they devised were performed everywhere: at Holyrood and at Trinity, at Greenside and at Orchardfield and the Netherbow, and induced children to laugh and their elders to hug them and each other. The great choral responsory created by Will Roger alone was performed before hundreds in the burgh's own High Kirk of St Giles, with the guilds and their flags standing each before its own altar. Dr Andreas arrayed himself with his flock before the glittering shrine of St Crispin, and for part of the ceremony, Anselm Adorne came to stand at his side, his eyes never leaving the master, or the choir beneath his two hands. Among the singers, robed and remote, were Adorne's niece Katelijne, and the man for whose great, solitary voice the anthem had been written.

Full of love, Adorne prayed for them both.

Then came the enemy sun; and it was spring.

Chapter 38

'Wnder the pane,' said he, 'to heid or hang
Thai ar commandit to revele it nocht.'

JUST BEFORE THE war began, Nicholas called on William Knollys, Lord Preceptor in Scotland of the Knights Hospitaller of St John. He went not to the Order's Edinburgh hospice, but to the grand old Preceptory at Torphichen, which lay to the west, halfway between Bathgate and Linlithgow. He took John le Grant with him. There, in the Preceptor's chamber, they were welcomed, seated and offered a choice of Rhenish, Gascon or Candian wine by Lord St John himself, in his robust, meticulous Scots. Then he asked, genially, if they had come to measure his shields, or to expose yet again – who would ever deceive an ex-banker? – some cataclysmic deceit over salmon?

To which Nicholas merely said, Neither: he wanted to talk about Alexander of Albany.

The wine-pouring slowed. 'Ah,' said Sir William. 'Deputed by whom?'

'I volunteered,' Nicholas said. 'There is a possibility that France and England may collude to install his grace of Albany in place of his brother. An English army would bring him. King James has not yet been told, and you will, I am sure, keep it secret. The Council simply asks for advice. If Albany came, would many support him?'

The Preceptor set out the cups. Done without servants, it looked friendly. His round Scots voice sounded friendly. Regarding his height and military bearing, men were reminded quite often of England's King Edward, although the Preceptor was five years older, and his hair was black and not fair. But both had the same middle-aged corpulence and the same appetite, evidently, for food and wine and sensual pleasures.

Only, in the Preceptor's case, the style was deceptive. William Knollys had never seen service on the island of Rhodes: his appointment had required special dispensation because of it. There was no army of Knights at Torphichen: there had rarely ever been more than one or two, and now there was none but himself, and the vast cohorts of his lay administrators and servants. He courted women and bred children, duly legitimised; but it was done for a purpose: from Aberdeen to the Borders there were men of his name – uncle, brother, four sons – who would act as his henchmen in business and as procurators in his innumerable law cases.

For the affable manner was misleading, too. To administer the vast network of the Hospitallers' properties; to collect his dues; to run his fleet; to sit in Parliament and on the Council of Judges; to please the King; and keep the Order in check with regular responsions, required something more than the simple attributes of a soldier. William Knollys was formidable.

Now he sat down, saluted, drank, and said, 'Would I support Sandy Albany? No. Would others raise him an army? Only a small one. Am I in touch with him? Yes. I have learned nothing of interest but the fact you have just mentioned. England has sent him an invitation. I have advised him to refuse it. I have told no one else about it. Whether he comes or not will change nothing, in my view, except his own fate. The issue is simply whether the King of England will be foolish enough to raise money and troops and invade. As I said in Parliament, I think that he will.'

Parliament had just met and, prodded by all those who knew, had addressed at last the prospect of serious war, and had provided for it. Nicholas said, 'I came, of course, to hear your position, and it is as one would expect. England's plans, however, may change. We have heard from Flanders today. There has been another death in the dukedom. The young Duchess took a bad fall in the hunting field, and has died. The Estates have taken her children, and may refuse her husband the means to go on fighting the French.'

'In which case,' said Knollys, 'the Archduke Maximilian applies to England for help with an immediate, pre-emptive campaign. If England agrees, she will have no time for Scotland. If she refuses, she will.'

'She'll refuse. Edward wants to keep his French pension,' John said.

'I think so. It means,' said Nicholas, 'that information from England will be welcome. The Abbeys are being very helpful, and you have already mentioned hearing from Albany. As you pass between Leighton Buzzard and Clerkenwell, you may hear other items of use.'

'I have been wondering,' said William Knollys, 'why this little conversation is taking place now, instead of at the council table with my usual colleagues. But now I see. You have friends in the Abbey of Newbattle, and especially among the Sinclairs?'

'Like yourself, my lord, I have friends everywhere,' Nicholas said. 'In Newbattle, perhaps, fewer than usual, since they harboured our mutual abomination, David Simpson. No. I have not come to grind a Newbattle axe; just to ask for your help. Simply, because of the King, news is best gathered outside the Court. If you hear anything, let me know and I shall come.'

'Or I shall have difficulty with my salmon?' Knollys said. 'But then, as a merchant yourself, you must know how prolonged – and expensive – a trade dispute can be. I should hate to incur one simply because there were no secrets to be had.'

'Fortunately,' Nicholas said, 'in my experience, there is always gossip where men are gathered. Did I not hear that one of the late Sultan's sons has promised the Knights total immunity provided they put him on his father's throne? Rhodes would become quieter than Scotland then.'

'I prefer Scotland,' said Knollys. 'The conversation is better. I was just about to partake of a meal. Will you join me? I feel we have hardly plumbed our relationship yet.'

At table, thank God, John le Grant found his voice and ended up arguing over Middle Eastern artillery and military architecture, not forgetting Cyprus, Constantinople, or the St Nicholas Tower in Rhodes. On all of these, their statuesque host was sufficiently primed to be challenging: he had, after all, been listening to individual Knights on the subject for fifteen years. When Nicholas deflected the conversation to the present Scottish war, the Preceptor was equally sure of himself. 'You heard the garrison numbers: too small; but the most that can be spared for the Borders.'

'And yourself?' Nicholas said. 'Will you be raising troops?' The Order had property everywhere. They were overlords, in the west, of Robin's family.

'In Aberdeenshire, yes, as I am sure you have heard,' Knollys said. 'The rest must wait on events. I have no difficulty in serving under others. I could perhaps help most on the east, but John Darnley is a good choice for West Warden. I hear your St Pols have gone back to Annan and Threave?'

'My St Pols?' He said it with amusement.

The Preceptor emitted a kind of sonorous snore. 'Only through being linked, of course, in notorious dissent. Eck Scougal told me how the lad Henry took your best horses. The colts are back in the stud under guard at the moment: that Liddell land is good grazing, but too tempting for soldiers.'

'Then, if need be, you move the whole stud?' Nicholas said. 'Where?'

'To various places. I have some of the horses here now. One you would give your eye teeth for. I'm proud of him. Come. Before you go, let me show you.'

The stables were buildings of splendour, and led to the kennels, and the mews. 'You must come hunting one day,' the Preceptor said. 'Once this Albany nonsense is over.' Outside, he wore his black robe with the spectacular cross. The great dog at his side nudged against him and he lifted his eyes. A groom, instantly responsive, whistled the animal off.

John le Grant said, 'Where have I heard that whistle before?'

'Probably at Blackness,' the Preceptor said. 'The Keepers get their dogs here. Lord Cortachy was asking the same. It's something to remember, I suppose. A Torphichen hound will only respond to one call, and will always remember its master.'

They had reached a gate, at which he turned gravely. 'I am very pleased that you came to the Preceptory. We have been under the same roof often enough, but it is not until you meet a man in his setting that you know him. Give my regards to our mutual seagoing friends. I hope we shall find our ships in the water next year, and for trading, not fighting.'

'I hope so, too,' Nicholas said. John remained polite, also, until they were out of earshot.

Nicholas listened, with half an ear, until they were both on the road. Then he said, 'I thought you admired him for his cheek.'

'I'd admire him more if he shed the daft accent. Aberdeen! That's a man with Norman roots if ever I saw one.'

'I dare say,' Nicholas said. 'But you know how they interbreed with the natives. His grandfather was sheriff of Berwick. The Order's vessels load there. Their hide and salmon would come equally custom-free under the English.'

'I know,' said John, calming. 'All frontier merchants face every way, and he may do the same. But he doesna like Archibald Angus, that I'd swear. And he likes Jamie Liddell's land in the Mearns a good deal more than he likes Jamie Liddell. I heard that from Julius. Julius thinks Knollys has Liddell watched. And what was that about Davie Simpson?'

'They were on opposite sides, he and Knollys. Simpson set the Newbattle traders against him.'

'And Adorne?' the engineer said. 'I've come to like the man well, but one of his sons is a Knight of St John, and there's always the thought that the Preceptor might have Adorne in his pocket. They were both lords in Council, remember.'

'The Preceptor still is,' Nicholas said. 'But if he sponsored Adorne, he didn't appear at his induction. I think Adorne is treading carefully. He does have friends with the Knights, and wants to keep the Pope's favour: he's in the middle of juggling Aberdeen prebends again for his sons. But I don't think he's in anyone's pocket.'

'I'd like to think that,' said John. 'Anyway, for what today's sounding is worth, I doubt if Knollys will risk backing Albany. Scotland's his personal milch-cow and it's giving him all that he wants.' He paused. 'At the same time, it would do his character no harm to be faced with a hint of a threat now and then, such as just now. You're a real treat to listen to, Nicol. And so smooth! Where did you learn it?'

'Tommaso Portinari,' Nicholas said. 'It was before your time. The greatest courtier of the age.'

'The Medici manager? But –' began John.

'I know,' said Nicholas. 'Married a girl thirty years younger than himself and went bankrupt. He kept getting painted.'

'What colour?' said John. Coming up to a war, John was never gloomy for long.

That same April, 1482, Alexander, Duke of Albany, brother of the Scots King James, Third of the Name, left France for Southampton in a Scots caravel captained by one Jamie Douglas, and by the fourth day of May was quietly lodged with his servants at the Hospice of the Herber, Thames Street, London, at the King of England's expense. The King of England had already, at Easter, raised an army of twenty thousand armed men against Scotland, to march north under the Duke of Gloucester his brother. An additional seventeen hundred men were to follow.

On the tenth day of May, King Edward ordered his army to prepare to march north, at fourteen days' notice.

By the third day of June, King Edward had covered a quarter of the distance to Scotland, arriving with his royal protégé in Northampton-shire, where he was joined at the old family castle of Fotheringhay by his brother Dickon of Gloucester, newly back from a probing raid into western Scotland. Thirty years ago, Dickon had been born here at

Fotheringhay. Over three hundred years ago, David of Scotland had owned the castle and all the lands round it. Now, in freshly built rooms, three men drew up a treaty; and King Edward went home. Nine days later, the army resumed its march north under the supreme command of Richard of Gloucester; and by the eighteenth of June, it had arrived at its halfway encampment at York, ready to join its northern contingent.

By then, news of its advance had been carried to Scotland, and the King was immediately told. Neither the public nor the King was informed of the possible implication of Albany. Edinburgh glittered with steel, and Julius hammered on Robin of Berecrofts's door.

The door was jerked open, not by a servant, but by Nicholas, breathing quickly. Behind him, Robin's voice died. Julius said, 'I heard you were here. I have to speak to you, alone.'

The voice behind resumed calling. 'Really? Can't you trust even cripples, these days? Take him away, Julius. I expect they're going to carry me off with the children in any case.'

Nicholas said, 'He's drunk. I'm sorry. You'll have to come in. How bad is it?'

Julius said, 'Too bad to risk having it known.' Robin was shouting again.

Nicholas said, 'I can't leave him. Come in. It's what he needs, to know that he's trusted.'

Julius said, 'You don't know what you're risking.' He was mortified. Robin and Moriz and John never stopped talking of war. Now it had come, he didn't see why Berecrofts couldn't pretend to behave like a man.

Nicholas looked fed up as well, and sounded it when he turned back to Robin. 'Have you stopped? Julius has come to us for help. It's a crisis. Do you want to hear, or would I be better off with the bloody children?'

It seemed a bit harsh, but Robin's voice stopped. Then he said, 'My cup's empty.'

'So it is,' Nicholas said. He jerked his head, and Julius followed him back into the house, closing doors. Robin looked terrible: his hair wet, his face rigid and white. He was sitting, propped up as usual, and Nicholas was refilling his cup. Nicholas said, without turning, 'You've heard something?'

'Liddell has heard something,' Julius said. 'He's asked me to pass it to you.'

He saw Robin's eyes open, and Nicholas himself turned slowly, nursing the flask. He said, 'He's realised what you're doing?'

'No,' said Julius. 'But he trusts me to be discreet. Albany is over from France. The English did invite him, as Kathi heard in the booths, and now he's marching with Gloucester. He's asked Liddell to give you a message.'

Robin's eyes were fixed on Nicholas, and Nicholas glanced down. Then he sat. 'What?'

'Albany wants to see you,' said Julius. 'In York. He's told Gloucester how you helped him in Dunbar. Gloucester wants information. What the garrisons are. What support Sandy can expect. How to get rid of the King.'

Robin said, 'I'm going to be sick.'

'I think we all are,' said Nicholas. He got a bowl and held it, helping Robin. He didn't look as if his mind was on what he was doing. He said, 'As we thought, then. England has invested in Sandy, but not just to help them take Berwick and one or two castles. He wants the throne, and they've promised to help him.' He put the bowl down and gave Robin a towel and sat again.

Julius said, 'According to Liddell, Sandy doesn't know what he wants.'

'Oh,' said Nicholas.

Robin said, 'No. *No*, Nicholas. Jamie Liddell and Sandy are both using you. Sandy can't make up his mind, and Jamie thinks you will help him. Liddell wanted high office for Sandy, but not fratricide.'

'A lot of people think the King has committed fratricide,' Julius said. 'Albany might get more support than you think. Or maybe you can persuade him to change his mind. He could get back all his old appointments and land, if he left the English. He could ask James for anything.'

'And the English would kill Nicholas if they dreamed that that was why he had come. No,' said Robin vehemently. He sounded cold sober, and frightened.

'No?' Nicholas said. He wasn't looking at Julius.

There was a silence. Then Robin said, 'You don't need to over-perform because I've been doing the opposite. No.'

'Were you performing?' Nicholas said. 'I didn't think so. You were faced with a situation, and you have now dealt with it. I am facing one, too. If I go, it is not because I want to. It is because I ought.'

Sometimes Nicholas sounded like one of Julius's Bologna lecturers, except that he stressed the wrong words. Julius said irritably, 'Well? I've got to go back with your answer.'

Nicholas turned to him. 'What do *you* suggest that I do?'

Robin was scowling. Damn Robin. Julius said, 'If spying wasn't supposed to worry Kathi or me, I don't see why you need to hesitate. Good God, man: you've played the fool in your time with every merchant in Bruges. Surely you can do the same with the English?'

'I expect so,' said Nicholas. 'Robin, I'm sorry.'

'No. It's all right,' Robin said. 'I knew you would. Go and tell Gelis. Kathi will be back directly. It's all right.'

Julius was glad to get out.

Adorne said, 'You've told Avandale and he *agrees*?'

'He hasn't much to lose,' Nicholas said. 'He thinks, as I do, that the message is genuine. England's used to agents, single and double. She's already bribed half the population of Scotland, and invited the remaining half to come into the fold. I might prove a waste of time, but I'm not a threat to them. They'll let me come back.'

'They may not harm you, but they may expect you to stay. And that's only half the story. What about your reputation in Scotland, if and when you come back?'

'There is some security,' Nicholas said, 'in the fact that you all know about it. That, and my honest face. And another thing. Andro Wodman has gallantly volunteered to come with me in secret. He'll lurk. If I can't get back myself, I'll try to send back what I find out. At least it should be obvious if they're splitting the army, or attacking only through Albany's land. And how long they're being paid for. That's vital.'

Of course, he was right. Up till now, an attack of this size would normally concentrate first upon Berwick, and then diversify to other Border strongholds. But with Albany there, the fall of Berwick, if it happened, might be followed by an invasion through the supposedly friendly lands of Albany's East March. And if that occurred, it was not enough to garrison the Borders, as they had done. The Scottish host would have to be called out. And the size of the Scottish host was in doubt.

They had talked through all these options. To summon an army to fight a pitched battle against far superior English numbers was good news for the poets, but little else. You might win by a ruse, but more likely you'd end up with smoking fields and dead men. Rather, you avoided general warfare. You negotiated.

On the other hand, if the attacks were to be limited to the Borders, the entire host needn't be drawn in at all. The frontier garrisons were tough. They might well hold out until the season had ended, or the English pay came to a halt.

If they knew what Albany was going to do, they would know how to handle the King. Once the King knew his brother was present, he would try to lead the entire army against him. And that, of course, was unthinkable. Whatever was in Sandy's mind, Gloucester was bound to want the King out of the way. Unambiguously and probably finally out of the way.

Adorne had allowed a long silence to develop. He wished he could say something different. Instead, he turned to Nicholas de Fleury and said, 'I do see. We need this information. I shall not try to dissuade you.' He cleared his throat. 'Kathi and I have to thank you about something.'

'No,' said Nicholas. 'Courage is like gold. It only needs to be burnished, now and then.'

Gelis said, 'It's like being ill: everyone has been so kind. Colin Argyll came and sat and told me how brave I was. And drank all my wine.'

'In Gaelic?' Nicholas said. It was late. The day seemed to have lasted for ever.

'Can you drink in Gaelic?' she said. 'Yes, I am sure that you can. Jordan will expect to go with you.'

'We have had that conversation,' he said. 'He has agreed to stay and look after you.'

They were sitting opposite one another. She said, 'You don't need to say anything. I know you. If you didn't do it, you wouldn't be who you are. When do you go?'

'Tomorrow morning,' he said.

She flinched. It was so slight, you would have had to know her very well to notice it. He added, evenly, 'I have to go quickly, or it's no good. It should have been tonight, but I said that I couldn't.'

When she still didn't speak he said, 'I just want to sit; and perhaps talk.'

'I know,' she said.

They talked; and presently, sat closer together; no more. Only very much later, in bed, did she sigh in his arms and say, 'Let me give you something to keep.'

He had not known, until then, that their marriage had so changed, and so deepened. Whatever became of him now, his decision had brought him this gift.

Before nightfall next day, he had forded the Tweed at the castle of Carham, and had given himself up to the garrison, who expected him. They did not expect or observe a companion, particularly one so adept in fieldcraft as a French-trained broken-nosed Archer. Wherever he went, Nicholas was sure that Andro Wodman would follow.

*

By then, the decision had been made to call out the Scots army, beginning with the farthest flung and most loyal contingents: those of Huntly and the Ogilvies and their friends who drew rents from the south, but whose homes lay in those rich, well-doing lands in the north and north-east. They were to arrive on the Burgh Muir just outside Edinburgh by the middle weeks of July.

On the March, the garrisons waited for orders. Some grew impatient. It displeased the Warden of the West March, in particular, to find that two of his Lochmaben garrison had left without sanction, riding east with a few mounted bowmen. Sometimes these men fought private wars. He hoped the father, at least, would have the sense to come back at once.

Chapter 39

Condampnit was as traytour thaim amang,
And was depryvit of his dayis mo,
Off his honour and of his lyf also.

FOREIGN MERCHANTS visiting York tended to know the taverns at the two wharfsides and, more officially, the guild-houses and the merchant adventurers' hall, and some of the churches where business was transacted. Nicholas knew about as much; rather less than he knew of Southampton or Newcastle or, certainly, London. He knew enough to be pleased when he was brought to St Mary's by means of a boat and the water-gate, which meant that someone thought his identity worth concealing.

It had not been a particularly pleasant journey. His escort had been told to be polite, but this was probably the twentieth defector they had brought south since King Edward's invitation, and the contempt showed, expressing itself in the officer's aloofness, and in a little unchecked rough handling from the soldiers. He knew the route reasonably well for the first day: he had fought over it. He didn't attempt to befriend anybody.

Most of the military leaders, he guessed, would be housed at the castle, or in pavilions close to the massed tents of the host, which he could hear and smell, but not count. The rumoured tally of twenty thousand did not seem unlikely.

The Duke of Gloucester was not in the castle, but enjoying the comfort of the Abbot's guest apartments in the richest monastery of York. His flag flew above the roof of St Mary's. There was no other flag, either ducal or regal. A wit brighter than Sandy's, Nicholas thought, might have put up the three legs of the lordship of Man. *See how I run.*

He was placed in a well-furnished room, and a servant unpacked his saddlebags and laid out fresh clothing. He shut the door when the man left, but there was another on guard in the passage, with the white boar badge on his arm. Nicholas achieved an automatic grooming and awaited the summons. It didn't take long to come.

He had never met Gloucester, but was prepared for the black hair, the jagged profile, the uneven shoulders. His voice was charming and so were his clothes: a soft brocade robe over a fine shirt, doublet and hose. There was a brooch in his hat. Sandy, seated on the same level, had the look of a man who has put on a lot of weight and lost it again. His auburn hair was elaborately shaped, but he had cut himself shaving. His pale, steady stare was defiant.

The room was handsome, and obviously used as an audience chamber. Against the walls there stood several servants: a chamberlain, a page, a man-at-arms. Closest to the chair of state waited a tall man wearing an expensive light robe over armour: Harry Percy, Earl and sheriff of Northumberland, and Dickon's partner in the north. Earl Harry's father had once burned Dunbar. Earl Harry's father had been a Lancastrian, in the days when the Lancastrian King had made his kingdom in exile at Bamburgh, and had fought and died for Lancaster at Towton. Then York had prevailed, and the family, after a spell in the wilderness, were back serving York. Or rather serving themselves, as all the great Border families were accustomed to do, on both sides of the frontier. Harry Percy was six years older than Gloucester, and had been the head of his house from the age of fifteen. Once, when Percy cancelled a March meeting, Sandy had been very annoyed.

Dickon Gloucester said, 'Do we need anything, Harry? No. Then perhaps Hugh will stay. We may call for the rest of you later.' Hugh was the man-at-arms, who placed himself by the wall. The rest left, except for Earl Harry and Gloucester.

Gloucester said, 'M. de Fleury, you know who I am. Let me present you to my lord of Northumberland, whom you will well know, by reputation at least. Harry, this is Nicholas de Fleury of Bruges, a merchant dealing in Scotland who fought and nearly sacrificed his life at the side of my sister's late husband at Nancy. I am only sorry that we meet him at this tragic time when her grace the Duke's daughter has also perished. You will have heard the news? Please, both of you, sit.'

'I have, my lord,' Nicholas said. He made the correct acknowledgements, and sat, as did Percy. He added, 'I had the honour of meeting the Duchess Marie several times, and my wife was fortunate enough to serve the Princess your sister. All who knew the young Duchess will mourn her. Indeed, it seemed possible that the bereaved husband might plan to renew his war against France, in his distraction. So, again, a single death may upset Europe.'

The Duke's sad expression did not alter. The Earl said, 'You mean pernicious rumours cause damage. The Archduke is not going to war.'

'But if he were,' said Dickon of Gloucester, 'would you have wished to join him, M. de Fleury? Had you planned to go back to Bruges?' He knew Bruges well. So did the Percy family. The Percy family had actually been members, in their time, of the Confraternity of the Dry Tree, of which the greatest recent luminary had been Anselm Adorne.

'I had often thought of it,' Nicholas said. 'I have the goodwill of the Duchess Margaret, as I have said; and of the merchant community. My opportunities in Scotland might seem limited. But there, too, favour has been shown me by many – by his grace at your side, and his sisters. With the right masters, I would have no fear of the future.' He looked directly at Sandy and smiled. Amazingly, Sandy smiled back. It almost looked natural.

'You don't get on with the King?' Percy said.

'He is unwell,' Nicholas said.

'You mean sick? Mortally sick?'

'The doctors think not. His grace here will have described his affliction. It makes for uneven behaviour, which deprives him of friends.'

Gloucester glanced at Sandy and turned back to Nicholas. 'You are saying that, put to the test, the people of Scotland would prefer someone in full health as their king, capable of making firm judgements, and without the perpetual need for elderly, perhaps senile advisers? And if that is so, how many would fight for their beliefs?'

The big question. What had the Douglases said, as they poured over the Border to join their exiled Earl? What had the Earl himself said, and that other exile, Jamie Boyd's grandfather? What did Holland suggest, or Jardine of Applegarth, who had fled with him? What did Sandy believe, who hadn't been in Scotland or near it for three years?

How long was the army being paid for?

Nicholas said, 'My lord Duke, the opposition to the King is underground, and confined to certain areas at present. It needs to be fostered. There is enough to smooth the path, as it were, of a new champion, but not enough to maintain him without help just at first. In six months' time, the helping force could be dismissed and the kingdom hold successfully under its new King. Of that I am sure.'

'Six months!' Sandy exclaimed.

'That is not what we hear,' Gloucester said.

Nicholas said, 'Perhaps, my lord, you have been speaking to the wrong people. The power in all this lies in the hands of the merchants.'

'Yours?' said the Earl of Northumberland. It was his function to say what the Duke preferred not to say.

'With the burghers and their officers, where the money is. Not with me, as my lord of Albany will confirm. If it were so, I should not be here. I should not wish to change kings, or dilute my profit.'

Percy grunted. Gloucester flashed him a glance and turned, smiling, to Sandy. He said, 'I like your man. He is not subservient. He is honest. I think he will be our good friend. We hope that, now that we know one another, he will further bear out all you have told us of him. Were we to cross the Border, what opposition might we find, in what castles? And what loyalties can we count on? You know of all his grace's good friends.'

His voice was still charming. He had just come from Carlisle. He had just attacked the West March and burned towns a few miles from Albany's Lochmaben Castle: he must have a good idea now of Darnley's strength in the west. Nicholas therefore didn't lie, or not much, about that. He said, for the rest, what Avandale and Argyll and Whitelaw had recommended that he should say, adjusted to what Tam Cochrane and John le Grant and a few others reckoned, and further adjusted in the light of some beliefs of his own.

He expected, and received, a number of questions.

'So few in Berwick?'

'The King has to pay for these himself,' Nicholas said. 'He feels deeply about Berwick. He would pour public gold into its defence if he could, but Parliament would allow no more than I have said.'

'That's true. I've told you,' Sandy said. Earl Harry glanced at him.

'And Cessford and Ormiston? Why so many?'

He explained. It all confirmed his conviction, as their questions continued, that the English army was not going to divide: that they were going to fling all their strength in one direction, provided he told them nothing to alarm them. He knew, as if he had been told, that whatever happened, they were going to make sure of Berwick. Outside the windows, somewhere, a horn blew.

The Lieutenant-General said, 'Ah. You came to us at the right moment, M. de Fleury, and I am only sorry that I must cut our interview short. Tomorrow we march. Where we march and how well we do will be owed, in large measure, to you and to his highness of Scotland, who thought to bring you here. You wish, if I have read you correctly, to return to Scotland, and await this new future?'

'Yes, my lord,' Nicholas said.

'They do not know of this visit, and therefore you may be able to send us more news?'

'I shall do my best, my lord Duke,' Nicholas said.

'Then God be with you,' said the Duke, getting up. Sandy jumped from his chair, and Earl Harry and Nicholas rose, side by side. Gloucester said, 'You have come at some cost to yourself in time and in trouble. I would have you know that we are not niggardly. My chamberlain will see you in the morning, and an escort will await you to take you safely back to the Borders. Meanwhile, you have all my gratitude.'

'My lord,' said Nicholas, beginning to move.

'No. We must go, my lord of Northumberland and I. Stay and talk to your King. You have been separated for a long time. There must be much you have to say to one another. Good night,' said Dickon of Gloucester. He left. Percy bowed and walked after, the man-at-arms following. The door closed.

Nicholas said, 'My lord, forgive me, but it has been a long journey. Would you object to somewhere less formal? If not so, of course we stay here.'

'My room,' Sandy said. 'No. I understand. You will be more comfortable in my room.'

He was learning. Nicholas supposed you couldn't live with King Louis and not learn.

Sandy said, 'They spy everywhere. Christ, what did you mean, six months before I get any support? I wish you'd never come. You're saying all the wrong things. I'll never get out of this alive.'

'You will. They'd rather have you on your own than have to deal with James and Avandale and the rest, or Buchan or Atholl as regent.'

He stood still and kept his voice calm while Sandy paced backwards and forwards. The sun had beat all day into the room and the air was stifling hot. Sandy was sweating, his creamy skin blotched. Nicholas said, 'Come on. You sent for me. If you don't want to tell me, I'll guess what the choices are, and suggest what I'd do in your place. Then I'll go.'

Sandy said, 'It's obvious, isn't it? My brother threw me out of the country, and France can't send an army to help me get back. England can, though, and they have.'

'Under Gloucester,' Nicholas said.

'Of course under Gloucester!' the Prince said. 'He's a king in these parts. Northumberland, Durham, Cumbria. Men rally to him, as they will to me. He knows what it's like to have a brother killed.'

Nicholas drew breath, and then left it. He said, 'So Edward is content to let him establish what power he likes in the north, add to his lands, perhaps, and win a few laurels. I would guess that his first objective has always been Berwick, but they've brought an army big enough to attempt other things. They might send it over the Border at several points, to take the strongholds they've demanded, like Lochmaben. Or if they think it might be successful, they'll start with Berwick, and hope to surge north through the whole of your East March, and set you on the throne. Or they may not have decided what to do until they get nearer, and weigh up their chances. What do you think?'

Sandy said, 'I don't need to think. I know. They're going for Berwick, and then straight through to Edinburgh. They've told me. That's why it was so stupid to talk of six months. It's going to be fast, and sudden, and irresistible. It'll be finished in twenty-eight days.'

A wasp, sweeping about, snarled past them both and slammed into the window. It dropped and lay, breathlessly buzzing. Nicholas said, 'That's Gloucester's contract time? That's how long his army has been paid to stay in Scotland?'

'The main army,' Sandy said. 'There'll be another seventeen hundred, a holding force, paid to arrive for two weeks next month when the other troops leave. I shall be on the throne by then. They know I'm coming. They'll be gathering secretly now, the men of the Merse and the Borders. My own Annandale, too.'

'Annandale isn't doing much to keep Gloucester pinned down at Carlisle,' Nicholas said. 'Sandy, you know this isn't true. Jamie Liddell himself must have warned you. It will take considerable force to put you on the throne, and a good deal to keep you there. And the more foreign help you need, the more you're going to have to concede for it. You would end up with less power than you had under James, and a struggle that could last the rest of your life.'

Albany said, 'You have a poor opinion of my popularity, it seems. Or my capacity as a ruler. What do you presume to know?'

'Only,' said Nicholas, 'that in the nature of things, the man in the saddle always has the advantage, and even a genius can't lightly replace him. We all know the King's failings. We also know that he is well advised, by men who have the good of the kingdom at heart. He sometimes escapes them and does foolish things. But in a prospering country, free of obligations to others, a prince who stands at his side can expect more from life than would a debtor to England, and a possible fratricide. For England might push you to that.'

'No,' said Sandy.

Nicholas looked at him. 'But you haven't mentioned that there are limits to what you would do. You haven't told them what your private plans are. You speak of your friends, but there are others in Scotland who know you, and who think that this is the way you have chosen to come back. You have induced the King of England to waste men and gold on a useless invasion. You will stay with them until they are trapped, and then turn to your brother – not as a supplicant, but as a man who can claim the reward he has earned. I imagine there is nothing the King would not give you, save the throne, and you would have that all but in name.'

The other man sat. He said, 'Did they tell you to say this?'

Nicholas said, 'The King does not know I am here. No one told me to say what I have said. It is obvious.'

The pale eyes stared directly at him. Sandy Albany said, 'He killed my brother. James killed my brother. He'll kill me.'

Nicholas said, using almost Albany's words: 'Did they tell you that? It isn't true. It was the opposite. John tried to kill the King, and had to be put under restraint. The fits got worse. He died in my own doctor's house – you remember Dr Tobias? I am sorry. I am sorry, Sandy, but John took his own life.'

'No one told me,' said the other man slowly.

'For his sake, James didn't announce it. But it happened. I was in Tobie's house the day your brother died. He had every possible care. He was ill, and you are not. Come home. Your life would be safe.'

Albany said, 'They would never restore what I had.' Then he said, 'Would they put it in writing?'

Nicholas said, 'Write it yourself. List what you want. I'll take it to them. I'll see you get a reply.'

There was a table, where a clerk had been working. Nicholas sat, and found paper, and wrote, at Sandy's dictation, in the neat, swift hand he had paid Colard to teach him, when first he had realised that he was leaving the coarse world of the dyevats for a world of fine clothes and fine manners, where your hands were always clean. Sandy signed it.

They talked for a while after that, of people and places. He didn't push Albany to make a decision: he had placed the choices before him, and a warning as well. He couldn't do more. Sandy must know Edward's character. He could not be as naïve as he seemed about Gloucester. They parted company, at last, and Nicholas found his escort outside, and was taken back to his room. The document was where once he had carried Phemie's letter, inside his shirt.

They locked him in overnight. It was what he expected, but it might imply, this time, more than a normal precaution. He knew a lot about building. Monastic property in public use was riddled with spy holes. It had been a risk he had had to take, and force Sandy to take. He was here to win Sandy over, or to discredit him. He would learn where he stood in the morning. They would never let him depart if they knew of that invoice for treachery.

He wondered where Wodman was. He had glimpsed him once or twice, reassuringly, at different stages of his journey, but knew, arriving in York, that he was on his own now. If he were allowed to leave, Andro must find him and be told what had happened. Then they would separate. That was the arrangement. If anything went wrong, one of them ought to get through; and if he himself didn't survive, at least Gloucester would think twice, now, about an invasion. That they might kill the Prince was also possible. It was something that Nicholas had made himself face, and accept. It didn't help that he was running the same risk himself.

He didn't sleep, but never required much rest in any case. It was not quite dawn when the quiet was blurred over by the sound of the distant rousing of many thousands of men. Whatever its destination, this immense army was now leaving York. Very soon after that, his door was unlocked, and he was told to dress and present himself again in the audience chamber. This time, Sandy was not present. Only the Duke of Gloucester occupied the chair by the guttering candles, with Henry Percy again at his side. The door shut on his escort and he stood, meeting the Duke's dark, cynical eyes.

'So,' said Dickon of Gloucester. 'I have not a great deal to say to you. You will hand me, please, the paper which you carry, presumably, on your person. Or if you prefer, I shall have it taken by force.'

'The lord Abbot enjoys the conversations of others,' said Nicholas. He drew out the paper, which the Duke leaned over and took, unfolding it to read at a glance.

He said, 'The Abbot may enjoy what he hears. I do not. Your purpose was to suborn your own Prince, denying him his right to the throne, and sowing mistrust between him and ourselves. The information you brought is of course useless, but we hardly depended on it. You might even like to know that we feel so confident as to proceed with our plan.

The host you hear stirring will be on the Borders of Scotland within a few days.'

Nicholas said, 'You cannot achieve this in twenty-eight days, my lord. What I said is true. There are many who are impatient with the present King, but the support for the Duke of Albany is uncertain. Whatever you take, you cannot reckon to hold.' He thought it worth saying, in that he might be believed, *in extremis*. For his own conduct, he had no excuses to make.

The Duke was studying him. 'What did you stand to gain? You won the regard of the Duchess my sister. Did England have nothing to offer, if Flanders had failed?'

It was an offer, or the opening for one. It was not a tune Nicholas de Fleury wanted to dance to. He said, 'I have already refused a pension from France. My family is settled in Scotland, and we are satisfied.'

'You are saying,' said Gloucester, 'that you have taken this trouble because, for you, the present régime is most suitable. You do not wish to change kings, but you would be happy to see my lord of Albany return to high office in Scotland?'

'That is so, my lord,' Nicholas said. He couldn't think what he had overlooked. The Duke was smiling, although Percy wasn't. Percy said, 'My lord Duke –'

Dickon Gloucester said, 'No. I am putting this to M. de Fleury because I wish him to see that his judgement is faulty and that his future might well lie where he did not expect, with a new and generous employer. M. de Fleury, you may know that a treaty was drawn up at Fotheringhay, between my lord and brother the King, and the Prince you call Albany?'

'My lord Duke!' said the Earl again. He sounded furious.

The Duke looked at him. 'Does this distress you? Would you prefer to leave?' He waited. As the other fell silent, he turned back.

'As I was saying. The Prince you call Albany, but who is now known, I have to tell you, as Alexander, King of Scotland, by the King of England's royal gift. Shall I go on?'

Show nothing. Do nothing. 'Please do,' Nicholas said.

'I felt you should be apprised. By this treaty, or rather indenture, King Alexander promised, on obtaining his crown, to do homage to England; to break the alliance between Scotland and France; and to surrender the town and castle of Berwick within fourteen days of entering Edinburgh. Equally, my brother King Edward has been promised, in return for his aid, possession of certain places – Berwick-upon-Tweed, Liddesdale, Eskdale, Ewesdale, Annandale and Lochmaben Castle, as I remember.

He has also offered the Prince his daughter Cecilia, provided the Prince can free himself from other wives.'

There was a thoughtful pause. Gloucester added, 'It is all well attested, of course. The Prince used his signet, and signed the document with his name, Alexander R, employing an extremely confident flourish. He had, I think, been practising.'

He stopped. His voice was solicitous, but his eyes hinted at a wicked amusement. He said, 'Thus, in whatever role the Prince re-enters Scotland, you may be sure that life there will not remain as it is. You may even wish to reconsider your future.'

He smiled. Nicholas could not bring himself to smile back.

Sandy. Bloody Sandy. Why? Because it was demanded, and he'd sign anything to get what he wanted? Did he not realise the damage it would do? Or did he really mean it all along? Blind Harry's Wallace had been a sham? All that nationalistic fervour just a means to gain himself popular backing, and a French army to return him as king . . . ?

But no. Emotion came naturally to Sandy. He had truly hated the English, at that time. Now he simply thought he was using them, and he could later repudiate anything. It wounded Nicholas, briefly, that last night Sandy had hidden all this, when he thought he had his confidence. Then he realised the illogic of applying logic to Albany.

Gloucester said, 'You are amused?'

'Is there any other way to take it, my lord?' Nicholas said. 'One man has subscribed to your treaty, but I doubt if anyone else would. Were I free, I should still stay in Scotland. While the war lasts, at least.'

'But alas, you are not free, are you, M. de Fleury?' said the Duke. 'You are an agent, a spy, an informer; and must submit to the fate of such men. You will prepare yourself in your room. In an hour you will march with the army. At the first halt, you will be brought to me to be tried. You may go.'

Nicholas bowed. Leaving the room, the last thing he heard was the Earl of Northumberland remonstrating with the Duke. He guessed why. Until Sandy became king, it was surely of vital importance that the Fotheringhay treaty stayed secret. Nicholas himself had been told, to induce him to change sides. The Duke had relished the telling. But since he had refused, Nicholas could not, of course, be permitted either to stand public trial, or to live.

It was hot, that July. Travelling south, Nicholas had been mounted. Returning, he tramped along with the foot-soldiers, far behind the drums and the cavalry, with the English commanders and King Alex-

ander IV (*rex hic*) in the lead. He had changed back into his travelling
dress of boots and plain doublet and cap. The clean shirt and hose were
the last he had. The rest he had left, with his spurs, in his room. His
weapons had been taken from him at Carham.

The man he was tied to was from Norwich, near where the Caxton
family came from. He knew some stories about them, and Nicholas
knew some others, from Bruges. The man couldn't read, but had picked
up a rare stock of ballads.

They got too friendly, and Nicholas was transferred to the stirrup of
a sergeant-at-arms who was riding alongside to marshal them. At the
next handy copse, the sergeant was summoned by nature, and Nicholas
found that the rope round his wrists had been carelessly knotted.
Invitation. He decided, in a burst of rebellion, to accept it. The marching
men passed, but he was masked by the bulk of the horse. Working fast,
he got himself free and started to run for the trees, just as the sergeant
appeared, but failed to notice him. They wouldn't kill him in plain
view, near the road. He was well into the wood and running really fast
by the time the outcry began.

Or he was, until somebody tripped him.

Nicholas swore, and rolled over, kicking.

'Hey!' said Andro Wodman, dodging. 'It's just that the north is this
way, if that's where you're going.' He had two horses. It was a miracle.

There wasn't time to embrace him. Nicholas flung himself into the
saddle and set off, Andro pounding beside him. The shouting receded.
They had come after him, he guessed, with a few horse and a handful
of foot, confident of riding him down in the trees. They would then
cast around briefly, unwilling to connect the tracks of two mounts with
his disappearance. Then they would be forced to believe it, and take
really serious action.

Nicholas changed from a resolute canter to a gallop.

'Whoa!' said Wodman after a while. 'Whoa! There's nobody after us
now.'

'That's what you think,' Nicholas said. 'I've just been allowed free
so that someone can ride after and kill me. Do you hear me?'

'Sadly,' said Wodman. He was galloping too.

'Good,' said Nicholas. 'So listen to what I'm going to say, memorise
it, and then go. One of us ought to get through, and they don't know
you exist. If you do get killed, just don't tell me.'

Chapter 40

The masonnis suld mak housis stark and rude,
To kepe the pepill frome thir stormes strang,
And be thai fals, the craft it gois all wrang.

WHEN, INCURRING Lord Darnley's displeasure, Simon de
St Pol of Kilmirren abandoned the fortress of Lochmaben
that summer to race east with his son and his archers, he
had no intention, as it turned out, of evading his service,
but was merely exchanging one Border keep for another. The captain
of Home Castle, the second son of Lord Borthwick, received the supplement to his garrison with surprise, but was prepared to make St Pol's
peace with the Warden. After nearly two months of standing to arms,
his sixty men could do with new blood. Simon de St Pol had had a
great reputation in his day, and his son was a fine-looking youngster.
Indeed, anyone of mettle would prefer to be here, near the action, rather
than under Tom Kilpatrick's command at Lochmaben. A good man,
Kilpatrick, but stolid. Borthwick himself was an artillery man. St Pol
was here because he wanted excitement.

It was a good enough theory, and one that Simon de St Pol encouraged.
In fact, he had left Lochmaben at speed for quite a different reason.
He had left with his son and his soldiers because he had received an
anonymous message. A well-substantiated, personal message to the
effect that Nicholas de Fleury was covertly leaving for York, ferrying
information to and from Albany. The dates were vague, but the place
of de Fleury's crossing was given as certain. He would use the ford that
led from Scotland to England at Carham, and would probably return
the same way. For he was not suddenly defecting to England. He was
already Albany's man, and England's agent in Scotland.

It was not surprising. It was what many suspected already. But to catch de Fleury shuttling to England would prove him a traitor. And one could do as one liked with a traitor. One could do anything, while capturing a traitor, and the law would turn a blind eye.

Henry agreed, after asking some questions. It was more than time that Henry was made to face facts. You didn't express doubts when pursuing enemies. You expressed enthusiasm.

The ford at Carham was no distance from Home. Home was only four miles from the river. Simon had sent two of his men there already. They knew de Fleury by sight. They would stop him. They would set up relays between them, night and day, and would catch him. Henry had wanted to tell all the garrisons and ask them to help, but Simon had explained that was futile. De Fleury fancied himself as an actor. He would deceive them. He would evade all the permanent guards at the ford. And if they brought in officials, there would be an official process once the man had been caught. A waste of time. A waste of money. A King's man like Simon could take justice, surely, into his own hands.

Henry had agreed in the end. It didn't matter whether or not Henry agreed, so long as he stopped interfering.

Once settled at Home, however, it was disappointing to obtain no result from their vigilance. Although St Pol took his men and made himself responsible for patrolling the river at several fords – Carham and Wark, Coldstream and Norham – there was no sign of de Fleury, and it began to seem as if he might have made the crossing already. In which case there was nothing for it but to wait for him to return. A journey between York and the Tweed would take several days in each direction, with a stay of unknown length in the middle. They might have to wait for ten days.

It was not so unpleasant, putting off time. June moved into July. The weather was warm, and the fishing less good than it should be, but there was other sport to be had. At the castle, they relieved the boredom with contests. As the most experienced jouster in Home, Simon had no difficulty winning the prizes, modest though they might be. And he had to admit that Henry also looked well in the saddle, with his brilliant armour, and the hair and eyes so like his own. One of the better archers was Constantine Malloch, whose estate was nearby; but his son had no style; and Henry seldom went near them these days. The girl had been the attraction.

There were quite a few girls in the township, and inside the castle they drank somewhat, and gambled and told stories. Henry was about all the time, but knew better than to interrupt. Occasionally Simon thought he looked sullen, and reminded him sharply how lucky he was. He was pleased when Henry won things. The day might come when, fit as he was, he himself would succumb to age. With Henry before them, people would not forget how his father had been.

De Fleury didn't come. What came was a messenger, bursting into the Castle with news. The bulk of the English army had left York, marching north. It was approaching Newcastle, Alnwick, Berwick. The captain called his lieutenants together, but Simon hardly heard what they said. Perhaps de Fleury's intentions had changed. Suppose de Fleury had stayed, and had joined the English army, marching with Albany. He couldn't get at him then.

Simon hesitated, and settled for remaining at Home. Back through the same route, the note had suggested. It might still be true.

Messengers also came regularly to Anselm Adorne, some of them from Lochmaben. About this time, with very few men, he left Linlithgow and rode quickly and quietly south to Upsettlington, where he avoided the laird's house, but entered the purlieus of the church. There, he made himself known to the Rector, Will Bell, who had attended St Andrews at the same time as Archie, now Abbot of Holyrood.

Adorne didn't stay long. By the time he left to go to ground, he had found out all he wanted, down to the beat of the river patrols. He had asked Bell not to speak of his visit, or not at least until he returned home. Very few knew that Adorne was due to come to the Tweed – Nicholas and Andro, and the Council in Edinburgh. Even Bell had not been told the true story. The negotiation with Albany was too delicate.

Unlike the St Pols, Anselm Adorne had the advantage of knowing exactly where Nicholas de Fleury proposed to recross the river. He was also better placed to calculate how long the double journey might take. If Nicholas had to return without help, it could take a long time.

A long time, but not too long, with any luck. An English army marching from York would take days to get to the Border, and longer to draw in its northern contingents. Even if it took Nicholas two weeks to emerge with his information – the army's numbers and plans, Albany's intentions – it would still be in time. News could be transmitted to Edinburgh and to all the relevant strongholds in hours. Anything Nicholas could tell them would be priceless.

Adorne could not hope to collect him from the trackless moors of the English interior, but he could be on hand to help when Nicholas and Andro came to the river. So, lying day after day, night after night, watching the river-mouth of the Till down from Norham, Adorne subscribed to a doctrine of patience. It served him for a while. But when the English army actually arrived on the Border, and settled on the Tweed opposite Berwick, increasing daily, Anselm Adorne began to lose his detachment.

He had known that Nicholas might not return: this large, calm man he had watched grow from boyhood and whose value, after many acrimonious clashes, he had learned to appreciate. The invitation to York, he now began to fear, had never been genuine. Nicholas had been killed because he was troublesome. To die in such a way was not ignoble. It was harder to accept that death was not reserved for grand causes. The countryside was full of masterless men who would kill for a horse.

In fact, Nicholas had lost his horse, by shattering mischance, just as he and Andro were about to part company. It was pure accident: it stumbled and fell on uneven ground, breaking its own neck and throwing him heavily. He got up and stood, intending to decide what to do once his head cleared. His head didn't clear, and Andro simply pulled him up behind him, jettisoning everything he carried except for his weapons and money.

The horse didn't like the double burden, and slowed. He must get another, immediately, or get down and let Andro go on. In town, horses were easy to come by. Here, there was nothing. He couldn't even remember seeing a farm: just a lot of warm, empty countryside with happy larks trilling too high to be seen. Lucky larks.

Andro, thinking along the same lines, said, 'Listen for cattle, or dogs. There. Do you hear it? Barking.'

Nicholas heard. It came from behind, and was blessedly some distance off. Fortunately, he didn't have to explain, because Andro had realised what it was. 'Bloody hell!'

He twisted round and stared at Nicholas, and Nicholas, who couldn't see very well, attempted to think. He had had concussion before. It wore off. But before that, they had to separate, fast. Wodman should stay with the horse, which could probably outrun the hounds with one rider. Gloucester's men couldn't detain him in any case: there was nothing to connect him to Nicholas. Nicholas himself had only to hide.

Wodman worked it all out for himself anyway. He made for and splashed over a stream, and then located a neighbouring peat bog at which he halted, dismounted, and manhandled Nicholas to the ground. From there, he pushed him down to the floor of the cutting and heaved the stack of peats thudding down over him.

'Will that do?' he said. He had hardly spoken throughout. The barking was now very much louder.

Nicholas said, 'Are you mad? Of course not. Good luck.'

Nicholas lay, as under a mound of heavy, cold, malodorous blankets, and listened to Wodman's horse squelch quickly away. The dogs arrived very soon after that, and he heard men's voices, and the tread of horses, and splashing. Then there came a shout, and more baying, followed by a concerted sound of hooves on the far bank of the stream. Presently, both the hooves and the barking receded.

Wodman must have laid a fresh trail. In any case, the water had baffled the hounds. The peat would have confounded them, too. Clever Andro. Clean Andro. Andro wasn't going to be dark brown and stinking for all the foreseeable future. The new Charetty colours: pea green and burnt umber.

He managed, in between vomiting, to improve on his covering, and give himself air. He hoped it wouldn't rain. He felt, in general, gloomy. He wondered if, having failed to catch Andro, the men would come back the same way. Or if, having caught Andro and tortured him, they would certainly come back the same way. He thought not. He thought of Andro these days as someone like Crackbene, or le Grant, whom he trusted to do what was right.

At any rate, Wodman now carried the family silver. The dispatch from the front. The report of all Nicholas had discovered. He hoped to God Andro remembered it. Part of it was simple enough: the probable size of the army at York; the numbers still to arrive at Durham and Alnwick and Berwick. First target: Berwick, employing heavy artillery, and allowing time to warn Albany's friends that he was about to make for the throne. Given enough popular support, they would then invade up the East March, and take the King. Alternative: if disappointed in Albany's friends and threatened by a Scots army, a probable pitched battle at Coldstream, with Norham prepared as a base.

At that point, Andro's reaction had been one of disgusted alarm. He had already expressed himself – they all had – on the subject of Albany's *volte-face* in his attitude to the English. 'So he does plan to usurp the throne, the little bastard. And that's the hell of an army. That's the biggest for decades. What's Edward thinking of?'

'His obituary, some say. There's more.'

'What?'

And so he told him. He remembered the sick look on Andro's face, turned towards him. 'After all that show of patriotism, he's bought himself the throne *by promising Scotland to Edward*?' And after a space he had said, 'Once they know that, no one will follow him.'

He had spoken with satisfaction, as if it hadn't occurred to him that few would follow Albany anyway, except for personal profit, and that these few might not care who was overlord. There had been no time to dwell on that; or on Albany's reasons, or his uncertainties; or what could be done about it. That would have to rest with the small group of dedicated advisers who knew the King and his brother through and through. Later, Andro had asked who else was with Albany and Nicholas had mentioned everyone he had noticed: not the Earl of Douglas; not Holland; but he had seen several Douglases, leaving York, and one of the two Alexander Jardines, who had ridden past him, kicking dirt in his face. For sure, this visit had done Sandy no favours. And he had seen – he thought he had seen – Jamie Boyd.

Andro had expressed disbelief. 'Jamie? The Princess's son? He's barely twelve!'

'Still,' Nicholas said. 'And someone called him Lord Boyd. The old man is dead. It must be Jamie.' Andro looked shocked, but not horrified Nicholas had been horrified, and still was.

In all this, he had made sure of one thing. If Andro got back without him, he was to repeat what he knew to no one except the innermost circle. It was too explosive. It could set off a wave of violence in either direction: a torrent of Anglophile traders with a good personal connection in Leighton Buzzard, or a host of Wallaces led by Blind Harry, baying for his former champion's blood.

Baying. There was none at the moment. Nicholas drowsed, and woke dizzily, and drowsed once again, vaguely aware of what was happening and annoyed by it. Finally he let go and sank into some sort of oblivion.

When he woke, it was quiet; and he felt both better and worse. His eyes had cleared, which was good, and so had most of the nausea; his headache was clangorous but not mind-deadening. He could think. At the same time, pushing his way from the peats, he found himself shivering. Whatever happened, he couldn't stay here for the night. Indeed, there was no point for, by now, Wodman would be dead or far away. He fervently hoped far away, on a fresh horse, and settling down to carry his information on the long, long ride by the route they had already decided, through northern England and up the Till valley to the Tweed, and Scotland, and safety.

There was no reason why Nicholas shouldn't follow him, once he had acquired a horse. No doubt later on he would also be the better of food, but he preferred not to think of that now. Anyway, for God's sake, he was resourceful. If he weren't, he would hardly have survived until now. The sooner he got out, the sooner he'd be back in the game.

The game. Once, it was the term he found reassuring to apply to almost everything that he chose to do: to trade, to war; to the moves and counter-moves, even, for the avoidance of war. But not after Nancy. Not now.

He forgot to be pleased that he had got into and out of York and had escaped both beheading and hanging. He began to fret over what might go wrong in Scotland without him.

In Edinburgh, just before the end of the third week in July, unauthorised news was brought to the King that the English army was fully operational in its camp at Tweedmouth and about to begin a bombardment of Berwick. The same messenger, awed to find himself with the King (he had been let in by mistake, at a shift change) confirmed that the English were led by their King's brother, Richard of Gloucester. He added, carefully, that he was sorry to report that early rumours seemed to be true, and that his grace the Duke of Albany had come from France to join the English attack, and was in the van of the army with Gloucester.

The shouting from the King's chamber brought in his ushers. His ministers of state were haled in thereafter. Within the hour, the proclamation had issued. The incomplete troop now assembling on the Burgh Muir was to march south to fight the Auld Enemy. And James of Scotland would command it himself.

The waiting was over; the period of grace had come to an end. Now they had to know Albany's intentions. Now, Nicholas de Fleury had to be found. A rider was sent, sparing nothing, to Upsettlington, to find and notify Anselm Adorne.

Home, besieged by messengers, only heard about Adorne's mysterious visit after he'd gone. According to a lieutenant from Wedderburn, Lord Cortachy had been conducting an ambush near Upsettlington with a handful of men. Verra secret, it was. A trap for the English, belikes. Now he had left.

Henry had been on patrol several times at Upsettlington. Simon sought him out. 'Did you know this?'

Once, Henry had had only three expressions: bullying, defiant, or sulky. In the last year or two he had acquired one which Simon detested: you could almost call it exasperation. Henry said, 'No, I didn't. No one mentioned it. Anyway, he seems to have gone home.'

'Has he? Because his tents are not there? I'm glad you're sure. I'm not,' Simon said. 'Have his horses gone, can you tell me? Are his tents really packed, or have they just been set up elsewhere? Do you know why I'm asking?'

'No,' said Henry.

Sometimes, he asked to have his face smacked. Simon said, with force, 'Because I can think of two explanations. Adorne has gone to meet de Fleury. Or he's gone to change sides like de Fleury. He's gone to join Gloucester's army.'

'You think so?' said Henry.

'Yes, I think so,' said Simon. 'And I'm going to find out which it is. I'm going to tell Borthwick the whole story, and he can give me a troop. Or if he won't, by God I'll find out for myself.'

Henry didn't argue: at least the Guard had taught him that much. Borthwick, a self-opinionated boor, professed to disbelieve unsigned messages, and poured scorn on the idea that de Fleury or Adorne might be traitors. At first, he forbade Simon to leave. He couldn't stop him, of course. When Simon de St Pol walked out with his son and his bowmen, the captain let him go. In a final, typical jibe, he said he had other things on his mind.

After that, Simon simply rode down to the river at Carham, and then followed it eastwards for seven miles, asking questions. If Adorne had joined Gloucester, he'd be at Berwick. If he'd crossed the river to one of the fortresses, he must have left traces. All the crossings were watched, on both sides.

He passed by the ford that led over to Wark. He examined Coldstream. Then he had his stroke of luck. Two of Borthwick's men came up with a prisoner: an English scout from over the river, where the Tweed was joined by the mouth of the Till.

The Till was a sturdy, small river which carved a long, wilful passage to the frontier, sometimes smiling between sloping banks, sometimes snarling at the foot of a winding ravine. Several keeps guarded its passage. The biggest, by name Castle Heaton, was heavily garrisoned, both to prevent Scottish inroads and to check would-be absconders. The garrison, bleated the scout, was at this moment looking out for a double agent who was on his way to Scotland from York. All the strongholds in the north had been warned.

He did not know any names. He had been given the agent's description: a very large man with two pits in his cheeks, and a Burgundian accent.

Simon de St Pol knew his name.

*

Since the River Till was the place of their rendezvous, Nicholas de Fleury shouldn't have been stunned to find Wodman there. He *was* stunned, but also grateful to see him alive, that went without saying. But he might have been less stunned and more grateful if they hadn't parted over two weeks before, and if Nicholas hadn't been persuading himself forcibly that Wodman was by now home in Edinburgh, and all the information from York safely delivered.

Nicholas, in a thumbed felt hat and cowled tunic, was one of a dust-covered group tramping the rough path that led to the hamlet above Castle Heaton. All of them looked like artisans, and the only one mounted and decently dressed had a set square sticking out of his saddlebag. Nicholas, walking cheerfully at his stirrup, was carrying a sack full of tool-shapes over one shoulder. Half his face was smothered in a bright yellow growth of new beard, and Wodman wouldn't have recognised him if he hadn't turned his head as he passed. Then Nicholas turned it away and walked on, but his smile had broadened.

The encounter was almost as much of a surprise to the Archer, but even more of a relief. He knew what could come of a blow like the one Nicholas had taken. For two weeks, he had thought of little else. And here Nicholas was, the ultimate survivor, large and capable and effortlessly in command of himself and probably everything else – except that he was not about to be understanding. From his point of view, he had risked his life to obtain information which Wodman had failed to deliver.

Wodman watched. At the little inn above the slope to the river, the rider dismounted; someone led off his horse, and the entire group wandered round to the side, where the benches were set out. After a while, Wodman got up and followed them, but to a different part of the yard, where some men he knew were already planted in front of their tankards. They cleared him a seat with a greeting: 'Aye, Fletcher!'

Making arrows was a skill Wodman had that he could take anywhere, especially close to a garrison. Fletchers were not all that common.

He had wondered what Nicholas would do, but he just looked up and sang out the same nickname, 'Fletcher!' Then, waving his mug, he rose and wandered over, as if they knew one another quite well. Nodding to him, he grinned easily round at the company. 'I said to myself, he won't remember Cuddie the Hod, but there, he did. Fletcher, how are ye?' There was no trace of French or Flemish in his voice. He was a hellish good mimic. And what he was doing, of course, authenticated them both. The English were looking for a single, displaced Burgundian whom nobody knew.

Later, alone in his primitive lodging, he got the flaming row he expected; then Nicholas calmed. It was for him that Wodman had gone back, once he had eluded the dogs. Then, finding him gone, he had tried to trace him. After that, it was a story much like that of Nicholas. Horses were not easy to come by. Like Nicholas, he had come most of the way on foot. He had only been there for a few days.

'I might have gone over already,' Nicholas said. He still sounded curt.

'Then you would have carried the message yourself,' Wodman said. 'I took the decision to wait. Gloucester's been sitting opposite Berwick for days. Everyone will know what his strength is by now, and it won't be hard to work out his plans. Your guess about Norham and Coldstream was just a guess.'

'No,' said Nicholas. 'That's why this squad of builders is here. We are to strengthen the bridge, in case they have to bring cannon from Norham.'

'I didn't know that,' Wodman said. He didn't ask how Nicholas had passed himself off as a mason's man. He had worked with Cochrane, and with Fioravanti in Moscow. He probably knew more than his master did.

'No. And what the Council needs to know about Albany isn't a guess either,' Nicholas said. 'Let me alarm you about that as well. We know Albany paid homage to Edward, and promised part of the Lowlands and Berwick, provided Edward puts Albany on the throne. Revolting. Dastardly. But how much does he mean it?'

'You think it's a trick?' Wodman said. He was sceptical. He was avidly fascinated.

Nicholas said, 'In anyone else, it might be. Sandy's mind takes one step at a time. Provided it turns into an easy, popular conquest, he'll let it happen. He'll lose face; he'll lose Berwick; but he may convince himself that the English can never afford to garrison the other lands, and the Borderers will take them back. If Edward dies, the overlordship will die, too, very likely. And meanwhile, Sandy is so well loved compared with James, that he'll be forgiven.'

'He believes that?' Wodman said.

'He wants to. Edward wants to as well. Edward wants, and has got, something on paper that justifies virtually anything he wishes to do, and redeems his prestige as well. But he's kept his fleet in the south, and he's only licensed the army, once they're mustered, for a total of four weeks in the field. That means he expects to win Berwick, for sure. Then Gloucester has to achieve something conclusive that will give him control in four weeks. A national rising for Sandy would do it, forcing the King to stand down, and then proving strong enough in itself to consolidate. The next best thing would be an actual conflict, in which the King is either captured or killed.'

'Will they rise?' Wodman said. He knew why he was being told. Now it really mattered.

'Sandy tells himself yes, but I think almost certainly not, in the numbers he needs. That leaves battle, and on the Border for preference; hence the artillery hereabouts. Otherwise Gloucester has to invade, with lengthening supply lines. The chance of success is much less, and he may have to cut loose and go home, with considerable losses and James still on the throne.'

'And Sandy?' said Wodman. 'Back to England, and wait for another chance?'

'Under a possibly dying King, and after an expensive fiasco? No. This is Sandy's sole opportunity,' Nicholas said. 'And ours. And Gloucester's. That brings us to the third possibility. If there is no rising, and no battle, and no captured King, then Sandy must become the prime mediator. Let him arrange Gloucester's peaceful withdrawal, and let James reinstate him in Scotland.'

Wodman stared at him. He said, 'Would you trust Albany to think of that?'

'I'd trust Gloucester,' Nicholas said.

'I see,' Wodman said.

Before any war, all the possibilities were discussed. Then, like this, they were abruptly reduced, and you knew where you were. And now only one thing mattered: to get the information over the river, and north.

The Archer started to calculate: how to get horses from Home; what route to follow to Edinburgh. Once they crossed the river, it could be done in five hours. He supposed if Adorne had ever managed to come, he would have cleared off from Upsettlington by now. Everyone must think they were dead. He said, 'We can't get out tonight. They had a man captured yesterday over the river, and they've doubled the watch.'

'All right,' said Nicholas. 'So, how?'

It was like a desperate comedy in the end. The Tweed was only a few miles away, and once they crossed it, they were in Scotland. But Castle Heaton was bristling with soldiers, occupying the low rises as lookouts, patrolling the distant steep banks of the Till as it darted headlong below, plummeting between mill-wheels and weirs on its crooked way to the smooth-running Tweed. And on the banks of the broad Tweed itself, the men from each nation were spaced out along either bank. Some were invisible; others were deliberately in view. Periodically one group or another would shout insults.

The bridge the artillery would use was between the Tweed and the castle, and just a mile from the mouth of the Till. Nicholas reported for duty next day with his friend Fletcher as a willing assistant, and helped drive the ox-wains there, with the mattocks and the sand and the limestone. The smell of dung steamed in the air: it had become breathlessly hot, with no wind. The river, dazzling below, looked like Paradise. 'After,' promised Hector the mason, a hard-working man with a kind heart. 'After, if you're good lads, you can strip off and give the lasses a treat.' It led to a lot of badinage, and kept them cheerful for a while.

It was hard work. The bridge was recent, a replacement for an old timber one, and put together in haste until a better could be built. Andro, heaving up buckets of water, could hear the master's diatribes, and Cuddie the Hod intervening and commenting. Nicholas did know a hell of a lot. Gossipy phrases floated down, to do with site-clearance, and quarrying contracts for ashlar. By the time the whistle went for a hunk of bread and a fill from the ale-cask, they were on to types of paving, and the length of the ideal abutment, and how to cut the cost of the iron and lead for the gates. He knew more about mortar, for sure, than Hector did.

It was just bad luck, Wodman thought, with a flash of yearning, that Nicholas wasn't alone, and able to put his expertise to real use. He had a wistful vision of the cannon lumbering over from Norham, and reaching the bridge, and falling clean through it. Then the whistle blew, and it was terrible, beginning again.

They were all bare to the waist, and slick with sweat, and his shoulders were stinging. Once, when the banging stopped, he heard a rumble far off to the south, and prayed it meant rain. He wondered, fuming, what the hell Nicholas was doing; then stopped himself. There was no way they could leave, just at the moment; and it was still only morning. Then there was another crack from the south that was loud enough, this time, to cut through the noise; and if you looked, the horizon was flickering.

After a while, Nicholas left the top of the bridge and came to work with his trowel near to where Wodman was mixing mortar. He made a joke, and then said, 'I'll suggest a splash in the shallow water at the next rest. We'll lose the chance if it rains.'

True. He hadn't thought of it. It was one of their simpler schemes.

Few men could swim at all, never mind underwater the way Nicholas could, taught by an African. And he wasn't so bad himself.

Dinnertime came, and they were indeed permitted to rollick about in the water, which was knee high. Cuddie manufactured a ball, and made up the rules, and they had shrieked themselves hoarse by the time Hector good-naturedly summoned them back. There had been no chance whatever to escape, and there wasn't to be one from that source. When the air cooled and the rain-clouds moved hazily in, Hector looked up at the sky and decreed a return with the wains to the village. If they were to go on, they'd need to build shelters.

Cuddie the Hod was struck by a helpful idea. 'If you'll give us the timbers, Fletcher and me'll put up a shelter, master,' he said.

Chapter 41

And for his kyndnes thocht he erar to de
Than tyne his fallow and he liffand be.

IT WAS THE noise of the water-sport, with its echoing voices, that drew the attention of Simon de St Pol as he lay with his son and two soldiers in the ruins of a hamlet on the English side of the Tweed.

They had floated across in the night, spinning and drifting on a raft strewn with weed, delicately steered by a paddle. Above them, the sky had been deep blue and full of inimical stars, and they had lain side by side, soaked in danger; silent as if about to hook a solitary fish, or kill a listening stag. When, safely arrived, Simon sank down to recline in this haven, he wanted to fling his head back and yelp aloud with relief and delight. Then he turned to his son, and met the twin of his glee in Henry's face. Moved by euphoria, Simon swung a punch and Henry answered it, their two arms aloft, jarring in comradeship, blue eyes ablaze into blue. Then they dropped, and Simon said, smiling, 'I suppose we should get some sleep.'

Just before dawn, they moved quietly to quarter the territory; locate the watchers; and explore the river-bank and the way to the castle. They were in hiding again by the time they heard the rumble of laden wains, and men's voices, and the work began on the bridge. They were strengthening it. Henry said, 'They're going to bring reinforcements from Norham. Artillery, even. We ought to let Borthwick know.'

'We shall,' Simon said. 'As soon as we've dealt with our traitor.'

It was a word he used often, as if Henry might be in danger of forgetting. De Fleury was a spy and a traitor. He had secretly visited the King's rebel brother, and was helping to plan an invasion. And Fate had chosen them to stop him.

Very soon after that, there came the noise, as if children were playing, and Simon sent Henry to look.

Splashing about in the gorge, and laughing like children, was a group of half-naked men playing ball. The man with the ball, clowning, was Nicholas de Fleury. And Andro Wodman was with him.

Henry lay for quite a long time, until the play finished and he saw that the two men belonged to the party of workmen. It was obvious that the builders didn't know who they were. He heard someone use the name Cuddie. It was a northern English version of Cuthbert. De Fleury was wearing a hat, and had let his beard grow, and seemed to have dyed his hair yellow. He was clever.

His father, when he got back, was both eager and captious. 'You should have fetched me! The builders don't know who they are?'

'I'd swear the labourers don't. I don't know about the master mason. And I don't understand. If they're on the English side, why the disguise?'

'To conceal their treachery,' said his father. 'De Fleury isn't supposed to be a double spy. You watch, he and Wodman are not going back to the castle. Unless we stop them, the mason'll try to slip them over the river. Then they'd reappear at the Scots Court as if they had returned by themselves, and no one in Scotland would suspect that they were still collaborating with Albany.'

'Except the person who warned you,' Henry said. 'Whoever it is, why didn't he come forward and help us?'

'Do you want a guess?' his father said. 'Because it's a man who wants de Fleury out of the way, but, knowing the King, doesn't want to be seen bringing him down. Someone close to the King. On the Council even.'

'Or the other Burgundian?' Henry said. 'You thought Adorne was joining de Fleury. Perhaps he's doing the opposite. Perhaps, all this time, he's been laying plans to get rid of him, without taking the blame.'

'Does it matter?' said Simon. 'We don't need any help now. We can capture or kill them, and no one will blame us. On this side of the river. On the English side.'

Henry didn't reply. Of course his father, like the unknown writer, would risk the King's personal displeasure, but he could hardly be punished for it. Grandfather Jordan ought to be pleased. This time, the St Pols weren't pursuing a private vendetta: they were legitimately protecting the realm.

It came to Henry, suddenly, that he knew who had sent that mysterious message; had set them the task that had brought them both here. It was his grandfather. His grandfather was testing them both.

A cloud lifted, and for the first time he felt calm, and confident, and glad to be here. He settled down by his father, and prepared to show his grandfather what he could do.

It wasn't simple. De Fleury and his companion were never alone. There was no way of taking them, and no safe way of killing them either, without being at once hunted down. Then as time wore on, the sky clouded, and the work on the bridge came to a halt.

'They're going back to the hamlet! Mary Mother, we'll lose them!'

'No,' said Henry, whose blue eyes were sharp. 'De Fleury and Wodman are staying. It's happened. We've got them, as soon as they're alone.'

Once, he had stood over Nicholas de Fleury; and had been invited to kill him. Except for an interruption, he would have done so. Some men knew when their time had come. Some men, without fathers or grandfathers, knew when their lives were no longer worth living. Henry, on the other hand, was a St Pol; and true to his line.

Sawing wood in the rain, Wodman was arguing in a murmur. The builders had gone. He and Nicholas were alone on the bank. Unfortunately, they were not entirely alone. At either end of the bridge paced its usual two duty sentries, returned now that the structure was vacant. To protect the pair of craftsmen still present, two more archers had come, perched on top of the carpenter's wagon of mallets and mattocks and timber and felt, and presently helping to unload it. When the wagon left they remained, sitting on a bit of tarred cloth, continuing a shouted conversation with the men on the bridge and the builders. One of them had a flask. They were there simply as a normal precaution, and it meant that there were only four Englishmen to dispose of instead of a squad. It was ungrateful, really ungrateful to complain. After thought, they had let the wagon go back. If it didn't, someone would come enquiring. They got on, cantankerously, with building the shelter.

Wodman, busily working and talking at once, was running through a number of excellent schemes. The common theme was that they should invisibly murder the pair on the ground, and purloin their bows to shoot the men on the bridge. Nicholas objected to this, on the premise that the bridge could be seen from upriver. Wodman pointed out that at the rate the river was rising, everyone would be running back to the castle and hamlet.

This was possible. A few minutes before, a silent wave had appeared round a corner and, coursing down, had swept past with a rumbling clatter, careering north to debouch into the Tweed. Another had followed. Here, the rain was at present haphazard. Somewhere far up the Till, the purple thunder-clouds had already exploded. It was unlikely that Hector would send his men back today. Bantering aloud, and arguing under their breath, Nicholas and Wodman agreed at least one thing. The shelter was so aligned that anyone inside its primitive poles and tarred felt would be unseen from the bridge or the opposite bank.

Desperate though it all was, the daft side, as ever, threatened to destabilise Nicholas. Shouting, murmuring, singing, thinking, calculating, hammering, passing the flask, he was working at full pitch, exuberantly, the way he and Kathi used sometimes to vie with one another in Scotland, in Iceland. Andro, wearing his oyster-seller grin, could just about match him. All they had to do, really, was get the shelter half up, and get the two bowmen into it. They had knives. The wetter it got, the easier it would be.

It was like that, edging up to success, when someone screamed. When one of the men on the bridge screamed, flung up his arms, and fell headlong down into the rising water, which began to bear him away.

Nicholas stopped. Beside him, Andro jerked and then also stopped, held ferociously by Nicholas's free hand. Beyond them both, the English archers sprang to their feet and started to run, appalled, to the river. The remaining sentry stood as if petrified. Then he turned, and began to run for his life to the opposite end of the bridge.

He might have escaped had the gate not been shut. They saw him reach it, and fling his arms over it, and then slide like a cloth to the ground. An arrow, fine as a toothpick, stuck out of his back.

Wodman said, 'Holy Mother.' It sounded entirely reverent, and his expression was awed. He said, '*Adorne?*'

Upriver, a bugle rang out above the thud of the water in a long, warning flourish that was repeated, closer at hand. It was too timely to be a coincidence. Nicholas had been right in his guess. The bridge had been under surveillance from the opposite side.

'Maybe Adorne,' Nicholas said. 'Anyway, someone who's going to be in trouble unless we do something, fast. Let's pick up those bows.' He began to run, Andro following, pelting down the side of the stream after the archers.

One was already dead when they came upon him, tumbled down the steep bank and half in the grip of the waters, his bow snapped and jerking. The next moment, a great bough swirled past, and took him into its tangle. On either side, the river was scouring high through the bushes, its lively roar melisma and counterpoint to the pedestrian thud of the thunder. The rain, hitherto desultory, began to drum down. The remaining archer turned and saw them, and whispered, 'Go back! You'll get killed. There are still some of them about.' He was crouching, his bow strung, below the lip of the bank and his face, glistening with water, had lost all the flush of his drink.

Nicholas descended beside him. 'How many? Where?'

'On this bank. They were shooting from four different places.'

'So maybe there are only four of them,' Nicholas said. He saw Wodman lift up his knife.

'Two, then,' said the archer. 'Davie got one. And the one that killed Davie, I got.' Then his eyes fixed in his face, for Wodman had thrust his knife home.

Nicholas himself might not have killed; but Wodman was not sentimental. They had to escape. And if they could do it still incognito, all the better.

The man slumped, and Nicholas seized his quiver and unclenched his hand from his longbow while Andro reclaimed his knife. Looking up through the fringe of rain from his hat, Nicholas tried, against the vibration and roar of the water, to listen for trampling feet on the bank, or any cries of pursuit from behind. High above him, there was a double flash, and the roof of the sky suddenly cracked in several places, producing a series of deafening reports. He was clinging to the slope of the bank, Andro behind him, when the river surged suddenly up to his waist and the archer's body had gone, leaving him to scramble up the bank as the water clawed at the sodden hide of his tunic.

He and Andro arrived at the edge of the ravine together, rashly confident of a welcome from whoever was there. With any luck, it would be the party which had killed the four guards, on the way to rescuing them both. Even if it wasn't, and some soldiers from Heaton appeared, they had no reason to harm two of Hector's men, fleeing unknown attackers. And if, best of all, the rescue party was there, and they all got away before the Heaton men came, the Heaton men would assume that their two builders had died with the guards, and all four had been snatched by the river.

It was with reasonable confidence, therefore, that Nicholas clawed his way in the drumming rain to the edge of the bank of the Till and looked about him at a landscape that at first appeared to be empty.

Behind, from the direction of Heaton, nothing moved but the river.

In front, it seemed at first to be the same. Then, far ahead, there was a glint between trees, followed by a deadly whicker close to his face.

Nicholas heard the arrow arrive, and the thud of its impact. At first, he did not know where he had been hit. Then he realised, from the gasp beside him, that it was Andro who had been struck, and who was lurching forward beside him in a welter of blood.

He thought at first that Wodman was dying. Catching him; rolling with him back over the edge of the bank, Nicholas determined that the wound was bad, but could wait for attention. It would have to. He took his bow and lifted himself along the lip of the bank, until he could see what was happening.

Four English guards had been killed. No one but Scots would do that. If they were now trying to kill fellow Scots, it was simply because they weren't Adorne's men, and didn't know who Andro was.

It was an interesting dilemma. If he stood up, they'd kill him before he had a chance to explain. If he did nothing, the Heaton men would arrive, bent on revenge for the four men they had lost. The Scots would die, and he and Andro would lose their chance of escape.

Andro, who still had his wits, was slowly binding a kerchief round his thigh, where the arrow had struck. The cloth became instantly red. Nicholas said, 'Could you swim?'

Wodman didn't even look up. Beneath the broken nose was a sketch of a grin. 'Not in that river,' he said.

'Nor any other,' someone observed. An elegant man, it proved to be, standing just within earshot on the same side of the ravine, with a bow in his hand. He wore no armour, but a plated helm on his head, the glint of which had caught the light when he shot and injured Wodman. Even though the thick, fair hair was concealed, there was no mistaking the carriage, or the man.

Simon de St Pol.

Four of them, the archer had said. Of whom the archer himself and his friend had killed two.

Nicholas closed his eyes, and then opened them slowly. Wodman said, 'He is there, Nicol. Henry is there.'

And so he was, stepping out to stand beside Simon, young and lissom and stern. You could see him draw breath; and it was as if he had made himself speak. 'We can't let you escape. You're a traitor.'

Simon turned his head to look, with resignation, at the speaker. 'You are proposing to talk to him, Henry?'

Nicholas said, 'We are your prisoners. We are not traitors, but that can be proved later. Take us with you. Bind our hands. We can't harm you.'

Simon laughed. 'You have a bow in your hands.'

'No,' said Nicholas; and, lifting it, turned to the river. Then he stopped, looking at Andro.

Andro said, 'Throw it.' Above the flattened nose and drawn skin, his eyes were open and clear. So Nicholas did.

There were boulders leaping and wheeling now in the torrent, and parts of whole trees. The bow vanished at once. The roar was as loud as the sound of their voices. Nicholas raised his, calling to Simon, but kept it even and calm.

'Let us walk towards you. There isn't much time. The Castle Heaton soldiers are coming.'

'Really?' said Simon. He sounded entertained. 'You must be terrified. If you are spying for Scotland, they'll kill you. Or will they? We saw you chatting. We saw you pretending to work. I don't think anyone from the castle is coming. Four men have been killed: who will notice, downriver like this, in this weather? Who will trouble when two more disappear? I think we can take all the time in the world.'

Nicholas said, 'No. They are coming.' His eyes were holding Henry's.

Simon said, in the same mirthful voice, 'Then there isn't time to come and tie you up, is there? You must, alas, be dealt with forthwith. Don't you wish, Claes, Claikine, young bastard, that you had stayed in your dyeyard? You would be safe now, if you had.'

Nicholas, motionless, answered; speaking to Henry with his eyes and his voice. He said, 'I am where I have chosen to be. I only wish we had longer.'

After a moment, he said, 'You are right. There isn't time; kill me. But let Andro go; your father would want it. And save yourselves.'

'We have your permission?' said Simon. 'How kind.' The bow in his hands was ready strung. He lifted and pointed it, fussily. 'And really, I don't think we wish to preserve witnesses. You have both died. We need not tell everyone how.'

Nicholas heard him, but let the words pass. He made himself look at Simon: at the comely, petulant face, no longer young, bearing even now, in his instant of triumph, the blight of dissatisfaction, the shallow vehemence founded on bitterness. He wished he could convey, in these closing moments, something of what he himself felt. *My father, my father . . .*

If you had taken me in, I would have come: I would have stayed bound to the furrow, and you might have found something in me that you were not ashamed of. We could have lived side by side . . . *neither for favour or reward, hate or love, but for the truth.* We could have found happiness.

But if that had transpired, what of Henry? If there had been no apprentice, Henry would not have been born.

He was thinking of his two sons, and did not watch as Simon's hand drew back, and steadied. So dissimilar, Henry and Jordan, and yet, in a shadowy way, there was something innate that they shared. He had imagined once or twice recently that a tolerance, even a friendship, was forming between them. If that happened, it might make this worth while.

Then he thought of Jodi, and the others he loved.

He had closed his eyes. He didn't hear, above the roar of the river, the Heaton bowmen streaming down from the bridge. He didn't see them slacken, drawing their bows, as they saw what was happening. He didn't see the arrows spurt, or the one that struck home. He only heard Henry's cry, and, opening his eyes, perceived the white face of his son, printed with amazement, at first looking at nothing. Then the blue gaze turned, passing over Nicholas de Fleury and coming to rest, bewildered and sick, upon Simon, as a child's eyes would dwell on its father. For a moment, nothing moved. Then Henry, shuddering, descended first to his knees and then, quicker and quicker, tumbled down the ravine and into the river.

Nicholas saw it, and leaped. The arm that held him back was inhuman: hard across his stomach; so unyielding that its force made him retch. And a voice – Wodman's – said, 'No. *Simon must do it.*'

Even Wodman's arm couldn't hold him for ever. Nicholas tore free, and jumped. But during that second's delay Simon de St Pol, with furious courage, had plunged to follow his boy down the slope at his feet, leaping and sliding until he, too, was seized by the torrent and spewed into the landslide of water that was the murderous flood of the Till.

Neither of them had the skills Nicholas had. No one had taught Henry to dart and swerve between rocks like a salmon; to duck and dive below floating obstacles; to ride the spume of a weir. No one had taught Simon either.

It would never enter Simon's head that what he was doing was useless. His son had made a blunder. He, Simon, would correct it. Had he been able to look, far behind, at the place where Nicholas plunged in to follow them, he would have been filled with cruel amusement. Wodman had been right, in his wisdom. The success . . . or the failure . . . had to be Simon's. To Simon, anything else would be intolerable. Anything else, good or bad, would leave Nicholas facing a murderous and illogical venom, worse than death.

That day no swimmer, hurled from rock to rock of the Till, could be sure of surviving. Luck came into it, as well as skill, and concentration, and the kind of blank stoicism that disregards shock and pain and fatigue, and thinks of nothing but what must be done. Sometimes, far ahead, Nicholas would glimpse the bared, darkened hair of the man who had never wanted him. Beyond that, and much less often, he witnessed the brighter head of his son. It lurched and soared with the billowing water, and Nicholas never saw a raised arm, or even the profile of a cheek with one dimple. That was when, deep within him, his heart started to fail.

But he swam, for as long as he could, and for as long, as it turned out, as was needed.

Andro Wodman, one-time member of the King of France's bodyguard of Scots Archers, one-time Conservator of Scots Privileges in Bruges, did not resist when he was found in the mud where he had dragged himself, under the overhang of the embankment of the Till. He had lain there for a long time, drained of blood and immobile, and even now was only half conscious. Then someone was holding him and calling his name. He thought it must be one of the English.

Then he realised that he was now on top of the gorge, not within it, and that the rain had stopped, and that there were no English masons or soldiers in sight. And that the man holding him was Anselm Adorne, in dark riding clothes. Within a close leather helm, his face was harshly indented and stern. He said, 'You're safe. The soldiers found no survivors, and left.'

Wodman lay, looking up. Other men of Cortachy's had arrived and were kneeling about him. So they had stayed at Upsettlington. Mildly indignant, Wodman reviewed the recent past, which he remembered quite clearly up to the point where they were repairing the bridge. He said, 'You took your time. Have you seen Nicholas?' He thought, with satisfaction, of the language Nicholas had probably used.

Adorne said, 'No.' He hesitated, and then said, 'Where is he? Do you know, Andro?'

Andro lay, looking surprised. He cast his mind back. Clearly, something had happened that he should have remembered.

Then he stopped breathing, for he had remembered.

Adorne said, 'I think I can guess. But tell me.'

Almost before he had got to the end they had scattered, running down the bankside, slinging rope, seizing branches for scouring-poles. The river was still brawling, and laden with rubbish, but the level had sunk.

Adorne said, 'We've searched the near water already, but not so far as the mouth. You say the boy was injured, and St Pol was not a strong swimmer? But Nicholas, following, was still alive when you saw him?'

'He couldn't have caught them,' Wodman said. He forced himself to sit up. It made him feel dizzy. 'Unless one of them was thrown out, or smashed and held by a rock. Nicholas had started from a few yards behind them, and they were all being swept along at the same rate. You couldn't swim. You could only ride the spate like a – like a –'

'Like a demon, perhaps,' Adorne said. 'Nicol can be one, at times. Don't give up hope. I haven't.' It was the first time he had ever shortened the name.

Then someone shouted, circumspectly, from far down the river.

In a flood such as that, swimmers of indifferent strength and ability would be carried at the same speed. Only the strong could diverge from the race, winning themselves the respite of calmer waters, or even forcing an exit to shore, if they were ingenious.

Several times, in his headlong career downriver that day, Nicholas could have abandoned his battle, and snatched at a chance to batter his way from the grasp of the water. He stayed, not because he could travel faster than the two men before him, but because luck sometimes took a hand in the game. A funnelling log could create its own unexpected diversion; a careering boulder could kill, but could also break the force of the flow. Henry might find some such haven, and Simon might join him there. He might come across both, idling and hapless, but requiring only his strength to draw them over to safety. He tried not to think of the cost: the broken bones, the crushed limbs, the dismembering gashes that they might have suffered by then, impaled upon the spears of snapped trees underwater. It was taking all that he knew to keep his own battered body intact, and fit for its purpose. But he persisted in hope.

He found no friendly backwaters, and they did not wait for him. Instead, through the leaden gloom and the rain, there rose behind him a pillar of water higher than any before, which arched its glossy neck and crashed down in foam at his back, together with all it contained. It hurled him forward, and he hit rock after rock and went under. Rising, retching and coughing, once more, he saw the whitened water travelling onwards with its own grinding roar. The boom of it was like the boom of taut sails in a gale. But this ship was without crew and without rudder.

He sank again, and hit his last rock. He didn't know, lurching backwards, that the afterwave was about to pick him up and throw him, half conscious, into just such a shallow lade as he had imagined. He lay there, half on silt, half in water. When he stirred, not long after, it was to find the rain had stopped; the water had loosened its grip; and the level was lower. Only the boughs of trees, high on the bank, showed where the last block of water had passed.

He did not think he could move, but he did; fanning into the water until the stream received him again, and he swam. He was close to the confluence when his gorged eyes perceived the cradle of boughs that had been cast up on the slope of one bank, and settled there, half out of the water.

Someone was sleeping there, lifted into it perhaps by a wave. Then he saw that there was not one person, but two.

It took a long time to reach them. He would think he had progressed; and then a surge would buffet his shoulders and snatch at his limbs and the nest would recede, so that he had to try all over again. When he touched the embankment, he could hardly climb to the ledge, and grasped at bushes as he made his way over and knelt. But by then, he knew what he would see.

Both men were fair, but he thought that nothing in life could ever approach the matchless purity of the young face, its fine bones upturned to the sky, the heavy lids closed, the soft lips parted a little, as if desiring to speak.

Simon lay on his breast, as he must have arrived, lifting himself with the last of his strength to gather the boy safe from harm; and then sinking down, his eyes open, to weep.

His eyes were still open, blue in the face which, at the last, had lost all its petulance. And Henry's gilt hair, loosed and fallen over his shoulder, was interwoven and mixed with the fair hair of Simon de St Pol. Both were dead.

Anselm Adorne climbed down before anyone else, and knelt in silence, his hand on Nicholas's shoulder. Then, having permission, he signed for his men. He and his captain drew Simon from the place of his finest passage of arms: the act of chivalry completed not for his own glory, but for the sake of another. But only Nicholas laid tender hands on the boy, and lifted him, and carried him uphill himself, aided by steadying arms. At the top, there were litters.

Andro lay in one, his eyes closed, but breathing still. Two more, drawn well aside, received those who were not. Men brought cloaks to cover the crushed and torn bodies. You could tell how beautiful they had been. Fair; so fair.

Nicholas's own clothing, too, was in shreds. As he knelt back from the pallet, he felt Adorne's hands on his shoulders, moving lightly to explore the bloody hacks and gouges and misshapen contusions that he could see but not, as yet, feel. Then someone, coming with cloths, began swiftly to tend them, and Adorne, who had gone to give orders, reappeared with a man at his side. 'Nicol, this is my courier. Tell us everything you know.'

Pain returned while he was speaking, and he began to shiver, and they brought him something to drink, and a rough shirt, and a cloak. He went through what he had to say twice, and then everyone vanished, and he was alone. The courier would leave now. The rest of them had gone to uncover the boats and prepare to cross while the Tweed was still running high, and the Till's flooding upstream held the soldiers' attention. Once across, Nicholas would be given means to take him to Kelso where, with fitting reverence, the crypt of the Abbey would receive Simon and Henry de St Pol for the interim, and where he could stay, if he wished. It was only an hour's ride away.

Adorne would not be with him. Adorne was to follow his courier north, taking Andro, for there were twenty thousand enemies at the door, and the King's brother leading them. Nicholas, said Adorne, had done enough.

Adorne would not greatly mourn Simon, who had been cavalier with his own son, and whose weaknesses he despised. Equally, he had had small time for Henry's undisciplined wielding of steel, although he had observed, perhaps, Nicholas's forbearance. Adorne's compassion was for Nicholas, and was rooted in those first days in Bruges when – to general derision – Nicholas had not only claimed the name of St Pol, but appeared to believe in the claim. Adorne had always been a humane judge. However baseless the contention, he was honouring it. For – he would argue – if Nicholas held it to be true, he was suffering today the loss of a father in Simon, and a half-brother and nephew in Henry.

He did not know more than that.

To an outsider, Nicholas had little cause to mourn Simon, a man who had shown him nothing but violence; who had stabbed and hounded him as a boy; who had, fatally, sent a man to oppose him in Trebizond; who had first sided with Gelis in her misery and then, persecuting her and Jodi, had come near to causing their deaths. Who had found it easy to blame Nicholas for the death of Lucia, Simon's sister, and had done his best to kill him just before, in an agonising fight stopped by

Adorne. Who had hoped to see Nicholas die in Madeira, and had taught Henry then, and ever after, to hate and despise him. So that Henry, too, over and over, had tried to cause harm to Nicholas, and to Jodi his cousin.

So an outsider would say. But a son would try – had always tried – to understand Simon, a man of divine looks and all the physical attributes of knighthood, whose rearing had been blighted by the lazarhouse that was his home; by his hated, too-early marriage; and, above all, by the brilliant, absent, acerbic father who mocked his intellectual short-comings and dispatched him rejected to Scotland, away from the golden arena of France.

And a father would feel love and pride and agonising pity for Henry, so alone and afraid, and beyond all but the most tentative touch of the lunatic happiness: the stupid, profligate de Fleury happiness that might have been his if he, Nicholas, had had the imagination to step out of his role and care for Katelina, study her, strive to understand her as he had learned to do, finally, with Gelis.

He had given Katelina happiness, too, in the end. Then she had died. *I leave you my soul and my son.*

He had tried. Because of this implacable feud, his path and Henry's had lain mostly apart. When they met, Nicholas had protected him as best he could, and tried to guide him a little, and staked his own life, as was only fair, in the process. It had not been sufficient. Henry would have been better with a father wiser than Nicholas, or more ruthless. The truth was that no rescue was possible while Simon lived, and his father. From these two, loved and hated and feared, Henry derived his coherent being: they represented all that he was, all he wanted to be. Subtracted from the St Pols, Henry would have found no highway to happiness. He would have ceased to exist.

He had ceased to exist.

On the pallet, his face was uncovered. Now, the features were stern: set in the timeless disdain of the dead. Before, the softness had said something different. Perhaps, with the last flicker of life, the boy had felt the touch of Simon's gathering arms, and had seen the face of his father, come for him.

The storm broke for Nicholas then. The black pillar of grief with its debris crashed upon him unawares, overwhelming in its ferocity; worse than the sorrow for his people at Nancy, for Godscalc or even for Umar and Marian; Felix; Zacco . . . reaching back beyond that, to a bottomless misery he could not remember; beating him down as he crouched. He wanted to scream. He could not keep silent.

Anselm Adorne, hearing, set his lips but did not come near. Andro Wodman, forced awake, clenched his eyes to shut out the anguish.

On the same day, Sunday, the twenty-first of July, 1482, James, King of Scotland, was riding south at the head of an army on his way to the Tweed, to confront the far greater army of Gloucester. He intended to save his proud town of Berwick. He was also responding, as royalty should, to the perfidy of Sandy his brother, who had joined the English he once claimed to loathe, and was leading them, insolently, cynically, against his own King.

On James's cheek was the red flush of his family; and behind him trod the files of yoked oxen dragging his guns, commanded by a bright-eyed Tam Cochrane, full of masonic fervour and deaf to the cries of his friends.

Towards the south, it seemed to be raining.

Chapter 42

A man in yr suld no pvnicioun mak,
For dreid that he exceid and tak a lak.

THE HEAVY RAIN dashed into Edinburgh that evening, pelting upon Adorne's courier as he raced with his dispatch to the Castle. He delivered it to Chancellor Avandale and the King's uncle Atholl, who was now Governor of the Castle and all it contained: its armoury and its seals; its charter-house and its treasure; its wells of sweet water and its cellars of ceiling-high stores; its defensible walls reverberating to the roar of the livestock within. This was according to plan. Immediately the King took the field, his officers of state were to disperse: some to spread about the Castle and burgh; some to accompany the King.

Indeed, the courier's first port of call on this journey had not been the Castle. An able man of Adorne's personal household, he had already been stopped, two hours south of Edinburgh, by the vanguard of the royal army, on its way to meet more troops at Lauder. The King was not yet with them, he was happy to find, so that he delivered his message, in full, to the Earls of Argyll and Huntly, with all the military detail he had memorised. He had Lord Cortachy's leave. Lord Cortachy had instructed him to convey his message to the King's statesmen and his commanders, but, under pain of death, not to the King.

He had also been asked, on a lesser matter, to say nothing yet of the death of St Pol and his son. It was of minor importance, except to the family, and Adorne had wished, humanely, to tell Kilmirren tomorrow himself. The courier respected his master, and said nothing of it, even when seized outside Huntly's pavilion by three Floory Land men – the priest, the doctor, the gunner – desperate for news of Nicol de Fleury. He told enough to set their minds at rest – that the man was safely back from his mission in England, but had elected to stay, reason unknown, on the Border. Master Wodman had taken a wound, but should be back in Edinburgh with Lord Cortachy in the morning.

The three had been silent at first and then, he suspected, had made straight for their men and the ale in a way that their leaders would not have approved. Or perhaps, after what he had told them, Argyll and Huntly would concede that there was something to celebrate.

They were pleased at the Castle as well, although they interrogated him for a long time, and he was glad when they let him retire, leaving the Chancellor and Archbishop Scheves and Master Whitelaw and the Abbot of Holyrood to assimilate what he had told them. He was particularly glad not to be at Lauder when the King finally got there. It hadn't looked much of an army to him: more of an arbitrary medley of companies from different parts of the country, all with different masters and different objectives and different grievances. They said, and he knew it for true, that you could hardly hold a burgh court in Scotland without a fight breaking out over something. They would never get near the enemy, that little lot. They'd be too busy fighting each other.

A few doors away, Avandale's voice had become very level. 'Darnley isn't there. The King is almost at Lauder and Darnley hasn't arrived. What has happened? They had enough warning?'

'Rain,' said the Archbishop. 'They have to come from Lochmaben. It'll slow everything down. Gloucester too. And the guns.'

Whitelaw grunted. There was nothing to say about the guns that had not already been said. The great ordnance, thank God, was still in the Castle. But despite all they could do, Cochrane had persuaded Cathcart and the rest to take the medium artillery with them. He had designed the carriages, and fashioned the balls, and planned the trajectories, just as he had constructed the defences of Berwick. Whatever anyone said, he was going to put his work to the proof. He was going to save Berwick for the King.

The fight over the guns had been lost. As a result, their artillery was exposed in the field, instead of where it would be needed. Darnley's absence posited an even greater disaster. The King was marching to war with a quarrelsome, incomplete army, and nothing between him and annihilation but the golden tongue of Argyll, the broad-spoken persuasion of Huntly, the short admonitions of Buchan his uncle, and

James's own understanding, if it ever dawned, of the odds now against him.

They had always known that he would hurl himself south without thinking. Given time, he would sometimes reconsider. It was thanks, one supposed, to the slowness of the guns that he had progressed initially no further than Soutra. By now, crawling to Lauder, he would be aware of the power of the English army and the sparsity of his own. And Argyll, fortified by the news from Cortachy's courier, could give him an honourable reason for retiring. Sandy was not the traitor he seemed. In return for little more than free reinstatement Sandy would abandon the English and come back to his brother. He had said so to de Fleury in York. He had written it down.

It might be enough. Taking counsel; setting his mind to what he was being told, James might well, at his best, take the responsible action of stopping the march and electing to return to his position of strength, there to negotiate. It was what they had hoped, even before de Fleury had supplied concrete evidence that it was possible. But since a nation's security cannot depend entirely on chance, the King's ministers had made a further provision, these many weeks past. If the King marched, and if the English attacked on the east, the Warden of the West March would bring his men to join the King's host. And if, having joined him, the Lord Darnley found the King's position untenable, and the King deaf to the advice of his officials, he would return him to Edinburgh by force.

John Stewart of Darnley had agreed. He had undertaken to perform, if necessary, what was an act of high treason because he, too, was a Stewart; second cousin to both King James and Avandale; kinsman to the three royal uncles; claimant to Lennox and grandson of the first seigneur of Aubigny. Darnley would bring with him men from the greatest families of Lennox and Ayrshire and Renfrewshire. Afterwards, he and they would be sure of indemnity.

But if he did not come, who would stop the King?

'Where is de Fleury?' said Whitelaw. 'Where is Adorne?'

'You heard the courier,' Avandale said. 'Adorne will be here tomorrow; de Fleury cannot be long delayed. Their usefulness, we agreed long ago, lies in Nicol's relations with Albany, and Adorne's with the King. This still obtains, whatever happened in York. We do not wish the Burgundians to play any part in removing the King into custody. They know this.'

'If de Fleury has disappeared, it hardly matters,' the Secretary said. 'So who will stop the King? You are confident that somebody will?'

'I shall make sure that they do,' Avandale said. 'A little more rain, Will, would help, if you are praying. A thunderstorm, even. Let's make it unpleasant for Dickon and Harry Percy and all those brave Englishmen crossing the Tweed. Come.' He slapped his hands on the board and stood up. 'Let's go to it. If we can't meddle ourselves, we can send someone who will. Archie, you spoke of de Fleury? Has anyone told his wife that he's safe?'

The Secretary got up, removing his spectacles. 'Adorne is coming tomorrow.'

'Of course. But he has achieved prodigies, Nicol, and has been lost to his folk for a month. Someone should tell them tonight.'

A chaplain went, braving the rain, and paralysed the de Fleury household by chapping insistently on the front door at midnight. When the door finally opened on a firm, compact man with a stick, the chaplain in turn was alarmed. Then the man, a superior servant called Lowrie, fetched his mistress, and the chaplain received his reward in Gascon wine and raisins (great grape, not currants), and a comfortable chair, and the anxious services of a tall, dimpled child with courtly manners, who put his arm round his smiling lady mother, and brought her a kerchief when her tears trickled into her smile.

Early next morning, forcing her way down the sluicing gutters to Kathi's house, Gelis presented her bulletin: Kathi's uncle was well, and would be back by late morning; Nicholas was safely in Scotland but still in the south; Andro Wodman was hurt and would be brought to the Floory Land by Adorne's men.

During all this recital, Kathi, sitting firmly by Robin, had gone very pale and then flushed. 'Damn you,' she said.

'I know,' Gelis had replied, with a scowl. Robin had given a laugh.

Jordan, who had come with his mother, looked surprised. Margaret was not there. Everyone younger than himself had been bundled off to their homes in the country, along with their valuables. Those who didn't have homes in the country sent their children to friends and dug holes for their silver. Some got permission to store their goods in the Castle, or one of the other stone towers. Robin was here because people thought him a cripple, when he was as capable as Jordan's father, or nearly.

Robin's wife said, 'I'll go across and prepare Saunders's household. Perhaps they'll let us have Dr Andreas from the Castle. Uncle will have to go there first.'

The demoiselle's brother was at Linlithgow. Dr Tobie was with the King. Jordan had wanted to march with the King, but he had promised his father to stay. He had been taught how to fight. Robin had trained him, and his friends. If the English army marched into Edinburgh, the militia would stop them. Jordan and his friends were in the militia. Rankin and Hob were still babies.

While the women talked, Jordan stayed with Robin. He wished to ask about hackbuts. Sometimes Robin's attention wandered, as it did when he was tired.

Andro Wodman arrived just before midday, brought to the Floory Land by one of Adorne's men, who immediately left. There being a shortage of fully grown men, Jordan crossed the road to help his mother and the demoiselle Kathi, who were putting Master Wodman to bed. Lord Cortachy had gone straight to the Castle, but was supposed to come soon, with the doctor.

Master Wodman had been hurt in the thigh, and was feverish. He kept trying to talk. He had grown a black beard, which made his squashed nose look worse, and his cheek-bones were red. He had saved Jordan's life once. He was the best man Jordan had ever seen with a bow, apart from his father and Robin. When he did manage to speak, it was to say what they already knew: that Jordan's father and the demoiselle's uncle were safe. He added that Jordan's father had been to York and back, and had spoken to the Duke of Albany and the Duke of Gloucester, and had found out what they were likely to do. It would be of great help to the kingdom, and Jordan could be proud of what he had done.

The demoiselle Kathi was sitting beside Master Wodman's bed, wiping his face. She said, 'You went with him too, and helped him to get out. That was pretty useful as well. I'm glad it was worth it.'

She was smiling, but not with her eyes. Master Wodman wasn't smiling: he was looking up at Jordan's mother with lines like bricks on his brow. Jordan's mother said, 'But there was a price to pay, Andro? You were wounded, and Nicholas hasn't come north?'

'He had something to do,' Master Wodman said. Then he suddenly shifted, and swore, and took Jordan's mother by the wrist so hard that she slipped from the bed quietly and knelt, her wrist still in his hand, looking down at him. She had beautiful hair.

Master Wodman said, 'You'll hear when Adorne comes. He wants to tell Kilmirren himself. Simon and the young lad – Simon and Henry are dead.'

Jordan frowned. His cousin Henry had gone to war with his father, as Jordan would have done, had his father been here. His cousin Henry's campaigns had always seemed rather grim, but he had never been wounded. His cousin Henry had bullied him once, but not now. Henry had belonged to the Royal Guard. He jousted. He sailed. Jordan said, 'Forgive me sir, but are you sure?' His mother looked at him.

So did Master Wodman. He released his mother's hand just as suddenly, and then gazed at her, and at the demoiselle, taking his time. Then he said, 'Forgive me. It's true, but that was no way to tell you. What happened was . . . There was a skirmish. Simon and the boy had come down to the Tweed to – to –'

'To scout,' Jordan's mother said. Her voice was quiet, the way it was when she was slowly tracing something wrong in the counting-house.

'To scout,' Master Wodman said. 'They had followed some rumour . . . They happened upon us just as we were escaping. The English shot Henry.'

'And wounded you,' the demoiselle said. The cloth in her grip was oozing water.

'And me. The river was flooding. The boy fell from the bank. His father drowned trying to save him.'

'Simon drowned?' It was his mother.

'Nicholas found them together. They were dead. He nearly lost his own life, swimming after. Simon did lose his life. He was brave.'

'And Nicholas?' his mother said. Transfixed with horror, Jordan hardly noticed what a long gap there had been.

'At the Abbey in Kelso. He left us to take the two coffins there. We don't know what he will do. Adorne said he must decide for himself.'

'He would be distressed,' Jordan's mother said. It was an odd, unmanly thing to impute to his father. His father wouldn't be upset over Simon, who had made such a fool of himself in that fight with the puddings. Jordan was distressed over Henry, but Henry was his cousin. Had been his cousin. And now he was suddenly dead, like Raffo, and Captain Astorre.

As it happened, Master Wodman didn't answer. The demoiselle, maybe thinking as Jordan did, abruptly said, 'Never mind. We mustn't tire you. Gelis, I think Robin ought to hear about this. Do you think Jordan might go and tell him? He and Robin understand one another very well. Jordan? Would you?'

Leaving, he tried not to show his relief. He blew his nose, crossing the road, and prepared what he was going to say. He thought again of the pudding fight, and unexpectedly remembered Simon's big sword, the one he had never been permitted to use. Now it was really his. He felt pleased, then ashamed.

He spent some time with Robin, and answered the door when Master Julius called to speak to the demoiselle. Jordan explained she was with Master Wodman and why, and asked him in, but he was in a hurry. Jordan watched him go, and returned to what he had been doing. Julius knew the St Pols. Jordan liked Julius. If his father was really upset, perhaps Julius could help him.

Across the road, Andro Wodman was sleeping. He had talked erratically for some time, relating the truth that he had kept from the boy, but would not withhold from Nicholas's wife, and Adorne's niece. Simon had gone to kill Nicholas. A malicious rumour had sent him – an anonymous letter, some said – but he would have seized any excuse. It had not only robbed him of life, but the lad had died too, believing the man they pursued was a traitor. And so the wilful feud had come to an apogee, with none but Nicholas and the old man still on the board, far apart, solitary: Nicholas tending his dead, and the old man, all unawares, about to learn that the house of St Pol was now finished.

How distressed would he be? How distressed had Nicholas been?

Andro knew. 'I have never before,' Wodman had said, 'heard a man's heart break with pity like that; and I hope I never have to again.'

Gelis had said in her low, contained voice, 'I hate Simon. I hate the St Pols. He is well rid of them all.'

And Kathi had looked at her and said, 'He will never be rid of them now.'

Neither of them had wept. Neither had said very much; they simply remained in the same room, in companionship. It was Kathi who was most aware of this aspect of their curious friendship: that the comfort that was useless to Nicholas they could bring to each other, at least.

Because of his years and his girth, Jordan de St Pol, lord of Kilmirren, did not nowadays lead companies of men into battle; he let his son and his grandson do that. But, hearing that the enemy was massing at Berwick, he chose to stay at his Edinburgh house rather than at Kilmirren, guessing that Simon and Henry would move east as well. He expected them to ride with the West Warden, John Stewart of Darnley, and either remain in force on the Tweed, or join the main host as it moved south from Edinburgh. He did not know that Darnley was expected at Lauder.

In common with half the town, late that Monday morning, he learned that Adorne had arrived from the Borders, and was now at the Castle. His men, sent to investigate, reported that Andro Wodman had appeared, wounded, at the same time. They could discover nothing but speculation about de Fleury, who had disappeared when Wodman did. Jordan de St Pol had expected Wodman to inform him of de Fleury's movements, and had been displeased when he did not. He had other agents, to be sure. To a powerful, inactive man, information was crucial.

When, therefore, a visitor was announced, the fat man expected it to be a Kilmirren fellow, with news or a commission from Simon. Serious news would have been brought by Adorne, who would have given his name, knowing what it would convey. When that tailor's dummy Julius of Bologna entered the room, astonishment and antipathy drove the old man to his feet.

'Indeed, sir? I cannot remember inviting you.'

'Then I shall go,' the man said. He had always been impertinent, trading on his mediocre good looks. 'But I expected some thanks for my wretched tidings.'

He still looked impertinent. It meant that he did have disturbing news, and was planning to impart it with relish. Jordan de St Pol said, 'In that case, I apologise. Please take a seat. You are about to tell me that poor jumped-up Claes, our mutual friend, has overreached himself at last. Is he dead?' Seating himself, he had signed to have the best claret poured. It came. He took a cup and drank.

The lawyer looked at him. 'I am sorry,' he said. Unexpectedly, he had sobered. He said, 'I know Nicholas meant more to your family than perhaps they wished to say. We watched him try to help Henry. It almost seemed that he and your grandson might become friends. That is' – the handsome features were earnest – 'I am right, am I not, in thinking that Nicholas was truly your grandson? A pity, of course, that Simon had to marry so young, to someone he came to dislike. But I suppose that the confusion over the birth gave the perfect excuse to renounce the marriage. Do you regret it? Nicholas's son is named after you, isn't he? If Nicholas had been legitimate, Jordan would make a fine heir. If, sadly, anything happened to Simon or Henry.'

The change of tone in the last words was slight, but St Pol heard it. He said softly, 'What is it to you?'

The lawyer looked down. His voice also was soft, even pleading. 'I have watched Nicholas fight this undeserved stigma. He never held it against you. We didn't always see eye to eye, he and I, but I knew and admired him for most of his life. I know how he yearned for your affection. My lord, tell the world he was legitimate, and honour hin and yourself.'

He had hurried a little. The door behind him was open. As he spoke, there had been voices, and the minor flurry of someone approaching.

Adorne, of course. All, all, all.

It was not Anselm Adorne in the doorway.

'Thank you, Julius,' said the man who was supposed to be dead. Claes stood there. Claes. The so-called Burgundian. De Fleury. The lawyer whirled round.

For the second time, St Pol forced himself upright. Planted, his legs did not shake. The blood mottling his vast face and neck withdrew, leaving him chilled, but with sense enough for what had to be done. He said, 'I see you contrived this moment between you. The apprentice pretends to be dead, and his underling is sent to coax forth lies and forgiveness.'

De Fleury said, 'Julius is not here by my wish. I have come on other business.' There was something stiff about his manner of standing. His flesh was swollen and mottled with colour, as if he had been set upon and kicked by a mob. One hoped, with fervour, that he had. His eyes were immense and, in any other man, would seem to be asking a question.

St Pol said, gratingly, 'So. Let me declare at once that which I have always declared, and which I shall maintain to the grave.

'*This man is illegitimate, and none of my blood.* He comes of an illicit union between an unknown man and the wife of my son. He is a bastard. This I will swear to before any authority. I shall repeat my affidavit if need be, before the highest courts of the Church; and it will stand for all time. Are you satisfied, both of you?'

He looked at the pair. The lawyer scowled. The look on the other man's face had not changed. St Pol felt his own expression alter before it. He heard himself say, 'Have you something to tell me?'

De Fleury stared at him. Then he turned to the lawyer, who smiled and gave a slight shrug. De Fleury spoke to him slowly and softly. '*You know?* You know; you came here; and you *haven't yet told him?*' He raised his arm. The man Julius flinched back. De Fleury's first, vicious blow took him under the chin and lifted him off his feet. The second flung him staggering back to the doorway, suddenly filled with running men. They gripped the lawyer and held him. De Fleury stopped.

St Pol spoke to his servants. 'Throw him out. Leave the other.' As they dragged the man Julius away, you could hear his voice, screeching at de Fleury. The old man sat down, pressing the arms of his chair.

The door was still ajar. When St Pol jerked his head, de Fleury went and moved it shut very slowly, the way he had opened the hall door at Beltrees. Then he came and stood before the high chair.

He said, 'Monseigneur. They are both dead. Simon and Henry. Forgive me for having to tell you.'

It was not news, now. He had guessed. He was ready.

'*Forgive you?*' said Jordan de St Pol. 'I forgive you nothing. They are dead, and you are alive.'

'They died bravely,' the other man said. 'They lie in reverent hands, in the crypt of the Abbey of Kelso. Monseigneur, I am here to take you there, if you wish.'

It was beyond belief an offence. '*Tais-toi,*' Kilmirren said through shut teeth.

'I was there. If you allow me, I can tell you –'

'*Tais-toi!*' He was shouting. It emerged as a hoarse double howl, still in French. '*How dare you!* The death of my son and my grandson, given to me by your mouth! Go from this room. Never come near me again. *I wish you were dead.*'

The brute went.

Outside, in the dripping core of a city preparing for war, laden wains splattered through mud, while sledges and barrows grated upwards, hauled by powerful women, or careered down to the Canongate in a curtain of water. Grooms hurried by, driving packhorses, or jostled by war horses and hackneys. Other animals trudged or trotted or scampered uphill and down, squealing, bleating and bellowing. Gulls screamed, children bawled, whips cracked, dogs barked and the rain rattled down on tiled roofs, while lines of thatched houses stood and piddled like sailors. It was unremittingly noisy.

Still, there were those who were quick enough to turn, as a man was expelled from the front door of old Kilmirren's house and, losing his footing, tumbled down the steps to lie sprawled in the dung at the foot, where Wattie's Pate was minding a big, well-fed horse. The next minute, the beast was stamping and clattering, because a much bigger bairn, emerging from the same doorway, had come down the stairs in three strides and facing the first just as he got to his feet, had knocked him staggering up to the height of the causeway. Then, following up, he hit him again with such force that the smaller one spun and half fell, with barely time to get his own fists up. Then he did, and blocked the next blow, and found his proper footing in time to pack in two shrewd dunts of his own, which fairly sent the big fellow tumbling over the stones.

And it was then, as he got up, that you could see that the big man, bless my soul, was Nicol de Fleury, his face covered in bruises, and the man he was attacking was the lawyer fellow that everyone's wife was slavering over except yours, although you wouldn't altogether mind if the lad lost a few teeth on some such occasion as this.

After that, busy and worried though everyone was, you would need to be blind not to crane about as you passed to see those two going at it like beings demented, or like one being demented, for the lawyer was fighting to defend himself. And it was all fisticuffs, too, although both were wearing good whingers, as if flesh punching flesh was the only satisfaction that was wanted. And it was as crazy a ruffle as anyone would ettle to see, with the pair of them rolling and staggering and ducking and swinging from the Butter Tron down to St Giles, up and down steps, into and out of closes, under the bellies of oxen and barrels, toppling crates and diving into the lapping basins of conduits and rolling down, down, down until they came to the steepest vennel that led to the Nor' Loch, and tumbled down that, fighting still.

There were those who followed them all the way, although others stood at the top, saying what a disgrace it was, surely, for two skilly, braw men to be wasting their powers on each other when they should be away killing Englishmen for their King. Nevertheless, when the lawyer, Julius, crashed into the water and floated there, there were enough well-meaning folk to haul him out and receive their due reward for collecting his horse and helping him, when he recovered, back to the Canongate.

By that time, Big Nicol, who had foundered on land, next to the leeks, had been picked up by somebody else, which was a crying shame, for he would have paid well. But you didna argue with Crown Office men.

The ceiling of Archie Whitelaw's uncomfortable guest-room was the first thing Nicholas saw when he woke, forced into teeth-shaking consciousness by a sequence of regular slaps to his bruised and misshapen face, delivered by someone he didn't know. By a servant. By a servant of the same Archibald Whitelaw who, he now saw, sat ensconced in the one chair. Nicholas uttered a protest.

'Ah! Some sign of life!' said the Secretary. 'That will do: he has deigned to awake.' And to Nicholas: 'What were you thinking of?'

'Idiotry and furiosity,' Nicholas said. It was an effort. He added, making another one, 'Necessitating *actio tutelae contraria*. I apologise.'

'*Actio tutelae directa*,' said the Secretary. 'Get up. Get up and come down. We are waiting for you.' His spectacles twinkled, advertising service by proxy. They had not expected him to survive York. Since he had, they did not wish him to slacken. Vehement medicine.

Tell the world he was legitimate, and honour him and yourself.

I forgive you nothing.

I wish you were dead.

Whitelaw left. Nicholas gathered himself, and got up. The same servant brought him clean clothes and steered him, presently, to join the others below – Avandale and Whitelaw, Scheves and the Abbot of Holyrood, Adorne and the Queen's man, McClery. And Tom Yare, the city Treasurer, who had once had a good house at Berwick.

None of them commented on his appearance, or his absence, or what had happened at Heaton. No one mentioned the public spectacle he had just made of himself. They merely looked up, and then included him in what they had been discussing, which was the much-debated switch from armed response to diplomacy. If the King came back and the army disbanded, Gloucester would try to take Berwick at once; or leave Berwick besieged, and invade. Whichever he did, he would be intercepted and invited to negotiate. The offer would not come in the name of the King, but from the senior officers of the Crown and the burgh of Edinburgh. It had always been planned, from the beginning, that their spokesman would be Nicholas de Fleury.

Now these same senior officers knew, from Adorne, the gist of what had happened in York. Nicholas had to help them decide what value he had as a messenger, and how Gloucester and Sandy would receive him.

He was not, as it happened, feeling suicidal. He had a great deal to live for: until recently, he had barely realised how very much. His personal situation didn't alter the obvious. Of the very few people qualified for this gambit, he was the only one these people could spare.

The meeting was quick: they had mostly achieved a consensus, and had only been waiting for him to recover from his idiotry and furiosity. To make sure he didn't repeat the performance, they put him back in the guest-chamber.

Indeed, he had to rest now, for he was at the limits of what strength he had. Yesterday, there had been the river at Heaton. Today, he had launched himself into a fifty-mile ride and a silly, senseless fight at the end of it. Tomorrow, he might have to travel almost as far. Meanwhile, God knew, there was no lack of urgent things to calculate and initiate and worry over, but there were others to deal with them, in a better condition than he was. Or so Whitelaw had kindly said.

Before they all left, the Abbot had climbed the stairs with something to say. Adorne had told Abbot Archie the truth about the St Pols' presence at Heaton. Nicholas wished that he hadn't, then altered his mind. He had always thought Archie Crawford a worldly man, but this time he said the right things. Kelso had prayed for Simon and Henry, but Holyrood spoke from the heart. It brought to mind Moscow, and that coarse man Ludovico da Bologna who, it turned out, possessed grace, and respected dignity, and had recognised, on another occasion, what was fitting to do.

He wondered who sat now with Jordan de St Pol of Kilmirren, and then realised, pierced with pain and with thankfulness, that he knew. Andro would have sent someone to tell her.

Everyone knew where Nicholas was, including Gelis and Jordan. They had been asked not to come, so that he might rest. There had been other reasons, with which he agreed. He missed them, but did not want help with this burden. It was his, and he would not impose it on others.

In any case, it was only late afternoon. The day was not ended yet.

Chapter 43

Quhen to the king chek in the feild is maid,
That is to saye in langage: 'Do me richt.'
Have he na reskew of sum vther knycht
He mon remofe, and gif he may nocht so
The feild is tynt and his victour ago.

FOR TOBIE, Moriz and John, that same Monday began before dawn in the camp of the royal army at Lauder. Darnley and his host from the west had not come; and the King, retiring to his pavilion the previous night, had let it be known that he would march on without him in the morning. He had flushed when they cheered him. The downpour had stopped.

Those who cheered were defiantly happy in the long twilight that night, roaring patriotic songs round the campfires, and encouraging others, less convinced, to join in. When Tobie expressed reservations about the inspirational qualities of Blind Harry, Wallace and Bruce, the priest and John le Grant sped to reassure.

'They'll fight all the better. Look at the Swiss.'

In retrospect, it was not a good analogy. The Swiss had caused half the slaughter at Nancy. Father Moriz offered a consoling rider. 'Mercenary companies are just as bad. Remember Urbino, Albania? Germans fighting Germans for money?'

It was too old an argument to pursue, and Tobie was silent. The difference was that, in this case, if their planning went wrong, people were about to die for an unreal cause. Some people argued, of course, that, if pursued fiercely enough, a myth – a dream – a misunderstanding – becomes real. Like Robin, hopelessly damaged, convincing himself and his friends he could manage. So, from today's half-illusory patriotism might emerge a fervour, in thirty years' time, that would bring a great national victory, rendering the next generation immortal, and sending songs of its fame round the world.

Moriz was watching him. Moriz said, 'Don't worry. There are more hard-headed merchants than patriots.'

John said morosely, 'Aye. But the patriots are bigger.'

By that time they knew from Adorne's courier that Nicholas was back, although still mysteriously in the south, and that Adorne would reach Edinburgh in the morning. By then, also, it had been reaffirmed to Huntly, Argyll and the other leaders that, whatever happened, the army was not to march beyond Lauder. The same leaders, observing orders, asked to be received by the King, who flew into such a passion at the suggestion of a halt, far less a retreat, that Tobie was sent for. He remained until the fit had subsided, having turned everyone out of the pavilion except for Hearty James the King's uncle, and the lord of Torphichen, whose fruity voice and packs of obedient tenantry had a soothing effect, no matter where his loyalties lay. He didn't try to shift Whistle Willie, the King's master of musical medicine, who had become very proprietorial in recent years. James, despite his uneven moods, was well liked by those who understood his enthusiasms.

Among these, it was already apparent, was the entire squad of gunners, who had rigged up lanterns in their part of the field and continued to cosset the guns, no matter what they were told. Tam Cochrane encouraged them. Tam Cochrane had been responsible for producing the gunstones and the gun-carriages and the gunpowder, and also, in one way or another, for the defences of half the fortresses in the south, including the town and castle of Berwick. If the King wanted an artillery battle against Gloucester, Tam Cochrane was his man.

John le Grant had gone to sort him out, and had come back close to speechless. 'He swears he's going to get the guns on the road before dawn. He's mustered all the Blind Harries to help him. And Leithie Preston, because of the wife. He's cocked a snook at Oliver Sinclair. Nobody says no to Nowie Sinclair. Who the hell do masons think that they are?'

'You have to ask?' said Father Moriz.

With the dark, some of the noise and movement abated, although not very much: oxen lowed; horses stamped in the lines; men coughed and talked in low voices; there came the lilt of a boat-song from the higher ground where the Highlanders lay, and below that the rushing continuum of the river, running full. It was still dark when the flap of the tent was moved aside, and one of Argyll's men spoke to them softly. Dawn was coming, and Darnley's force was not here.

John and Moriz had already agreed: when the moment of decision came, Tobie would be their spokesman in council. He was already dressed. It was five minutes' work to follow other dark, silent figures across the meadow to the little building with its row of lit windows: the church of Lauder where the commanders of the King's army were to decide, without the King, what was to be done.

Stratagem after stratagem: of course this, too, had been foreseen by Nicholas and his seniors in the long hours of planning that had preceded this war. Nicholas was not here: if and when he came north, his task, like Adorne's, would be to advise the temporary administration now established in Edinburgh, using all his knowledge of Albany. But Colin Argyll was here, Master of the Household and King's protector, whose daughter Darnley's son was to marry. And George, second Earl of Huntly, husband in the past to the King's aunt Annabella, who had brought the other great lords of the north – Ogilvy and Arbuthnott and Forbes; Erroll, whose daughter was Huntly's present wife; James Innes, who was uncle by marriage to the late Phemie Dunbar, whose lover's land, Cortachy, lay in that same wealthy region, centre of the famous salmon cartel co-ordinated by the ingenious mind of Adorne's fellow Burgundian. The salmon that filled the King's coffers with tax money, and helped to bring little George Robieson also to Lauder, with his chest of money from the Great Customs of Edinburgh, for the use of the King's soldiers. There might be many here who were tolerant of England, but there were also many who were filled with anxious loyalty for the King.

The sky beyond the river had paled by the time Tobie returned to the tent where Moriz and John were waiting. This time, not only their own men but others were clustered on the churned mud, watching also. Tobie had pulled off his cap, so that his fine hair flew about his round, naked head, and his eyes glinted in their cavities. He spoke loudly enough to be heard by them all.

'You will all hear in a moment. We have word from England. Gloucester is here not just to take Berwick, but to kill the King and put the Duke of Albany on the throne. This army is too small to stop him. The King is being advised to disband and get back to Edinburgh.'

John said, 'He refused yesterday.'

Tobie said, 'It is life or death for him now. If he refuses, he will be overruled. A delegation is going to tell him so.'

'Led by what brave man?' asked Father Moriz. But, of course, he knew. Whatever great lords were there – Seton and Lyle, Hepburn and Lord Grey – the volunteer was going to be the same energetic Earl of

Angus whose ill-advised raids into England had virtually started the war, and whose present wealth was largely due to the English exile of that other Douglas whose lands he now held. Archibald Douglas, fifth Earl of Angus, had proclaimed that he, and he alone, would bell the cat.

'Bell the cat?' had repeated Father Moriz, in a puzzled German way. It was a reference to a fable, he learned. For the sake of the common good, a mouse might brave a cat for such a purpose. So Angus would brave the King, and reverse the fatal advance.

Father Moriz nodded, with every appearance of attention. As they spoke, he could hear single voices, and then others speaking out across the dark meadow, followed by a sporadic rustle of movement. The host was being told. And it was not only the King whom Angus was about to have to bell.

Tobie said, 'I must go.'

When a king went to war, the appearance of the royal pavilions was a matter of pride to the master workmen who created and cared for them, from the masts and gilded vanes and turned tops to the ornaments on the canvas and the banners that flew overall. Lit at night, the housing of the Dukes of Burgundy had seemed strange and magnificent as a city in fairyland. The strong pavilions of the King of Scotland – the hall and the kitchen, the bedchamber and the closet – were not of that order, but were seemly within, floored with timber and lined with silk, shimmering in the candlelight, with the King's campaign bed hung with embroidered cloths against draughts, and his coffers placed to hand, with a table for dining, and fine, two-thread towels on the hat-stand, and a handbasin and jug of chased silver.

When, on a night such as this, he could not sleep, his pages would read to him or sing, or his gentlemen would amuse him with dice or with cards. Tonight, he had Master Roger himself playing softly on the lute, sometimes well-known fragments, sometimes a new work of his own. And to sing he had Johnnie Ramsay, one of Will Roger's prize performers, who was not strictly a page, but the sprightly (probable) nephew of one of the wealthy Napiers, who happened to be married to one of Nanse and Thomas Preston's relations. It occurred to the King, listening, to wonder where Thomas Preston might be. Leithie, they called him. A man with the Preston temper who certainly traded with the English but who, like Tam Cochrane, could never be accused of disloyalty. James really thought they would do anything for him.

The King smiled, and then realised that his eyes had closed. Sleep at last. He would let the lad finish the song, and then dismiss him and Roger to bed. Tomorrow – today – would be a great day.

Will Roger, watching the King, had also decided that this song would be the last. A boy's voice, not quite settled, should never be worked too much when tired, however much he himself enjoyed studying it. He had jotted down a piece for two voices that had been developing recently at the back of his mind, set specifically within Johnnie's best range, and exploiting the smooth bridge between registers which was one of his gifts.

The other part had been written for Nicholas de Fleury, but the bastard was away so often just now that you'd be in your grave, or he would, before ever he sang it.

It was only as the song came to an end that the voices outside the pavilion became really audible. The King heard them too, and roused to frown at an attendant, who wordlessly slipped from the tent. He returned, looking ruffled.

'It was nothing, sire. My lord of Angus requested an audience.'

'Why?' said the King. 'Ask him!'

He found out soon enough, when Archie Douglas was brought in and sank to his knees, his stepfather from Lochleven behind him. It seemed that Sandy's perfidy was public knowledge at last. Spies confirmed it. This invasion wasn't a ruse; a silly ploy to get back his lost honours. Sandy had come to take James's throne.

The doctor, Tobias, was standing watchfully now inside the entrance, but the news didn't bring back James's frenzy. It was what he had always suspected. It vindicated that early decision to begin calling in troops. It meant he could raise his banner today and march forward, his unified army behind him, to punish his brother, and show Gloucester who was King of this realm.

He had begun to declare as much, ringingly, when that stupid man Angus jumped to his feet. Master Whitelaw had always said that Earl Archie had no head for power, but enough land to remind him who his friends were. He had attacked the English with Sandy. Unlike Sandy, it would suit him to keep attacking them now.

So said havering schoolmasters. Here was Archie Angus declaiming the opposite. Standing in front of his King. *Interrupting* his King. And announcing, if the ears were to be believed, that a Scottish attack was out of the question. That the army did not wish to advance. That to preserve his serene highness's life, the King must retire with his forces to safety.

It was a lie. His army was loyal. Brave men did not cringe before a superior force. They used guile, and gallantry, and could win. He knew. He had fought in the Highlands with Colin. Where was Colin?

'Here, my lord,' said Argyll, from the door. He knelt, as was proper, and his accent had become very strong, as it did under stress. He said, 'The Earl of Angus is right. George Huntly is here, and Grey and Lyle. They will tell you the same. To take this army against twenty thousand armed men would be suicide. But we would do it, if we knew, in the end, that our King would be safe. My lord, it is your death that they want. We cannot let you go forth to martyrdom.'

Then, hearing that, James found it hard to breathe. He was stabbed with pain: in his chest, in his belly, while the heat surged into his face. He rose, swaying. He saw the doctor starting to move, but Will Roger was nearest. His grey hair wild, his long face furious, he caught the King by the arm and shouted, 'Are ye Lapps, or Tartars, or children? This is your King, who asks you to follow him! Will you destroy him here, in his tent, out of misery at your cowardice?'

Argyll spoke quickly. 'Will. The doctor will see to him.'

'*I* will see to him,' said Will Roger. He had no weapons. There was a whistle stuck in his doublet.

The King said, 'Then come!' and with the musician's hand still at his arm, dashed through the tent and out between his servants into the half-light outside, and the crowds that surrounded the pavilion. He saw a crate, and leaped on it, Roger still at his side. He drew a great breath.

'To me!' the King said. 'Who will fight at my side! Who will march to England, with me, today?'

He realised then that the roar of assent, that the masses shouting his name were far off, and that the armed men about him were Huntly's, and Campbells and Ogilvies. And that, as he watched, the disssenting parts of the army were moving against each other, pikes in hand, so that screams began to be heard over the shouting. Until then, no one had laid hands on him but Roger, and even now, the commanders stood back. It was the young men – he recognised them – the firebrand Lindsay, the mad Fleming heir – who thrust forward and seized him, while all his own servants were knocked out of the way. He saw Will Roger fighting ineptly to reach him, until Fleming turned aside and flung him into the arms of his men who passed him back, like a struggling sheep. He saw the whistle fall into the mud. He even heard, as they dragged him back into his splendid silk tent, the great shout that rose from the riverside, followed by an even greater roar from the bridge.

*

John le Grant was already at the brimming river by that time, gazing at the gouged mud and deep tracks where the ox-teams and the gun-carriages had been. Moriz, battling through the crowd on his short legs, heard him repeating, 'The bastard! The bastard! The bastard!' It was unlikely that he was talking of anyone but Cochrane. Big Tam.

'He's started off south,' Moriz suggested. 'With all the guns. Without telling us. And he'll attract all the King's men in the army.'

'All the Blind Harries,' said John le Grant bitterly.

'Men willing to die for their country,' Moriz said. 'To mock is unfair.'

'I know it is,' John said. 'But it makes me feel better. Well, Tam won't get very far.'

'Why not?' said Moriz. But, sinkingly, he thought that he knew.

'Because I doctored the wagons,' said John. 'I've a knack for it. They'll get so far on the road to Coldstream, then stick. In fact' – there came a great roar from ahead – 'it sounds as if they already have. Come on, come on.'

He was a decent man, John; just single-minded. He looked eager. He looked almost pleased.

'Just the place for a pitched battle,' said Moriz.

Within the silken pavilion, in the battlefield that was Lauder, the King had ceased to struggle and shout and was sitting, restrained by many men's hands, weeping from anger and weakness. Colin Campbell, kneeling bareheaded before him in cuirass and surcoat, was saying over and over, in Gaelic, 'My lord; my lord; my lord.' Colin Campbell, Master of the King's Household, whose men were swaying shoulder to shoulder with others outside, blocking the way to the King, striving to hold off the men who wanted to rescue him, and have him lead them to victory against England.

Argyll knew it himself: bowing his head, he got to his feet and looked over the King's head at Tobie. 'I must go. Can you ease him?'

'He has had no sleep,' said Tobie.

'If you can calm him?' Argyll said. 'For a little. He will have nothing but love and respect. It is for his own sake.' He spoke with authority. But he had been moved to tears himself, a moment before.

He left. The King, who was thirsty, took what Tobie gave him and slowly descended into sleep. They put him to bed, in a tent pink with dawn, outside which several thousand men were still milling in turmoil, disputing the half-completed exodus to the south and the east. The King's supporters, if not stopped, would march along the Coldstream road, securing the way, in advance of freeing the King. Cavalry was now playing a part: Tobie could hear the drumming of hooves and marshalling orders. He thought of Moriz and John. He thought of the guns. He shut his box, once the King settled, and tried to talk his way out of the tent, which was lined with armed men. The refusal was vehement enough to make him realise that if he walked out, his life would be in danger. To some, he was one of the enemy, having condoned the detention of James.

To some, but not everyone. Vociferous though they were, less than half the army – less perhaps than a third – was still intent on marching off, in the time-honoured fashion, to resist the Auld Enemy. And most of these, by the sound, were leaving what remained of the camp and had begun to fight their way south.

It came to Tobie that they might not have the numbers, but that they might very well have the guns. And he did not know which side Big Tam would end up with.

He escaped a few minutes later, slithering under the rear of the tent, and finding the Napier youth, Ramsay, beside him. Will Roger had gone with the first of the mêlée, the boy said, and he wanted to find him. Tobie grunted. Without his box, with a woollen cap low on his brows, he hoped no one would recognise him. The youth, in a cloak, looked like anybody else. Neither Moriz nor John, unsurprisingly, was where he had left them. The gun park was empty, but you could see the tracks of the guns. Swearing and stumbling, Tobie followed them.

They had gone to the bridge. They were still on the bridge. The bridge and its approaches were crowded with struggling men, and the rising sun glittered on steel helms and mail-shirts; on swords and axes and pikes, knives and maces. The noise came in great throbbing waves, drowning all the natural sounds of the country. The knights like Archie Douglas and Innes didn't have banners or surcoats: there hadn't been time; and they were disciplining men of their own side, who knew them. Tobie didn't see Moriz, or John, or Cochrane, or Whistle Willie. What the hell was Whistle Willie doing in the middle of this?

Then he saw that they were trying to turn the guns, to point back to the camp, to the King's captors.

Later, he thought that Angus and Buchan and Grey would have managed to stop them: the cavalry threw itself forward, and there was a sudden and effective deployment to cut off the bridge from the rest of dissentients. In response the crowd round the bridge seemed to thicken, and the noise increased yet again, the thud and squeal of weapons being punctuated by bouts of frenzied cheering. There were men – gunners? – clambering up on the carts, head and shoulders above the fighting about them. Two of them fell, pierced by arrows, and after a moment the others began to climb down. It was the first indication that the anti-war party might be prevailing. Driven by fear, Tobie forced his way up to the bridge, dodging weapons and ducking between horses. He heard Ramsay following. Then, suddenly, he caught sight of Moriz and John. They were in the thick of the mob by the guns, and were being set upon. Moriz was protecting his head; John was laying about him, and losing. 'Here's another!' his assailants were yelling. 'Hang him over his guns!'

Hang him over his guns?

'You bloody fools!' John was screeching. 'I don't want to fight! I'm the one who jammed the gun-carriers for you!'

'That for a tale!' someone roared. They'd wrapped a belt round his neck.

Tobie arrived. The impact, in the person of a middle-aged medical man who did not observe his wife's dietary regimen, had all the violence of one of Tam's thirty-three pounder gunstones. 'Stop! He's on your side! He can disable the guns! He can help you!'

They did stop, for a moment, being winded. Then, disregarding all he was yelling, they laid hands on him, and Johnnie Ramsay as well. Running out of baldricks, they were cutting up harness. John was continuing to shout. He was shouting, 'No! No! Listen! Look! Wait!' And all the time he was trying to point. Tobie looked.

Five years ago, he had experienced something like this; not in summer, but in winter; not in this country but in Lorraine, at the start of the battle that had obliterated the fine little company he fought with, and rendered Robin a cripple, and brought Nicholas home with barely his life. Then, it had been Swiss horns, not trumpets. Then, the snow had turned black beneath the massed hooves of the enemy cavalry, thundering out of its hiding place. Now, the red July sun lit the steel of a different horde distantly pounding towards them: a horde that came from the west, and so could not be English.

It was not English. Its banners were those familiar in Ayrshire, Renfrew, the Lennox. Its commander's pennant, unreeling its six ells of rain-sodden taffeta, bore the chequered device of John Stewart of Darnley.

At last. At last; and at the same time, Tobie Beventini suspected, too late.

Halfway through the long hilly journey to Lauder, breasting swollen rivers and stumbling about broken bridges and bogs, Darnley had known that he could not reach the King's army by Sunday, and that someone else would have to try to stop James. Approaching his destination at sunup on Monday, he was thankful to detect, from the noise, that the whole force was surely still there, even if in fierce disarray. Someone, he guessed, had announced the retreat against the King's wishes, and the army had split.

Topping the rise, he saw that this was the case: soldiers who had been clearly encamped in the meadow were now scattered between Lauder and the bridge, where fighting was taking place. All the tents seemed to be empty or struck but those of the King, which were closed, with a squad of armed men surrounding them. They looked surprised as he brought his troop down: as he suspected, his advance riders had failed him. It didn't matter. He reported to Buchan, his counterpart, spurring up towards him, and then both made with speed for the bridge. The guns were there. He wondered how the hell the warmongers had got them away from Tam Cochrane. He had three of Tam's relatives among the lairds and their men at his tail. They would give him the hard time he deserved. But first: secure the bridge with his spears and his bows, and they could reduce the rest of the trouble at leisure. He set to gallop, with Rothesay Herald and his trumpeters blaring beside him. That would stop it.

It did. The struggle in the field was coming to a halt even before he thundered through it; and the barrier of men preserving the approach to the bridge let them through into the only quarter where steel was still flashing. The bridge was packed, the guns rising in the midst two by two, like water-horses stuck in the Ark. As in the field, though, the war party was now outnumbered by those intent on halting the advance. Among the fallen were men wearing the tool-satchels of gunners and carpenters. Angus's men and the rest had made it their business to strike first at the foundations of the advance: to reduce the services without which it could not take place. To render useless the smiths and the weapons; to abstract the gold that was to pay for its provisions and wages; to corral the quartermasters and the team of experts whose business it was to handle and furnish the King's pavilions, and the acres of canvas required by the army. All such men were huddled under guard, Buchan had said; Dod Robieson and Jamie Hommyll among them, and where Dod's treasure chest had gone was anyone's guess.

Darnley kept his horse moving in the throng on the bridge, his sword drawn, shouting orders. He was a big, fleshy man, from a military family, and knew how to fight and how to manage others. He left his men to deal with the hand-to-hand scuffles and didn't interfere, even when some youth screamed his name; even when it was reinforced by a second voice. Then someone tugged at his arm and he saw the latter belonged to the King's mediciner, Dr Tobias, who certainly should not have been there. Beside him were three other men, one of them with a strap round his neck, and one just rising, bleeding, from a series of blows. The injured man, the boy who had screamed, was the heir of a Napier, and thus remotely his kinsman. Darnley called in return, and sent over his men to extricate the four from their attackers. It didn't take long. When they staggered out, he pulled the boy, as seemed only friendly, into the saddle behind him, while the other three were accommodated by others. It transpired that one of them, John, was a gunner. Ned Cochrane, leaning over, addressed him.

'So? Where's Big Tam, the deil?'

The gunner looked round. His neck was black with bruising, and his face was mottled and glistening with white and red bristles. When he spat his answer, it was to Darnley, not Cochrane. 'Where he wouldn't have been, if you'd come when you said. I hope you have an excuse you can sleep with, you bastard.'

'Where is he?' said Darnley. His voice was quiet. As the fighting died, his other men gathered about him.

'Oh, ye haven't far to look,' said the man. 'Just glance over the parapet. Mind you don't get dizzy, of course. It's a fair distance down to the water.' His words, cut from Aberdeen granite, occupied the space where all the drubbing and shouting and clattering had been, and then stopped, so that you could hear the sound of the river, and the jingle and snorting of horses, and the murmur of massed men in the distance.

John Stewart of Darnley dismounted, leaving the boy, and walked to the parapet, and looked over.

Three dead men hung there, swaying lackadaisically in the updraught from the river. Being the heaviest, Big Tam Cochrane had an ox harness bound round his neck, and there was still a trace of surprise on the suffused face above it. To one side of him depended his argumentative kinsman by marriage, Leithie Preston. And on his other side, his throat sealed in perpetuity by the bite of a thong, hung Will Roger.

Chapter 44

All commoun offis suld the massour zou schaw,
And by this purs the customeris ze ken.
Befor the knycht ar situat sic men,
For to this knycht as capitane of the tovne
Thai suld obeye in absens of the crovne.

LATE THAT MONDAY, trembling with fury and weakness, James, King of Scotland, was brought to the Castle of Edinburgh and there delivered to its Governor, his half-uncle Atholl. His other half-uncles also remained with him. So did his captor and escort, John Stewart, Lord Darnley, with sixty-six chief men of his train, including Maxwells and Drummonds, Muirs and Douglases of Morton, a Semple, a Crawford, a Fleming, a Wallace, a Brown and three Cochranes. And, of course, more Stewarts than anyone, including Walter, the half-brother of Avandale.

So quietly was it done that no one realised at first that the King had come back. The horses were left outside the town: only the King and his immediate circle had been mounted, and their animals had been immediately sent out. The rest of the army had already disbanded. Knollys returned to Torphichen. Some leaders – Nowie Sinclair, the Prestons – went back to their castles, taking their dead. Some had set out for their properties in the south, including Alexander Home, grandson of the bailie of Coldingham, sweetened beforehand by Huntly, who had lands down there by Gordon, of which Alex Home was now bailie for life. Others went east, to Haddington, the traditional muster-point for the region between Edinburgh and the east coast. The eastern muster, which included Archie of Berecrofts, had not, of course, been asked to set out for Lauder. Its part had still to be played.

For Tobie, the ride north was wretched, almost as the long journey from Nancy had been grim. The sick man this time was the King, who depended on Tobie, and yet recoiled from him as a traitor. Nor was it a relief, having arrived at the Castle, to relinquish his patient to Andreas, for even Adorne's physician was tainted, in the King's eyes, by his presence in what was a prison. By then, the King was in no doubt that his nobles, paid by England and Albany, had turned against him, and that he might end as Johndie had, dead in the care of his doctors. At present, there was no safe way of comforting him.

Leaving the Castle, the participants had been briefly thanked for their part in the stratagem, and asked to remain out of public view until morning. Colin Argyll had already gone, having taken no part in the physical delivery of the King to the Castle. So far as the outside world was concerned, the King's other ministers had never left Edinburgh, and were innocent of any complicity. The same was true of Nicholas and Adorne, who had been in the Borders, and nowhere near Lauder.

Amid all that farrago of half-lies, it seemed to be true that Nicholas had somehow followed Adorne back to Edinburgh. About to join Moriz and John at the Castle gates, Tobie had turned back, on an impulse, to confirm it. After all the hapless, miserable losses at Lauder, the return of Nicholas would be something to exult over, at least. It struck him, abruptly, that Nicholas himself would not yet have heard about Lauder.

As he had hoped, John Stewart of Darnley had the information he wanted. Nicholas was back. He had had business in Kelso. Since it was no longer private, Darnley mentioned, regretfully, what de Fleury's concerns at Kelso had been.

For a while, Tobie stayed in the Castle, speaking to no one, and doing nothing in particular. Then he walked slowly down to the guardroom, where John and Moriz were waiting.

They looked angry and anxious. John said, 'So, what? Couldn't you find out? Has something happened to Nicholas?'

'No. He's here,' Tobie said.

John said, 'Well, where? We ought to find him. I don't want him hearing the news from just anybody.'

'The news?' Tobie said. He felt ill.

Then Father Moriz said, 'Of Lauder. Of the death of his friends. Tobie? What is wrong? What have you heard?'

Tobie looked at him. He said, 'Darnley just told me why Nicholas didn't come back with Adorne. He has been at Kelso all night.'

'Kelso?' said John. Moriz was silent, but he had taken his crucifix unthinkingly in his fingers.

'Kelso Abbey,' Tobie said. 'Simon and Henry de St Pol both died yesterday, drowned in the Till during a skirmish. Nicholas brought them away, and carried them both to the Abbey. They are still there.'

'And *Henry*?' Moriz said. His fierce face was drawn. Of course, Moriz knew. He was one of the few people who knew. John did not.

John's mouth had opened. He said, 'Nicholas was coming from York. How could Simon be there, on the English side, at the same time? No one was supposed to know where Nicholas was crossing.'

'Except Adorne,' Tobie said suddenly. 'Adorne was on the Borders, and knew. If someone arranged this, I am going to find him and kill him.' Then he broke off and said, 'But, dear God, that is the least of it.'

Father Moriz closed his eyes. He said, 'To Nicholas, certainly. This, to Nicholas, is more than the death of a handsome man, and a . . . beautiful stripling.'

John said, 'I suppose he'll never find out, now, whether he was Simon's son. It will stop Julius's prying, at least.'

'It hasn't,' said Tobie. 'This very afternoon, apparently, Nicholas knocked him off the steps of Kilmirren House, and kept at his throat all the way down to the Nor' Loch. Julius has been put to bed in the Canongate, and Nicholas has been removed from public view by his disapproving superiors. He isn't at home.' He sneezed. It felt like a cramp in the vein of his heart.

'Bless you,' said the priest gently.

Tobie took out his kerchief and blew his nose. He couldn't remember when he had last felt so sick, or so helpless. He said, 'So you see, we have nothing so momentous to tell Nicholas, have we? Nothing, by the divine pity, so terrible as the darkness he is walking through now.'

Far distant from the mishaps that beset every grand plan, the complex strategy of the King of England's campaign unfolded: half evolved by its own leadership, and half dictated by changing circumstances, which, however exasperating, were proof of a Scottish incompetence of truly marvellous proportions. By the evening of that same Monday, the memorable twenty-second day of July, it was known to the English command that the advance against them had stopped. That, for some shameful reason, the King of Scotland's army had revolted at Lauder, and had refused to march further south. An hour later, and they heard that it had disbanded.

To Sandy Albany, hedged about with English magnates, the news was pure bliss. 'They refused to fight me! The people want me! Now we can march!'

Smiling, Dickon of Gloucester agreed. Now they could march. Not (had he not mentioned?) across the entire Border, but across the eastern part of it, certainly, where Sandy's loyal supporters were to be found; leaving a good, solid siege in place at Berwick, just in case anyone thought of relieving the town. But with what fervour the rest of the army would pour over the frontier on a front as far west as Coldstream and, marching in parallel, would leave their mark upon all those dis-affected rich regions where lurked Sandy's enemies, the Homes and the Sinclairs and the rest. Upsettlington would feel their displeasure; and Hutton Hall and Kimmerghame, and Auchencrow, and all the places belonging to Coldingham Priory. He was sure Sandy would agree that they might find a good few acres of crops and inflammable buildings round Coldingham Priory.

In private, with Percy and Dorset, Stanley and Woodville, the Duke did not disguise his true feelings. 'These giddy, lamentable Scots! A cowardly army, and a King so weak that he cannot control it! So what now? He is under arrest in his own Castle. We can neither fight him nor treat with him.'

Dorset said, 'We could enter Edinburgh and starve them out of the Castle. We have twenty thousand.'

'We have three weeks,' said Neville. 'Then the money runs out. And the supplies.'

Dickon grunted. Percy said, 'Is it possible . . .'

'What?'

'Is it possible,' said Harry Percy, 'that this is deliberate? That they know how short a time we can stay, and have removed the King for that reason?'

'How could they know?' Gloucester said. 'The only one who knew all our intentions was the Burgundian, and I am assured that he drowned in the Till.'

Cannily protecting this particular asset, Master Secretary Whitelaw permitted Nicholas to sleep until the night was half over, and then sent for Gelis, his wife, who had not been allowed to see him since his return from York. By that time she knew, as Nicholas did not, what had happened at Lauder, having given beds to three of its warriors. Coming to Whitelaw's, she left John and Moriz but brought Dr Tobie, who chose to remain tactfully out of Nicholas's room until called, sitting on an uncomfortable chair and falling asleep from time to time, neck askew.

Had he been there, he would have seen nothing of intimacy; none of the fever that had marked other reunions. When Gelis entered, Nicholas had exchanged his bed for a chair, and was standing beside it, wrapped in a robe. When she crossed to him, he touched her elbows, drawing her close for his kiss, and then set her as gently apart. His face was open and grave and quite steady. 'Cry mercy,' he said. *Be kind. Be guided.*

She said, 'Andro described it all. There is nothing you need to say, unless you want to. Or only one thing. Adorne says someone betrayed you?'

'It was going to happen,' he said, 'whether someone betrayed me or not. It isn't important. Gelis, I know you are concerned, but I should be a poor pupil if I ran crying from this. I can carry it.'

'I think you can,' she said. She touched his face, and he took her fingers and kissed them, but did not keep them. She said, 'We all can.'

She tried to speak with conviction. She, too, had learned patience. She had learned how to keep her afflictions to herself, as he did. She had also learned to give up her privacy sometimes, because it bore too hard on others. But he had to think of that for himself.

She said, 'There is only one thing I want to say. Don't blame Simon. Don't blame yourself. I have never seen anyone work as hard as you did to redeem Henry, but I don't think you could or maybe even should have succeeded. And don't imagine that you have failed Katelina. She made the wrong choice. She didn't give you a chance to recognise or rear your own son. She committed you both, out of foolishness, to a deception. If you can forgive her, then you must forgive everyone, including yourself.'

'Everyone?' he said. 'No. I know what you mean. Let's leave it at that. Thank you. I knew you would say something wise.' His eyes rested on hers, and she returned his gaze. She couldn't tell what he was thinking. She was taking such care that her breathing kept lapsing.

There was another chair. She slowly sat, and after a moment he resumed his own, with a smoothness that she could see was deliberate. *I have recovered.* And, behind that, *I can ride. I can leave. I am sorry.*

She supposed then that the shutters had closed; and that she no longer had the chance to tell him anything else. Instead, he said suddenly, 'What does Jodi think?' He had used the little name, to keep the old man out of the conversation.

She had not lost the chance. She didn't know whether to take it. Her throat aching, she answered his question. 'Robin explained that soldiers die, and Jodi is thinking about it. We all have to do that, about different losses.'

As she had learned to read him, so he read her. She said only that, and saw his face change. He said, 'Something else has happened? Something at Lauder? *Tobie?*'

She spoke quickly then, as he would have done. 'Tobie is downstairs.

John and Moriz are at home. No.' And as he stared at her, she said, 'There was trouble over the guns. Big Tam lost his head, and Leithie stood up for him. Anyone who got in the way was liable to be attacked. The army was defying the King. Men were frightened.'

'Gelis?' he said. 'Tam Cochrane and Leithie Preston are dead? And who else?'

'And Will Roger,' she said. 'He loved the King. You risked your life in York. He did the same, going to war. You happened to survive, and he didn't.'

All her concern was for him. The only measure she had of Roger's importance was the measure Nicholas gave it. She should not have been surprised when he looked at her and said, 'What have I to do with it? The world has lost him.' Then he said, 'Tobie is here?'

'I'll call him,' she said.

It was the correct decision. The least sentimental of men (as he said himself) Tobie delivered an accurate account of the day's events with speed and belligerence and then proceeded, encouraged by Nicholas, to seek and extirpate the truth of what had led to the hangings. For, of course, Tam Cochrane had not been killed solely because he had blindly obeyed the King's desire to send his guns to defend Berwick. He was killed because his particular skills and abilities were essential to and penetrated every aspect of Scottish affairs, including the shipping of the necessary materials for war and for peace. And from that had stemmed the reciprocal exports, of salmon and timber, whose success had aroused jealousy against all its agents, including Leithie Preston who, like others, had so notoriously traded with England.

And there was much more, of course, to dislike about large, rich men who came from your neighbourhood and whose father you had known. Mint masters were casters, and casters were gunsmiths, and gunsmiths, like Will Goldsmith the Halfpenny Man, employed Big Tam Cochrane to build their stone cunzie houses and import the skills and tools and even the metal they needed to mint their bloody black money, which had ruined the kingdom; in return for which, they supplied guns. Gibbie Fish of Berwick used to work with Tam Cochrane. No wonder Tam Cochrane wanted to hang on to Berwick.

Gelis said, 'So Tam was always going to die, so many wanted rid of him. But why Will?' Nicholas had become rather white but Tobie, in the heat of the argument, had ceased even to sneeze.

Tobie said, 'He was English, wasn't he? He had St Leonard's Hospital once; he was given Traquair, until the King transferred it to Buchan. The King was fond of him: he might have restored him all that. But most of all, Will was blamed for the King's dream of a great chapel of music, to be financed out of Coldingham Priory, and hence wrecking the sinecures of the Home family. Not every Home is for Albany and England, but none of them want to lose Coldingham.'

'So he was always going to die, too,' Nicholas said. 'Does Kathi know?'

Gelis knew that she did. Tobie had slipped away to break the news to her and to Robin. Kathi had brushed aside Tobie's sympathy, speaking of Roger. 'What do I matter? The world has lost him.' She had asked who would go and tell Nicholas.

Now Tobie said, 'I have told her, and Jodi, poor lad. Tam Cochrane was a hero of his, with all those wonderful drawings. Which reminds me. Kathi tells me you gave a beating to Julius.'

Nicholas said, 'He also gave one to me.'

'But you started it. What got into you?' Tobie said. 'You know he's an inquisitive idiot. Now he's in the Floory Land, swearing to get his own back. You ought to see him. If you can't see him, Moriz says he thinks he can calm him.'

Nicholas said, 'I was upset. I'll put it right when I get back. I was going to tell Gelis. I am about to be launched into the arena for another public calamity.'

'Well, that was part of the scheme,' Tobie said briskly. Behind the briskness, there was worry. 'I assumed you would go, in due course, if you were in shape for it. A lot of people like Gelis and Robin and Abbot Archie have put in some hard work convincing the town what to do next. We're lucky we've got Tom Yare and Wattie Bertram to deal with. Everyone knows everyone else, and they've argued it through with the Council.' He broke off. 'But you're not going at once?'

'In the morning.' Nicholas was looking at Gelis. She returned the look with what she hoped was wry acceptance. Anything else would make it unbearable. She saw, with sudden misgiving, that Tobie's agitation had grown. She tried to send him a message. Please, no. Leave it.

Tobie said, 'And when will you be back? Nicholas, I don't want to assail you with it just now, but you have just lost your son. Gelis and I know it, and Moriz. Are you going to leave Henry to be committed without you? Not only committed, but unclaimed?'

Cry mercy, Nicholas had said. But Tobie had rights as well. There was a space. Then Nicholas said, 'All through last night, he was mine. The old man should have them both now.'

'And Henry will be buried as Simon's son?' The pupils of Tobie's eyes were sharp, and black, and fierce. 'You know what else I am saying?

Publish the proof that Henry is yours, and you also prove to the world who you are. It can't harm anyone now. If your son was the image of Simon, then you must be Simon's legitimate son.'

There was another silence. She could only imagine what answer Nicholas would choose. He said eventually, 'No. If Henry is at peace, let his mother rest there as well. I am destroying the evidence.'

Tobie had paled. He said. 'I have a copy. So has Moriz.'

Nicholas said, 'You are my friend. I am not threatening you. I can only ask if you will do the same.'

Tobie said, 'Dear God. Nicholas? Let me ask Moriz.'

'I think you will find,' Nicholas said, 'that Moriz will agree. But ask him. I have to go very soon.'

His voice was flat. Tobie said, 'What doctoring have you had since the river? Let me look.'

Few had the courage to refuse Tobie that kind of demand. Nicholas submitted, and when it was over, Tobie left, taking Gelis. Despite himself, Nicholas held her for a long time, silently, at the door, before he relinquished her finally. When he returned to his chair, he found it beyond him to sit down, whether with studied ease or without. But that passed.

He was to establish himself at the commandeered Priory at Haddington tomorrow, but did not expect to stay long. He had not seen his son Jordan. He had asked Gelis to have him kept safe.

Different men; different sons. He remembered the words of de Lannoy's wistful prayer (*Your praise, my perfect joy*) to his son.

Your praise, my perfect joy; and may we go together to Paradise, at the last.

They tried to stick in his mind, but he would not let them.

By the day following his crass fight with Julius in the High Street, the English command knew that Nicholas de Fleury had not died in the River Till but was alive, and could be assumed to have passed on all that he had found out in York. The Duke of Gloucester, hearing that, turned pale with rage. 'I cannot believe this. De Fleury is alive, and no one knew? No one told me? We have crossed into a country where all our plans are already known; our strength; our intentions? Send me the man who said this fellow is dead. He will answer for it!'

Two servants limped, hurt, from the room, and Harry Percy, Earl of Northumberland, had to force himself to be silent, or come to blows. At the same time, Percy had to agree, it was bad news. He was not enjoying this war.

Three days later, encamped in the blazing uplands round Coldingham, the Duke had recovered his temper, but Harry Percy was losing
patience with Albany. The southern commanders had had none to
begin with, but he had been asked by Dickon Gloucester, in his most
winning manner, to do what he could. They needed the man. Only,
quartering the March north of Berwick, they had been treated every
few miles to a fresh complaint – these farmlands belonged to Jamie's
cousins; that church provided income for Ellem; if they burned that
township, they would alienate John, Sander's father. Albany had
destroyed all the joy of destruction. And to cap it, he was shocked to
the point of disbelief at the amount of support he wasn't getting. He
had always maintained that, once they saw him on the road, East March
lairds – and the Middle March, and the masters of Annandale – would
flock to him. Even Dickon had compelled himself to believe it, or he
would never have got the money out of the King. But it wasn't true. There
were English sympathisers – there always had been. There were men who
thought the King was madder than Albany. But there were more who
trusted not just James or his brother but the tight circle of men who were
James's advisers. And it was not clear, yet, whom they favoured.

Or at least that had been the position until recently. Then a message
had come, originating in Haddington, and addressed to the right noble
and worshipful lord, his grace Richard, Duke of Gloucester. The sender,
an accredited herald, asked leave for himself, with a temporary Usher,
to join the Duke for an informal parley, under flag of truce, at a place
of the Duke's choice. Coldingham, then two days away, had been
suggested. The name of the Usher was not mentioned. It was signed:
Marchmont Herald.

The Duke had quizzed Albany. 'Who is Marchmont Herald?'

Even when told, he was not much the wiser. The man was called
William Cumming, and had business in the north-east and Fife, and
lodgings in Edinburgh. His alliances were with the rich merchant
families: the Prestons, the Napiers, the Bertrams, the Meldrums, the
Errols.

So. A royal herald, but not from the King, since the King was
immured and this message had not come from the Castle. It could be
anything. It was worth taking further. A message was sent back, agreeing, and the men who carried it were followed discreetly to Haddington.
Watchers reported that the sender was indeed Marchmont Herald, and
that he had immediately set out, with two grooms and an official
companion. Someone with good local knowledge and better eyesight
reported who the accompanying officer was.

Hearing, the Duke of Gloucester sent for Harry Northumberland. His face was dark. 'The effrontery! They are proposing to send Nicholas de Fleury to parley!' His voice sharpened. 'Let him come. We shall send them our reply with his head.'

The Percies all had reddish-fair hair and tall brows, which wrinkled when they were perplexed. Northumberland said, 'Certainly, my lord, de Fleury deserves to be killed. He has escaped punishment once. His arrival now would be an insult to England.'

'But?' the Duke said.

'But, however tempting an execution might seem, it might be best to forgo it. I would advise that you refuse to receive him. If de Fleury came, Albany would be involved. And we cannot be sure what the Prince would find tolerable.'

The Duke looked at him. 'We shall never be sure of Albany under any circumstances,' he said. 'As for de Fleury, I suspect that he is being sent as a warning. We are being invited to think again, since they know all our plans. This is a cynical message, sent not by the King, but by clever men. *We all have options*, they are saying. *You can pretend to leave. Albany can pretend to stay. As matters develop, you can continue to bluff, or find the money and men to do something quite different. So may we*'. He fell silent, discontented.

'You will let him come?' Percy said.

'I fear so. We do not have to appear overjoyed. But you are right. We do not harm him, or Albany cannot credibly play Trojan horse, if he has to.'

Accustomed to the nervous protocol of the field, Marchmont Herald was not alarmed to be waylaid halfway through his journey by a group of silent, hard-riding men bearing a paper, sealed by Richard of Gloucester, which invited the herald and M. de Fleury to accompany them. Artlessly, de Fleury was mentioned by name. It was done discreetly, and they agreed without fuss, continuing south by the steep, broken cliffs in virtual silence. Sometimes, the herald wished de Fleury would speak. Then, eventually, he saw by the black smoke in the distance that they were close to the invading army.

It was obvious that the English wouldn't spare Coldingham land, that was for sure. The Priory itself was a different matter. Big as a city, it was capable of housing royal retinues of many hundreds, and of defending itself with the contents of a formidable artillery store. Whatever Gloucester's intentions, he wouldn't waste effort and time on trying to take Coldingham Priory. He would destroy its assets instead, and place his men in the area, under canvas. Which he had done.

The audience tent, in this instance, was as lavishly equipped as that of James, but with a battered air, as if much on campaign. The Duke of Gloucester occupied a state chair, with Sandy Albany on another beside him. The rest of the captains stood on either side, watching. De Fleury, executing his reverence, made quite an impression. His grace of Albany's face was a picture, even though (de Fleury had said) they would have been told to expect him. To be honest, it was all a bit heady; but it was up to a member of the Lyon Court to keep calm, and do his duty, and honour his profession, even though he was not representing the King.

They were offered seats. Folding stools. The Duke of Gloucester said that he trusted his magnanimity would be noted, to wit that he was receiving a man – he would not say a gentleman – who had come to York as a supposed friend, and had been exposed as a spy. The Duke of Albany said that he had appealed to his grace to throw out the turncoat, but had been overruled. The Duke of Albany added that he did not see the point of conferring with a dog who would serve any man for a shank.

Marchmont coughed. He remarked that he would not presume to discuss affairs of state with their highnesses, but that he was here, on the contrary, to arrange such a meeting, if their highnesses willed, with his lords.

Who were?

Who were the Primate of Scotland, William Scheves; Colin, Earl of Argyll; Andrew Stewart, first Lord Avandale; and James Livingstone, Bishop of Dunkeld. In other words, the inner council that once served the King, who was now removed from their reach and imprisoned.

Indeed. And these lords were willing to come to this camp? Or were inviting their highnesses, perhaps, to meet them in Edinburgh?

These lords were proposing a meeting, with hostages, at an agreed place of neutrality, with equal forces in attendance on each side. The place was open to discussion. The time was to be in six days or less.

And the matters to be discussed?

Marchmont introduced Nicholas the Burgundian, who spoke.

They were not answered at once. They were escorted out, after an hour, and were brought back after an uncomfortable spell in another tent, being plied with over-rich food in a parody of subservience. The second time, they were asked many more questions, always returning to the same point. Why was the English King's brother expected to confer with mere ministers? Why was the King still in custody? Once these lords had set to and freed their own King, other Princes would listen. To which Marchmont and de Fleury in turn each gave the same patient answer. The King had been imprisoned by misguided rebels. He was immured in a castle which could withstand a long siege. To obtain a quick resolution, the lords were acting in the King's name. Thereafter, however long it might take, the lords themselves would set siege to the Castle, and gave their word that the King would be freed.

No one liked this reply. The English command objected for a long time. But in the end, they agreed to the meeting.

Riding home, quivering with emotion, Marchmont rehearsed their triumph over and over. '*They agreed!* Twenty thousand men, unopposed in enemy territory, with the King cut off from his army, his ministers, his Parliament, and the King's brother and potential successor in their hands! And they agreed to stop attacking and parley!'

'We were very persuasive,' de Fleury said. He had always been a very jolly fellow up north, but had been disappointingly quiet on this trip. He was quite right, though, with that sardonic remark. After all, Gloucester had really been bound to agree. He was not in the strong position he seemed. He couldn't stay long. He couldn't get the King out. There were few short-term benefits to be had. If he wanted Albany as a puppet, he would be unwise to wreck the lands of his friends. If he was willing to be bribed, he shouldn't offend the princes, ecclesiastical or mercantile, who might arrange it for him. He was vulnerable. The Scots were anxious. If they wanted a meeting, it was obvious that a bargain of some sort was in the wind. If they followed the mild double-talk of de Fleury, they could now at least guess at its nature. Provided his own safety was assured, and it was, Gloucester had nothing to lose.

Marchmont said, 'You must have been glad not to be alone in the dark with poor Sandy. I think he's going the same way as Mar. Anyway, you can present yourself in correct style another time. The Unicorn is a valuable honour. I don't like not wearing my tabard, myself. I shan't be happy until the King is out of there, and we can follow proper practice again.'

It was good, then, to find de Fleury smiling suddenly, in the old companionable manner, and saying, 'It won't be long. We took the first step towards it today. Are you as thirsty as I am? There's a tavern.'

Marchmont protested a trifle, for they ought to return as fast as they could. But he found the idea appealing, and he was pleased with what they'd done, and he was cheered, too, to find that he liked the man after all. Nicol. Nicol, he took to calling him. And the title. He should use the title, a clever man like that, bowing in the Burgundian style.

Gelis said, 'I expected you sooner. Drew Avandale received this peculiar message, urgently dispatched from an ale-house in Yester. The brewster who brought it swore he had been told to say just one word: Yes. Or Yesh, I gather it was.'

'That's why I was late,' Nicholas said. 'I had to tell Drew what Yesh meant.'

They were in their own house, in their own room and nearly in their own bed. It had been rather precipitate. She said, 'Gloucester agreed? You've got what you wanted?'

'Not yet,' said Nicholas crossly.

'From Gloucester.' She couldn't breathe. Her anxieties fled.

'He wouldn't have been any good,' Nicholas explained. 'He doesn't have those little –'

'The meeting?' she said. But she was just teasing now, and was punished for it. At the indisputable end of the tournament, when all the turbulent contestants had left, he roused from a long, waking dream to ask something. 'Where is Jordan? When can I see him?'

Jordan, the man of the future; not Jodi.

'He's with Robin in Adorne's house,' she said. 'Waiting to see you.'

She had been anxious. When he reached to kiss her damp eyes without words, she knew he understood why. But although she waited, he didn't bring his losses into the open; either then, or when they moved, later, downstairs.

The great wound, the deaths of Simon and Henry, was beyond touching at present; but she had expected, by now, to hear him speak of the others, about the friends who had been close to them all. Yet, although she was given a detailed account of the political consequences of Lauder, he didn't mention Big Tam, or Whistle Willie, or Leithie. It was like dealing with the survivors of Nancy again, except that Nicholas was very different from Robin, and the murderers this time had been from his own side. Hence there was not only grief, she suddenly saw, but boiling anger and shame. His friends had died, and he had not been there.

But he was saying nothing about it, as he had dismissed the fact that someone had betrayed him to Simon: *it isn't important*. But, of course, it was.

She interrupted him then, without compunction. 'Nicholas? Are you planning something? Are you planning to run down the men who perpetrated those hangings?'

He looked at her. His hands lay at random and loose, and you had to guess at the effort that kept them so. He said, 'Why? Do you think they should escape?'

'They may be dead already,' she said. 'The underlings, anyway. Tobie saw fallen men from both factions. As for their masters, they can wait. You'll spoil everything if you hound them down right away.'

'So I have been told,' Nicholas said.

'Who told you? What?'

'That the principals will suffer for it in time, but not now, when their very guilt could be an asset. That Tam and Leithie's families, of course, will be lavishly compensated for the delay.'

'And you have agreed to hold back?'

'Yes. It is my misfortune to live with the knowledge that I have neither defended them nor avenged them. It would be a greater misfortune if I put my own feelings first.'

'But?'

'But if the law does not deal with them later, then I shall. I think that would be allowed.'

'Allowed by whom?' she said again.

'By ghosts, largely,' Nicholas said. 'Forget them. We all need to talk about what we have lost and, of course, between us, we shall. I'm only in temporary exile, quelling my impulses. I should like to know about the funerals. Can you tell me?'

She wished she could match him. She could only do her best. She said, 'Yes, I can. Big Tam's will be over. They took him to Renfrewshire, to the family church. Will is at Soutra. The Master and Edward Bonkle took him there. He always wanted to go back to Traquair and Yarrow. They will bury him there, and there will be a service at Trinity. Leithie has gone to the Prestons.'

She broke off, studying his face. He was resting propped in the window, a favourite seat. He said, 'You are telling me that the Kilmirren funeral is over?' His hands had shifted together, their crusted lesions now glazed and pink.

She said, 'In fact, it isn't. Monseigneur left for Kelso as soon as you'd gone. He's had the caskets brought back and set in the Abbey at Paisley. The funeral Mass will be held as soon as the English crisis is resolved. You said you didn't want to attend.'

'I said I wouldn't attend,' Nicholas said.

'Still?'

'Still.'

The ghosts, she deduced in silence, had had no opinion to proffer. No. It was Monseigneur who had proffered the opinion. She tried to show nothing. After a while she said, 'Bel will be with him. Kathi is going, and Robin's grandfather. Men, of course, from the Guard. Someone will arrange to take Wodman. Julius wants to go.'

'Does he?' Nicholas said.

She said, 'He's in Adorne's house, with the rest. They've all moved from the Canongate meantime. Moriz talked to him about the fight you had. Andro as well. You know Julius. He understands you were sick; but wants to know why, if you really thought Simon your father, you kept trying to stop him from proving it.'

'But he has stopped now,' Nicholas said. 'Hasn't he?'

'He's been told to,' she said. 'I'm not going to Paisley. I'm staying here.'

He came over and knelt. He said, 'Go if you want. You don't have to be here. Wherever I am, you are with me.'

Out of turmoil, a testimony. Below death's tattered wings, the glimpse of a marriage, still standing firm.

Part V

Thir men of craft suld kepe a gret lawté,
Off fallowschipe and frendfulnes to be,
Off countenans and word of suthfastnes,
And keip thar promys boith to mor and les.
Ta keipe frendschipe it semys weile thaim till,
And fro discord set baith thar mynd and will.
Frendschip and luf encressis aye the tovne,
The commoun gud discord it puttis dovne.
No thing in erd is swetar for till haif
Than is a frend in traist attour the laif.
Bot for his frende the wys man neuer stud
Agane his aith or zit the commoun gud.

Chapter 45

Now of the merchand suld we saye sum thing.
This popular suld stand befor the king,
That gold and gud be redye at his will,
For his knychtis for to dispone thaim till.

WHEN NICHOLAS LEFT home that day, and those that
followed, Gelis had no need to ask where she would find
him. Now that the orderly fuses were lit and the actors
were charged with their tasks, nothing was left to the
architects of the nation's affairs but to assemble with their servants,
their clerks and their couriers in the Tolbooth, that strong irregular
building, parliament hall, court and prison, next to the church of St Giles
in the High Street, which had become the unofficial council chamber
of Scotland. Now the hired rooms were empty of hucksters: the cells
had become offices serving those larger spaces which acted as meeting
halls, or refectories, or even emergency dormitories. The merchants
who entered these rooms were the chosen representatives of their burgh
and community, members of the grim and anxious consortium of able
men now awaiting news of the events they had caused to unfold.

Outside, on the crown of the hill, the Castle remained sealed; its
drawbridge up; its walls manned by the men of John Stewart of Darnley
and Atholl. No one threatened to enter, but the empty, uneven slope
attracted the curious, who came and stood in small groups, debating
anxiously, or occasionally shouting daring obscenities. There was no
sign that they had been heard; but after the first day, Avandale set a
light guard on the hill, to discourage unseemly conduct.

On the Thursday after Nicholas came back from Coldingham, a
rich cavalcade left the town and rode east, picking up an armed force
from Haddington as it went. It returned the next day, preceded by a

fast-riding courier who burst through the gates of the Netherbow and spurred up the steep, winding hill to the Tolbooth. The resulting conference at the Tolbooth stayed in session until dusk, when men began to emerge, and their torchbearers leaped up to claim them, from the drift of dark, chattering figures waiting in the warm August air. Nicholas, calling good night to Tom Yare, made a decision and walked not to his home but to the High Street house of Anselm Adorne, now host in his absence to some of his colleagues and friends from the Canongate. Julius was there. Young Jordan had recently stayed there too, with Kathi and Robin, but now lived at home with his parents.

Gelis had been right, of course, in her instinct. For Nicholas, to celebrate the love of one son on the heels of the death of another had seemed wrenchingly disloyal at first, until he collected his own thoughts and feelings into some sort of order. After that, opening his door for the first time to Jordan, Nicholas had not, as he had bitterly feared, found it intolerable to see a boy of thirteen, not twenty-one; with plain brown hair instead of gold, and grey eyes for blue. He saw only that the grey eyes were ringed, and the young face pale, and that there was a dam of questions which had to be brought to breaking point and then past it; and that this was his job. The deepest distress, it emerged, had to do with Whistle Willie and Tam. Jordan had known them best of all, although he had admired Henry, in spite of the nonsense at Eccles. Nicholas told him how Henry had outfaced the English and fallen, and how his father had jumped in to save him.

'But he couldn't,' Jordan had said. 'One person can't swim faster than another in that sort of river. You couldn't have saved me in the Findhorn. You have to run along the bank first.'

'You can't do that either, if it's a ravine,' Nicholas said. 'Anyway, the first instinct is to jump. Anyone would.'

He stopped, thinking about it, and found Jordan's eyes fixed on him. Jordan said, 'You did? You jumped in after Henry as well?'

He had told no one that. Neither had Wodman or Adorne. Nicholas said, 'It is an instinct. I couldn't save him. I couldn't save either of them.'

Jordan said, 'Did they know you jumped in?'

'Simon did,' Nicholas said, after a moment. 'Henry's father. Henry just knew that his father was trying to save him, which was all that mattered.'

'But,' had said Jordan, 'you would be glad that you had. That you tried. It wasn't your fault that they died. They were fighting a war. They could have died anywhere.' He paused and said, 'I think you would have felt worse, like I do, if they had died somewhere else, and you just heard of it. You wish you could say goodbye. I wish I could have said goodbye to Whistle Willie.'

'So do I,' Nicholas said. He didn't know how he appeared suddenly to be receiving counsel instead of giving it. He said, 'But people part all the time, without saying anything special. You can't. What is important is that the other person should know you are fond of them. Whistle Willie didn't need to be told that. And he's happy. He had a great, frenzied sunburst of a life, in a place that suited him, and he only suffered for moments at the end of it. You and I are really sorry for ourselves, as much as for him.'

'I'm sorry for him,' Jordan said. 'And for Tam. I would be sorry if anything happened to you.'

'Well, I'm glad of that,' Nicholas said. 'Things do happen. Everyone is taken away, sooner or later. I know how I would feel if I lost you. But you have to live through it. You are your own person, not anyone else's.'

He had left soon after that, leaving Jordan, contented, behind him. He felt much the same. In trying to heal Jordan's hurt, he had somehow crossed the next barrier himself.

That exchange had been private. Tonight was Crown business. This unscheduled visit to Adorne's house was to discuss, with those working with Nicholas, the latest turn in the English negotiations. Undeniably, there was a personal element as well, but that was nothing to be afraid of. He hoped.

Adorne was not in the house. Now, he divided his time between the Tolbooth and Linlithgow, although he had spoken to Nicholas since his return, and his had been one of the aforementioned cautionary voices. Don't rock the boat. Don't seek vengeance, not yet. Adorne had said the same to Father Moriz and Tobie and John, and eventually to Robin, when he fell into one of his rare, uncontrolled rages on Kathi's behalf. 'We are here for the good of this kingdom. Let us deal with that first.' Since Lauder, Nicholas had never been alone with Kathi to talk about any of it, nor had attempted to be. Adult comment (as it had transpired) had not been what he required.

Now, it was Tobie's wife Clémence who opened the door, and accorded him the fond smile he hadn't merited when she was Jordan's nurse, but which he had earned as Tobie's friend. Then he was in the parlour, and all seven of them were there, as he hoped, including his sparring-partner from Kilmirren House, whom he hadn't seen since their fight eleven days before, and who stared at him, grunting, before he sat down. Kathi, her face winsomely blank, said, 'You've come to apologise to Julius.'

Nicholas inspected Julius briefly, without enthusiasm, and returned his gaze to the others. 'No,' he said. 'I've come to tell you the news. Avandale and Scheves and the other two are just back from their meeting with Gloucester. He was, of course, amazed at being asked to negotiate, but ended by discussing the terms on which he might remotely consider ending the campaign. Some were agreed on the spot. The rest will depend on what happens on Sunday, when Wattie Bertram and his burghers go to meet him. It looks promising.'

'What was promised?' said John. John, who had no personal life, felt uncomfortable with others who had, and did not wish to talk about Henry, which suited Nicholas.

Nicholas said, 'What we agreed. The surrender of Berwick-upon-Tweed. The return of Sandy to Scotland, fully pardoned, as the King's most powerful subject, with all his lands and honours restored. Gloucester made a little speech about how sorry they would be to lose him. There isn't, of course, the local backing to support Sandy as King, or not yet.'

No one spoke. These were the terms painfully thrashed out beforehand. It was no less painful to see them about to be ratified. John said, 'And the Provost's offer on Sunday?' Again, they all knew what that was. To save their country, the Council had given up Berwick, and offered their power to Albany. The merchants of Edinburgh, on their part, had beggared themselves to create the final, golden inducement that would save Gloucester's face.

Nicholas said, 'We can only wait. But the feeling is that it will be accepted.'

Kathi said, 'You must have been glad to see Drew and Colin and the other two back. That was dangerous.'

'They're brave men. It was a gamble,' Nicholas said. 'But we had to take it, not Gloucester. He's the King's brother. He doesn't come to a parley that would expose him to kidnapping or murder, or even risk losing him Sandy. Wattie and Tom will be in less danger, we think. They'll want to keep Berwick men sweet.'

'So what comes now?' It was Julius, gazing down his Roman nose; acting the schoolmaster.

Nicholas said, 'Nine griping days. If he's going to do it, Gloucester has to disband by the eleventh: that's when the pay runs out, and the season is starting to close. Then we welcome back Albany. Then we reconcile Albany and the King. What will Liddell do, Julius? Will he welcome Sandy back as well, or has he been juggling the ledgers?'

'He'll weep for joy. You know that,' Julius said. 'He's Sandy's staunchest supporter. After you, of course. That's why Sandy brought you to York. Now he's about to get everything that he asked for. If Sandy's uncrowned King, you're going to be uncrowned Prince.'

Father Moriz said, 'I think Nicholas has more sense than to believe that. Indeed, Julius, you have proved a friend to Liddell, and know as much about Sandy as anyone. I see a role for you in all this.'

'That's what I told the Council,' said Nicholas. 'I also had to say that he and I weren't speaking to one another. Are we?'

'No,' Julius said.

'Well, that's all right,' Kathi said. 'We've finished speaking. Is anyone hungry? Nicholas, what do you eat at the Tolbooth?'

'Each other,' he said. He and Julius were still staring at one another.

Robin said, 'Nicholas, why don't you and Julius go and help Kathi and Clémence? We've no servants left since the children went.'

'I'm not standing over a hot spit with Julius,' Nicholas said. 'Not unless Julius is on it, and turning.'

Neither did he, of course. Instead, he found himself standing in a small room alone with Julius, helping Kathi by tasting her wine. After a moment, he sat down, and so did Julius. Julius said, 'You bastard. I was trying to help you, and you just about killed me.'

'Trying to *help* me!' Nicholas exclaimed. 'You made the old man so wild he bloody disowned me.'

Julius said, 'Dear me! Then you'll have to explain, Nicholas; you really will. First, you don't want me to prove you a St Pol. Next, I'm told to forgive you because you were so upset at the drowning of Simon. Now you're rounding on me for getting you finally barred from the family. Who do you think that you are?'

'Nicholas de St Pol of Kilmirren; grandson of Jordan de St Pol, and son of Simon. Who else?' said Nicholas. 'I don't have proof. If I did, I wouldn't use it, for it would bastardise the son of my marriage.'

He had finally silenced Julius. He had meant to. Julius said slowly, 'You could have young Jordan legitimised. You could get dispensation for any other children you have.'

Nicholas said, 'We don't seem to be about to have other children. And I'd rather have Jordan grow up without his legitimacy being questioned.'

'But Kilmirren?' Julius said. 'Diniz is disinherited. The old man has no other heirs. Will you let it fall back to the Crown when he dies?'

'Yes. There really is no proof, Julius,' Nicholas said. 'You must have realised that. Certainly no papers. And nothing to show that between my mother's first child and my birth she came to Scotland, or Simon went to join her in France. There is only my own unshakeable belief, and the bond I've always felt for them all. So I lost my head when we met. Also, whatever you think of the old man, it was cruel not to tell him the truth.'

The brawl seemed to have slipped Julius's mind, which was following a different track. He said, 'Did you know he was a raving beauty when young? Fat Father Jordan? They said young men swooned in his company.'

Nicholas refilled their cups. He said, 'There was a rumour that he liked boys.'

Julius lifted a brow. 'And you, his grandson, believed it? Not a bit. Don't you remember Diniz being whisked off from your evil presence in Cyprus? And later, Tilde lost her first child from the shock, when the old man was raging about, accusing you and Diniz and Nerio of unnatural practices? No. He didn't like pretty boys. He had a horror of them. That's why he brought up the next generation to be as randy as hell with the opposite sex. It was just as well that Simon couldn't manage much in the fatherhood stakes. Didn't you realise any of that?' He was looking curious.

Nicholas said, 'I suppose I should have.'

'Get the Archer families to tell you. Andro won't, he's too mealy-mouthed. But Johnny Darnley remembers his grandfather's stories – the first Lord Aubigny, whose troops became the French royal bodyguard, that Kilmirren belonged to?' He broke off, considering. 'I suppose it's not surprising, with all those French connections, that Darnley didn't want an English conquest of Scotland. I wonder what he really wants?'

'Supper,' said Kathi, coming in. 'I see you liked the wine. I wonder if we have any more?'

Later, leaving, Nicholas walked with Kathi to the door. She said, 'A reconciliation?'

'More a kind of regal pardon,' he said. 'But thank you, from both of us.' In the distance, Julius, happy, was shouting something to Robin. Close at hand, something sighed. Nicholas stopped.

Kathi had halted as well, her eyes dark in the lamplight. She said, 'Tobie brought the lute back from Lauder. Other things, too. In that closet. You were to have what you wanted.'

He fingered open the door. Drums. He knelt by the nearest, his lips close, and spoke. It replied. When he rested his cheek, it became slowly still, but not deadened. He thought it simply resumed listening. He rose.

'Yes. Soon,' he said to Kathi; and smiled; and left. When he turned, she was standing still, as if listening, too.

On Sunday, the fourth day of August, Walter Bertram, Provost of Edinburgh, together with representatives of the merchants, burgesses and community of the burgh, rode out of the town and proceeded to the appointed place to confer with the Duke of Gloucester, guarded by equal numbers of armed men, as if none was aware that within easy reach was the vast English army, come north last week from Coldingham. The offer on the table was eight thousand marks of English money, disguised as a refund of the Princess Cecilia's dowry, should King Edward decide not to proceed with her wedding to King James's heir. Both were, of course, children; and the wedding contract had long since grown cold.

The delegation returned in safety, as predicted. They brought a conditional agreement. The Duke wished to consider his position overnight.

In the Tolbooth, merchants and noblemen waited in company for whatever was to befall. The windows, set open because of the heat, relayed to them the muted sounds of the High Street, empty of children and treasure, with all its steep, crooked closes blocked by stacked turf and locked gates. The weapons – and there were weapons – were out of sight. If something went wrong – if Gloucester changed his mind; if some contrary order reached his pavilion through the network of relay stations that connected him to the south – some resistance at least would be offered. But against a determined attack, Edinburgh the town could not survive, any more than Berwick had. On the other hand, this was a citadel that would not surrender.

The officers of the Crown and the town slept in the Tolbooth that night: some in beds; most on mattresses. The following day, a herald arrived from the Duke.

It was not, of course, capitulation. It was an intimation that, given confirmation of certain assurances, Richard, Duke of Gloucester, proposed to withdraw, having decided to conclude his campaign. Upon reaching the Border, he expected to receive the surrender of Berwick-upon-Tweed.

It was necessary to receive the news calmly, and to treat the herald and his suite with the ceremony his office required. Clerks were sent for. An official statement was written out, rewritten, agreed, and finally ratified with all the appropriate seals. The herald was feasted, given presents, and finally sent out of town with a guard of honour, a wallet of papers, and a train of packmules laden with precious articles which the Provost and community of Edinburgh wished to bestow on Duke Richard and also, of course, Duke Alexander and their captains.

Even then, no one hurled his cup into the air, or ran screaming into the streets. It had yet to be proved that the army would leave, and that it would attain the Border without destruction and pillage. And that the reduction of Berwick would take place in a civilised manner, as the Council had promised the men of Berwick, in confidence, long before. Berwick had always been the one, attainable prize in this war. The trick had been to save the rest of Scotland from falling as well.

Bit by bit, it fell out as designed. The Duke's pavilions were struck and his host began to move south, briefly escorted by Albany to the limits of his own land, where he stopped. The Duke continued to the frontier, the Tweed, where (reported relays of palpitating riders) he honoured his commitment to disband all his army, save for an extra force which he then took to Berwick. The town was already his. The citadel now prepared to surrender, and, in due course, the Governor and garrison were told that they would be allowed to march out without hindrance. Berwick was about to be English again.

To the worn men in the prison of the Tolbooth, it was the culmination of the second part of their plan, as the King's arrest at Lauder had been the desperate end of the first. They did celebrate, for the loss of Berwick was nothing compared with the saving of the kingdom. Colin Campbell, as temporary host, distributed the best of the food and the wine they had left, and speeches were made which were far from trite, for they paid tribute to the efforts of every man there who had risked his life, his honour, his goods, to reach this miraculous point.

They were still wearily there, in their creased doublets and shirts, in the fumes of the room, when the fresh message arrived: the one which reminded them that the departure of the conquering army had been obtained at a price, and that a different struggle was pending.

From south in the Lammermuirs, the Duke of Albany wrote to his brother's lieges in Edinburgh to command a royal escort for himself and his train, now that he returned to his land with open arms, hoping and expecting to embrace his royal brother.

'Nicol?' Avandale said.

'No,' said Nicholas.

'The rest of us, of course, will also go: it must be an escort of honour. Fresh clothes, horses, harness, heralds, trumpets. A suitable apartment for the Duke: at Archie Holyrood's, or the friars, or James Dunkeld's palace of delights in the Cowgate. Or the house of Sir James Liddell, his factor, if the Prince would prefer it. Liddell, of course, will come with us, but I also wish men I can trust to bear-lead this young man. You and Master Julius, as you suggested.'

'That was when I could still walk and talk,' Nicholas said. 'You are bearing in mind that, before he parted with Gloucester, Sandy will have reaffirmed all his Fotheringhay vows? Whatever they say, Gloucester expects Sandy to make himself King, and acknowledge Edward as his superior.'

Avandale said, 'We all know the situation, I think. Sandy will stay if it suits him, and cross back to England if it doesn't. Your task is to tell us what he is thinking. For example, you still don't believe he'll harm the King?'

'He'll try to discredit him. I don't think he would physically harm him, but others might. Anyway, no one's going to release James or the instruments of power, are they, until we learn a bit more? Whether Gloucester will be made to come back next year and try harder; whether Sandy wants a crown for his Bourbonic son? And in any case, the King shouldn't be rescued too promptly. If his indignant subjects set siege to the Castle, could it hold out forlornly for a month?'

'Their main affliction,' said Avandale, 'would be progressive obesity. But we are in agreement. The King should stay out of reach. The person Albany has to see is the Queen . . . Nicholas?'

'I heard you,' said Nicholas.

Visiting the Queen was never a chore for Drew Avandale, who regarded her, sometimes, as his creation. He couldn't recall whether it was himself or Whitelaw or Argyll who had hit on the idea of presenting that great Scandinavian Queen, another Margaret, as her model. Two generations ago, the other Margaret had ruled Denmark and Norway and eventually Sweden, either herself or by proxy. She had come to power at twenty-two, a clever, ambitious woman, and never relinquished it till she died, aged nearly sixty. Margaret Two was not thus preternaturally endowed, but she would do, and she had been fourteen years on the throne. He trusted her, at twenty-six, to carry off this, the most difficult act of statesmanship in her life. And in his own, very nearly. Bringing Albany to the Queen was a device that could either pull them out of this mire, or sink them for good.

The Duke of Albany's Grand Entry had gone off well enough. As demanded, the escort of honour had ridden south to receive him and bring him to Edinburgh. The streets had been unblocked and swept and there was a lot of dutiful cheering: since the English army had recrossed the Tweed, the children had come back to their homes, if not all the money. Albany had wanted to storm up to the Castle and solicit his brother to come out and greet him, but de Fleury had talked him out of it, and they had settled in Holyrood, with Archie Crawford at his most sincere and disarming. There was no one contentious in Albany's train. The less acceptable supporters had presumably gone straight to Dunbar, now vacated by Murray, the King's man. And Jamie Boyd, if he had marched north with the army, had discreetly left it before it turned south. A few days ago he had turned up, all innocence, in his mother's household, and was now with the Princess in Stirling. Both the Princesses were in Stirling, with the Queen. Sandy was to be made to feel at home.

Using Nicol de Fleury had been a wise move. Sandy's face, seeing him there at the rendezvous, had been a study: the princely hauteur giving way to something less cool, even through the formalities. De Fleury cleverly had not presumed; but had presently been called out to ride at Sandy's side. On his other side, of course, was Jamie Liddell, whom Albany had greeted with a wet-eyed embrace. It was the sentimentality in Sandy that made him vulnerable, as de Fleury had certainly counted on.

Over five continuous years, Drew Avandale and his colleagues had all come to appreciate what they had been given, when Nicol de Fleury chose to turn his back on the turmoil in Flanders, and then extended his stay. They had assumed he was hoping for power, but such power as he had – and it was real enough – was all indirect. He had not even laid claim to the St Pol inheritance. The family funeral was due to take place this week, just as they were setting out on this visit to Stirling, and de Fleury was here, and not in Paisley. Of course, he and Kilmirren were at loggerheads. It was natural. Two prize bulls in one pen. Guts, and guile, and intelligence; but the one with fewer scruples would win.

The Queen had chosen to wear her portrait hennin and gown, and the jewels with a name. The rest of the Court, including the King's sisters Mary and Margaret, were also in heated splendour: it was still August, and warm. From the windows of the audience chamber, looking down and abroad upon the silver links of the Forth, the flowery plain, the hills of the Highlands in the distance, the entering breeze was hardly cooler than the crowded room. The Queen kissed her brother of Albany, and greeted Drew himself, and the Archbishop, in full panoply, and Colin Argyll, who sometimes displayed his independence (if it were ever in doubt) by dressing unsuitably, and would only have been outdone by Archie Whitelaw, had he been here. However. And also, of course (correctly attired) there was Nicol de Fleury, but without Master Julius, who, it was said, had gone to the St Pol interment.

Albany's sisters, who had received the privilege of an earlier, more private meeting, cast flushed smiles at their brother and sat. Mary, the oldest, had recently begun to look her age, which was thirty-one, a year older than the King. Meg, the youngest, had become quite alarmingly plump since her unfortunate lapse into motherhood, and seemed unaware, her eager gaze fixed on Sandy, of any reserve in his face. While elsewhere, perhaps, Sandy had felt closer to the girls and his poor brother Johndie than he found himself now. Yet his siblings had always represented his strength: the four of them impatient of James, whom accident of birth made their ruler. To them, James and the Queen were now the enemy. To keep to his plan, Sandy had to make the most of it.

And to keep to their plan, the Queen had to maintain, as she was doing, a calm and friendly manner, enquiring about Sandy's health, his marriage, and his little son John. She had a child of the same name herself. And here was her oldest son, eager to embrace his loving uncle once more. James?

Thus the Queen, calling forward the boy. She sounded confident, but you could never quite tell what James, Duke of Rothesay, would do. God knew, he had been well enough brought up, but at nine, he sometimes went his own way. On those occasions, his eyes became round and his hair, thicker and redder than his father's, seemed to take on a life of its own. Avandale suspected that James didn't like dear Uncle Albany. Albany's discarded son Andrew shared a tutor with James. If Andrew was in the castle, he wasn't on view. Nor was Jamie Boyd, who had been in York, de Fleury said. At this point, Lord Avandale became aware that the Duke of Rothesay, aged nine, had actually smiled, and was now proceeding to say more or less the right things. The person he had been smiling at, of course, was the same person that Jamie Boyd and Princess Mary his mother used to smile at: Nicol de Fleury. For a moment – only a moment – Andrew, Lord Avandale, experienced a childish twinge of annoyance. No, God save us, be truthful: of jealousy.

The first of the meetings, when it came, was a small one: the Queen, the three lords and Albany, with Master McClery taking notes. The Queen was thankful that the English threat had receded, and was indebted for the part her dear good-brother had played. Her husband, when he knew the facts, would feel the same. Alas, did she not wish, like Sandy, that the King could be freed? But the uncles would not allow it. The uncles – Lord Darnley as well – had imprisoned James for his own good. The uncles – Buchan and Atholl and Andrew – feared the hired assassins of Gloucester. The King himself, she believed, was held back by an entirely unfounded fear of Sandy himself. He feared that Sandy would wish to depose him. He feared that Sandy wished to see her son James on the throne, with Sandy himself as his Governor. And while such a thing, in the long run, was not impossible, there was no chance that the King would place himself in such a position just now. Rather he would die in the Castle.

The Queen's eyes, at the height of her earnestness, betrayed a slight cast.

But, pointed out Sandy (after a moment), was it not necessary for the King to emerge, with the royal seals, if Parliament were to be called? And was it not true that, unless Parliament were called, all the gracious offers to restore his honours and accede to his modest requests would be in vain? In the eyes of the law, until then, he was a criminal.

In the Queen's oval, artlessly painted face could be detected nothing but sympathy. She understood the dilemma. So did her lords. Let them seek a solution together. And, of course, there were gifts within her own competence which she might wish to bestow, and which would not require the ratification of anyone else.

Over the next two or three days they sought a solution, and found one. It was, fortunately, the one already reached, beforehand, by themselves, the Queen and the merchants of Edinburgh. Parliament was to be called. The new situation of Alexander, Duke of Albany, would be placed before it, and his future secured. And in order that Parliament might be properly summoned, with the usual forty days' notice, the freedom of the King was to be achieved by a kindly deception. They discussed the deception, and Sandy agreed.

After the Queen had retired, they sat drinking with Sandy that night, while Nicol treated them, by request, to a number of excruciating tales from his repertoire, followed in due course by Colin, who had a barbed, sleek wit of his own, in both Gaelic and English. Heavy with relief and contentment, Sandy seemed willing to stay there till dawn, and when his servant finally took him away, he was calling for Nicol to go with him, but unsuccessfully, for Nicol had fallen asleep.

When the door shut, he woke up. 'Well done,' said Avandale. 'Well done, everybody.'

A tolerant man, Will Scheves smiled. 'Especially the Queen,' he remarked. Avandale returned the smile. Grimly, as the Great Margaret would have done, the Queen had made her personal contribution to the effort of pleasing the siblings. It meant losing some land, and she had required a little persuasion; but they had laid the matter before her, and she had agreed after a number of talks, some of them with de Fleury in private. Henry Arnot and Adorne had been right: she had taken to Nicholas de Fleury, and so had the young Prince. Because of the Queen, they had been able to promise Darnley a fee for what he was doing, as well as immunity. Because of Will Scheves, they had an inducement to offer the King's uncles. To the public, Edinburgh Castle was sealed, with the monarch inside, but of course there had been constant secret communication between those who occupied it and those who were holding the kingdom together outside. As soon as he, Avandale, got back to Edinburgh, he and the King's uncles would meet, and the King's freedom would be arranged.

It would take just over a month. Beginning immediately, the Castle would be placed under siege by the Provost and leading merchants of Edinburgh in the name of Albany, who had spurned England to seek the love of his brother. And during the month, someone had to persuade the King that he was in no danger from Albany. He trusted the merchants. He was already unsure of the motives of his half-uncles and Darnley. When, in due course, the uncles would (tragically) be driven to surrender, James should be reasonably glad to emerge. It might be, by that time, that someone like Darnley could explain what was happening. *This is the price of Gloucester's retreat. Pay it, for now.*

Or possibly, of course, pay it for ever. Albany's first condition for returning to court had been the prior departure of Argyll, Scheves and Avandale himself, 'who had so nobly held the breach, but who must now be allowed to return to the peace of their estates'. Albany did not wish the King's veteran Councillors, the men who had known him as a boy, breathing over his shoulder. They were being permitted to install him, that was all.

They had agreed. It had been foreseen. It was why they had left Whitelaw behind. They were all leaving for Edinburgh in the quiet of the evening tomorrow. As soon as they had conferred with the uncles, Will and Colin and he would disperse. Not too far, naturally. God knew, they would still require to confer and to meet. But of the old inner Council only Archie Whitelaw would remain, and James of Dunkeld to watch out for the Church, and Nicol de Fleury to watch out for everyone. If Albany was Gloucester's Trojan horse, then de Fleury was theirs.

Colin's mind, obviously, had been running along the same lines.

Stirring, flushed, in his shirt-sleeves, Argyll said, 'Niacal, *fhir mo chridhe, fhir mo chridhe*, do not in any way get yourself killed this day or another, will you then? Your country needs you.'

The Queen's friend was still flat on the floor, but not asleep. 'Which country?' said Nicholas de Fleury.

Colin Argyll unfolded, quick as a polecat. He said, 'The one you are fit for, to be sure. Go where you please. *Foghnaidh salann salach air im roineagach.*'

They were glaring at one another. It must have been quite an insult. Avandale sighed, but not audibly. He said, 'MacChalein has had a few bottles, Nicol.'

'I know,' said de Fleury. 'Otherwise he would never have invited me to his bed.'

'Will you accept?' Avandale said. He was entertained. Colin's fair face was purple.

'Why yes!' Nicholas said. 'I don't mind a bit of *roineachd*.' But before he finished the word, Colin was on him, and they fought with some intensity, for a bit, until they fell apart, satisfied.

Chapter 46

*This king askit at his brother gif he
Wald tak his stait and as a king to be.
Plesit he was and held him weile content
The kingis stait that he mycht represent.*

THE FUNERAL AT Paisley Abbey was unlike that of Lord Hamilton, and when it was over, children did not compete in dangerous races with sledges. Of such a pair, one had now come to his grave, and the other, tall and grey-eyed and solemn, had today been cursed by the dead youth's grandfather and told to get out of the church: *'They brought you here to gloat!'* But young Jordan had stood without moving, and so had Gelis his mother behind him, while the Abbot hastened forward with others of sense and compassion: Robin's grandfather; neighbour Semple of Elliotstoun; the lord of Torphichen; the young men of the Guard who had come to carry Henry's coffin. In the end Andro Wodman, helped by his stick, had taken the fat man by the arm and turned him away, while Bel went first to Jordan, and then to Kilmirren.

Julius, standing by Kathi, had wanted to help, but she had kept him back, to stay beside Gelis. Since Nicholas wasn't here, Gelis should be supported. Kathi had also brought her own daughter Margaret, but not for Gelis's sake. Young as she was, Margaret was a stout friend to Jordan, even though he had left their house now, to prepare for his higher studies elsewhere. Once he had gone, Margaret would miss him, Kathi knew.

The ceremony ended. Afterwards, no one wished to stay there for long. The neighbours and the men of the Guard were offered hospitality, as was proper, but Kathi made her excuses and left, and Julius left with her. Gelis and Jordan had already departed to spend the night with

Tam Cochrane's kinsmen, and she had allowed Margaret to go with them. Kathi wondered how sorely Gelis was remembering her last visit to Beltrees, when Robin had been the bait, and David Simpson had died in Nicholas's place. Someone still wanted to kill Nicholas, and had caused the tragedy they were mourning today. But if today had been perceived by anyone as a lure, it had failed, for Nicholas wasn't here. It struck Kathi to wonder whether Gelis had come in part for that reason: to observe anything or anyone out of the way. But what brought her of course was more than that. Henry had been her sister's son, and her sister had been married to Simon.

Bel of Cuthilgurdy had also left. She had wept at the funeral: something rare for that small, composed woman; and when Kathi had gone to speak to her, she discovered that Bel was not returning to Kilmirren. It did not surprise her. After three weeks as the self-appointed mainstay of that obese, stricken, bitter old man, she was exhausted. Now that Andro was here for Monseigneur, she said, she felt free to go back to her home. Stirling was a short ride away: she would sleep in her own bed tonight.

Kathi, returning to her other children and Robin in Edinburgh, had been more than ready to alter her journey and come with Bel instead, but Bel, after hesitating, had refused. Then, Kathi didn't try to insist. But when Julius set out with her presently, and they came across Bel's small cavalcade on the road, Julius asserted himself. Of course Bel should not return home alone. He and Kathi had to spend the night somewhere. They would diverge to Stirling, and travel to Edinburgh tomorrow. If Bel didn't want him, he would stay at Cambuskenneth, with Abbot Henry.

Julius, when he liked, could be irresistible. Bel agreed, even knowing, Kathi supposed, the inquisition she might be inviting. But, in fact, it did not come. It was a thirty-mile journey, and they were weary. It was more than that. Although she had watched Julius and his insatiable curiosity at work, even here, Kathi knew he realised now that it was fruitless to try and legitimise Nicholas. She had learned of St Pol's explicit denial from her own kitchen: *You made the old man so wild he bloody disowned me.* Since then, she had thought of Julius more kindly. However wrong-headed he might be, he had tried to help Nicholas, over and over. For all they kept quarrelling, he must be the oldest friend Nicholas had. And his greatest pleasure, still, was the excitement he found wherever Nicholas was.

They were within sight of the Burgh Port of Stirling after a hot, tiresome journey when, without warning, their way was blocked by a group of dark horsemen. The men who stopped them were faceless: they wore expensive weapons and armour but carried no emblems. Their own men, of course, were also armed: Julius, never backward, was already offering battle to the opposite captain, who neither answered nor shifted. At the same time, Kathi noticed, there had issued from the Burgh Port in the distance a troop of well-guarded horsemen, riding sedately. They, too, bore no distinguishing marks, and their cloaks hid the quality of their dress. As the gates closed behind them, they began to string out, moving more quickly. Of them all, only one glanced across.

Julius had seen him as well. He called out in surprise, turning aside so that one of their captors, thinking him about to escape, leaned across and seized his reins roughly. The mysterious cavalcade continued regardless. Then the man Kathi had already noticed leaned over, speaking to someone, and the next moment detached himself and trotted over. The captain threw down Julius's reins and went to meet him. They spoke. A moment later, the soldiers detaining them saluted and went, following their fellows along the Edinburgh road. They were free.

Their rescuer approached, and pushed back his hood.

'*Nicholas?*' Julius said.

It was, of course. He was wearing his stand-by expression: one of tranquil authority. 'Kathi? Mistress Bel? I'm sorry. They were under orders to hold everyone back. Let me take you into the town. You're going home?'

'We've come from Paisley,' said Bel. 'Do you have to follow your friends, or can you spare us a night? You'd be welcome.'

'I hoped you'd ask me,' he said. His face, the versatile face, had given way, for a moment, to something he hadn't controlled; and you could see the same attrition, for a moment, in Bel.

Julius said, 'You look terrible. You've spent the night drinking, you dog. What was all that about?'

Julius. What could you do with him?

Often, in her dealings with Bel, Kathi had felt herself under scrutiny, and had realised very soon that this applied to any person of either sex who was connected with Nicholas. She believed she had passed the invisible test, whatever it was, and found proof, if it were needed, during the night and morning they all passed in Bel's house in Stirling. They had come to support Bel, but the situation was made bearable, in the end, by the presence of Julius, whose few observations on the funeral were entirely prosaic, and who preferred to talk about other things. For him, Nicholas outlined, on promise of secrecy, what had clearly been a momentous meeting between the Queen and the Duke of Albany; and watching Bel's absorbed face, Kathi was relieved that she, at least, had received a respite from the burdens of the day.

Bel had a well-ordered house, trained to deal with any contingency. Julius, content in mind and in body, lingered at table, and left it deep in strenuous argument. 'Why not simply kill Albany?'

Nicholas, sharing a settle with Kathi, had treated it seriously. 'The purely practical reasons against? Because the King doesn't want it; and, at the moment, couldn't be blamed for it anyway. Because it would consolidate the faction that already exists behind Albany and his two sisters, who might well invite England to come back, get rid of the King, seize the Prince's guardianship from the Queen and rule in his name, probably through the half-uncles, throughout young James's entire minority.'

'And the less than practical reasons?' Bel said. She had eaten nothing.

'Because we promised him – I promised him – that we wouldn't.'

'He's an idiot,' Julius said. 'So why not kill the King, or free him on condition he abdicates?'

'Same reason,' Nicholas said. 'Civil war, bloodshed, with the weaker party bringing back England. As it is, we've got peace; the King ruling with Albany's help, and a council of sorts to advise them, even if it isn't as strong as the original one. And the Prince is still safe, in the Queen's custody.'

'And you'll be at his side,' Julius said. He had said that before. His slanting eyes gleamed with satisfaction and mischief.

Nicholas said, 'No. You'll be at his side. If he's daft, he needs someone about him who's dafter.'

Julius swung a desultory punch and Nicholas answered it, mildly. The marks of excess (Julius had been right) had receded, and Nicholas had behaved, once in Stirling, as if this were a day like any other. Indeed, he had made only one untoward reference in Kathi's hearing, and that had been a question to Bel. He had said, 'How is he?'

He hadn't mentioned a name. Bel, round and taut as a tabour, had answered immediately. 'Vindictive. Otherwise he wouldn't have survived any of it. He pitched into the boy, into your son, in the Abbey. Gelis will tell you. Like he pitched into you, Julius tells me, in his house. You may not have enjoyed it, but it was a God's blessing to him.'

'I am glad to have been of service,' Nicholas said.

Then Julius came along, and the subject was dropped. But it was the only reference. And it pertained to Fat Father Jordan.

Tobie had talked about the odd, tenuous relationship between Nicholas and Bel. Tobie had found out quite a lot about Bel, and believed that Nicholas knew at least as much. Tobie had investigated the young woman at Chouzy in France, whom Tobie and Robin had once met, and whose *nom de fille* was Claude d'Échaut, or Shaw. She was Bel's daughter. There seemed no doubt about that; or that her father, also called Shaw, must have been Bel's second husband, or lover. And then you had to remember that the wife of Fat Father Jordan, and the mother of Simon and Lucia, had been called Aleis Shaw.

Which connected it all to the St Pols, and accounted for the silence of Nicholas. Whether or not it had anything to do with his birth, he never volunteered anything about the St Pols. And it was time, whether he wished it or not, that that changed. Abbot Henry had said as much, and her uncle Adorne. If only Julius were not there, she would have broached the subject herself.

But Julius, being there, had found topics even more interesting. 'So what about the stupid business at Lauder? I could have told you Tam Cochrane would go his own way. You should have been there. Someone said you had drawn up a blacklist of the killers. Do you want any assistance?' Kathi looked at Bel, and Bel closed her eyes.

Nicholas said, 'I'll tell you if I do. At the moment, we don't want to antagonise anyone. Anyway, we don't really know who they are.'

'I heard Fleming and Crawford and Alex Home,' Julius said. 'And Will Knollys has a finger in most things. And what about the message that told Simon you were going to York? Who sent that? It was meant to kill you. It was just luck that it drowned Simon and Henry.'

'Yes, wasn't it,' said Bel, heaving herself up. 'Kathi, hen, I'm for bed. Will you see me upstairs?'

In her chamber, Bel put Kathi into a chair, and sat down herself. She said, 'Now, now. He's not a frail reed, our Nicol, and he knows Julius through and through. Let them be. Julius will keep treading on toes, just to see what will happen, and Nicol will give as good as he gets. Sometimes a good hearty blow does more for a pain than a tickle. Have you and he spoken about Will Roger yet?' She knew everything.

'Yes,' said Kathi. 'Indirectly. He will come to it, later.' She shook herself. 'I'm sorry. I forget that he can deal with these things now.'

'Oh, he needs us as well,' the small woman said. 'Especially Gelis and you. I think we've turned out a good man, between us.'

'And the future?' said Kathi. 'Who wants him out of the way, Bel? Who sent that message to Simon?'

The colourless eyes studied her. 'Some say it was your uncle,' Bel said. 'Even sober men like John and Tobie and Father Moriz were wild enough to consider it. But there's Andro to say that it wasn't: that he saved his life when he could have killed him, there at Heaton. And for the same reason, it wasna Andro himself.'

'You know it wasn't my uncle,' said Kathi. She felt frightened.

'So does everyone else. It was but a rumour. Like Nicol, he is envied. Your troublemaker may be someone like that: just a man who resents the Burgundians.'

'But he had to know that Nicholas was going to York,' Kathi said. 'Only we knew that, all of us: the House of Niccolò, if you like. Us, and the high-ranking men who arranged it all – Avandale and Argyll and Whitelaw, and Liddell and Albany – whose entire plan depended on Nicholas coming back safely. No one else . . .' Then she stopped, seeing where she had been led.

'So it couldn't have been Simon's father,' Bel said. 'I could have told you that. When Jordan embarks on a piece of wickedness, he takes pleasure in signing it. Or if he doesn't, I can usually tell. No: Jordan de St Pol wasn't the author of the sad, sad thing that ended today.'

She got to her feet. 'Lassie, we both need our beds. Tell me, is your uncle about?'

Kathi jumped up and took the small, puffy hand she was offered. 'He's in Linlithgow with my brother. Why?'

'Tell him to come by and see me one day,' said Bel of Cuthilgurdy. 'And give me a wee cheep as you go. You're a grand lassie, Mistress Katelijne Sersanders of Berecrofts.'

The door gently closed. Carrying to bed the small, dry kiss that was her wee cheep, Kathi heard, from below, the comfortable flow of men's voices: Julius and Nicholas, disputing languidly over something. Bel had been right. While Nicholas had such friends, he was safe.

The elaborate, difficult programme, object of so much anxious thought, slowly began to unfold. The semi-avuncular Earls of Buchan and Atholl and their younger brother, the near-Bishop Andrew, stole out of the Castle, and reached a satisfactory understanding, part of which involved the retiral of Scheves, and the promotion of Andrew to be Archbishop of St Andrews, with the financial help of the town. The uncles returned to the Castle (leaving behind a certain amount of unexplained luggage), and the lords Avandale, Argyll and Scheves vanished from Edinburgh.

The Duke of Albany and the Provost laid polite siege, with a small force, to the Castle of Edinburgh, accompanied by a number of cannon and some handguns, but no ammunition. Carriers of wine and provender were stopped on Castle Hill and requested by bowmen to go away. The Governor of the Castle issued a furious complaint, followed by an order to lift the siege under pain of artillery fire. The Duke of Albany and the town bravely repeated their demand that the King's grace of Scotland be instantly released. The Governor (the Earl of Atholl) refused with equal firmness, but did not fire his guns, which was as well, since they would have flattened the town.

After a siege of over a month, in pleasant weather, the Castle found itself starving, and sent its thinnest envoy to announce its surrender. The date was Michaelmas, that time in late September when the Dozen and the Heid Court went about the business of choosing Provost, Dean and officers of the Guild of Edinburgh for the following twelvemonth. In the final, flamboyant act of his term, Wattie Bertram, in the clean doublet and sark brought by his wife in a basket, rode by my lord of Albany's side into the Castle on the newly let-down drawbridge, and after an interval emerged again with a pedestrian escort of honour, at the head of which rode Sandy Albany, with the King sharing the saddle behind him. The King had a fixed smile, but Sandy's was large and damp and looked genuine. They rode together all the way down to Holyrood between cheering crowds, briskly assembled, and feasted together all night. The King, it was seen, was not hungry, but Sandy made up for it.

Adorne said, 'You wanted to see me?' The day after the feast, it was the first opportunity he had had to ride to Stirling.

Bel said, 'Aye, I did. There's something I want you to know. There's something needs doing, and I don't know who else to turn to. Forbye, it's in your own interests.'

Adorne said, 'You don't need to say that, Mistress Bel. You only need to say, as I am sure you can, that it is for Nicholas.'

Later, leaving the house, he thought to call on the young lady Bonne, placed these several months in the august home of the late Sir William Charteris. His widow, by birth a Stewart, was perhaps too well connected to produce husbands for impecunious foreigners, and none had so far appeared. The nun, Sister Monika, was permanently settled in Elcho, and had washed her hands of the whole affair. The girl Muriella, a handful, was now with Malloch cousins in Edinburgh, in a bleak farm on the far side of the Nor' Loch. She had sung, with her brother, in the memorial service held in the Collegiate Church of the Holy Trinity for Will Roger. Adorne had been there. So had Kathi. So had Nicholas.

Thinking of it, Adorne found himself again moved, as he had been moved to tears by that glorious, unbearable ceremony. And if he felt so, he could not imagine how Nicholas had felt. Years ago, lost in the toils of his miserable plot, Nicholas had sat there, in that beautiful church, and denied the music that Will Roger had made for him. Then Roger had forced him out of his isolation, and had given him in return a burnished talent, and a pass-key to happiness. Next had come the great Marian work they had created together, and after that, alone or with Nicholas, Roger had been spurred to compositions, from sacred to lyrical, that he would never have troubled to create on his own, enriching the lives of all his hearers, whoever they were. If much of the inspiration for the church had been Flemish – through Bonkle, through vander Goes, through Adorne and his friends – then much of what had followed was owed to Will Roger. The foundress, the Dowager Queen lying in her Trinity tomb, had died too soon to know it; but in the north aisle lay someone who did – Bishop Spens, who had also built nearby, and had become one of the sardonic circle of Will Roger's admirers.

All those living were there, although only some, like Nicholas standing apart, were able to offer the dead not only their grief and their love but their voices, floating aloft, traces of the mind of God in the sky. They had sung the *Stirps Jesse* again, from Willie's marvellous responsory, and all the other music was his. At the end Nicholas, adopted into the body of singers, had disappeared in their company, leaving unexplained the last piece of music, performed with John Ramsay and written, you would say, with all the beauty of Nicholas's voice and that of young Johnnie in mind. The text was not elegiac, nor was the singing, which was triumphant.

Now, in visiting Bonne, Adorne was minded to perform a service for Nicholas de Fleury if he could. They had been at odds in the past, with good reason; but now, all that was done. He braced himself a little.

Bonne, the subject of dutiful visits from M. de Fleury, but few from her stepfather Julius, was flatteringly grateful to have the company of a well-born, worldly-wise man who could speak of Flanders and Germany. 'Would you prefer to go back?' Adorne asked.

Encountered outside the cloister, Bonne von Hanseyck was a handsome girl, solidly built, with well-brushed brown hair and a sharp blue gaze which might disconcert weaker mortals. She said, 'I think not. As someone pointed out, my presumed father's family have shown no eagerness to accept me. I begin to fear I am unclaimed goods, like M. de Fleury.'

'He has managed well enough,' said Anselm Adorne. 'Enough at least to have time and money to set aside for someone carrying his mother's name. But it would spare him, of course, if you knew who your real father might be. You are less sure that it might be the Graf? Is there nothing you can remember?'

He listened. It had never been easy to piece together Bonne's past. Once, her self-proclaimed mother Adelina had professed that Bonne was the daughter of Marian, Nicholas's first wife, born in secret and adopted and brought up by Adelina. Adorne was willing to believe that Adelina was not the mother of Bonne, but not the rest of it. All the proof, all the probability was that Marian had borne a dead child, and concealed it from Nicholas to spare him unnecessary grief. Whoever Bonne was, she had been gallantly claimed by the Graf before he married Adelina. And nothing Bonne could remember had ever explained where Adelina had found her.

Nothing she said now added to what Adorne had already heard. Adelina had introduced Bonne as a love-child of the Graf's when she and Julius first met. It had been in Germany, in Cologne, and Gelis, who had been there at the time, had the same impression exactly. So had Father Moriz, who had made later enquiries. After so long, no one was going to remember events in quite the same way, but in one particular they agreed: Bonne's parents were unknown, and likely to remain so. But Nicholas, none the less, was taking the responsibility for her.

It made Anselm Adorne think of his Efemie, who was five, and old enough now to live with her nurse in one of his houses in Linlithgow, with her cousin Saunders to entertain her. Adorne, also, came almost every day to visit his daughter, as he had omitted to do with the children who were now grown up in Bruges, and who sent him admonishing letters from convents. It was not their fault. He had been negligent. But there was the humbling example of Nicholas – Nicol – who had grown up fatherless and virtually motherless, and yet could open his heart to care for Phemie, and for everyone's children, not just his own. When in Edinburgh, Lord Cortachy made a point of talking to young Jordan, when calling on Gelis; and spending some time in the Canongate with six-year-old Rankin, Robin's newest trainee and heart's joy. Rankin was never relinquished to accompany his mother's uncle, but occasionally Adorne would borrow Margaret, the boy's older sister, and take her to stay with Euphemia.

His heart went out to them both: his little deaf daughter and his great-niece, just two years her senior, with her long lashes and quick smile and tapering fingers, so like his own. When, one day, he would no longer be there, he trusted his nephew Sersanders to look after them; setting aside any other entanglements he might have. But he liked to think of the two girls growing to womanhood with the infinite blessing of Nicholas's care, and that of Katelijne. It was too late for Jan and Antoon and Arnaud and the rest, but with these children, he could make a fresh start.

He spent some time with Bonne, and then left, having achieved, he thought, very little. But his expectations had been low. He became immersed in certain preoccupations of his own and was not necessarily delighted to hear that Prosper de Camulio of Genoa was coming to Scotland to take up his bishopric in this, the non-fighting season of winter. Adorne's connection with Genoa was past. He had begun to think that Bruges might be behind him as well. Lodged in an alien country, itself on the edge of rebellion, he had found a place where his experience could make a difference; a kingdom he could help make effective. He had concluded, quite recently, that this was the way he wished to finish his life.

He had also realised that he owed much of this decision to his regard for Nicol de Fleury. It was important to him that de Fleury should equally make this commitment to stay, and that he should not be impeded by any faceless threat to his safety. Adorne wished to trace the perpetrator of the slaughter at Heaton. Mistress Bel had concurred – had indeed felt uneasy enough to approach him. Kathi, when told, had been less eager to revive what had happened. Adorne had mentioned his interest to no one else. As a magistrate, he had tracked down lawless men often enough. These investigations took time and patience and dedication, but he had all of those. It was a wry atonement to Nicholas for all those well-deserved beatings, long ago.

Nicholas himself, who would have stopped him, was at Holyrood all through October, shut off from his wife and his family; locked into the sequence of events, deadly, farcical, that he had helped set in motion. Even had he desired to leave, Albany would not have allowed it. Albany had received certain promises, and was waiting, critically, to see them carried out. Only then – when restored to all his former lands and offices, when the King had bestowed upon him his dead brother's earldom of Mar, with more honours to come – only then did Sandy's face lose its starkness, and his daily bouts of camaraderie with the King begin to sound natural. The King, by contrast, was losing whatever ability or willingness he once had to respond. Filled with fear and bewilderment, surrounded by men he did not trust, James did what was asked of him, quite simply, lest he be killed.

A simulacrum of majesty was provided. The nationwide call to a December Parliament was sent out; but for lesser matters, where James lacked the Privy Seal or the Signet, he had recourse to his ring of the Unicorn which, it had to be noticed, was singularly similar to that often used by Adorne. By letters sealed with the unicorn, John, Lord Darnley, was thanked for his care of the King, at a time when His Majesty feared for his life, and he and all of his followers were exonerated from any suspicion of improper conduct. Lord Darnley was invited to depart, confiding the Castle to Governor Atholl, or his representative. Thus, with skill, the various factions of the garrison were exculpated, and could prepare to move out with impunity.

The besiegers received separate thanks. For the faith, loyalty, love, goodwill and cordial service which the office-bearers of the burgh of Edinburgh had, with his brother Alexander, Duke of Albany, rendered His Majesty, at the peril of their lives, by freeing him from prison in the Castle of Edinburgh, His Majesty gave, granted and perpetually confirmed to them the office of sheriff within the burgh for ever, and equally their enjoyment of the customs and moneys arising from the Port of Leith. Special prizes for good behaviour seemed to appear every day: Wattie Bertram alone got a forty-pound pension for losses sustained in the King's name, and Dod Robieson had had his lost treasure made good, and Alex Lauder, who had removed it (to order) commanded to make restitution.

The King, it was implied, was among friends. While some had bravely detained him for his own safety, others had tried to create a climate into which the King might safely step. He was now reassuring his well-meaning captors that they would suffer no harm.

Grindingly, all the other promises were realised. On the fourteenth day of October, the Princess Mary was given life-rent of the barony of Kilmarnock, the barony of Dalry, and other Ayrshire lands which had belonged to the Boyd family of her first husband, the same to descend in feu to her son James, second Lord Boyd. No mention was made of the fact that these belonged of right to the eldest son of the King, and were presently held by the Queen as part of her dower; or that the lands of Tealing and Polgavy, which she also received, had once belonged to Anselm Adorne.

By the twenty-seventh of October, the King of England had made it known that he proposed to cancel the marriage arranged between his daughter and the Prince of Scotland, and advised the town of Edinburgh that he awaited the return, as arranged, of the dowry money. The town pledged itself, in the vestibule of the church of St Giles, to fulfil its promise. At about the same time, it constituted Procurators to appear in the banks of Rome, Venice, Florence, Bruges and others following the Court of Rome, there to speak for the sum of six thousand gold ducats, on the security of Edinburgh's income and property, in case of the promotion of Andrew Stewart, the King's youngest half-uncle, to the Archbishopric of St Andrews. At a meeting attended by the three half-uncles and Jock Ross of Hawkhead, the future Archbishop, having at present no money or credit, promised to reimburse the town in due course.

So the merchants, the producers, the shipmasters, the agents with their foreign credit, their kinsmen, their acumen became the kingdom's bank and its bulwark in time of disaster.

Plunged into the feverish company of Albany, Nicholas negotiated each day with all the skill at his command. To help him, he had his own servants and Julius, but not Sir James Liddell, who had disappeared. Newcomers from Glasgow filled Avandale's post and that of the Clerk Register Inglis, but there were also familiar faces: those of Bishop Livingstone of Dunkeld, under whom both Inglis and Scheves had held office; and the two Archibalds, the Abbot-Treasurer and Master Secretary Whitelaw, who kept him advised about the temper and mood of the King.

Nicholas's first audience with James was not pleasant. Until Whitelaw intervened, in a rattle of waspish humility, Nicholas found himself regarded as a renegade who had courted Gloucester in York, who had given away Berwick, and who was in the process of wrapping up the rest of the kingdom as a present for Albany. In the end the King professed to accept that it was all done in the nation's best interests, but he clearly still entertained doubts.

Had he been a better actor, they could have been frank. They had hoped to be. As it was, no one dared hint that the Duke of Albany's present ascendancy might be temporary, given certain felicitous conditions. For the moment, Sandy must be coaxed into thinking that everything he wished was now in his grasp. And, of course, he might be right. There might be no alternative. The King might end as a figurehead, while Sandy held all the power.

Just before Nicholas left, that first time, the King had thrown him a question. 'We are told you have seen the Queen's grace?'

The royal chambers at Holyrood were not large. Standing in front of the dais, Nicholas looked directly into the gaze of the King. He said, 'I had that honour, my lord. Her highness was in the greatest anxiety. It was through her kind offices that the arrangement was made which allowed your grace to leave the Castle. I am sure others have praised her devotion.'

'But you left her in Stirling?'

Nicholas said, 'She remains in Stirling, my lord, because it is the safest place for herself and the Prince in these changeable times.' He tried to convey what he meant (Be thankful: she, not Albany, is the guardian of your children). He tried to conceal what had happened (Albany wants you to abdicate, but your Queen found a way to prevaricate).

'You have leave,' said the King. (Go away.)

The short English truce, created to cover the Duke of Gloucester's retreat, expired at the beginning of November, and was not renewed. The King of England was not pleased with his brother, who had spent a great deal of money and achieved Berwick, which might be nice for Harry Percy, but Harry Percy didn't have to pay for its upkeep. Edward, booming, was even less enchanted when the King of France, with whom he had had a secret truce for over a year, forgot himself and referred to it openly. Even when bed-ridden, Louis could make himself felt.

It indicated, to the wise, that the said truce was about to come to an end. It confirmed, in Scotland, why France had let Albany go to England in the first place. It opened several possibilities for the future.

The sweetness and light within the Abbey of Holyroodhouse became further obscured, and a messenger arrived for the Abbot, who sent for Nicholas. Surveying him, he said, 'Are you as harassed as you look?'

'Yes,' said Nicholas. 'I've been hunting all morning and trying to lose at a board game. What has happened?' He was beyond being worried. He knew, in any case, that nothing was wrong with his friends. With an abbot as collaborator, there was little to stop a man of ingenuity from infiltrating from the Canongate into Edinburgh now and then. Otherwise he would be looking rather more harassed.

The Abbot said, 'Sir Oliver Sinclair has sent to ask you to visit. Sandy would allow it. It's Roslin, not the Edinburgh house.'

'Freedom!' said Nicholas.

'No. Just a day away from James and Sandy. Well, freedom,' the Abbot agreed.

Chapter 47

This brother seid: I am in sic a dreid
Off zone scharpe swerd that hingis be zone threid,
That all blythnes in erd is reft fra me.
I will na mair of sic a dignité!

THE MASONS' PART of the hamlet at Roslin was empty, but
the rest of the cabins were full and busy. The Sinclairs
created plenty of work, and they had just finished the fair of
SS Simon and Jude, which did well, despite Jude's being a
hopeless-cause man, without much to say, you would think, to a Sinclair.
Nicholas returned a few amiable greetings but continued down to the
castle, passing on his left the memorable collegiate kirk, dedicated much
more suitably to St Matthew, farmer of taxes.

So the Sinclairs were rich and cheese-paring. But they also fought at
the battle of Bannockburn, and signed the Declaration of Independence,
and one of them had been chosen to carry the heart of Robert the
Bruce to the Holy Land. The first Sinclair to cross to England from
St Clair-sur-Epte had fought at the Battle of Hastings under William
the Conqueror, who was his cousin, and descended from the same
Orkney Jarl.

The selfsame blood had run in Phemie. You could understand why the
Sinclairs had had no objection to Phemie's courtship by the well-born
knight and judge and councillor from Burgundy. To aid the King they
served, they were prepared to plunder men from any culture and any
country: gunners and doctors, teachers and churchmen, builders and
miners and carpenters, moneyers and metal-casters. Clever agents and
administrators like Sersanders and, he supposed, himself. And if they
married and settled down, so much the better. Nicholas crossed the
bridge and was cordially received by the chamberlain and taken to Sir

Oliver Sinclair's big chamber. Nowie rose. So did the three men sitting with him. One was Anselm Adorne. One was the young nephew Henry, whom Nicholas had last met in Orkney. And the last was Prosper Schiaffino de Camulio de' Medici of Genoa, the newly made Bishop of Caithness, that part of north Scotland that stretched from the Pentland Firth to the Dornoch Firth, and from the west sea to the east. Caithness, of which Nowie's younger brother was Earl, Justiciar, chamberlain and sheriff. Naturally.

They had last met when Camulio was Papal Legate, here in Edinburgh at Blackfriars five years ago. Since then, the Legate had been in prison, had lost his Procurator David Simpson (who had probably helped to put him there), and had been ranging Europe on curial business on a route which had just failed to cross that of Nicholas three years ago in Bruges. He had, however, met the former Franciscan friar, Ludovico da Bologna. So had Nicholas, Camulio understood. What a character!

He appeared just the same, with over-rich clothes and over-smooth skin, and a sly, busy look to him that always made Nicholas feel cheerful. Adorne, behind him, looked suspiciously grave. Nicholas said, 'Where is the Patriarch now?' He had heard nothing since he had seen him in Cologne with Moriz.

The Bishop sat, and so did everyone else. His robe was pure silk and his crucifix was quite glorious. He said, 'I wish I knew. The Emperor and His Holiness had each prepared urgent tasks for him, but he failed to appear.'

'He was ill?' Nicholas said, a little sharply.

'Not so far as anyone knows. Unless it is a sickness – perhaps it is – to send word that you may no longer fulfil the demands of your masters, for God has called you to do something else.'

'And had He?' said Adorne. He turned to the Sinclairs. 'We speak of a singular priest, who has travelled the world for his faith. If the Deity deigned to address anyone, I should think Ser Ludovico da Bologna would be the man.'

The Bishop remarked, 'I am prepared to believe that He did, although I trust that, if so, Our Lord used the vernacular rather than Latin. The Patriarch mentioned Ethiopia.'

'Ethiopia?' Nicholas said. The young nephew – Henry – looked at him.

The Bishop said, 'You went there with his encouragement once? Or part of the way?'

'Part of the way,' Nicholas said.

'I thought I was right. He spoke of taking another route, and doing better this time than you and the priest. I am sorry. He did not mean to be harsh. Indeed, he had set aside a memento he wished me to give you.'

It was a stout battered rosary, chipped and mended and caulked with what appeared to be fragments of food. You could almost imagine it smelled.

Nicholas suddenly laughed, moved by that affection which can sometimes alleviate grief. He said, 'Oh, he meant to be harsh.'

With Nowie for master, no meeting ever wasted too much time on the personal. The first encounter between Nicholas and Camulio had been in Bruges, long before Africa, and had taken place during the last days Nicholas had been vouchsafed with Marian, his first wife. Camulio had known Adorne and Julius then, and now brought messages for them both from Genoa and Bologna, and news of Gregorio in Venice, and Tommaso Portinari and Maria and the six children, struggling to survive without their Medici credit; and, of course, from Diniz and Tilde and their family in Bruges, whence he had just come. These he was allowed to deliver, and some account of his journey. Then Nowie stepped in, with an interrogation which found an equally ready response.

The French-English truce? Genuine enough at the time, the Bishop thought, but now being used to trap larger fish. 'Maximilian is horrified. He now knows that England has been cheating him, and never intended to help him with archers. More, he knows he can never defeat France on his own, for the Estates of Flanders will now refuse him men and money. So – who will take a wager? Maximilian and France will make peace.'

'And England will take her revenge on France, or on Scotland, or on both?' Adorne said.

Camulio said, 'We are not speaking of England, but of Edward. Edward is impulsive and angry and, I am told, not very fit. Sick men take risks.'

Adorne said, 'They may, but Parliaments are more cautious. I doubt if Edward will be allowed to attack France, but he might send Gloucester back north in the spring. And if he does, what will Albany do? Nicholas? We need a report from the interior.'

'Then I need one from the exterior,' Nicholas said. 'Where is Liddell?'

Nowie Sinclair smiled. His nephew – Henry – who had been watching in silence, stretched suddenly and smiled also. Since Orkney, it had become clearer that this was one of the Sinclairs to watch. He was contracted, by God, to marry the granddaughter of Princess Joanna.

Nowie said, 'Sir James Liddell is back in Dunbar. But you are right. Sandy sent him to London. He was escorted by Dickon's own servant, and they paid him forty pounds for his trouble. My reading is that Gloucester demanded to be reassured that Sandy's intentions and loyalties were unchanged, and Sandy obliged. Also, Sandy wanted some encouragement for Bell-the-Cat.'

'Bell the cat?' said the Bishop of Caithness. They were talking, for his benefit, mostly in Latin and French.

'The Earl of Angus,' Nicholas said. 'He got the nickname from arresting the King. He lives in a very large sea castle close to Dunbar, and Albany would like him as a possible ally. Angus is holding back, because he may lose land to a rival branch of the family favoured by Gloucester. I think he'll still hold back, just as Sandy is watching the honours roll in, and weighing his chances. My report from the interior says that Sandy will have decided by Christmas whether he wants to oust James, or will be content with what he has. My prediction is that he will be content, provided that James remains calm. There are a few hotheads in Dunbar, but Liddell isn't one of them.'

'And what is your view of the King?' Nowie asked. 'We are so fortunate, Nicol, to have someone like yourself in constant company with him. You have not told him, for example, of his brother's secret undertaking at Fotheringhay, for that would lead to immediate civil war. So long as you avoid telling the King, Gloucester may deduce that we lack the means to overthrow Sandy. It may encourage him to come north in strength.'

'Or it may not,' Nicholas said. 'He cannot be sure. We may have the power to dispatch Sandy, but prefer to win him to stay here, in his own country with his brother. Or we may not have the power to dispatch Sandy now, but news of his treachery would soon change the balance.'

The nephew – Henry – said, 'So why not take the risk and announce it now, during the winter, when England can't interfere? Then all those who don't want Albany as King, or England as overlord, will cross to help you.'

He was young. Also, Albany had divorced his aunt, and bastardised his three cousins. Nicholas drew breath, but Adorne replied. 'It is possible. On the other hand, men have committed a great deal to this peace. In breaking it, lives would be lost, and the Stewart family split, perhaps needlessly. Events overseas may lift the pressure from Scotland, and give us time to shape a new order. I think, with Nicholas, that we proceed slowly, and change what we can, and tolerate meantime what we cannot.'

'A Christian sentiment,' said the Bishop of Caithness.

'A humane one at least,' Nowie said. 'I hope we can afford to maintain it. So. You think, Nicol, that the King can tolerate it as well, so long as his friends keep him calm? But at the same time, the lords you can depend on will keep their men close to Edinburgh and prepared, through the winter? Good. And now to more pleasant things, my lord Bishop. I trust we have not marred your felicitous arrival. These are difficult times.'

'There are princes,' said the Bishop, 'who would weep with joy to have no more to contend with.' Nicholas avoided Lord Cortachy's eye. If anyone knew, it would be Camulio.

Returning, Nicholas did not pass the church of St Matthew but, by arrangement with Nowie, was met there and admitted by a servant who then left him alone.

Candles had been lit. St Bartholomew flourished his flaying-knife. St Roche showed the plague-spot on his leg. Amid the reptilian mass of stony grotesqueries, it was obvious that all the pillars were solid; none more so than that by the Lady Chapel, with its merry capital of blowing, plucking and drumming musicians, including the determined man with the bagpipes, *cibalala durie*. It was necessary to view these things with good-natured acceptance.

A door creaked. Adorne's voice said, 'May I join you? Or not?'

Phemie's bier had lain there, below the east window. Nicholas said, 'More than anyone else.'

Adorne came forward: a spare, graceful man with clear eyes. He said, 'I have been here many times. This is your first, since Tam and Will died?'

Nicholas said, 'They were both here, the day I came to see Phemie.' There were garlands as well as demons round the pillars, and upside-down flowers thick within the towering vaults of the ceiling, forty feet over their heads. He added, 'We sat and drank and told stories round the fire in the sacristy. It didn't feel like sacrilege.'

'A dear man, Tam; and mild as a novice in arms, except when in thrall to his latest enthusiasm. It can happen to anyone. Have you ever wondered,' Adorne said, 'what Archie Holyrood does with the Abbey treasure in time of war?'

He had seated himself on the step to the Lady Chapel. Nicholas let himself descend to the floor among dragons. 'Treasure? No?'

'Yes. He puts it in the Castle, of course, if he can, or locks it away in the Tolbooth, or with Wattie Bertram, or Swift. If Edinburgh's barred, he'll spread it around. Craigmillar, Blackness, Newbattle and, of course, here. That's when masons come in useful.'

'I didn't notice anything,' Nicholas said.

'You wouldn't. They were also doing some genuine work. But I shouldn't mention it to Knollys,' Adorne said. 'You know he was Lord High Treasurer himself for a year? Thirteen years ago. He has a secure house at Torphichen, and remains glad to rent out its strong-rooms; but I don't think Archie wants to be badgered. Nowie, of course, esteems the Preceptor as we all do, but with personal reservations. You have been told to leave Knollys alone?'

'I have been told to leave everyone alone,' Nicholas said. 'For the moment.' As time went on, the white heat of his anger over Lauder had died, as the killers had probably done, on the spot. That put the blame on the men the killers were trying to please, and the mad and glorious folly that had sent Tam on to the bridge, and Leithie to help him, and Will to gallop about getting angry. Anyway, no one had been punished because it was not a time to make enemies. And some recompense had been made: Leithie's young Archie would probably get the good land at Cousland that the Prestons and Cochranes held under the Sinclairs, and Leithie's widow had been given the prize money Leithie had earned bringing the wine-ship back from Orkney. It had angered Nicholas, to begin with, that the few lands of both men had been forfeited, as if they deserved to die. But unless that happened, of course, the law would have to be invoked. And the King would re-grant them, in time.

Adorne was speaking again. 'Nowie feels protective over his tenants. You may find that, in the long run, he has forestalled you. I have to tell you that I have been interfering as well. Mistress Bel knows. I have set myself to search out the man who put the St Pols on your trail. I want him caught for your sake, of course, but there are other considerations. Whoever he is, this man also knew more than he should about Sandy. He could create a rift between Albany and the King.'

'He won't,' Nicholas said. 'I don't think he was interested in Sandy or me. All he wanted, surely, was to hound the St Pols into danger. Otherwise, why drag them in? He could have got rid of me by himself. Look, it's over. I don't want to know who did it. It's four months ago; I can't think there is any more danger. And if there is, I'd rather risk it than have Simon's private affairs dragged into the open. Tell Bel, and anyone else.'

'Only Kathi,' Adorne said. 'But we think there is nothing shameful about it: nothing that would reflect on the St Pols. You must trust us.

We don't agree with your theory, but we're not as gallantly perverse as Julius. We think the message came from the Border country; from a resident, even, with friends over the river. We think you were the target. Perhaps he thought you a traitor to the King. Perhaps he knew you weren't, and wanted you out of the way. Plenty of Borderers have a good understanding with the English. And he needn't dirty his hands: the St Pols' dislike of you was well known.'

'It's a nice theory. But why pursue it?' Nicholas said. 'Some small two-facing laird in the Borders isn't going to damage the King's trust in Sandy. He won't get near him, for a start; that I can promise you.'

His voice had sounded, he thought, as it usually did. Despite that, the other man's face altered in the flickering light. Adorne said, 'The King wants you with him through Yule? To entertain him?'

'And Sandy. And Mary. Everyone will be at Court but the Queen and the Princes. It is the crucial time. If they are going to live and work together, the foundation for it has to be laid now. As you can imagine, it won't be especially delightful for me, but there are other players and other musicians, besides Will. It won't be as fine, but nothing ever will be as fine, and they won't notice it. And it will free me to help in other ways.'

Adorne said, 'You think that excellence will never return, but it will. Nothing ever stays still. A branch dies, and the sap gathers, and bursts forth elsewhere. Would you rather be preached at by Camulio?'

'I don't think Camulio would convince me,' Nicholas said. 'And I couldn't ask him the favour I am about to ask you. Would you and Bel and Kathi save your theory until after Yule, and meantime leave it alone?'

'And after Yule?' Adorne said.

'I don't know,' Nicholas said. 'Perhaps my mind will have caught up with my emotions, or the other way round. The graves are too fresh, just now.'

Adorne's eyes were full of pity. He said, 'I have just told you. I think this had nothing to do with the St Pols.'

The bagpiper played, silently, placidly. The wild men leered. There was a beautifully scrolled Latin legend above the stairs to the sacristy which, translated roughly, stated that wine was strong, the king was stronger, women were stronger still, but truth conquered all. The present conversation, elegantly scrolled, would make just as much sense.

It wasn't Adorne's fault. Nevertheless, Nicholas replied with uncharacteristic savagery. 'Of course it had to do with the St Pols. It killed them.'

*

It seemed, at that point, as if a steady nerve would carry everyone through the precarious journey that lay ahead. The threatened conflagration had been quelled and a kind of template produced which might steer them clear of another. Nicholas returned to the Abbey, but Anselm Adorne, saying nothing, went straight to the comfortable, well-appointed house in the High Street where Nicholas was once to be found and spoke to Gelis alone.

Something about him must have startled her, for she closed the door and seated herself and him at once. 'Something is wrong?' She knew they had both been to Roslin.

'With Nicholas, no. With myself, perhaps. That is why I am here. Gelis . . .'

He hesitated, and she sat quite still, watching him with that pale, Arctic gaze below the heavy van Borselen brows. Once, he had thought her cold, but now knew that it was self-control he was witnessing. He said, 'I do not have his full confidence. I hope that you have.'

There was a silence. Then she said, 'I know all that matters. I wouldn't expect to be told everything.'

'This matters,' said Anselm Adorne, 'but he is concealing something about it. He is a good actor, but I have known him from boyhood. I need to know what he is not telling us. There is no stain on his own life; I am sure of it. He is lying to preserve someone else. There was nearly a tragedy – there was a tragedy – over Adelina. It must not happen again. He cannot protect all the world.'

'He thinks he can,' Gelis said. 'So why is it important?'

Again, he hesitated. Then he said, 'I have been trying to find out who told Simon that Nicholas was secretly going to York. I have a clue: the message came from the Borders. Nicholas will not listen, and has asked me to halt the enquiry. He either knows the answer, or means to pursue it himself.'

'He will know,' Gelis said. She spoke with unemphatic certainty. He had been acquainted with Nicholas from boyhood, but Gelis had fought to understand him, on and off, for eighteen years. She added, 'You are saying that you – and perhaps others? – have had to promise to leave it alone, but the rest of us haven't?'

'That,' he said. 'Or I hoped the name of the spy might suggest itself.'

She said, 'No. I don't know, and if Nicholas has asked you to stop, it's for a reason. Whatever it is, leave it to him.'

'Do you think he is infallible?' Adorne said. 'Simon and Henry died. Nicholas himself would have died, had I not been there. He is one of the most remarkable persons I know: a doer of startling works; a man who finds wisdom through his mistakes. But there is one area where he is still blind; you may say heroically blind. He has still to learn that life is not a noble fable for children; that honour is not sacrosanct; and that, for the desirable good, one may be forced to walk naked of the garment of loyalty.'

She said, 'I don't want you to teach him.'

They looked at one another. Then he said, 'No. But I would rather he learned this lesson from a friend; and I would be that friend.'

He wanted her to know how grave it was. He was using her to warn Nicholas that he was reneging. He had considered the possible hurt, and the danger, and had weighed it against the public good. It was what Nicholas ought to have done, and had not.

On a Monday in early December, the Parliament of Scotland met in the Tolbooth of Edinburgh for the first time since March. The monarch led the procession of state from the Abbey of Holyrood, filling the winding defile with banners and singing and incense, silks and velvets and furs and fine, gentle gems. It was reminiscent of the wedding cavalcade of the Queen, except that the King rode with his brother; and Avandale, Scheves and Argyll were now missing. So also, it transpired, were the small lairds who normally made up the tally. The assembly, when it finally settled, numbered only fifty-eight. It was sufficient, however, to appoint the committee which was to consider the new offices proposed for the right high and mighty Prince Alexander, Duke of Albany. The committee sat down to its deliberations, which they were to complete for the Three Estates in ten days.

The Queen in Stirling, sadly debarred from these events by ill health, was well enough by the Saturday to attempt a recuperative sail with her eldest son and her suite. It took her to the Governor's jetty at Blackness, where she was met by that gallant poet and jouster Sir Jock Ross of Hawkhead, once a favourite of her late father. Within the hour, she had arrived at her own Palace of Linlithgow. It was the seventh day of December, the eve of the fifty-eighth anniversary of the birth of her Keeper, Anselm Adorne, Baron Cortachy; which occasion his sovereign lady had chosen to mark with a feast.

Considering what this had entailed, Lord Cortachy and Saunders his nephew looked as marvellous calm as two pax-boards to the many guests from Linlithgow who counted them friends. Of course, when you got up to the hall, everything would be of the best. With Seaulme directing, the wagons from Stirling would have been stripped in a trice, and the linen, the staff, the provisions all punctually dealt with – none of your beans with their pods on, or windy meat here. Even the Master Cook would have to keep his mouth clean, or dip his hand in the swearing-box. There! What did I tell you? Wax lights. And the Queen's own patterned hangings. And linen napkins, all new-chopped from the roll.

Of course, his lordship's own house in Bruges was a palace with its own kirk, and his cousins were doges in Genoa. That was why the Genoese Bishop was here, on top of Nowie Sinclair and Will Knollys and a few others you wouldn't expect in the same room – as well, of course, as all the ones you would. Kathi, the spunky wee niece, chatting with Jock Ross and the comfy widow that once had Cuthilgurdy. The bald Italian doctor, him that was a dab hand at itch of the purse; and the unchancy one, Andreas from Vesalia, that some people thought dabbled in magic.

Julius, the lawyer from Bologna who looked so rich and grand, but could keep you roaring over a wine-cask. The Scandinavian shipmaster, Crackbene, with the fine armful of a wife, jabbering away at the Queen in her tongue. Big Nicol's clever lady, as good as a man in the warehouse, and the laddie their son, a well-mannered wee loon, standing listening to the young Prince. And the Prince glancing at Big Nicol, who had not been the same since Will Roger lost his head – or, to be sure, had it half cawed off him – at Lauder. Yon was a shame. The two of them on the fiddle and drums, late at night, fleeing with Danzig beer, and making up verse about every bastard at court, so dirty and daft you could shite yourself. Those were the days.

'Poor Uncle,' said Kathi. 'Doom threatens the nation, and he has to give a party for himself. We thought you wouldn't come.' It sounded challenging. She added quickly, 'Not for personal reasons. I know you advised against this.'

'I was probably wrong,' Nicholas said. 'And your uncle deserves to be honoured.'

Her uncle deserved to be honoured, and so she hadn't protested; but she understood Nicholas's unease. The truth was that the supper was more than it seemed. It was an excuse to bring together men who could not appear in Edinburgh, but could inform the Queen of what was happening there. Avandale, Argyll and Scheves were all privately here, and Avandale's kinsman recently departed from Edinburgh Castle: John Stewart, Lord Darnley, who had commendably saved his young kinsman Johnnie Ramsay at Lauder, and who had daughters contracted to the heirs of Argyll and Jock Ross.

The feast for Adorne was thus, in part, an excuse for the Queen's faction to meet without being identified. In the wrong quarters, such a concourse might seem like a second Court, a duplicate of the King's. In reality, it *was* a second Court. The Queen was the legal guardian of the heir to the throne. If the King died, hers was the power, and these might be her ministers.

Nicholas had thought it naïve, Kathi knew, to expect to hide such an event. On the other hand, hearing of this, Albany might well become cautious. If he threatened the King, demanded too much, the realm had another alternative.

Nicholas was speaking. 'Bel is here?' He had come with Tobie and Julius and Andro, now healed and back in the Canongate. John and Moriz were among those left behind. And Robin, of course.

Kathi said, 'The Queen likes her. Bel's staying in Edinburgh for Christmas with Fat Father Jordan and Bonne. *Belle, Bonne et Sage.*' She broke off. It was not the way to talk about a bereaved father. But he deserved it. He deserved it.

'Bonne? Whom no bridegroom has yet received, veiled and blessed? She isn't here, is she?' said Nicholas. He spoke as if he didn't know. He didn't perhaps realise that she had seen the list of all those specifically debarred, of whom Bonne was one.

Bel was coming over, and with her was Abbot Henry of Cambuskenneth. Bel stood before Nicholas, her gaze strict, and did not raise her arms. After a moment he bent instead, and kissed her raised hand. There was a ripple of silver: the trumpets were about to announce their procession to the table of honour. Once, Nicholas had stood in this same banqueting hall and invited the mockery of the Court, for his own ends. Now, no one here would mock him, nor he them, except from affection.

Kathi smiled at the thought, and then realised how meaningless it was as a yardstick. Yesterday was the Feast of St Nicholas. This year, no one had marked it. Another year, she had heard, the King of Cyprus had honoured Nicholas at his table, beside all the lords of that name in the land. He had been a Knight of the Sword before he became a Knight of the Unicorn. He was attending a banquet for her uncle in a modest palace in a small country; but he was capable of making his name anywhere, and always had been.

Henry Arnot said, 'It is a new fanfare. Tell me what you think of it; and of the music at the end. All harmony is not finished, you know.'

'For some it is,' Nicholas said.

He stayed as long as he should, and added his lifelong accumulation of awe and admiration and gratitude to the praise presently heaped on

Adorne. And Adorne, in his answering speech of wit and grace, included the name of *Nicholas vander Poele, or de Fleury* in the long list of those whom he in turn thanked for their friendship, while his prosaic niece smiled through her tears. Then the tables were cleared, and the music began for the dancing, which was led, with the sweep of her train, by the small, erect Queen on the arm of her husband's first Knight of the Unicorn. She looked like her picture. Camulio had brought over the rest of the altar-piece, in boxes from Bruges. It had been quite a nuisance.

The other Knight of the Unicorn waited so long, and then made his discreet exit. Pursued, to his surprise, by a page, he let himself be conducted to a guest-room. He expected an emergency meeting: the morning had been devoted to conclaves, but new disasters unfolded by the hour. He entered the room. The door shut. But instead of Avandale or Argyll, he faced the solitary figure of a woman. It was Bel of Cuthilgurdy. He revolved.

'I told them to lock it,' said his elderly captor. 'That is, I hope ye werena on your way to the necessary. But there's a place over there, if ye were.'

He made a sound of despair that was almost a laugh, and sat down. Her face, round as ever, had acquired no structural elegance with the passing of years, but the thick, fair skin was unblemished and the brown gaze as amiably critical. Being at Court, she had exchanged her usual coif for a full head of sail with pearls in it, and her shapeless portly-sleeved gown was still shapeless, but cut out of velvet trimmed with black fur, and set off with a necklace of hawsers and hatch-lids. The hawsers were gold, and the hatch-lids were set with cabochon rubies. He had observed them at the start of the evening, and knew what he was being told.

She said, 'Struck dumb?'

'Yes,' he said. 'But you have not been so afflicted, I suspect.'

'Aye. I spoke to Julius,' she said. 'About myself and St Pol. It was time. He had half the story: some from Wodman; some from Stewart of Darnley.'

'And you told him the rest,' Nicholas said.

'It was going to come out. I told you. All the Archer families knew of the famous Jordan de St Pol, who once commanded the French King's Archer Guard. They knew he had a wife. If they went to Chouzy, as you did, they'd find my daughter there, and learn from her name who her father was. So tell me what you know. Ask me questions.'

'I don't need to,' he said. 'Years after St Pol left the Guard, you were living in France in the Scottish Princesses' household, and mixing with the Scottish Archers of the day. You were a widow, with a young son at school in Cambuskenneth. You met and married Perrelet d'Échaut, whose father had been granted a seigneurie at Chouzy. When d'Échaut died in his thirties, he left you also to care for the daughter you bore him, and for his own sister Aleis.'

She was looking at him with compassion, as if he had lived through it, not she. She said, 'You know most of it, then. Peter and Alice Shaw, just, they were called: my second man and his sister. It was no great drama, Nicol. He was a grand man, my Peter, and brave with it. So was his sister. She was five years older than Peter, married Jordan de St Pol at fourteen, and bore him two children, Simon and Lucia. Then she was stricken with the trembling illness, and lost most of her sight, and her senses. Jordan was a trusted man at the French Court by then: he couldna nurse her. He found it hard: he was bitter at times; but he was loyal; loyal; and stood by her till she died many years later. That is why I don't leave him, Nicol, nor him me. Don't mistake me. I can see the worst of him better than anybody. Whiles we canna thole one another. But our lives are bound together. And mine is a voice that sometimes he'll listen to. Mine and Andro Wodman's.'

Of course. Wodman had become an Archer of the Guard before Bel left France. And he, too, had protected this clever, cruel man. Nicholas said, 'He tried to rape Gelis's sister.' He couldn't let that go unsaid in the presence of anyone trying to excuse Jordan.

Bel's colourless eyes studied him. The compassion was still there. She said, 'But he didn't, did he? Don't you think that says something? A big, powerful man can usually get his own way. He did get his own way. He lays plans, Nicol, like you do. I tried to tell you that, once. He follows a plan, and won't drop it. Now he has disowned you, you are disowned, and for ever. I have no family claims: he will keep me by him for comfort, but that is all. There is no one else. There is nothing more, in my view, for anyone to fear.'

They looked at one another. 'And you have told the others?' Nicholas said. 'Since, as you say, it was half known already?'

'I have told them all,' Bel replied. She drew a long breath. 'Mind, the old man won't like it. He was never fond of me being known as his wife's brother's widow. He thought I'd tattle, maybe, about Alice. He persuaded himself that I was with him and Lucia because I needed the shelter. I'm tired of that, now.'

'Hence the vulgar display of rude wealth. Julius will want to marry you,' Nicholas said.

She smiled. He said, 'Why else are you telling me? St Pol made it clear he never wants to see me again.'

She said, 'Think what he had just lost. He may always feel the same, or he may not. I told you because I hear that this winter is dangerous for you and your friends. Seaulme Adorne went to confession this morning and wrote out his will: did you know?'

Gazing at her, Nicholas swore, and then apologised slowly. He said, 'I knew this assembly was wrong. I knew it.'

She said, 'If he is in danger, then so is everyone attending tonight, including yourself. But he may be over-cautious, thinking of Efemie. He was worried, too, that Saunders would leave and set up house in Lille, now his lady's husband has died. But you are not meant to know that.'

'Everyone knows that,' Nicholas said. 'Also that he is shipping her and her daughter over here. There would be someone to bring Efemie up, apart from Phemie's sister in the north. There is Kathi, and all of us.'

'Nicol,' she said. 'If one of you dies, you may all die. There is something grievous ahead. Andreas feels it. I think you feel it, too. It is not just your own loss, is it, that made you flee from the music? Kathi said that you would.'

'It was the very, very bad man on the viol,' Nicholas said. 'No. It was just because it was music. I don't have any fearsome premonitions. I never do.'

'You once had, for others,' Bel said. 'It seems to me, from what Gelis has said, that you expected to know, wherever you were, if ill had come to her, or the bairn.'

Nicholas said, 'That was then, close to the years of divining. I didn't have the gift before, and I don't have it now. I don't want it, especially not for myself.'

Bel said, 'Because you have no fear of death. Is that it, Nicol? Still? You have family, friends, a cause you are making your own; but your own end is of no importance to you?'

Nicholas looked at her. 'You should have a talk with Prosper de Camulio. Am I not blessed, who am fulfilling every Christian exhortation? I am content. I am resigned. I am not pestering the Almighty with demands for my survival. I just don't want to hear that bloody viol playing again.'

There was a long silence. Then she said, 'Oh, come to me here, my poor, silly bairn,' and held him, her hand tight on his hair, when he came.

After a time he spoke, without moving. 'Once I thought that perhaps –'

'– we were kin? No. Of the heart, maybe.'

'I think so,' he said. He didn't look up. When he spoke again, it was with a steadier voice. 'Bel, I am so sorry about your own family. Both your husbands, and then your one son. I wanted to say so. I didn't want to make it difficult between you and St Pol. And I am so grateful for this.'

'But?' she said. He had stirred, to look up at last.

'But please don't make it hard for me, either,' he said. 'Please, Bel. Please.'

Chapter 48

Two rokis maye a king allone put dovne
And him depryve of his lyf and his crovne.

THE GATHERING AT Linlithgow dispersed, and no one appeared to have taken note of it. Four days later, Parliament met, and announced its final enactments. The word flashed from the Castle to the Canongate inside the hour.

FIRSTLY, it is ordained, avised and concluded that England is to be asked to renew the truce between the two countries, and revive the marriage between England's Cecilia and Scotland's James, for the pleasure of God and the common weal of both realms. And if England refuses, such will not lead to an effusion of Christian blood, save in defence of the realm; in which event our sovereign lord will fight in honour and freedom, as his noble progenitors have done in times begone.

'Blind Harry,' said Robin.

'No. Wait! Wait! What are they thinking of? England won't agree to a truce. The bloody wedding's dismembered already. I ought to know. I had Wattie Bertram's corns in my lap for a month, getting picked out for free while he thought about raising the money.'

'Lucky you. Tobie, be quiet. It's a device. Go on, Nicholas,' Gelis said.

SECONDLY, since the Borders are daily invaded, and his noble highness should not put his person in danger, his grace should ask his brother the Duke of Albany to be Lieutenant-General of the realm,

*and advise in what manner he is to be supported, to bear the great cost
of the office.*

'That's the highest power in the land,' Robin said eventually. 'And
the money to go with it, added to everything the King's allowed him
already. Did we promise Albany that? Did you promise him, Nicholas?'

'I expect so. Also a new set of buttons, and a bag of ginger at
Christmas. Of course he wanted the post, and Gloucester had to believe
he was getting it. He might. It's up to the King. Parliament can advise,
but only the King can appoint him.'

'So he has to be careful with the King. Was that all?'

'I've left out the bit about rallying the nation for war, just in case
England gets silly ideas, and the licence to kill people who import corrupt
wine. There were some sensible measures as well. Wattie Bertram is
going to Paris. You must have fixed his feet.'

'Why? Ostensibly why?'

'Ostensibly to demand justice for ill-treated merchants. Actually to
find out if the English alliance has died, and if the King is going to die
too, and what they all think about Sandy. Wattie voted himself for the
trip, and I think he deserves it. It won't make much difference to Sandy.
It takes a King's man out of the way, and he'll have his own agents in
France.'

'So Sandy is happy?'

'My God, I hope so,' said Nicholas.

Two weeks – fourteen days – fourteen tense days to Christmas.

The Court officially moved to the Castle, swept, scoured and garnished
so that nothing brought to mind its recent custodial function. As Yule
approached, the higher nobility – Huntly, Seton, Arbuthnott, Sinclair
and Angus and Crawford – gathered in their Edinburgh houses, if they
had ever left them. Those deposed stayed away, but the new officers of
state presented themselves daily, as did the Treasurer, and Master
Secretary Whitelaw, and the Lord Preceptor Will Knollys. The Chancellor, a former Vicar of Linlithgow, was not very well, and spent much
of his time with the two resident physicians, Andreas and Tobie. The
three half-uncles also lodged in the Castle; and the disgraced and
undisgraced Princesses with their households, and the Duke of Albany,
in chambers next to the King.

With Sandy were his confirmed friends, such as Sir James Liddell
of Halkerston, and less prominent friends, such as Bailie Alex Home

of that Ilk, who still held Huntly's favour. Other admirers came to the Duke's bidding, although some fell prey to the unseasonably mild weather, and found themselves confined to bed with a hoast; while others were detained by unfortunate accidents, such as the death of an aunt, or a court case.

England's official response to the olive branch was not as yet known. Since, in theory, it might lead to peace, there was as yet no basis for appointing a Lieutenant-General for Scotland, and the King had not done so. The King of England (unaware of the coming olive branch) had long since given the equivalent English post to the Duke of Gloucester, and was rumoured to be offering to present him with Cumberland, and a petty Scots kingdom of everything that Richard might manage to conquer next year in the south-west. This situation could be regarded with horror, or as an indication that Edward, unwell, was willing to do anything to keep his brother out of the way.

There was a rumour, which proved to be true, that France had made peace with Maximilian of Flanders and Burgundy, and had excluded England from the pact. One or two men from the East March left Edinburgh, and others from the Merse and Lauderdale failed to appear. Sandy wanted to know when the bloody women were coming to Court, or were they all supposed to be eunuchs? And what was Nicol doing? In bed at home, without doubt, and no question what he was doing. Nicol's pleasure was Nicol's first thought, same as everybody's. When the chaplain tried to moderate Albany's intake of wine, he nearly found himself knocked down the stairs.

Noble ladies, as a matter of course, arrived at Court, while others less noble were pressed into Albany's service, and occasionally the King's. Nicholas, who was already spending half the day with the King, apologised to Gelis, with whom he had had very little opportunity to do anything, and moved himself to a room in the Castle. He took Jordan with him, but explained beforehand about the King's brother. 'Don't be shocked. He will be rude, perhaps cruel. He is disappointed and unhappy and unsure. It seemed to him once that he might be King. He might not be a bad King, but I don't think he will be given the chance: it is better if the present King rules. Also, he has no family to depend on. His offspring are scattered – a son in France, a daughter and other sons here. He has a French wife, and a Scots one discarded. He has no one to depend on but friends, and they in turn may have other loyalties.'

'Are we his friends?' Jordan had said.

And Nicholas had said, 'We are trying to work for the good of everyone.' It was evasive, because the answer was complex, and Jordan was not old enough, yet, to be burdened with it. He had to forget it, through all the hours that followed, when he and others sat and chatted to Sandy, and entertained him, and put up – to a degree – with his tantrums. As he hoped, Jordan behaved quietly and well, and sometimes Sandy would adjust his behaviour, but usually didn't.

The rest of the time, Nicholas made himself available to the King, in much the same way. He had brief, invaluable meetings with Whitelaw who, used to treading this tightrope for decades, largely ignored him in public. The Bishop of Dunkeld, another invalid, was capable of shrewd advice. He was on guarded terms with two of the half-uncles, but continued his long-standing, not unfriendly relationship with Buchan. Their cousin, Euphemia Graham, Prioress of Eccles, was at Court, released to her family from her temporary exile in the Priory at North Berwick, on the sea coast east of Edinburgh.

The Prioress remembered Dr Tobias with pleasure, greeted Nicholas and Jordan with suspect eloquence, and asked after the lawyer, Master Julius. Her predatory gaze kept returning to Nicholas. He remembered their discussion about St Pol's forgotten sister Elizabeth, just before they all went off to Malloch. Eccles was almost on the English frontier. It had seemed a wise idea to empty it. He hoped no one was going to rush to send the Prioress back, and wished he hadn't mentioned where Julius lived, although, with any luck, Kathi would regulate any encounter. For the present, Nicholas tried, but signally failed to avoid the venerable lady's company. He wondered if Adorne had been afraid of the Bishop her brother, but decided that Adorne and Kennedy were two of a kind. The Prioress frightened him.

He was not required to arrange much in the way of festivities: this was to be a Christmas of pronounced spirituality, involving grand ceremonial, and conveying the Court from the Abbey of Holyroodhouse to the Church of the Holy Trinity, and from the kirk of St Giles back to the Castle. The community, impressed and disappointed at once, began to suspect that the mummers and singers of January were about to be banned, and the Uphaly Day guisers done down. Nicholas carried their objections to what he called *the medical diwan*, the rule of Tobie and Andreas which presently controlled all he and everyone else did.

The rivalry between the two doctors was long over, although they still disagreed. Primed by late, companionable sessions in their room, Nicholas had revived what Arab medicine had taught him of uroscopy. From the beginning, a glance at Tobie's face had been enough.

'*Inopos?*'

'Pure liver-colour. You are right. The anxiety of the present situation is provoking the illness. The King is not well.'

He had not been well since Lauder. A strong man, by now, would be feeling the strain. The King's painful, recurring sickness was tightening its grip. Nicholas said, 'Would he retire to bed? Or is that undesirable?'

'It is undesirable in that rumour will at once have him dying,' Andreas said. 'We are already hearing gossip since Dunkeld became unwell, and now Laing. If it isn't pestilence, then it's poison.'

'Could it be either?' Nicholas said. The answer was no; but that didn't solve anything. He thought of Craigmillar. He said, 'I think, all the same, I'll get Sandy's food and drink tasted, and the King's. That should stop any false accusations, or real ones, for that matter. Is there anything else I can do?'

'Have your own food tested,' said Tobie.

Nicholas stared at him. 'Well, of course. If someone wants to kill the King or his brother, then clearly I'm next. Everyone will appreciate that.'

'I didn't say,' said Tobie, 'that it would be for the same reason, or that you should take precautions in public. Your pendulum would tell you. You've used it for poison before. You've used it for other things that maybe you ought to return to. We need all the help we can get.'

'But not that kind,' said Andreas. 'I agree with Nicholas. Let the pendulum rest.'

He would not say why, and Tobie dropped the subject, annoyed. To begin with Nicholas, too, preferred to leave it alone. Then he changed his mind and sought out the astrologer. 'Will you tell me why?'

As always, Andreas of Vesalia had no air about him of mystery; no hint of the occult in his large-hewn, positive face or garrulous tongue; nor in his romantic history, about which gossip was rife. But he took the question seriously enough – more seriously indeed than Nicholas expected.

'Why do I think you shouldn't divine? Because in ordinary hands, the wand or the pendulum are just tools, but sometimes they are more. It seemed to me that you were in danger of becoming the possessed rather than the possessor: the moments of dislocation were increasing. For any good you might do, you might harm yourself more. I should leave it.'

'Of dislocation?' Nicholas repeated.

Andreas looked at him. 'You told me once. Gelis also described it.

You see something familiar that cannot be familiar, for you have never been there before. Does that still happen?'

'No. Or hardly ever,' Nicholas said. He had just realised it.

'No. And you do not want to encourage it,' said Andreas.

He said, 'Why not?' Bel had talked about fear. He felt fear now. He added, 'Is it because the events I thought I saw – the fires, the terror, the deaths – were all about to happen to me? None of them has.'

'I have been wondering,' Andreas said. 'It seemed to me that what you were seeing was not your own life, but another's. I was concerned enough to go further. My conclusion so far is the same as your own. The moments of great emotion are not yours, but belong to some other person. You may not even know who it is. They may live in the past or the future. But they must be related. No other bond could be as strong as this one must be.'

He waited. Andreas was good at waiting, when he thought it worth while. Nicholas drew a long breath. Then he said, 'Might it be the lady my mother?'

The astrologer looked at him, not without sympathy. He said, 'You would like to think so? But do the experiences match? That lady lived most of her life in one place. These happenings indicate many different scenes, some of them violent; or so your friends say. There must be many more that only you know of. Was this the life of Sophie de Fleury?'

No, it wasn't. It fitted no one he knew. The mind he had felt behind all these random, formidable pulses was not that of a woman. He saw that now. It was a man's.

Then he thought of Umar, and was transformed, until he saw that that was impossible, too. The long, polished library table; the swooping eagle had no place in the life of a European slave, or an African judge. Whoever it was, the sender was not in his present life. He could not be reached, and the unconscious messages, whatever their source, would now fade.

Instead of fear, Nicholas felt desolation. He said suddenly, 'Perhaps I should use the pendulum. It detects poisons. It told us about Robin.'

Then Andreas stood up and said, 'Nicholas. This is dangerous. Dangerous for you, and perhaps even for the sender, whoever or whatever he is. Leave the pendulum. Appoint me your surrogate. Let me use what arts I have. When I have the answer, whatever it is, I promise to tell you.'

Nicholas said, '*Whatever* it is? Good or bad?'

'You have my word,' said Andreas.

*

Then it all came to an end, because of Leithie Preston.

Thoughtlessly aggressive as he had always been, Leithie himself would have enjoyed it. No one else did. For all their elaborate preparations, no one expected it. As the Day of the Nativity approached and then dawned, it seemed to all those charged with the safety of the kingdom – the legislators, the controllers, the administrators, the men who had not experienced normal life for six months – that the reverence and joy of the season had brought its own temporary peace, overlaying anger and fear and resentment with its solemn language and slow, familiar rituals. The calm face of the Church moved through the streets and into great chambers; men listened, and prayed. Nowie Sinclair, who had brokered the deal, was not even present when Pate Leitch, Alex Inglis's successor, crossed to the King as he changed dress in his chambers in David's Tower, and reminded him that Ruthven and his son required to get back to St Johnstoun of Perth, and there was a charter to sign.

It was a moment when the three uncles were absent, but Chancellor Laing could be reached with the Great Seal, and there were enough people for witnesses – Constable Erroll, the King's friend Davie Lindsay, now Household Controller, and three or four others, including a peely-wally James of Dunkeld. Master Whitelaw had a table brought in. Pate Leitch, a Paris-educated man, had been Rector of the University there sixteen years ago and, despite his crisp style, was on good terms with the King, as were most of the men there, including the beneficiary. James knew the laird of Ruthven of old, and his son, and the charter was simple enough, handing back to young Ruthven land that the father had once leased to the late Thomas Preston, known as Leithie.

It seemed to James, then and now, that both Cochrane and Preston had deserved commendation, not forfeiture. They had been trying to march with the guns and save Berwick. He was not supposed to say so aloud. His limbs were aching; he had just swallowed the latest of several libations to soothe them, and he felt like saying so aloud. It came out with satisfactory vehemence, perhaps because his brother Sandy had just entered the room. James lifted the parchment and waved it at Ruthven. 'Do you need this land, Will? Do you? I say, let it go to Tom Preston's widow and son. Cochrane, the best Constable I ever had at Kildrummy. And Preston: brave man, brave man. They didn't turn on their sovereign lord and put him in prison.'

Master Whitelaw, pen in hand, gazed at the King over his spectacles. 'No, my lord, they didn't. They did what they thought was for the best.

But the rest of us knew that you would have been captured or killed by the English. It was my lord of Albany there who saved us all by crossing back to your side, and hastening the English army out of the realm. The Preston family have had their reward, and will never notice the loss of Middle Pitcairn. Whereas it's in the middle of the barony of Ruthven and ought rightly to return there, as your grace will remember. Here's the pen.'

The grating voice, pitched in the way it had been pitched for the last twenty years, saying, 'I told you. Remember?'

He supposed he did remember. If it came to war, the Prestons would fight against England, no matter what. So indeed would the Ruthvens, but, given their strategic connections, a little extra encouragement was being offered. He put down the parchment and stared at it, unwilling to appear to give in. Sandy, leaning over his shoulder, said, 'Come on, James. Shall I sign it after you?' He smelled of wine, and spoke in a way that brought back their boyhood. It was Christmas Day, after all. His brother was here, and his sisters not far away. They had all been to the Abbey; it was time for eating and drinking and dancing, not for huddling over a board stinking of ink and vellum and wax.

He had better sign it. The men standing behind him, in discreet low conversation, were waiting to add their own names. The King dipped the pen he was given, wrote his name and rose, leaving seat and pen to the others. Across the room, his gentlemen waited with his hat and great robe. His jewelled collar lay on a chest, with a folded packet lying across it. He picked up the paper and opened it, while they were dressing him.

At the table, the Chancellor's clerk dusted the last of the signatures, and the Lord Clerk Register and Master Secretary Whitelaw shared a glance of mild satisfaction. Sandy Albany and the Bishops shook William Ruthven and his son by the hand, and the older Ruthven was slapped on the back by his kinsman by marriage, Earl Davie. They waited, as courtiers must, for the King, whom they could see, standing motionless, now attired in his robe. Then he started to move. He came towards them, his mouth open, his face red, his gown surging behind him, crashing between stools, chests and chairs and oversetting the table in a great swathe of glistening ink. Then, sweeping up to Albany, the King knocked his brother to the ground and, standing over him shouting, kicked his half-dazed body until his toe was red with his blood.

By the time the doctors were there, Crawford and Erroll and Borthwick had pulled back the King, and Kennedy and Leitch had lifted Albany and prevented him, as he recovered, from rushing in his turn upon his brother. The words the King was shouting were incoherent, but the paper crushed in his hand was quite explicit. The doctors recognised it, because they had privileged information, as had Master Whitelaw, and Nicholas de Fleury, sent for and arriving at speed. Sandy Albany himself knew it better than anybody:

> *The Duke of Albany, styling himself Alexander, King of Scotland, promises to do homage to the King of England when he obtains his realm of Scotland, to break the alliance between Scotland and France, and to surrender the town and castle of Berwick within fourteen days after entering Edinburgh.*

It was the first of the treaties signed at Fotheringhay Castle in June, before the army of the Duke of Gloucester marched upon Scotland. Below it was the second, detailing the Scottish lands the King of England would acquire, and offering Albany his daughter Cecilia.

James, his arms held, had fallen into a chair and was choking with laughter. 'What did you say? *It was my lord of Albany there who saved us all by crossing back to your side.* Oh, he saved us all. He crossed back to kill me. He crossed back to take the crown. He crossed back to become a vassal of England, and give England whatever she wanted. Kill him.'

You could see Sandy, his face bleeding, fighting his rage. He said, 'They are forgeries.'

He was looking at Nicholas. And Nicholas, steadily returning the look, said, 'My lord Duke, forgive me. I know, as you do, that they are not forgeries, but a promise exacted from you, which you did not intend to keep.'

Albany's lips opened, but he did not speak. The King said, 'You knew? De Fleury, you knew and said nothing?'

James was shivering. Tobie released him, and glanced at Andreas. Someone – Whitelaw – made a movement. Nicholas said, 'I said nothing because it was only one of many plots and counterplots. To publish them all would have done nothing but cause alarm. In the event, my lord Duke did make it possible for the English army to leave Scotland without greater damage. Nothing could have saved Berwick.'

'So you say,' said the King. 'And now he is here, he will be content to be Duke of Albany? Or does he not plan still to become Alexander Rex?'

'Your grace must ask him,' said Nicholas. He sounded calm and reliable. Tobie, kneeling by the sick King and waiting for the next outburst from the Prince his brother, thought of Johndie Mar, and all that Nicholas, with his patience and self-control, had done and tried to do for this family. If ever a man had made good his mistakes, it was this one. And he was taking the blame. Whatever the King might suspect, he must not have his confidence in his senior ministers destroyed. And, somehow, an illusion about Albany must be maintained, if humanly possible. Anything that would stop civil war. Or nearly anything.

Sandy Albany didn't have either patience or self-control. He stared at his brother and turned. 'You want that madman James for a King? When he killed my brother? When you saw him try to kill me? I beg your pardon, but you must excuse me from serving him. I am going to my own. If you want me, send for me.'

He waited, breathing quickly, until the King, shouting, had again been restrained, and then turned and limped to the door. The ushers stepped in his way, but Nicholas came between them and took Albany by the arm. 'Let me come.'

For a moment nothing happened. Then the Chancellor nodded, the doorway cleared, and the Prince handed himself through, half-supported by Nicholas, and stumbled down to the open air, and his servants. There, he shook himself free and stood, swaying. His lips were tight, as if they wanted to shake. 'Well, de Fleury? On both sides as usual. What do you want?'

'To serve you both,' Nicholas said.

Albany looked at him. 'No. You must choose. A future King, or a killer.'

'I see neither here,' Nicholas said. 'I see a sick King and his brother, who could help him. I see a sick country, with the means of healing at hand.'

'What do you know of us? You are a Burgundian,' the Duke of Albany said. He mounted and left, with his men, and without looking round.

Within a matter of days, every trace of the Duke of Albany's presence had vanished from Edinburgh, as had all his supporters, among whom was Lord Home's grandson Alexander, bailie of Gordon. By the time December came to an end, the kingdom had two centres of power. One, occupied by the King, was the burgh of Edinburgh and its suburbs. The other, occupied by his brother, was the castle of the Earls of March at Dunbar, massively fortified, and blessed with daily increments to its company, as Albany was joined by Lord Crichton and Douglas of Morton, Lord Grey and Alex Home, Archibald Angus, together with Applegarth and the Tantallon Douglases, and finally by young Jamie Boyd and his great-uncle Hearty James Buchan. In recent days, such men had lingered at home, but now conscience called. Three years ago, aided by witchcraft and abetted by the Burgundians and their doctors, this half-crazed King had killed Johndie Mar. Now it had happened again. Now all the world knew how, desecrating the holiest feast of the year, the King had attempted – had vowed – to murder his one remaining brother, and the hope of the kingdom.

In reply to which, there was only one really popular solution.

The Prioress of Eccles, at present in the convent of North Berwick, wrote to Anselm Adorne's niece, inviting her to bring her children for a short stay, away from the distress and anxiety of the burgh. The shipmaster Mick Crackbene offered to transport the demoiselle Kate-lijne and her baggage by sea, provided the January weather allowed. It was a very short distance. Accepting, Kathi decided to bring Margaret and Rankin, leaving four-year-old Hob behind with his nurse and his father who, after hesitation, had firmly agreed that she should go. To help her, she took two good-hearted maids and – at the suggestion of Gelis – the willing person of young Jordan de Fleury.

By then, the winter snow had begun, and the country, to those who had time to look at it, became singularly beautiful, rather like the fields around Nancy.

Chapter 49

Without iustice quhat is a kinrik than
Bot thift and reif with foull slauchter of man?

AFTER JORDAN HAD gone, Gelis closed her residence and moved to the Canongate, where the House of Niccolò and the Floory Land had become one.

As in the great moments of crisis in the Bank, after Albany's departure no one touched or importuned Nicholas for three weeks, as he moved about daily: from Adorne's house to the Castle, and from there to the secret houses in the burgh where the inner Council and burgesses met, unknown to the King. From there, Nicholas always returned to the Canongate for, as statesmen resorted to him, so he made use of the combined experience of the men who had set him this trial and then, by following him, had adjudged him to have passed.

These days, the connecting door to the Berecrofts house stood permanently open. Robin had brought his remaining family to live there, for the present, with his father. Occasionally Sersanders, Kathi's brother, visited from Linlithgow. Since Kathi left, Tobie and Clémence had also crossed the road to become part of the group in the Floory Land upon whom Nicholas would descend at untoward hours, rarely sitting; more often ranging round the room, eating, talking, listening. They argued as they had always argued: John and Julius and Tobie, Moriz and Gelis, to whom no one made concessions because of her sex. Sometimes Wodman would join them from Adorne's house.

From him, they learned that Fat Father Jordan was still with Bel at his High Street house, where Bonne had joined them for Christmas. Nicholas had avoided the subject of Bel since he had met her in Stirling and again at the Castle. It made Gelis uneasy. She would have called on her valiant friend, or sent a message, but Nicholas had asked her if she would wait. What for, she didn't know, but she gave in, as they all did. He was carrying enough. Keep to essentials.

They knew, from the thin stream of reports from the Council's agents, of the reinforcements at Dunbar, and the land gifts with which Sandy was rewarding his new adherents, notably the bailie of Gordon, Alex Home of Home, damn the man. They also brought back lurid rumours of plots against the King's life. One of these, with the horrifying facility of the Fotheringhay treaty, reached the ears of the King, who instantly commanded the dispatch of batches of letters begging armed help. The letters were written, but remained with Whitelaw unsent, while Andreas and Conrad prepared soothing draughts. The aim was to avoid confrontation, not to provoke it. As for the person who left the Fotheringhay treaty, or spread the rumours, no one could trace who it was.

The physicians had other patients: Chancellor Laing was succumbing to his long fever, and Dunkeld, taking his duties, was poorly himself. It was as well that, discreetly meeting in the Cowgate or the High Street, Avandale and Argyll and Scheves and their burgess supporters were in vigour. Since confirmation of the peace between France and the Archduke Maximilian, Wattie's French trip had been postponed. There was something else. Edward of England was not only furious with France, he was ill. If he was mortally ill, his brother Gloucester wasn't going to linger about northern England, waiting to encourage Albany.

About this point, as January moved through its second week, Julius became restless. 'Shouldn't we know whether Albany has heard about that? Shouldn't we make sure he knows that he can't count on English help after all?'

It was one of the times that Nicholas was there. He said, 'Yes. How?'

'Let them capture a messenger.'

'Hard on the messenger.'

'Send them word of it direct.'

'They wouldn't believe it.'

John said, 'They would if Julius took it. He's well known to Liddell.'

'All right,' said Nicholas. 'So long as you pay his ransom. I'm not raising it.'

Julius reddened. He said, 'I'm not proposing to get myself captured, thank you. But I'd write the thing, and put it in the hands of someone local whom Liddell trusts. I could get near enough Dunbar to find someone.'

'Well, that's all right, then,' Nicholas said. 'But in fact we can manage without. I hope to tell Sandy myself fairly soon. We've written to him suggesting a meeting.'

There was a silence. Talks; bribes; dialogue through intermediaries: they had all been discussed, but foundered on the issue of safety. Sandy would never place himself in danger of capture and sentencing. And King's agents would hardly come unsupported, and risk death or capture for the King.

Tobie said, 'It's a trick? You've found some way of trapping Albany?'

Nicholas said, 'No. It's the suggestion of a very brave man, willing to speak for the King, unsupported. Do you remember when Pope Pius visited Scotland?'

So that was it. Gelis said, 'Before he was Pope. When he survived a near-wreck, he kept his vow to walk barefoot to the shrine of St Mary at Whitekirk. Ten miles, he said. Tobie's uncle not being as brilliant as Tobie, his feet were never the same.'

'A healing well and a very fine church,' Nicholas said. 'Also a large number of cabins for pilgrims and others. The Abbot of Holyrood holds his courts there: it comes under the regality of Broughton, which makes Archie Crawford little King of Whitekirk. Adorne is proposing to walk from the Abbey kirk and cloister of North Berwick, unarmed, without servants, and meet Sandy at Whitekirk. Adorne will apologise for the King, excuse him on the grounds of sickness, and ask Sandy to come back on the same terms as before, and with no charges against him. He will also explain to him what has happened abroad, and why he can expect no help from England. He might even offer to have the King himself come, if Sandy asks.'

'Would he?' said Father Moriz.

Nicholas said, 'Probably not. But it might help to safeguard Adorne's life in the meantime.'

John said, 'But it's a trick. The King hasn't relented. You say you talk to him daily, but he's still enraged.'

'We all talk to him,' Nicholas said. 'He will come to agree, when he is calm. Until then, we are fending off war. We're not trying to trap or cheat Albany. He can stay away if he likes: perhaps he will. Or he may want to come with a fully equipped cavalry troop. Regardless, Adorne will be there, and on foot, and unarmed. There will be no hidden soldiers. If Albany loses his head, or takes bad advice, he may simply kill the King's envoy. But it would be a very bad move. Think how bad.'

'So Adorne is really safe?' Gelis said. She spoke like an enemy. She knew Nicholas.

Father Moriz looked at her and then back to Nicholas. He said, as a statement, 'You are going with him.'

Nicholas was still holding Gelis's eyes. He said, 'Yes. We all have a better chance if I go. Adorne, and Albany, and the country.'

He didn't add anything. He didn't ask her forgiveness, or say he didn't do such a thing lightly, or explain at all. She understood.

No one spoke. She supposed they were all struggling with the same realisation. Then Julius said, 'You're mad.' He sounded resigned. When he continued, it was with mild decision. 'All right. They'll kill you, but they might hesitate if they've heard from me beforehand. I'm still going to send Liddell that letter. I'll even add, if you like, that you really will be unarmed.'

Tobie drew breath. Nicholas said, 'What's got into you? You just want to get out and build snowmen. All right. But if they capture you, I'm not paying more than I won off you last night at cards.'

John released his breath. He said, 'Christ. That'll get about one finger back.'

'Well, why not?' said Nicholas illogically. 'The Pope turned his toes in for nothing.'

Later, he got hold of Julius.

'You don't need to go. Look, I've chosen this country, you haven't. If all this becomes hopeless, you can go back to Germany, or give Gregorio or Diniz a hand.'

'How exciting,' said Julius.

Nicholas sighed. 'Sugary pastries? Embroidered doublets? No Bonne?'

'So why don't you go back?' Julius said.

He tried to think. He tried very hard to think of an answer that Julius would understand. In the end he just said, 'I don't know.'

Julius left. Alex Home of Home, to the general amazement, sent a messenger to the Netherbow Port asking leave to enter with his company of kinsmen and friends. It seemed that he had become disenchanted with Albany's chances, and wished to return to the King. The King, his emotions assiduously tended by his doctors and friends, agreed to see him, forgave him, and promised him Chirnside in Berwickshire, which at that moment belonged to the Duke of Albany.

John said, 'Julius must have got his letter in, and they believed it.'

Nine days later, they had stopped joking about Whitekirk, since the insubstantial proposal had suddenly solidified. Albany had replied to the approach to negotiate. He had accepted the rendezvous and expressed no antipathy to the envoys, who were to be the Baron Cortachy, the merchant Nicholas de Fleury and (a late suggestion) that well-known exponent of papal diplomacy Prosper de Camulio, the most reverend Bishop of Caithness. The date was to be Thursday, the twenty-third day of January, three days hence.

The day the reply came, Nicholas went and sat with Robin, away from the others. Recently, they had not spoken much to each other. Now Nicholas said, 'About North Berwick.'

Robin flushed. He said, 'I knew you would have a plan. You are bringing her out?'

Kathi was still at the Priory, with Margaret and Rankin. It should be safe. It was on the coast, and at least five miles from Whitekirk. If Robin required further reassurance, he might recall that Jordan de Fleury was there.

Nicholas said, 'I meant to have her brought back before, but the weather's too rough for a boat, and I won't risk it by land. But I did make a contingency plan.'

The spark had returned to Robin's gaze. 'Naturally.'

'Yes. Mick Crackbene has been there from the beginning, with a squad of ten men. I'll take a few more. There are also relays of couriers. Adorne and I go to North Berwick on Wednesday, and will be with her until we set off for Whitekirk next morning. We shan't take the soldiers to Whitekirk, but if we don't manage to return, the Priory could withstand an assault almost indefinitely. I don't think it will get one. It would be ridiculous for Sandy to attack a Cistercian foundation and have all the rest – Melrose, for God's sake, Newbattle, Coupar Angus, Haddington, Culross – turn on him. He'd lose all the noble families who support them, and it'd destroy him at Rome.'

Robin said, 'I am not sure if I believe you, but I forgive you, for Jordan is there. Did Kathi know there might be some danger?'

'She may have suspected.'

Robin's eyes were still clear. 'Yes. She took Margaret and Rankin, but she left Hob for me.' He waited. 'You must know that we think something is wrong. With you, not with the others.'

'Yes. I know,' Nicholas said. 'If I don't come back, you will know what it is.'

'But not before?'

'No. Everyone should have a last chance,' Nicholas said. 'And this, I can tell you, is Albany's.'

He was not sure, then, whether or not he would see Robin again before he set out with Adorne. They had parted so often, all of them, that the grand farewell (as he had tried to say to his son) would have been trite. Nicholas knew what Robin felt: the extent of his love and gratitude had never been hidden. Nor had the truth. 'Go,' Robin had said, on one such occasion. 'Come back, if God wills it. And if God offers a choice between my fate and death, then choose as I should have done.'

Nicholas had shaken his head, but said nothing. He felt the pain still, as if the earth had shown him its gold, and then, cracking further, the price of it. The price and the value of the high ground. The value of valour and the cost of pride, of the kind that had lost him eight years. The value of loyalty, honesty, patriotism. And how to divine when the price was too much.

Nicholas left, with Anselm Adorne, and Bishop Prosper, and the retinue which they would abandon at North Berwick. The day before they departed, Adorne rode to Linlithgow, where he spent some time privately in the church, before going to his own house to speak to his nephew Sersanders and to see his daughter Efemie. Bel of Cuthilgurdy had come to visit her for a few days, as she sometimes did when the old man was unusually difficult. It was good for the child; Sersanders did not mind, and Adorne himself had grown fond of the small, grey-haired lady, who was only four years older than himself. She came down to see him ride off, hoisting the child for his kiss, and setting her down to feed oats to his horse, her small palm spread dutifully flat. The child had no fear of horses, or of people, and had known only love. He could not regret having decided to see her.

Nicholas cancelled everything, that last night, to spend time in his chamber, talking, and then ceasing to talk with the angry rebel he had married, who had become this clever, beautiful, self-contained person, admired by women and men who did not suspect that in private, she was still clever and beautiful, but not self-contained in the least. Or perhaps – smiling at him broadly some mornings – the denizens of the Floory Land did guess, although on what evidence he couldn't quite see. And Gelis, if she could have told him, did not.

Nicholas left, with Adorne, the next day. Four hours later, a Sinclair man raced into Edinburgh with news. It was said – by a fisherman you could usually trust – that a party had left Albany's castle to sail to the south. He said it included Angus and Liddell and Lord Grey, and its purpose was to assure the English King of Albany's loyalty, and to ask him for three thousand archers.

It sounded feeble enough. As an appeal, it would almost certainly fail. That, however, wasn't the issue. The fact was that the Whitekirk meeting tomorrow was pointless: Albany had only agreed in order to squander some time.

'So we send to tell Adorne to come back,' said Will Scheves, at the rushed meeting called to consider the news.

'Do you think so?' said Avandale. 'He should be told, of course; gallant friend, it is disappointing to say the least. But why don't we suggest he goes to the meeting as planned? Albany may not trouble to come. Or he may come, out of curiosity, but defer a decision. If his delegation has just left, it may be three weeks before it returns from Westminster. Sandy won't want to close every bolt-hole before then, nor would he be wise to harm Adorne. The meeting should be safer than we expected.'

'You have the truth of it,' said Colin Argyll. 'Leave the plan as it is, but have someone ride to North Berwick now and tell this to Adorne. He can decide on his tactics tonight, and set out for Whitekirk, if he thinks it expedient, tomorrow. Whom shall we send? Shall I go?'

'Colin, you forget you are indispensable,' said Drew. 'Why don't we ask Alex Home to go to North Berwick? With Chirnside under his belt, he ought to be willing.'

'And having deceived Albany, he ought to be vigilant. Casting his left eye askance like a tunny. Aeschylus,' offered Master Archibald Whitelaw, holding his spectacles up to the light.

That same afternoon, a number of visitors called upon Jordan de St Pol at Kilmirren House, benefiting from the brief absence of Bel, his formidable hostess, in Linlithgow. The Preceptor of Torphichen stayed merely to exchange the news of the day, but other calls were more personal. The Mallochs, father and son, came to express friendly concern for Monseigneur, since the tragic deaths of his son and his grandson. His handsome grandson, so missed by Muriella.

The Borderer chatted pleasantly with the old man, while his son renewed his acquaintance with the young demoiselle Bonne von Hanseyck, so happily discovered to be residing in the same house. Naturally, there was a hired chaperone, but the demoiselle, rescued from atrophy, made him positively laugh at her accounts of the Charteris household, and Sister Monika's Cistercian tattle.

Bel, returned rather wistfully from Efemie's tight clasp at Linlithgow, found the visitors gone, and the old man mysteriously missing as well, having ridden out with his servants, Bonne said. It was then mid-afternoon, and the short winter day close to its ending. Bonne could tell her no more of her host, but was willing to regale her with an account of all the events she had missed. She was glad, she observed rather thankfully, to have Mistress Bel's company again.

'Aye,' said Bel. 'Well, I'm just away again, lassie. I need to call on a friend with a message. But I'll be back for my supper, so get the board out, and the pieces, and I'll play ye for who gets the box of marchpane I was given by Saunders.'

It wasn't pleasant, when already chilled from a ride, to step out into the gloom of the High Street and slide and squelch through the filthy snow down through the Netherbow to the Canongate. But the steps of the Floory Land were all swept and dry, the lantern powerful, and the big windows lit and warm-looking. As soon as the door was pulled open, Bel could hear the busy, familiar voices inside. Andro Wodman came out of a room and stopped, looking surprised and then pleased, but Bel didn't smile back.

She said, 'I've come for advice. Alex Home is on his way to North Berwick, and that great fool Kilmirren has joined him, and maybe Knollys and Malloch as well. It doesn't sound right. I don't like it. I jalouse Adorne and Nicol and the rest of them could do with some help.'

They heard her out, and then sent for their horses. She thought, to begin with, that it was just going to be the men of the Land – Tobie and John and Andro and Moriz and Archie of Berecrofts, with maybe the doctor, Andreas. But then, at the last minute some news came, and suddenly there were others as well: the Earl of Huntly, for example, with a lot of his men, and others who had lands south of the Forth as well as in the north-east. And merchants and agents who had dealings with Adorne and Nicholas, like Dob Cochrane and Henry Cant, and Sir Jock Ross and Tom Yare.

It worried Bel, for you couldn't go by informers, and to attack Whitekirk would destroy all their plans. But they said they weren't going near Whitekirk: they would just make sure the Priory was all right.

She saw them off, and then went in with Clémence to sit beside Robin and wait. She thought about Malloch, and she thought about Knollys, former Rector of Whitsome, which was halfway between Chirnside and Upsettlington. Will Knollys and one David Ramsay had both been Procurators for the Priory of North Berwick, in the days when the Prioress was a Ramsay. And Jordan de St Pol had gone off with the same princely warrior-monk Knollys, whose bastard son Robert had married the cousin of young Johnnie Ramsay whom Darnley, they said, had saved with some reluctance at Lauder. Knollys, a former chaplain to Hearty James, Earl of Buchan, who was now in Dunbar, supporting Albany.

She thought about it all for some time, and then, presently, sent to tell Bonne that she was staying the night in the Canongate, and would see her tomorrow. It was then more than six hours after noon, and pitch dark.

Immured in the Cistercian Priory of St Mary of North Berwick under the rule of two Prioresses, Katelijne Sersanders would, under normal circumstances, have devoted her first week or so to observing, with joy, the silent power struggle between the two ladies: the dainty steel femininity of the resident, Elizabeth Forman, in opposition to the commanding personality of Euphemia Graham, her elderly semi-royal cuckoo from Eccles. The Master and chaplain, she gathered, had both promptly absconded to quieter foundations, and the nuns on each side, much reduced, had been in some disarray until a *modus vivendi* was found and the house settled down to a régime remarkably close to that of a double-sex monastery. Jordan, who was not effusive with Kathi, nevertheless showed from time to time that he, too, appreciated the joke. He was teaching Margaret to draw.

Under normal circumstances, the Priory of North Berwick was not a bad place in which to pass a few weeks in January. In size second only to Haddington, it reared its bulky components on the slopes between the sea and the freakish volcanic cone of North Berwick Law. Snow seldom reclined on the hill or the undulating descent to the shore: the salty east wind, fresh in summer and devastating in winter, saw to that. But inside the mellow red-ochre buildings, warmed by the great fires, the inmates entertained one another and praised God with a reassuring regularity.

Mick Crackbene was also still there, although he lived with the lay officers and servants in the service buildings, and only came to the conventual table on invitation. Much of the rest of the time, he was working outside, repairing something, or labouring on something for the nuns. Often he would take Rankin or Margaret with him, but his most constant companion was Jordan. The solid friendship between the lad of nearly fourteen and the taciturn Scandinavian warmed her heart, for Jordan's sake, and the sake of his father. She wondered whether Crackbene remained because the weather was bad, or because he knew more than she did. She hesitated to ask, until the day Rankin jumped into her room, alight with some tale of a distant bothy full of mail-shirts and weapons. Did his mother suppose that nuns wore them?

Or the servants that slept over there? There were ten of them, big men like sailors. Could he fight with the axes? asked Rankin.

She gave him a lying, sensible answer, and went to seek Crackbene. The Prioress Euphemia was with him. The Prioress said, 'I believe your son has noticed the soldiers. We should talk. Come, Master Michael.'

As was only right, the chamber of the Prioress Elizabeth had become the chamber of the Prioress of Eccles. North Berwick might be supported by Formans and Ramsays, but Euphemia Graham was the granddaughter of a king and the niece of another; half-sister of the late Bishop Kennedy; cousin of the King's three uncles and of the Princesses Eleanor and Annabella and Joanna and their powerful husbands; cousin of the first wife of Wolfaert van Borselen, and so related to Gelis. Related to everyone, but now isolated on the stark rock of age, and reft from her present charge because of its suspect situation.

Entering her room, Kathi sat, Crackbene beside her. Dame Euphemia, elevating her chin, had indeed some resemblance to an article on a rock: perhaps a malignant heron. She said, 'You should have been told. I assured your M. de Fleury that you were the niece of your uncle, and could withstand a little anxiety. You were brought here to remove one of you from temporary danger. To make doubly sure, M. de Fleury also provided the armed guard found by your son: it is not desirable that others should know of it. It is merely an extra precaution.'

Crackbene said nothing. He had obviously known. It wasn't worth being angry. If Nicholas and Crackbene had arranged this, then they trusted the Prioress. Unless, of course, the Prioress and Crackbene were lying.

Kathi said, 'I am glad you think I can stand the truth, for I should now like to have it. Who was in danger?' She thought she knew. Now, unexpectedly, it crossed her mind that it might be herself, from someone who wished to influence her uncle.

The Prioress said, 'I thought you and your friends had discussed this. There have been serious attempts against the life of M. de Fleury, and his son is thought to be another possible victim. It is safer here for Jordan than Edinburgh.'

Kathi said, 'How did you hear of this, Reverend Mother?'

The chin tilted again. There was a wart on it. 'From M. de Fleury and your uncle,' the Prioress said. 'Your uncle has been seeking the man – disloyal to the King – who contrived the sad conflict at Castle Heaton. He suspects that man, or the person who paid him, to be the cause of other disruption. A paper found in the King's chamber, apparently.'

'But my uncle doesn't yet know who it is,' Kathi said. 'Or not when I saw him last. Do you perhaps know, Dame Euphemia?' Her heart had started to thud. In the Floory Land – away from the Floory Land – so many arguments, so many angry discussions. Who was it? Who was it?

And cravenly, now, to herself: You didn't want us to know. I don't want to know. I don't want the responsibility. Don't tell me.

The Prioress gazed at her, buckled into starched linen, her brows formidably arched. She said, 'Certainly, I believe that I know. Your uncle discovered that M. de Fleury's visit to York was known beforehand to the Duke of Albany's most fervent follower, Jardine of Applegarth. He was at York. He has land in Lochmaben, and his father owns Jardinefield, three miles to the north of Upsettlington. Applegarth has always suspected Lord Cortachy and M. de Fleury of subverting the King. He regards M. de Fleury, especially, as having betrayed Albany's friendship.'

'But –' began Kathi.

'But, you would say, this does not accord with the picture of long aggression against M. de Fleury, and even his son. Therefore, there must be at least two culprits: Applegarth and the man who encouraged him. Have M. de Fleury or Master Julius reported some information I gave them at Eccles? About, I am sorry to say, the birth of a child to a nun?'

Crackbene sat, unsurprised, his fists on his knees. She could have slapped him. 'No,' Kathi said. She listened, fuming. Nicholas and Julius had known all about this, and had said nothing. At first, of course, it seemed understandable: the story was common enough. A nun had transgressed, and died giving birth to a child. The child's father had also died young, and the fate of the child was not known.

'So?' Kathi said. She had become tired of saying Reverend Mother.

Crackbene spoke. (Marvellous.) He said, 'The name of the nun was not a secret: she had stayed at both North Berwick and Eccles. The name of the father was unknown. Since we came here, the Prioress and I considered it advisable to find it. This is one of the safe houses for treasure. When the English raids started, the Eccles rolls were brought here, and so was the cartulary from Coldingham. I happened to know what was relevant in the Coldingham papers. I found them for the Prioress, while she sought and showed me the records from Eccles. These completed the story. The nun's name, as we knew, was Elizabeth

Semple. The father's name was Andrew, half-brother of Robert Liddell of Halkerston. Their child was a son, and a cousin therefore of Jamie, the present Liddell of Halkerston.'

'But not his heir,' Kathi said.

'No. Sir James has a son of his own, and is of comfortable means, but not wealthy. The Semple family, on the other hand, has chanced to generate great wealth through one of its members, and has much to offer its young.'

'Elizabeth Semple?' Kathi repeated. She tried to think of all her acquaintances of Elliotstoun.

'Try Elizabeth de St Pol,' Crackbene said. 'The disowned sister of Jordan de St Pol of Kilmirren.'

Fat Father Jordan. She stared at the stolid, sea-weathered face, thinking wildly. Kilmirren's siblings, including this poor girl, had long since died. His two children and one grandson were also dead. A second grandson, Diniz, was removed, by his own wish, from the succession. Nicholas, who claimed to be a third, had not proved his claim, and Fat Father Jordan had repudiated him also. But Kilmirren could change his mind. Proof might be found. Nicholas and Liddell, Elizabeth's son, if he lived, were the only possible remaining heirs of Kilmirren. With Nicholas and his family out of the way, Elizabeth's son would be the only claimant when old Kilmirren died. Claimant to Kilmirren, and claimant, he might expect, to whatever fortune his second cousin Nicholas left.

Kathi said, 'So what happened to the son, Liddell? Is he in Scotland? Living secretly somewhere, perhaps being helped by Sir James?'

Crackbene said, 'It's a small country. I know of no one called Liddell who fits. I don't think, either, that Sir James is involved, or even knows there is such a person. His uncle died before Sir James was born, and he has always been well disposed towards Nicholas. No. We think this Liddell has changed his name: gone abroad maybe, and returned with another identity.'

He was speaking slowly. The Prioress's brows had gone up, tall as razor shells. She had said she knew who the man's parents were, not that she knew how to find him. She made no comment, nor did anyone for a long while. Then Kathi gritted her teeth, for cowardice was not for a Sersanders. She said, 'When did Elizabeth die?'

The date was a long time ago: over fifty years. It didn't help. You forgot that Nicholas was so much younger than anyone else. Within the House of Niccolò, and her uncle's circle, and among their associates, Kathi could think of six or seven men who could be the right age for

Elizabeth's son, even if they claimed to be older or younger. She was no nearer to knowing. She was glad. She remained glad even after she left the room, and took Crackbene to task for his duplicity, and wished she could vent her annoyance on Nicholas as well.

She actually believed, then, that Crackbene had told her everything. She knew better, a few days later, when the Prioress (it was Elizabeth Forman this time) drew her into her room to tell her that his lordship the Bishop of Caithness was about to honour them with a visit, and that her uncle Lord Cortachy was to accompany him, together with his countryman, Nicholas de Fleury. They were arriving tomorrow.

The Bishop of . . . ?

Camulio.

And her uncle and Nicholas? Why?

The Prioress told her.

It was not the Prioress's fault, and Kathi should not have described the proposed confrontation with Sandy at Whitekirk as lunacy, and its promoters as fools. Then she apologised, and stormed off to find Crackbene. It transpired that Mick had known about the scheme for ten days, and didn't think anyone could change her uncle's mind, so why worry. He improved his position slightly by volunteering to tell Jordan himself, and provide a colourful version for Rankin and Margaret. He had children at home.

In the long run, the younger children regarded their great-uncle's forthcoming engagement as some sort of contest, with prizes; but Jordan was left with no such illusions, for Crackbene told him the truth. Accordingly, Jordan understood that his father and Lord Cortachy and the Genoese Bishop were coming tomorrow, and would stay overnight. The morning after, they would all three walk unarmed to Whitekirk to meet the King's brother, whom the King had tried to kill, and who had threatened to kill in return. Master Crackbene explained that some things had to be done, and only great men, the best men, could do them. He would not say there was no danger, for there was; but you could be sure that the King would not send out a bishop, a lord and his father without being fairly sure they would come back. Jordan, perceiving that Master Crackbene was doing his best, made it easy for him, and agreed. Kathi watched it, and watched Crackbene take the lad off to finish some task or other. Then she found a task for herself.

Better than most, she knew the history of Sandy's friendship with Nicholas. He had treated Nicholas, through the years, as a servant, and a confidant, and an intermediary. Now he was being persuaded by others that Nicholas was the King's man, not his. It might be the last time Jordan would see his father. And back in Edinburgh, Gelis and Robin must be among those taking farewell of Nicholas now. It was right, she now saw, that Jordan should know the reason for the sacrifice, and its extent.

What Anselm Adorne was doing was offering himself for something that he believed in, and that he thought might succeed. He would not endorse, mindlessly, a cause that was hopeless. Neither would Nicholas. She tried to forget that these were the two men who, with Robin, made up the core of her life, and attempted to view the matter objectively. For example, if Prosper de Camulio was coming, it must be safer than it appeared.

In this, she underestimated the Bishop, who was a man of education and ability, as well as being an inveterate meddler. In a life filled with running battles throughout Europe, and including at least one spell in prison, Prosper de Camulio had never shown himself averse to inviting trouble, or helping a friend, as well as himself. Besides, he had known both Adorne and de Fleury (young vander Poele then) from his various sojourns in Bruges, even before his later visit to Scotland; and had been well acquainted, from the same days, with the Scottish Bishop James Kennedy. There were a few soldiers, he had heard, at this Priory. And if there were to be none on the journey to Whitekirk, yet a Bishop might be deemed to be safe. No one would risk the Pope's wrath over a Bishop.

He chatted, therefore, in gasps, throughout most of the fast coastal ride to North Berwick, undeterred by the relative silence of the other two. When (duly preceded by an outrider) they arrived within the precincts of the Priory, he received the reverence of the resident Prioress first, as custom demanded, but found a little extra warmth for the dear late Bishop Kennedy's sister. The curtsey of Dame Euphemia, addressing his ring, was gratifyingly respectful, if you did not observe, as Kathi did, the impatient glitter in the downcast black eyes.

Anselm Adorne, waiting behind, smiled at his niece, just as Jordan, his hat a shade above hers, was bestowing one of his intent, lavish smiles on his father. Nicholas acknowledged him, and Kathi herself, but his first glance, she had seen, was for Crackbene. Then he crossed to his son, throwing his gloves into Jordan's safe hands and swinging off his furred cloak lumped with ice to carry on his own arm. For a moment they stood talking together: the large, tranquil man with the dimples and deceptive, wide gaze; and the stalwart boy, already broad-shouldered and tall, with worship plain in his eyes.

As, however long they might live, Rankin and Robin would never now stand face to face, although they each had fine looks, and the love between them was as great.

It was still early, two hours before noon. They didn't have to leave for Whitekirk until the following morning. There was time to talk to Nicholas, and to her uncle. Or so it seemed, then.

Chapter 50

And at his belt his keyis suld he beir
Of lokkis, to kepe his gestis geir.
And to thar gestis suld thir folk be leile,
Thar gudis kepe, and thar secret conseile,
And to defend thar gestis at thar micht,
And supplé thaim in thar quarell richt.

T HAT AFTERNOON, the wind dropped and it snowed, calming the seas and presenting, enduring for once, a tranquil landscape of white hill and plain and clustered cabins, among which was set the sturdy sprawl of the Priory. It would have been possible, then, for a boat to set off on the grey, surging sea that they could glimpse but not hear. Adorne and Nicholas decided against it, for it would have meant losing Mick Crackbene, and exposing vulnerable women and children to risks greater than those they ran in this solid building, with their ten soldiers, and the six more that Adorne had brought.

They did not then know of the changing situation in Edinburgh, or of the meetings in Avandale's home, or Kilmirren House, or the Canongate; but they had considered most of the probabilities and were fully aware of their danger. It was the vital meeting at Whitekirk, tomorrow, that occupied all of their minds, when they allowed it.

That afternoon, Anselm Adorne did not allow it, but – strategy defined and orders given – laid himself out to please and comfort the religious whose hospitality he was receiving; to speak at length to the Prioress Euphemia; to walk round the grounds and allow himself to be snowballed by Kathi's children, and watch them make snowmen. Passing through the cloisters, he smiled, observing outside in the garth a well-tried sledge, and a once-painted barrow, and a child's spade stuck in the snow. He talked for a long time to Jordan and saw, and was pleased by, his friendship with Margaret, his great-niece. Between, he walked with the nuns to their church and prayed there, while Bishop Prosper administered the sacrament in Genoese Latin and heard his confession in Genoese. A worldly man, come late to the priesthood, Camulio was not a bad choice for a man of Adorne's stature. Nicholas attended the services, but did not confess.

Throughout the strange afternoon, Jordan was close to him. They had been apart once, when Kathi had asked to say something in private. It was about Applegarth, which was all right. Then it was about Andrew Liddell, and it wasn't all right at all. Mick's patience had clearly run out, and the bastard was taking a hand. To hell with Mick, and the Prioress.

Nicholas said, 'I heard about Applegarth, too. It isn't unlikely that he had that unsigned message sent to Simon at Lochmaben. He works with Davie Purves, another firebrand. I don't think you need look for anyone else.'

She said, 'Nicholas. Don't be stupid. Who is Elizabeth's son?'

'How should I know?' he said.

Darkness fell between three and four, over a black sea and a moon-coloured land blinking with light. By five, the younger children had supped in the kitchen and Bishop Prosper visited them there for a while, teaching Rankin some words of Italian, while he kept Margaret beside him, and made her laugh. He had a son himself, were it known, in the service of King Ferrante of Naples. Women liked Bishop Prosper. The kitchenmaids and the nuns sat round him, their faces rosy in the light of the fire. He had really come, he said, to see what was for supper; and let them take him to the great larders, and the bakehouse, and the brew-house, and the row of barred storerooms, each with its low vaulted ceiling, which held their less edible stores. He was sorry to go, he said, when someone from above came to fetch him.

Adorne was in the Priory parlour, with Katelijne Sersanders and de Fleury. He looked calm. 'Prosper. We are receiving word of a cavalry skirmish not far off. They have found trampled snow and some blood, and tracks that seem to point to Dunbar. Now our lookout tells us that two armed horsemen are coming this way. Crackbene has taken men to intercept them. We should know soon who they are.'

'Sooner than soon,' said the young woman. 'Jordan is up on the roof, and I suspect Rankin is trying to join him.'

'Sooner than soon indeed,' de Fleury said.

The door burst open upon his son, streaked with peat-soot. His son exclaimed, 'Father! It's Master Julius, covered in blood; and Monseigneur de St Pol of Kilmirren is riding beside him!'

'Ah,' said de Fleury. The girl looked at him, but he was gazing at Adorne. De Fleury said, 'It sounds as if they're in trouble. How fortunate that we are still here to help them.'

Familiar with the detritus of battle, the nuns were not shocked, but dealt efficiently with the wounds of the handsome man with the slanting eyes and pleased smile, by name Master Julius. He was in better shape in some ways than the lord of Kilmirren who, though unhurt, was not of the age or the build for strenuous skirmishes. He had been on his way to the Priory with a troop led by Lord Home's own grandson, he said, when they had been attacked by a superior force from Dunbar. Master Julius (a lawyer) had been travelling with the Homes for security, and managed to get himself and the old man away. The rest had been captured.

'Really?' said M. de Fleury, who had lain in contented repose in the window-seat ever since the two gentlemen were brought in. 'Couldn't you save them, too, Julius? You mean Alex Home is now back in Dunbar, a prisoner of his own former master, and facing all those men he threw over when he crossed to the King? That was unkind.'

'I felt unkind,' said the lawyer. He was testing his arm-sling and smiling. 'I think, like you, that he had a hand in what happened at Lauder. Anyway, it's over. Reverend Mother, Sisters, how can I thank you?'

The ladies withdrew, with reluctance, leaving the gentlemen to their affairs. Some expected the demoiselle to depart also, but she remained by her uncle, who had seated himself beside the fat lord. The old man, almost recovered, was staring at M. de Fleury, who gazed tranquilly back. M. de Fleury said, 'I hope you thanked Julius. You threw him out last time you met.'

'It was a mistake,' the lord of Kilmirren said.

The door closed. Inside, no one spoke for a moment. Then Anselm Adorne said, 'We are glad to see you both safe, but perhaps we ought to be quick. My lord, why were the Homes coming here? Do you know?'

Kilmirren stirred. In his mid-seventies, he no longer wore armour. His only protection today had been a jerkin of leather beneath his jacket and cloak, and a helm on his head, which he had taken off, leaving a strapped cap beneath, set into the descending cataract of his jowls. His dress was stained, and his chest rose and fell still with hard breathing. Julius, encountered by chance, was dressed more for hunting than battle, and his sword-cuts were all on his arm.

Kilmirren said, 'Fortunately, I can tell you all that Home could. Albany is renewing his service to England. Avandale suggests you go to Whitekirk tomorrow, but the chances of an agreement are slighter than they once were.'

He expounded, with concision. It came to Kathi that she had often heard his voice raised in mockery, or provocation, or with some lancing taunt, but never in the mode he must have used all his days as a skilled commander; as a minister whose advice King Louis, of all men, respected. It struck her to wonder whether half the mischief in his life had not sprung from boredom. Then she recalled the days when he controlled his own merchant fleet; when he secretly ran the great company called the Vatachino, which he created to crush and shame Nicholas. He had been just as cruel, then.

She listened, pondering on what he was saying. Liddell, the moderate man, was now absent in London. It confirmed Crackbene's impression that Liddell had no direct hand in the campaign against Nicholas: he was not managing the affairs here of some unknown and vindictive cousin. Liddell's absence also helped to explain Sandy's aggression. The foray against Alex Home, just before Whitekirk, had not been wise. Liddell would have advised Sandy against it.

Absent, too, was Bell-the-Cat Angus; but he had lost political courage after his gesture at Lauder, and his personal backing for Albany might not have been fierce, had he stayed. The same couldn't be said of his unruly, leaderless Douglases, now filling his fort of Tantallon. And Tantallon was close. The red, cliff-top bulk of Tantallon was here, on the doorstep; three miles from where they were sitting, and closer to Whitekirk than that.

Applegarth. Someone was mentioning the name. Nicholas, in course of pursuing some point with Kilmirren. His voice throughout was neutral. The last time they met, he had just come from Kelso, and the fat man had spurned him. 'Monseigneur, why were you here with the Homes?'

And the fat man answered. 'Shall I tell you? Yes. I am here to do what the Crown is afraid to do: to uncover the man who plotted against my son and my grandson, and kill him. I know his name.' He turned to Adorne. 'You fear I shall upset the delicate balance tomorrow. I shall not. I shall seek this man out myself, when you have gone. Dunbar is full of informers.'

He hadn't mentioned a name. Nicholas did. Nicholas said, 'Applegarth is in Tantallon.'

There was a little silence. The fat man said, 'How do you know?'

And Nicholas said, 'North Berwick is also full of informers.'

There was another silence. 'But you will not touch him,' the fat man said, speaking distinctly. 'You will not help him escape me, you will not take him prisoner, you will not kill him. He is mine.'

A third person spoke. '*I* would kill him,' he said. 'He lied to Henry. He called my father a traitor.'

Jordan. Jordan, Kathi saw with a pang, standing defiantly before the obese, elderly man as a much younger child had once stood, in scratched silver armour, defending his family. In the window, Nicholas had stiffened. Now he must be thinking as she did. How much had Jordan overheard, guessed, been carelessly told?

The yellowed eyes stared at the grey. Kilmirren said, 'And how many men have you killed?'

Jordan's gaze did not move. He said, 'As many as Monseigneur, perhaps, at the same age.'

'And,' said St Pol of Kilmirren, 'you imagine you could kill a man more successfully than I?'

'I have your son's sword,' Jordan said.

There was another space. She could not look at Nicholas. At length: 'I remember. Perhaps that was another mistake,' Kilmirren remarked. 'Perhaps one day you will challenge me with it. Shall I take it back?'

'If my lord wishes,' Jordan said. He had brought it with him, Kathi knew. He slept with it over his bed.

'No. You will have blunted it,' Kilmirren said. 'So let us return to men's affairs. Cortachy, what is your plan for tomorrow?' She wondered what her uncle would do; but he simply looked at the other man quietly, and spoke.

What he said was not welcome. Kilmirren had been in no doubt that Adorne, abetted by Nicholas, proposed to trap and kill the Duke of Albany by some superb act of Burgundian villainy. He found it beyond all belief that there should be no plan at all, and that Adorne meant to do just as he promised. It was perhaps the presence of Camulio that made the lack of deceit so unlikely.

She registered all of that, but her heart and soul were with Nicholas, who had stretched out his arm and taken his son to sit beside him.

The Ultimate Supper (as her uncle wryly named it) was simple but stately, the two inadvertent guests being outshone by the splendour of the Bishop, not to mention the King's other envoys, attired in the court dress and chains they would be wearing tomorrow at Whitekirk. The Prioresses, returning the courtesy, were dressed in long, simple robes of double Caspian silk, with some important ecclesiastical jewellery. Kathi just wore her best.

Sitting next to her, Nicholas duly admired it. He added, 'Are you fasting from fright, or from religious conviction?'

She hadn't spoken to him since Jordan's outburst. As soon as the conference finished, the old man had gone off to rest, and Crackbene and Nicholas had been locked in discussion with Julius. Adorne had gone to walk in the cloisters with the Genoese bishop. She knew that his faith gave him relief, and was glad. For herself, she had just spent a vociferous two hours in fierce games with Rankin, ending in an attempt to steer him towards bed. Margaret, as ever, was more successful with her winsome sibling than anyone. Vying with her two handsome children, one a Berecrofts, one an Adorne, Kathi refused to admit to cowardice. But certainly she had come to receive comfort from them, rather than give it.

Nicholas guessed as much, of course; hence his present bland question. She *was* fasting from fright. She suspected that the vast calm of Nicholas also covered something other than lethargy. She said bluntly, 'I don't like tonight, and I can't stand the thought of what is going to happen tomorrow. And now you have St Pol to think about as well.'

'He could be an asset,' Nicholas said. 'If there was an attack after we'd gone, for example. He'll be here, and the soldiers, and Crackbene. And Jordan isn't bad, or at least his master-at-arms cost enough. Do you remember the provision cellars, the ones Prosper investigated today?' Perversely, he was answering as if she were afraid for herself.

She stared at him. 'Do you *know* how long we've been here? Is there a blade of grass that has escaped me?'

'Don't pretend: you've enjoyed it. If anything awkward does happen, you should take the children to one of those vaults. They're locked and barred, and no one could easily see you. And there's plenty of food. Casks of wine and bags of raisins for weeks.'

'So Dame Euphemia said. It was one of the first things she suggested,' Kathi said. She watched his face. 'That worries you?'

'Not necessarily. She came here from Eccles because someone thought she was spying,' Nicholas said. 'The Bishop her brother lived with the young Sandy in Bruges. But in other ways, as you've mentioned, she's been helpful.'

Kathi gazed at him. 'She should be. She's one of Efemie's god-mothers,' she said. 'Didn't she tell you?'

'No,' said Nicholas, and gave a grunt halfway between appreciation and laughter. The Prioress, who had been watching them, sent him a sardonic smile, but no more. Nor did she impose herself on them when, at the end of the meal, her six principal guests resorted to the day-room they had been given to make their final plans before morning. Kathi returned to her children, stopping on the way to reconnoitre the cellars. There were four, and their doors gave on to the garth. The keys, trustingly, were all in the locks. She left them there, but noted the cell she would choose. It was a precaution. She was not afraid of what might happen after Nicholas and her uncle had gone. She was blinded with terror and pain over what Nicholas and her uncle would be facing at Whitekirk, tomorrow.

Outside, the snow gleamed in the dark. Behind the kirk and cloister of St Mary's, North Berwick, six hundred feet up on the Law, Crackbene's lookout saw the stirring of movement beyond the Heugh, but at first put it down to stray sheep. A moment later, he grasped that he was looking at a large force of armed foot-soldiers in white, travelling in the direction of the Priory, and accompanied by some twenty white-shrouded cavalry, their harness muffled and their hooves silenced by snow. He leaped to raise the alarm, but the advance scouts had climbed the hill earlier, and attacked him from behind. A moment later, and he was lifeless. A dog barked, and then stopped. The other animals had already been silenced. The troop, of two hundred foot and eighteen cavalry, was composed of Douglases and other men who called them-selves supporters of Albany. It included John Douglas of Morton, David Purves, Gifford of Sheriffhall and the second Lord Boyd, who had been born in Anselm Adorne's house, and who believed that he was simply preventing tomorrow's meeting at Whitekirk, which might lure Sandy back to the King. His captain, Alexander Jardine of Apple-garth, held the same view precisely, in a slightly different form.

Through the falling snow, at four hours to midnight, St Mary's lay warm and secure behind its high walls; below a sky ikon-gold from the lamps from its chapel and kitchen and little infirmary; from the dormitory and the rooms of the Prioresses; from the occasional window in the range of guest-chambers and the cabins where the house-servants lived. There was a haze of smoke, and the smells of peat mixed with spiced food and incense.

It looked secure but was not, for the main gates stood unbarred, and the superb inner door had already been opened, from the inside.

Of the two hundred unmounted soldiers, only fifty slipped past the lodge at the gate, which was unguarded. With two exceptions the gentry, with the horse, stayed outside. Of the fifty, most deployed themselves quietly along the inner wall, in what cover they could find; while six of their number, bent low, ran across the outer precincts and followed their leader noiselessly into the Priory.

Upstairs, in the day-room, Mick Crackbene returned to his chair beside Nicholas, having deposited Julius in the infirmary, where he was being re-bandaged by one of the prettier nuns. Adorne looked up, and then returned to the mild conversation he had initiated with the Bishop and St Pol of Kilmirren. Jordan said, 'It's snowing!' Crackbene's flat cap was wet.

'Maybe, but you're not going out,' Nicholas said. He glanced at Crackbene. 'Unless there's anything you'd like me to do?'

'Such as what?' Crackbene said.

'Only a suggestion,' said Nicholas.

A short time later, the door opened again, on a tap, and Dame Euphemia's servant stood there, looking round till she found my lord Cortachy and M. de Fleury, both of whom were wanted, she said, in the Prioress Euphemia's room.

Bishop Prosper, who had not been invited, bent a friendly eye on the woman. 'Why not ask the lady Prioress to join us all instead? Go and ask her, my dear.'

Adorne rose and stretched. 'She may have in mind something private. If not, I'll bring her back. Nicholas?'

'It *is* something private,' said the maid.

Jordan looked at his father, who grinned. 'I'll tell you later, if it's anything interesting. Meanwhile, do as Mick tells you, or else.'

He walked out after Adorne. The servant had vanished. The quiet way to the Prioress's room was empty as usual. Outside her door, Adorne turned to him, his face shadowed. Nicholas said, 'I have no regrets,' and received a resigned grimace, with no bitterness in it. When Adorne knocked, and obtained leave to enter, Nicholas followed. He would have shut the door, but it was wrenched out of his hands by two men who immediately blocked it, unsheathing their blades when he jumped. When he turned, he saw that Adorne had continued steadily forward and stopped, as if before a tribunal, at the place where the Prioress sat, her clasped hands on the table before her, her black eyes trained first on him, and then Nicholas.

Adorne said, 'You sent for us, Reverend Mother.'

'No,' she said. 'No. A frightened servant sent for you, induced by a group of silly ruffians. They think you will obey them to save me. You will not. If I see you weaken, I shall take my own life, with the full permission of God. Do you understand me?'

A man had stepped out from the shadows behind her. He had a knife in his hand. Nicholas said, 'Jardine of Applegarth.'

'So I deduced,' Adorne said. 'The gentleman who sent the unflattering message about you to Lochmaben, and who would prefer to see the Duke of Albany on the throne, with English overlords. I am right?'

'Well enough put,' said the man. He sat on the desk. He didn't look crazed, or evil, or personally vindictive. He just looked like a swarthy, unshaven man with a permanent, puzzled frown. He said, 'It seems better than a mad King with two Burgundian overlords. Others think so as well. I've nothing against the Prioress or the Priory. I've just come to make sure that neither of you can interfere in this country again.'

'Interfere?' said the Prioress. She sounded amused. 'How can two foreigners of this kind interfere?'

Applegarth glanced down. 'By manipulating the King,' he said. 'That's what Adorne does. By killing Johndie Mar with magic and poison. That's what Master Nicol and your Dr Andreas do. And by enchanting Sandy Albany away from his duty tomorrow. But you won't do that now.'

'Three against two?' Adorne observed with mild sarcasm. 'Impossible odds.'

The man smiled. 'What do you think that I am? A man with a grudge and six cronies? There are ten more men inside these buildings alone. And if anything happens to me, there are five hundred outside, with orders to enter and burn down the Priory.'

'Two hundred,' chided Nicholas. The Prioress pursed her lips. Behind, he heard one of the door-keepers shuffle. 'And none inside, I'm afraid. You didn't know about our fifty soldiers? It has been quite an exciting few weeks for the nuns.'

'Nicholas?' Adorne said.

The Prioress said, 'Curb your tongue.'

'No,' said Applegarth. 'Let us hear more. Where are these invisible warriors? You have a lookout, I accept. But you can't have believed we would be able to walk into the convent. If you have any men, which I doubt, mine will have killed them by now.'

'How did you walk in?' Adorne said. 'Someone climbed over the wall?'

Applegarth smiled. 'Someone let us in. I told you that others think as I do.'

'I don't believe you,' said Adorne.

'Would you like to meet him?' Applegarth said. He raised his voice. 'Open the door.'

The two guards were still there. One of them brought out his sword, and the other jerked open the door. Mick Crackbene was standing outside it, holding his sword with its point on the floor. The blade was red. He surveyed the room, beginning with Nicholas and Adorne, and ending with Applegarth. He said, 'I was just coming to tell you. All the bastards are dead but these two.'

Grinning, he lifted his sword. The grin, swinging round, was for Nicholas. The sword was for the first of the doormen, who took it through the chest, just as Nicholas kicked the legs from under the second, and Crackbene dispatched him as well. Adorne made a move to the desk, and then stopped.

'Very clever,' said Applegarth from his perch. 'And do I kill the Prioress now, or will you let me escort her to the gate? I think you should. As I said, unless I appear, my whole force will make themselves very unpleasant. And some of them, I fear, are vigorous men of the land, with primitive urges.'

The Prioress said, 'And the Duke of Albany is employing men like yourself? It saddens me.' The knife laid at her throat unflatteringly reflected the wart on her chin. Her expression, of faint distaste, didn't change, but her eyes had moved from Nicholas to the door, and back again.

Nicholas stirred, in an unthreatening way. He said, 'I don't suppose Albany knows that he's here.'

He had barely got out of the way, when the door swung open quietly. 'Oh there you are,' Julius said and, walking forward, cast the knife in his hand straight at Sander Jardine of Applegarth. It sank into his chest. Jardine's eyes and mouth opened. For a moment, his knife continued to stand against the Prioress's neck, then it slackened, and Applegarth fell.

Nicholas sprang round the desk. Adorne was already there, between the Prioress and the body. After a moment he rose and turned to care for the Prioress. The anonymous note-sender of Lochmaben was dead.

Nicholas stood gazing at Julius, whose face, after a number of false starts, could be seen as conveying nervous pleasure. 'I wish you hadn't done that,' Nicholas said.

'I know. Kilmirren wanted the privilege. I'll confess that I did it, not you. But that solves it, doesn't it?' Julius said. 'Once they know Applegarth's dead, that mob will go home.'

'Will they?' said Adorne. Below his eyes, Dame Euphemia was kneeling, gravely, her hand on the brow of the dead man.

Crackbene said, 'They might. We took one hostage. Jamie Boyd is here, Nicholas. Jordan is keeping an eye on him, with Bishop Prosper and Kilmirren. Applegarth's men wouldn't want to face Albany without him.'

Jamie Boyd was younger than Jordan. Jamie Boyd was the second Lord Boyd, the King's nephew, who admired his uncle Albany, and had been persuaded to join this grandiloquent foray.

Adorne said, 'Very well. Then I think we have an announcement to make to Applegarth's troops. Their captain is dead, after breaking into the Priory and threatening to kill the Prioress Euphemia. The Law and the Church will hold all his companions equally accountable, if they remain. They are therefore ordered to leave. If they do so immediately, no further steps will be taken, and no harm will come to Lord Boyd, who is at present here, in our custody.' He looked from Nicholas to the Prioress, and to Julius. 'Does that seem suitable?'

'It sounds convincing,' Nicholas said.

'Then we do it. Returned by all the black beans. Who would best act as our orator? I think Prosper. Don't you think, Nicholas? The Bishop will speak for us.'

Chapter 51

His procuratour he was and maid him trew reknyng
And gud payment of all this forsaid thing.

ONLY PROSPER DE CAMULIO, man of diverse experience, would have taken so calmly a request to walk into the dark and order two hundred armed men to depart without protest. Adorne went with him to the door, and he was preceded by a Priory servant with a flag. Nicholas was not there, having been told to go and speak to Jamie Boyd.

The lad was in a room, under guard with his own son, and Fat Father Jordan was installed with them both. The boys, when Nicholas entered, were not speaking, but both were flushed. St Pol of Kilmirren, on the other hand, looked merely bored. 'Ah,' he said. 'The expert with children. Hale in hide and hue, despite everything. And who gave you the right to kill the man Applegarth?'

'Julius killed him,' Nicholas said. 'The Prioress was quite pleased, although she might have preferred her throat cut, had she known how annoyed you would be. Jamie? Are you all right?' The boy, his mouth shut, was glaring.

'You won't get a reply out of him,' Kilmirren said. 'He thinks the Whitekirk meeting is nothing but a trick to kill Albany. In other words, the good Lord Cortachy is a rascal, which, of course, my young Lord Boyd and his mother ought to be able to judge better than anyone.'

'He's the King's man,' said the boy. He spoke with contempt. Young Jordan looked at him, then at his father.

Nicholas sat down with a thump. 'Well, that's true,' he said. 'But it doesn't mean Lord Cortachy hasn't come in good faith. If you think of it, why in God's name should he choose this elaborate way to kill Albany? And what would it gain him, other than coalesce all the opposition against the King? And if that doesn't make sense, look about you. There is a small band of trained soldiers here, and a number of holy persons, and six fairly experienced men, like Adorne. At Whitekirk tomorrow there will be three. But even if we cheat and smuggle in everyone, including the nuns, they're going to be outnumbered by his grace of Albany's men, armed to the teeth, to any degree that he wishes. Does that sound like a trap?'

No one spoke. The boy's face was bloodless. He was a nice enough lad, but had yet to come into the virile attraction that went with the heavy Boyd build. There was red in his hair from the Stewart side. Then he blurted, 'You'll bring in reinforcements.'

Nicholas said, 'Do you see them? Don't you think they would be here by now? No, we shan't. That would endanger the nuns – and my own family if you like. Jordan is here, and the demoiselle Katelijne, did they tell you? And the children. Struggling a little, as we all are, to do the right thing. I'd like her to be safe.'

'Shall I fetch them?' said Jordan. 'She's in . . . She went somewhere safe with the children, but I expect it's all right now.'

So she had gone to the cellars. Nicholas said, 'Let's be sure first. We have to await Bishop Prosper's triumph.' And, to the boy, 'I'm sorry it happened like this. But if it's any consolation, you may have prevented some very wretched things happening in a holy place, which really wouldn't help the Duke's case. Without a leader, men sometimes get out of hand.'

'David will lead,' the boy said. 'Master Purves. He was Sander's friend. He'll be angry.' Then he broke off, for he heard, as they all did, the shouting below.

'I am afraid,' the fat man said. 'Dear Nicholas, I am afraid that my lord Boyd is right.'

Then the door burst open on Crackbene and Adorne, escorting a flushed Bishop Prosper.

His exhortation had been thrown in his face. Far from accepting the chance to escape, far from bargaining for the release of Lord Boyd, Master David Purves had produced a demand of his own. He asked for the persons of Cortachy and de Fleury. Unless he got them at once, he would attack. And should he be forced to attack, Purves had added, the Bishop would have to answer for the nuns' fate. Two Sisters had already strayed into their hands. He could not speak for their safety.

'Is that true?' said Kilmirren. 'Of the nuns?'

'Yes,' said Adorne. 'One went to get her dog, and the other to find her.'

Kilmirren said, still to Adorne, 'You must make up your mind. But if you go, they will kill you.'

The Princess's son raised his voice. Since the Tolbooth, it had started to break. He said, 'This expedition was to take and imprison my lord of Cortachy and M. de Fleury. That was all.'

'I am glad that you thought that was all,' Nicholas said. He was conscious of his son's eyes.

Adorne said, equally gently, 'The Prioress will tell you that Master Jardine's plan was more radical. His friend may share his view.'

The boy said, 'So you told Master Purves to go away, or I would suffer.'

And Adorne said, 'Yes, we did. It was less than honest, for I, for one, would see that you came to no harm. Perhaps Master Purves has realised as much. As you heard, he has said that he will still attack, despite your presence, unless I give myself up.'

His voice was deprecating, for it was not a pleasant thing to convey to a young man, a Princess's son, that he appeared to have been jettisoned by his own side. He waited, and then said, 'I am sorry. The captain is obsessed by a single idea, and can think of nothing else. Also, as I said, he probably saw through the deceit. That being so, we have no need now to keep you. If you wish, you may walk out and join him.'

The Bishop looked startled, and Nicholas looked sharply at Adorne. Then he saw that he was right. Released, Jamie could report on their defences, for what that was worth. But, more to the point, he could repeat something of what had been said to him. If he had been half convinced, he might find his doubts shared.

It was a gamble. Everything had been a gamble, from the moment they had refrained from closing the traitorous gates, and so tempted Applegarth to try and abstract his victims. Applegarth's effort had failed. With luck and some guile, this new threat might have been countered. Then, in theory, the troop would march off rather than attack a Cistercian priory. An assault, whether it succeeded or not, would be political madness.

But there had been little luck, and perhaps not enough guile, and, sadly, Sander Jardine and David Purves were political madmen. Furthermore, the gates were still open, and two hundred men could be deployed round the outer precinct with longbows and crossbows and swords; with maces and axes and battering-rams. And inside were women. And outside, it seemed.

Adorne was speaking quietly 'Nicol? Mick? As we planned. We haven't long. We should start.'

'And I, if you please,' said the fat man.

They were agreeing, without words, to fight.

It was the last gamble, of course. They were in a strong place, which was also a church. There was a chance that among the attackers, there were those who would waver. It was worth trying. It was perhaps not worth more than that. Fortunately, there was not much time to think.

Most of them had been in battles like this, where there were few choices, and all of them harsh. Nicholas and Crackbene and Adorne had all seen action together in the past, and they worked well together. Crackbene had charge of the soldiers, deployed high in the attics and within the penthouses attached to the walls. Julius helped him, with his one active arm. Kilmirren, rendered static by age and obesity, could still command; and however little he made himself liked, his advice was worth listening to. For the rest, young Jordan stayed with his father, and the Bishop, stripped for action, displayed an alacrity that endeared him to Crackbene at once.

During all the swift preparations, Nicholas ran downstairs, once, to visit the cellars where Kathi, wrapped in three blankets, was playing cards with her two children, similarly cocooned. Her nose was blue. Nicholas said, 'I'm sorry. It is safest, if you can stand it. They've turned down our offer, so we're preparing to fight.'

With Kathi, he never had to spell anything out. They were here, in the cold shuttered dark with a candle, because they might be overlooked if the Priory fell. Then, men would make for the chapel, where the treasure was, and the brewery, and the warm kitchen and refectory and dormitory where the nuns and servants would be gathered. You might say that she ought to be there too, sharing the risk, helping the others. She had not done so because of her children, and because of Robin, and because of Nicholas.

She said, 'You don't think you can hold out.'

No one had put that into words. In battle, one never did know. He said, 'Your uncle will decide.'

Rankin was trying to get his attention, and Margaret was reproving him, with all the authority of eight over seven. Their mother said, 'Adorne is the person they want.'

Nicholas said, 'If something is worth buying, it is worth the fullest extent of its price.'

'I see,' she said. Then she said, 'And what about Jordan? Young Jordan?'

Always straight to the core. He said, 'Crackbene will look after him.'

'Against whom?' Kathi said. 'Have you told Crackbene who it is, Nicholas? You have to tell someone now. Who is more important than Jordan?'

He was silent. She said, 'Nicholas. You've seen obsession in others. Now, at last, you are being forced out of yours. You have done all you can; all you should; all that anyone could ever expect of you. Now you tell someone, or you let my uncle walk out alone. They will take Lord Cortachy. They will allow Nicholas de Fleury to stay. They may even suspect that if you stay, someone will kill you for them.' She waited. She said, *'Who is Elizabeth's son?'*

Rankin was showing him something: a tile with a bird on it. He made a comment and gave it back with a smile. Then he looked up at Kathi. He said, 'I have left a sealed note with the Prioress, and asked her to give it to Crackbene when we have gone. He will decide what to do.'

She drew in her breath. She didn't comment. What he was doing, without words, was passing to Crackbene the task he could not do himself. If that was the end of an obsession, then so be it.

She said, 'So you and my uncle will go out together.'

'Yes. Of course,' he said.

Of course.

She said, 'Tell him I love him, and always shall.'

'He knows,' Nicholas said.

They were not going to be able to hold out. It was the nature of the assault that finally determined it. For a while, the attackers fought by the rule, hoping to achieve a quick, tidy success that would escape public censure. Unfortunately, success proved elusive, and too many men were being picked off from high vantage points by extremely talented professional archers. The enemy command, its temper frayed, decided to descend to rough tactics and finish it. The accessible penthouses were sent up in flames; fires were built under walls; and the two nuns were brought out into the light and subjected to the humiliating first stages of something increasingly brutal.

Anselm Adorne, seeing that, laid down his bow and said, 'No.'

Nicholas was within earshot, as he had been for the last ten minutes. He also laid down his weapon, and turned to look at the other. Then, because it was such an obvious decision, he gave a large smile that came of its own accord, from sweet relief, and said, 'Shall I get Prosper? He's good with announcements.'

He was good with that announcement: it stopped the trouble at once. By then, everyone knew that Adorne had resolved to surrender. Nicholas had not seen St Pol, but knew that he had consented. Naturally. He himself had discussed it briefly with Crackbene, who had been remarkably taciturn, and would be even more so, he supposed, when the Prioress gave him his note. Then Nicholas had gone to his son. There wasn't much time, but he had seated himself on the floor, by the window at which Jordan had been kneeling, and said, 'They are going to injure the nuns and perhaps burn down the Priory, so Lord Cortachy and I are going to do as they ask, and let them take us away. They don't want us to go to Whitekirk tomorrow, and they think we are plotting against the Duke of Albany's life. Once they find that we are not really a threat, they'll let us go free. In the meantime, you will behave as you usually do, obeying your mother except on the occasions when you have to tell her she's wrong. You'll have plenty of help; you aren't being burdened for life; and if you ever want to go somewhere else, then do that: no one is indispensable.'

'You are,' said Jordan. 'And you're going somewhere else.'

Nicholas said, 'My mother went somewhere once, without telling me, and didn't come back. I understood later that it wasn't because she didn't want me, or like me. She didn't want to go, but thought it was better for me if she did.'

'Is this better for me?' Jordan said.

'I don't know,' Nicholas said. 'If I don't go, everyone here could be hurt. If I survived, I would feel I had killed them. You might come to feel the same. Anyway, it's only prison. Parrots don't mind them at all. Come and teach me a new word now and then.'

They walked out in procession, he and Adorne; with the Bishop, robed, striding before them. They paced over the snow, shoulder to shoulder, and the torchlight illumined the velvets and furs they would have worn as the King's envoys at Whitekirk, and roused the gems flashing in their gauntlets and hats, and the golden links of the Order they both wore, with the white and gold Unicorn himself, trapped and chained, swaying below. Adorne was smiling a little, but Nicholas was wearing the mask that obliterated all else, and beneath it could have been either remote or most violently aware.

Now, the precinct was less full, as most of the attackers were assembling outside the walls. At the gates stood the party awaiting the prisoners:

a small band of horse led by Purves, and flanked by foot-soldiers with torches. To one side stood a groom between two riderless horses. No, not a groom, but a youth: James, second Lord Boyd, regarding the approaching procession with a stern – indeed, a proprietorial air.

Far behind, standing with the rest at the door of the Priory, Crackbene let his breath go. Young Boyd had been right. Purves had settled for taking the King's envoys prisoner, to prevent the meeting, and protect the future of Albany.

It might, up to that point, have been true. Adorne thought that it was, and smiled at Jamie, who almost smiled back. Nicholas, attuned to every change in the flickering darkness, was the first to sense the heads turn on the other side of the gate, and then to hear the rumour of sound they had heard – the faint percussion of a very large body of cavalry travelling fast from the west; from the direction of Edinburgh. A force much too large to be casual. The kind of force a foreign trickster would need if, having proposed a rendezvous without arms, he was secretly introducing his men for a killing.

The soldiers round the Priory of St Mary's realised that, very quickly.

The cavalry might be approaching at speed, but there was still time for betrayed men to retaliate. Jamie Boyd started forward, his face blanched, and then, with a look of bitter hatred, flung himself off with the riderless horses. The men already inside the compound, now shouting, had begun to hurry, some drawing their swords. One of the nuns started to run and was killed outright by a vicious slash from a rider; the other was hurled to the ground. Some of the foot-soldiers snatched up the torches and began to fling them against whatever would burn, or took their bows and shot randomly as they made for the gates. In the upper floors of the Priory, the few bowmen still left snatched up their weapons and began to shoot downwards. Below, the Prioresses stood rigid, until pulled back, with a curse, by Kilmirren. Crackbene thrust his way out and started to run towards Nicholas, but was immediately set upon by two men. St Pol drew his sword and proceeded, calmly, to help him. Jordan, who had been standing transfixed in the doorway, disappeared and returned, panting, with Simon de St Pol's sword on his shoulder. Then he looked for his father.

It was a long way from the door to the gate, where escaping men were thrusting past their own captain. The Bishop, nearest the van, had scorned to run when the unrest began but, setting his teeth, had lifted the long, solid weight of his crozier and brandished it threateningly. A pike, dashed through the air, had sent him flying. Next, before they too could run, Adorne and Nicholas had been seized and forced before Purves.

In fact, Adorne had made no attempt to escape. He had looked up and spoken clearly and simply. 'I don't know who they are. We have kept faith. So has the King.'

Purves had gazed down. Another firebrand, Nicholas had called him. Although unlike his friend Jardine in feature, there was a great similarity. The face, the dogged, sick face of the fanatic. Purves did not even draw his own sword. He simply said, 'Kill them,' and turned, and spurred his horse out of the gate.

The men who laid hands on Adorne were of the simple kind Applegarth had described: solidly muscled and greedy. Nicholas was a big man, trained to war, and at present possessed, to the point of insanity, with one purpose. They cursed, overthrown at first by his strength, and he almost got to Adorne. But then three or four more fell upon him, with blow upon blow to his body and head, and held him upright as he struggled still, tearing off everything of value he had; but without as yet using their axes. Axes caused damage, and were kept for the last, against valueless flesh.

They had done the same to Adorne. The collar of honour had gone, and the furred robe and jewelled jacket beneath it, and the Unicorn ring, so like the King's, but for the small difference: *Para Tutum*, in legend. The King, for whom the ring's owner was dying. They threw their victim to the ground when they had what they wanted, slashing his lower limbs first, so that he couldn't have risen. Lying face down in the dark, in his torn shirt and hose, he must have been only half conscious by then, and perhaps hardly felt the stab over the shoulder-blade that travelled inwards and down, to the heart. Then they rolled him over and opened his skull with one blow.

He lived for a moment, before the blood rolled down and closed the eyes looking at Nicholas. The look held everything he was trying to say, although he only breathed two words. 'I wish . . .'

The men drew back. Nicholas didn't see them. He stood in the grasp of his captors and was aware of nothing until he heard a great scream, in his son's voice. Then he wrenched his head round.

Calling his name, Jordan was running towards him, his face lowering and white, Simon's great sword held two-handed, pointing forward. Arrows were falling. Other men were running with weapons. Some were only intent on escape, but some were veering towards him. Crackbene seemed to be wounded, and was struggling to rise from the ground. Nicholas found his voice then: the voice of final authority that had always stopped Jordan, wherever he was. With all the power of his lungs, he delivered his order. 'Jordan! *Turn round and go!*'

But Jordan now was a man, and made his own decisions. He continued to run. He continued to run until the elder Jordan, rearing behind him, slammed him into the ground with the great tumbling mass of his body, and pinned him there, helpless beneath him. Then the rags of Applegarth's army ran past without pausing, for the ground had started to shake and the distant drumming of hooves had turned into low thunder. At the same moment, the men grasping Nicholas loosed him and ran, their booty clutched in their arms.

Prosper's voice said, 'Is he alive? Oh, dear God.'

'Pray for him,' Nicholas said, and got up and went to his son.

The arrows had stopped, but the ground between the walls and the Priory was still dangerous with running men, slashing at anything in their fear and frustration. The torches had mostly burned out, but you could still see, among the brown and red slush, the bodies of the men the archers had killed, and of the two nuns. The Priory door had been closed, against refugees this time, instead of marauders. Jordan, half pulled free from the old man, was gasping, 'I'm all right. Are you all right? You're not going? You don't have to go?' And then: 'Is he dead?'

Nicholas glanced across, and said, 'Yes.'

'No. I know. Is Monseigneur dead?' Jordan said. 'They shot an arrow at me.'

The old man's eyes were closed. There was no sign of an arrow, but there was a bloody tear where it had been. Nicholas eased his son from below him, and bent to look at the wound. The old man opened his eyes. 'I shall survive. Take the youth away. He has been quite feckless enough. Where is your Nordic friend?'

'Over there,' Nicholas said. Crackbene was standing, now. Of those who had come out, no one had died but Adorne. With a silent gasp of internal anguish, he remembered Kathi.

The old man said, 'What is this company that frightened them off?' They were very close now. Beyond the wall, most of Applegarth's men had now gone, running and galloping.

Nicholas said, 'I don't know. Friends, I hope. I have to go inside. Can you manage?'

'I'll help him,' said Crackbene. 'Jordan can lend me a hand. Was that Adorne?'

'Yes,' said Nicholas. 'They thought we had cheated them. They probably meant to kill us both anyway.'

'It's the end of Albany,' Crackbene said. 'Whether he knew about it or not; that's the end of him.'

*

In the cellar, the change in sound was odd enough to cause Kathi to put out the candle and attempt, by opening one shutter, to see beyond the bars into the precinct. The air outside was raw, and she shivered. Rankin, lucky Rankin, had fallen asleep.

She had been prepared for the reduction in shouting, once the surrender had been accepted. She had been prepared for the ironic cheer, which must have accompanied the appearance of her uncle and Nicholas. She expected a pause, while they were mounted and taken away, and then a period during which the troop collected its weapons and dead and prepared to depart in an orderly manner. Instead, there seemed no order at all, but a hubbub, as if some disaster had happened. There would have been no such reaction had her uncle and Nicholas been killed, which was the other pattern of sounds she had been waiting for. There would have been, her imagination told her, an abashed silence followed by jeering. That hadn't happened. Then, very soon, she heard the reason for the dismay, which was the sound of a large troop approaching.

That was when she opened the shutter and saw men running, and realised that the intruders were going. Then someone screamed, and she knew the voice: Jordan's. A pause; and then from several voices she picked out others. Crackbene. And Nicholas. Nicholas was there. The attackers were leaving, and Nicholas was still there, and perhaps even her uncle. They had been allowed to stay, or had escaped in the panic.

Margaret said, 'What is it? Is Great-uncle there? That's the shutter that squeaks. Rankin will waken.'

'I don't care,' said Kathi defiantly. 'I think it's good news. I think everybody should waken.'

Nicholas was alive. He was outside. When he came inside, she knew the first thing he would do. He would look for and destroy the letter he had left for the Prioress.

Kathi said, 'Margaret?'

'No,' said her eldest child. 'Whatever it is.'

'It isn't much,' Kathi said. 'I've got to go out for five minutes. I'll be back. Lock the door from the inside, and I'll close the shutters. It's for Uncle Nicholas.'

'He isn't Uncle Nicholas,' Margaret said patiently. 'Or Jordan would be our cousin.'

'All right. I agree. Lock the door.'

'I heard you,' said Margaret. Kathi left.

*

In the cellar, Margaret was bored. She laboured at whistling a tune. When that failed, she opened the squeaky shutter, and Rankin woke. He was entranced to see out of the window, and watch the men running about. There were very few now. He said, 'I want to fight.'

'You will, when you're a big boy.'

'I'm big enough now. That bar is broken. Look. I could get through.'

Margaret inspected it. 'You couldn't. Anyway, we're not to go outside. It's dangerous.'

'I can fight. I can punch,' Rankin said. 'I could go and help Uncle Nicholas.'

'He isn't Uncle Nicholas,' Margaret said.

'He's my best friend,' Rankin said. 'I could get through that hole.'

The trouble was that he did; and so she had to go after him. It took longer, because she was bigger, and he had already run off laughing. Rankin was always escaping and laughing. She caught up with him just as the big horse came round the corner, and someone bent down and hit at them both. Rankin did no punching at all, although she screamed at him, and then stopped.

Chapter 52

Sic is the douchter as the moder beyne.

WITHIN THE PRIORY, it was not at first clear what was happening; except that a miracle had occurred, and a force was approaching which would put their assailants to flight. They could see, from their windows, the panic among the soldiers outside, and the running men, and the ominous mounds of the dead in the flickering dimness, where torches were dying and fires were guttering within dark, drying pools in the snow. They knew that their two poor Sisters had not survived. Also, someone had seen Lord Cortachy fall. Dame Euphemia feared the worst, although she did not say so, especially as the demoiselle Katelijne had not yet been told. She relied on M. de Fleury to break the news gently. Moving from place to place, comforting her charges, she dwelled, troubled, on the thought of her god-daughter, Efemie.

Hurrying over the garth, on her way to Dame Euphemia's room, the demoiselle Katelijne's chief concern, at the time, was to avoid M. de Fleury. It seemed likely, from the noise outside, that he was still in the grounds, dealing with stragglers and welcoming the incoming party. She was still agitated enough to squeak when someone slammed into her in the dark, hurrying in the opposite direction. It was only one of the company archers from Edinburgh who had held the ramparts so nobly all day. He said, 'Mistress! Have you heard? It's our own people, Master John and Master Tobie and everyone, come to relieve us!' Then he stopped and said, 'Is Monseigneur all right?'

'Monseigneur?' she said. She had started to rush on, but halted.

'Monseigneur de St Pol of Kilmirren. He stopped an arrow. They've taken him to the infirmary.' In the uncertain dark, she thought his face changed again. He said, 'We're all desperate sorry about your uncle.'

Then she came back. 'I haven't heard. I'm sorry. Will you tell me?'

He didn't do it very well, in his distress, and she had to hold herself in check until he finished. Then she thanked him and started away, and turned back. 'We've been in the cellars. I've left my children. Would someone bring them out when it's safe?' He looked puzzled, agreeing. He probably thought it strange that she didn't turn to look for her uncle. Her principal feeling was the same as before, only intensified. If this was the end of something good, then it should also mark the end of an evil. She would not think, yet, beyond that.

The Prioress's room was empty, but for Julius. It was not surprising: those appointed by God had work before them this day. On Dame Euphemia's desk there was no sign of a letter. It had several drawers. Julius rose. He had been sitting heavily on one of the coffers. He said slowly, 'Kathi? Have you heard? I'm most desperately sorry.' He looked worn, and dirty, and cold, as they all did. For her, the ordeal had been going on since this morning, when her uncle and Nicholas arrived. The last five hours, since Julius and Kilmirren escaped the Home ambush, since Jardine of Applegarth had arrived, had been as bad as the last days in Bruges, when her uncle faced possible death.

Now he had died, in Scotland, for someone else's quarrel, and someone else's King.

Dismiss it. Don't dwell on it now. Now she, too, was walking in danger, but she was also surrounded by friends. It was only heartbreaking that the dearest of those was someone she must defeat.

She said to Julius, 'I wanted somewhere to come and be quiet. I'm sorry. Would I disturb you?'

He came and took her hand, and made her sit down in the Prioress's chair. Even smeared with dirt and full of compassion, the sculptured face kept in its bones all the traits that had persisted since he and Nicholas had been boy and young man together: the charm of the student, the Venetian merchant, the artist in flamboyant escapades. He had thrown off his sling during the siege. He said, 'Dame Euphemia asked me to meet her here, I don't know why. Look. Let me get you some wine. She must have a flask.' His voice was troubled.

Kathi said, 'I've seen it, I think. Over there.'

It took him a while to locate it, since it was not where she pointed.

It kept his back to her for long enough for her to open a drawer, and immediately find what she sought. It was intact. The outer wrapper, without ties, was addressed to Dame Euphemia in Nicholas's clear, fluent hand. The inner letter, bearing Mick Crackbene's name, bore a rough seal. Writing fast, Nicholas had placed it there, out of sight, where the Prioress would find it after he and her uncle had gone. In a moment, when he was able, he would come back to remove it.

She broke the seal with one hand, still within the half-open drawer, and skimmed the few lines on the page. They were plain, and jotted down without drama, like a singer's working notes between staves. The unheard song was one she was glad to be spared. Here was the name of the man against whom, year after year, Nicholas had safeguarded his family. The man whom he, in his turn, had protected, for he was of his own blood. Elizabeth de St Pol's bastard son, who had indeed prospered, and acquired a new name. The name of the man in the room with her now. The name of Julius.

He was turning back with the wine. Before he brought it to her, the drawer was closed. Her hand shook, taking the cup, and she set it down. She said, entirely truthfully, 'I think I may be going to be sick. I think I had better go.'

His face expressed genuine anxiety. She must look as ill as she felt. He said, 'Of course. I'll find someone to take you. You should be with the nuns.'

She stared at him, her mind blank, her eyes sightless. His voice boomed. She was used to the phenomenon: it had happened often before she was married, when she attempted too much and exhausted her strength. Or so Dr Tobie would have it.

Dr Tobie. Tobie had been full of theories about the invisible traitor. So had Moriz and John. So, latterly, had her uncle, when he had determined, at last, to compel Nicholas to admit what he knew. None of them had made the proper deduction. None of them knew enough about Elizabeth's son.

The papers about Elizabeth's son and her lover, Andrew Liddell, were somewhere in this room. That was why Julius was here. He wasn't waiting for the Prioress: he had been searching. He was Andrew Liddell's missing bastard, now legitimised; and the time was coming when he wanted to prove it. He had asked Bishop Prosper to bring him some scrolls from Bologna. He had been interested in records from Paris. He had befriended James Liddell from the beginning. He had chosen Albany's side. He had been the man behind Jardine of Applegarth, and the secret messages to the King. He had caused the death of her uncle; and of Simon and Henry de St Pol; and nearly of Nicholas. Oh, many times, nearly the death of Nicholas.

He was holding her. Her mind was quite clear, but something seemed to have happened to her limbs. His clasp, although one-sided, was quite comforting. He must have been an attractive husband to Adelina, even though she only married him to use against Nicholas.

But he must have known that. That must have been why he married her. That was why Tasse had to die, because she would have recognised who Adelina was. All those other shame-faced suggestions they had tossed about in the Floory Land in Julius's absence – that he had traced her by using Adorne's name at Montello; that he had lain in wait for her at Cologne, not the other way round – must be true. Moriz had thought so, based on something Bonne had said, which Gelis had substantiated. But all the embarrassed speculations about Julius had always petered out in rejection and ridicule, for he was the lifelong friend of Nicholas, and had saved Nicholas's life, over and over.

And so he had, when Nicholas was young, and full of well-concealed, brilliant promise, and on the threshold of building the golden kingdom which Julius, and Julius alone, would step in and inherit.

And Nicholas, all the time, had known, and had said nothing. And Julius had no idea that he knew.

Julius said, 'How do you feel? The wine will help, really.' There was a thread of impatience in his voice. If the papers were here, this might be his last chance to find them.

The wine, thought Kathi, had better help. She had to scotch all this, quickly. She emptied the cup, banged it down and got up, wavering slightly. She said, 'I should like to go now.'

'Then let me take you,' said Nicholas from the doorway. He hardly looked at Julius. He was wearing hose, and someone's doublet over a torn shirt. He had a sword. He said, 'I'm sorry. I hear someone told you about Anselm. You don't want to be here, on your own.'

'She was just going,' Julius said.

Plain Sersanders obstinacy, as sometimes it did, conquered the fear and faintness and horror. Kathi picked up her cup, walked to the flask, which was beside Nicholas, and poured and drank off more wine. Then she said, 'I've changed my mind. I'll wait till the Prioress comes.' Then she sat down, still beside Nicholas.

Nicholas said, 'She isn't coming.' His eyes were on the desk. There was nothing to see. Julius was still standing beside it.

Kathi regarded Julius. 'You said the Prioress was coming.'

'She must have been held up,' Julius said. He looked at Nicholas. 'She hasn't been well. She ought to be with the nuns.'

'I didn't know she hadn't been well,' Kathi said. 'I think she's wonderful for her age. Mick Crackbene thinks the same. Did I tell you about all the papers they found, from Eccles and Coldingham?'

'Come on, you're drunk,' Nicholas said. After the first second, it was just like his usual voice. She wasn't drunk, and he knew it.

Julius said, 'Wait a moment. Tell me more. Juicy scandal?' He wasn't nearly such a good actor.

'You'd need to ask Mick or the Prioress. I don't remember the details. It was all in the papers. Julius? Is my kerchief over there?'

'Where are the papers?' Julius said. 'Your kerchief? No.'

'I left it somewhere,' Kathi said. 'Try the top drawer.'

She looked up as she said it. Nicholas was standing quite still. Then he looked down and met her eyes.

Julius said, 'The drawer's empty. Look, take mine. So where are these papers?'

Beside her, Nicholas let out a long, slow breath. Kathi said, 'No, it's all right: My kerchief's here after all. The papers? Goodness, they burned them. Far too juicy, as you said.'

'*Burned* them?' Julius said. 'Burned a conventual record of births? They'll excommunicate the lady.' He had begun by smiling, and then had ceased to smile, although his voice was still rallying.

'Is that what they were?' Kathi said. 'You'd better report it to the Cistercians, or Bishop Prosper. Although he isn't very reliable either. He wanted to bring you your Bologna papers, but someone else had got rid of those, too. It's mysterious, isn't it? It's like Nicholas, really. Without records, people just don't exist. And if they don't exist, they can't claim anything.'

'What is she talking about?' Julius said.

Nicholas lowered the back of his hand to her neck, and let it rest there, half curled, as if in gentle admonishment. His eyes had changed to the look that was hers, mixed with other things. Understanding. Compassion. He said, 'She *is* rather drunk. What do you think she is saying?'

'I don't know. I think we'd better all go,' Julius said.

Nicholas didn't move. He had given her the initiative. It was the greatest gift he had ever given her. Kathi said, 'I was talking about identity. And the habit of killing. All those hunting mishaps in Poland. The dove in the church – do you remember? Ludovico da Bologna had his doubts about that. Do you think he removed the papers at Bologna? Or was it even Bessarion?'

Although an educated man, Julius had never been excessively quick. He was just coming to realise what she was telling him. He had not yet fully grasped what he was being told about Nicholas. He said, 'Poland! I'll tell you what I remember about Poland. I recall lying between life and death because that fool tried to kill me.' He flung himself down in Dame Euphemia's chair with an angry half-laugh. 'What *is* all this?'

Nicholas said suddenly, 'That was true. I did try to kill you. Most of the time, though, it wasn't worth while. Avoiding you was a game. I didn't mind, or not much. But sometimes, you and Adelina together were insufferable. Did you tell her, before you killed her, that you always knew who she was? Just as I'm telling you now?'

He had come into the open. *Avoiding you was a game.* He would know that Julius would never stand for that. At last, at last, Nicholas was compelling Julius to confront him. And before someone else. Before her, a witness.

It was no time to be morbidly thankful. It was time to attack, even with guesses. Kathi said, 'And the fight in the High Street, the other day, Nicholas. You knew Julius had tried to kill Simon before, and that he had hounded his sister to death. But you didn't denounce him before, and you didn't then, even though you had just carried Simon and Henry to Kelso. You had just come from Kelso, and yet you didn't call him to account! Why? What excuse could you possibly have?'

She waited. When he answered her, he didn't look at her at all, and the answer wasn't for her. 'I had made a promise,' Nicholas said. 'To someone who was trying to spare me, she thought, from a lifetime of conflict. I was also arrogant enough to think that I could lead him away from it. But he couldn't leave it alone: it was too exciting. Wasn't that the way of it, Julius?'

'What are you saying?' said Julius.

Nicholas said, 'What Kathi knows. What everyone will now get to know. That you and I are second cousins. That you have been trying to extinguish my family, and I have done nothing about it. Until now.'

Julius frowned. He had flushed with surprise and resentment. He said with open belligerence, 'No one will get to know unless you two leave the room.'

Kathi said, 'Open the second drawer. That's the outer cover of a note Nicholas left when he walked out to surrender to Purves. The letter names you. I found it, and I've given it to everybody.' She fixed him with a cold, hazel eye. She had had no chance to give it to anyone.

It was stuck in the cuff of her sleeve. She prayed that he couldn't see it.

Julius's face never changed very much. He stood, looking angry and peevish, and then said, 'You just said: it was a game. So we stop. You keep your promise. I'll go away.'

Rigid, she waited. The hand at her neck turned, and smoothed her shoulder, and dropped. Then Nicholas said, 'No. Kathi will leave, and you and I will conclude this between us.'

'She'll bring help,' Julius said. But his eyes gleamed.

Nicholas turned. 'Will you?' he said.

'No,' said Kathi. 'If something is worth buying, it is worth the fullest extent of its price.' Then she said, 'But his arm?'

'If he can lay hands on a bow, he can manage a sword,' Nicholas said. He looked at her, and she left, to go to her children.

Outside, in the rest of St Mary's, an army of four hundred picked men were brought in from the cold and settled under the roofs of the huddled buildings and halls of the Priory. They came from Edinburgh and its surroundings, and represented all the great families loyal to the King, and owing friendship to Anselm Adorne and his companion who, together with a Genoese bishop, had offered their lives on the King's business, and whom (they had heard) a renegade troop proposed to attack. They arrived in time to catch the brutes on the run, and pursued and cut down more than a few, before their leaders called the hunt off. Then, turning back to the Priory, the men from Edinburgh had learned for the first time of the death of Cortachy, and how it had been done. At that, their wrath had been so great that Huntly had had to use threats and brute force to prevent them from issuing all over again to chase and kill the whole band. Cold anger was better than hot, and would help make the most of this weapon that Albany's rash friends had provided. Time enough for retribution after that.

Meanwhile, silent and sobered, the Sinclairs and Prestons, the Arbuthnotts and Gordons and Ogilvies, the sea captains and merchants and the burgesses found themselves quarters for what was left of the night, and the seven men from the Floory Land went to seek Nicholas, and found Jordan and Crackbene. Soon, they were installed in the single big day-room with pallets. Nicholas, it seemed, had gone to do something, and Julius and Kathi had disappeared.

Tobie said, 'They'll be in the chapel.' They had been carrying the dead there, with Camulio's help. Huntly had given his own cloak to cover Adorne, and Andreas, from the moment he came, had not left him. Tobie hadn't yet been to the chapel, or brought himself to visit Fat Father Jordan in the infirmary, although Wodman had gone. Tobie, like the rest of them, wanted to see Nicholas, and was worried about Kathi. Then he thought to ask where the children were.

Kathi had placed them in one of the cellars, but they weren't there now. Presumably, they would all be together, Kathi and Margaret and Rankin, possibly in the kitchen, or the dormitory, or somewhere else warm. A small party set off and split up to find them – Kathi's brother Sersanders, and the children's grandfather Archie of Berecrofts, and Father Moriz and Tobie and Jordan. It was bright inside the buildings and cloisters, where the lamps had all been renewed, but dark outside the garth. It was a little while before Father Moriz called something, and the searchers all went to look.

He was outside, upon that stretch of ground between the Priory and the walls, where the row of barred cellar windows threw their scalloped light on the snow. One of the bars of one of the windows was missing, leaving a very small gap, but one large enough for a child. And outside, and not far away, were two children lying together, one protecting the other, in a turmoil of hoof-marks. The boy, lying below, was unconscious. The girl, her arms stretched around him, was dead.

Leaving Nicholas, Kathi ran. She had been away for half an hour instead of a few minutes. Outside, she could hear voices and horsemen: it was hard to tell what was happening. She wondered at first whether to go to the cellars, but decided that the archer would have brought out the children by now. Margaret and Rankin had lived here for more than two weeks; they knew all the nuns and, with Tobie about, they would be in the best possible hands. She would find them. And then she would go to her uncle. She wondered if her brother and Andreas were here, and recoiled from imagining what they must be feeling. As she felt. As she would feel, doubled and redoubled, if something happened to Nicholas.

She came across Jordan, Nicholas's son, sitting on the ground in the garth, weeping openly. She glanced about, saw no one else, and dropped beside him. 'Jordan?' It couldn't be about Adorne, although Jordan had admired him, she knew. He couldn't know what his father was doing. She couldn't leave him like this, when word of any kind might emerge from that room. She imagined she could hear the swords biting and clashing from here. She said, 'Jordan, what is it?'

He jerked his head up. She caught the glare of two distended grey eyes; then he cried out in a voice of appalling, of unrecognisable stridency. 'Your son killed her! Your stupid son ran away, and she went too, and it *killed her*!'

Tobie's voice said, 'Jordan, go and stay with Mick Crackbene. Kathi, come with me.'

She resisted. She said, 'Who was he talking about?'

But she knew. And everything else left her mind.

Behind her, Nicholas had locked the door of Dame Euphemia's room and drawn his sword. Julius, still behind the desk, had laid his sword on its surface and was looking at him. Unlike Nicholas, who had thrown off his borrowed garment, Julius still looked dapper, even though his well-cut doublet was stained and slashed, and his hose were unembroidered and smelling of horse. He said, 'This is silly.' He was smiling.

'No,' said Nicholas. 'Pick up your sword.'

Julius said, 'You didn't even know how to fight when we first met. Or to ride. It didn't stop us from enjoying life.'

'No,' said Nicholas. 'Pick up your sword.'

Julius said, 'So what put this idea into your head about Andrew Liddell? You didn't have it in Bruges.'

'I had it in Fleury, aged seven,' Nicholas said. 'My mother knew. I knew when you dropped into Geneva, after you finished in Paris. Then you went to Bologna – did it never strike you that people like Bessarion and Fra Ludovico sometimes read records? Next, you came back to Geneva, and followed me eventually to Bruges. I asked Tobie to lock up his poisons in case you used them on Jaak and blamed me – but instead, you simply waited for me to ruin Jaak for you. Proof that you were a Liddell as well as a St Pol? Crackbene saw your early papers in Coldingham, or Ada did. And there was proof, wasn't there, in the Liddell grazing ground at Dunbar, which mysteriously belonged to the St Pols?'

'Ada!' Julius said with derision.

'She's quite a good witness. But there are others; either already in place, or soon found. Lucia's death? Jock Ross can tell about the hound you borrowed, and that you didn't come back to Blackness when you said you did. Adorne nearly killed Simon, he told me, by being given the wrong lance. There was an arrow at Venice which wasn't from some outraged Muslim source: Umar traced that, and told me. And even today – Alex Home told Kilmirren that Applegarth had betrayed my visit to York, and you know Applegarth well. He wasn't surprised when you entered this room. You killed him so that he wouldn't compromise you, in case you had to come back.'

It was odd, watching the expressions crossing Julius's face:

impatience; defensiveness; hurt disbelief; peevish annoyance. At the end, annoyance mostly prevailed, although he persisted – out of habit, you would say. 'That's in your imagination, but even if it wasn't, didn't we have good times together? And why are we fighting if we're kin? Am I not Simon's full cousin? Come on. This is nonsense.'

Nicholas said, 'I could only be related if I were Simon's son.'

'Well, of course you are,' Julius said. 'Only there's no proof. I've searched, but there isn't. Not, of course, that you mind. What hurt and mystified you was the rejection. Why should anyone hate you so much that they hounded everyone near to you? Don't you know?'

'It doesn't matter,' said Nicholas. He didn't want to hear. Especially, whatever he guessed, he didn't want to hear it from Julius.

Julius looked him up and down. 'Well, surely. Wodman could tell you what all the old Archers knew. Simon got your mother pregnant, and since she was wealthy and titled, your grandfather forced him to marry her. When the child was born dead, Simon was delighted. But meanwhile his father had found out about the peculiarities of Jaak de Fleury, and he was told that old Thibault was the same. When you were born, it gave him a perfect excuse for claiming adultery, and repudiating both the marriage and you. He thought you were tainted.' He paused. 'You thought that was just an excuse? It wasn't. He loathed you. You must feel the same about him. So do I. I'm your family, Nicholas. Now we can say so. Now we can kill the old man together.'

There were voices everywhere outside, now. The window flashed with gold from newly lit lanterns. Voices echoed through the rest of the building: only the Prioress's wing, where they both were, was quiet. He had been told only what he had already guessed. This was the man who had brought about the deaths of Simon, and Lucia, and Henry, and who had tried to get Adelina to kill him in Moscow. This was the man whom Kathi had valiantly brought him to confront.

'No,' said Nicholas. 'Pick up your sword.'

He should have remembered that Julius was adept with a knife. It came flying, just before the thrower vaulted forward, sword in hand, and followed up with a swing of the blade. Nicholas ducked. The knife struck the panel behind him and, before he could grasp it, shot skittishly behind a great cupboard. Staring after it, Nicholas barely saved Julius's blade on his own, and hurriedly twisted away, moving nimbly sideways and backwards, among all the furnishings whose places he had memorised: the stools, the coffers, the towel-stand, the lectern, the haphazard piles of books. A globe. A crucifix fell, shattering the flask of wine, and Julius laughed. It had begun.

It had begun like the Floory Land battle with Simon, except that this was a much smaller room, and Nicholas had no dear acolyte, now, to push trestles into the other man's way. Then, Julius had been unaccountably unable to help him. Then, he himself had exulted in the childish joy of the fight. Now, if he did not weep, it was only because he was too old to weep.

It didn't matter. It had to be done. Nicholas lifted his sword.

He wanted steel between them: that was his mistake from the beginning, given the size of the room. Julius had a one-handed sword but Nicholas's was of the kind that fitted his height and his build: its blade three feet long, its grip suited to his large hands, the right close to the quillons, the left settled next to the pommel. With that kind of weapon, you fought with your arms fully extended, the point facing forwards. A downwards cut from a sword of that weight could slice through cheek, neck and shoulder. A horizontal sweep, one hand pushing, one pulling, could cut a man nearly in half. Since he meant to kill Julius, that was how he intended to do it. It was simpler in that neither of them wore armour. Julius had an open doublet over his shirt, and below that, only hose and light boots. Nicholas was dressed in two garments only: his hose and the shreds of his shirt. His feet were unshod, which was why Julius had laughed when the glass smashed.

He knew, of course, that Julius was shorter, and lighter, and had a more flexible sword. He also had the wit to use the terrain: to make a rampart of a desk; an impediment of every light piece of furniture. He took particular care, where he could, to limit the space where a great sword could be swung. Julius could not afford to be struck, even once. He began, quite effectively, to secure himself.

'Poor Goliath!' he said. His blade darted and flickered. 'Do I see regret on your face? Do you wish you had told the girl to bring help? You could call, but I fear no one would hear you.'

He had his back to the window. Nicholas said, 'Take a good look. It's too high to jump, and there are too many people.'

'My dear boy!' said Julius. He moved, and his blade came from the right and the left. Nicholas parried the first, and flung himself out of the way of the other. Before he could lift his sword, his way was blocked by a prie-dieu. And as he thrust that aside, there was a sudden, unbelievable blow on his steel that almost wrenched it out of his hand. With his free arm, his injured arm, Julius had hurled something – a heavy box – at it. And now, his arm soaked in blood, he was leaping at Nicholas.

There was no time to bring the heavy sword up. He left it and rolled, gritting his teeth. Julius's blade cut down to where he had been and then dragged itself out of the wood as Julius, gasping, kicked the great sword out of reach.

'As I was saying,' said Julius. 'Who has need of a window? All I have to do is kill you, unlock the door, and escape.' He brought his sword down again, hard, as he spoke, and it screamed across the surface of the Prioress's best silver tray, snatched up a second before to deflect it. Then, because there was no alternative, Nicholas did what his young son had once done. What Gelis had done for him, twice. He slammed the great candelabrum to the floor and then, before Julius could move in the darkness, swung the full weight of it against the other man's injured arm, and then against the opposite wrist. Its fingers opened, and Nicholas dragged the sword from them.

'Escape where?' Nicholas said. Julius had moved, crying out. Nicholas turned. The dim rectangle of the window revealed itself to his widening eyes. He could see nothing yet inside the room. Holding Julius's sword in the darkness, he was as handicapped as he had been with his own. Then he heard the other man's irregular, painful breathing.

The blow had hurt. Julius, swordless, was twisting his way to the door. He hadn't answered; but Nicholas knew what he was doing. Once outside in the glimmering chaos, he could make his way to the shore and a boat. There were countries other than Scotland.

Nicholas said, 'The key isn't there.'

He heard Julius rattle and slam at the door, and curse; and then begin to make his way purposefully back, avoiding the flecks of light from the window. His footsteps stopped on the way, and then resumed. He was quite close when half the timber ceiling was lit by a sudden new glare from outside, and Nicholas saw his handsome, stark face, and his hand, sweeping up the deep box of sand from the escritoire. Then the grit struck Nicholas in the eyes, and he was blind, as men are in the desert, when the sand-demons come.

He cast down his sword, and Julius flung himself upon him.

Now, against all his instincts, there was no steel between himself and Julius, and no space. It was as it had been in the salt-pans long ago, fighting with Simon. It repeated, flesh to flesh, the moment when the blood tie had spoken. And added to that, in this place, was the worth of twenty-five years of silent, unending guardianship. Nicholas had recoiled from his father. Now he did so from Julius; and Julius struck his neck with the edge of one hand, and then used the heel of his hand on his chin. His injured arm held in reserve, he was setting himself quite industriously to kill. To redeem, in his view, twenty-five years of tedious injustice.

The sheer, blinkered conceit of it suddenly cut through all that had seemed complex, and roused Nicholas from his stupor. He conceded that it might well be too late: that Julius had an advantage that could not be overturned. He thought it worth trying. He took a second to scrub an arm across his closed, streaming eyes. Then he set to respond to the attack: to evade the chopping, gouging, strangling hand and the the agile, oppressive body. He reached some conclusions. In the glow from the window, some of the furniture would be visible to Julius. Nicholas was blind. Sightless, his head ringing, his bruised muscles protesting, he was fighting not only a man but a room: crashing from one punishing obstacle to the next as he struggled to rise, to evade the strong fingers and the dragging lock on his limbs. Julius might be bleeding, but he could see, and his brain was clear, and he had, by his position, prevented his adversary from using, so far, his advantage of weight.

So that had to be dealt with. Nicholas couldn't see, but he could devise a strategy against the holds he could feel and, gathering himself, did so. The surge that brought his shoulders from the ground thrust Julius backwards; the next effort twisted the lock on his lower limbs until the untoward pressure actually threatened to snap Julius's own leg. For a moment, it almost seemed that Julius, wild with indignation and anger, was about to hold on through the pain and let it break; but he fell back at the last moment, gasping, and Nicholas pulled free.

And bumped his head against something.

And, rising half stunned from that, met Julius's flying body again, and crashed with him to the floor, rolling over and over in what space there was.

Then it became very dirty and difficult.

They both knew the tricks of the trade. They knew each other. From rough sport, from contests, from war, Nicholas was familiar with every inch of Julius's body; as Julius knew his. Only he had the advantage of knowing how Julius's mind worked. Unable to detect incoming blows, twice Nicholas invited them, moving his guard so that Julius made for his face or his neck, offering a chance to grip his hand or his wrist. After that, Julius was wary. In turn, Julius protected his arm, and made the most of his spread hand and his elbow, his knees and his booted feet. The two men travelled all the time: sometimes on the floor, sometimes half risen, sometimes upright; hand to hand; shoulder to shoulder. Once Nicholas, tumbling, found a towel under his hand and clawed it briefly into his eyes. After that, he kept his lids screwed as before, but he had some sight on one side. He could see the window, and objects between it and him. He wrestled back towards the door, enlarging his view, and profiting from it a little, as if by accident. It brought him close to the glass on the floor, but at least he could see well enough to rock with the long, grazing kick that was meant to end with a stamping jump on his toes, which would have brought him to his knees.

Listening, it seemed to him that Julius was tiring, and knew it. He had lost blood. Even with Nicholas dead, he still had to find the key: he had had chance enough to confirm that Nicholas had it nowhere about him. It would take him a while: it lay out of sight on a very high ledge. Now, Nicholas could almost feel the resolve with which Julius gathered himself, and came at him.

The window had brightened. Without that, Nicholas would never have seen the gleam on the floor that was his dropped sword. Julius noticed it at the same time. On his face there flashed the look that all his friends knew: a distillation of greed, and satisfaction, and boyish pleasure. A wish, even, to share the success. You felt, even now, that he longed to tell someone, and laugh. He stooped.

Nicholas lifted his powerful arms, his hands united as if in intercession, his gaze on the nape of the other man's neck. His shoulders widened. With all the force of his body, Nicholas de Fleury slammed his palms down on the other's bent head, driving his face as with a mallet towards the knee set like a coining-iron to receive it. Then, as Julius staggered, bloody and crouching, Nicholas pulled his head back, and struck him down to the floor. He used the edge of his hand on his throat, as had been done also to him. But he was stronger than Julius.

In extremity, Simon had still kept his looks. Julius, his face ruined, had not. That it so happened had not been intentional. It was a fact, if it mattered, that Julius would not have cared to live with a face that was less than agreeable.

Nicholas, standing above him, strained his sight and was able to distinguish that Julius was not quite unconscious, but lay frowning up at him, breathing irregularly. Even then, behind the pain, there was no real awareness in his look: just disappointment and anger.

Nicholas lifted his sword, and finished what he had done, with one clean, competent stroke.

He had taken the life of a cousin of Simon's. It was like killing Simon. There was no difference at all.

That was when he remembered Tasse, who had served Esota de Fleury and Thibault his grandfather, and who had nursed Marian his wife when she died. And he thought that perhaps he was wrong; and there was a difference.

*

Because the nuns worked carefully, it was some time before the chapel was fit for its mourners, and the Mass was ready to start. They had placed Anselm Adorne nearest the altar, and his great-niece not far away. Eight and fifty-eight years old, the faces bore no particular family resemblance, except that lent by death, and the chill of the snow. Margaret's features, with the loss of colour and life, appeared still and flat. Of Adorne's, nothing was visible but the firm chin and sensitive lips, the straight nose and the tips of his lashes. The rest was swathed, to conceal what had spilled on the ground.

Halfway through the Mass, the slow, brooding voice of the choir found a new luminosity. Kathi, her face in her hands, filled her palms with tears, in thanks for something she did not deserve. She passed Nicholas, as she left at the end, and looked to see if he was hurt, but he did not seem to be. He was wearing a cloak. Outside, he caught up with her, and she stood still. Around her, others hesitated, and then left them alone. The snow had started again. She felt like part of the snow, looking up at his face in the darkness. She saw then that his face was marked, and his eyes veined with blood, as if recently recovered from injury. He said nothing. Then she saw that she must make him speak. She said, 'Is Julius dead?'

And he found some sort of voice and said, 'Yes. I killed him.'

She tilted her head. When she spoke, it was as a juror, delivering a verdict. She said, 'We both made mistakes. I should have left the children secure, or not left them at all. You should have stopped playing God with Julius and Adelina long ago; but, Heaven knows, you were thinking of them, and not yourself. And what led to my uncle's death was pure, selfless courage on his part and yours. It has probably saved the kingdom.'

'It has been a triumph,' he said.

Then she said, 'We agreed. Everything has a price. Sometimes you cannot be sure if you have paid enough, or too much. But I think this could be a triumph, if you allow it to be.'

He said, 'With these two dead?'

And she said, 'Nicholas. You gave me Robin, and he gave me Hob. Put that in your ledger.'

'I can't,' he said, and walked away. He had not said anything else about Julius. That, too, should be put in the ledger. But tonight, for God and profit, the blood and the ink were too fresh.

Chapter 53

Conzeour, wislar, resaver to the king,
And all thir folk suld kepe thaim our all thing
Fro awaris, danger, and of det,
And thar promys kepe withoutin let.

IN THE CANONGATE, evening passed into night. At midnight, several hours after Tobie and the others had left, Mistress Clémence excused herself and went off to bed. Bel and Gelis remained in the hall chamber, sometimes silent, sometimes talking to Robin, who rested in his wheeled chair at the side of the fire, which blazed and spat with the snow. At two hours after midnight, the rider came with the first of the news. The Priory had been attacked. The great force from Edinburgh had been too late to save my lord of Cortachy, and – forgive him – Master Robin's young daughter. Today's meeting at Whitekirk had been quashed, and all but my lord's family would be returning, soon after first light. And he was to say that Master Julius had died. Of that, he didn't know more, and left quickly.

There was no comfort in the bare facts. Even to think of the survivors was painful, when you could not thank God aloud, before Robin. The news of Julius had brought a gasp of dismay, and then uneasy silence. Perhaps he had ended his life as nobly as Anselm Adorne. Perhaps not. No one speculated. In time, Clémence, who had been summoned to hear, sent Bel and Gelis to bed, and stayed with Robin herself. Finally, as he fell into weary slumber, she allowed herself to nod in her chair until the household awoke, and she and the others prepared for those who were coming.

Gelis had known that Nicholas would not be among the first to arrive: that he would be obliged to report to Avandale and Whitelaw and Argyll; and to the Abbot at Holyrood, under whose jurisdiction Whitekirk lay.

She also guessed, as it turned out correctly, that he would keep Jordan with him. Nicholas, in time of misery, was the best companion any young person could have. And it would spare Robin, for a while, the worse misery of pretending to welcome someone else's live, healthy child. It was, blessedly, Robin's father who came back first, with John and Tobie and Father Moriz, and from them they heard the whole story of the attack. Later, Father Moriz told them how and why Julius had died.

Bel gazed at him throughout. When he ended, she spoke into the silence. 'And Nicol killed him. In a sad, sad day, there is a tragedy, I can tell you, to match the worst of it.'

'A *tragedy*!' Tobie cried. His worn face was flushed. 'You talk of Anselm Adorne in the same breath as Julius? A man who lied to us all; who took all we gave him and used it to deceive and betray us; who killed, or got others to kill for him, again and again? Who pretended to be Nicholas's friend while he was planning to get rid of him and his family, and all but succeeded in having him labelled a killer and traitor himself? Who tricked him into fighting – into losing his own . . .'

'Tobie,' said Gelis. He stopped.

Father Moriz stirred. He said, 'You are right. So is Mistress Bel. Julius was all of that. Mistress Bel began to guess it before most of us. But what you have to remember is that Nicholas knew it. He always knew. And he chose to keep quiet, as he chose to give Adelina a chance. They were his family. He thought them redeemable. So the killing yesterday was terrible, as Mistress Bel says. It was an admission, for him, that he had been wrong. And that, in turn, meant that he had let us all down.'

'He had,' said John le Grant. 'He let the country down. Julius was a traitor.'

Gelis said, 'Do you think, any of you, that Nicholas didn't think of all that? He took a decision. He protected us, his family, by keeping us separate from Julius, whatever it forced him to do; wherever it forced him to go. And in everything else, including this country, Nicholas gave himself as a shield against Julius, as he did at North Berwick. If Julius was an example of petty selfishness, don't you have something there to set against it? Something that might not have been there but for Julius?'

She was shivering, the cool golden Gelis. Clémence, seated beside her, took her hand.

Moriz said, 'I think you have it. This is not Good against Evil: a piece from the Holy Book done in verse on a wagon. It is as you said: the tale of a small spirit that has enabled a greater to grow. But now, what shall that spirit do? He has failed us. He has failed himself. He has reached the top of the mountain, and someone must help him to choose.'

No one spoke. Then John le Grant said, 'Then we show him he hasn't failed us. I was wrong. You were right. Julius has gone. We don't speak of him; we don't care what he did. What we care about is what Nicholas is going to do, and if he will want us to join him.'

'Do you want to join him?' Gelis said. Her eyes were wet.

'Will he want to have us?' said Tobie. Then his face changed. He said, 'Why are we talking of Julius, or even Nicholas, when we have lost what we have lost? Archie; Robin; I'm sorry.'

They talked, after that, of what mattered: eight friends, coming to terms with what Bel had rightly named as a tragedy.

Adorne, in that calm, handwritten will, had asked to be buried in Linlithgow, where the Queen had made him captain and Governor of her Palace, and where his small, deaf daughter was. Kathi and Sersanders and Andreas had stayed with him and with Margaret, and the Bishop would presently help to bring them to St Michael's, the church of Linlithgow.

Gelis had asked how Kathi was.

'Dazed,' said Father Moriz. 'There is a blessed numbness, at times, when terrible events first come to pass. And there are arrangements to make. The child Efemie is to be under the guardianship of Kathi's brother, who is likely to follow as captain of Linlithgow. All the Scottish property will be hers. But Bruges has not been forgotten. His first family are grown, but he has asked his surviving siblings to care for them, and for his heart to be placed by his wife. I do not think Phemie would mind.'

Bel spoke. 'And I hear that Kilmirren survived. I was right, then. He went?'

Tobie said, 'Yes, and he'll live. Wodman is bringing him home. The cantankerous bastard wouldn't stay with the nuns any longer.'

Bel sat up. 'He'll *live*?'

'You didn't know he was injured? An arrow. You heard that Julius tried to shoot young Jordan, the boy, from above? The old man stood in the way of the arrow. I've seen him. He'll do; as well as a man of that bulk will ever do.'

Bel said, 'What did Nicholas say? Did he realise how Kilmirren came to be wounded?' Her voice was composed, but her hands had shut together.

Tobie sneezed. Below his round eyes were circles like blisters, and he had pulled his hat from his sun-spotted cranium. Once Clémence would have sighed. Now she gazed at him through watering eyes. Tobie said, 'I told Nicholas what the old man had done. He didn't say anything. The place was in an uproar. Anyway, he'd just . . . ended the business with Julius. He wasn't in the mood to visit the sick.'

'He refused,' said Father Moriz with Germanic bluntness.

'But St Pol saved Jordan's life?' Gelis said. Then she remembered, and stopped.

No one had saved Margaret's life. Margaret was dead, and she ached for both Kathi and Robin. But the greater grief that she felt was for the other death: the one that would bear hardest on Nicholas, on the day that Julius, also, had died.

The death of Anselm Adorne, the wise, courteous mentor of his boyhood.

The death of his boyhood.

Entering Edinburgh, Jordan de Fleury was allowed to call with his father on the Abbot of Holyrood, but had to wait in the antechamber of the grand houses they visited next. Master Crackbene kept Jordan company, and Master Yare, whom he knew from Leith and Berwick as well as Edinburgh. On the journey, they had talked quite a lot about Berwick. When he was young, sailing there with Master Yare and his father and Henry, Jordan had thought it a splendid place, and envied Master Yare his great house in The Ness, and longed to fish, and to live in the castle.

Now it had gone to the English, but no one appeared too depressed. It seemed that the English were complaining already about the extra taxes to pay for the garrison, and all the casks and baskets of coal expected by loyal merchants in their new homes. And here was Scotland, to hear Master Yare, with its trade and its harbours adjusted, a war averted, and nobody very much worse. Certainly not Master Yare, who was Treasurer of the burgh of Edinburgh. Or Gibbie Fish, or Wattie Bertram, or Will Scheves, or Humphrey Colquhoun, or Lauder of the Bass, the whilk, said Master Yare, ye didna notice renting out their candlesticks, did ye?

'Poor Sandy,' had said Master Yare, jogging along. (He said Pooh.) 'He might have been a nice enough lad, but no gumption, ganging or coming; and awfu' blate [bhate] about asking advice. He should have lent heed to your sleekit da, Jordan.'

'You sound as if you're sorry for Sandy,' said Jordan. He had never called the Duke Sandy before.

'After what happened at the Priory, you mean? Sure enough, it happened because of him, whether he had a hand in it or not. But in the end, he'll be worse off nor us. Mind my words,' had said Master Yare. 'If your own brain pan is wanting – and I'm sure it's not – mak' siccar you buy someone else's.'

They talked to Jordan a lot, both on the journey and after, and told him things about his father he hadn't known. Jordan wasn't likely to forget Margaret, or the rest that had happened, but he felt more normal by the time the morning was over, and Master Crackbene and Master Yare had gone home, and he was alone with his father. He felt hungry.

The house was quiet, by the time Nicholas brought Jordan home. The talk was over, and most of the tired men who had been at North Berwick – Tobie and Moriz and John – had for the moment dispersed. Bel had gone, returned to Kilmirren House to wait for St Pol. Gelis wondered what she would tell Bonne; and how Bonne would receive the news that her stepfather was dead, and that Nicholas had killed him. With indifference, she thought. Then she regretted the thought.

Jordan, coming over to kiss her, had a little air of soldierly brashness that degenerated, for a moment, with his embrace, and then reasserted itself. It seemed mostly genuine. Nicholas looked extraordinarily tired, but spoke and acted as he always did. He had a bruise on his face. He said, 'You've probably heard all the news. Could Jordan go and get himself dinner? I've had all the refreshments, and he's had all the hard work in the antechambers. And we could both do with some sleep.'

It was said for Jordan's sake. She knew that it would be a long time before the day would be over for Nicholas. He would have to go to the King.

Jordan went, and Nicholas sat. They were alone. The fire flickered. Then he put his face in his hands.

His chair was not very near. He had taken the first one he saw. She didn't rise and cross over, or move. She didn't speak for a long time. Then she said, 'What did Avandale say? And the others?' She didn't care what they said. She was only reminding him that soon, someone would come; and that he had to continue to think, and to act, to give the sacrifice meaning.

He said, 'Avandale?' and took his hands down. His eyes, large and deep and heavily lidded, were dry as sand. He said, 'You can perhaps imagine. As a man, he regrets Adorne's murder, of course. But really, nothing more opportune could have happened, and the world is to hear of it at once. How the King offered fraternal friendship to Albany, and his emissary was done to death on his way to the meeting. Or put even better, how his envoy gave up his life to deter Albany's men from committing sacrilege.'

'It is what happened,' she said. 'We feel bitter, I think, because a friend's death can be turned to advantage, and this seems to detract from the tragedy. But what would Anselm have wanted? He had chosen a King. He would surely want to serve him in death as well as life? And it also allows us to praise him. Think what he was.'

'Oh, we have done that,' Nicholas said. 'I can tell you precisely all that he was, and which factions will be asked to respond to his murder with horror. He was the envoy of the little Duchess of Burgundy to Scotland, and had been her father's emissary to Poland. His daughter served the English King's mother; his wife was honoured by the English King's sister. He was a friend of Caxton, a patron of architects, music and art. He and his family were judges and councillors to the Dukes of Burgundy, and related to the Doges of Genoa. He was a merchant trader, and Conservator of the Scots Privileges in Bruges. He was burgomaster of Bruges. He was a champion jouster and a leader in war, but also a man of devout faith. He went on pilgrimage to the Holy Land, and was welcome in Rome. He beautified his family's Jerusalemkerk, and was patron of hospices, almshouses, churches. He was a Knight of the Sword, of Jerusalem, of the Unicorn. He was a man whose death will perform a small service, but whose life would have ennobled a country.'

'Then others must do it,' she said.

There was another silence. Then he said, his voice closer to normal, 'Of course, we must talk, you and I. But not now. Sweetheart, I'd better eat, too. And wash the dirt away. And find some . . .'

'There are clothes ready laid out,' she said, when he hesitated. He and Adorne had been robbed of everything, Tobie had told her. Everything he wore had been borrowed.

He wore a ring on his right hand. She had never seen it before.

His eyes followed hers, and for a moment she thought he would cover it. Then he lifted his hand, and let her see it. He said, 'Adorne left it with the Prioress Euphemia. He had willed it to her half-brother thirteen years ago, when Bishop Kennedy was still alive. Seaulme asked the Prioress, yesterday, if she would mind if he left it to me.'

'He hadn't told you?'

'No,' Nicholas said. 'He probably hoped I was going to die first.'

It wasn't even black humour; it was just a necessary denial of feeling.

The stone was a sapphire. In size and colour and brilliance, it surpassed anything Gelis had ever seen. It was meant, as he said, for a Bishop's ring. It came as a bequest from a man of deep convictions to another who, on the surface, had few. But Adorne had been a wise man.

She said, 'You had best make a start.'

He said, 'All right,' and stood up. He hadn't touched her. He knew, better than Jordan, what was too sweet.

Later, he went to Robin, and knelt, and talked. Then he went to the King.

He thought at first it was going to be like six years ago, when he came back in wild February weather from Flanders, and was so circumspectly reintroduced to the monarch by the three men who had since become part of his life. This time, there had been no wild escapade on the way. Oysters had come to mean something else. Henry was dead. Andro Wodman was in self-exile, serving a sick and evil old man in Kilmirren House, which Nicholas had no intention of visiting.

It was closer to six years ago than he expected, for men had reappeared: men like the former Archbishop Will Scheves, whom he had not seen at Court through the autumn. Andrew, the King's half-uncle and prospective Archbishop, was missing, but Davie Lindsay was there, and Leitch, and Master Secretary Whitelaw, whose spectacles Nicholas had cleaned, with difficulty, just that morning. But, of course, no Johndie Mar, and no Albany, now in Dunbar. No Princess Meg at Court now, since Crichton her lover had joined Albany. And no Lady Mary today, with her newly regranted Boyd lands, and her Boyd son equally caught on the side that was suddenly wrong: caught in Dunbar Castle with Albany.

The King said, 'We are displeased.'

'My lord, I am sorry,' said Nicholas.

The King said, 'We are reprimanding you. We should be reprimanding our Baron Cortachy, but for the tragic events of last night. They would not have occurred, had you followed our orders. We gave you no leave to mediate with our brother. You heard his threats. You saw his conduct. You heard of his traitorous dealings with England. Does it do us honour, after insults such as these, to be thought to be sending to *treat with* the villain?'

One followed the moves of the game. Nicholas said, 'My lord King, we were concerned for your highness's safety. We believed the Prince spoke in anger, and would repent. But until we were sure, we wished to give him no cause to harm you.'

'And you think he cannot harm us now?' said the King.

'My lord, he has put himself so far in the wrong that he dare not. I think that my lord of Cortachy's death has strengthened your grace's throne.'

'That is what they tell me,' said the King. 'I wait to be reassured. It is also true, I am told, that you shared his danger?'

'I came to no harm,' Nicholas said. 'But I fear I have lost the Duke of Albany's trust. I cannot expect to serve the King's grace as usefully as I have in the past.'

The King said, 'What are you saying? You are leaving? Before the funeral Mass of your countryman? That we cannot permit.'

'No, my lord. Nor would I wish it. I shall be there,' Nicholas said.

The King was staring down the long nose. 'You have some plea, some complaint? The murderers will be brought to court. The criminals will be justified. My lords assure me of that.'

'I am glad,' Nicholas said. 'No, I have no complaint, sire. Events have moved rather quickly, that is all. I should like a little time to consider my future.'

He was aware that it sounded like a well-worn stratagem for advancement. He was too tired to care. The Lords Three knew, at least, that he had simply spoken the truth.

The King said, 'We are told that the robbers purloined the chains of our Order. Is that so?'

Nicholas said, 'Yes, my lord.' He wondered if he were about to be asked to replace his. He wished he could go.

The King said, 'We shall have a replacement made. Two. My lord of Cortachy shall not go to his tomb without our recognition. Does that please you?'

He said something, and made all the standard gestures, and went. Nowie Sinclair walked a few steps with him outside. 'Are you as ill as you look?'

'No. I'm tired,' Nicholas said. 'Was there something?'

'I rather think not,' Nowie said. 'Perhaps in a day or two, when you feel better. I share your grief over that splendid man, Cortachy. And the small maid, of course. And the quarrel, as I understand it, within your own family. But such things occur to us all. We are foolish to take them too seriously.'

Nicholas stopped. He said, 'I am sure that, whatever it is, I can deal with it now, as well as I shall in a day or two. So?'

They were on the slopes leading down from David's Tower. The old lodge of the King's Guard was not far away. It was cold. Nowie said, 'Very well. Was Will Knollys with the troop that came to your rescue in North Berwick? Or any of his bailies and their men?'

'No,' said Nicholas. He should have remembered that Nowie never wasted anyone's time, especially his own. He found it hard to be interested.

'He was supposed to be,' said Nowie Sinclair. 'Huntly wouldn't like that. Nor would a few other people. You couldn't say, of course, that the Order of St John was supporting England: all that was long ago. But it is getting greedy. Over-demanding about rents and tithes. Extortionate, even. People are talking about taking the law into their own hands, and recovering what they've paid over the odds.'

'He would get it back,' Nicholas said.

'Maybe,' Nowie said. 'But it would cost him time and trouble. Especially if it weren't just money.' He produced the slow smile that people compared to a squeezed loaf of bread. He said, 'Of course, you shouldn't take part. It's people like the Johnstones of Linlithgow, and friends of the Prestons and the Cochranes and the Russells who have the grievances. Heriot of Longniddry, and Gullane of Newbattle. Even one or two clients of Adorne's nephew.'

Nicholas looked at him. 'When?'

The squeezed slice widened. 'Oh, about the time of the funeral might be appropriate. Don't you think? The Lord Preceptor has quite an amount of property close to Linlithgow.' He patted Nicholas on the arm with his manicured fingernails. 'I'll tell you afterwards. It might help you to make up your mind.'

'About what?' Nicholas said. As often happened after seeing Nowie, he felt slightly better. Slightly.

'But, of course, the weather is depressing,' Nowie said, as if he were producing an answer. 'You must take absolutely everything into account.'

On the day of his funeral, the *endeclocken* tolled for Anselm Adorne, Baron Cortachy, in the church of St Michael's, Linlithgow, as they would, a month hence, in his own church of the Jerusalemkerk, Bruges. As he had asked long ago, his body was wrapped in fifty-two ells of fine linen, to be gifted eventually to the poor; and among his bequests was one of a fine painted window for the monastery of the Charterhouse in St Johnstoun of Perth, that had held the heart of the first royal James, and had once assisted Maarten, his son. His other sons, the canons of Lille, the absent recipients of the prebends of Aberdeen, were not there;

but his friends were, and the great and powerful friends of Phemie, the companion with whom he might have ended his days.

The King rode in procession from Edinburgh, and brought with him Mary his sister, the noble and mighty Princess who had once sheltered in Adorne's great mansion of the Hôtel Jerusalem, and had borne her first children there. Her son James was not present, nor was her brother Alexander of Albany; but the lady Margaret attended, withdrawn and silent as she had been for that other ceremony, for the burial of Margaret of Berecrofts, whose mother had once been her handmaiden. The sovereign lady the Queen had also come from Stirling for both, and had brought James, her son.

The church, hung with cloths, pinned with the arms of Adorne and his family, was a place of splendour. The robes of Will Scheves and his Bishops glittered and blazed, as did the gowns and jewels of the King and his nobles. On the catafalque lay a new Collar of the Unicorn Order, one of a pair made in a single workshop by two rival goldsmiths, sleeping by turn. There were only two living Knights of the Unicorn present, of whom one was the King. The King was replicated again, in solemn profile, on the reverse of the glowing altar-piece behind the Archbishop, loaned from the Holy Trinity church to link Scotland with Flanders, and to honour Hugo vander Goes and the man who commissioned it, and the man who had advised its commissioning: Adorne, friend of artists, who, long ago, had recommended van Eyck to the Duchess Isabella, and had pursued Memling's painting to Danzig.

The anonymous painted prince at this altar, piously kneeling, was not nine-year-old James, stiffly standing between the Queen and Abbot Henry. Nor would anyone ever admit, now, that it might be Albany, possible heir to the throne. Adorne's death had brought what the lords had foreseen, a landslide of revulsion. The vacillators would never join Albany now. Burgundy and dying France would hold back. England, whatever promises it made, was also facing an empty throne, and a fight for the succession which would leave no time or inclination for new northern empires. Albany would never become Lieutenant-General, and would be expected to impeach his friends, and sever all his treasonable bonds. And like a common criminal bound by a Constable, he would not be allowed within three leagues of his King.

It was over. And the King was alone.

Dirige Domine gressus meus . . . The antiphone, the work of a dead man, was glorious. Anselm Adorne's daughter Efemie did not hear it, but trotted out at the end, hand in hand with her cousin Saunders, while her other cousin Katelijne steered her softly from behind.

As she passed, the lady of Berecrofts glanced up at Gelis, who returned the look as if from the wastes of the sea. Nicholas neither spoke nor glanced round, and no one would have recognised the look on his face.

Returned with Katelijne Sersanders and her family to Edinburgh, Dr Andreas saw them all settled and then, obeying orders, crossed the Canongate to the Floory Land to find Gelis. 'Where is he?'

'Nicholas?' she said. She looked wind-wrung, as she had in the church. She said, 'Can you help him?'

'*Help him?*' repeated Dr Andreas with comfortable contempt. 'God bless and preserve him, all that man needs is a porridge stick up the arse. Women! What did you think you were looking at, but a finished example of unfettered cowardice?'

She looked startled. She had not observed, as he had, that they were no longer alone. '*Confiteor,*' said Nicholas from the far end of the room. 'You had better come with me, via the kitchen.' But instead of a porridge stick, all they picked up in the kitchen was a lavish provision of wine, which they took back to a quiet room and drank.

The conversation that then ensued was quite different, naturally, from the consoling pap envisaged by laymen. It began, certainly, with the loss of Adorne, of the child Margaret, and of the man Julius, but moved beyond these matters of transient importance. Dr Andreas did not, of course, belittle the dead, or suggest that one should not experience grief. He had spoken for Adorne's life in Bruges, and stood beside him in the chapel in Roslin; he recalled the aftermath of Nancy as well as or better than Nicholas de Fleury; had been affected as had de Fleury by the hangings at Lauder; had understood some of the tragedy of the River Till. Now he was simply placing these matters in context. Perspective. De Fleury appreciated perspective.

At first, de Fleury had been reluctant to turn to the future. He did not want to think of his own. Andreas put him right about that.

'Not your own. We spoke of this before. You stopped your divining because of it.'

'You want me to resume?' de Fleury had said. There was an edge to his voice.

'No, I do not. I told you that I felt it was dangerous. Now I am sure that it is.'

'You want me to live a long, happy life,' the other man said.

Andreas looked at him. He said, 'You may die tomorrow, and it would affect nothing now. Oh, the kingdom would suffer: I give you that. You would be mourned. Your family would be desolate.'

'I should like to think so. But if my death doesn't matter, why not divine?' Then, at last, he used his intelligence, and answered himself. 'Because it affects someone else? You thought it might?' And then: '*You know who?* You have found out where the illusions come from?'

'*Come* from?' Andreas said. 'You have had more?'

He was disconcerted. 'I'm not sure. There was something, with Julius. As if I were being forbidden to fight him.'

Andreas watched him. Then he said, 'It was someone else's resistance. Someone else's dilemma. You took what was the right decision, for you. But it is better if you receive nothing more. I think, in the end, you won't regret it. You may even meet him one day.'

It was a mistake. Nicholas de Fleury cried out. 'Then he is in this life? Where?'

It was necessary to quell that at once. 'No. Never. You will never meet him in life. Later, perhaps. That is why I suggest you protect your life, so far as you can. You have a long time to wait. So has he.'

But when de Fleury said, '*But who is he?*' the astrologer did not give a direct answer. 'Ask me what he is,' Andreas said. 'Some of that, I can tell you.'

Presently, he forced a digression, and filled his own cup and the other, many times.

Later, when Andreas had been assisted back over the road, Gelis went and sank into his place beside Nicholas. 'Well?' she said.

He sat and gazed at her. He looked warm, and rather shaken, but not drunk. 'Oh,' he said. 'He used a hogspear.' He went on gazing at her. He said, 'He admired the sapphire. Seaulme had left him his Unicorn Horn.'

'And?' she said. 'What did he tell you?' It was not like before, a stone wall. He was struggling to think of two things at once.

'He didn't tell me anything,' Nicholas said. 'What are doctors supposed to be for? He just said that I would continue to blame myself for a long time for just about everything, and that it was damned right that I should. He said that since I had dragged everyone over here, I should either tell them what I was going to do, or let them go away and forge their own lives.'

She could see why he looked heated. She said, 'I rather agree with all that, or most of it. So?'

He now looked mildly harassed, but not angry. He said, 'What do you think? Where do you want to go?'

She stared at him. (Dr Andreas? What have you done?)

She said, 'I don't know. Perhaps we should make a shortlist. Persia? No. It's still split over Uzum's succession. Turkey? They've just retreated from Italy. The new Sultan is pro-Venice and promising, but is against Italian art: poor Bellini. And of course, Rhodes is grooming a supplanter. Cyprus? No. Not after what the Venetians did to Zacco. Venice? A new House of Niccolò, Venice?'

'Gelis,' Nicholas said.

'No. Wait. Venice? It's Gregorio's now. Going back wouldn't be fair. Africa? It's less safe than before, and the English are racing the Portuguese for the gold. Poland? You liked it a lot, but you'd have to spend all your time fighting. I rather think Muscovy would be the same. The Tyrol? No. The Duchess is dead, and I don't care for Sigismond. Spain? They're driving the Moors out of Granada. Umar wouldn't have liked that at all. France?'

'Gelis,' Nicholas said.

'No. Wait. France? You liked Louis, but he's dying, and the next King is a boy. You've had enough of bear-leading boys, and I can't see you joining Lorraine, although old King René might have suited you well. Burgundy? The heirs are two children, and the Archduke is an unlikeable youth who didn't stop Seaulme's indictment, and is disliked by both Brabant and Flanders. Diniz can handle it. You've done enough. Milan, Naples, Genoa, Florence – do we wish to follow in the bankrupt footsteps of poor Tommaso, even though his vander Goes altar-piece is magnificent, and Filippo Strozzi has opened a third branch in Rome? Or,' said Gelis, 'we could go to Egypt. We could go back to the monastery on Mount Sinai, and see where Seaulme signed his name beside Jan's. The King still has the book he wrote, hasn't he? I wish Fra Ludovico had gone there instead of Ethiopia,' Gelis said. 'And perhaps, every few years, a monk would land here, rather soiled, with some dubious habits, raising funds for a new pair of sandals.'

She was crying. 'A monk would land here,' Nicholas echoed gently. The dazed air had gone, and he was smiling a little. He said, 'The monk would come here, because this is where, all the time, you were really sure we would be? Am I right?' They were still at arm's length, but he had laid one hand on her arm, and was studying her.

She said, 'I told you before. I will be wherever you are.'

'Then will you be with me in Scotland?' he said.

She looked at him. She had spoken out for Nicholas to John and the rest, because she thought sometimes that no one knew his stature as she did, who had fought so hard to be his equal, and had learned to accept that she was not.

She knew now what strengths she possessed, and how they complemented his own. The joy of their physical life was very real, but it was also the curtain that protected the other life which continued behind: the deep partnership that showed itself in all the work they did together, in their aims and their ideals and how they fulfilled them.

There were other parts of his being that she did not enter, or could not enter because, as with music, she did not have the key. But others did, and he was a man who could find harmony in more than one love, and still maintain loyalty, as his sweet, sardonic honour from Zacco had proclaimed. Yet again, there were privacies which he protected against every intrusion. Umar represented one. He had not confided to her what he felt about Simon and Henry, or about his own mother. He had kept the secrets of Adelina, and of Julius, and of his feelings about them both until the end.

Tonight, he hadn't refused to speak about Julius, but had reduced the silent struggle of twenty-five years to an obedient résumé. He had expected Julius to change. He had felt responsible for him, as a relative. He had tried to ensure that no one else would suffer, until it became apparent that this was no longer possible. The end had been difficult, and he didn't find it easy to speak of, although he blamed himself for allowing Julius to act as he had. He apologised to Gelis for that; but not for his own reticence.

It still hurt, that absence of the ultimate trust, but not as much as it had; and it made it easier to know that he confided in no one. To deal alone with such things was the source of a great deal of his strength. She believed Ludovico da Bologna was responsible for some of that; and could not regret it.

Now: 'You want it?' she said. 'You want to live your life in Scotland? Are you not weary? Are you really prepared to spend your days like these tired, patient men, supporting such a King?'

He said, 'MacChalein Mor isn't tired, nor Whitelaw nor Huntly nor Lindsay nor Darnley nor Scheves. Neither am I. Neither will Jordan be, although he must choose for himself. And there is the Queen, and the Princes growing up.' He drew her to him, in a manner of gentle persuasion.

'Those countries are part of our past. That is what you were thinking? But we haven't left them: we have brought them with us, as every merchant and student will go on bringing them here, Jordan included. And if we fail, if all the patient men fail, it's because no one can plan for quite everything as, God knows, you and I learned. There are always happenings beyond our control. There are always *people* beyond our control: personalities so wonderfully compelling that, right or wrong, whole countries will follow them. History is made by individuals, not by masses. The art of directing the future is the art of choosing and grooming the leader.'

She was in the crook of his arm, thinking. She said, 'Did Dr Andreas tell you that?' and felt him laugh.

He said, 'There are some things I don't need an Andreas to teach me. Gelis, I haven't been fair to you. I shall probably be unfair to you again. It's a lack in me, not in you. Will you forgive me?'

Help can take many forms. She was beginning to forgive him when the door banged open and John and Tobie strode in. Tobie said, 'Oh. I'm sorry.'

'I'm allowed to kiss her. I'm married to her,' said Nicholas fretfully. 'Come in, now you're in. What is it?'

He was acting. The next moment, miraculously, he was not acting, for they brought news which, on that day, should not have seemed so irredeemably comical. Further, as a scion of the Knights of St John, John le Grant should not have so revelled in telling it, in full legal vernacular.

It was a case of Spontaneous Spulzies, attributable to gentry who should have known better. The Order's Preceptory at Torphichen had been overrun (would you credit it?) and three more of their places attacked. Abstracted to the Preceptor's prejudice had been beasts (yowes, tupps and stirks), and farm graith, and oats and hay by the chalder, and fine stores of coal and peats and cheese and malt, down to a barrel of tar. By violent intrusion into the Order's own houses, the callants had made off, in clear wrangous spoliation, with iron chimneys and noppis beds with their cloots and their arras, a Flanders kist and a great shrine, for shame. They actually claimed the villainous haul was their due, owing to the Order's retention of deceptorious overpayments. The Order! Deceptorious anything! Surely not!'

'Torphichen, Lochcotes, Fauldhouse and Liston,' repeated John, reverting to normal speech, his pale eyes shining in the reddened skin and foxy hair. 'And you haven't heard the best of it yet.'

'Tell me,' said Nicholas. He had kept his arm around Gelis, and she could feel all the high spirits suddenly surging back.

John had become unexpectedly sober. He stood looking down at the two of them, and the expression on his face was almost reverent. He said, 'Listen. When the Johnstones and the rest got into Torphichen, they found this crate with the mark of David Simpson. Knowing him dead, they broke the thing open. It was gold, Nicol. Your African gold.

Davie lied. He didn't spend it all on Beltrees. He stored it with the last person we'd think of, his unfriend the Preceptor. He knew Knollys would take it, for if anything happened to Davie, Knollys could keep it himself.'

Tobie wore a satisfied smirk. Gelis looked at Nicholas, who sat gazing at John. 'So why hadn't he used it? Oh, I suppose he couldn't flood the market with illicit gold: he'd have to find some way to get it out piecemeal. Do I understand that Knollys wasn't there while all this was happening?'

'No. He was at the Mass, didn't you see him? And he came back to his Edinburgh house after that. Gibbie Johnstone thought he'd better get me, knowing we knew Davie Simpson. So I went, and I took it away.'

'You did?' Nicholas said. He looked worried. 'Then I suppose I'd better start dividing it up. Gelis and I have just decided that we are staying in Scotland. I dare say Tobie will want to get back to his printing-presses, and Pavia, and yourself to the fighting, wherever it is?'

Tobie flushed. His short mouth set, and his nostrils curled like small beans. He said, 'Is this a way of saying you don't want us? We can move out of that house.'

'No, it wasn't,' said Nicholas with interest, 'but it's an idea. Where would you move to?'

John said, 'Calm down, Tobie. He's back to normal. You can't trust a word that he says. Well, thank God. We all thought you'd gone daft. If you're staying, then we are.'

'You mean,' said Tobie, 'he was sane before, and now he's gone daft again. All right. We have talked about the future, as John says, and we all felt the same, Moriz included. We're staying. Provided –' He stopped.

'Provided?' said Nicholas.

'Provided you don't do this sort of thing ever again. Keeping all that about Julius to yourself. And Adelina and the rest. Is there anything else we don't know?' Tobie said.

'A fair amount, by the sound of it,' Nicholas said. His eyes, no longer bloodshot, were extremely wide. 'When not to interfere, for one thing.'

Gelis sought the eyes of John. Before anyone else could speak, Tobie swore. He said, 'She said I wasn't to say that. But damn it all –'

'Who said?' Nicholas asked.

Tobie looked surprised. 'Clémence,' he said. 'She said that she hadn't said she knew Bel, and Bel hadn't said she knew the Duchess Eleanor,

and John and I hadn't admitted we were trying to find out about
Adelina, and Moriz hadn't confessed that he was asking questions
everywhere about Bonne. She said if we wanted you to be open, we'd
have to be open as well, and she thought the loftier heights of virtue
beyond us.'

'I'm sure she's right,' Nicholas said. He looked shaken. He said, 'I
can't remember any major subterfuges at the moment, but if I do, I
tell Clémence?'

'That's the idea,' Tobie said. His tone was one of embarrassed relief.

'And what will she do?' Nicholas said.

'Put you on a physic to flush out your bowels,' said John sombrely.
'I tell you, I'd rather have a good penance from Moriz any day. Is that
some wine?'

'No,' said Nicholas.

'And another thing,' Tobie said. 'While we're on good behaviour.
That old man St Pol isn't going to live many months. You have to
thank him. You wouldn't have Jordan, but for him.'

Nicholas said, 'Did Bel ask you to ask me?'

Tobie said, 'No. Wodman did. You know Tom Swift has been given
his and Adorne's job? Very suitable. Conservator of the Privileges of
the Scots Nation in the Low Parts of Burgundy they call him, as from
now. Andro Wodman's helping transfer all the papers. Wodman wants
to see you. Then he wants you to go to the old man.'

'The old man doesn't want to see me,' Nicholas said.

'How do you know?' Tobie said. 'Anyway, what will we buy with
the gold?'

'Another room for you to sit in?' said Nicholas.

Chapter 54

And sen the wanis pvnsing of the man
Is lyk in armony, him nedis than
The richt mesur of musik for to haf
To knaw the wanis pvnsing with the laif.

ISITING JORDAN DE ST POL of Kilmirrcn was, Nicholas
believed, the last ordeal he faced, once he had made known to
the lords the decision that he had just reached: to commit
himself and his life to the country that Anselm Adorne had
considered worth choosing. To become his memorial.

When he left Avandale's house, his thoughts were on Scotland, and
the place he and Adorne held in it. In concrete form, there was little to
mark the other man's sojourn. His life-rental of Cortachy had ceased,
and the land been effortlessly reabsorbed into the lands of the Ogilvies.
His houses in Edinburgh and Linlithgow were rented to provide an
income for Efemie, who stayed with her big cousin Saunders and
possessed her own loving household.

The same was true, Nicholas supposed, of himself. He had no land,
unlike Robin's family, with their acres at Berecrofts and lucrative
near-baronial land at Templehall, which two growing young sons would
inherit. In town, their trade in Leith and the Canongate flourished, as
it should, with all their prodigious connections. It was not everyone
who was great-nephew, like Robin, to the Lord High Treasurer of the
realm. They had also a new small domain, bought by Robin for Kathi
in Yarrow, which she said Nicholas might share if he wished. It was
the land Will Roger had loved, south of Traquair, and not far from
where he was buried.

After Beltrees, Nicholas had no hunger for territorial possessions,
other than the houses he already owned. His business was well placed

and thriving, and now his presence was permanent, he could expect to be bound into the fabric of the royal *familia*, with all the extra emoluments that implied. And there was music with Arnot and others, and the chance perhaps to continue what he and Whistle Willie had begun. Go on, Andreas had said. Use your life to the full.

He had come to that point when, walking quickly, he found himself stopped. He had forgotten that the nuns of the Cistercian Priories had a house in the High Street of Edinburgh, and that the Prioress Euphemia might be there. It had never crossed his mind that Bonne might be there too; removed as a maiden without legal protection from Kilmirren House. He had killed Julius, her guardian. If that were to be endorsed as a just execution, he might be regarded as having some say, at least, in her future. He had been related to Julius's late wife, Bonne's supposed mother.

She did not seem, when he was ushered into the parlour, to be mourning her stepfather. Prioress Euphemia, seated beside her, displayed the air of aggressive self-possession that had barely changed since their encounter at Eccles. Following the attack on North Berwick, he had seen her in passing, at funerals, as he had seen Bonne. He had avoided them both.

Which had been unfair, he realised. He greeted them and was seated, without benefit of refreshment. The Prioress said, 'There is no need to look quite so abashed. Nor am I about to recommend that you should replace the late unfortunate gentleman as the demoiselle's tutor.'

'I am sorry. Then, yourself?' said Nicholas rather wildly. Bonne was studying her lap.

'She may stay with me, if she so wishes. It will not be for long. She may also enjoy the spiritual guidance of Father Moriz. I wished to speak to you about her support in the meantime, and about the terms of her dowry. Assuming, of course, that you approve of the match.'

'The match?' Nicholas said.

'She has not had an opportunity to tell you. But the lady of Cuthilgurdy appeared to think it quite suitable, and I am sure that Sister Monika will approve. The Charteris household was certainly unproductive of offers. You know the young man, of course. The son of Constantine Malloch.'

'John Malloch,' said Nicholas rather blankly. The child singer in his play eleven years ago. The brother of Muriella. The half-brother of Muriella, rumour went; born remarkably soon after his mother's marriage but, naturally, accepted as his own son by Conn. It happened sometimes. He spoke to Bonne. 'Are you happy?'

The hard, bright eyes surveyed him. 'Of course. Would I have accepted him otherwise?'

The Prioress continued. 'The family is, of course, modest in means, and not well placed, so close to the Border. But the maternal uncle was a merchant, and there are connections abroad. Bonne may find herself pursuing an interesting marriage in other countries.' She refrained from adding the obvious. Bonne had no money. This was the best she could hope for.

Nicholas said, 'If she wants it, then of course I agree. Might I discuss it with her?'

'Of course,' said the Prioress, and rose. She left the door open.

Nicholas reseated himself, and Bonne looked up. Nicholas said, 'This isn't too hasty a decision?'

Her smile was tolerant. 'A recoil from the death of my stepfather? No.'

'You have never thought of finding a husband in Germany?'

'Why?' she said. 'The Graf, I fear, was not my father. I doubt very much whether my mother was Adelina de Fleury. I think Father Moriz came close to proving that she was not. And if she was not, then who am I?'

'I don't know, Bonne,' he said.

'And if you did, you wouldn't tell me. You don't want me as your daughter, M. de Fleury?' the girl said. 'That was one possibility, wasn't it? That I was born to your first wife at Damparis?'

'I am sorry,' Nicholas said. 'I have tried to find out; so have others. It seems to have been a mischievous suggestion, no more. There is nothing to support it.'

'Tasse knew the truth,' the girl said. 'She was at Damparis. Later, Julius had her killed.'

Her voice, mildly informative, had not changed. He remained, outwardly, equally calm. He said, 'So I believe. How did you know?'

'I overhear things,' she said. 'I pick locks, if I have to. We unprotected maidens cannot afford to be unduly decorous.'

'And so,' he said, 'you made some discoveries.' He had expected anger, resistance, certainly challenge. Instead, it was danger he sensed.

She said, 'Certainly, I knew more than you did. I knew Julius and my so-called mother were using each other. I didn't know you had guessed. Why didn't you kill him?'

'I did,' Nicholas said.

Again, the contempt. She switched back. 'Tasse. I had some sympathy for Julius when I found out. I guessed he didn't want his wife recognised.

But I didn't expect him to have Tasse killed before he could question her. Tasse would know if Marian had borne a daughter who lived, and even perhaps what had become of her. I might be your legitimate heiress, and Julius my guardian. But he didn't want that. He would rather know nothing at all than share his prospects with me.'

Nicholas said, 'How do you know he didn't question her?' He didn't want to be in the same room.

'Because nothing happened,' Bonne said. 'If I had no claim, he would have made sure, these latter years, that I knew. If I had, he would have tried to get rid of me. Although, in a convent, that isn't easy.'

'So you knew what he was like,' Nicholas said. 'You didn't think to warn anyone? If I had died, would he have supported you?'

'What do you mean? I didn't know anything,' the girl said. 'No one could prove that I did. Of course, if I had had some evidence against him, I could count on his support in the long term. As it was, it was simply a case of waiting to see who would win: you or Julius.'

'You didn't mind which,' Nicholas said.

She considered. 'Personally? Julius was handsome, but not very clever. You are quite a kind man. Reflect, if you will, on who gave Mistress Bel the information that sent your friends to help you at North Berwick.'

He met her eyes. She did not look away. He said, 'Because, of course, you were going to need funds for a dowry.'

'Of course,' she said.

He didn't want to talk to her any more. He said, 'Where do you think you will live?'

She laughed. 'You won't have to meet me. John's uncle had friends in the East. In Rhodes and Zakynthos. Is that sufficiently far?'

For him, it was. Leaving, he forced himself to think of her, and to persuade himself that she might have grown differently, in different hands. But she wasn't like Henry. It had taken more than a mismanaged childhood to produce Bonne von Hanseyck. And he did not have the skill, or the desire, to put it right.

Standing in the High Street after that, with the thatch and the orchard-twigs flying, and the wind twisting his cloak, Nicholas did not want to go to Swift's office to see Andro Wodman; and especially he did not want to go, after that, to Kilmirren. He wished he had no sense of duty. He remembered, painfully, what had just happened and resolved to do the best he could, this time at least.

He saw Wodman alone, and accepted ale, and talked about Adorne, who had saved Andro's life, as well as his, by Castle Heaton. From there, Nicholas went on to speak of Jordan de St Pol.

'You know him, Andro. He risked his own life, it seemed, to save my son from being shot at North Berwick. I haven't thanked him, partly because I'm not sure that he'd wish me to, and partly because I'm not sure that I could. It seems to me, from what I heard recently, that I myself owe him remarkably little. I might enjoy telling him so, but it would only cause pain to Bel.'

Wodman was drinking ale from a chopin. He put it down. 'What have you heard? Something you didn't know? Who could tell you something new, now?'

And so Nicholas told him what Julius had said.

At the end, the Archer was quiet. Then he said, 'I heard all that. I don't know much more. I can tell you something of his loathing of Jaak; and of anything to do with men's relationships with each other, or with children. It was an obsession that pursued him all his life, because of his beauty. Maybe you can still see what he was, beneath all that bulk. The fat is protective. Whether he invited it deliberately or not, I don't know. But before he put on weight, he was as handsome as Simon, with twice the intelligence. Some of the Archers are married, but it is a closed community, as armies tend to be, and he was constantly pestered.

'He also reacted too strongly. I don't know, but I suspect he had already experienced something like it at home. I never met Alan, his brother. It became a competition, to try and captivate the magnificent Jordan, or tempt him at least. Even after he left the Guards, it dogged him, for he still lived in France, and within reach of them all. By that time I knew him, and I knew he would kill someone one day if it continued. As it was, I tackled the next man myself, and challenged him to a sword-fight, and he died. It was why I left the Guard. St Pol gave me work, and Simpson contrived to join me.'

'But wasn't he a liability too?' Nicholas said. He kept his voice quiet.

Wodman said, 'I warned him not to try and attract the old man, or he would be either thrown out or killed. Most of the work filtered through me. With my looks, I was considered reliable.'

'I'm not surprised,' Nicholas said. He tried, as he always had done, to look at what had happened objectively, as if it had occurred to someone else. That it had been a forced marriage was known at the time; and so was Simon's dislike of his wife: far older than he was; kept long unmarried by some doubt or timidity no one had plumbed. Sophie's second child had arrived when he had long been out of the country, and the dates of birth had never been properly proved. There was only one certainty: that Simon had not been near his wife between the two births. Eager for any excuse to end the marriage, Simon would find, to his delight, that he suddenly had his father's full agreement. His father had belatedly found that the taint he abhorred existed in Simon's wife's family, and was now harboured, no doubt, in the child. He intimidated Sophie. He menaced the life of her son. He threatened to ruin Jaak's business, and the reputation and business of Thibault, unless the child was brought up as a bastard, and did not bear the name of St Pol. He continued to threaten her until, alone, without any hope of help from her invalid father, she became afraid that she would make some mistake, and so offend her oppressor that her son would die. She thought it better to remove herself from her son's life.

That had been the hardest part to accept. Once, Nicholas had said something of it to Jordan, but nothing to anyone else. It went too deep. As his understanding had grown with the years, so had the torment. He had lost many mothers, many times. The mother who left without warning because he disappointed her; because she never cared for him; because he was wicked. The mother who took her own life – died – because he had failed her. The mother who took her own life – committed her soul to eternal misery – for his sake. Because she was afraid that, scared and hounded, she would do or say something that would harm him.

And, finally, the mother who loved him; who sacrificed herself for him; and yet could not trust him to help her; could not talk to him; could not envisage that he, even at seven, was staunch, determined, agile: a small bulwark, maybe, but there, only for her.

Marian de Charetty had seen all those things, no more than three years after that, and had trusted him. It was why he had loved her. It was the source of the greatest pain, that he stood between Marian and his mother, with all his mortgaged love, and no one to help him apportion it.

Wodman went on explaining. It fitted with what he already knew. The consequences of Sophie's death could be imagined. When she died, Jordan de St Pol was out of the country. Thibault's keepers knew nothing suspicious about Jaak. When St Pol returned, he found the child, apparently contented, performing menial work in the home of the same Jaak de Fleury, abuser of children. It confirmed all St Pol's fears. It made it intolerable when, as the child grew, it became apparent that, however deprived, however unprepossessing, it was endowed with all the intelligence that his own son Simon lacked; and the power to attract affection, and happiness. After that had come the bitter scarring;

the cynical whim of throwing Simon and Nicholas together, base coin and silver, to see what would happen. For by then, Monseigneur had also realised that the joyous lusts of the artisan Claes were not of the same cadre as Jaak's. All the girls in Flanders seemed able to prove it.

One listened, and breathed. 'And so he hit on the idea of setting me to vie with Simon?' Nicholas said. 'Let the best man win? What a large part of his life he seems to have devoted to this. I find myself wishing he had picked some other sport.'

'Go and see him,' Wodman said. 'He won't change his mind. He'll never confess to the truth now. But if you want to punish him, show him finally what he has lost by repudiating you.'

Nicholas said, 'Julius said much the same. I might be assured that I was Simon's son, but there was no proof, and St Pol would never admit it.'

'Does it matter?' said Wodman. 'Monseigneur knows who you are. So do you. You have no need of his name or his property. Go and see him. Tell him what you think of him: why not? But keep in mind how it started. It took a lot of misery to bend a man's nature like that.' He stopped. He said, 'You are very like him, you know. The way he should have been, maybe.'

'So I have been told. I am trying not to believe it,' Nicholas said. He thought of Bonne. He wished this day would end.

Bel of Cuthilgurdy opened the door, when he crossed the road to the house of his grandfather, and he hesitated, even though he had been prepared. Within, Mistress Bel stood in her hall, arms almost folded, and snapped.

'I hear it was Katelijne that made ye face Julius. So you might as weel ken it was me that sent Tobie to help. Adorne might be alive if I hadn't.'

'No,' Nicholas said. 'They were going to kill us both anyway. Because you sent the army, I escaped.' *Because of Bonne.*

'But not wee Margaret, and not Julius,' she said. 'Andro told ye that Jordan is dying?' Then she added quickly, 'My Jordan, not yours.'

Now that the child-name Jodi was shed, he found it odd that both his son and his grandfather should answer to Jordan. It was Gelis who had so named their son, during the war Nicholas and she had then waged. He had thought she meant only to hurt, but he had been wrong about her again. When no one else did, she had believed that Nicholas was a St Pol.

Nicholas said, 'Is he too ill for a visitor? Should I trouble him?'

'Nicol,' she said. 'He'll injure you sooner than you'll injure him.' Which was true. He went in.

A beauty like Simon's, he had been told. You could only look for it in the symmetry of the features within the gross folds of fat; in the breadth of shoulder pressed into the pillows, and the length of the body beneath the handsome coverlet. Now that St Pol wore plain head-linen, you could see the line of white hair on his brow, of the purity that comes from golden fairness. Nicholas's own beard, when he grew it, was yellow. His eyes were grey. St Pol's were blue, as Simon's and Henry's had been.

Bel had followed him in. She said, 'Here's Nicholas come to tell ye how his son does. He's not to stay long. Ye havena finished your drink.'

'And I'm not going to,' said the old man. 'Go away.' She had nursed his wife for years. She had nursed his wife, and helped to look after Lucia. Nicholas supposed she knew now how Julius had driven Lucia into the river at Berecrofts, thinking that she was her brother. He remembered begging Adorne not to let Simon leave on his own, certain that Julius would kill him outside. He remembered having to use his sword on Adorne, in his anguish.

The skin on St Pol's face was mottled, and his lips were a cold-looking blue. He said, 'Young men don't pay calls, these days, to thank their benefactors? Next time he can suffer the arrow.'

'I'm sorry,' Nicholas said. 'We have been in Linlithgow. I am here to thank you on his behalf. Is the wound very painful?'

'No. Or I should not be lying back as I am. I have no desire for a visit by you. Send the boy.'

'Why?' said Nicholas.

It was Bel who answered, from her chair in the corner. 'Because St Pol has an offer to make.'

'Dear me!' the fat man said. 'Did I ask for an audience? No. I asked you to go away.'

'Then this is me refusing,' said Bel. 'Go on, Nicholas. Ask him what it is.'

'I don't know if I want to,' Nicholas said. 'In any case, if he had one, he'd have to make it to me. Jordan is in his minority.'

The gross face appeared bored. 'I had noticed. In that case, I shall ask him, and you will stand by and listen.'

'There isna time for that,' Bel said with continuing calmness. 'Nicol, Monseigneur wants to make Jordan his heir. Not you. Him. And on condition he changes his name to St Pol.'

'No. To Semple,' said the fat man. 'There is no style these days in things French. The Madeira land is being sold. If the family is to stay in Kilmirren, then it reverts to the Renfrewshire name. Jordan Semple, Master of Kilmirren, for the present. Semple of Kilmirren in time to come. And he will move in with me now.'

'I'm afraid not,' Nicholas said.

The old man laughed. 'Why? In case I turn him into a Simon or Henry? There is not quite enough time for that. He comes to me now. The papers have been properly drawn up and notarised. You will have what you always wanted, dear Claes. A son following the St Pols in Kilmirren. And legitimately, without having to prove your own birth. For if you proved to be a St Pol, the boy would be a bastard, would he not? You and your wife would be shown to be related, and your marriage therefore null from the start. Such a trial.' Although smiling, he was breathing more harshly.

Nicholas continued to stand at the foot of the bed. He said, 'You misunderstand me. There is no question of Jordan coming to you, for there is no question of his being your heir. If he is not both the natural and the legitimate heir, and he is not, then I have no wish for him to be granted your estate as a gift. He has no need of it, and he is worthy of something far better.'

'You would buy him a title?' said St Pol. His face was full of contempt.

'I could. I have just recovered my African gold. But I prefer to think that de Fleury is a name he is proud of, and that he will grow up to inherit my property, and add some of his own.'

'De Fleury? The name of a small French vicomté now defunct? What weight will that carry in Scotland?' St Pol said.

'What weight does St Pol carry?' Nicholas said. 'Alan, Simon, Lucia, Elizabeth. Julius, on his mother's side – you heard about him? Diniz is the only other man of worth, and he has rejected you. Once you have gone, the tarnished shield can drop from the wall.'

'Nicol,' the woman's voice said behind him. From the bed, the breathing was hurried.

The eyes, however, had not changed. St Pol said, 'You don't mention Henry. Does he escape your litany of inadequate failures? Or did you beguile him into your bed as well as your house? I never did quite find out.'

Nicholas said, 'I think you know the answer to that.'

'I wonder,' said the fat man. 'Well, if not for that reason, why omit him? He was as puerile as Simon, and as vicious, and as vain. A St Pol to the core, you would say. I think I can guess, after all, why you don't choose to have Jordan follow him. The upright Jordan must not be compared to such trash.'

Bel was letting him speak. Certainly, the fat man's voice was suddenly stronger, and his breathing reflected no worse than an angry contempt. It was Nicholas who stood still, his breath choking, as he detected the terrible game, the subtle, terrible game he was being invited to play.

He had always wondered. Now he need wonder no more.

He said, 'You knew who Henry was.'

'You said something?' said the fat man.

Nicholas said, 'How long have you known? Since I sought him out? Since before that, when he was young? Or since –' He stopped.

'Dear Katelina,' the fat man said softly. 'She was so very shocked. When she thought I was you, she flirted quite prettily. But when I took off my mask – ah, no, no. But unflattering though her disgust was, I suppose it made her all the more compliant when true love came along, if somewhat frayed from Jaak de Fleury's attentions. It was true love, my dear Claes, wasn't it? Or was it, more sadly, more realistically, just another well-born young lady curious to experiment in the byre? Oh, yes' – and he smiled – 'I knew Henry was your son, poor vicious Henry. I virtually begat him upon you.'

'Thank you,' said Nicholas. Behind him, Bel made a sound. Nicholas said, 'So then you allowed him – encouraged him – to dislike and despise me, and later to kill me if he could. There is, by the way, the question of how Jordan emerges so upright and Henry the opposite? Their mothers were sisters. What, does anyone remember, was the result of that experiment with the twin dogs? *La nourriture passe nature*, more or less? So the evil was yours; the fault is yours that you lie here without sons, and die childless.' He laughed, without joy. 'Even your son and your grandson were killed by a St Pol. Through Julius, son of Elizabeth, the sister you and your brother ignored.'

St Pol was staring beyond him. He said, in an angry voice, 'Help her.'

Her?

Nicholas whirled round.

The small woman had slipped from her chair, her face blanched, her brow contorted with pain. She said, 'Henry, Nicol? Ah, not Henry!'

She knew so much. She hadn't known Henry was his. She lay, half on the floor, gazing up at him, and he dropped to his knees. He had gathered her like this in Africa. He had carried her, sick and ill and valiant, and sung to her, and helped make her well. Love and music. Bel? Bel? Don't go. Listen?

He held her. She was not fully conscious. He held her, and followed a thread of song in his mind, as if he could induce her to hear it. Her hair was thick and grey under the gauze, and her face was round still, and still bonny. She had a daughter in France, and a grandchild. They were not going to lose her. Nor was he. He spoke to her, in a murmur. He spoke about Henry.

'Come along, Bel. Come, Bel. It's over. It was Simon he loved, and his grandfather, and now he's at peace. We remember him, and so does his brother. They were halfway to becoming friends, Henry and Jordan. It wasn't all loss.'

Her eyes were open on his. Presently she shook her head, and attempted to smile, and he drew her up into the chair. She was cold, so he laid his jacket around her, and turned to the bed-chest for a blanket.

The coverlet was upset. The fustian wool hangings were as neat as before, and the carpet laid on the steps, and the table set to one side with its tin flagon of physic and cups. But the coverlet was crumpled, and one of the pillows tumbled askew; and half sunk in its depths was the frozen face of Jordan de St Pol, caught as it was when he dropped, wild with frustration, at the height of his effort to rise. His mouth was a little open and his eyes reflected the light as Henry's had done; but no one had held him as he died.

Sent for, Tobie brought Gelis with him. By then, the staff of the household had come and ordered the room, while Nicholas took Bel away. She wouldn't go to her room, but sat with him in the parlour, where Nicholas had first met his son Henry, the golden child, and the golden man he thought was his father. Then Tobie came, and went to the bedchamber, while Gelis walked in and kissed Bel and sat beside her, her hand at her back. Bel was weeping, her face immobile; the tears running ceaselessly into her kerchief. Nicholas, without very much colour, moved quietly about, responding to questions, giving low orders to the same servants who, six months before, must have witnessed his struggle with Julius. Now they simply obeyed.

Presently, Tobie came to sit with Bel and Gelis, and Nicholas joined them, and answered his questions as well. He might have kept something back, but Bel had a mind of her own. Discovering that the others knew about Henry, she questioned them steadily. Then, against Nicholas's silent resistance, she brought in the name of his living son, Jordan.

It was over, what had been said in that bedroom. No one had to know, least of all Gelis, that St Pol had wanted to make Jordan his heir.

Nicholas sat, looking at no one, while Bel told all that had happened.

At the end, he glanced up, and found her watching him grimly. 'I told him ye wouldna. I told him ye'd be too thrawn to take it, even if it was for the bairn.'

'It was too late to make amends,' Nicholas said. Gelis said nothing.

Tobie frowned. 'But he saved Jordan. Didn't that count? The gift was for Jordan.'

'It was for the succession,' Nicholas said. 'It was why he saved Jordan. Without Jordan, Kilmirren was lost.'

Bel blew her nose. She said, 'I think his reasons were more praiseworthy nor that. You know what I hope? I hope he heard the last words you said, Nicholas. About Henry's love for his grandfather and Simon. About Jordan and Henry becoming friends. Ye thought that worth doing. Might he not have thought the same? And even if he didna, would your hopes for Henry not be carried out if Jordan went on in Henry's place? I would want that. I would want that to remember my Jordan by. Otherwise my hale life has been wasted on someone worthless. And to me, he never was that.'

There was a silence. Then Gelis said, 'So you wanted Jordan to have Kilmirren, Bel?'

'Aye,' she said. 'I got St Pol to write the gift out and sign it, just in case he lost the knack, or fell out of his senses. I have the paper there yet.'

Nicholas was looking at Gelis. She said, 'It is your decision.'

He said, 'No.' His gaze had moved. When he spoke again, it was slowly. 'Bel? What would Father Godscalc have said? He knew who Henry was. Tobie and Gelis and I have kept the secret all these years. When Godscalc was dying, he spoke of him, but he also spoke of us all, and how he wished us together. He asked us to make him our bridge. Is this what he meant?'

'You would do it?' she said.

'Not for St Pol,' he said. 'But I would do it for you, and Gelis, and Jordan – our Jordan – and in memory of the friends we have lost, whom it might have made happy. What would Adorne have said?'

'*Property. Take it.* And Tam Cochrane,' said Gelis. 'He would be there with his slate and his ruler before anyone said a word about garderobes.'

'And Whistle Willie,' said Tobie. 'You'd have an organ in no time at all.'

They were talking heartily, out of shock, but they meant what they said.

Nicholas said, 'Then, Bel, we will take your paper, and Jordan shall have his inheritance. And he will be Semple and we shall be de Fleury, which will keep him explaining until the end of his days.'

Later, he went upstairs alone, and stood by the bed, his gaze resting on the grey, silent bulk of his grandfather, whose beauty had altered his life. They had left the great ring, now immovably part of his finger. St Pol could not hurt him with it, or pass it on to him now.

Bel had hoped that his last words had been heard. Now, he thought that he could wish the same thing. Today, he had rejected a gift, and Fate, it seemed, had determined to thrust it upon him. As he had recently said, one could not depend upon plans.

He had never thought, long ago in his own flat country of Flanders, in his own well-loved burgh of Bruges, that one day he would abandon it all for a small, mountainous land, at the behest of a man whose ill-will had dogged him for most of his life.

But no. That was not accurate either. He had already decided to stay.

Bruges was part of his life. So was Marian. So was her family. That would remain. As for Bonne, he felt no obligation; no wish to know more about her, any more than she did about him. She would marry, and that would be the end.

For him, this choice seemed right. It simply meant that now there might be descendants of his who would choose to work in this country that had welcomed him, and perhaps gather about them a circle as various, as eccentric, as fond as the one of which he and Gelis were part.

He had found Gelis, and happiness. The other element in his life he had also, for it took nothing from others. He had a great deal of love to give, and was fortunate in attracting it, he had discovered.

He remembered the gold, and wondered, with slight irritation, how he was going to spend it. He had a feeling that someone would tell him.

He walked downstairs, not to begin a new life, but to continue the one that was already his, with his friends.

Epilogue

And I beseik him, lord of all, Iesu,
The ground of grace, the well of all werteu
To send ws grace, that sic werteu we haf
To serf him so that our saulis he saif,
And bring ws to his kinrik and his blys,
Quhar lyf but end and ioye eternall is.

                                Amen, amen.

HERE YOU HAVE a spiritual pronouncement. We astrologers are not necessarily attuned to the work of the Almighty and His servants, although I have time for Will Scheves. My concern is the Future, thus capitalised – not my own; not even that of the men and women in this tale; but the Future in which some of their children or grandchildren may take part. And, of course, my descendants. I have great hopes of my daughter, Camille.

My efforts have met with some success. I had a glimpse of something, just about the time of which you have been reading. I cannot remember what medium I used – the beryl, the tray of ink? (ink is so expensive) – but I can tell you the vision was short, and I could not say what year it represented, although I recognised where it took place: a pretty spot in France, which I happen to know very well. Nicholas de Fleury was there – indeed, he was my unwitting intermediary.

It is a sobering thing, to occupy the mind of another. The *amour propre* may find itself damaged. In this instance, Nicholas appeared to regard me with due respect, which is something. Some of the persons connected with him were visible, but there is no reason to suppose that harm had befallen those who were not. It was merely a glimpse. All I can say for certain is that I perceived the children more clearly than ever before, each with its thread to the future now firmly held in its hand.

Here is what I saw.

*

The river was broad, and full with the summer flood. It was not yet the season for vintage, but the scent of the fruit drifted in the soft air and filled the senses like music.

Nicholas stood, without seeing. Far off, he could hear voices. If he turned, he would discover them: Bel's family, Kathi's family, and his own, taking their ease in the woodland and orchards of Chouzy, in the vale of the Cisse and the Loire; renewing, as he did every year, their old acquaintance with France.

He would see Bel's son-in-law, Bernard, seigneur de Chouzy, a little frail for his years, smiling at Isabella, his fair, his bewitching young daughter. And never far off, he would find his own tall son Jordan, brown-haired, loose-limbed and inventive, with a flute stuck at his waist, or plucked out to amuse Isabella. Apart, the younger children would be playing: Camille dominating young Hob, unless her father Dr Andreas intervened. And behind them somewhere in the grass, Gelis and Kathi were certainly talking: Gelis lying back, her eyes screwed against the sun; Kathi sitting up collecting something, or shelling something, or unpacking the baskets. And halfway up a very tall tree, with a flower stuck in his hair, Kathi's other son, whose childish name had been Rankin.

Seeing the way things were going, Nicholas had asked Bernard de Moncourt recently about the future of Chouzy, and he had smiled. 'You don't fancy managing it? Then have no fear. It will last my time, although Isabella's husband, when she has one, and her family may have other ideas. The King's advisers have sent to ask if this is for sale.'

'Chouzy?'

'No. The vineyards. This land we call Sevigny, by the river. The Crown wishes to build. A château for the monarch, or his guests, or to lease to privileged commanders.'

'Will you sell?'

'I might. I am not poor, as you know, but it would bring considerable wealth to my family. We could remain here for my lifetime. But if the Crown eventually tired of the building and sold, my heirs need not stay, and suffer a string of new neighbours.' Then de Moncourt had smiled. 'If the château is built, you may wish to advise about architects.'

'I used to know a good Italian,' Nicholas had said.

The river ran, singing. Life was full of surprises. He had never truly wanted to shorten his own, even when things were at their worst. He had not needed Andreas to warn him: fill your life. There is a long time to wait. Don't make it longer.

He wondered how long it would be, and where he would wait, and what it would feel like. He wondered if anyone else had this happiness, to know what death was going to mean. He understood and was reconciled to the fact that he must not shorten the interval; must not call home that other, unknown life before its due span. The world had a right to its servants; and echoes must remain only echoes; the shell remain shut, with its music, until the time came.

Until the time came.

Someone touched him. 'Come and join us,' said Kathi. She took his hand to lead him to Gelis. Now that he looked, it was all as he imagined, except that Isabella had snatched the flute and was running, laughing, from Jordan. A flower dropped on his hair. He looked up.

Blue eyes, golden hair, framed in the leaves of a tree. Kathi's son, bright as a fawn, his face dirty. He sang out, and Kathi looked up with resignation and said, 'We notice. You will, of course, fall. But wait until we have left.'

Walking with Nicholas again, she unexpectedly spoke. 'You don't mind?' She glanced back at the tree. 'You don't mind what he is called?'

She had not asked him before. She was offering to speak of it now, as an expression of faith in his strength, his self-discipline, his ability to recover, even, from something she had seen in his face. Nicholas opened an arm and, walking still, Kathi took his hand over her shoulder. He said, 'You disguised it well enough, didn't you? No, I didn't mind.'

'It began as Franskin,' Kathi said. 'Just a pet name, but hard for a little person to say. When he was born, Margaret couldn't pronounce it.'

He said, 'There wasn't much she couldn't do.'

'No,' said Kathi in thoughtful agreement.

He had given Margaret a pearl. Kathi had asked him to keep it. Nicholas had no daughter, but might have a granddaughter one day, who might have a daughter in turn. Its story would live.

They walked. Then Kathi resumed in the same tone. 'The name for our son? Robin wanted this one as much as I did, and asked Gelis. She said she gave it to us as a gift from you both. She had made a journey to Dijon. She had found it engraved in the crypt.'

'I thought so,' he said.

Gelis had never told him. His hand clung to Kathi's, and hers to his. She spoke gently. 'The child in the tomb. He was your twin, who died before you were born?'

Rankin; Franskin; Francis.

'Yes,' he said; and by his voice, closed the subject for ever.

Was; and is; and will be.

He looked back. The lad had swung himself from branch to branch to the ground, lissom as once his father had been. A handsome boy, with springing blond hair, and features fine as if fashioned in porcelain.

This was a soul that he knew, gifted and eager and generous; beloved of many; destined surely for fame; and determined, as Robin was, to follow a man he thought worthy. A noble child of his race, Francis Crawford of Berecrofts. Francis Crawford of Templehall, it would be, one day.

But this was not the piercing spirit, clear as a snowfield in sunlight, for whom Nicholas de Fleury was waiting. A being fiercer than this: far more passionate, far more vulnerable, with far more to give to a world which would not know, at first, how to receive it. A spirit that would always lead; that could never be a disciple.

The other half of his being, come again.

Kathi's son left the tree and came running, and Nicholas turned the flower into a dart and flung it, with comradely venom. The lad, laughing, ducked.

Ahead, the pretty, fair girl ran on, but Jordan had glanced round, and was looking. Nicholas waved to him, with his free hand.

Here ended the picture.

Heir endis the buke of the ches.

December 15, 1998 – November 5, 1999
EDINBURGH